Saddle The Wind

Jess Foley was born in Wiltshire but moved to London to study at the Chelsea School of Art, then subsequently worked as a painter and actor before taking up writing. Now living in Blackheath, south-east London, Jess Foley's first novel *So Long At The Fair* was published in 2001, followed by *Too Close To The Sun* in 2002.

Praise for Jess Foley

'If all sagas were as convincing and exuberant as this, the world would be a better place. I loved it' Monica Dickens

'Jess has really captured the sense of a family united against great odds. The heroine is strong but flawed as all good heroines should be and as we follow her triumphs and trials we see her change from a girl to a woman in the most dramatic and satisfying of ways' Iris Gower

'A compulsive and well-paced story' *Wiltshire Times*

'An earthy tale of love, longing and tragedy' *Swindon Evening Advertiser*

Also by Jess Foley

So Long At The Fair
Too Close To The Sun

SADDLE THE WIND

Jess Foley

arrow books

Published by Arrow Books in 2004

3 5 7 9 10 8 6 4 2

Copyright © Jess Foley 1989

Jess Foley has asserted the right under the Copyright, Designs
and Patents Act, 1988 to be identified as the author of this work

First published in the United Kingdom in 1989 by Grafton Books

Arrow Books
The Random House Group Limited
20 Vauxhall Bridge Road, London, SW1V 2SA

Addresses for companies within The Random House Group Limited
can be found at: www.randomhouse.co.uk offices.htm

The Random House Group Limited Reg. No. 954009

www.randomhouse.co.uk

A CIP catalogue record for this book
is available from the British Library

The Random House Group Limited supports The Forest Stewardship
Council (FSC), the leading international forest certification organisation.
All our titles that are printed on Greenpeace approved FSC certified paper
carry the FSC logo. Our paper procurement policy can be found at:
www.rbooks.co.uk/environment.

Mixed Sources
Product group from well-managed
forests and other controlled sources
www.fsc.org Cert no. TT-COC-2139
© 1996 Forest Stewardship Council

ISBN 9780099517924

Typeset by Palimpsest Book Production Limited,
Polmont, Stirlingshire
Printed and bound in Great Britain by
Cox & Wyman Ltd, Reading, Berkshire

For Glen and Bev

PART ONE

Chapter One

'Are you sure?' he asked. His voice had the burr of the West Country; a voice usually soft but now touched with a note of weary disbelief. The woman raised her eyebrows and answered in a tone of angry impatience.

'Of course I'm sure.'

He shook his head. 'Jesus Christ. Why did this have to happen? As if there's not enough to cope with already with four small mouths to feed.' In a sudden display of anger he slammed his fist onto the table top, making the cheap shade of the oil lamp rattle on its metal base. 'Damn it!' he said bitterly through gritted teeth. 'Damn and blast it!'

Sarah stood very still, watching him. She knew that with her words she was shattering what little of the dream remained.

'How d'*you* feel about it?' he said at last.

She didn't answer. 'No,' he said, 'you haven't got the responsibility of providing, have you? Oh, yes, you bring in a few shillings each week with the washing, but how far does that get us?'

Remaining silent she turned away.

'Have we *got* to have it?' he asked. 'Have we?'

There was a little silence, during which only the ticking of the clock could be heard, then Sarah said, 'Yes, Ollie, we have. There's nothing to be done about it now.'

'Nothing?'

Briefly she closed her eyes, sighing. 'What are you

3

asking, Ollie? What do you want me to do?' She had no need to ask, of course. She knew what was in his mind. The thought had been in her own at the beginning, but then the memory of her mother had come clutching at her and she had thrust the thought aside. She could never risk that happening to her. 'We'll manage somehow, Ollie,' she said, then added a little more forcefully: 'We must.'

Glancing up, she looked at the reflection of his face in the mirror beside the range. A cheap glass, it distorted his image so that his features became as seen through water, an ugly parody of those she knew so well. After a moment he came around the table, stood behind her and raised his hands to her shoulders. At his touch she shook him off. 'Please,' she said, '– don't ask me again. It's no use.'

'Well, we've got to do *something* about it.'

Turning back to him she said, 'We're not doing *anything* about it, Ollie. Nothing. So you can forget that. I'm not taking the chance of leaving my children without a mother. It happened with my own mother. It won't happen here.'

'That's foolish talk,' he said. 'You'd be all right. For God's sake, Sarah, we haven't got enough to live on as it is.'

'I know, but –' She shook her head hopelessly. 'I'm sorry, Ollie.'

'Look,' he said, '– it's the only thing to do – with four children already – you must see that. They're more than enough to cope with. Damn it, we can't afford another child. We can't even afford the ones we've got.'

'Well,' she said quickly, 'you should give that some thought when you start coming at me like some damned bull, not to be denied.'

He stared at her for a moment then raised his hand and struck her hard across the face. With a little cry she

4

put a hand up to her check then turned and ran from the room.

In the small thatched cottage there was not far she could go before she reached the limits of the interior. Now, with the tears starting in her eyes she ran up the stairs and into the front bedroom, the one she shared with Ollie. There in the dark she closed the door behind her, moved to the bed and sat down, the worn springs giving a whine of protest under the weight of her small frame.

As she sat there she made an effort to choke back the tears. She wouldn't cry. Anyway, what good would it do? There was no room in this life for indulgences. Besides, she had brought it on herself. For those moments downstairs she had so wanted to hurt him. And she had succeeded. The stinging imprint on her cheek was proof enough of that; he had never struck her before. But *she* had been hurt too. Not by the blow from his hand – no, not that – but by his reaction to the news of the baby. But she had known what his reaction would be. Which was why she'd put off saying anything until tonight. She'd been sure about the baby for more than a fortnight now, but she had been afraid to tell him. And so she had put it off. She'd kept on putting it off.

After a while she heard the sound of the front door closing. He was going out. Leaning closer to the window she pulled aside the thin curtain and, in the moonlight, saw him move from the front gate and start off along the lane. He would go to the Wheatsheaf – and probably wouldn't be back till it closed.

She sighed, took up the matches and lit the candle that rested on the chest of drawers next to the bed. With the candleholder in her hand she got up and moved to the door and stepped out onto the narrow strip of threadbare carpet that covered the tiny landing. There she stood listening outside the children's room. All was quiet. Softly she opened the door and went in.

Inside the room she stood in the wavering light of the candle flame looking down at the nearest bed, in which slept the boys Ernest and Arthur.

Ernest, her first born, was eight years old. Arthur was four. Both boys had dark chestnut hair – her own colouring – but it was there that any likeness between the two ended. Ernest, the picture of health, slept soundly, his face slightly flushed from the past day's sun. Arthur lay a little apart, his head further up on the pillow, as if unconsciously reaching for air and space. And while Ernest's breath came sweet and even, Arthur's sounded slightly laboured, coming only through his open mouth, evidence of the problems that had plagued him from his earliest days. All his life Sarah had had to give him that extra bit of care.

His lack of physical strength, though, only made her love him the more, she realized; those imperfections – his weak chest and lame right leg. And such a tiny, feeble creature he'd been at birth. She could remember so well when Ollie had first seen him. It had mattered not at all the encouragement in her voice as she'd said, 'A son, Ollie. You've got another son to help you out.' She had seen the expression of disappointment on his face.

And he had never shown affection for the child; merely toleration. And there were times, of course, when she was sure that Arthur was aware of it. How could he not be? And how could Ollie withhold his love like that? Not that he showed that much affection for the others – apart from Mary. How could it be, she wondered, that a man with so much feeling in some ways could be so lacking in it in others . . . ? Perhaps, though, she said to herself, there just wasn't that much love in his heart; perhaps it just wasn't there to give –

the way some people had no sense of smell; or like Arthur with his own lack – his inability to walk or breathe as he should . . .

And it was partly that, too, Sarah knew – Ollie's lack of love for Arthur – that turned her own heart even more strongly towards the boy. So many of the tears she had wept had been for Arthur. Those nights when she had held him in her arms as he had lain gasping for breath, or on those bright afternoons when, looking from the steamed-up scullery window, she had seen him hurrying, dot-and-carry, in the wake of his adored, agile, elder brother.

She sighed again and, moving silently, stepped around the end of the boys' bed to the window where she parted the curtains and gazed out.

On the very outskirts of the village of Hallowford, the thatched cottage was the last in a row of three pairs of cottages that flanked the northeast side of Coates Lane, the narrow way that met with Gorse Hill to the south and, to the north, joined up with Elm Road. It comprised a front parlour, kitchen and scullery downstairs, and two bedrooms upstairs. The rear bedroom window at which Sarah stood looked out over the yard with the shed and the privy, and, beyond them, the garden, a narrow little strip of land bearing two small apple trees and the vegetables that Ollie had planted. The view hardly differed at all from that of the neighbours, the Hewitts, on the left. Raising her eyes slightly Sarah saw beyond the garden the dark shape of the Ridge rising up, a high cliff, its sheer, chalk face gleaming faintly in the May night.

She sighed and let the curtain fall back into place. She was tired, and her back ached from all the pails of water she had had to carry from the pump that day, from all the stooping over the washtub. Turning, she looked at the two girls asleep in the second bed, next to the wall. Mary, her elder daughter, was seven. Beside her slept Agnes. She, the youngest of all at not quite two, lay with her dark hair next to Mary's blonde curls, her arm across her chest.

Sarah's eyes shifted back to the peaceful face of Mary and lingered there. Mary . . . Yes, Ollie loved her all right, and had done so right from the moment she had been placed, red and lustily squalling, in his arms. And as the child had grown, so his love for her had grown too, quickly outstripping his lukewarm affection for Ernest, and the other two who came after. *She* was his if no one else was. His girl. His Mary. Of all the children only she it was who seemed truly able to reach his heart.

As she stood there the thoughts and memories came crowding in and she pictured Ollie as he had been when they had first met. He'd been beautiful – like those sculptures he'd taken her to look at that day before their marriage. That had been in the early spring of 1871. Nine years ago. And he hadn't changed much, really. His body was still tall and strong, his face still good-looking, his corn-coloured hair still as thick, his eyes still as blue – bluer than any eyes she had seen before or since on anyone, except perhaps Mary. And yet, she thought, Ollie's eyes were different now. Now they were without that spark that had been there, that reflection of promise. Though he was still young. Thirty-two years old. It was the poverty that was doing it to him, the responsibility of providing for a wife and children on the little he earned from his work on the gardens of Hallowford House and the little she brought in with the washing.

But why wasn't it bearable for him? she asked herself. And the answer, she knew, lay in his dreams. If you had no dreams, no aspirations, then you could be content; there was no wanting to get in the way.

8

Turning her head, she gazed around her. On the top of the small chest of drawers she could see the little tin box holding Mary's cheap paintbrushes and paints. There too were the magpie's feather and the robin's nest that Ernest had found, and the boat he had made for Arthur. Above the girls' bed hung an oil-painting depicting people picking blackberries. A second painting, a still life of apples and flowers, done on an old piece of wood panelling, hung beside the door. Ollie's pictures were all over the house – oil-paintings of all sizes done on bits of old canvas, boards and panels, paintings on which he lavished so much concentration and quiet passion in the few spare hours his working life allowed and when he could scrape together enough spare money for a paintbrush or the odd tube of paint.

It was that that had first attracted her to him, his passion for artistic things, a sensitivity that had made him different from the rest. And, she was sure, it was that same sensitivity – blunted now by circumstances – that had got in the way of any real happiness he might otherwise have found.

As she had been so often in the past she was touched now by the warmth of pity for his wasted talent. For he had talent, she was quite sure. And it was a *great* talent, possibly. But his painting could not be anything more than a hobby. Not now. There was no place in their lives for dreams of anything more grand, not now – if indeed there ever had been.

She could understand his resentment, though. And she could well remember how at the very beginning she had encouraged and shared his hopes. Yes, she had said, yes, she would help him in every way she could. She would help him earn the money for his materials, help him find the time to paint, to establish himself so that eventually he could leave his work on the land and make a living from his painting. And together they would build the kind of life they wanted, with a good home, and, eventually, children.

The children, though, had come along first, and with their arrival fame and fortune had had to take a back seat. And so all those plans made in the earlier days had never become anything more than hopes – mere pipe dreams, and as substantial.

Sarah minded much less about their poverty than Ollie did; she'd known that for a long time now. Perhaps it was because she no longer had any real dreams of her own – for herself, anyway. In the face of day-to-day reality she tried to be content with that reality and as a result had come nearer to accepting her lot and resigning herself – perhaps too readily, she sometimes thought – and now sought her only happiness through her children. Not so Ollie. It was different with him. For him reality was something to be avoided.

She had had her own dreams once, though. With a good education from her English mother – once a schoolteacher – and a little grit from her Scots father, Sarah, orphaned at eighteen, had found herself a post as governess to a doctor's children in Trowbridge. She had thought then that the whole world was open to her. She could marry anybody, she had told herself – shopkeeper, teacher, lawyer . . . But then in Trowbridge one morning she had met Ollie, a young man rich only in his dreams – and her own dream had changed; he had become a part of it.

Ollie had been a stockman then, caring for the cattle of a local farmer. It wouldn't be for always, though, he had said; before too much time had passed he would have left the farm to set up on his own, as a painter of pictures. In those days his hopes had been untainted by experience and he had been certain that it would be only a matter of time before they became reality.

She could remember so well that moment when she had first realized the extent of her feelings for him. They had been walking in Trowbridge one Sunday soon after they had met. It was a winter's afternoon and they had stopped to look in a shop window. Ollie, standing beside her, had taken his hand from his pocket and written something on the glass with his finger. She asked him what he had written, but, smiling, gently shaking his head, he had said, 'Oh, no – can't tell you that.' When she had looked at the glass she had been unable to see anything, and a moment later he was taking her arm and they were moving away. But then, when they had gone just a few yards she had broken away from him and stepped back to the window. There, putting her face close to the pane she had breathed upon it and had seen appear the words: *Love me, love me, Sarah Keane.* In that moment any lingering thoughts of teachers, doctors or lawyers had vanished, disappearing in the cold air like the breath vapour from her mouth. She had known in that moment that she loved Oliver Farrar and would marry him.

The candle, burnt very low, sputtered once or twice, its suddenly flaring, wavering flame lighting up the shabby room so that the shadows danced and darted. She was aware of a pin escaping from her hair and falling onto her collar. She retrieved it and moved to stand before the small discoloured glass that hung on the wall beside the fireplace. Bending slightly she peered at the image before her. Her dark chestnut hair was woven into a thick, heavy plait coiled about the crown of her head and which now, following the blow from Ollie's hand, had come loose. Setting down the candleholder on the mantelpiece, she took two or three more pins from her hair and readjusted the plait. In the feeble light she continued to gaze at her reflection. She looked her

11

thirty-one years, all right, she thought. Her face, once so pretty, was already settling into maturity, while the hand that brushed back the wisps of hair was rough against the softness of her cheek, irretrievably broadened, coarsened by the constant wringing out of wet washing; by endless hours' immersion in water.

Her hands moved down her body. The growing child within her had not yet begun to change the shape of her belly. Soon, though, she would be all too aware of its presence, and then, come December . . .

And it was true what Ollie said: they couldn't afford it; they couldn't afford another demanding mouth to be fed, another body to be clothed. But they would have to; and somehow they would get by.

The cottages in Coates Lane were owned by John Savill at Hallowford House, a large Georgian house that stood a little less than a mile away to the southeast, on the top of Gorse Hill. Secluded from passers-by on the road, the house was set back behind immaculate green lawns, its wide front door approached by a carriage drive that led from tall wrought-iron gates and curved through and beyond a screen of trees, yew, rowan and flowering cherry. Built by John Savill's great-grandfather in 1782, it was large and well-proportioned, its tall, elegant windows at the front facing out over the village in the valley, at the back over the yard, the stables, outhouses, formal and kitchen gardens, orchard and meadows.

John Savill was a wool clothier, owning one of the few remaining successful mills in nearby Trowbridge. He had married his wife Catherine, the daughter of a Bath solicitor, a little less than two years before; his first wife having died some five years earlier, the only child of the marriage, a daughter, dying in infancy. As the gentry went, John Savill was quite well regarded in the village. For one thing he kept his servants much longer than did most of the other employers in the larger houses in the area, and also he had the reputation of being more considerate than most where his factory workers were concerned.

It was from the Savills that came all the money that entered the Farrar household. Ollie, on his marriage to Sarah, and with her encouragement, had given up working as stockman for a Hallowford farmer in order to take on the slightly less demanding job of assistant gardener to the Savills, at which time he and Sarah had moved into one of John Savill's cottages in Coates Lane. As a stockman Ollie had had to work almost every day of the year, whereas the job of gardener allowed him all his Sundays off – days he could put to good use, not only in and around the cottage, but also at his painting. Sarah's income from the Savills came by means of the laundry she did for them each week. She had been doing it for several years now, the washing being brought to the cottage regularly every Thursday by two of the Savills' maids, the girls making the return journey with the laundry that Sarah had finished.

Like most of the other villagers, Sarah viewed the Savills with a mixture of awe and respect. Throughout her years of doing the household's washing she had never had occasion to exchange more than a few words with Mr Savill – at which times he had been distantly polite – but with his young wife she had spoken several times and had taken a liking to her. Whereas Sarah had found the first Mrs Savill almost unapproachable in her imperiousness, the present Mrs Savill had shown that beyond the usual formalities that marked the difference in their stations there was a genuine warmth and understanding.

Now, this July of 1880, when the Savills' maids had

come to the cottage with the week's washing, Sarah learned from them that Mrs Savill was expecting her first child and that it would be born towards the end of January.

Soon after the maids, Emmie and Dora, had left to return to Hallowford House with the freshly ironed laundry Sarah herself prepared to leave the cottage. Just before the harvest season each summer Ollie would be taken from his work on the gardens to help with the haymaking in Mr Savill's fields, and on some of the days during this time Sarah would take his dinner to him where he was at work. Now into a basket she placed half a loaf, a small basin of beef dripping, an onion, some cheese and a small flagon of cider. Then she called Mary, Arthur and Agnes to her – Ernest was out somewhere with his friends – and set off along the lane, up the hill and across the fields. It was an errand she undertook with pleasure, enjoying the walk and the chance to relax for a spell with the children and take a brief respite from the endless round of washing and ironing.

The July day was hot and on the hills herds of grazing sheep were dull white masses, hardly moving – reminders of the source of John Savill's wealth. Most of the land round about his own acres – apart from the few fields with grain crops – were given over to sheep farming. When at last Sarah and the children reached the edge of the wide field where the men were at work, they waited until the foreman gave the call to signal the dinner break and then walked across the stubble, catching up with Ollie as he retreated from the sweltering sun to rest in the shade of an elm.

A few minutes later, sitting beside him, watching as he ate the bread and dripping, Sarah thought of the happiness at Hallowford House at the prospect of a child. *That* child, the Savills', would be born into wealth and comfort, cared for by parents who could dedicate their lives to its well-being. Her own child, on the other hand, had very little waiting for it – nothing more, really, than the love that she was so ready to give.

She had hoped that the passing of time would melt Ollie's resistance, but it had not. As the baby had grown within her so it seemed had Ollie's resentment. He made hardly any reference at all to the child she carried, acknowledging it generally only by a surly muteness. He was angry, too, she was aware, over the fact that she discouraged any advances he made to her at night; something else he held against the unborn child.

In truth, though, her reluctance was not only on account of the baby. It was because of Ollie himself. In the past he had been so tender with her, but over more recent times he had seemed to give no thought at all to her own wants or desires. Rather she felt that he had simply used her. What for? As a release? – a means whereby he could somehow gain forgetfulness for a few minutes and blot out the reality of his existence?

She watched as he drank some of the cider, then looked across the fields to where the back of Hallowford House was visible beyond the orchard wall. 'I hear that Mr Savill's to become a father too,' she said. 'In January, so Emmie told me.' She waited but he made no reply. After a little silence she added, 'Emmie says he's just about over the moon.'

Ollie nodded and said shortly: 'Ah, well, that's fine for him. He can have as many children as he likes. He won't have any trouble feeding 'em.' There was a short pause, then he went on, 'And if he's as keen as you say he is, perhaps he'd like to take on an extra one. God knows we've got no use for it.'

Sarah said nothing. After a few moments she got to her feet, called the children to her and started back over the field. By the gate she stopped and turned and looked back. Ollie still sat in the elm's shade, eating the bread and drinking the cider. There was no reaching him these days.

She worked right up to the time the baby was born.

During the afternoon of Friday, December 10th, she had just finished washing some of the Savills' underwear when she felt the first pangs of her labour. She put down the petticoat she had just wrung out, stood quite still and tried, calmly, to analyse the little darts of pain that stabbed dully at her body. Aware that it was no false alarm, she wrung out the few remaining items and placed them in a large bowl. Then, calling Arthur and Agnes to her from the kitchen she took them to the adjoining cottage where she asked her neighbour, Esther Hewitt, to look after them for a few hours and to send her son Davie for Mrs Curfee, the midwife.

When Mrs Curfee arrived a little over half-an-hour later she let herself in and moved her considerable bulk up the narrow stairs; she knew where to go. Entering the bedroom she found Sarah lying on the bed and after satisfying herself that Sarah's time was close asked if Ollie should be told. Sarah shook her head. 'No, leave him be. He's working. He won't thank you for bothering him.'

Mrs Curfee clicked her tongue disapprovingly and raised her eyes to the ceiling, silently speaking volumes of men in general and husbands in particular, then got to work. The baby was born just after half-past-five.

'You got a lovely little girl,' Mrs Curfee said, smiling into Sarah's sweat-damp face.

'Is she all right?' Sarah asked. Into her mind had flashed a sudden image of Artie. Mrs Curfee smiled at her. 'Yes, don't you worry. She's a perfect little mite.'

When the baby had been bathed Mrs Curfee laid her

in Sarah's arms and began to tidy the room. As she worked she said over her shoulder: 'You timed it just right. If you'd left it much later I wouldn't 'ave been 'ere. I'm off to join my son and 'is wife in Bath in a few days – to spend Christmas with 'em.'

Sarah nodded. 'When'll you be back in Hallowford?' she asked.

'Soon as Christmas is over, I reckons. Or maybe after New Year's.'

'In time to look after Mrs Savill's baby, then.'

Mrs Curfee shook her head. 'No – I doubt I'll be needed there. They'll be 'aving the doctor and a monthly nurse, that's for sure.'

When Mrs Curfee had gone, with a promise to look in again the following day, Sarah lay in bed with the baby at her side. She felt surprisingly well, and at peace. The baby was beautiful and perfect. Ollie would be sure to love her in time.

Later, when Ollie came in from work he was greeted by Mary who told him excitedly of the new baby. He went up the stairs and stood at the bedside looking down at Sarah as she lay with the baby in her arms.

'Look at her, Ollie,' Sarah said. 'She's going to look just like you.' She watched him, waiting for his reaction.

He nodded noncommittally. 'How are you feelin'? All right?'

'Yes, I'm all right.'

'Good. I'd best go and get on with dinner for the others.'

'Thank you, Ollie. I'll be back downstairs soon. Just give me a little time.' With her words she recalled how once she had read in a copy of *Cassell's Household Guide* that no mother should get up before nine days after the birth of her child. *Nine days*. Where did she have nine days to spend lying in bed? *Cassell's Household Guide* hadn't been written for the likes of her. 'I'll be up tomorrow, Ollie,' she added.

He nodded again and started towards the door. Sarah called after him:

'– Ollie?'

Stopping in the doorway he turned his tall frame back to her. 'Yes?'

'What d'you think we should call her?'

He shrugged. 'I don't know. That's up to you.'

'Oh, come on, Ollie . . .' She wanted to evoke some positive response from him; anything was preferable to this dull indifference. 'What d'you think? You must have some idea. Isn't there some name you'd like?'

'No.' He refused to be mellowed. 'I'll leave that to you.'

After a moment she said, 'What d'you think of the name – "Blanche"? I mean – she's so fair. Like you, Ollie.'

'Blanche? Don't you reckon it's a mite grand?' He paused. 'Still, why not. It'll be about the only thing about her that is. Like the rest of us she'll never have more'n two ha'p'nies to rub together.'

'Oh, Ollie . . .' Sarah's disappointment showed on her face. Ollie shrugged again. 'You call her what you like. It's your decision.' He turned and went from the room.

As his descending boots sounded from the stairs Sarah lay back on the pillow and looked at the baby. How could Ollie be so sure that the poor little thing would never have anything? And to damn a child's existence like that from the moment of its birth . . . All right, perhaps she and Ollie didn't have anything, but it didn't have to be that way with the children. It could be different for them. It *could*, yes – and whatever she could do to make it so, then that she would do.

Chapter Two

Snow had been falling all day long, blanketing the earth and sealing in the house. Inside, though, beside the glowing fire in the library, it was warm. Glancing over at Catherine, Savill saw that she had just awakened. Now she smiled at him from her chair, one hand on the round swell of her belly. 'You slept for a while,' he said.

She sat up and reached down to the knitting basket beside her chair. As she did so Prince, the small King Charles spaniel that lay near her feet, lifted its head and looked at her. As Catherine took up the knitting Savill got up from his chair to turn up the flame of the oil lamp on the wall above her head. At fifty he was nineteen years older than his wife. Of medium height, he was straight-backed, with a lean, fine-featured face, grey eyes and thick grey hair. As the lamp flame burgeoned Catherine raised her head, dark eyes wide in the oval of her face. 'Oh, John,' she sighed. 'I'm so impatient. I want the time to go by.'

He nodded, smiling. 'I too. But it won't be long now. Five weeks or so; they'll pass quickly enough.'

'Not for me.'

He turned, moved to the window and drew back one of the curtains. Putting his face near to the glass he gazed out.

'Is it still snowing?' she asked behind him.

'Yes, heavily.'

'I hope Mrs Callow's all right.'

'Yes, she'll be all right.'

Mrs Callow, the housekeeper, had gone into Trowbridge that morning to visit her elderly mother. After her departure the snow had really begun to come down again, quickly adding to that which had already blanketed the area during the past two days. Many of the roads would be unpassable again. 'She'll be staying overnight,' Savill added. 'She won't try to come back in this.'

He let the curtain fall, sat down and took up the remaining newspaper; the one he had read lay on the carpet near his slippered feet. After looking at the paper's front page for a couple of minutes he set it aside again. Folding his hands over his stomach he looked at his wife as she bent her head over her knitting, a slight frown of concentration on her brow as she negotiated a particular stitch. He had a sudden image of her in an earlier time, in the spring, seeing her lying naked beneath him, her brow damp with sweat . . .

Catherine had brought into his life a happiness and contentment that in earlier years he had never expected, never looked for. And now she had brought to him also so much promise. He looked past the knitting in her moving hands and took in the swell of her body. In five weeks, come the end of January, the child would be here . . .

Glancing up, Catherine caught his gaze and smiled at him. She lowered the knitting, stretched, then leaned forward and looked up at the clock on the mantelpiece. Almost ten-thirty. 'I won't do anymore,' she said. 'I think I'll go on upstairs.'

He nodded. 'You must be tired. I'll put out the lights and follow you soon.'

Dropping the knitting into the basket she got up from the chair. The dog arose, stretched, stood there for a moment and then followed her to the door and out into the hall. When the door had closed behind her Savill put his hands behind his head, closed his eyes and, deep in his contentment, leaned back in the warm, snow-wrapped silence.

From the library, Catherine crossed the hall to the stairs and started up. She moved slowly. She was tired and her back ached. As she reached the little landing where the stairs turned she saw that one of the window catches had sprung and that snow was coming in through the crack. She clicked her tongue in annoyance and tried to pull the window closed again. She couldn't do it, though, and after a moment she turned and moved back to the head of the stairs. There she hovered briefly, wondering whether to go back down and tell John, or trust that he would notice it when he came by in a few minutes. She turned away; he would see it himself. But then the next second she was saying to herself, yes, she would tell him. Turning quickly, she moved to step down, and suddenly, in a split second, she realized that the dog was right before her, beneath her descending foot. The realization came too late. She snatched at the banister rail, missed it, and the next moment she was falling, crashing down the stairs in a flurrying, rolling blur of blue woollen skirts and white petticoats, coming to a halt at the foot of the stairs in the hall below.

She groaned lightly, sighingly, her breath catching as though she was trying to stifle screams welling up inside her. Pressing her hand to her side she moved her pained gaze to her husband as he bent to her, his grey eyes filled with sudden tears of shock and despair. She lay on the carpet, one leg twisted around, the foot raised and resting on the lower step of the stairs.

Savill had roughly pushed the dog away and now knelt beside her, hands moving impotently, wanting to touch her, to hold her, but afraid to do so. 'Oh, God . . .' His head moved from side to side in his distraction. He could see the waves of her growing pain reflected in her eyes, hear it in the sounds that came from her parted, drawn-back lips. 'Catherine,' he whispered hoarsely. 'Catherine . . .' And then he was straightening again, hurrying towards the rear of the house. He started to call up the back stairs for the housekeeper, Mrs Callow, then broke off, remembering that she hadn't returned. Then, throwing back his head he shouted for the other servants. 'Emmie! Dora! Come quickly, for God's sake!' A pause and then again: 'Emmie! Dora! Florence!' his tone falling as he added, 'For God's sake where are you all?'

Hurrying back to Catherine's side he bent beside her.

'John . . . help me up . . . please . . .' Her words came stuttering in his ear and he gave a small cry of anguish. Then, her voice very low, she added: 'Take me upstairs.'

He nodded, lifting her up, holding her swollen body to him and turned to make the laborious ascent of the main staircase, her head on his shoulder, her dark hair close to the grey of his own. As he got to the landing, panting and out of breath, he saw Emmie come hurrying towards him from the direction of the rear stairs. He could hear the tears of fear in her voice as she cried out to him, 'Oh, sir – sir –!' She wore slippers, and a dressing-gown over her nightdress.

'Quick,' he gasped out, cutting off her words, 'open the bedroom door, Emmie. My wife has had an accident.' And then Emmie was moving past him, towards the door of the master bedroom.

As he entered the bedroom Emmie moved from turning up the flame of the oil lamp and stepped forward to turn back the bedclothes. Catherine's hair had come undone and as Savill laid her down it flowed like jet across the pillow and lay stark against her cheek, emphasizing her pallor. Turning to the maid he said sharply, 'Quick – get dressed and run to the stables and wake James. Tell him he must take the phaeton and go at once for Dr Kelsey.' Then, as the girl hovered for a moment in panic he rapped out, 'Now! Go now! Quickly!'

While the sound of Emmie's hurrying feet faded along the landing he tucked the covers more closely about Catherine's trembling body. 'I've sent Emmie to find James,' he said. 'He'll be off to fetch Dr Kelsey any second.' He tried to force a note of calm into his voice, but the fear overrode it and he suddenly found himself repeating over and over, 'Don't worry, don't worry, don't worry . . .' He was like the parrot in the conservatory. Sitting on the edge of the bed he leaned over her and with shaking fingers brushed the hair from her cheek. 'Don't worry,' he said again, 'it's going to be all right.'

It seemed an age before at last Emmie knocked and came back into the room. This time she had the other housemaid, Dora, hurriedly dressed, at her heels. 'James, sir,' Emmie said, gesturing out through the door, ''e wants to see you. 'E's waiting down in the 'all.'

'Christ!' John Savill shook his head in exasperation, then motioned towards his wife. 'Stay with her,' he said gruffly, and hurrying past the two girls he went out onto the landing to the top of the stairs. There he looked down to where the groom stood nervously in the hall below, gloved hands clenching his cap.

'What in God's name are you standing there for, man?' Savill said sharply. 'Get off and fetch Dr Kelsey!'

The younger man helplessly shook his head. 'Sir, the snow's so deep. I'll never even get the carriage out of the yard.'

'Then go without the carriage! Take the mare alone. But go!' Then when the groom still hesitated Savill cried out: 'God damn you, man, can't you understand me? Go! And tell Kelsey to get here as fast as he can.'

'Yes, sir.' The young man turned, thrust his cap back on his head and hurried away.

Returning to the bedroom it was obvious to John Savill that neither the seventeen-year-old Emmie, nor her fifteen-year-old companion Dora would be much help and he sent Dora scurrying away to fetch the cook, Florence, the one remaining servant who was resident in the house that night. She arrived some minutes later, in her dressing-gown, breathless and distressed. By this time the perspiration was beaded on Catherine's forehead and tendrils of hair clung to her skin. Periodically her back arched and she clutched at herself as the pains struck at her.

'My wife – I think she's having the child,' Savill said as the older woman followed Dora into the room. 'Dr Kelsey's been sent for but we can't depend on him getting here yet. If only Mrs Callow were here . . .' His thoughts were spinning. Turning to Florence who stood with her mouth open he said abruptly, 'We're going to have to do something till the doctor arrives. We've got to.'

It was soon established, however, that none of the three women before him knew much about childbirth. Something had to be done, though; it was clear to anyone just looking at Catherine's drawn, pain-touched features that things were terribly wrong. In his ears he could still hear the echo of her cry, the sound of her fall; in his mind's eye still see her as he had found her a moment later, lying at the foot of the stairs. He thrust the picture from him. His hands moved aimlessly for a moment and then he said quickly, 'The midwife – of course,' and turning to Emmie he rapped out: 'Emmie – quickly –

24

put your coat back on and go and fetch the midwife. Mrs Curfee, isn't it? She'll know what to do until the doctor gets here.'

Emmie shook her head. 'Sir, she've gone away. Gone to Bath for Christmas.'

'Are you sure?'

'Yes, sir. Mrs Farrar told me only yesterday when I went to get the washing.'

'Mrs Farrar . . .' He nodded. His mind was racing. Mrs Farrar – she was the wife of Oliver Farrar, one of the gardeners. She did the family laundry. Catherine had spoken of her on one or two occasions.

'Mrs Farrar – she has several children, I believe, hasn't she?' he said.

'Yes, sir. And they got a new baby, born just a week ago.'

'Go and fetch her,' he said, '– if she can come out. Bring her back here. Tell her it's a matter of life and death.'

The hall clock was striking eleven as Emmie, without her gloves but otherwise dressed and muffled against the cold, let herself out of the house. She could have saved seconds by using the front door and going down the drive but habit survived even such a crisis and she took the long way, leaving by the back door and going across the yard. The snow was driven in such a fury that for a moment it blinded her and took her breath away, but pressing forward she made her way to the narrow door next to the side gates where she drew back the bolt and let herself out. Holding high the lantern she started off along the narrow lane that ran beside the house. She could see no sign of any hoofprints of the mare ridden by James; already the snow had obliterated them.

At the end of the lane she came out onto Gorse Hill and set off down towards Coates Lane where the row of cottages stood. Reaching the first cottage she hurried around to the back where she saw to her relief that there was a light in the kitchen window. Moving quickly to the scullery door she rapped upon it, making her bare, cold knuckles sting. When no answer came she knocked harder, and then at last she heard the sound of Sarah's voice calling softly to her from inside:

'Yes? – who is it?'

'It's me – Emmie – from Mr Savill's.'

The door was opened a moment later and Sarah stood there holding a lighted candle and wearing an old coat over her nightdress. 'Emmie –' She peered at the girl, frowning. 'I was just on going to bed. What is it? What's the matter?' Without waiting for an answer she beckoned to her to enter. 'Quick, come on inside.' Hurriedly kicking the snow from her boots Emmie stepped into the scullery while behind her Sarah closed the door against the wild night. 'Dear God, Emmie,' Sarah whispered, 'what brings you out on a night like this? It's not fit for man nor beast.'

'Mr Savill's sent me,' Emmie cried out, and Sarah raised a hand urging her to speak quietly so as not to wake the children. Bringing her voice down to a whisper, Emmie blurted out the reason for her errand. 'Oh, you must come, Sarah!' she finished. 'Mrs Savill – she looks that bad, I tell you. And none of us knows what to do.'

Sarah didn't hesitate but simply said, 'Come into the warm,' and turned and led the way from the scullery into the darkened kitchen where the range was giving out the last of its heat. 'Wait here.' Moving to the hall door she opened it and hurried out of the room.

Upstairs in the bedroom she stood above the bed

where Ollie lay asleep, then leaning down she put her mouth close to his ear and softly called his name.

'Ollie . . . ?'

She waited for a second then called his name again and after a moment he opened his eyes and turned to her.

'What's the matter?' he said sleepily.

She held the candle a little higher. 'I've got to go out,' she said.

'*Go out?*' He frowned. 'What's the time?'

'Getting on for half-eleven.'

'In God's name, girl, what're you talking about – go out?'

'I must – now. Mrs Savill's had an accident and Mr Savill's sent for me to help till the doctor comes.' She put the candle-holder on the chair at the bedside and began to take off her nightdress. 'Just keep an eye on the children till I get back. I'll try not to be long.'

'The baby,' Ollie said, '– she'll wake and want to be fed.'

'No, I've just fed her. She'll be all right for a while yet. She'll sleep soundly if she's not disturbed.'

When Sarah had put on her dress and fastened the buttons she stood for a second looking down at the crib in which the baby slept peacefully, blonde hair gleaming dully in the light of the candle. Then, turning away, she moved out of the room and down to the kitchen where Emmie waited, warming her cold hands at the range. There Sarah put on her coat and pulled on her boots. Minutes later she and Emmie had left the house and started up the hill.

The way was difficult as they struggled through the deepening snow, their heads bent against the biting wind that struck their faces like shards of glass, rocked them in their tracks and seemed to enter through every fibre of their clothing. Like Emmie, Sarah was without gloves, and the hand she held to keep closed the collar of her coat was soon almost numb with cold. Then at last, after what seemed an age, they reached the side door of Hallowford House, entered and made their way across the yard. When they reached the rear of the house Emmie opened the back door, and Sarah, after kicking the snow from her boots, followed her inside. There Emmie took Sarah's coat, shook it free of snow and hung it up.

The scullery was the only part of the house Sarah had ever seen before and as she followed Emmie into the hall she couldn't help but be aware of the elegance of her surroundings. The soles of her old, worn boots sank deeply into the soft pile of the carpet and the thought went briefly through her mind that the whole house where Ollie and the children now lay sleeping would have fitted into this hall alone.

Seconds later she had reached the top of the stairs and was following Emmie across the landing to the door of a gaslit bedroom. There on the threshold she stopped as John Savill came towards her. He reached out to her and took her cold hands in his. 'Thank God you've come,' he whispered. Turning, he led her into the room. 'Help her,' he said, his voice breaking on a sob. 'Please – help her.'

Sarah moved to the bed and looked at the young woman as she lay on her back, wincing and biting her lip as waves of pain racked her body. 'I'll do whatever I can, sir,' she said.

On the landing outside the bedroom John Savill stood motionless as he waited, his face pale in the gaslight and looking older than his fifty years. Inside the room the fire was banked high, and the atmosphere was humid.

The sweat shone on Sarah's face as she bent over the young woman while beside her the elderly Florence leant over and gently dabbed at her mistress's forehead with a cool, damp cloth. At the same time Emmie and Dora, who had already brought in towels and steaming kettles of water, hovered, ready to help, waiting for instructions. The group of women was like a tableau; they had been like this, their positions hardly changing, for over an hour.

The long, long minutes continued to drag by, and then all at once from the bed the woman's breath began to come even faster and suddenly she gave a scream and arched her back. Sarah saw then that the top of the baby's head had begun to appear. 'It's here!' she whispered. Then, slowly, so slowly, the tiny baby made its way out into the world and at last lay limp and seemingly without life in Sarah's bloodstained hands.

'It's a girl . . .' Florence breathed while Sarah, after quickly clearing the baby's nose and mouth of the matter that had lodged there, lifted the deathly still form, holding it by the ankles in her left hand. Then with her right hand she gave it a small sharp slap on the buttocks. There was no reaction and she tried again. Still nothing; the small body just swung there like some lifeless doll. Sarah became suddenly aware of the stillness of the room, a stillness broken only by the sound of breathing and the occasional crackle from the fireplace. She was aware too of the women as they gazed, awed, and of the pale face of the child's mother as she anxiously looked on.

Raising her hand again Sarah struck the child once more, and this time she felt the tiny body convulse in her grasp as it sucked the room's warm air into its lungs. Then a moment later it began to squall and she cradled it in her arms and smiled at the woman on the bed. 'Yes,

29

you've got a daughter,' she said to the young woman. 'A beautiful daughter. And she's perfect.'

Turning back to the infant, she tied the cord, cut it, and with warm water washed the little body clean of the signs of its ordeal. It was such a tiny creature, but for all its lack of size it seemed healthy. Quickly, tenderly she wrapped it in a sheet and shawl and placed it in Florence's waiting arms.

Mrs Savill, watching intently, gave a sigh, a sound full of heartfelt relief and satisfaction and half-turned her head to glance towards the door, beyond which her husband waited for news. Sarah nodded to Emmie. 'Go and tell Mr Savill he's got a fine daughter. And tell him not to worry about Mrs Savill. We'll do all we can to make her comfortable till the doctor gets here.'

As Emmie hurried from the room Sarah turned her attention back to Mrs Savill. She looked so much better now, she thought. For a while there she had been very worried. She had the feeling now, though, that everything would be all right. And anyway, soon the doctor would be here and he would take charge of the situation.

In a bowl of warm water on the table at her side she wrung out a flannel cloth and then moved to Mrs Savill. 'How are you feeling, ma'am?' she asked.

The young woman gave a faint nod. 'I shall be all right now,' she murmured. Her face and body were bathed in sweat and she looked exhausted. Gently Sarah began to clean her, wiping away the blood, and as she did so Mrs Savill reached out a hand and laid it on her arm. 'Thank you for what you've done,' she said. There were tears in her eyes.

Sarah shook her head. 'You've no need to thank me, ma'am. I've done very little.'

For brief moments the two women faced one another,

sisters in their shared relief, and then Sarah turned back to the bowl to rinse and wring out the flannel again. As she did so she was aware of Emmie slipping quietly back into the room. The baby had stopped crying now and lay sleeping in Florence's arms. Glancing at the servants Sarah saw their faces reflecting her own feeling of growing calm. The worst was over now; they all felt it. Turning back to Mrs Savill a moment later she saw the same look of peace on the woman's face as she looked fondly towards the sleeping babe.

No one was prepared for what happened next. One moment Mrs Savill was smiling her happiness and the next moment her face had become suddenly distorted in agony while her mouth opened in an ear-piercing scream. At the same moment a great spurt of blood shot out from between her spread thighs, spraying Sarah's breast and shoulder crimson and spattering the chest of drawers behind her. Momentarily shocked into immobility by the sudden horror, Sarah watched open-mouthed as the woman screamed and clutched her hands to her lower belly, her eyes wide in fear. At the same time the blood kept coming, pumping out in a steady pulsing action that threatened in no time at all to drain the woman's body of every drop within it – already it was saturating the sheets. Mrs Savill, seeming to grow paler before Sarah's eyes, continued to cry out, while Dora and Emmie moaned and Florence turned away, the child, squalling again, clutched in her arms.

'*Oh, God, help us.*' The muttered words came from Sarah's drawn lips as she hovered, and then a moment later she was quickly stepping forward, and while the pulsing blood drenched her arm she made her left hand into a fist and thrust it up into the woman's body. There up inside she could feel the ruptured artery as it pumped hot against her knuckles. Then, quickly bringing her other hand to the outside of the woman's belly, over the same spot, she pressed down.

The bleeding, or most of it, was at once stemmed. Sarah felt she could have wept with relief. Raising her head she said sharply to Dora, 'Go and see if Dr Kelsey's coming.' Then, her voice breaking, she added, 'He's got to get here soon. He's *got* to.'

Dora, her face ashen, turned and dashed out of the room, and as Sarah remained bent awkwardly over the bed she was suddenly aware that Mrs Savill's cries had stopped and that she was lying still. 'Emmie!' she whispered, her heart lurching, 'is she all right? Listen to her heart,' and Emmie stepped to the bedside and leaned down, laying her head on the woman's chest. 'Yes,' she gasped. 'She's all right, Sarah. I can feel 'er 'eart beatin'. She've fainted.'

Her knees suddenly weak, Sarah supported herself momentarily against the side of the bed, and as she did so she became aware that John Savill had entered the room and was standing gazing in horror at the scene. In the middle of the blood-soaked bed his wife lay with her face chalk-white and her mouth loosely open. 'She's fainted, sir,' Sarah whispered. The next moment there came the sound of feet on the landing outside and then the doctor was in the room.

Robert Kelsey was a tall, lean man in his mid-thirties. He had shed his topcoat and hat in the hall below, but traces of snow still clung to his boots. Without saying a word he put down his bag and moved to the bed, as he did so taking in the position of Sarah's hands. Watching his face as he quickly assessed the situation Sarah didn't miss the little flash of fear that darkened his eyes. Coming to a stop he stood still for a brief moment then turned and looked into the stricken eyes of the other man. 'Please – Mr Savill,' he said, his voice brisk but gentle, '– I think it would be better if you waited outside.'

Savill nodded dully, stared down at his wife for a second then made his way from the room. Kelsey turned to Florence who was holding the crying child. 'Is the baby all right?'

'Oh, yes, she's fine, sir.'

'Good.' He nodded. 'Take her outside, will you? Give me some breathing space.' As Florence moved out of the room he turned to Dora and Emmie. 'You girls – stand aside – but be ready in case I need your help.'

While Dora and Emmie stepped back in the room he leaned over and laid a hand on Mrs Savill's forehead and then lifted one of her eyelids. After that he took her wrist and felt for her pulse, at the same time bending low and putting his head to her chest. 'She fainted,' Sarah said, 'but at least I managed to stop the bleeding. Will she – be all right?'

Kelsey raised his head. 'No,' he said wearily, and then gruffly added:

'She's dead.'

Chapter Three

When Kelsey had broken the news to John Savill he turned his attention to the baby. After making sure she was all right he left her in Dora's care and instructed Emmie to get the nursery ready. Emmie was up there now, making up the bed and the baby's crib and lighting the fire. Florence was busy in the kitchen, making tea and sandwiches. James, so soon after his return from fetching the doctor, had been sent off again – this time to the village to bring back Mrs Coolidge, the undertaker's wife.

Sarah had cleaned her dress as well as she was able for the present and now sat in the hall, waiting in case the doctor or Mr Savill should need her. At the moment they were in the bedroom. She had been sitting there for what seemed a long time, and then at last she heard the bedroom door open and a moment later the sound of Kelsey's voice.

'Mr Savill, there's nothing you can do. Why don't you get some rest.'

There was silence again, but then after a few seconds there came the sound of footsteps on the stairs and John Savill appeared, slowly making his way down. The doctor followed a few steps behind him. When Savill reached the hall he stood for a moment as if lost in a dream then moved off towards the drawing room. Sarah looked at him as he passed her by. His face was pale and drawn, his reddened eyes hollow and haunted. As he disappeared from sight the doctor moved across the hall. As he reached Sarah's side he looked in the direction the other man had taken. He shook his head. Then, turning to Sarah he said:

'Where's the baby now? I must go and see her.'

'Dora took her into the library, sir.' She got to her feet. 'There's a fire there.'

He nodded, gave Sarah a sad little smile of approval. 'Well, your work here is over. Thank you for all you've done.'

'Oh – sir, I just wish I could have done more.' She began to put on her coat.

'You did all anyone could do – and more than most.'

Sarah gave a helpless little shrug. 'Well . . .' she said, and then: 'I suppose I'd better get back home.'

Kelsey nodded. After a moment Sarah asked:

'Sir – what about the baby? Will she be all right?'

He paused. 'Poor little thing,' he said. 'Five weeks premature. It's not the best beginning for her. She's going to need the best care possible. Mr Savill will need to find a good nurse for her. But if she's well looked after she might just be all right.' There was no conviction in his voice. 'She'll need to be fed in a few hours,' he added. He gave a rueful smile. 'We can only hope she'll thrive on cow's milk or goat's milk or gruel. To give her the best chance she needs *mother's* milk, of course, but I'm afraid wet-nurses have rather gone out of fashion. In any case, how could we get one here now, in this weather?'

When she got back to the cottage Sarah found Blanche awake and hungry. Ollie was awake too and voiced his relief at her return. As she fed the baby she told Ollie of all that had happened at the house. Later when he and the baby were asleep she lay in bed, gazing into the dark. She kept thinking of the tiny, new-born Savill infant and of what the doctor had said.

Next morning, after Ollie had gone to work and the three older children had gone trudging through the falling snow to school, Sarah asked her neighbour, Esther Hewitt, to come in and stay with Agnes and the baby for an hour while she went out. A few minutes later she left the cottage and set off back up the hill to Hallowford House.

Florence opened the back door to Sarah's ring and Sarah kicked the snow from her boots and entered. As she did so she asked how the baby was.

Florence sighed as she closed the door. 'Poor little mite. Emmie spent the night with her in the nursery. Though I don't think either one of 'em got much sleep. The doctor's due back any time now. He said he'd call and see how the baby was getting on.'

'Would it be all right if I go up?' Sarah asked.

'Oh, I'm sure it would.'

Florence moved with her to the foot of the back stairs and directed her up to the nursery on the second floor. As Sarah set off up the stairs she soon realized that she could have found her way without the cook's directions, for the sound of the baby's crying came floating down to her. Reaching the nursery door she knocked and entered. Emmie was sitting by the fire with the crying baby in her arms. Seeing Sarah she said quickly,

'Oh, Sarah, thank the Lord you've come. I just don't know what to do.' She looked to be on the verge of tears.

Sarah took in the scene for another second and then proceeded to take off her coat. As she did so Emmie said over the sound of the baby's crying: 'Is there any sign of the doctor yet?'

'No, not yet.'

Emmie said despairingly, 'I wish he'd get 'ere. We just can't feed 'er properly. We did what the doctor said – Dora and me. We've tried ordinary milk and when that didn't work we tried 'er with thin gruel. But she won't 'ave none of it. And what she do get down 'er she brings right up again. And she just keeps crying all the time.'

'Does Mr Savill know?'

'Oh, yes, and he's that worried. But 'e's as much at a loss as we are. 'E don't know nothing about babies.'

Sarah laid her coat down across a chair and stepped forward, holding out her arms. 'Here – give her to me.'

With a heartfelt sigh of relief Emmie allowed Sarah to take the baby, and she watched as Sarah settled herself in the chair and unbuttoned her dress. In just seconds the baby's cries had ceased and it was sucking hungrily at her breast.

After a few moments there came the sound of footsteps on the landing. Then the door was opening and Dr Kelsey was standing there. He looked at the scene. The room was silent but for the sounds from the baby's sucking mouth. Kelsey smiled and gave Sarah a little nod. 'Thank you,' he said softly.

'She's got to be fed, hasn't she, Ollie?'

'Well, yes.' He frowned, shaking his head. 'But does it have to be you who does it?'

'There's no other wet-nurse around, and the baby needs the proper milk. She's got to have it to have any chance at all. What else can I do?'

Leaving the new baby fed and sleeping in the nursery, Sarah had spoken to the doctor who had then gone to see Mr Savill. When Kelsey had returned to speak to Sarah she had put on her coat and come out in search of Ollie in the gardens of the house. She had found him in one of the greenhouses. Now she stood facing him.

Outside beyond the glass the snowflakes swirled down out of the leaden sky. Inside, all around them in the oil-heated interior, the plants grew green and succulent, filling the warm air with their pungent scents.

'Did Mr Savill ask you?' Ollie said.

'No, it was Dr Kelsey. Just now – in the nursery. I just couldn't say no, Ollie, could I? Not after what's happened.' She shook her head. 'Mr Savill ask me? No – poor man, he's going round as if he's in a dream. I don't think it's struck him yet – the reality of it all.'

Ollie said nothing for a moment, then he said, 'That means you'll have to stay here at the house, doesn't it?'

'Well, yes – because of the night feeds. But after a while I won't be so tied to the place. Anyway, they might get another wet-nurse soon. Till then, though . . .' She reached out, laid her hand on his arm. 'Say it's all right, Ollie, please. Say it's all right.'

He said: 'So you'll have to bring Blanche up here along with you, won't you?'

'Oh, yes, of course. I can look after both of them here. It won't be difficult.'

'Maybe not – for you or the babies. But what about the rest of us? – Mary and the others – and me?'

'I know.' She nodded sympathetically. 'I'm sorry, Ollie, but – well, I'll try to make sure that you're not put out too much. When I get back home I'll see Esther and ask her to come in in the mornings and get you your breakfast, and see you off to work with your dinner. And I'll get her to feed the children and get them off to school too, and keep an eye on Artie and Agnes when I can't be there.' She pressed his hand. 'It won't be that bad, you'll see. I shall be able to get down home for short spells during the days and also when you're coming home in the evenings. So with a bit of luck I can have your supper ready for you and see to the children a bit too – be able to spend a little time with them before I come back up here for the babies' next feed.' Watching his face in the cold light she thought that he looked suddenly lost. 'Oh, Ollie, we'll work it out all right. But I've got to help the baby. I can't refuse, can I?' She gave him a little, pleading smile. 'Don't worry, you won't go hungry – neither will the children. And as I say, it won't be for too long a time.'

'Not for too long a time? It'll take months till the baby's weaned.'

'Well – yes. But if they get another wet-nurse –'

'They won't get another wet-nurse. You hardly ever hear of 'em nowadays. It's not like years ago when they were advertising in the papers all the time. And what makes you think Esther's going to be ready to come in and look after us while you're up here?'

'Well – she'll be paid for her trouble, of course.'

'Out of what? You won't even be able to do the washing now.'

'No, maybe I won't, but – listen, I talked all this over with Dr Kelsey and he's had a word with Mr Savill. Afterwards he said – Dr Kelsey – that I'll be paid well enough so that I can let Esther have something for her trouble. I don't doubt she'll be glad of it.'

'Ah, I daresay she will.'

'And Mr Savill will pay me well – so the doctor says. It might help us all, Ollie.'

'Yes, it might.' His tone was grudging. He picked up a trowel that lay on the bench beside him. 'Anyway, I've got to get back to work.'

'Yes – and I must get back home and see to Blanche and the others.' She looked up at him entreatingly. 'You don't mind too much, Ollie, do you? Please, say you don't.'

He shrugged. 'Doesn't matter much whether I mind

or don't mind. And seeing as Mr Savill pays my wages there's not a lot I could do about it if I *did*.'

When she reached the foot of the hill Sarah didn't go straight to the cottage but went next door to the home of the Hewitt family. Knocking on the scullery door she found Esther cleaning the floor. In the warm kitchen Blanche lay asleep in a nest of cushions and pillows while Arthur and Agnes quietly played nearby. Esther made tea. She was a small, round, agreeable woman with red cheeks and a broad smile, the wife of Jack Hewitt, a shepherd in John Savill's employ. They had one son, David, who was Ernest's age. An older son had died of scarlet fever some five years earlier. As the two women sat at the kitchen table Sarah, keeping her voice low, told Esther of what had transpired, ending by asking for her help in the situation. Esther readily agreed and by the time the teacups were empty the matter was settled between them.

Sarah then did her best to explain matters to Agnes and Arthur as far as they were able to understand. They protested at the news that she would be sleeping away from home for a while, but after assurances that she would be coming back to see them during the daytime they came nearer to accepting the situation. She left them then to go next door where she packed the things that she and Blanche would need. Then, returning to Esther's cottage she wrapped Blanche warmly against the cold and, with kisses and goodbyes to the children and promises to see them soon, set off back up the hill towards the house.

That night in the nursery at Hallowford House she lay in the bed beside the crib in which Blanche and the Savill baby lay sleeping. It wouldn't be long, she knew, before they were awake and demanding to be fed.

The pillows beneath her head were softer and fuller than those at the cottage and, like the sheets that were drawn up to her throat, were without darns.

As she lay there in the silence she thought of the children at home in their own beds, and of Ollie. It was an odd feeling lying there alone. It was the first time she and Ollie had slept apart since their marriage. She missed the warmth of his body beside her and the ever present feeling of the children being in the next room. Stranger than the strange bed and the strange room was her separation from everyone.

Chapter Four

With Arthur and Agnes beside her, Sarah walked up the hill towards Hallowford House.

August had gone out, and now they were in September. On the heathland over to her right the late-flowering heather was in full bloom while the bracken was turning sere, the hawthorn berries red, and the tall, pink blossoms of the rosebay willowherb had changed almost overnight into candles of cotton-wool-like seeds that drifted away and floated on the breeze like snow. Another summer was dying. Time passed so swiftly. At the end of the previous year Britain had gone to war, fighting the Boers in the Transvaal. It had ended quickly – with Britain's astonishing and humiliating defeat, a defeat soon followed by the granting to the Boers of 'complete self-government' – subject to several attached strings and Her Majesty's suzerainty.

To Sarah and many like her some of the events happening in the world outside Hallowford might have been fiction rather than fact. Information came with the newspapers, but the events rarely touched her. There was always so much to occupy her mind and her time.

As the trio drew closer to the top of the hill Agnes skipped on ahead. Sarah looked down at Arthur as he limped along at her side. Gently she squeezed his hand. As they exchanged smiles she listened for any warning in the sound of his breathing. He had had several bad attacks over the past few weeks and this was the first time in nearly a fortnight that he had been outside.

When they reached the brow of the hill Sarah paused to look up at the sky. The sun was bright but clouds were beginning to move in from the east and the breeze was growing fresh. She gave a sigh for the vanishing summer. Eight months had passed since the birth of Mr Savill's daughter and now here they were on the rim of autumn again. Most of the harvest was in, and over on the distant hills she could see areas of blackened earth, scorch marks left by the burning of the stubble. It made her think of the painting Ollie was working at back in the cottage scullery. The thought of Ollie brought a momentary frown of preoccupation to her brow but she thrust the thought aside and moved on. She was going to Hallowford House to bring Blanche home to the cottage.

In her desire for the baby to get to know her family – even if only to some limited degree – Sarah had done the same thing almost every Sunday since the spring, wheeling Blanche down to the cottage in the old perambulator and taking her back again later in the afternoon. This Sunday was different, though. Today Blanche was coming home for good.

Reaching the side gates of the house Sarah went across the yard and entered the house by the back door. There, leaving the children in the kitchen in the care of Florence she went upstairs to the second floor where she knocked on the nursery door. The nurse, Ellen Jessop, answered the knock at once. As Sarah entered the room a moment later she saw that the two infants were lying on cushions on the thick carpet, enclosed in a square pen.

Indicating the pen, Ellen said, 'Mr Savill had it delivered yesterday. There's no keeping them still for long these days.'

Sarah murmured her approval. Blanche had been crawling for three weeks now and the Savill baby, Marianne, had just begun. Looking at the neatly made pen, Sarah thought how very different it was from the makeshift fence they now erected on Sundays in one corner of the kitchen at home.

Sarah packed Blanche's few belongings in the old shopping bag she had brought and slipped the handles of the bag over her arm. As she did so she heard children's voices and moving to the window she looked down onto the stable yard where she saw Agnes and Arthur following James the groom as he carried feed to the horses. 'I'd better go,' she added, 'before they get up to mischief.'

She moved then to the pen in which Blanche lay contentedly on her stomach next to Marianne. Blanche's curls were very fair, while Marianne's straight hair was as dark as her mother's had been. Lifting Blanche up, Sarah settled her securely in the bend of her left arm and moved across the soft carpet. In the open doorway she stood and looked back. She didn't expect to see the nursery again.

Bidding the nurse goodbye, Sarah, with Blanche in her arms, left the nursery and closed the door behind her.

Downstairs she settled Blanche in the perambulator, said goodbye to Florence and let herself out. Arthur and Agnes came towards her as she emerged into the yard. As they reached her side she heard a voice call to her:

'Mrs Farrar . . .'

Turning her head she saw John Savill coming towards her. She waited. Since that night last year when Marianne had been born and Mrs Savill had died she had seen him only on those occasions when she had been in the nursery and he had come in to see Marianne.

Now, coming to a stop a couple of yards away, he wished her a good morning. She returned his greeting, smiling shyly at him. Then she watched as he lowered his glance to the two children who stood beside her, their large, solemn eyes gazing up at him.

'And who have we here?' he asked, smiling at them.

The children remaining silent Sarah released a hand from the perambulator and gently cupped the back of Arthur's head. 'Go on – say "How do you do" to Mr Savill – and tell him your name.'

Arthur shook his head, though, and pressed closer to Sarah's side. 'No?' She looked from him to Agnes on her left. 'What about you, Agnes? Aren't you going to say "Good morning" to Mr Savill?'

Agnes lowered her eyes and moved nearer to her mother. Sarah shook her head and said with a little shrug, 'We're not going to get much out of them, sir. I'm afraid they're shy.'

'So it seems.' John Savill eyed them kindly for a moment or two and then dipped a hand into his trousers pocket, brought out some coins, sorted through them and held out two pennies. 'Here – one for you . . .' he held it out to Agnes, '– Agnes, isn't it?'

Agnes nodded and, shyly thanking him, took the coin. Then Savill turned to Arthur. 'And what's your name, young man?'

'Arthur.' Arthur whispered the word, and a second coin was held out.

Arthur thanked him, clutching the penny. Then as he and his sister gazed at one another, eyes wide with wonder at their unexpected gifts, John Savill raised his eyes to Sarah again.

'You're taking Blanche home, are you?'

'Yes, sir. Home to stay, this time.'

He nodded. 'I'm sure you'll be glad to have her back

with the family.' After a pause he added, 'But you must bring her back here sometimes – to see Marianne.'

'Yes, sir, I will. Thank you.' Sarah smiled at the gesture, although she knew that now that Blanche and Marianne were parted they would remain so.

Another little silence, then Mr Savill said:

'I've never really thanked you for all you did that night . . .'

'Oh, sir –' Sarah protested, 'there's no need . . .' And it was true; he had no need to put his gratitude into words; he had shown it in so many different ways since that night. Not only had he paid Sarah for her services as wet-nurse, he had also instructed the cook to provide the Farrars with numerous items from the Hallowford House pantry from time to time. In addition to this he had informed his rent-collecting agent that rent from the Farrars was no longer required.

'You did a great deal.' He raised his head and looked up towards the nursery window. 'Without your help I might have been left with nothing. Instead –' he lowered his glance again and smiled, warmly, '– I have my child, my daughter. Thanks to you. And each time I look at her I think how easily she too could have been – lost.'

Sarah said nothing. He stepped closer and bent to peer down at the sleeping baby in the perambulator. 'Your little girl – Blanche – she's a beautiful child.'

'Thank you, sir.'

He straightened and reached into his pocket again. A moment later he was reaching out. 'Here . . .' Taking Sarah's free hand he put a coin into her palm. 'Something for Blanche too.' He smiled. 'Just a token – of my grati- tude. After all, she played her own special part, too.' Then, before Sarah could thank him he was wishing her a good morning once more, smiling a goodbye to Agnes and Arthur and, turning, was moving away across the yard.

When he was out of sight Sarah opened her palm and saw a gold sovereign there.

'What did Blanche get, Mam?' Arthur asked. 'Did she get a penny too?'

'– Yes.' Sarah nodded as she lied. 'Yes, she got a penny too.' She dropped the coin into her pocket and, with the two children beside her, set off for the gate.

Outside, beyond the shelter of the high wall that encircled the stable yard, the strengthening wind whipped at her skirt. There was a chill in the air now, too, and she bent to Arthur and pulled the collar of his coat more closely about his throat. 'Come on, we're going home now.'

Home. The word echoed in her mind and the sudden thought came to her that the cottage was home for herself and Ollie, and Ernest, Arthur, Mary and Agnes, but it wasn't for Blanche. Home for Blanche was the nursery at Hallowford House. That was the only real home she had ever known. Oh, yes, there had been the Sunday visits to the cottage, but Sarah couldn't pretend that such brief episodes could have counted for much in the baby's experience of life. And, she reflected, just as Blanche really knew only the nursery of Hallowford House, so, too, she was truly only familiar with those faces she saw around her there – Sarah herself, the nurse, the nursemaid, Lizzie, and the other baby, Marianne. And even Mr Savill to a degree. Compared to Blanche's familiarity with those faces, her father and brothers and sisters must be almost like strangers to her.

Strange, Sarah thought, the changes brought about by the birth of Marianne and the death of Mrs Savill. They had affected her own life and that of Ollie, and Blanche and the other children. The lives of all of them had been altered to some degree or other.

At the very beginning Sarah had spent most of her

time at the house, feeding the two infants, being nurse to them and sleeping beside them in the nursery. Then with the arrival of the nurse proper she had moved into the little bedroom next door. Her brief visits to the cottage had been made between the babies' feeds. She had looked forward to those times. Ollie and the children had missed her presence and resented her absences – particularly in the evenings when they were accustomed to be all together.

But gradually things had grown easier. After a period when the changing pattern of the infants' feeding gave her more time she had been able to get down to the cottage more frequently, there to clean and cook for Ollie and the children and generally spend more time with them. Also she was able to resume her old task of doing the Savills' laundry, doing it in the scullery of Hallowford House.

And now things were returning to normal. Both babies were completely weaned now. Even the laundry had been done back at the cottage over these past couple of weeks.

Earlier, though, the situation had brought problems. Not with the children – she didn't think they had been harmed by her temporary absences – but with Ollie. There was no doubt that at the start it had prolonged and strengthened the estrangement that had developed between herself and him.

There had been no sexual closeness between herself and Ollie for some time while she was carrying Blanche, and afterwards, following the baby's birth, when things might have begun to grow easier between them, she had left to spend her nights with the two infants, only seeing Ollie for brief periods in the evening and at weekends. And then at those times there had always been work of one kind or another waiting for her, added to which the children had always been around. As a consequence she and Ollie had rarely found themselves alone for more than a few minutes at a time. So there had been no real opportunity for them to regain anything of their former closeness, and they had remained apart, like polite strangers, as if each of them was afraid to make the first move.

The situation had continued throughout the winter, until at last, in May, there had come the time when the two babes could go through the night without the need for food and Sarah was free to move back to the cottage each night and sleep in her own bed once more.

She could recall so well that first evening. Leaving Blanche at the house she had returned to the cottage just before eight, in time to see the children into bed and hear their prayers. Then, somewhat self-consciously she had gone back downstairs into the kitchen where Ollie was sitting sketching. He had looked up as she entered, and put his sketchbook aside, and she had realized suddenly that his hair was neatly combed, that he was freshly shaven and that he had put on a clean shirt.

She made tea for the two of them, and they sat drinking it, facing one another beside the range, talking of this and that. The conversation was awkward, though, both of them aware that they would be spending that night together. They spoke of the children's school work, of Ollie's painting and his work on the land, of Mr Savill and the folk up at the house. But no mention was made of what was uppermost in their minds, and Sarah began to fear that they had gone beyond some point of no return, beyond the point where they could relax again in each other's company, and be close. And perhaps they would continue like this, she said to herself – except that as time went on they would grow even further apart. Then, moments after the thought had come to her mind, the desultory conversation dried up altogether and they were left sitting there, avoiding one another's eyes and unable to think of anything else to say.

Sarah felt she could weep. They had been so close once, and here they were like strangers meeting at the market. She stared at the range for a minute or two until, unable to sit there any longer, she got up, put down her cup and went out into the hall. There she stood in the silence, purposeless. After a few moments she opened the door to the little parlour and went in, closing the door behind her. Moving to the upright piano she lit the oil lamp on its top, sat down on the stool and lifted the lid.

The piano was very old. It had been given to Sarah's father in lieu of payment for some long outstanding debt when she was a child. She struck a chord. The instrument had been out of tune for so long.

She began to play, softly, Mendelssohn's 'On Wings of Song', a piece she had learned as a child. After a while she began to sing, her light contralto almost whispering in the little room:

> . . . Bear thee to regions enchanted,
> Where joy fills the rapturous day . . .

She became aware that the door had opened and closed again and that Ollie had come into the room. Self-consciously she broke off the song and turned to him with an awkward little smile.

'Don't stop,' he said, moving to stand beside the piano.

'Oh . . .' She shook her head. 'We're both so out of tune these days – the piano and me.'

'No, don't say that.'

They remained there, she sitting on the piano stool, he standing, looking down at her. She dropped her eyes beneath his gaze.

'Sing "Comin' Thro the Rye",' he said.

It was a favourite song of his. Soon after they were married he had taken her to a concert at the old Trowbridge Town Hall where a soprano had sung the song. Ollie had never heard it before and, much taken with it, had tried to recall snatches of the words and the melody as they walked home. When they had got back to the cottage Sarah had sat down at the piano and, to his surprise and delight, had sung the song for him. 'You know it,' he had said, laughing. 'How? How do you know it?' 'From my father, of course.' 'You didn't tell me you knew it. You've never sung it before.' She had shrugged, smiling up at him. 'Well, I've sung it now.'

Now she said, avoiding his eyes, 'Oh – that old thing. No – I can't . . .'

'Yes, you can. Please . . .'

'Oh – well – it's so late, and the children . . .'

'They'll sleep through anything, you know that.'

Making no reply she sat in silence for some moments, and then her fingers began to move softly over the keys. After a few chords she began to sing.

> Gin a body meet a body, comin' thro the rye,
> Gin a body kiss a body, need a body cry.

She sang the song quite slowly, investing the words with the brogue she had learned from her Scots father.

> Ilka lassie has her laddie,
> Nane they say ha'e I.
> Yet a' the lads they smile at me
> When comin' thro the rye.

She sang the song through to the end while Ollie stood in silence, unmoving. When the last notes had

51

died away she stood up and put out her hand to close the lid of the piano. At the same moment he stepped towards her, his hand reaching out and closing around her wrist. She didn't move for a second, then, turning, she looked into his face and saw that his eyes were tight shut. Still with his eyes closed he murmured her name, the diminutive that he had been accustomed to use in the past.

'Sare . . .'

She remained where she was, held in the position of slightly bending. And then he opened his eyes and placed his other hand on her wrist, as if to prevent her escape. He didn't meet her glance. Giving a little shake of his head, he said:

'Sare . . . Don't – don't keep away from me – please.'

'Oh, Ollie . . .' She breathed the words, feeling her heart lurch.

'I can't bear it – for us to be like this.'

It was what she had wanted to hear. 'No, Ollie, no. I don't want it either.'

He looked into her eyes. 'I know what I was like sometimes in the past, but –'

She broke in quickly: 'Don't talk about it. They're gone, those times.' She thought of the hard words she had said to him that night after she'd told him she was expecting the baby. 'Let's forget it, can't we?' she said.

'Yes. Yes.' He drew her hand to his mouth and kissed it, then gently drew her to him and held her close. She was so aware of the feel of his arms about her. It had been so long since they had touched like this. He kissed her mouth, gently at first, but then more insistently, and she returned the kiss with gladness and relief. After a few moments he held her back from him a little and gazed at her. He gave a little nod, as if of confirmation.

'Ah, Sare,' he said, 'you're a grand, beautiful woman.'

He drew her to him again and his large hand came up, touched her breast and closed over it. He stroked and kneaded her soft flesh for a while, then his hands came higher and he began to undo the buttons of her bodice. She helped him, aware of the sound of his breathing and of her own. When she was naked before him he knelt and clasped her around the waist, his face pressed to her warm body. She felt one hand release her and then come moving between her thighs, higher, higher, to where she waited for his touch. She gasped, tipping back her head and closing her eyes.

'Ollie . . .'

After a while he pulled away, and urged her onto her back. Moments later she felt the hard shape of him entering her eager body. She gave herself up to him, wrapping her arms around him, holding him prisoner as he moved inside her, filling her burning warmth with his own.

When it was over they lay together on the rug, at peace. Ollie's arm lay across her while in her ear the sound of his breathing grew quiet again. After a time she turned her head, gazed on his closed eyes, and gently kissed him on the mouth.

As she entered the lane at the foot of the hill she saw Esther Hewitt moving away from the pump with a pail of water. Esther, turning, seeing her, came to a stop at the Farrars' gate and waited.

'So,' she said as Sarah reached her side, 'our Blanche is comin' home, is she?' In her voice was a faint note of resignation which Sarah didn't miss. While Sarah had been away from the cottage Esther had been so glad of the little extra money she had been able to earn by helping out in the Farrar household. Blanche's return to the cottage spelled the end of that extra income.

'Yes, coming home,' Sarah answered, and Esther nodded. 'Well, it'll be nice for you to be all together again.'

They stayed chatting for another minute or two and then Esther took up her pail while Sarah opened the gate and went around to the back of the cottage. There Arthur and Agnes left her to go and join Mary who was playing in the garden and she called after them not to dirty their clothes. As she moved to the scullery door a moment later she thought of Esther's words: *It'll be nice for you to be all together again.* Would Ollie think the same? she wondered.

Pushing open the scullery door she went inside, pulled the perambulator after her and set it near the wall. Ollie, as she had left him, was sitting at his easel. He turned and smiled at her. She returned the smile and then bent to the baby. Blanche was lying quietly for the moment. She would leave her there for now while she got the dinner.

'Is Ernest still out in the fields?' she asked Ollie as she took off her shawl and moved towards him.

'Yes.' He nodded briefly then turned and gave his attention back to the painting before him. The canvas depicted a number of men burning the stubble after the harvest had been gathered in. The scene was one of quiet drama. In a lowering, stormy sky clouds streamed out like grey, shot-riddled banners above a field in which the stubble burned in long lines of brilliant flame. The men, tension evident in every line of their muscular bodies, concentrated on containing the fire, while the smoke swirled about them before being carried up towards the clouds above.

Sarah stood at his shoulder for some moments, looking at the canvas, then she said, 'Ollie, it's magnificent.'

He turned to her, pleased. 'You think so?'

'Oh, yes. *Yes*.'

'It's not quite finished yet,' he said. 'But I'm hoping to get it finished today – if I get the time before the light goes.'

Since the spring Ollie had become much calmer, far more at peace. And it wasn't only because the two of them had grown closer again, Sarah knew. It was also partly because of his painting. It was a similar pattern every year. During the short days of the winter the hours he could spend at his easel were limited, and there were always so many other things, more important things, to be done. With the lengthening days, though, he was able to find more opportunity to work at his painting, and any odd hour that he could squeeze in between his other responsibilities found him either at his easel or working on sketches in preparation for the painting that would follow. At such times, doing what he loved best, so much of his frustration seemed to vanish. He was clearly so much happier.

The picture now before him he had begun several weeks ago, working at it every Sunday, his one day off in the week. Today he had been sitting at his easel since eight o'clock that morning. When he was painting, Sarah kept the children out of his way as much as she could – easy on fine days but more difficult when they were confined to the house. This afternoon, she decided, after the children had got back from Sunday school, she would take them out for a walk if the weather stayed dry. That would give Ollie a little more time on his own.

Into her contentment a thought nagged faintly. She hadn't told him that Blanche was home to *stay*. The thought stayed with her; Ollie's relationship with the baby was a constant source of quiet melancholy in the back of her mind. She felt that he had still never truly accepted the child, and that he was relieved that she spent most of the time up at the house. He rarely showed any interest in her, or referred to her when she was absent. It was almost as if during the time when she was away she ceased to exist for him. It was true that on those Sundays when Sarah brought Blanche back to spend some hours with the family he made token gestures to show a kind of affection, but, Sarah felt, they were only gestures; nothing more.

As she entered the kitchen to begin preparing dinner she suddenly thought of her meeting with Mr Savill in the stable yard. From the shelf above the range she took down an old broken teapot. It held a brooch that had belonged to her grandmother, and her mother's wedding ring. Taking the sovereign from her pocket she placed it along with the other treasures.

When Ernest returned from his excursion in the fields they had dinner. Blanche slept peacefully afterwards and while Ollie returned to his easel Sarah got the three older children ready for Sunday school. Then, with Agnes and Blanche going along for the air, they set off for the church hall.

Ollie was still working when she returned, and while Agnes sat down to play with her doll she took Blanche – becoming restless back in the house – and laid her on a blanket in one corner of the room. To prevent her from straying she arranged a couple of chairs and a piece of wood to form a makeshift barrier.

Agnes grew tired after a while and Sarah put her upstairs in bed to sleep for a while. Then, with Blanche still crawling about behind the chair-fence, Sarah washed the dishes, tidied the room and put kettles of water on the range. When the water was hot she undressed herself and, standing in a wide tin bowl, washed herself from top to toe. When she was dry she went upstairs and put on her second-best dress – the one for Sundays – undid her hair, brushed it and re-plaited it and then coiled the heavy plait around the crown of her head and pinned it in place.

As she went back down the stairs a few minutes later she heard the sounds of the children returning from Sunday school. Looking out at the sky, she saw that dark clouds had gathered and rain was beginning to fall. The thought of any walk was out of the question now.

After tea Ollie went back to his painting while the children went to play quietly in the front parlour. When Blanche began to grow fretful Sarah took her up into her arms. The baby wouldn't settle, though, and she was crying loudly when Ernest came in from the parlour to get one of his books. After listening to the baby's crying for a moment or two he said, 'She always becomes a misery at this time of a Sunday, doesn't she? She wants to go back up to the house. She doesn't like it here.'

Sarah was about to make some angry retort when Ollie appeared, paintbrush in hand. Looking down at the baby he said: 'Isn't it time you took her back to the house?'

Sarah looked at him over the head of the crying child. 'She's not going back anymore, Ollie. Marianne's weaned now, and there's no longer any need for us to go there.'

'Oh – I see . . .' He nodded, then gave a shrug and turned back into the scullery.

Half an hour later, when Sarah sat alone with the baby still crying in her arms Ollie came back into the kitchen and sat down.

'Have you finished?' Sarah asked.

He shook his head. 'No, not yet.'

'You taking a rest from it for a while . . . ?'

'No. I reckon I'll stop now.'

'I thought you wanted to finish it today. The light's still good enough, isn't it?' The rain had stopped now, the clouds had passed over and the sky was bright again.

'Oh, yes, there's nothing wrong with the light.'

There was a little silence, broken only by the fretful sounds of the child, then Sarah said, frowning, 'It's Blanche, isn't it?' She shook her head distractedly. 'Oh, Ollie, I'm sorry. But she'll be all right soon. I just don't know why she keeps crying the way she does.'

He gave a little smile. 'No? Perhaps it's true what Ernest said – perhaps she'd rather be up at the house.'

As they sat there Blanche's crying began to grow louder and more piercing, and after a while Ollie got up and went into the front parlour to join the children. Sarah remained sitting there with the crying baby in her arms.

Chapter Five

Marianne lay in her crib while Dr Kelsey bent over her. After examining the infant he straightened and turned to John Savill.

'Well, she has no fever. I can't see any obvious sign that she's sickening for anything.'

Savill's expression remained one of concern. He had arrived home after spending several days in London on business to find his daughter fretful, listless, and refusing to eat, and her nurse, Ellen Jessop, worried and at a loss to account for the situation. Now, with the nurse being questioned by the doctor, it emerged that Marianne's condition had developed over the past three or four days.

'But what's *wrong* with her?' John Savill said. He added, 'As you know, Mrs Farrar has been here wet-nursing her. She took her own baby away just the other day. Could it be that Marianne was weaned too early? Perhaps she wasn't ready.'

'No.' Kelsey shook his head. 'I'm sure it's not that.' He was silent, then: 'You say Mrs Farrar only recently took her baby home?'

'Yes,' Savill answered, to which Ellen added,

'A week ago exactly, sir.'

After a moment's thought Kelsey said, 'When I've called at the house in the past they've always been together – Marianne and the Farrar child. Did they sleep together too?'

'Oh, yes, sir,' the nurse answered, '– here in the same crib. Miss Marianne always slept better like that.'

Kelsey nodded. Turning to Savill he said, 'Then I should think that's your answer. I can't be sure, of course, but it seems to me that your daughter misses the other infant. She's pining for her.'

'Pining?'

'Yes, if Marianne has spent almost every minute of her life with the other baby then she's bound to miss her enormously. I've seen the same thing in the past, with twins – when one of them dies.'

Savill frowned. 'And – and what happens?'

'To the pining child? – the survivor? Oh, usually it gets over it all right – though I've known it to take quite a time.'

'– You say the child *usually* gets over it. What does that mean?'

'Well, the pining in itself isn't dangerous. It's just that its effects can sometimes – cause problems.'

'In what way?'

Kelsey shrugged. 'Well, according to the nurse the baby's not eating properly – which commonly happens when a child pines. And of course at this very tender age a child is delicate and needs to be properly nourished. If not, it starts losing weight and then, of course, becomes far more vulnerable to any illness that might be lying in wait.'

Seeing the deepening concern in John Savill's face the doctor quickly added, 'Look, I don't think you need to start worrying. The Farrar baby has only just left. Marianne will probably get over it in a few more days.'

'And if she doesn't?'

'Then you'd do well to try to get the other child back for a while. It's like weaning a baby from the breast. Sometimes a child needs to be weaned, slowly, from the companionship of another infant.' The doctor fastened his bag. 'Look,' he said, turning back to Savill, 'I suggest you wait a day or two and see whether Marianne begins to get over it. If she doesn't then perhaps you can get the Farrar child back to stay with her for a time. If you do that then I warrant that your daughter will pick up again in no time.'

A few minutes after Kelsey had gone from the house Savill was downstairs and reaching for his coat. 'I shan't be long,' he said to Mrs Callow, the housekeeper, 'I'm just going down the hill to see Mrs Farrar.' He wasn't prepared to wait to see whether Marianne began to grow accustomed to the Farrar child's absence. Where Marianne's health was at stake he wasn't prepared to take any chances.

Sarah Farrar was drying her hands as she opened the front door to John Savill's knock and it was clear to him that he had caught her in the middle of her work. After he had wished her a good afternoon he said apologetically,

'Mrs Farrar, I'm sorry to disturb you. I wanted to talk to you for a minute – but it looks as if I've chosen the wrong time. I'll come back when you're not so busy.'

She smiled ruefully. 'Wait for then, sir, and you'll be waiting a very long time.' As she spoke her small daughter – he remembered that her name was Agnes – came to her side and stood looking up at him with wide hazel eyes, curious to see him again. The woman spoke again.

'Please, sir – come in.'

Urging the child to stand aside, she stood back from the door and John Savill thanked her and stepped into the little hall. Then she opened a door to a room on the left and gestured in. 'Please, sir – do go in and sit down.'

As Savill entered the room she turned to the child and said softly:

'Go into the kitchen and try to keep Blanche amused for a few minutes, Agnes, will you? There's a good girl. Mr Savill wants to talk to me.'

The child protested at once, shaking her head: 'Oh, must I?' and quickly the woman lifted a finger to her lips. 'Not so loud,' she whispered. 'You'll disturb your brother. He was awake all night and he needs his sleep.'

As the child turned and moved into the kitchen the woman followed, and John Savill heard her say, 'Now make sure you keep an eye on her. And don't let her get up to any mischief.'

He knew a sense of reluctance as he stood there, feeling that he was intruding on the woman's privacy. He looked around him. He had passed by the Coates Lane cottages countless times but he had rarely been inside any of them. Now, standing in the Farrars' little front room he realized how very small the buildings were. And in the tiny, cramped interior the Farrars were raising a family of five children. His eyes wandered about the small room, taking in its cleanness, its neatness, the pictures around the walls. He noticed to his surprise that there was a piano. In the silence the solemn ticking of the old grandfather clock sounded unusually loud. He saw that the time was almost half-past two. The woman's husband, Oliver Farrar, would be working in the gardens up at the house. He wondered briefly what life was like living with Farrar. He saw him from time to time going about his duties, and according to the head gardener he was a good worker, conscientious and efficient. Savill recalled how he had given him a rise in wages a while back, but that had been less for the man's efficiency than for the inconvenience he had suffered in having his wife up at the house for so long.

Before that, soon after Mrs Farrar had gone to stay up at the house, Savill had made a point of seeking Farrar out, going into the garden where he was working and making known his appreciation of what he and his wife were doing. Farrar had politely replied that they were glad to do what they could. In the brief conversation that followed Savill had found the man to be intelligent and articulate, and his voice surprisingly pleasant. When Savill had left him some ten minutes later, however, it was with the feeling that he didn't know him much better than he had before. The one thought that had stuck in Savill's mind was that in spite of the man's efficiency at his job he nevertheless seemed somehow a stranger to it, as if in a way some part of his mind was on other things.

The woman came back into the room, closed the door behind her and, a little shyly, asked him to sit. Thanking her, he took a seat on an old sofa, holding his hat between his hands. She looked nervous and a little worried, he thought, as she sat in the chair opposite. Then, before he could speak she said quickly:

'You wanted to see me, sir. It's – is it about Oliver, sir?'

'About your husband?' He shook his head. 'Oh, no, not at all.'

He suddenly realized that he had never really looked at her before. He had only ever seen what she stood for in his mind – a strong, intelligent woman, the woman who had so willingly come out in the snow that night to try to help his wife – and to be his daughter's saviour. And somehow, because of her strength of will at that terrible time, because of the spirit she had shown and all that she had done since then he had always seemed to see her as a tall woman. And he could see now that he was wrong. She was quite small. It was partly her

63

carriage that gave the impression of height, he realized; the way she held herself, proudly erect as she faced him, as if her spirit alone might be shield enough against misfortune.

The thought came into his mind that at one time she must have been beautiful. Now, though, much of that beauty had been worn away, leaving just a shadow of what had once been there; worn away by child-bearing, hard work, care and worry. Even so, enough remained to show what she must have looked like as a girl. Her hair, a rich chestnut colour and plaited about the crown of her head, still looked thick and luxuriant, and her hazel eyes, in spite of the faint lines that now lay beneath them, were wide and clear. Her features were well-shaped and finely boned, though her hands were broadened and coarsened with hard work.

He smiled gravely at her.

'Mrs Farrar,' he said, 'I've come to see you about your little daughter.'

'Blanche . . . ?' Her frown deepened.

'Yes – Blanche.' He hesitated for a moment and then began to tell her of Marianne's pining and of what Kelsey had said. When he came to a stop the woman said nothing, waiting for him to continue. After a moment he went on:

'What I'm asking is – is whether you would allow Blanche to come back up to the house for a while – to live there again – just to be with Marianne . . .'

'I see.' She paused. 'For how long did you have in mind, sir?'

He shook his head. 'Well, I can't say exactly – but I'd hope it wouldn't be for too long. As the time goes by I'd think we could begin to keep the two babies apart more and more, so eventually we can separate them completely – without Marianne fretting.' He paused. 'I need hardly add that I'll pay you something for your – temporary loss.'

She moved her hands in a little gesture of protest. 'Oh, sir, I wouldn't want to be paid for such a thing. And you've already done so much – what with the rent and Ollie's rise in pay.'

He shrugged. 'Well – anyway, you'd have the consolation of knowing that Blanche would be well looked after. She'd have the best of everything, I can assure you. And, naturally, I'd take full responsibility for all her expenses – her food, clothing, any doctor's bills – everything.' He waited while the woman sat in silence. Then he said gently,

'Well, Mrs Farrar – what do you think?'

After a moment she said, 'Yes, Mr Savill. We can do what you want, I'm sure.'

'You think your husband will agree?'

She gave a slow nod, then she said, 'I don't need to ask Oliver. I know what his answer will be. It'll be the same as mine.' She smiled, an uncertain smile, then added, as if forcing a positive note into her voice, 'Yes, sir, if you need Blanche up at the house for a time then you must have her.'

A few minutes later when all the arrangements had been made he prepared to go. Standing before her he reached out and took her hand. 'Thank you,' he said. 'Thank you, so much.'

As he withdrew his hand his eyes were caught again by the pictures around the walls, and suddenly he was aware of a significance that had previously missed him. 'It's just struck me,' he said, '– your pictures – they're original oils – they're not prints.' Then immediately he regretted his remark, afraid that it might have been taken to imply that people in the Farrars' situation shouldn't have original paintings. The woman merely smiled, though, and said, 'Oh, yes, sir, they're all original.'

He shook his head in a little gesture of wonder. 'It's like a picture gallery,' he said. He paused. 'I'm no expert, but they look to me to be of very fine quality.' He noticed then that not all the pictures were framed – and that the frames that had been used were mostly very old and shabby or else had obviously been cheaply and simply made.

He took a step closer to the painting on the wall immediately to his right. It showed a tranquil scene of a shepherd and a flock of sheep on a hillside. He gazed at it for long moments then moved on a step to look at the next picture. It depicted a harvest scene, the workers, men, women and children, gathering up the stooks and placing them in rows. The scene was drenched in sunlight. Savill could almost feel the sticky, almost airless, heat of the day. Who could have done such work, he wondered – and then his eye caught the signature, written small in the lower righthand corner: *Oliver Farrar* – and beside it: *1879*. He turned to the woman.

'Your husband,' he said wonderingly, and shook his head. 'They're done by your husband. I had no idea he had such talent. They're beautiful.'

At his words he saw pride in her eyes. She smiled. 'Thank you, sir. I'll tell him what you said when he comes in. He'll be pleased.'

He turned and gave his attention to the paintings again, looking at them one by one as he moved slowly around the small room. There were nine of them altogether, landscapes, still-lifes, portraits, and studies of figures in domestic scenes.

'When does he find the time to do them?' he asked.

'At the weekends – on his time off on Sundays. Just about any spare minute he can find.'

'Does he sell them?'

She raised her eyebrows in surprise. 'Sell them, sir? How would he do that?'

'Well – I should think he'd be able to. And perhaps for quite considerable sums.'

'– Really, sir?'

He nodded. 'I would think so. I don't know. I'm no expert, but I should think he could take them somewhere. To the city. To Bath or somewhere – or even up to London. There must be somebody there who would be interested.'

She smiled. 'It needs time and money to go traipsing off like that, sir.' Then she added: 'Though it doesn't stop him – not selling them, I mean. I should think whatever happened he'd still go on painting. It's all he thinks about.'

Savill thought again of the time he had gone to talk to Oliver Farrar in the garden, and suddenly, now, he could understand him better. If a man had such a thing as this inside him – this talent eating away at him with no real outlet for it, it wasn't to be wondered at if he gave the air of having things on his mind apart from gardening.

After a moment Savill prepared to leave and the woman opened the door. He thanked her, said he hoped he hadn't taken up too much of her time.

She shook her head. 'Oh, no, sir. There's a while yet before my other children get back from school.'

'D'you have to go and meet them?'

'No – Mrs Hewitt, my neighbour, will do that when she meets her own boy.'

'I see.' He hesitated on the threshold of the room. 'Did I understand from what you said earlier that one of your children is in bed?'

She nodded and glanced upwards. 'Yes, my little boy

Arthur. You met him the other day when I was up at the house.'

'Yes, I remember . . . Is he ill?'

She nodded. 'He has asthma. He's had it since he was a baby and – well, I'm afraid he's not – not as strong as the others.'

'I see. He's been having some bad attacks lately, has he?'

'Yes, he has.'

'Have you had the doctor to him?'

'Yes. But he's never able to do much.'

'Which doctor do you have?'

'Dr Harmon.'

'I don't want to interfere,' Savill said gently.

'It's all right, sir.'

Her voice sounded overly bright. It didn't convince him, though. She might be strong and proud, he thought, but where her children were concerned she was very vulnerable.

When John Savill had gone Sarah got the baby ready, left her in the makeshift pen and went upstairs to the children's bedroom. There Arthur lay in the half-light that came in through the thin curtains. As she bent over the bed he smiled up at her.

'Hello, Artie,' she said softly. 'Did I wake you?'

'No, I was awake.'

'How do you feel now?'

'All right.' He nodded his head on the pillow.

In spite of his assurance she could hear the slight wheezing in his breath that signalled the obstruction there. He had been awake for so many hours in the night, and to prevent the other children being kept awake too, Sarah had brought him downstairs until the worst of the attack had passed. Now, gently, she laid her hand on his forehead, leaned down and kissed him on the cheek.

'I've got to go out for a few minutes when Ernest and Mary come in from school,' she said. 'But Mrs Hewitt will be coming in from next door while I'm gone. I'll try not to be long. And when I get back I'll make you something nice for your tea.' As she straightened she heard the sound of children's voices from below. 'There's Ernest and Mary now,' she said. She moved back to the door. 'You're sure you'll be all right?'

'Yes.'

Downstairs she found Ernest and Mary insisting, as usual, that they were hungry, and she quickly made them sandwiches of bread and jam while she told them that she had to go up to Hallowford House with Blanche.

'What for?' Ernest asked.

'Because she's going back there to stay for a little while.'

'Why?'

'Because,' she said, 'Mr Savill's little girl is missing her, and wants her back again.'

At her words she saw a look of disbelief appear on his face. To his nine-year-old wisdom such a notion was incredible – the idea that anyone could actually *want* the company of a crying baby was beyond him.

Mary asked then if she could go as well and quickly Sarah washed her face and made sure she was presentable. As she combed Mary's hair she said to Ernest, 'Mrs Hewitt is coming in to mind Artie for a while.' She urged him towards the door. 'Go and see her now and tell her we're ready to leave, will you?'

A minute later Ernest was back with Esther following, and Sarah took up the baby from the rug and put her into the perambulator. Then, with Mary and Agnes beside her, she set off up the hill.

On reaching Hallowford House they crossed the yard to the back door. There in the little room just inside, Sarah left the perambulator and lifted Blanche, now crying, up into her arms. Then, leaving Mary and Agnes in the kitchen with Florence, she went upstairs to the nursery.

Ellen Jessop was expecting her. When Sarah went into the room she found Marianne lying on cushions within the pen near the window. Sarah placed Blanche, still crying, in Ellen's arms. Marianne, disturbed by Blanche's noise, began to cry. 'Do you want some help with them?' Sarah asked.

'No, thank you. I'll manage all right.' Ellen guarded her task jealously, and now Blanche as well as Marianne was her responsibility. 'It's time Miss Marianne had her sleep,' she said. 'I'll put Blanche in the crib with her. They'll be all right once I get them settled together.'

Sarah nodded and moved back to the door. In the doorway she said, 'I'll go on downstairs, but if you don't mind I'll look in again before I go – just to see that Blanche is all right.'

Blanche was still making her irritable little crying sound as Sarah went from the room.

In the kitchen Sarah found Agnes and Mary sitting at the scrubbed, wide table eating slices of fruit cake and drinking glasses of milk. Agnes looked up at her with the milk painting white her upper lip and Sarah grinned at her. For the next fifteen minutes Sarah remained in the kitchen talking to Florence then left to go back upstairs.

There was silence this time as she stopped outside the nursery door, and she hesitated before tapping lightly upon it. A few seconds later the door was opened and Ellen stood there with a warning finger up to her lips. She stood aside then and very softly Sarah entered.

There was no sound now from Blanche or Marianne. Whispering, Ellen gestured towards the crib. 'Go and look at them.'

Sarah moved silently across the room to the crib and looked down at the two infants. They were sleeping soundly, Marianne's head close to Blanche's.

A minute later Sarah whispered goodbye to Ellen and let herself out. When she had closed the door behind her she stood for some moments on the landing. No sound broke the quiet.

How would Ollie feel when he learned that Blanche was back at Hallowford House? she wondered. But, as she had known the answer to that question when Mr Savill had come to see her, so she knew the answer now. Ollie would probably be relieved to have Blanche away from the cottage again for a while. Since her return home there was no doubt that her crying and fretfulness had disturbed him and got in the way of his work.

Sarah turned her head, listening. Still no sound came from behind the nursery door. For the time being Blanche was content and had ceased to have any need of her. But there, she told herself as she moved towards the stairs, Blanche had rarely seemed to belong to her since the moment of her birth.

When she got downstairs she called Mary and Agnes to her and they said their goodbyes to Florence and left the house. In a basket over her arm Sarah carried several items that Florence had given her. There was the remainder of the fruit cake the children had been eating and a piece of ham and a large slice of game pie; also, and especially for Arthur, a little vanilla-flavoured junket in a basin.

As the time wore on towards Ollie's return from work Sarah became more and more certain that she should have discussed with him the matter of Blanche's return to the house before taking any action. It was too late now, though, and she could only wonder how he would react to the news. Then, when he walked into the cottage just after six she could see at once that he already knew. Of course, she realized, he had learned of it through the servants. Moments later her belief was confirmed.

'I understand that Blanche is back with Mr Savill's daughter,' he said.

Sarah heard quiet anger in his tone, and quickly began to tell him of Mr Savill's visit and of her decision. When she had finished he frowned, his mouth grimly set.

'You should've waited,' he said.

'Yes, I know I should have, Ollie. I'm sorry. But I thought it was the right thing to do.' She paused. 'Would you have had me do differently?'

'That's not the point. You should have waited.'

He fell silent then, and remained so as, later, she served him his supper. She put the piece of game pie on his plate, saying:

'Florence up at the house gave it to me. And there's a lovely piece of ham for you to take with you tomorrow.'

'Oh, ah.' He nodded, sullen and indifferent. When he had finished eating he sat back in his chair looking ahead of him. Sarah, pausing in the act of clearing the table, said to him placatingly, 'Oh, come on, Ollie.' And then: 'Listen, why don't you light the lamp and do some sketching for a while . . . ?'

He shook his head. 'No,' he said shortly, 'I don't think I'll bother with any drawin' tonight.' He got up from his chair. 'If you don't mind I think I'll go down the lane for a little while.'

He left the cottage then, bound for the Wheatsheaf, and soon afterwards Sarah sat down to her mending while the children gathered around the kitchen table. Arthur had come downstairs earlier and now in the pool of light from the central lamp he sat cutting out pictures from a magazine. Beside him Ernest sat reading, while Agnes was trying to sew and Mary was drawing a picture. Just after eight o'clock Sarah told them to get ready for bed. As they prepared to go upstairs she looked at the picture Mary had been making.

'It's for Papa,' Mary said.

Coloured with cheap chalks that Sarah had got for her from the market, the picture showed a man sitting before an easel, painting.

'It's Papa – doing his painting.' Anxiously Mary watched Sarah's expression. 'D'you think he'll like it?'

'Oh, yes, indeed,' Sarah said enthusiastically. 'It's lovely, it truly is.' Mary's artistic talent was developing so rapidly, she said to herself. Inherited from Ollie, of course; and yet another strand to draw the two of them even closer to one another.

'Mam, can I stay up till he comes in?' Mary said. 'I want to give it to him tonight.'

'No, I'm sorry, dear. You wait and give it to him tomorrow.'

The children went upstairs then and Sarah heard their prayers and saw them into their beds. Coming back downstairs she waited for Ollie's return. When he wasn't back by ten she prepared to go to bed herself and, leaving a candle burning on the kitchen table, went upstairs. She went first into the children's room where, holding high the candle, she looked down at them as they slept. Arthur, she saw, was sleeping peacefully, and the sound of his breathing was clearer than it had been all day.

As she straightened and moved towards the door she heard a voice whisper:

'Mam . . .'

73

Turning she saw Mary raising herself in the bed. 'Lie down,' she said softly, stepping back to the bedside. 'You'll wake the others. And you should be asleep.'

'Is Papa back yet?'

'No, not yet. He'll be in soon, though, don't worry.' She reached out and brushed the thick blonde hair (so like Ollie's) back from the child's forehead. 'Now, come on – lie down.'

Frowning, Mary laid her head back on the pillow. 'I wanted to give him his present,' she said.

'I told you – you'll have to give it to him in the morning. Now, go to sleep.' Bending over her, Sarah kissed her on the forehead. 'Goodnight, my love.'

'Goodnight.'

Sarah crept out of the room, then went into the room across the landing and climbed into bed.

It was almost an hour later when she heard from downstairs the closing of the scullery door. She hadn't been asleep. She could never sleep knowing that Ollie was out somewhere. After a while she heard his footsteps on the stairs, and a moment later he came into the bedroom. By the moonlight that shone in he undressed, but then instead of getting into bed beside her he sat down on its edge. She could smell, faintly, the scent of ale.

He was just sitting there, not moving. In the pale moonlight she could make out his profile as he sat hunched over, staring into space.

After a while she took her hand from beneath the covers and laid it on his bare knee. He started very slightly and her heart went out to him. In so many ways, she felt, he was as much a child as any of the children. She saw him at times as transparent as spring water and in other respects as difficult to read as some foreign tongue.

'Ollie,' she murmured, '– come to bed.'

He said nothing.

'Mary's been asking for you,' she whispered. 'She made you a present. A little picture. A picture of you.'

At her words he gave a bitter little smile and his head sank lower. Sarah pulled herself up in the bed and lit the candle. In the stronger light she could see anguish in his face.

'What is it, Ollie?' she said. 'Please – tell me.'

He said nothing for some time, then raising his head slightly he looked over at the empty crib.

'We should bring her back,' he said.

'– Bring her back? You mean – Blanche?'

'Yes.' He turned to face her. 'You let her go back partly for my sake, didn't you?'

She shook her head. 'No, Ollie. I told you what Mr Savill said.'

'Yes, but I can also guess what was in your mind.' He paused. 'I've been thinking about it all evening. And I realized tonight what I'd done. Turning my back on her like that.'

'No, Ollie, no.' Leaning closer, she put her arm across his shoulder. 'Don't say that.'

'That's why I was angry,' he said. 'It was – guilt, I suppose. I wanted too much out of life, that's the trouble. That's why I took against the baby as I did – because of what I wanted.'

There was a little silence. Sarah felt a tightening in her throat. Ollie went on:

'I used to wonder what was to become of me. And of course the answer was – nothing. But I couldn't stop wanting, hoping. I couldn't see anything but that – some wonderful future.'

'And why not,' she said stoutly. 'You're a very talented painter. Mr Savill said so when he was here today.'

He turned to her at this. 'He said that?'

'Yes, he did. He looked at all your pictures. He thought they were beautiful.'

He thought about this for a moment or two and then turned away again. She gazed at him. She had never seen him like this before. He had never before got this low; somehow he had always retained a spark of hope – enough to keep him going. After a moment she said, 'You're a talented man, Ollie, and you must keep on with your painting.'

He sat in silence for a while, and then got into bed. Sarah lay back on the pillow. He didn't lie down beside her immediately, though, but sat up. 'We'll have her back, shall we?' he said at last, '– Blanche.'

'But – why, Ollie?'

'I – I think we should.'

'No, Ollie – leave her where she is for the time being. She's doing some good there – and apart from that she's better off.'

'You think so?'

'Oh, yes. How can you doubt it? Staying up at the house – having the best of everything. Of course she's better off.'

He gave a little sigh. 'I hope you're right.'

He blew out the candle then and lay down, and Sarah moulded her body to his back, arms around him, nestling into his warmth. After a time they slept.

Chapter Six

One fine Sunday morning in that October of 1881, Sarah, as she often did after washing the breakfast dishes, took the children out into the fields for a walk. She had suggested to Ollie that he accompany them, but instead he had gone up to Hallowford House to work. Lately he had taken to giving up a good deal of his spare time in order to work up at the house for extra money or to do odd jobs for the neighbours, often giving up his painting time in order to do so. She had not asked him why, though she was curious.

Now, nearing the cottage again towards the end of their walk, Sarah observed the children. How fast they were growing. Agnes, three years old that summer, had just started school, while Arthur had had his sixth birthday only a few days ago. Ernest would be ten years old in a fortnight and in the new year would be leaving school to start work.

She looked at Ernest. A tall boy, he was high-spirited – and clever, too – like Mary having a quick mind. Though while Mary had an artistic, creative bent, Ernest was more analytical. He was fascinated by the whys and wherefores of everything in the countryside about him, and was never happier than when observing some particular animal or bird or conducting some simple little experiment with plant life.

Sarah recalled how a few days previously she had heard him telling Arthur that one day he would be a doctor. And hearing the enthusiasm in his voice she had realized with a sinking heart how trapped they all were by their situation. There would never be the money to send him to any doctor's college or anything like that. There wouldn't even be enough to apprentice him to a carpenter or glazier or any other tradesman.

From Ernest, Sarah's glance moved on to Mary who skipped along at Agnes's side. Eight years old, she spent every spare moment she could find with her stubs of pencils and chalks, drawing on any odd scrap of paper she could find. She was the only one of the children who seemed to have inherited Ollie's talent, and as a result Ollie gave her as much help and encouragement as he could.

The reason for Ollie's doing extra work up at Hallowford House and for the neighbours was revealed one November night a few weeks later. The children were in bed and Ollie had just come in from doing over-time up at the house. As he sat down, obviously tired from his labours, Sarah asked him what was the purpose behind it all – for certainly none of the extra money was coming her way for the management of the house-hold. At her question he looked at her in silence for a moment then said:

'It's for Mary.'

'Mary?' She frowned, not understanding.

'For God's sake, Sarah,' he said, 'haven't you seen how the girl can draw?'

'Well, yes, but –'

'She's got such talent,' he broke in. '*Such talent.* It's far out of the ordinary, believe me. If you think *I* have ability – well, Mary's got so much more.'

Sarah had never really thought that much about Mary's artistic ability, seeing it only as a developing interest that took up more and more of her time. That

Ollie had been viewing it with such seriousness took her by surprise.

'But what's Mary's drawing got to do with your working overtime,' she said, 'and doing all these odd jobs?'

'– I've got hopes for her.'

'– Hopes?'

He nodded. 'Yes. I never really had a chance to do anything with my ability – such as it is – but it's going to be different for her. I want her to have the chance to make use of it. That's why I'm doing the extra work. And any extra cash I can get I'm putting on the side. Then, when I've got enough I shall go into Trowbridge and open an account in the post office. I'll add to it regularly. And the money's to stay there, no matter what else might happen. The money's for her. Then perhaps when she's older there'll be enough to enable her to have some training – to study with the right people. She's going to have the chances that I never had, I'm determined on that. And if she doesn't it won't be for want of effort on my part.'

'But Ollie – how can a girl make a career in painting? It's hard enough for a man; but for a woman . . .'

'It can happen.' There was no doubt in his voice. 'If she's got the talent then it can happen. When the time comes I shall make the necessary inquiries and find out the best way to go about things.'

Sarah sat silent for a few moments, then she said, 'Ollie – you've got other children too. What about *their* chances in life? Ernest – he's a clever boy. He deserves an opportunity. And Agnes and Artie. They might not be quite as bright as the others – it's early to tell – but they deserve their chances too, don't they?'

'Of course. And if it's possible they shall have them – Ernest and the others. You tell me where we can find the money and we'll send them all off to university or wherever.' He reached across the table and laid his hand over hers. 'Sarah, it's impossible, you know that. My God, it's going to take every effort to try to make sure that Mary gets some sort of a start – and even then I can't guarantee that I'll be successful. But if we *are* able to scrape together enough to give just *one* of them a chance then shouldn't we do that? Isn't it sensible to give one of them a chance rather than deny them all? If we deny Mary any opportunity that comes along it's not going to help the others, is it?'

And nothing, Sarah found, would move him from his new obsession – for that was what in her eyes it became. He scrimped and saved in every possible way, and every spare penny and farthing he could find went into the old, cracked, earthenware jar that he kept on the chest in the bedroom. It was Mary's money.

While Ollie worked on the gardens up at the house and did other odd jobs that came his way Sarah continued with her laundry work, at the same time making regular visits to see Blanche. She never stayed very long on such occasions, though, feeling somehow that she was intruding in the running of the nursery. During the time she was there, however, she played with Blanche and talked to her. At other times she took her out in the perambulator – which was what she preferred – either taking her down to the cottage or around the lanes. At those times she felt that the child was hers again.

Early one Sunday afternoon in mid-December there was a knock at the front door. In the kitchen Sarah and Ollie looked at one another. They weren't expecting visitors, and particularly anyone who would use the front door. Sarah, after answering the knock, returned to tell Ollie that Mr Savill was there to see him.

'Mr Savill?' Ollie looked puzzled.

'Yes, I've shown him into the front room.'

'What does he want? Did he say?'

'No.' She paused. 'Ollie, is there something wrong? Something you haven't told me about?'

He shook his head. 'No, nothing.'

'Are you sure?'

'Of course I'm sure.'

While the children gazed at him, Ollie went into the scullery and washed his face. Then, after running a comb through his hair, he went into the front parlour.

Conscious of the room's coldness as he went in, he saw that Mr Savill, wearing his coat, was standing before one of the paintings. At Ollie's entrance Savill turned and smiled at him. Ollie automatically raised his hand to his forelock. 'Will you sit down, sir?' he said.

Savill shook his head. 'No, thank you, Farrar. I shan't be long. I hope you don't mind my calling . . .'

'No, sir, not at all.'

Turning, Savill gestured to the paintings on the walls. 'I've come to see you about your pictures,' he said.

'My pictures . . . ?' Ollie gazed at him.

'Yes – I saw them back in September – when I called on your wife. I thought I'd like to see them again if you don't mind.'

'No, sir. Of course not.'

Savill cast his eyes around the room. 'Have you any others?' he asked.

'Yes, sir. There're some more upstairs. Would you like to see them?'

'If it wouldn't be any trouble . . .'

'Not at all. I'll get Ernest, my eldest boy, to give me a hand – if you don't mind waiting a few minutes . . .'

Back in the kitchen he hurriedly whispered to Sarah the purpose of Mr Savill's visit and then called Ernest

81

to him. Together then they began to bring some of the remaining paintings from upstairs. After some minutes a number of other pictures had been added to those already in the front room – the additions being set to lean against the furniture and the lower walls. That done, and with his job completed, Ernest backed out of the room, leaving the gentleman and his father alone.

Ollie stood nervously watching while Savill surveyed the pictures. The older man looked at them for what seemed a very long time, in the end returning to one of the paintings that Ollie had brought downstairs. 'This is a very fine picture,' Savill said.

The canvas showed the scene of a river bank in early summer. Much of the view was in a shadow, cast by the leaves of weeping willows and other foliage that hung over the water. A warm, bright sun was evident by its brilliance on the higher leaves and the way it dappled the water and the grass in the foreground. In the cool shade sat two children, a boy and a girl. The figure of the boy as he sat holding his fishing rod was deeply shadowed, while the top of the girl's blonde hair was caught by the sunlight as it poured through breaks in the foliage above.

John Savill stood before the painting, studying it intently. 'It's really beautiful,' he said. He turned to Ollie. 'It *is* all your own work . . . ?'

'Oh, yes, sir,' Ollie said. 'Indeed it is.'

Savill smiled. 'I'm sure it is. It's just that – it's hard to accept somehow.' He studied Ollie. 'Where is the talent?' he asked. 'Is it in your hands? In your head?'

Ollie shrugged. 'I reckon it's in my head, sir. I used to feel that if I lost the use of my hands I'd just have to use my feet.'

Savill smiled again, gave a little nod and turned back to the painting.

'Is it for sale?' he asked.

Ollie stared at him. 'For sale, sir?'

'Yes. Is it?'

'– Well, yes, sir, I suppose it is . . .'

'Good. How much are you asking for it?'

Another silence. Ollie shook his head. 'I don't know, sir. I've never given it any thought . . .'

'Well – would you like to give it some thought? And then when you've made your decision let me know.'

Ollie excitedly gave Sarah the news as soon as John Savill had left the cottage, but for all their discussion he couldn't settle on a price to ask for the painting.

He had still come to no decision the next day when, at work on one of the herbaceous borders in the front garden of Hallowford House, he heard Mr Savill call his name. Turning he saw Savill coming towards him from the gates astride a chestnut mare. As Ollie straightened and touched his cap Savill brought the animal to a halt and said, 'Well, Farrar, did you decide how much you want for the painting?'

Ollie shook his head. 'No, sir . . .'

'What's the problem then?'

Ollie helplessly spread his hands. 'Sir, I've never sold a painting properly before. I just don't know how much to ask for it.'

Savill was silent for a moment then he said, 'Listen, I want to give you a fair price for the picture. What do you say to two guineas?'

Ollie was briefly tongue-tied. He would never have dreamed of asking so much. 'Yes, sir,' he said, 'I reckon that'd be fine.'

'You're sure?'

'Yes, sir.'

'Good, then perhaps you'd be good enough to bring

the picture up to the house this evening. I'll pay you then. Come as soon as you've finished work, will you?'

Ollie hurried back to the cottage after work that evening and while he washed, shaved and changed, Sarah carefully wrapped the painting in paper and a blanket – which latter she gave instructions should be brought back again. Then Ollie, with Ernest equally neat and tidy at his side and the wrapped picture beneath his arm, set off up the hill.

Going through the yard to the back of the house they were asked in and shown into the library to wait. When the maid had gone Ollie carefully placed the painting on the carpet, leaning it against the corner of an easy chair. Turning to Ernest he found the boy looking back at him with wide eyes, silently communicating with his glance the wonder of their surroundings. Ollie was equally overawed. Neither had ever before been inside a house of such grandness, and they gazed around them, trying to take it all in.

On the highly polished floor lay a wide carpet with an Eastern-looking design. There was a large, polished desk with a leather top on which pens, pencils, papers and ledgers were neatly placed, while on either side of the huge fireplace in which crackled a log fire was an elegant bureau bearing fine porcelain ornaments. And the books. Ernest had never seen so many books and he stood and stared at them. The shelves all around the room were full of them, row upon row upon row.

They were still looking about them when the door opened and John Savill entered. He smiled at Ernest and then said to Ollie:

'Good, you've brought the picture.'

'Yes, sir.' Ollie took up the painting, unwrapped it and placed it on the carpet again. For some moments John Savill just stood there looking at it – until Ollie began to think that perhaps he was changing his mind and wasn't going to take it after all. But then Savill, giving a smile and a nod of satisfaction, brought a purse from his pocket and took from it some coins.

'Two guineas, I believe was the price . . .'

'– Yes, sir, thank you . . .'

'Thank *you*, Farrar.' John Savill placed the coins in Ollie's palm. 'The painting is to be a Christmas gift,' he added. He looked back to the picture. 'Yes,' he said, 'and I'm sure I've made an excellent choice.'

As they neared the foot of the hill on their way back Ernest pointed over to the high chalk cliff that rose up at the back of the cottages. A few villagers had gathered there.

'Something's happened, Papa,' Ernest said and, leaving Ollie's side, he ran to where the little group stood together at the foot of the cliff. Known as the 'Cut', that part of the cliff had the appearance of having been formed by some giant spoon that had scooped out the chalk of the cliff's side and base.

Joining Ernest a minute later, Ollie saw the object of the onlookers' gaze. In the hollow beneath the towering bank five black-faced Suffolk sheep lay dead, the blood from their mouths running out and starkly staining the chalk on which their broken bodies lay. Arkham, another of the tenants from the lane cottages, came to Ollie's side and told him that a stray dog had run amok among Savill's sheep and driven five of them over the precipitous drop.

The sight of the dead sheep lying there was like a sudden cloud across Ollie's particular sun. He touched Ernest's shoulder. 'Come on,' he said, turning from the sight, '– let's go on home.'

Entering the lane moments later he thrust the memory of the incident from him. In his pocket the sovereigns and the shillings were real and hard.

Chapter Seven

That Christmas was one of the best the Farrars had ever known. Not only did the extra money make a great difference as regards the things they could buy, but the happening itself had brought to Ollie a feeling of well-being that he had not known for a long time.

A week later, on Monday, January 2nd, Ernest started work as assistant stockman for Harker, a Hallowford farmer. His hours were long, and he could have earned more by working in one of the Trowbridge factories, but he preferred the open air.

The following day Sarah was in the kitchen ironing when there came a knock at the front door. Quickly she straightened her apron and smoothed her hair. On opening the door she found herself facing a tall, elderly man in a well-cut coat. He took off his hat to her and, after ascertaining that she was Mrs Oliver Farrar, handed her a card and introduced himself. His name, he said, was James Heritage, and he wished to enquire as to when he might be able to see Mr Farrar. When Sarah said that Ollie was out at work and wouldn't be back till just after six o'clock the man said he would call again just after six-thirty if it was convenient. Yes, she said, of course. As he was about to turn away she asked: 'Could you tell me, sir, what you want to see my husband about . . . ?'

'Yes, certainly,' he smiled. 'Perhaps you'd be good enough to tell him that I own an art gallery in Bath, and that recently I've seen one of his paintings, and that I was most impressed with what I saw. *Most* impressed.' He paused then added, 'And who knows – if Mr Farrar is agreeable we might be able to do some business together.'

He went away then and Sarah was left to try and calm her growing excitement and try to get on with her work.

A little while before Ollie was due back she stopped work, changed out of her old clothes and put on her best dress. A few minutes later when he came in he looked her up and down and asked, 'What's the matter? Why are you all dressed up?'

'Quick, Ollie,' she said, 'you must get changed too. We've got a visitor coming in a few minutes.' Giving him Heritage's card she told him of the man's visit. 'He's coming to talk to you about your paintings,' she added.

Ollie stood there gazing at her in surprise. She shook her head impatiently.

'Don't just stand there,' she said. 'Hurry up and get ready. He'll be here any minute.'

With a bewildered nod he quickly began to take off his jacket. As he did so Sarah added: 'I've made a fire in the front room, and lit the lamps – so you can show him your pictures in there.'

It was just after seven when Heritage reappeared and Ollie, looking fresh and spruce, asked him in and showed him into the parlour. In the kitchen Sarah kept Ollie's dinner warm while the children were ordered to be on their best behaviour. They, awed by the presence in the house of the elegant stranger, willingly complied.

It was almost an hour later when Sarah heard the visitor depart, and as his carriage moved away down the lane she went into the front room where Ollie stood in silence, gazing down into the fire that crackled in the small fireplace. She stopped before him and stood waiting. When at last he turned to her she saw a strange, excited look on his face, an expression not quite like any she had ever seen there before. His eyes shining, he suddenly gave a little laugh.

'Oh, my God, Sare,' he said. Reaching out to her he put his hands on her shoulders, drew her to him and held her close. He laughed again, the sound muffled against her hair.

'What happened?' she said, then quickly added, 'I told you to offer him some tea. Did you forget?'

'What? Tea? No, I didn't forget. He didn't want any. He just wanted to talk. And he didn't have much time; he had to get off again.'

'Tell me what he had to say.' She drew back so that she could look into his face. 'Does he want to buy a painting?'

He shook his head. 'No – not that.'

'Then what?'

He hesitated, teasing her, then said:

'He wants to take all my pictures – or most of them – and put them on show in his picture gallery in Bath. And they'll be for sale, and people will come to the gallery to buy them. He'll take a commission on any that he sells – and the rest of the money will come to us.' He drew her close again. 'Oh, Sare,' he breathed, 'things could change for us.' He spoke with wonder in his voice. 'Things could really change.'

The exhibition of Ollie's paintings would open in early April, Heritage had said. Ollie had agreed that he would supply him with the paintings in the cottage – there were just under thirty – and that if he was able he would do one or two new ones in addition. To pay for any canvases and paints Ollie might need Heritage advanced him a guinea which, he said, he would deduct from any monies finally due from the sales of the works. In the same way, Heritage undertook to frame all the paintings, the cost of which would also be deducted later, when the exhibition was over. The prices of the various canvases he and Ollie would decide between them. 'But what if I don't sell any paintings?' Ollie asked him. The thought of being left with an enormous bill for the framing and the painting materials was daunting. 'Don't worry,' Heritage told him, 'that's a risk *I'll* take. All you have to do is supply the pictures. If you don't sell anything you won't owe me a farthing. But don't worry –' he reassuringly pressed Ollie's shoulder, 'I'm certain you'll sell a good number. If I didn't think so I wouldn't be taking the chance.'

Ollie asked him then how he had come to seek him out.

'Oh, I thought I'd mentioned it,' Heritage said. 'I saw a painting of yours – of children sitting beside a pond. It was in the house of a friend of mine in Bath – Mr Harold Savill. It was given to him by his brother – who's your employer, I believe.'

'– Yes – at Hallowford House.'

Heritage nodded. 'As soon as I saw it I made it my business to find out about the artist.'

The next morning at Hallowford House as Ollie left the kitchen after delivering vegetables he saw Mr Savill moving across the yard. Quickening his steps he went after him.

'Mr Savill – sir . . .'

The older man came to a stop and turned to him. 'Yes, Farrar. What is it?'

'Excuse me, sir, but – I just wanted to thank you.'

'Thank me? For what?'

A little hesitantly, Ollie told him of the visit from Mr Heritage, and of the coming exhibition of his work.

'Well,' Savill said, 'that's good news. That's excellent news.' He shook his head. 'But I don't see why you have to thank me for any part in it. My brother wrote and asked me about you and where you could be found – and I told him. But anyway I'm delighted that something has come out of it. You're a talented man, Farrar, and it's always a good thing to see talent recognized.' He smiled as he added, 'And I wish you luck.'

Following the meeting with Heritage Ollie spent every spare minute on his painting while Sarah did her best to ensure that he was not disturbed by the children or anyone or anything else.

In the period from Heritage's visit to near the end of February Ollie completed one further picture. A few days after it was finished Heritage came with an assistant and packed up all the paintings and took them away.

When the two men had driven out of sight Sarah stood looking around her. How strange the room looked without Ollie's pictures on the walls.

On the following Sunday morning Ollie put a fresh canvas on his easel. He was going to paint Mary's portrait, he said. And this one, he added, would not be for sale. He got to work soon after, with Mary sitting before him, her chair and his easel over to one side, well away from the clean laundry and the table on which Sarah was working.

From where Sarah stood near the window she could see Agnes and Arthur as they played in the garden. There had been heavy snow for much of January but of late the weather had greatly improved and the two children, well wrapped up, had been encouraged to get outside and take advantage of the day's mildness. Ernest was nowhere to be seen; he was off somewhere with Davie Hewitt. This was his first day off since starting work earlier in the month and he was making the most of his time off.

As she worked Sarah reflected on the differences that were touching their lives. For one thing she and Ollie had grown closer. And it was hope that had done it – hope that life could change for them, could change for the better.

The previous night in bed Ollie had lain with his arm around her. After a while he had whispered into the dark, 'Sare – are you awake?'

'Yes . . .'

'I was thinking – what it will be like for us . . .'

'With your paintings in the gallery, you mean?'

'Yes. I keep thinking about it. You know, if things go well – if I sell my pictures – well, it could be the beginning for us – for all of us.'

'Yes, I know.'

'A real beginning – of a better life . . .'

He began then to speak of the money that could be realized if the exhibition of his work proved successful, and the figures he spoke of were beyond anything she had ever dreamed of. 'And another thing,' he said, '– we'll get Blanche back as soon as we can. I know it's nice for Mr Savill's daughter, having her up there at the house – but after all, she belongs here with us.'

Ollie's voice went on, murmuring soft in the silence of the room. If all went well and the exhibition was successful, he said, he should be able to leave his work on the gardens – and in time they could move to a bigger place, where he could spend his time just painting. Listening to him, Sarah realized that she didn't dare think about it too much. Somehow even with the promise writ large the possibilities were too remote, too fragile.

'I'm afraid, Ollie,' she said after a while. 'It's all too – too wonderful to be real . . . I feel it can't really be happening to us.'

'Well, it *is* happening to us,' he said. 'It *is*.'

After a while the confidence in his voice began to settle a warm contentment within her. But it was more a contentment for the present – not for what was promised for the future. Perhaps this is the best time of all, she said to herself, turning, burrowing gently into his warmth – this time of hope, this time when hope is everything, this time when everything is before us and everything is possible.

Then, holding onto the contentment and settling into the comfort of Ollie's body, she had slept.

Now, today, standing ironing at the scrubbed-wood table, that contentment was still on her.

She worked silently, listening to the sounds of Arthur and Agnes from the garden and the occasional words that passed between Ollie and the child: 'Mary, please don't keep moving your head, there's a good girl.' Then Mary's reply: 'All right, Papa.' And then after a moment, Mary's voice again: 'Will it soon be finished, Papa?' 'No, of course not. Be patient.'

There was no impatience or irritability in Ollie's voice, though, and likewise there was none in Mary's. She regarded it as no hardship to sit still for him. Silently observing the two of them, Sarah reflected that Mary would do just about anything for her father.

The canvas Ollie was working on was relatively small compared to some of those Heritage had taken for the gallery. He was working left-side-on to the window, getting the best of the north light over his shoulder onto the surface of the canvas. Mary sat about four feet away against the wall, in the old grandfather chair which had been propped up on a makeshift dais of old boxes.

Although it was winter, she wore her best summer dress. Made by Sarah it was of blue linen with a lace collar taken from an old dress of Sarah's own. The fact that it had been made for the summer had made no difference to Mary, and although Ollie had wanted to paint her in the old brown dress and pinafore that she wore around the house she had been firm in her choice. Ollie had not insisted and Sarah had merely made her put on extra underclothes. Now, dwarfed by the grand-father chair, Mary sat with the light from the window on her face, her blue eyes shining, her blonde hair, tied up with an old, but newly pressed ribbon, tumbling to her shoulders. Her gaze was directed past Ollie's head and out through the window where, beyond the garden in which Arthur and Agnes played, she could see up onto the hills.

Sarah, glancing up from her ironing every now and again, watched the progress on the picture, while faintly came from the garden the murmurs of Arthur and Agnes. Sarah thought she had never before known such a time of peace. It didn't matter about getting rich and moving to a big house, she said to herself; she would be content if they could remain as happy as they were right now.

'Oh, Papa – look . . . !'

Into the quiet Mary's voice came as she straightened in the chair and pointed out past Ollie's head. 'Mary, please,' he protested. Then, sighing, he turned and looked out and up to the hill, above which a tiny shape dipped and soared on the wind.

'It's a kite, Papa,' Mary said. She sat there for some moments watching as the kite dipped and rose, then she added, 'Oh, it's like a bird. It's just like a bird.'

Ollie turned back and looked at her as she sat gazing out, rapt. 'Would you like a kite too?' he asked.

'Oh, yes!' She moved her eager gaze to him. 'Could I? Could you make me one?'

'I don't see why not.'

'When?'

'Oh – soon.'

'Will it be like that one, Papa?'

'Like that one?' He shook his head. 'Oh, no – much better. Much, much better. You shall have the best kite in all of Wiltshire.'

She was silent for a second or two. Then she said:

'Papa, it's my birthday soon. Could I have it for my birthday?'

He nodded, smiling. 'Yes, you shall.'

'You promise?'

'I promise.' He stepped forward and gently adjusted the position of her head. 'Now,' he added, 'd'you think we might get on with the picture?'

The following Sunday Ollie returned to the painting, working on it for another two hours, after which he set aside his brush and told Mary that she could get down. The cottage was empty but for the two of them. Ernest was out with friends while Sarah, with Blanche in the perambulator, had taken Arthur and Agnes to Sunday school.

Mary stretched, sighing with relief. 'Is it finished, Papa?'

'Almost – not quite.' He checked his hands to make sure they were clean then lifted her down from the elevated chair. 'There's just a little more to do on your dress and the back of the chair. That won't take long. We'll finish it next Sunday.'

'Next Sunday's my birthday.'

'Ah, yes.' He nodded. 'Well, then, the Sunday after if there's no time.'

She stood there looking up at him. 'You haven't forgotten my kite, have you?'

He smiled. 'No, I haven't forgotten your kite. Don't worry – you'll have it.' Then urging her out of the scullery, he added, 'Now go and change your dress, as your mother told you.'

When Sarah returned she left Blanche in Mary's care while she took off her coat and went to look at the work Ollie had done. She gazed at the painting for a long time, then, turning to Ollie who had come to stand at her side, she said, 'Oh, Ollie, it's beautiful.'

'It's not finished yet, mind.'

'Even so.' She paused. 'They're going to be after you to sell this one, too – you see.'

'Ah, maybe. But I won't part with it – ever.'

He began to clear his brushes and materials away then and as he did so there came a knock at the front door. 'I wonder who that can be,' Sarah said as she moved into the hall. A few moments later she was back to say that Mr Heritage was there. 'I showed him into the front room,' she said.

'Mr Heritage?' Ollie smiled at the news, then quickly running his fingers through his hair he went from the kitchen and into the hall.

Entering the front room a moment later he smilingly greeted the man. Heritage took his hand, but did not return his smile. Instead he looked at him gravely. Ollie, seeing the man's set expression, felt his own smile die away and a little tremor of nervousness begin suddenly to flutter in his chest. There was a moment of silence between the two men, and then Heritage shook his head and said:

'Mr Farrar – I had to come and see you . . .' He broke off and turned away, as if unable to meet Ollie's eyes.

Ollie stood in silence, waiting, then, frowning, he said: 'Mr Heritage – what is it?' He felt his heart sinking. 'It's – it's the exhibition, isn't it? Is it the exhibition?' *It's not going to happen now*, the thought went through his mind. *He's come to tell me that it's cancelled.*

Heritage shook his head and turned his eyes back to Ollie's anxious gaze.

'It's your paintings,' he said.

Ollie forced a smile to his mouth. 'Don't you think they're good enough now? Don't you think that –'

Heritage broke in before he could go on. 'They're gone.'

'*Gone*? My paintings? What do you mean?'

'Oh, God.' Heritage gave a kind of groan.

'Tell me – please. What is it? What's happened?'

Heritage hesitated for a second or two and then said dully, 'There was a fire last night. In the workshop of the picture-framer. I'm afraid everything was destroyed.'

'And you mean – my paintings were there . . .'

'I'm sorry. I'm so sorry. Not only *your* paintings but others too – not that they're any concern of yours.'

Ollie turned away. He felt a sick feeling rising from the pit of his stomach. With his back to Heritage he stood gazing unseeingly from the window. After some seconds he took a breath and said: 'So – so it's all finished.'

'I'm sorry – there was nothing left. Nothing.' A pause then Heritage added: 'And he was not insured.'

Ollie turned back to face him. 'So it really is finished, isn't it?'

Heritage put a hand to his forehead. 'I would have given anything for this not to have happened.'

The two of them remained standing there. After a

moment Heritage said: 'All I can say – if it's any consolation at all – is that if you can get to work and produce
some more paintings I'll exhibit them as I planned to
do with the first ones.'

'Do more paintings?'

'Yes. You have my word on that.' Heritage put a hand
into his pocket. 'In the meantime – perhaps you'll accept
something towards your – your loss.' He held out his
hand and Ollie saw some gold coins in his palm. He
made no move to take them. After a moment Heritage
turned and placed the money on the top of the piano at
his side. 'I wish I could fully recompense you for the
paintings you lost,' he said, 'but I'm afraid I can't. That's
beyond me. I'm not exactly a wealthy man.'

They stood in silence again for some moments, then
Heritage gave a sigh and said, 'Well . . .' He took up his
hat, ready to make his departure. Ollie remained
standing there as if in a dream, then after a second he
straightened and followed the man into the hall.

At the front door Heritage turned to him again. 'I'm
sorry. I'm so sorry,' he said.

Ollie said nothing. Heritage went on:

'But remember what I said – if you can do some more
paintings . . .' He left the rest of the sentence unspoken,
hesitated a moment longer then put on his hat and
moved out onto the front path.

After Ollie had closed the door on the sound of the
departing phaeton he remained in the hall for some
seconds before turning and moving stiffly back into the
front parlour. There he came to a stop in the centre of
the little room and just stood there. His paintings – they
were gone. Every single one of them. All of them
destroyed.

'Ollie . . . ?'

Vaguely, through his numbing thoughts, he became

aware of Sarah's voice behind him. He turned towards her.

'I heard the front door go,' she said. 'What did Mr Heritage –' Her words broke off. 'Ollie . . . what's the matter . . . ?' Putting a hand on his arm she looked up into his face. Under her gaze he turned his head away.

'Ollie,' she said, 'what's happened? Tell me.'

'It's all gone,' he said. He barely opened his mouth as he spoke, his words only just audible in the little room. 'My pictures – they've been burnt. There was a fire. They're gone.'

Sarah stared at him in horror for a second as if hardly able to believe what she was hearing. The sound of a sob welled up in her throat and quickly she choked it down. Raising her hand she laid it against his cheek, her other arm going around him. He stayed without moving in her awkward embrace. As they stood there there came the sound of footsteps and the next moment Mary was standing in the doorway. Looking at the two of them she sensed at once that something was wrong.

'Papa,' she said, 'what's the matter?'

Neither Ollie nor Sarah spoke.

'Papa, what's the matter?' Mary said again. Her safe world was threatened and there was the sudden sound of tears in her voice.

Forcing a smile to her lips, Sarah turned to her. 'It's nothing, my dear. Nothing. Please – you go on into the kitchen and watch over Blanche, there's a good girl.'

Mary gave a slow, reluctant nod and, with a single backward glance, turned away and disappeared from sight.

After a moment Ollie said quietly:

'He told me – Heritage told me – that if I do some more paintings he'll put them up in his gallery.' He gave a hopeless shake of his head and a bitter smile. '*Do more paintings . . .'* His voice was heavy with irony. 'The ones I had took me years to do. *Years*. A lifetime.'

Sarah tightened her arm about him. 'Don't,' she said. 'Don't . . .'

'Do more paintings,' Ollie said again. 'Easy for him to say.'

A moment later he was aware of her releasing him. She stepped to the piano and took up the coins. Ollie said:

'He gave them to me to help make up for my loss – as he put it.'

Sarah looked at the money in her hand. 'Five sovereigns, Ollie,' she said. 'Five sovereigns. It's a lot of money.' She raised her palm for him to see but he didn't look. He only shook his head, the bitter smile back on his lips.

'Five sovereigns,' he said. 'He could have afforded more than that – even though he *says* he's not a wealthy man. But what does it matter to him? It matters nothing at all to him – not for all his show of sympathy.' He gave a little groan that pressed Sarah's heart. 'Five sovereigns,' he said. 'What I was expecting was a future.'

Chapter Eight

In the dark of the bedroom Sarah lay awake, waiting for Ollie to come home.

He had been gone for hours, leaving the cottage not very long after Heritage's departure. Standing there with the sovereigns in her hand she had watched him go, not asking where he was going and unable to say anything that would keep him by her side. Later she had put Blanche in the perambulator and, with Mary, Arthur and Agnes beside her, had taken her back to Hallowford House. Coming down the hill on her return she had quickened her steps, hoping that on her arrival she would find Ollie at home. Entering the cottage she saw at once that he hadn't returned.

Now, Sarah sat up in bed and lit the candle. After some moments she got out of bed and put on the old coat she used as a dressing-gown. Taking up the candle-holder she moved to the door, quietly opened it and started down the stairs. A candle was burning on the table near the window in the kitchen and she blew out the candle in her hand and settled herself in a chair to wait. It was just after eleven-thirty. A wind had sprung up and was keening around the thatch, creeping in through the cracks in the window frame and making the candle flame shudder and dance. The fire in the range had died and the room was cold. She drew her coat more closely about her.

It was just after midnight when she heard Ollie's

footsteps at the back door. She heard the door softly open and close and then moments later the kitchen door was opening and he was standing there facing her. After a second or two he closed the door behind him.

'I saw the light of the candle as I came round the back,' he said as he turned to her. Then he added. 'You shouldn't be waiting up for me. You should be asleep.'

She shook her head. 'Oh, Ollie, I couldn't sleep – not knowing where you were.'

'Are you angry?' he said.

'Angry? No, of course not.'

'I walked,' he said. 'I walked for hours. And then I went to the Wheatsheaf.'

She shrugged. '– Just so long as you're home.'

'I had some drink. I wanted to get drunk but – it didn't seem to make any difference – however much I had. Afterwards I walked again. I've walked miles.'

He stood before her in the pale light, his form splintered by the tears in her eyes. She blinked them back. 'Sit down,' she said. 'I'll make you some tea.'

She was about to get up but he came towards her and stood above her, looking down at her. She remained in the chair. Then with a little groan he sank to his knees and laid his head on her thigh. His head was turned away from her and she couldn't see his face. But then suddenly she was aware of the shaking of his body and she reached out and laid her hand gently on his cheek and felt there the wet of his tears.

'Oh, Ollie . . .' She whispered the words chokingly as her own tears sprang into her eyes again. 'Please don't. Please. I can't bear to see you cry. I can bear everyone else's tears but yours.'

His tears continued to flow, as, unspeaking, the two of them sat there, she in the chair, bending over him, her hand on his cheek, he on the floor, his head against her thigh. After a while his silent tears ceased, but still he sat there, the only sounds in the room the sounds of their breathing, the ticking of the clock and the sighing of the wind as it roamed about the cottage. After a long time he said quietly into the silence:

'I can still hardly believe it's happened.'

She said nothing but moved her hand and gently stroked his cheek. He went on:

'It's his fault, of course – Heritage's. He's the one who's – who's liable. They should have been insured – my paintings.'

Sarah nodded. Then she said, '– Well, then, perhaps he should be made to pay you what they were worth.'

'How?'

She gave a faint shrug. 'I don't know. The law, perhaps.'

'The law,' he scoffed. 'It takes money to go to the law. You mean hire some fine lawyer? Lawyers are rich men. How d'you think they get rich?' He shook his head. 'No, it's no good. I've been through it all, over and over. There's nothing to be done. Nothing at all.'

She was silent for a few moments then she said, 'But there's one thing, Ollie – at least you know now that people will buy your paintings.'

'What good will that do me? I've got no paintings to sell.'

'No, but – well, perhaps – you *could* do some more, couldn't you? I know it'll take a long time, but –'

'Years. Years and years to get together as many as that again.' He shook his head, sat there for a moment longer then got slowly to his feet. With his back to her he said:

'I don't think I could do it, Sare. Having it all so close and then seeing it just – snatched away – right when it was almost in my grasp. I don't think I could do it again.' He paused. 'I haven't got the heart for it.'

She remained silent, not trusting herself to speak. After a few moments she got up from the chair. 'I'll make you some tea,' she said.

'No, thanks. I don't want anything.'

She nodded. Moments of silence went by. 'Come to bed, Ollie,' she said softly.

'Yes.' He turned to her. 'Oh, God, I'm so tired.'

In the wavering light of the candle she could see how weary he looked, how defeated. 'Come,' she said, 'let's go to bed.'

He sighed and slowly began to take off his jacket. As he did so he came to a stop and Sarah saw that he was looking at the little picture on the wall beside him. It was the picture that Mary had made for him, her portrait of him sitting at his easel. He had framed it and hung it on the wall beside the kitchen range. Now with his jacket half off he stood gazing at the picture as if he had never seen it before. After a minute Sarah said:

'Mary was asking for you tonight. So many times. She was worried about you.' She smiled, shaking her head in wonder. 'That child loves you so much, Ollie. She worships you.' She paused. 'Remember, Ollie – whatever might happen, you've got us. We love you.'

The following evening when Ollie came in from work he ate his supper in silence and afterwards sat before the kitchen range, an open book in his hands. He was not reading, though. Often Sarah would glance his way and see him just gazing before him, as if his eyes were fixed on some distant vision.

When the children were on the point of going to bed they said their goodnights to Ollie and went upstairs – except for Mary, who lingered at his side.

'Papa,' she said, 'what's the matter?' She took his hand. 'You look so sad.'

'No – I'm all right.'

'Are you?' She paused. 'You have to finish my portrait soon, remember.'

He hesitated for a moment then said, 'Yes, of course.'

'But not on Sunday, though. There won't be time.'

'No?'

'It's my birthday – have you forgotten?' She frowned. 'Papa, you forgot.'

'No.' He shook his head. 'I haven't forgotten. I wouldn't forget a thing like that.'

Mary kissed him and then followed the other children upstairs. A few minutes later when Sarah came down from seeing them tucked up in bed she found Ollie sitting at the kitchen table with paper and pencil before him. She stood watching him as he worked. After a moment he said, without looking up:

'I promised Mary a kite for her birthday. I'd better get started.'

Every evening that week when Ollie got in from work he waited until the children had gone to bed and then got on with the business of making Mary's kite. In the kitchen by the light of the lamp he worked carefully, meticulously, with balsa wood, paper and glue. Sarah, pausing occasionally to look up from her mending, would ask how he was getting on. 'All right,' he would answer. 'All right.' When it was time for him and Sarah to go up to bed he took the unfinished kite with him, in the bedroom placing it carefully on top of the old wardrobe out of sight.

When the construction was finished he took watercolours and painted on it roses of yellow and pink, Mary's favourite colours, after which he attached to the lowest point of its diamond shape a long tail of string with paper bows at regular intervals. Nine of them, one for each year of her life.

It was finished on the Friday evening.

On the Sunday morning, over breakfast, Mary began to receive her birthday gifts and good wishes. Arthur had drawn her a picture of a sailing boat – something he had never seen in his life, and Agnes, not to be outdone, had also drawn a picture – but of lambs.

Ernest had gone off for his morning's work at the farm, but he had left for Mary a little book on famous painters that he had bought in Trowbridge. Sarah had made her a little bag, embroidered with her name, in which to keep pencils and chalks. Inside she had placed a new pencil and a small piece of indiarubber.

When Mary had looked at her presents and thanked the givers Ollie got up and went out of the room. Two minutes later, standing outside the kitchen door, he called out for her to close her eyes. Then, assured by Arthur that she had done so, he entered, cleared a space on the table, and placed the kite before her.

Ernest returned to the cottage just before eleven and at once he and Ollie and the children got ready to go up onto the hill. In the meantime Sarah set off for Hallowford House to fetch Blanche down to the cottage to spend the afternoon and join in Mary's birthday tea.

Soon after Sarah had left, Ollie, Mary, Ernest, Arthur and Agnes set off from the cottage. Ollie carried the kite. The day was still bright but it had become very cold and they were wrapped up against the keen wind. Arthur, pointing up to the high chalk cliff that rose up behind the cottages, said, 'We can fly the kite from there, Papa.' But Ollie said, 'No, we need space. We'll be better up on the hill.'

It was even colder up on the hill and in no time the cheeks and noses of the children glowed pink and they were pulling their hats down over their ears.

Spring was close, though. The signs were everywhere. Clumps of primroses dotted the banks, the gorse bushes were all in bloom, and in the centre of one of them Ernest found a pair of yellowhammers building a nest.

It was a perfect day for flying a kite, Ollie said, and once up on the very top of the hill he managed, after one or two attempts, to get it off the ground and soaring up on the wind. As the children stood at his side watching the yellow and pink diamond rising up, he glanced down at Mary and saw the excitement in her wide eyes and in the clenching of her hands. Her hair, escaping from beneath her old woollen hat, streamed out in the wind.

After a little while when the kite was safely aloft, Ollie handed the winding card to Mary and showed her how to let the string out and draw it in again. Then, following his directions she loosed the string and sent the kite even higher. A little later, when the kite had come diving down to earth again, coming to rest in a gorse bush, she handed the string to Ernest.

He took it eagerly and after getting the kite in the air again began to walk backwards along the hill's crest, playing out the string. Agnes and Arthur walked with him, as usual, like acolytes following their priest. And soon the kite was riding on the wind again, soaring up, higher and higher.

Standing together, hands linked for warmth and for closeness, Ollie and Mary gazed up as the kite rose and dipped above their heads on the bitter wind, watching the diamond bank and halt and then come plunging down towards the earth in sudden, breathtaking dives, only to swoop up again to swing and drift on the currents. The string in Ernest's hand was taut. Glancing back at Mary, Ollie saw the pride and happiness in her upturned face. Every hour spent making the kite had been worth it.

Later when it was time to go home they set off along the top of the hill towards the path that would take them down. Ernest led the way with Agnes and Arthur on either side of him, their hands linked, while Ollie followed with the kite. Behind him Mary had stopped to gather some primroses.

At the spot where the path led down, Ollie came to a stop and waited while Ernest, Arthur and Agnes walked on ahead. After a few moments Mary came running to Ollie's side, a bunch of primroses in her hand.

'Here, Papa.'

She was holding the flowers up to him, and he thought, *I would like to paint you now. Just as you are now – your cheeks reddened by the wind, your hand reaching up with the flowers . . .*

'Are they for me?' he said.

'Yes, of course. You like primroses, don't you.' It wasn't a question.

'Oh, yes, I like them. Thank you.'

'But you mustn't be sad anymore, Papa.'

'– No, I won't be.'

She smiled up at him until he smiled back, then she turned and pointed off.

'Look, Papa – the cottages are so small from here . . .'

He followed her eyes to the row of thatched cottages in the valley. 'Yes, they are.' They were small from any distance.

Turning her head, Mary sought out Mr Savill's house at the top of Gorse Hill.

'– Not like Hallowford House,' she said.

He smiled. 'No, not at all.'

He stood there without moving for long moments,

and then she said, pulling at his hand, 'Come on, Papa, let's go home; I'm getting cold.'

He didn't seem to hear her. 'We'll have a place like that one day,' he said.

'Like Hallowford House?'

'Yes.'

'Truly?'

'Truly.'

'When?'

'One day. You just wait. Just wait a little longer.'

And perhaps it could happen after all, he said to himself. Perhaps he *could* start all over again with his paintings. Yes. And he would work even harder at it this time. And he would find a gallery where he could show them, and sell them.

He glanced down at the child as she gazed across the hilltop. He would do it for her, for Mary – for Mary and for the others.

With the thought it was suddenly as if their future was as clear and as real to him as the panorama that was stretched out below. He had lost sight of it, but now he could see it all again. Everything. In time his painting would bring to them what they wanted. It would take longer now, but it would happen. In time. He just needed to be patient, and in time they would have everything. There would be a fine house. For Sarah there'd be no more doing other people's laundry. For himself no more working on Mr Savill's gardens. There'd be no further need to scrimp and save to put away the odd penny for Mary's future. His painting would make certain that her future was assured. As would be the futures of all the children.

He lowered himself, crouching before the child. Then, placing the kite and the flowers at his side he reached out and put his hands on her shoulders and gazed into her blue, blue eyes.

'Trust in me,' he said gruffly. 'Believe me. We'll have a good life soon.' He nodded and laughed suddenly out into the wind. Then, leaning forward he kissed her on the forehead and drew her small slim body to him. As he held her he silently murmured: *I vow it. For your sake, I vow it.*

Chapter Nine

After dinner Sarah got Mary, Arthur and Agnes dressed in their best clothes and, settling Blanche in the perambulator, took them off to Sunday school. Ernest who, now working for his living, was no longer obliged to accompany them, went off to join some of his friends. His only part in the others' Sunday-schooling would be to meet them and bring them home when it was over.

On Sarah's return from the church hall she set Blanche down in the makeshift pen in the kitchen. Blanche had been walking for three months now and was also starting to talk. Leaving her there, for the moment happily playing with various old toys, Sarah turned to Ollie where he sat in his chair. He had appeared so much brighter earlier on when he and the children had got back from flying the kite. She looked at him closely.

'How are you?' she asked.

He hesitated before he answered. 'Fine. Almost – now.'

'Good.' She reached out and gently brushed his shoulder with her fingers.

'I've decided,' he said after a moment, 'to go on with my painting.'

'Oh – I'm so glad, Ollie.'

'Yes.' He paused. 'Next week I'll get Mary to sit for me for an hour or two – then I can finish her portrait. After that – I'll start another picture.'

'Oh, Ollie, it makes me so happy to hear you say that.'

He nodded. 'I won't be beaten, Sare. I won't.'

A little while later, taking advantage of the children's absence, she began to prepare water for a bath, filling kettles and saucepans and putting them to heat on the range. Ollie, meanwhile, brought in the tin bathtub from the shed. A little later, while he was lighting the Sunday fire in the front parlour, Blanche began to cry. Sarah took her onto her lap and talked softly to her. Blanche went on crying for some minutes longer, but then at last she became quieter and, lying back in Sarah's arms, drifted off to sleep.

Gently, Sarah laid her in the perambulator, loosely tied the rag cords to stop her falling out, and stood gazing down at her. She was a year and three months old now. She was a beautiful child. Her closed eyelids were rimmed with the densest lashes, while her softly curling hair, unusually thick, was, like Ollie's and Mary's, the colour of pale corn.

Since Blanche had been taken back to Hallowford House to ease Marianne's pining six months had gone by and there had been no word from Mr Savill regarding the question of her leaving the nursery and returning to the cottage. He was well content, it seemed, for the situation to continue and, as Sarah had said nothing to him about it either, the situation had gone on. Blanche now had spent practically all her life at Hallowford House, Sarah reflected. And, she realized with a pang of guilt, she had not really missed her. Not because she didn't love her – she did. But there had been no time to miss her with all there was to do. Besides, she had seen her regularly, making it a rule to visit her once or twice each week and bring her back to the cottage almost every Sunday when the weather permitted. It was important that Blanche's ties with her family were maintained; she mustn't be allowed to forget them.

But Blanche *was* forgetting.

Sarah had seen the signs over the months and she had tried to disregard them. It did no good, though; it had to be faced; just as Mr Savill's daughter had been unhappy at being separated from Blanche, so, it appeared, Blanche was unhappy when she was away from Hallowford House. She always became fretful when she was kept away for any length of time, and when she did settle in the cottage the peace was usually an uneasy one.

Sarah thought of what Ollie had said about bringing Blanche back to live at the cottage again. And that's what they should do, she knew. Blanche should be where she belonged, with her family – before she grew even more accustomed to her present life . . .

When the water on the range was boiling Sarah left the baby and drew the curtains while Ollie poured some of the water into the tub and added cold to it from the pails he had brought in from the pump. Then while he refilled the kettles and put them back on the range Sarah got undressed and stepped into the tub.

When she had bathed she got out and washed her hair. Then, while she dried herself and wrapped herself in a towel Ollie renewed the water and got in. After a minute or two Sarah knelt beside the tub and washed his back, her soapy hands moving over the smooth, muscular shoulders – she could feel the tension there – then down to his narrow, tapering waist. Ollie was the only man she had ever seen naked and the sense of wonder that had first touched her had never quite left her. It was there now as she moved her hands over his body.

Without either of them speaking Ollie got to his feet

in the tub and Sarah took a towel and began to dry his back. When she had finished he turned to face her and she began to dry his front. Stepping back a foot she looked at him as he stood there. How beautiful he is, she thought. Bending her head she kissed his chest and then pressed her face against his loins, feeling against her cheek his hardness, the coarseness of his damp pubic hair and the soft firmness of his lower belly.

When she straightened a few moments later he stepped out of the tub and drew her naked body to his.

'Oh, I do love you, Sare.'

'I love you too, Ollie.'

Gently, he kissed her. 'It's going to be all right,' he said against the softness of her damp, sweet-smelling hair. 'It's going to be all right. It will.'

'Yes, I know.'

'We're going to be happy, all of us.'

'I am happy, Ollie. I'm happy now.'

He kissed her again, a long kiss this time, and as she felt his lips on hers, soft, warm, she knew that she had never loved him more than she did now. She became aware of him growing harder against her belly and then a moment later she felt his hand, low down, as his fingers moved between her legs. Then his lips left her mouth and he said softly, urgently, 'Come on – before the children get back. They'll be home before we know it.'

Taking her hand he began to lead her from the kitchen and into the little front parlour. 'Wait – one moment,' she said, and went back to the scullery and wheeled the perambulator with the sleeping infant into the kitchen. 'There,' she said, '– we'll hear her if she wakes and cries.'

Ollie had pulled the curtains closed and as she turned the key in the lock he spread a blanket on the rug before the fire. They lay down together on the blanket and, putting off the prize moments, kissed and fondled one another. Time had gone by, though, and all too soon they could hear the sounds of the children's return. Sarah sat up. After a moment there came the sound of the door handle being tried and she got to her feet and moved to the door. 'Don't wake the baby,' she whispered loudly and then added, 'What do you want?'

'Can we come in?' Ernest's voice came whispering in reply.

'No – not right now.'

Ollie came and stood at Sarah's side. 'You and your sisters go and play outside for another ten minutes,' he said.

'Oh, Ollie,' Sarah whispered to him, 'they'll be all right in the kitchen.'

'No,' he replied, 'they'll wake the baby.'

Sarah nodded and then called softly through the door: 'Do as your father says – but don't get dirty.'

The children went away then and, hearing the silence in the house again, Sarah moved back to where Ollie was settling himself on the rug once more.

After closing the scullery door behind him Ernest quickly started off along the lane. When Mary called after him, asking where he was going, he answered that he was going into the village to rejoin his friends. Mary shrugged, without interest, but Arthur started forward, eager to join him. He was too late, though; in just another moment Ernest was turning the corner out of sight.

'You can come with me if you want to,' Mary said to him as he came back.

'Where to?' he asked.

'Up on the hill.' Mary smiled. 'We'll go and fly my kite.'

With her words she turned back to the cottage, went

round to the back and softly opened the door into the scullery. On the table lay the kite with its pattern of pink and yellow roses. In a moment it was in her hands and she was letting herself out again. She smiled triumphantly at the other two as she rejoined them in the lane. 'Come on,' she said. 'We mustn't be long.'

At the end of the lane she came to a halt and gazed up at the hill. This morning, with her father at her side the hill had not seemed so far away. Now the distance was daunting. After a second she turned and looked off to the left. 'No,' she said with a shake of her head, 'we won't go up onto the hill. It's too far. We'll go up there – up on the Ridge.'

'Oh, no, Mam'll be angry if we go up there,' Arthur said. 'And Papa will be, too.'

As Agnes voiced her agreement Mary quickly said, 'Papa won't be angry with me – not on my birthday.' She paused. 'And anyway, we shan't be up there very long.' Then without waiting to see whether they were with her she left the lane and started up the steep, winding track.

Holding the kite carefully in her hands Mary led the way up the steep, meandering path, Arthur and Agnes, anxious not to be left behind, following close on her heels. The wind was stronger and colder the higher they climbed and at any other time Mary would have wanted to turn back. Today, though, was different. Today was her birthday and she had the kite. Also, in the absence of Ernest, she was the eldest of the three children.

It took much longer to get to the top than she had anticipated and when they were there the wind buffeted them, snatched at their clothes and tugged at the kite in her cold hands. They wouldn't stay long, she decided, just long enough to fly the kite once. Then they would go down again.

It was strange up here, and she felt a little afraid. They were very high up. Over to the right beyond the pathway stood the spindly little trees and shrubs that marked the edge of the Cut. Above was nothing but the sky. Moving closer to the edge she could see beyond the trees, down below, the thatched roofs of the cottages.

'I don't like it up here,' Agnes said. 'I want to go home.' Her voice had a faintly nervous ring to it.

'Oh, Aggie, not yet,' Mary quickly replied. 'We haven't flown my kite yet.'

'I don't care,' Agnes said. 'I want to go home. Besides, I'm cold.'

'Oh, please, Aggie.' Mary's voice was pleading. She didn't want to be left up here alone, and at the same time she didn't want to lose face by appearing too anxious to get back down again. 'We'll fly the kite just once and then we'll go back, all right?'

Reluctantly Agnes nodded and Mary quickly began to unwind some of the string from the winding card. When she had unwound a good length she played out a little of it the way her father had shown her and then started off at a run, at the same time throwing the kite up into the wind.

And, miracle of miracles, the wind caught it at once.

Arthur and Agnes gave little whoops of joy while Mary cried out ecstatically, 'Look! Look! It's flying!'

Coming to a stop on the turf she let out more of the string until the kite was drifting high up above their heads. Proud, jubilant, she watched as it swayed in the air, swinging from side to side, a diamond of pink and yellow roses, straining at the string she held in her hand until, to make it easier to hold, she wound a little of it around her wrist.

And then all at once the kite did a somersault and began to dive downward. Mary gave a little cry of despair and, in an effort to keep the kite aloft, leapt forward, turning as she did so, running backwards across the turf.

In the same moment that the wind snatched at the kite and flung it high into the air once more, Agnes and Arthur squealed out in horror. A second later, while their cries were still ringing in the air, Mary's own shout of jubilation turned to a scream as her scampering feet took her out over the edge of the Cut.

To the terrified eyes of the two watching children it seemed that for a moment Mary hung there in the air, her arms and legs thrashing the wind, her mouth and eyes open wide as she shrieked in terror and surprise. The next moment she was gone.

For seconds Arthur and Agnes just stood and gaped. And then as one they reached out and groped for the other's hand. Then, fearfully, slowly, they moved forward, creeping towards the chalky edge where the ground fell sheer away.

Five yards from the edge they stopped, too afraid to go nearer, and hands damp in one another's grasp they stood there, white-faced in the teeth of the wind. Then after a few moments they turned and, shrieking out into the cold air, began to run back down the path towards the lane.

Chapter Ten

The bath water had been emptied away and the bath tub put into the scullery, there to wait until the children had their baths that evening before going to bed. Ollie, dressed again and wearing his worn old carpet slippers, sat in his chair beside the range reading a book. Sarah was laying the table for tea. Blanche was still sleeping. The cottage was peaceful.

Sarah was just setting out the bread when Arthur, with Agnes running screaming behind him, suddenly came bursting in at the back door, through the scullery and into the kitchen. 'Quick! Quick!' he yelled out. 'Come quickly!' His tear-filled eyes were wild and he was gasping for breath.

'Easy, easy –' Ollie started up from the chair, while Sarah put the bread down on the table and stepped forward. Blanche, disturbed by the noise of Agnes's hysterical shrieks, awoke and began to cry. Arthur reached out, snatching Sarah's hand. 'Oh, Mam, come quickly – it's Mary!'

Ollie's book fell to the floor as he moved towards the boy. 'Mary?' he said. 'What about her? Where is she?'

Agnes went on screaming, automatically now, as if she was no longer in control, and with the baby crying too it was hard for Sarah to tell what Arthur was trying to say as he sobbed and babbled incoherently against the din.

Thrusting Sarah aside, Ollie bent to the boy. 'You say

Mary fell down?' he shouted. 'What d'you mean, she fell down?'

'The Cut!' Arthur cried out. He turned and pointed off. *Mary – she fell over the edge!*

Ollie's face went chalk-white, and lashing out he struck the boy hard across the face. Then, even as Arthur reeled backwards Ollie was turning. A moment later he was flinging himself out of the door.

As the children had run towards the cottage their horror-stricken cries had attracted attention and now as Ollie ran along the lane some of the neighbours came from their doors to see what it was all about.

As Sarah emerged from the cottage moments afterwards she saw Esther Hewitt at her gate and she called out, her voice breaking with fear, 'Oh, please – Esther – will you come in and stay with Blanche for a minute?'

'Yes, of course.' Esther nodded and began to hurry towards the Farrars' gate. 'What's the matter?' she asked.

'It's Mary. Something's happened to Mary.'

'Oh, dear God . . .'

Sarah dashed on past and, with Arthur and Agnes running crying in her steps, ran after Ollie along the lane.

By the time she reached the foot of the Cut there were several people already there. They were standing motionless, silent, watching Ollie scramble down into the wide shallow basin at the foot of the great chalk cliff and pick his way across the rocks and rubble. Peering past him Sarah could see a little dark blue shape lying between him and the face of the cliff. It showed up starkly against the white of the chalk.

Sarah's head swam and for a moment the sight receded and wavered before her. She could feel her heart thudding in her chest and her knees were so weak that she felt they might give out beneath her. She had started to climb down into the rocky basin when she felt a hand snatch at her sleeve. Turning, she looked into the frightened, crying faces of Arthur and Agnes. 'No – no,' she cried out, her voice breaking, 'go on back. Go on *back*!'

She was dimly aware then of Jack Hewitt standing there, and as she turned away she saw him bend and put his arms around the two children. Then, unsteadily, and feeling as if she were in some kind of nightmare, she stepped down into the basin and, in Ollie's footsteps, started off across the rough, uneven surface.

She reached his side as he knelt down beside the little dark blue shape.

Mary's body lay there like some rag doll, as if her limbs had no bones in them. She lay oddly twisted, her face pressed into the chalk floor, one arm flung out sideways and the other bent beneath her. Stripped of all dignity in the dying her skirt and petticoat had risen up around her waist so that her darned and patched drawers were exposed to the eyes of the onlookers. Her woollen hat had partly come off and her blonde hair streamed out over the chalk, now turning red beneath her head.

Silently Ollie bent and scooped the limp form up into his arms. As he lifted her up her head fell back and the blood poured out of her mouth. Her hat hung there briefly and then fell to the ground. Ollie remained standing there for a moment as if transfixed and then raising his head he opened wide his mouth and howled out, a long, hollow cry, like some animal in torment. Then, slowly, he sank down again until he was kneeling on the chalk, rocking backwards and forwards, Mary's body held close to his chest, his right hand supporting her shattered skull.

Standing before him, blinded by her tears and feeling that she might choke on her despair, Sarah fell to her knees and reached out her arms. Ollie, without even looking up, tightened his grip on Mary's body and shrank back.

He stayed there for some seconds, bending over Mary's body, and then he rose and began to move slowly away across the basin of the Cut. As he did so Sarah saw a pink and yellow shape moving behind him, trailing along in his wake. For a moment she didn't know what it was, but then she realized that it was the kite, dragging and dancing over the rough ground, still held by the string around Mary's wrist.

Chapter Eleven

The leaden days that followed seemed to Sarah to pass by without recognizable shape or pattern. Later she would look back and see it all as a blur of shifting images, a series of incidents that stood out in her mind like pictures in a book. Somehow over that time things were taken care of. Somehow all the necessary jobs were done. She didn't remember when, but at some time that evening Esther Hewitt took Blanche back to Hallowford House, and somehow Sarah set a part of her numbed mind to feeding the children. Life had to go on.

Someone had sent for Dr Harmon, but he was not at home, so word had gone then to Dr Kelsey. He came at once and went straight to Ollie and Sarah's bedroom where Ollie had placed Mary's body on the bed. There Kelsey found that, apart from the child's broken skull, her neck and spine had also been shattered. There would, of course, have to be an inquest, he said, but it would only be a formality.

He went away then saying that he would set in motion the necessary wheels for the inquest and also send for the Coolidges, the undertaker and his wife who would come and lay out the body.

Mrs Coolidge came soon after the doctor's departure. She had heard the news and was waiting for the summons. On her arrival she was shown up to the bedroom where she began to lay out the body.

As Mrs Coolidge worked upstairs James Carver, Mr

Savill's groom, came with a letter for Ollie. There was no answer required, James said, and Sarah thanked him and he went away again. In the kitchen Sarah went to Ollie where he sat beside the range. He made no move to take the letter, nor showed any interest in it. After a moment she opened it and read it aloud. Mr Savill had written of his great regret at their sad loss and then gone on to say that Ollie need not report for work until he was ready to, and that his wages would not be affected. Ollie made no comment.

Later, when Mrs Coolidge came down into the kitchen to say that she had finished her work, Sarah made her a cup of tea. Ollie went back upstairs to the bedroom.

He didn't come down again that night, even for his supper, no matter that Sarah went up and tried to persuade him. Later, after she had seen the children in bed she returned to the door across the landing and found it locked. Trying to make as little noise as possible she shook the handle a few times and, with her mouth close to the keyhole, softly called.

'Ollie . . .'

There was no answer. After a moment she called again. 'Ollie – please – open the door and let me in . . .'

He still didn't answer.

'Ollie . . .' she whispered again at the keyhole, kneeling there on the tiny space of the landing. 'Ollie, please . . . Ollie, don't shut me out. She – she's my child too . . .'

On the other side of the door Ollie made no sound, and eventually, choking back her tears, Sarah went back into the children's bedroom. There, taking Mary's place, she got into bed beside Agnes.

She didn't sleep for a long time, but lay wakeful in the darkness, the sleeping Agnes's breath like a caress upon her neck. In the other bed Arthur and Ernest slept soundly. The tears from Sarah's eyes ran down onto the pillow.

The inquest, held at the Three Tuns tavern was, as Kelsey had said it would be, a mere formality. It was soon over, bringing the expected verdict of accidental death. No members of the Farrar family were present.

Mary's funeral was planned for the following Friday, and up till then Ollie spent much of the time sitting beside her body, first up in the bedroom, and afterwards, when she had been placed in her coffin, down in the front parlour. On the Thursday night he sat polishing the brass coffin handles.

On the morning of the funeral he and Jack Hewitt brought out the coffin and, followed by Sarah, the children and other mourners, hoisted it onto their shoulders and set off along the lane towards the village churchyard.

In the cemetery Mary was laid in the earth. Nearby a flowering cherry was bursting into bloom and around the boles of the silver birches the daffodils were out, standing up straight and brilliant yellow in the newly springing grass. Around the grave Sarah and the children stood weeping. Ollie's eyes were dry.

Later, back at the cottage, Sarah set about getting dinner. When it was ready she called Ollie and the children and he took his place with them at the table. He had hardly eaten anything since Mary's death and Sarah was astonished at how gaunt he had become in such a short time. She watched now as he picked at the food for a minute or two and then put down his knife and fork.

'Ollie,' she said softly, '– please try to eat something. You'll be ill.'

'I'm not hungry.' He didn't look at her as he spoke.

That evening after the children were in bed the two of them sat together in the kitchen. For the most part they were silent. Sarah sewed by the light of the lamp while Ollie stared into the fire. Outside a fierce wind had sprung up, howling around the chimney, throwing itself at the windows and rattling the front door. On the table beside Ollie's chair stood a small jar holding the primroses Mary had given him that last morning up on the hill. They were dead now, but he wouldn't have them moved.

Into the quiet of the room Ollie said:

'It was my fault.'

'– Your fault? Ollie, what do you mean?'

'I told you to send them outside to play. If I hadn't done that she'd still be here.'

'Ollie, you musn't say that. You musn't think such a thing.'

He nodded, as if in confirmation of his words. 'Now she's gone. She's gone and I don't know how I'll manage.'

'Ollie, don't . . .'

'It was for her – the painting – all of it. It was all for her.'

Sarah felt tears start in her eyes and a lump rise in her throat. 'Please, don't say that. You have other children. Ernest, Arthur and Agnes and Blanche – they need you – and your caring. So do I.'

He turned his gaze from the glowing coals and looked at her. There was a strange haunted look in his face and his hollow eyes seemed to burn into hers. Then on his mouth came the ghost of a smile.

'I love you, too, Sare. And I love the children. I truly do. But – I don't know – somehow with Mary it was . . . it was like she was a – a part of me – and I don't know how I'll manage properly without her. She was all I ever wanted in a child.' He shook his head. 'I expect as time goes on I'll get used to it. I'll be able to live with it and get over it. I mean – people do, don't they? Till then – I suppose all I can do is try to get through the minutes.'

Over the following days Ollie spent his time in the cottage or walking in the lanes and the fields around. When he was at home he would sit silently in his chair, sometimes getting up to look at Mary's unfinished portrait on the easel in the scullery.

Although it pained Sarah to see him so utterly desolate, she was glad when he stayed about the cottage. When he went out she worried until the time of his return, which was often late in the evening when the children were asleep. She herself could never go to bed until he was indoors, always waiting until he was home and safe.

On the Friday, a week following Mary's funeral, he stayed out late again and Sarah once more sat waiting for his return. The high wind was back and was moaning about the cottage walls. Then, at last, close on midnight, he was there.

He came into the room, looked at her for a moment and sank down into his chair. He was still wearing his coat. From the opposite chair Sarah gazed into his thin, hollow-cheeked face. His eyes were dry, and the thought went through her mind: *If only he would cry . . . if only he would let go and give vent to his misery . . . He had wept over his paintings, but not a tear had he shed over Mary.*

They sat there in silence while he stared into the fire's embers and she fought the urge to go to him and wrap him in her arms.

After a while she murmured to him that it was time to go to bed. He nodded.

'Are you coming, Ollie?' she asked softly.

'Yes, in a minute or two,' he said. 'You go on. I'll be up in a little while.'

'All right. You won't be long, will you?'

'No, I won't be long.'

She went on upstairs then and got ready for bed. Later, lying in the light of the candle she heard his soft footsteps on the stairs. Then the door opened and he came in. He had taken off his coat and boots. He stood for a moment looking down at her then sat on the bed at her side. She reached out and pressed his hand. 'It's such a wild night. Come to bed . . .'

'Ah, in a minute. I want to see Arthur . . .'

'Arthur? What for?'

He closed his eyes for a moment. 'I hit him,' he said. 'When he came into the kitchen that day and told us what had happened, I lashed out and hit him. It's been on my mind.'

'Oh, Ollie, I'm sure he understood that you – you weren't yourself. Anyway, he'll have forgotten it by now.'

'I doubt that.' He rose, took up the candle. 'I must go and see him.'

'Ollie – he'll be asleep.'

He paused momentarily. 'He'll soon get off again.' Moving out onto the landing he closed the door behind him, leaving Sarah in darkness.

Softly Ollie crept into the children's bedroom, moved silently between the two beds and put the candle down on the chair between them.

Turning to the bed on the left he looked down at the sleeping form of Agnes. She lay almost buried under the bedclothes, only the top part of her head visible. He put his hand over her head, just a fraction of an inch from touching. A little blessing, and then he turned and looked over at the other bed.

Arthur slept on the nearside, Ernest beside him. Ollie stood looking across at the elder boy for some moments, silently mouthed some words and then moved his glance to his younger son. After a second he crouched and whispered the boy's name.

'Arthur . . .'

Arthur stirred briefly and then settled again into sleep.

'Artie . . .'

Ollie whispered his name once more, closer to his ear. Arthur stirred again and this time awoke, opening his eyes.

'Papa . . .' he whispered, and then, frowning: 'Is something the matter?'

Ollie gazed back at him for some seconds, then finally shook his head.

'No, it's nothing at all, son. Go on back to sleep. I'm sorry I woke you.'

He straightened, Arthur's eyes, puzzled, still upon him. Ollie stood looking down at the boy for a moment then reached down and brushed the boy's cheek with the back of his hand.

'Goodnight, Artie.'

When Sarah heard Ollie leave the children's room she relaxed a little, expecting any moment that he would return to her. Instead she heard the faint sound of his feet on the stairs. Then in a moment the sound faded away again, drowned by the wind as it buffeted the house.

The sound of the wind was somehow soothing. And she was so tired. Lying there, waiting for Ollie, she closed her eyes. She thought of Mary. She had loved her with all the power that her ability to love had allowed, but somehow, somehow, they had to go on. Somehow they had to try to begin, no matter how slowly, to pick up the threads of their lives again . . .

She lay still, listening for any sound of Ollie downstairs, but she could hear nothing but the wind. She pictured him sitting in the kitchen before the dying fire, staring into space. He needed time to get over it. But he would do it in time.

Exhaustion from tension and grief lay like lead weights on her eyelids. After a while she fell asleep.

There was a noise coming from down below. Something banging. It sounded like one of the kitchen window shutters. She sat up in bed, realising as she did so that she was alone. Ollie hadn't come back upstairs. She turned and reached out to light the candle, and then remembered that Ollie had taken it. She remained sitting there in the dark for some seconds then pushed back the bedclothes, swung her feet onto the floor and got up. Wrapping her old coat around her she opened the door and, in the dark, made her way down the narrow stairs.

When she opened the kitchen door a few moments later she found the room in darkness. She lit the lamp and looked at the clock on the shelf. It was just after quarter-past-three. There was no sign of Ollie. Moving to the window she secured the banging shutter and then went into the front parlour. That too was empty. Entering the scullery a moment later she discovered that Ollie's boots and coat were gone. She found also that the easel was bare. He had gone out somewhere, taking the little unfinished portrait of Mary with him.

With panic rising in her breast she went from the back door and around the house to the front gate. There she gazed up and down the lane while the wind tugged at her coat and whipped at her hair. There was no sign of him anywhere. After a time she went back into the kitchen and lit the range, then sat down beside it, waiting and watching.

When the dawn came up she was still sitting there.

PART TWO

Chapter Twelve

Sarah glanced at the clock as she put on her coat. Almost twelve-fifteen. Agnes would be back from church at any moment. After fastening the buttons Sarah stood before the glass where she touched at her hair and adjusted her bonnet. As she did so Arthur came in from the back garden with some yellow chrysanthemums he had just cut.

'Will these be all right, Mam?' he asked. 'There's not much left.'

She turned to him. 'Oh, yes. Thank you, Artie, they'll be fine.'

Arthur took a piece of newspaper and wrapped the flowers in it. He was fourteen now. Like Ernest before him and Agnes after, he had left school at ten, though with his disabilities it hadn't been easy for him to find and keep employment. At first Mr Savill had offered him work in the mill but Sarah had declined on account of the dust in the atmosphere, which, she was afraid, would only worsen the boy's condition. Later, when his health had improved somewhat, she had secured him a job at the Woolpack Inn in Trowbridge where he cleaned the knives and the guests' boots and shoes, and did any other of a hundred odd jobs, each day walking the four miles there and the four miles back. He had kept it up for some time, but then had fallen ill and the job had been lost. Afterwards he had found work as odd-job boy for a wealthy family in the next village, but again lost it through sickness. And so it had continued. But then, miraculously, over the past year his attacks had lessened in their severity and in the frequency of their occurrence, and eventually had ceased altogether. Gradually he had become stronger, and had put on weight, with colour coming to his cheeks. The job he had found then, as assistant to the local butcher, Grill, he still held after more than a year.

As Sarah gave a last touch to her collar, Agnes, wearing her coat and bonnet, came through the door. She was eleven years old now, and often when Sarah looked at her she could see herself so clearly. Agnes had the same smile, the same wide hazel eyes, the same tilt to her chin.

At this particular moment Agnes had an air of excitement about her, and was slightly out of breath.

'Well?' said Sarah. 'How did it go?'

Agnes laughed. 'Oh – Billie Norman on the organ pump – I think he must have fallen asleep – or else he got carried away with the singing.' Her laughter rang out. 'The organ died dead away right in the middle of "Jerusalem the Golden"!'

While Arthur joined in Agnes's laughter Sarah said, 'But your solo. How was that? Was it all right?'

Agnes nodded, her eyes shining. 'Oh, yes, it went well! Oh, but Mam, I was that nervous to start with, I tell you! My heart was poundin' away like a hammer. But it was all right, it really was – and after the service the vicar stopped me and said how nice it was.' She gave a breathless little laugh and hugged herself. 'Oh, but I was ever so pleased afterwards. It really did go well.'

'Good. Well, I shall be there tonight to hear you. You *are* to sing it again tonight, aren't you?'

'Oh, yes!'

Today was the day of Agnes's first choir solo. She had

joined the church choir just over a year ago, after appearing at a concert held in the village at the Temperance Hall. That evening, holding a pink rose and wearing a white muslin dress that Sarah had made for the occasion, she had sung 'A True Little Heart and a True Little Home'. Sarah had almost wept with pride. Afterwards the church choirmaster had come to Sarah and asked whether Agnes would like to join the choir. She had a remarkable voice, he said, particularly in one so young.

Agnes had left school just that past summer. Sarah would like to have kept her there a few years longer in the hope that she might eventually have been equipped to find work as a governess somewhere, but there just wasn't the money. And anyway, apart from a passion for music, Agnes had no real aptitude for studying and book work, and where the competition for such employment was so fierce there was no guarantee that at the end of her studies she would have been able to make a living for herself – particularly when, even at the best of times, the pay for such work was so poor. So, she had found a job with Thompson, the village baker, helping in the bakery and the family house, fetching and carrying from seven in the morning till four in the afternoon. She didn't enjoy it, but it would do until something better came along. Any spare time she had she spent with the choir or playing the old piano in the front parlour.

'Was Blanche there this morning?' Sarah asked.

Agnes nodded. 'Yes, with Marianne and a woman I've never seen before.'

'Ah, yes, one of Mr Savill's friends. Blanche mentioned them.' Sarah paused. 'I'm glad Mr Savill heard you sing.' She glanced up at the clock. 'Listen,' she said, 'I must go. There's not much for you and Arthur to do – just set the table and keep an eye on things. I shan't be long.'

With her words Sarah took up the flowers and left the cottage.

As she made her way along the lane the November day was cold and damp and the last of the morning fog was still hazing the trees beyond the hedgerow. Dead leaves scattered beneath Sarah's feet as she walked.

As she drew near the church she saw that the time on the church clock was just after half-past-twelve. She always chose this time, in the period of quiet after morning service when all the worshippers had gone home to finish preparing Sunday dinner. Now as she entered the gates she saw that there was just one other person in sight, an old woman, who bent over one of the graves. She recognized her as Mrs Perkins, the widow of a gardener who had once worked with Ollie up at the house. Sarah quietly exchanged greetings with her then made her way over the grass to the grave beneath the cherry tree, almost bare now of its leaves. There she laid the flowers on the grass and took up from the grave a chipped earthenware pot. The roses that she and Arthur had placed in it two Sundays before were dead and she took them out and dropped them in the rubbish bin near the hedgerow. Then she moved to the rainwater butt, filled the pot again and returned to the graveside.

When she had put the chrysanthemums in the pot she placed it back in the earth, straightened and looked at the headstone. Mr Savill had paid for it. On the stone were engraved the words:

MARY
BELOVED DAUGHTER OF
OLIVER AND SARAH FARRAR
BORN 19TH MARCH 1873,
DIED 19TH MARCH 1882
AGED 9 YEARS

Beneath the inscription for Mary a further inscription had been written:

AND OF OLIVER FARRAR
BORN 4TH FEBRUARY 1848, DIED 1ST APRIL 1882
AGED 34 YEARS

Mary would have been sixteen now. Oliver forty-one. So much time had gone by. Seven years, when at the time Sarah had thought she could not survive another seven hours. But she had managed, somehow. Life had gone on. There had been the children to care for, and somehow the days had been got through.

After Ollie had gone from the cottage that wild March night Sarah and Ernest had searched for him along the lanes and roads leading out of Hallowford. They had found no sign of him. As the days had gone by Sarah had tried to convince herself that he would return. But then three days after his disappearance someone had found on the river bank, a mile or so from the cottage, his jacket and boots. Along with them had been the painting of Mary. His body was discovered later that same day, fetched up at the weir further down river.

Sarah remained there for some moments longer, looking down at the grave, then, turning, she moved away. It was time to go to Hallowford House and bring Blanche home for the day.

As Sarah made her way from the churchyard John Savill stood at the window of Hallowford House looking out over the lawn. From behind him came the voice of his friend, Edward Harrow:

'You're quite sure Gentry's going to be no trouble, John?'

Savill turned from the window. 'Indeed not. And it'll be good to have him here.'

The two men, now both aged fifty-nine, had been close friends since boyhood, first meeting as pupils at boarding school, and later attending university together. Over those early years they had found a friendship that was now so well established, so comfortable, that they never now questioned but that it would last for the rest of their lives.

Edward Harrow was a tall man, and broad, his large form filling the armchair in which he sat. He was handsome still, in spite of his age and the grey of his hair. His skin had about it the slight richness of inherited tan that told of Mediterranean blood in his ancestry, his dark eyes adding another sign. He was part Sicilian, his father having married the wealthy daughter of a prominent Sicilian property-owner and soap-manufacturer, and settling in Messina, Sicily, where Edward had been born, later going to England to be educated.

It was while he was at Oxford that he had met Alice Gentry, the daughter of a Berkshire doctor, after their marriage settling in Cornwall where he worked in the management of the tin mine left to him by his father. Both their children had been born there, first a daughter, Joan, and then, much later, when they had both given up hope and expectation of further offspring, a son – named Gentry after his mother's family.

Now, in 1889, it was a time of change for the Harrows. With their daughter having married and gone to America, and Gentry, now fourteen, away at boarding school in Brighton, Edward and his wife were leaving England.

The tin-mining industry had been in decline for many years now, and Edward had decided to cut his losses, and sell up. Now he and Alice had given up their home in

England and were moving to Sicily where Harrow planned to concentrate on the Sicilian interest, taking over the business from his ageing, now widowed, mother, at the same time investing in it what he had realized from the sale of his tin mine interests.

It was their son Gentry who was the reason behind the Harrows' present visit to Hallowford House. While his parents went to Sicily together Gentry was to remain in England to continue his studies. Previously the boy had spent all his vacations with his parents. From now on, though, that would not be possible; he would be able to see them only during the summer holidays and, possibly, at Christmas times. Savill, on learning of the problem, had at once insisted that the boy stay at Hallowford House during the shorter school holidays. The Harrows had gratefully accepted the offer and yesterday had arrived to make any necessary arrangements and to say their goodbyes. They would be leaving next Friday.

Savill had met Gentry on a number of occasions over the years, either when visiting the Harrows or when they had brought the boy to Hallowford House. He had last seen him a year ago, a long-legged young man, tall for his age, with the dark eyes and black hair of his paternal grandmother. Now, smiling at his friend, Savill shook his head. 'The only likely problem,' he said, 'is that Gentry will find it all rather dull here. I'm afraid he's going to find Hallowford a good deal quieter than Brighton.'

Harrow waved a dismissive hand. 'Don't worry about that. It'll do him good to slacken his pace a little. And he needs to be with someone with a keen eye and a restraining hand. If he's left at school for the holidays I'm afraid he'd only get up to mischief.'

'Eddie, the boy's only just fourteen,' Savill said. 'What do you expect from someone that age?'

'That's true. His mother worries, though. One or two reports from his school have upset her considerably.' Harrow gave a short laugh. 'Listen to me! Keep on like this and you'll change your mind. But it's not that there's anything malicious or wicked in him. He's just a little wild, I suppose. As you say, like most boys his age.'

'Stop fretting,' Savill said. 'He'll be perfectly all right here. You and Alice can rest assured on that. Believe me, there's not much mischief he can get up to in a place like Hallowford – and if there is I'd very soon know about it.'

The conversation moved on, and they spoke of the latest gruesome murder in London's Whitechapel district which had been reported in that morning's papers. They spoke briefly too of the influenza epidemic that was sweeping Russia, and Harrow read from the newspaper a report of the mounting death toll. After a while the talk turned to the West Country's wool industry, and Savill spoke of Britain's urgent need to invest in new machines. If something wasn't done soon, he said, they were in danger of being overtaken by the European market.

As they talked there came a sound of voices out in the hall and a moment later the door opened and Alice Harrow entered with Marianne and Blanche.

Marianne and Blanche would be nine years old that December. Marianne's hair, full and heavy and, by dint of the governess's work, falling in ringlets to her shoulders, was as dark as her mother's had been. In contrast Blanche's soft, flax-coloured curls looked even paler. Marianne's hair was set off by pink ribbons, the same colour echoing in the braid that trimmed her crimson velvet dress. Blanche's dress was of the same design, but differently coloured, the body dark blue, trimmed with a pale blue braid, her hair ribbons of the same shade.

Savill smiled now as Marianne came towards him, then bent and kissed her. 'Did you enjoy your walk with Aunt Alice?' he asked.

'Oh, yes, Papa,' Marianne said. 'We fed the ducks on the pond.' Then she added, 'Don't forget, this afternoon I'm to go and have tea at Blanche's house.'

Savill nodded. 'Yes, we know all about that.'

Blanche spoke up then. 'Ernest says he'll take us to the woods if we like,' at which Marianne added, 'Oh, good, I like it when Ernest takes us out. It's better than when we go with Miss Baker! When we're with Miss Baker we always have to keep to the wretched paths.'

The Harrows laughed while Savill said: 'Well, wherever you go, you just make sure you behave yourself. Otherwise Mrs Farrar won't invite you again.'

A moment after he had spoken the door opened and Miss Baker was there holding Blanche's coat and saying that Blanche's mama had come to take her home. Also, she said, it was time for Miss Marianne to get ready for lunch. With her words she held out her hands to the two girls and they moved across the room to her side.

When the trio had gone from sight Edward Harrow put the paper aside, got to his feet, stretched, and said that he too had better go and get ready for lunch. As the door closed behind him Alice smiled and said, 'John, your Marianne is such a pretty child. She's going to turn some heads when she's older, there's no doubt.'

Five years younger than her husband, Alice Harrow was an attractive woman, tall and slim, with graceful movements.

Savill smiled at her words and said, 'And young Blanche too, don't you think?'

'Oh, yes, indeed.' She paused. 'I must say,' she went on, 'that when we arrived I was surprised to see Blanche still here. I thought she would have returned to her family by now.'

Savill nodded. 'Yes,' he said, 'and I suppose she would have done but – well, I still feel some responsibility for her. After all, it was partly through me that her father lost all his paintings that time and – and everything went so wrong.'

'Oh, John,' Alice said, 'you can't blame yourself. No one could foresee what was to happen.'

'No, but even so . . .'

'How's the family managing now?'

'As regards money? Well, the two boys are working. And Mrs Farrar is too, of course. And, I think, the eldest girl as well now – Agnes.'

'The one who sang in church this morning.'

'That's right.'

Alice nodded. 'Such a sweet voice. With a voice like that that girl could have a future.'

'Yes . . .' Savill's voice was doubtful. 'Oh, but they haven't got the money to spend on anything like that. Even with the three children working there can't be much money going into the house.' He sighed. 'I shall always be in Mrs Farrar's debt for what she did for me – and this – looking after Blanche – is one way I can repay her. She won't accept any money.'

'She's quite proud, is she?'

'Oh, yes. When it all began I managed to persuade her that I could manage without her rent for the cottage, but that's as far as it went. Still – it's not only that – a case of repaying Mrs Farrar . . .'

'No?'

'No, I have my own selfish motives too.'

'Oh? And what are they?'

He said, 'Well – it's just so good for Marianne to have Blanche here. I mean, Blanche *could* have gone back to her own family ages ago and, of course, Marianne would have got used to her absence after a while. Children are very adaptable. But with Marianne having no mother – well, at least with Blanche here she always has company. I suppose Blanche is like the sister Catherine and I would have chosen for her.' He smiled at some image in his mind, and Alice said:

'They get on well, don't they?'

'Oh, indeed they do. Blanche is such good company. She's bright and clever and attractive. She's a spirited child, too. And that's good for Marianne as well. Marianne is naturally rather – shy – like Catherine – and inclined to be reserved and even a little – timid. But somehow Blanche has a way of counteracting that. I've seen it. In Blanche's company Marianne becomes a little braver – a little more assertive. Oh, having Blanche here has made all the difference in the world. I hear the voices of the pair of them, laughing and talking away, or I listen to them at their singing lessons or their piano lessons and – well, I'm just – very glad of Blanche's presence. I know it sounds sentimental, Alice, but this house is a happy place. It really is. When Catherine died I never imagined I'd ever be able to say that again, but it's true.'

She nodded. 'I'm sure it is. And also it's quite obvious that Blanche herself is very happy here.'

'Oh, indeed. And it isn't as if she's left her family. She spends time with them – on Sundays, like today, and occasionally at odd times during the week. Oh, yes, I think she's happy – I've no doubt about that.'

'And no doubt she never considers that it might not last.'

Savill looked at her in silence for a moment then said:

'D'you think perhaps it's a mistake? That what I'm doing is wrong?'

143

Alice shrugged. 'Oh, John, I don't know, I'm sure. I was just thinking – one day it will have to end for her, won't it? All this – living here, getting the best of everything.' She paused. 'What will she do then?'

Chapter Thirteen

The leaden skies of the morning had cleared and now the November sun shone clear and bright. Soon after two o'clock Miss Baker brought Marianne to the cottage. Sarah invited the governess in, but Miss Baker politely declined and remained on the doorstep only long enough to instruct Marianne not to dirty her clothes or get her feet wet, and to be back at Hallowford House by six-thirty. With that she went away again.

When Sarah had closed the door on Miss Baker's departing back, she took Marianne's coat and ushered her into the front parlour where Agnes sat at the piano playing 'Little Brown Jug'. Blanche and Arthur were sitting on the sofa just finishing a game of Beggar-my-neighbour. As Marianne entered Blanche threw down her cards crying, 'I won! I *won!*' Then, looking up at Marianne, she smiled: 'Ah, here you are. Ernest and Fanny will be here soon.'

'That's right,' Sarah added. 'Ernest's going to take you girls out for a walk while I get the tea.' As she lingered in the doorway, her glance on Blanche and Marianne, a familiar little feeling of doubt came to nag at the back of her mind. She gazed at the two girls for a moment longer, then turned and moved away into the kitchen. As she busied herself over the range the doubt was still with her. Something had to be done, she said to herself. It was time she made a decision.

During the past few weeks the problem had been on

her mind constantly. What had begun so long ago simply as a temporary measure to solve immediate difficulties had become a way of life. It couldn't go on, though. There had to come a time when Blanche's stay at Hallowford House came to an end and she returned to the family. And what then? Right now Blanche was happy and content, never questioning the situation. She lived the major part of her life at Hallowford House, coming down to the cottage at weekends and at various odd times. But although Blanche got on well with her brothers and sister, still Sarah could not escape the feeling that over the years the child had been steadily growing further and further away from her family. And it was time it was changed. Sarah knew that she would never be able to offer Blanche the comfort she found at Hallowford House, but now Agnes and Arthur were earning regularly, as well as Ernest, and they would manage all right. Other families did.

'Here we are, Mam. Are the girls ready?'

Ernest's voice came breaking into Sarah's thoughts as, followed by Fanny Greenham, his young sweetheart from the village, he entered from the scullery. Sarah smiled at him. 'Yes, they're waiting for you. They just have to put on their coats.' Turning, she called Blanche and Marianne to her and, aided by Ernest, got them into their coats and hats.

Ernest had turned eighteen just two weeks earlier. He had been at work for almost eight years now, and still was assistant stockman at Harker's farm. He was a tall young man. Although his colouring was her own Sarah could see Ollie so clearly in his features. They were echoed in his straight blunt nose; his wide, sensitive mouth with its finely sculptured upper lip; the round jawline and the sometimes thoughtful preoccupation in his eyes.

146

Sarah had realized lately that she had come to depend on Ernest more and more as the years had gone by. In so many ways he had taken Ollie's place, and in some ways had proved to be more dependable than his father. Whereas Ollie had never really been a practical man Ernest had shown a more pragmatic side to his nature, and as he had grown so he had shown a strength and reliability in his makeup that Sarah, to her surprise and relief, had found she could rely on. Not that she could expect to depend on it forever, she sometimes told herself. One day he would want to get married and make a home of his own. Perhaps, in time, with Fanny.

With the thought, Sarah moved her gaze to the young girl. Fanny, seventeen years old, was the daughter of a local villager who, as did Fanny and her three sisters, worked at one of the cloth factories in Trowbridge. Fanny had red-gold hair, freckles, and a pert, pretty face. She and Ernest had been walking out for over a year now and it was clear to Sarah that he was taken with her. Still, Sarah said to herself, they were both still too young to think about marriage; if it happened it wouldn't happen for a long time yet.

Ernest and Fanny were late bringing the two girls back to the cottage and it was almost a quarter-to-seven when Sarah eventually set off up the hill towards Hallowford House with Blanche and Marianne at her side. As they neared the gates of the house she saw a dim shape coming to them from the darkening shadows. As the figure drew closer she saw that it was Miss Baker.

'It got so late,' Miss Baker said, frowning as she came to a stop before them. 'I was wondering what had happened.' Sarah began to apologize, saying that the children had got in late from their walk, but Miss Baker wasn't listening; her attention had been caught by the state of Marianne's coat and boots which were stained with mud.

'What on earth have you been doing?' Miss Baker said to Marianne.

Sarah began to explain that on the walk Marianne had tripped and fallen, but before she had finished the governess took Marianne by the hand and, wishing Sarah a goodnight, turned away. Hurriedly Sarah bent and kissed Blanche on the cheek, then stood watching as she ran off to catch up with Marianne and the governess.

It was Friday and the Harrows were leaving.

Blanche had gone downstairs with Marianne to wish them goodbye. Now, leaving Marianne in the hall, she had come back up to the schoolroom on the top floor where, standing at the window, she stood looking down onto the drive where James was loading the last of the luggage onto the carriage. Mr Savill was to drive with the visitors to the station to see them off. They were going to Sicily to live.

After a few moments she saw Mr and Mrs Harrow come in view as they moved to the carriage, then Mr Savill appeared and got in behind them. A minute later James climbed up and took the reins, and then the carriage was moving away. Blanche followed its progress along the drive and out between the tall gates where it turned onto the road and was lost to sight.

'Where will the carriage go to now, Miss Baker?' Blanche asked without turning from the window.

'To Trowbridge. To the station.' Miss Baker's voice came from behind her.

Dorothy Baker was thirty-six years old. The daughter of a clergyman, she came from Taunton in Somerset. She was red-haired, short and plump, and wore glasses.

This was her sixth post and she earned thirty-five pounds a year. Like most of the thousands of governesses who advertised in *The Times* and *The Lady* she taught mathematics, English, geography, history, music and needlework. She also offered French and Italian – which additional subjects had helped her secure the post at Hallowford House. She had been there now for just two months, replacing Miss Sanderson, the previous governess.

Blanche wasn't sure how she felt about Miss Baker. She only knew that she liked Miss Sanderson better. What Miss Sanderson's shortcomings might have been, Blanche didn't know; she only knew that Miss Sanderson had been warm and jolly, and fun to be with. Miss Baker was different. She was unfailingly pleasant and polite to Marianne, but with Blanche herself, Blanche felt, there was always something else.

'And then what will happen?' Blanche said.

Miss Baker gave a little sigh of irritation at Blanche's questions. 'Mr and Mrs Harrow will catch the train for London,' she said, '– and there, I imagine, they'll take the boat train for the Continent. From there they'll go to Sicily – which is an island in the Mediterranean.'

'Yes, I know. It's part of Italy. I looked it up in the atlas.' Blanche paused. 'Is it a nice place?'

'I have no idea. I imagine it is.'

Blanche sighed. Travel was exciting. She had learned that much from the little she had done. During each of the past three summers she had gone with Marianne and Mr Savill on holiday to the seaside for two weeks, once to Weston-super-Mare in Somerset, and on the other two occasions to Weymouth in Dorset. Before that, in 1887, she had been taken up to London to see some of the Queen's jubilee celebrations, also with Marianne. And there had been other trips here and there. To go abroad, though, to another country, that would be something quite different. 'I'd like to go to Sicily,' she said with another sigh. 'I think I will – one day.'

Miss Baker said nothing, just lifted her head and looked at her.

'One day,' Blanche added, with a little nod, '– if I like.'

'Really? Well, perhaps you shall and perhaps you shan't. It costs money to travel.' There was no humour in Miss Baker's smile. 'And perhaps in the meantime you might like to complete your English exercise.'

Blanche moved back to the table she shared with Marianne, sat down and got on with her writing. After a few minutes the door opened and Marianne came in. As Marianne sat down and took up her pencil Miss Baker looked at her and smiled.

'Have Mr and Mrs Harrow gone now, Marianne?'

'Yes, Miss Baker.'

When the English lesson was over they turned to geography, after which it was time for lunch. The girls ate with Miss Baker up in the schoolroom. When lunch was finished they rested for a while before beginning the afternoon lessons, which they began by taking out their history books. After the history lesson they took up their needlework. They were learning to embroider, sewing squares of linen with brightly coloured silk thread. Now, with their embroidery still before them, Miss Baker began to talk of foreign languages. She would make a start with Italian, she said, beginning with a few simple Italian words.

Blanche pushed her embroidery away and sat up straighter in her chair. Listening intently as the governess began, however, she soon found that the lesson seemed to be directed solely at Marianne. She said nothing, but continued to listen, and then watched as Miss Baker turned and wrote on the blackboard. A few moments later Miss Baker turned back and said to Marianne:

'*Io.*' She stressed the first syllable. 'It means "I". Repeat it after me. *Io.*'

'*Io,*' Marianne repeated.

And then Blanche spoke up:

'*Io.*'

'No, no, Blanche,' Miss Baker said. She frowned vaguely in Blanche's direction then forced the hint of a smile to her lips. 'This is just for Marianne, dear. You carry on with your embroidery.'

Puzzled, Blanche frowned in return. 'Why?' she asked. 'Why is it just for Marianne? Why isn't it for me too?'

'Now, Blanche,' Miss Baker said. 'Don't begin with all your questions again. We really haven't got time for them. Please – do as I say. Just go on with your needlework.'

'But – but I want to learn to speak Italian too.'

'Please, Blanche . . .' Miss Baker eyed her for a moment then turned back to Marianne. 'Now, Marianne, repeat after me the word –'

'I don't want to do my needlework,' Blanche said. 'I want to learn Italian like Marianne.'

Miss Baker ignored her. 'Marianne,' she began again, 'please repeat –' But Blanche broke in again, now with rising anger in her voice:

'Why can't I. *Why?*'

Then Marianne spoke up as well. 'Yes, Miss Baker,' she said, 'why can't Blanche learn it too?'

'My dear child,' Miss Baker said, 'there wouldn't be any point to it, would there? It takes time and there's so much for us to learn, isn't there? We can't afford to waste time, can we?'

While Marianne frowned, not understanding, Blanche pushed back her chair and stood up. 'Why wouldn't there be any point to it?' she demanded. 'Why not?'

Miss Baker took no notice. Blanche said sharply:

'Miss Baker, I want to learn Italian like Marianne. I want to. Why can't I?'

Miss Baker continued to ignore her for another moment, then she gave a sigh, turned back to Blanche and stepped towards her.

'Sit down, Blanche,' she said evenly.

Blanche hesitated for a moment then sat down.

'The simple reason,' Miss Baker said, 'why there's no point in your learning a foreign language is that you'll never have a need for it. Do you understand?' She turned and smiled at Marianne. 'It's different for Marianne, of course. She'll travel to other countries when she's older, so she'll need to be proficient in other languages, won't she?'

'And *I* shall too!' Blanche said sharply. 'I shall too!'

'No, dear,' Miss Baker said with a humourless little smile touching one corner of her mouth. 'You must remember that we should concentrate on learning only those things that will be useful to us in our lives.' She bent and pushed towards Blanche the piece of embroidery the child had been working on. 'Now you would do yourself a service,' she added sharply, 'by concentrating on your sewing.'

'But I don't want to do my sewing,' Blanche said. 'I want to learn Italian, like Marianne.' She paused. 'Why can't I? I've got a right to.'

Abruptly Miss Baker's demeanour changed. '*Right?*' she rapped out. 'You say you've got a *right?*' Her voice throbbed with fury. '*No!* You do *not* have a right! You have *no* rights here!' Her voice rose. 'Now – get on with your sewing and let me hear not one more single word from you!'

For a moment Blanche just glared at the governess, and then suddenly her feelings of anger and injustice erupted. 'No!' she shouted into Miss Baker's face. 'I won't! I won't! I *won't*!'

In the next moment, as the room still rang with the echo of Blanche's defiance, Miss Baker stepped forward and, eyes blazing with fury, raised her hand and struck Blanche across the face.

The force of the blow rocked Blanche almost off balance and she reeled. Recovering herself, one hand moving involuntarily to her cheek, she gazed with stricken eyes at the governess. Then, impotent in her hurt and anger, she snatched up the embroidered linen from the table and began to wrench at it in an attempt to tear it in pieces. It wouldn't be torn, though, and with a choking cry of fury and frustration, she drew back her hand and hurled the fabric into the governess's face. Miss Baker gasped, recoiling in shock. Then, lashing out, she struck Blanche again, so hard this time that Blanche fell backwards onto her chair.

'How dare you!' the governess said, her face white with anger. 'How dare you do such a thing!'

As Blanche faced the governess she could feel the pricking of tears in her eyes. She fought them back. She wouldn't cry. She would *not*.

'Now.' Miss Baker's voice was icy cold as she pointed down to the floor where lay the piece of embroidered linen. 'Now come round here and pick this up.'

While Marianne, white-faced and sobbing, gazed from her friend to the governess, Blanche slowly stood up from the chair. On her cheek the marks of Miss Baker's palm were clearly defined.

'Now, come round here at once and pick this up,' Miss

Baker said, pointing again at the linen. 'And then you will apologize to me for your behaviour.'

Blanche, not moving, remained silent.

'Did you hear what I said?' Miss Baker asked.

Blanche said nothing.

'Did you hear me?' Miss Baker said.

'Yes.'

'Then do as I say.'

A little silence, then Blanche said:

'No.'

There was a pause, then Miss Baker said quietly:

'What did you say?'

'No.'

'Are you defying me?'

'Yes! I'm not going to pick it up. And I'm not going to say I'm sorry. I'm *not* sorry. I'm *glad*.' The tears sounded in Blanche's voice now, but still she fought them back.

Miss Baker glared at her while her lips twisted in a sneer. '*Italian*,' she said witheringly. 'Miss Blanche Farrar says she wants to learn Italian. And no doubt she would like to learn French too, and German and Spanish and Russian. She's obviously intent on travelling the world.' Her eyes cold, she bent slightly, leaning towards Blanche. 'You are going nowhere, little girl. Nowhere.' Her words were measured. '*Nowhere*. Who do you think you are? I've learned a little about you and your family, and that was enough for me to know that this is as far as you'll ever go. You were born with nothing and that's all you'll ever have. *Nothing*.'

'Stop it!' Blanche cried, and suddenly the tears overflowed and ran down her cheeks. 'Don't you say that to me. It's not true. It's *not*!'

'Not true? Of course it's true.'

'*Stop it!*'

'No, I won't stop it. You'll have to learn it one day, and the sooner you learn it the better.'

Choking on her sobs, Blanche cried, 'I hate you, Miss Baker.' Then, her voice rising, she added, 'You've got frizzy red hair, and you're ugly, and I hate you!'

White rage flashed across the governess's face for a moment, then she gave a short, hard laugh.

'And *you* – you come from the gutter, child – which is where you belong. You certainly don't belong in this house, living here with Marianne, taking your lessons with her.' Contemptuously she shook her head. 'Mr Savill might insist that you wear as good clothes as Marianne, but don't think for a moment that that makes you as good as she is. And it's the same with your lessons. If I'd wanted to teach children like you I would have gone to the Ragged School. Which is where *you* should be. But, fortunately for you, Mr Savill, out of his kindness, sees it differently, and takes pity on you. And that's all it is – *pity*. He feels pity for you. Still if that's what he wants, then . . .' She shrugged, leaving the rest of the words unspoken.

Blanche stared at her, eyes wide with horror. Miss Baker gave a little smile, then added:

'You've got a shock coming to you, Miss Blanche Farrar – a very rude awakening. Someday soon you'll be saying goodbye to this house and you'll be going home. How shall you feel *then*?'

Speechless, Blanche gazed at her for another moment and then, with the tears streaming down her cheeks, she turned away, dashed across the room and out of the door.

Chapter Fourteen

John Savill was just coming from the library when he heard from above him the patter of descending feet. As he turned to the sound Blanche came running down the stairs. He waited as she reached the hall, expecting her to stop, but she did not. Without pausing she turned and ran on towards the rear of the house. She was crying. He called after her.

'Blanche! What's the matter?'

After a moment he crossed the hall and started in pursuit of her, making his way to the kitchen where he found Florence sitting at the table, scraping carrots. She looked round at the sound of his step.

'It's all right, Florence,' he said. 'I just looked in to see if Blanche was here. She ran by me in tears a moment ago.'

'I heard someone go by just now, sir, though I couldn't say who it was.' She gestured with her knife.

He nodded, turned and left the kitchen. As he emerged into the rear passage he heard a sound from the scullery next door. The door was partly open and he moved to it and pushed it open wider. Blanche was standing by the large stone sink. Little crying sounds came from her.

'Now, now, what's this?' he said.

She turned and looked at him, then turned away again, her crying growing stronger. Savill moved forward, bent to her and laid one hand on her shoulder.

'Blanche – what's the matter? What are you crying for?'

She shook her head.

'Aren't you going to tell me?'

She shook her head again.

'– Where's Marianne?'

She pointed up.

'In the schoolroom?'

'Yes.' Her tearful voice was muffled against her arm.

'Come on, then. Let's go and join Marianne again, shall we?' As he finished speaking he reached out but Blanche cried out, 'No!' and shrank away from him.

'You don't want to go back to the schoolroom?'

'No.'

'Will you tell me why not?'

Another shake of her head. 'I – I can't.'

He straightened, stood there for a moment then said, 'Well, I'll tell you what – you come with me into the kitchen and stay with Mrs Acklin for a minute – all right?'

She didn't answer but allowed him to take her hand and lead her from the scullery into the kitchen. There he handed her over to Florence then went back to the front of the house and up the stairs.

At the top of the house he knocked on the schoolroom door and entered. Miss Baker looked up from her table and smiled nervously at him. He nodded to her and then his eyes went to Marianne who was sitting at the other table, bent over her school exercise book. As she looked up at him he saw that there were the marks of tears on her cheeks. He turned back to the governess.

'Miss Baker, I just found Blanche downstairs – crying, and refusing to come back up here. And now it appears that Marianne has been crying too.' He paused. 'Perhaps you could tell me what's been happening.'

'Oh, sir,' Miss Baker said, with a little shake of her

head, 'I'm afraid we had a little upset, and I found it necessary to rebuke Miss Blanche.'

'I see. What had she done?'

'Well, sir, she refused to do her work. And in addition to that she was very rude to me. I told her that I wouldn't stand for it.' Then, looking over at Marianne, she added, 'And I'm afraid Miss Marianne got rather upset at all the fuss.' She beamed at Marianne. 'Still, I think we're all right now. We've dried our tears now.'

'Good.' He nodded. 'Well, I'm sorry to have disturbed you, Miss Baker.'

'Oh, not at all, sir. It's time we stopped work, anyway.' She turned to Marianne. 'You may stop work now, Marianne, and go and wash your hands. Tea will be ready in twenty-five minutes.'

Silently Marianne put down her pencil and closed her school book. Savill held out his hand to her. Eyes downcast, Marianne got up from her seat, moved to him and took his outstretched hand. A moment later they had left the room together.

Savill took her down to the library where he sat her in a chair at the side of his desk.

'Well,' he said as he sat down facing her, 'perhaps you'd like to tell me what that was all about?'

She didn't answer at once, but then after a little prompting she gave her story.

'And apart from striking the child, I understand you also told her that she is here only because I pity her. Is that so?'

Marianne had gone from the library and now the governess stood facing John Savill as he sat at his desk. Miss Baker said nothing for a moment to his question but then, shaking her head, she said:

'Mr Savill, sir, I'm afraid tempers got a little frayed.

It all became rather heated and – and somewhat unfortunate.'

'I didn't ask you that,' he said. 'I asked you if it was true that you told Mrs Farrar's daughter that she was only here owing to my pity. Did you tell her that?'

'Mr Savill, she threw her embroidery at me. She threw it right in my face. And she was defiant. She wouldn't do the work I had told her to do.'

'Which was, I understand, according to my daughter, this piece of embroidery you speak of.'

'Yes – that's right.'

'Whereas you were starting Marianne on Italian, I believe – beginning to teach her some Italian words. Is that correct?'

'Yes.'

He was silent for a moment, then he said, 'When I employed you, Miss Baker, I made it perfectly clear that Blanche was to be treated in exactly the same way as my daughter and that –'

'Oh, but sir, I –'

He held up his hand. 'Please, let me finish. As I said, I made it perfectly clear to you. It was not for you to decide that one child should learn one thing and the other something else.'

'– I only did what I thought was best, sir.'

'But I had made it clear to you.'

'Yes, sir, I know – but I thought, in the circumstances, that I was doing what was best for her – Miss Blanche, and –'

'Were you really thinking of Blanche, Miss Baker?'

'I beg your pardon, sir?'

'Judging by what I've been told by my daughter, it seems to me that you had no other thought in your mind but humiliating the child. If so you certainly succeeded in doing it.'

Miss Baker drew herself up a little under his cold glance. 'Not at all, Mr Savill. As I said to you, I was merely doing what I thought was the best thing for her. If I may say so, sir, I'm not exactly – inexperienced as a governess. I've taught many children over the years. Children of good families, naturally. Although, I must confess, I haven't taught any of the – the poorer children in the past, nevertheless it doesn't take long to learn certain things about them. And with all due respect, sir, they are not like Miss Marianne. She's a dear child, sir – sweet, clever, obliging and –'

'Quite,' Savill broke in. 'But we're not talking of my daughter.'

The governess gave a little nod. 'No, well – the – the poorer children, the lower classes . . .' She came to a stop before his penetrating gaze.

'Yes?' He prompted her.

'Well – they have to know their place, sir. They have to.'

'I see.' He nodded. 'You keep referring to "they". Who exactly are "they", Miss Baker? I take it you're meaning Blanche.'

'Well – yes.' Then, taking a half step forward she went on: 'Mr Savill, if I might say so, I do not take my position as teacher lightly. On the contrary, I take it very, very seriously. I have made studies of all the great educationalists of the past – and of their methods. And I'm quite certain that it's a mistake to educate a person out of his class. As Mr Lowe said, "the lower classes –"'

'Mr Lowe?' There was a note of impatience in Savill's voice. 'Who is he?'

'Mr Robert Lowe, Minister for Education under Palmerston.'

'Oh, *that* Mr Lowe.'

'Yes, sir. He said the lower classes "ought to be

educated to discharge the duties cast upon them". And as a conscientious teacher I try to keep his words in mind, sir. That is one of my aims as a teacher, to fit a child for the life and the world that is before him.' A little pause then, taking another step forward, she said, 'Mr Savill, forgive me if this sounds impertinent, but with all due respect, I've known a good many more children than you have, and I tell you, sir, it is a mistake to allow one's better nature to be – be taken advantage of.'

'I see.' He nodded. His expression was unreadable.

The governess ventured a little smile and shook her head. 'Oh, I do regret very much that this has happened, sir. Believe me, I do. And I will admit that I was a little – hasty. But the child – Blanche – is very forward and extremely self-willed – traits one mustn't give in to, of course – and I'm afraid as a result things got a little out of hand. But it's all just a storm in a teacup, sir, that's all. I'm quite sure that in another day or two she – Blanche – will have forgotten all about it.'

'Really.'

At his tone Miss Baker nodded uncertainly, peering anxiously at him through her spectacles. 'To tell you the truth, sir,' she went on, 'in my opinion Blanche is not – well – not the best company for Miss Marianne.'

'Oh? Why do you say that?' He sounded interested.

She shrugged. 'Oh, I know there's no denying that Blanche has a certain – cleverness, but nonetheless I don't think she's exactly the – the ideal company for a girl like Miss Marianne.' She came to a stop.

'Please – go on.'

'Well, sir, for a start Blanche is inclined to be mischievous – and she leads Miss Marianne into things.'

'Such as?'

'Well, only last week, for instance, they just –

vanished from the house, right after lunch, and I found out quite by chance that they had gone down to Blanche's home. I went after them and met them on their way back. They said they had gone to look at some rabbits belonging to one of Blanche's brothers. I don't mind telling you, sir, I'd been very worried.'

Savill said nothing. Warming to her subject, the governess went on:

'And yesterday, sir, when you allowed Miss Marianne to go to tea at the Farrars', she came back with mud all over her coat and boots. She told me she had gone out for a walk with Blanche and her brother, and that she had slipped and fallen whilst crossing the heath.'

'She wasn't hurt, was she? She didn't mention it to me when I saw her before she went to bed. According to what she said she had had a very enjoyable time.'

'Oh, no, she wasn't hurt, sir. But I just think that – well, to be honest – I think it was a mistake to have allowed her to go in the first place. I hope you don't mind me saying this, sir, but – after all, as Marianne's governess, then naturally I do have certain – views.'

'Naturally.'

'And I've felt the same thing on the few other occasions you've allowed her to accompany Blanche back to her home.' She shook her head. 'It just doesn't seem somehow – fitting.'

'You think the Farrar home is – beneath Marianne, do you?'

'Well, in all honesty, sir – yes. I don't really think it's the ideal place for her to go. You know what some of those places are like, sir.'

He nodded. 'Some of them, I do – yes . . .' He paused. 'Have you been inside the Farrars' home?'

Miss Baker shook her head. 'Oh, no, sir. Mrs Farrar asked me in but I – I declined.'

He was silent for some moments, then he said, 'I don't know what the sum of your experience is, Miss Baker, but whatever it is I don't want it imposed on my daughter. If you recall, I told you at the start that although I wanted Marianne to have every care, I did not want her to be wrapped in cotton wool.'

'Oh, yes – of course, sir . . .'

'And as regards Blanche, it appears that you've made up your mind that because she's from a poor background she is not fit company for Marianne and, in addition, only deserves some kind of inferior education. It was not up to you, though, to make such a decision. On the contrary, it was your responsibility to treat her as you would any other pupil – my daughter or any other in your care. It was not encumbent upon you to make the child feel different or inferior. I gave you your instructions at the beginning and I expected them to be carried out. If they were not – and I made it clear to you – then you would have to find yourself another post.'

'Sir – Mr Savill – I'm afraid this is all the result of a – a foolish misunderstanding.'

'Oh? But you assured me that you understood me perfectly.'

He continued to gaze at her for some moments then looked down at his desk and took up some papers. The governess remained standing there. After a few moments she said:

'Do I take it that I am dismissed, sir?'

He looked up and nodded. 'You do indeed, Miss Baker. This time, it seems, there is no misunderstanding.' He paused. 'I will give you references if you require them, of course. You may leave as soon as you wish, and I trust you will find your next position more suitable than you've found this one – and that you're not faced with the problem of having your duties conflict with your beliefs.'

When the governess had gone Savill rang for the maid and sent her to fetch Blanche to him. He was still sitting at his desk when there came a light tap on the door. He called out, 'Come in,' and the door opened and Blanche entered.

'Hello, Blanche.'

'You wanted to see me, sir.'

'Yes, Blanche.' He got up, went to her and led her to the chair where earlier Marianne had sat to answer his questions. When she was seated he pulled up his own chair before her and gave her a grave little smile.

'Are you all right now?'

She nodded. 'Yes, sir. Thank you.'

'Good. You mustn't be distressed any more.'

She shook her head. 'No.'

'It's all over now, all that – that foolish business. It's all finished with.'

'Yes.' She paused, then a frown touched her brow. 'What did Miss Baker mean when she said all you felt for me was pity – and it's the only reason I'm here?'

'Now – listen . . .' He paused, searching for the right words, then, leaning forward, he took one of her small hands in his. 'I want you to forget all that Miss Baker said to you up in the schoolroom today. She didn't mean it – and anyway she was mistaken. You're too young now to understand everything, but one day you will and then you'll see that people have all kinds of reasons for doing the things they do.'

She gazed at him solemnly out of her wide blue eyes. He went on:

'And I don't only mean Miss Baker. I mean every-body. You – and me – and Marianne . . . Like your

164

coming here to stay with Marianne. When you first came it was for *her* sake – for *our* sake – not for yours.' He paused. 'Do you understand that?'

She nodded.

'Good. And you must remember that. You didn't come here for what *we* could give to *you*, but for what *you* could give to *us*. D'you see?'

'Yes.'

'And that went on for a long time. And we were very – very glad – and thankful to you.'

'Oh.' A faint smile touched the corners of her mouth.

He was silent for a moment, then he went on again: 'And if things change – the reasons as to why you're here – then you must remember that however much they change it's still only because of what happened at the beginning – because of what you did for us.'

She nodded. The nod came too quickly, though, and he realized that she didn't understand.

'When you were small, you and Marianne – when you were both very small she – she needed you.' He shrugged and smiled. 'And because she needed you – you came here to stay with her.'

'Ah, yes . . .'

'And because of all that happened at that time, so long ago, you stayed on with her. And let me tell you that we're very glad that you did. Both Marianne and I.'

Blanche nodded.

'One day, of course, you'll be going back to your own home – to live all the time with your family again.' He paused. 'You do realize that, don't you?'

She said nothing to this, just looked at him. The frown touched her brow again and he could see a little shadow of concern in her eyes.

'You do understand that, don't you?' he said gently.

After a moment she nodded. Then she said, 'Miss Baker said that I –'

He broke in: 'Look, never mind what Miss Baker said. Just remember what I'm saying to you now. And remember that you will only return home when your mother decides. It's up to your mama. Until she decides she wants you back then you'll stay – and while you stay you must remember that we want you here. D'you understand?'

'Yes.'

'Good.' Gently he pressed her hand. 'Now you go on back upstairs and join Marianne. She'll be wondering where you are.'

Blanche stayed where she was. 'Miss Baker is upstairs too.'

'Don't worry about Miss Baker. She won't say anything to you. Now, run along upstairs.'

After a moment she got down from the chair, moved across the room and opened the door. In the open doorway she turned back and looked at him. He smiled at her.

'All right now?'

'Yes, sir.'

'Good. No more tears?'

'No.' She paused then added, 'I wish I hadn't cried this afternoon.'

'Oh – don't think about that. We all cry at some time.'

She thought about this for a moment. Then she said, 'Anyway – I'll never cry for Miss Baker again.' She shook her head. 'I won't cry for a hundred Miss Bakers.'

Chapter Fifteen

The new Trowbridge Town Hall had been opened earlier that year, 1889, by the Duchess of Albany to mark the Queen's golden jubilee, two years before. Now at its imposing entrance Ernest and Fanny stood reading the notice there.

THE PHONOGRAPH COMES
TO TROWBRIDGE!
Tonight at 7.30 pm, Saturday, 16th November an exhibition of the lastest marvel of science

Hear, captured for eternity by means of the Phonograph, the voices of the famous! Listen to the voice of Madame Patti as she sings 'Una Voce Poco Fa'. Listen to the voice of Tennyson as he recites: 'O! for the touch of a vanished hand, and the sound of a voice that is still . . .'

Come Inside and Witness a Demonstration of Edison's newest invention, as presented by Mr Lloyd, who will also give a versatile and interesting account of the uses of this fascinating and beautiful machine.

Admission 2/- 1/- 6d

'It's a wonderful thing,' Ernest said. He stood with Fanny's arm linked with his, she standing back slightly, a little removed from his enthusiasm. He gave a slow, wondering shake of his head. 'To think of a machine being able to hold a human voice – and then to be able to give it out whenever you want.' He had read of the machine when it had first come out over a year ago, but this was the first time it had been seen in Trowbridge. He began to read the notice again, but Fanny gave a little sigh and pulled on his arm.

'Oh, come on, Ernie,' she said. 'It's 'alf over now. And besides, it's too dear.'

He nodded. 'Yeh, I s'pose you're right.'

'Anyway,' she added, her tone dismissive. 'It's only another nine days wonder. Do they truly think folk have nothing better to do than sit down and listen to machines all day long?' She pulled on his arm again, and reluctantly he turned and they moved off.

Trowbridge was the usual venue of those from the nearby villages who wanted a more alert, lively atmosphere than that found on their own doorsteps, and Ernest and Fanny were no exceptions. Finding little to do in Hallowford on a Saturday night they had walked the four miles from the village. They knew Trowbridge well, particularly Fanny who, like her father, worked as a machine operator at the Castle Court Mill where the world-famous West of England broadcloth was produced.

From the Town Hall they crossed Silver Street into Fore Street where they stopped to spend an hour over coffee in a small coffee shop. Outside again they strolled hand in hand, passing by the cattle market-place where a brief, pale smell of dung came to them on the November air. They made their way on down Castle Street, coming at last to the bridge over the Biss. There they stopped, standing side by side in the light from the gaslamp, looking down into the dark of the moving water below. Now, very faintly on the breeze, came the smell from the malthouse. Straightening and moving nearer to Fanny, Ernest put his arm across her shoulder and drew her closer to his side. She gave a little sigh and briefly laid her head on his shoulder. He turned her to him and bent his face to hers.

'Ah, Fan,' he murmured, 'I do love you so.'

'I love you too, Ernie.'

He kissed her, lightly at first and then more insistently. After a few moments she drew back her head. 'It's too public in the lamplight,' she said. 'Someone'll see us.'

'Ah, to hell with 'em.'

She chuckled. 'All right for you to say that.'

Ernest and Fanny had seen one another about the village for most of their lives, during which time they had barely taken notice of the other's existence. But then in the late summer of last year they had found themselves together at a village dance. Since then they had spent more and more time together, meeting two or three evenings during the weeks and at weekends.

Now, in a sudden rush of affection, Ernest drew her to him, kissed her again and then stood looking down into her face. Sometimes lately he felt hardly able to believe his luck. Fanny was just about the sweetest, prettiest girl he had ever seen. Coming up to just above his shoulder, her neat, trim little figure was dressed in a woollen coat of olive green with a paler green braiding. On her red-gold hair she wore a little bonnet of green velvet, trimmed with ribbon. Her eyes, laughing up at him now, were a greenish-grey. She had a short, pert, freckled little nose and a soft, pink little mouth that turned up at the corners and which, when she smiled, as now, set tiny dimples in her cheeks. It was no wonder at all to him that Charlie Durbin from Hallowford, and Tim Higham who worked near her at the factory, should both be trying their luck with her. Neither one of them would have her, though; he was determined on that score.

He kissed her again and she returned the kiss. Then as they broke apart she said with a sigh, 'I suppose we'd better get back home. There'll be ructions if I'm late.' She pulled up the collar of her coat and sighed again. 'Oh, I wish I didn't have to live at home.'

'Why?'

'There's no privacy – no room. Having to do what you're told all the time. I 'ates it.' She shook her head. 'I'd like to go away from Hallowford. There's never anything to do there.'

'Where else would you live, then?'

She shrugged. 'Well, I wouldn't mind livin' here in Trowbridge. Would you? For a start you could get a better job. One that paid better.'

'Work in the brewery or in one of the mills? No, I wouldn't want to be cooped up all day long in some factory. Anyway, I like Hallowford all right.'

'But you wouldn't want to live there after we're married, would you?'

Fanny had brought up the subject of marriage on several occasions over the past few weeks. Ernest wanted marriage, but it just wasn't possible yet. They were too young.

'When d'you think it'll be, Ernie?' she said, '– our getting married?'

'Oh, Fan – we've got some time yet before we seriously start thinking about that. It's too soon yet.'

'I don't know why you say that,' she responded quickly, '– Robbie Soames is getting married – and he's only eighteen, same as you.'

'Yes, maybe, but perhaps Robbie Soames can afford it.'

'Well – I don't think 'e's got that much in the way of money.'

'No, and ain't got that much in the way o' sense, neither. Anyway – I couldn't leave our mam yet. She depends on me.' He shook his head. 'No, I'll 'ave to wait a while till the others are a bit older. Our Arthur's earnin' a bit now – and our Agnes, too, so maybe after a while, in two-three years –'

'*Two-three years?*'

'Don't say it like that, Fan. It's not a lifetime. It'll soon pass.'

'Oh, ah, for you, per'aps. Anyway,' she said with a sigh, '– we'd better get on back home.'

Soon after eleven-thirty the next morning, Sunday, Sarah called at Hallowford House to take Blanche down to the cottage. As they made their way down the hill towards the lane Blanche walked slightly apart, silent. Sarah studied her, seeing the preoccupied expression in her eyes. Something was wrong; she had realized it as soon as she had seen her that morning.

Later, when midday dinner was over Agnes cleared the table while Arthur took Blanche to Sunday school. A little while after Arthur's return Fanny came to the cottage and Ernest put on his coat saying that he and Fanny would meet Blanche from class and take her for a walk before tea. Agnes said she would go with them.

When Blanche emerged from the small church she found the others waiting, and with Ernest determining the way, the four set off. They went first into a small wood where they tramped over the fallen leaves down to the river. There Ernest enthusiastically pointed out a family of coot, thirteen of them swimming in the water, and then, high up in the sky above the water meadows, a kestrel hunting for food. While Agnes showed interest in it all, however, Blanche remained silently detached and seemed to pay little heed.

On the way back they followed a bridle path at the edge of a field and joined the road halfway down Gorse Hill. As they emerged through the stile in the hedgerow Blanche came to a stop and looked up towards the hilltop where, beyond the rise and the trees, stood Hallowford House. Ernest, turning beside Fanny and Agnes, called back, 'Come on, Blanche – let's get on 'ome for tea. I'm getting hungry.'

But Blanche remained where she was and after a moment Ernest left the others and moved back to her side. Crouching down before her he looked into her eyes.

'What is it, Blanche?' he said. 'What's the matter?' He had always been able to reach her.

She shook her head, saying nothing.

'Aren't you going to tell me?'

'– There's nothing to tell.'

'Are you sure?'

She didn't answer. He looked at her standing there, preoccupation in her face – and some other expression of concern – out of place in a child so young. He sighed and said, 'Well, we'd better get back to the others.' He was about to get up then, but Blanche reached out and took his sleeve.

'I don't want anyone to feel pity for me, Ernie,' she said. 'Not ever.'

'No, of course you don't.' He frowned, smiling at the same time. 'But why should they?'

She was silent for a moment, then she said, 'You know, Ernie, it's very different up at the house. It's very different from at the cottage.'

He nodded. 'Ah, I daresay it is, Blanche.'

'Yes. We haven't got all the nice things they've got there, Ernie. Why not? Why can't we have those things too?'

He put his arms around her. 'Oh, Blanche – I'm afraid we just can't afford 'em. That's the truth of it.'

'It's not fair, is it?'

He shrugged. 'No, maybe it's not, but we 'aven't got the money, and that's all there is to it. I'm afraid we're not rich like Mr Savill.'

'Yes – he's rich, isn't he – Mr Savill?'

'Ah, I reckon so.'

She nodded. 'Yes. I never thought about it before. But I've been thinking about it – since Miss Baker went yesterday.'

'Miss Baker? What's she got to do with anything?'

'People can't help being poor, can they?'

'No, I don't suppose they can. If they could they'd do something about it.'

'What would they do?'

'Well – get rich, I s'pose.'

'Yes. That's how you get a fine house, with carriages and horses and all those things. That's how you're able to travel, isn't it? To go to London and Sicily and those places.'

He wondered what Sicily had to do with anything, then he said, 'Yes, you need a lot of money for those things.'

She nodded; then: 'D'you like looking after Mr Harker's cattle, Ernie?'

He gave a short laugh. '*Like* it? Well, I can't say as I like it that much. But it's better than some things.'

'It's not better than being a doctor, though, is it?'

'– A doctor. Oh, no, I reckon that'd be much better. Why d'you ask that?'

'Agnes told me that you want to be a doctor one day.'

'Ah, well, that was a while back – when I didn't know

173

any better. I didn't realize then that you need a lot of money to learn to be a doctor.'

'If you were rich like Mr Savill, though, you'd be able to, wouldn't you? – learn how to be a doctor.'

'Yeh, I reckon I would. But we're not, so I'll just have to be a stockman, wun I?'

'Mr Savill doesn't have to work nearly every day like you, you know. Lots of days he doesn't work at all.'

'No, well, lucky for 'im.'

Blanche stood in silence for some moments, taking in his words, then, her voice resolute, she said, 'I'm going to be rich one day too, Ernie. And when I am I'll give you the money to go and learn about medicine and being a doctor. I'll have the money to do whatever I like. I'll have a house like Mr Savill's, with lots of rooms and nice furniture. I shall. And I shall have lots of nice clothes, and servants, and friends who come to call on me in their carriages.'

'Will you indeed?' Ernest said, smiling. 'Well, I hope one day you will.'

'I shall, Ernie, I shall. I'll have anything I want, and I'll do anything I want to do.'

He chuckled and gently touched his hand to her cheek. 'Maybe, maybe. But you're gunna 'ave to saddle the wind before you can ride it, my dear.'

The sound of the piano came to them as they entered the cottage on their return. They took off their coats, hats and boots and went into the front room where Sarah was sitting at the piano. To her accompaniment she and Arthur were singing 'I Will Meet You in the Twilight'. Ernest, Fanny and the two girls sat on the sofa. When the song had ended Ernest called on Sarah to sing again, to which Arthur added, 'Yes, sing "Comin' Thro the Rye".' 'Oh, no,' Sarah said, '– not that old thing.' She opened before her a piece of sheet music, played the introduction and began to sing:

> Lucy and John from the village,
> Were in love and engaged to be wed:
> But up went the nose of sweet Lucy,
> At what John of some other girl said.
> John smiled, much given to teasing,
> Then softly he started to sing,
> Till Lucy with rage growing warmer,
> Threw down their engagement ring.

Ernest, getting up and moving to Sarah's side, joined in the song, taking the man's part. Taking alternate lines he and Sarah sang:

> 'I won't be your wife,' said Lucy,
> 'Thank goodness for that,' said John.
> 'I hate such a brute,' said Lucy,
> 'But other girls don't,' said John.
> 'I'm going back to the dairy.'
> 'Perhaps it's as well,' said he,
> 'But I hope you will come to the wedding
> Of Molly Malone and me.'

There was laughter at the end of the song and then Sarah called on Blanche to come to the piano. Blanche, who sang and played well for her age, usually joined in with the music at the cottage when she came down on a Sunday. Today, though, she shook her head, remaining where she was. After a moment Agnes got up and took Sarah's place. She played while she sang in her light, clear soprano, 'The Stream in the Valley', Ernest, Fanny and Arthur joining in the chorus:

Oh, stream in the valley, so lovely and bright!
I wander beside thee with joy and delight!

Sarah, moving to the doorway, turned and looked at Blanche as she sat in silence; then she left the room and went into the kitchen.

She was setting the table when Ernest came out to her. He told her of his conversation with Blanche. Sarah stood still, listening in silence. Then she finished preparing the tea and called the others in from the parlour. At her voice they left off singing and came into the kitchen. All except Blanche. Sarah, going back into the little parlour, found her sitting on the sofa gazing out of the window.

'Blanche,' she said, moving towards her, 'aren't you coming to have your tea? I made you a vanilla cake – your favourite.'

Blanche said nothing.

'Blanche – what's wrong?' Sarah said. 'You're unhappy about something. What is it?'

'Nothing.'

A little silence went by, then, putting some brightness into her voice, Sarah said,

'So – what shall you be doing tomorrow?'

'I don't know. Mr Savill's going to find us a new governess.'

'Yes, Ernest tells me that Miss Baker has gone. You never mentioned it. When did she go?'

'Yesterday.' Then vehemently Blanche added, 'I didn't like her. I'm glad she's gone. I'm *glad*!'

'– Why didn't you like her?'

'She wasn't nice. Still, Mr Savill said I must forget all about it – the things she said.'

'– Oh? What did she say?'

'She said Mr Savill pitied me, and that was the only reason I was at the house. Because he felt pity for me.'

'– She said that?'

'Yes, but Mr Savill said it wasn't true, and that I wasn't to think about it.' She shrugged. 'Anyway, she's gone now, and I'm glad.' She sat in silence for a moment then added: 'She said I belonged in the gutter.'

Sarah felt herself go cold. With sudden tears starting in her eyes she reached out and drew Blanche to her. For a moment she held her in her arms, and then Blanche broke away and started towards the door. 'I'd better go and have my tea,' she said.

For a few minutes after Blanche had gone from the room Sarah continued to sit there. Then with a sigh she got up and followed her into the kitchen.

When tea was over Sarah went out to the scullery where she began to wash the dishes, joined a moment later by Agnes. As they stood there Ernest came out, took the dish towel from Agnes's hand and said to her, 'You go and get ready for church, Aggie. I'll do this.' At his words Agnes readily relinquished the task and went away. Ernest began to dry the plates. After a few moments he set down the dish he had just dried, closed the door leading into the kitchen, then said to Sarah,

'I wouldn't worry about Blanche, Mam.'

Sarah sighed. 'Oh, Ernest, she's so unhappy. Though after what the governess said to her it's hardly to be wondered at. It's more than that, though.'

'Oh? – what is it?'

'I think now she realizes that she's only a – a guest up there at the house. She's not a part of it.' She shook her head. 'And in a way I'm glad. It's time she was aware of the situation. All the while she's been there it's just been setting her further apart from the rest of us.'

'She'll be all right again as time goes on.'

'No, that's the trouble, don't you see? Too much time has gone by already.'

Later on Sarah and Blanche set off up the hill. Sarah's thoughts were in a turmoil. After a while they reached the house, entered by the side door and started across the yard, Blanche a little ahead. Sarah observed the slight air of eagerness in Blanche's steps and called after her.

'Blanche . . .'

Blanche came to a halt.

'I want to talk to you for a minute,' Sarah said.

'What about?'

Sarah shook her head. 'Not here.' She looked about her then nodded in the direction of the garden. 'Let's go over there for a minute.'

Blanche shrugged, took the hand that Sarah held out to her and together they walked across the yard.

Sarah led her towards the kitchen garden. There in a little area screened by the shrubbery she came to a stop. Blanche stopped beside her and looked up at her in puzzlement.

'I just wanted somewhere where I could talk to you in private for a moment or two,' Sarah said; then: 'Are you warm enough?'

'Yes.' Blanche frowned. 'What is it, Mama?'

Sarah gazed at her in silence for long moments, trying to find the right words, then she said simply:

'I want you to live at home again, Blanche.'

Blanche stared up at her for a second then cried out loudly, 'No! *No!*'

The words felt like a wound in Sarah's heart and she felt tears well up in her eyes. She blinked them away. 'I'm sorry, Blanche. I know how you love it here but – well, it's time you came home.'

'No, please . . .' Blanche shook her head from side to side. 'Please, Mama, no . . .'

Sarah shrugged. 'I'm sorry . . .'

'But I like it here. I do.'

'I know that. But you've already been here too long. And it's time you came home.' Raising her head slightly, Sarah could see the roof of the tall house above the shrubbery in between. 'You don't belong here. You belong with us at the cottage.'

Blanche looked away. 'Mr Savill said that one day I would have to go back home again. I didn't think it would be yet.'

Sarah said nothing. Blanche turned back and looked up at her. 'Is Mr Savill sending me away?'

'Oh, no, no. Mr Savill is very fond of you.'

'Then – why?'

'I told you – you don't belong here. This isn't your home. Your home is with us, down at the cottage.'

'Does Mr Savill know – that I have to leave here?'

'I haven't spoken to him about it yet.'

A pause. 'When do I have to go?'

'Well, I thought – oh, wait another four or five weeks and come back in time for Christmas. You'll be nine years old then.'

'What about my lessons?'

'– We'll see about those.' Sarah stood looking down at the little stranger who was her daughter, then bent to her and put her hands on her shoulders. 'Listen to me,' she said softly. 'You've been living here for many years now, Blanche. But it's not your home.'

'No – I know, but –' Blanche's brow creased with worry, '– but you get used to things, Mama.'

'Yes, I know.'

Blanche gave a deep sigh. 'I didn't think it would change. I thought it would go on for ever.'

'Yes – I'm sorry.' Sarah gave a little shake of her head. 'Oh, I know that at the cottage we haven't got all the nice things there are at Mr Savill's, but – even so, we shall be happy together. You, me, Ernest, Arthur and Agnes. We'll all be together, and – and that's how families should be. You'll be happy, I promise you – you wait and see. Just give it a chance.' She looked into the child's blue eyes. 'Will you?'

Blanche nodded her head. 'Yes, Mama.'

A few minutes later as Sarah walked back down the hill she felt her spirits lifting. The decision had been made, and Blanche, in spite of her initial reaction, had accepted it. It was going to be all right. Just another month or so and Blanche would come back to the cottage – and this time it would be for good. And, yes, it would be hard for the child at first, but she would settle. She would accept the change, in time.

Sarah suddenly thought of Blanche's question regarding her school lessons. She would take care of that too. She would go and see Mr Savill during the next two or three weeks. Perhaps he would agree to Blanche still going to the house for her tuition for a time. That way Blanche's education could continue and the strain of her leaving would be less severe.

Sarah smiled as the growing promise and contentment warmed her, and she quickened her step.

After tea Marianne had joined her father in the library where they now sat together at a small table making a jigsaw puzzle. Marianne wasn't accustomed to being on her own and during Blanche's absence that day Savill had tried to spend more time with his daughter. Soon the girls would have a new governess – and in the meantime Savill had hired an elderly woman from the village to fill the breach. Miss Timperley, a retired governess herself, would begin her duties in the morning.

As they sat there there came a tap at the door. Savill called, 'Come in,' and Blanche entered. 'Ah, Blanche,' Savill said, smiling, '– you're back. Good.' He rose from his chair. 'You're just in time to take over this job from me.'

Blanche joined Marianne at the table and as the two of them worked at the puzzle Savill moved another chair and took up his newspaper again. There was mention of the Spanish influenza having now reached England. According to the report it appeared to be a particularly virulent strain and already a number of people had been stricken with it. When some excited exclamation from Marianne took his attention from the news he looked over the top of the paper at the two girls as they sat side by side. It was true what he had said to Alice Harrow, he thought; the girls were like sisters ... And then he found himself wondering what would happen when Blanche went back to her family for good. How would Marianne feel? There was no doubt that she would miss Blanche enormously. And surely such a time couldn't be very far away; he had been expecting it for some time now. Over the years he had never once spoken to Mrs Farrar about Blanche's absence from her home; he had kept silent on the matter, content to have Blanche there as long as it suited Mrs Farrar. But Mrs Farrar had said nothing either. And if she continued to say nothing would the situation continue? But it couldn't go on for ever. As the situation was it was causing problems for the child herself. He thought in particular of what Miss Baker had said to Blanche – that she, Blanche, was at the house solely as a result of his own feelings of pity. And Blanche, with a foot in both camps and belonging to neither would very likely continue to be a target for such comments.

He watched Blanche now as she snapped a piece of the puzzle into place and then lifted her eyes to Marianne. There was something rather melancholy about Blanche's expression today, he thought; or was it his imagination? He studied her. There was no doubt, he said to himself, that she was a sensitive, clever and intelligent child – the kind of child any man would be glad to have as a daughter.

Chapter Sixteen

'I want to adopt her – legally.'

John Savill sat at a table in one of the upper rooms of the New Inn on Trowbridge's Silver Street. From around him came the clink of glasses and the murmur of voices from the other Freemasons who had gathered there. The monthly meeting of the Lodge of Concorde at the new Masonic lodge in Yerbury Street had just ended and, as was the custom, some of the members had come to the tavern's private room to relax, to talk and drink for an hour or so before going to their homes.

On Savill's left sat Dr Robert Kelsey, on his right Harold, John Savill's brother, manager of his mill in Trowbridge. Eight years younger than John Savill, Harold looked little like him. Whereas John Savill was tall and slim, Harold was somewhat below average height and of stocky build. Their colouring was different too; John's once dark hair had long ago turned grey, while the little grey in Harold's sandy hair was hardly noticeable.

At Savill's words the doctor sipped at the whisky in his hand and gave a slow nod. 'You've obviously given it serious thought,' he said.

'Oh, indeed, yes,' John Savill replied. 'And it's not such a new idea of mine. I mean. I've toyed briefly with it from time to time over the past couple of years.' He paused. 'I really do think it's the best thing to do.'

'Have you spoken of it yet to the girl's mother?' Harold asked.

'Not yet. But I intend to see her about it during the next couple of weeks.'

'How do you think she'll respond?'

'I really don't know. I just hope I can make her see the – the wisdom of it. I'm quite sure it would be the best thing for everybody concerned. It would ensure Blanche's future – which at the moment is as uncertain as it is for the rest of Mrs Farrar's children – and also it would relieve Mrs Farrar of a certain amount of responsibility. And it isn't as if things would be that different as far as Mrs Farrar's concerned. As it is she only sees Blanche two or three times a week. And she'd still see her, of course. That wouldn't change.'

With a smile Harold said, 'Altruism isn't dead, then.'

Savill frowned. Quite often he found himself regarding his brother with disapproval. But they had never been close, notwithstanding the fact that they often spent time in one another's company. Now Savill said with a trace of exasperation in his voice,

'It's not altruism, Harold. Don't be cynical. I'd be getting a great deal out of it.'

'Such as?' Harold said.

'Well, in particular Marianne would have a sister – *legally*. And I must confess I'd like that for her.'

'You don't wish to continue with the arrangement as it is?' Kelsey said.

'I don't see how it *can* continue as it is – for much longer. It's got to change in one way or the other – and fairly soon, I'd imagine.' Savill took a drink from his glass and shook his head. 'No, it's got to be settled – and before much more time goes by. The girls will be nine next month.'

'Well,' Harold said, 'just don't be too impetuous. Perhaps you should give it a little more thought before you rush in.'

John Savill moved his hand in a gesture of impatience. 'I'm not *rushing in*. I've given it a great deal of thought.'

At John's tone Harold raised his palm as a shield. 'All right,' he said, 'I just think it's important that you consider everything.' He shrugged. 'Anyway, it's none of my business, is it?' Then, changing the subject, he turned to the doctor and said:

'I imagine you've been reading the reports on the influenza, Doctor?'

Kelsey nodded. 'It would be difficult to miss them, wouldn't it? It appears to be more severe than it was in the last outbreak, three years back. The number of dead in Europe and Asia is really astounding.'

While Savill shook his head in sympathy Harold said disparagingly, 'They said at first in the papers that it had reached Britain in a milder form – that it wasn't nearly so dangerous as it was abroad. They didn't seem to treat it with that much seriousness.'

'I know,' Kelsey agreed, 'but they have to now. With so many having been stricken over the country, and upwards of twenty deaths in London alone last week they've had to change their views.'

'Do you think it will get to the village?' Savill said. 'Though I suppose there's not much doubt about that, is there?'

'It already has,' Kelsey said. He shook his head. 'I've already got two cases amongst my patients.'

'And how serious are they? I mean – isn't it possible that by now it's losing some of its virulence?'

Kelsey gave a shrug. 'Well, one always hopes for that. But it's a bit *too much* to hope for, I'm afraid. No, the cases are serious, believe me.'

The conversation moved on to other topics, and a little while later the doctor rose from his chair, wished them goodnight and went away. Over his beer Savill observed his younger brother. Harold would be fifty-one years old in August, and Savill silently remarked that there was about him a rather restless air. It had been evident for several months now. Perhaps, Savill mused, it had something to do with the loss of Harold's wife, Jane, who had died the year before after a long illness. The couple had not been that happy, but nevertheless she had been a stable influence in the marriage.

Harold now was talking about the motor car industry. He was vaguely toying with the idea, he said, of selling his few remaining shares in the Trowbridge mill, adding the proceeds to his savings and investing the lot in one of the new automobiles that were so firing the imagination. Savill advised caution; for God's sake, wait, he urged, before doing anything rash; make sure first of all that such a venture is viable. In reply Harold insisted, a little impatiently, that he was not about to take any impulsive decisions.

'Now *you're* telling *me* not to be impulsive,' Harold said. Putting down his empty glass, he added: 'Are you serious about adopting the little Farrar girl, John?'

'You obviously have some doubts, Harry,' Savill said.

'Oh, well, I just think – oh, I know that she's pretty and bright, and well-mannered and –' Harold shrugged. 'I mean, it's all very well to talk of her being a sister to Marianne, but she can never really be that, can she?'

'Why not?'

'Well – what about her background?'

Savill frowned. 'I'm not certain I understand you.'

'Oh, John, you know what I mean as well as I do. I'm just thinking of the old saying about silk purses.'

Savill sat in silence for a moment, looking at his brother. Under his gaze Harold gave a little laugh. 'I think I've said too much,' he said.

Savill shrugged. 'Well, it won't be the first time you and I haven't seen eye to eye, will it?'

Reports of the progress of the influenza were becoming increasingly disturbing. The outbreak of three years before had caused a great many deaths, and now it was beginning to appear that the present one might be even more serious. In London and other large cities the death toll was mounting at an alarming rate, while the newspaper accounts frequently gave reports of whole families being affected. A number of schools throughout the country had closed down through high incidence of the disease among the pupils and staff alike. In other quarters to prevent the disease from spreading, public meetings in many towns were being cancelled. And now the disease had reached Trowbridge and the surrounding areas. In the town that Tuesday morning Savill had seen a notice outside the Town Hall advising of the cancellation of a forthcoming meeting of councillors: 'Until further notice, due to the prevalence of the Influenza . . .' while at the mill the numbers of absentees had increased over the previous week. On Wednesday Savill received a letter from Edward Harrow's son, Gentry, from the school in Brighton where he was a boarder, telling him that the influenza had broken out in the school and that a number of the pupils were affected. He himself, however, Gentry said, had so far remained free of any symptoms.

On Friday, by the second post, came another letter from Gentry. Beneath the school's address he had written:

5th December, 1889

Dear Uncle John,

   I have to write and tell you that due to the influenza epidemic the school is to be temporarily closed. I hope you are at home as I am to leave for Trowbridge tomorrow morning, Friday. I shall be travelling via Southampton, Salisbury and Westbury and if the trains are on time I should arrive at Trowbridge at 2.10 pm. I shall be grateful if you can send someone to meet me, otherwise I'll walk or try to get a cab.

Yours,
Gentry Harrow

That afternoon James took the phaeton to Trowbridge and just before three o'clock arrived back at Hallowford House with Gentry and his box. After Gentry had been shown the room prepared for him on the first floor, Savill took him into the library while Florence went to get him some lunch.

In the library Savill stood by the fireplace facing Gentry who sat in the wing chair, his long legs stretched out before him. The boy was tall for his fourteen years and a good deal taller than when Savill had last seen him. Studying him, Savill peered into the boy's dark eyes. 'Are you sure you feel all right?' he asked.

'Oh, yes, absolutely, Uncle John.'

'Are you sure? No trace of a headache, no beginnings of a cold . . . ?'

'No, really, I'm fine.'

'Good.' Savill nodded, though he sounded unconvinced. 'What about your schoolfellows?' he asked.

'Over forty of the ninety-two boys have gone down with it,' Gentry said. 'And two of the masters. Those boys who are too sick to travel are all in sick-bay, in isolation. The rest have all been sent home.' He grinned, showing white, even teeth. Savill watched the grin, smiled and said:

'Oh, I can see that it's not that unwelcome to you –

to get a holiday from school, but it's a very serious business all the same, young man.'

'Yes, I know that, Uncle John. But, as you say – it's nice to get an unexpected vacation.'

'Yes, of course it is. Though I don't know how you hope to spend it.'

Gentry shrugged. 'Oh, don't worry, I'll find something to do.'

Savill gazed at him for a moment in thought, then he shook his head. 'Well,' he said, 'I'm afraid you're going to be disappointed if you're looking forward to getting out much.'

'I'm sorry, Uncle John – I don't understand.'

'It's simple, my boy. You must understand, this is a deadly disease. It's not something to be taken lightly.'

'No – of course not.'

Savill nodded. 'So, I'm afraid there'll be no going out for you, no mixing with anyone in the village. Apart from my responsibilities to you, I've got two children in this house and I must protect them. To that end I intend to do everything I possibly can. I don't want you to think I'm being hard on you, but for a few days you'll have to go into isolation.'

Gentry stared at him. 'Isolation?'

'Yes. This is not some mild little head cold going around. This is a killer. People are dying of it. Don't you read the news?' Savill took up the newspaper and riffled through its pages. 'Look at this.' He slapped the page before him. 'In Waltham Cross, look – a mother, her daughter and two sons, all dead within seven days.' He looked at another column. 'In Sweden one small town has had twenty funerals in one day. At Kimberley in South Africa – more than a thousand deaths. Over six hundred so far in Budapest.' He glanced up from the newspaper. 'Shall I go on?'

'It's not happening here, is it?' Gentry said.

'No, it's not.' Savill shook his head. 'But there's plenty of time.'

When Arthur arrived home that Friday evening, it was with the information that Mr Grill, his employer, had come down with the 'flu and had spent most of the day in bed.

Ernest returned from the farm a little later and after he had washed and changed and eaten, Fanny came round. They had arranged to go out for a walk together. Soon after her arrival Ernest put on his coat and they left the cottage.

They walked along Elm Road, Peters Lane, along Bridge Street and around the green. As they approached the back of Fox Lane Fanny said,

'Did you think any more on what we talked about?'

'– About – getting married, you mean?'

'Yes.' When he didn't answer she prompted him, 'Well, did you?'

He shook his head. 'We're too young, Fan. We are, you know that.'

'Oh, we're not, Ernie. We're not.' She came to a stop, Ernest halting beside her. 'Think how it could be, Ernie,' she said. 'We'd find our own little place. A home of our own. And we wouldn't have to stay in Hallowford if we didn't want to.'

He smiled. 'You're really set on goin' away, ain't you?'

'Well – why not? Anywhere's better than here. Trowbridge, Bristol. Maybe London.'

'London?'

'Why not?' She paused. 'Tim Higham says he's going to London soon.'

'Tim Higham, that bloke who works with you at the factory? Well, you can believe that when it 'appens.'

'How can you say that? You don't even know 'im.'

'No, but I've 'eard about 'im. I've seen 'im, too – all that macassar on 'is hair. I shouldn't think 'e needs any more oil – not by the looks of 'im.'

Fanny smiled. 'It couldn't be that you're jealous, could it?'

'Jealous? Me? Of that masher?'

'Ernie, I think you are. Come on now, own up.'

'Nah, I ain't jealous. Why should I be jealous about 'im? Besides, he's too old for you. He's ten years older than you at least.'

She shook her head. 'Ernie, you don't know anything about him, really.'

'No, well, maybe I don't.'

'He's been to London. He was tellin' me all about it. He said I could get a really good job there if I wanted. I could go into an office and work a typewriter machine. He makes London sound a really wonderful place and –'

'Yeh, wonderful,' Ernest broke in. 'If Jack the Ripper don't get you the 'flu will. They're droppin' like flies there.'

'Oh, well, if you don't want to be serious . . .' She turned away and began to walk on. Ernest hurried after her and took her by the arm.

'Fan, don't get all like that,' he said as he turned her to face him.

'Ernie, you say you love me, but sometimes I get the feelin' that it's only talk.'

He felt a little rise of panic within his chest. 'No, Fan, don't say that.' He drew her to him. She came unwillingly; he could feel her resistance. 'I do love you, Fan,' he said. 'I do. You know I do.'

'Ah, so you say, but talk's cheap.' She pulled away from him and moved towards the rear gate of her home. 'Anyway, I must go in.'

'Ain't you gunna say goodnight to me?'

She closed the gate and looked at him over the top of it. 'Goodnight, Ernie.'

'I mean *properly*.' He reached out for her over the gate, but she stepped back out of his reach.

'I must go. Really I must.'

'– Well, shall I see you tomorrow?'

'I don't know.' She gave a shrug. 'We'll see.' Then she was turning and moving away up the path.

As the evening had worn on Arthur had begun to complain of not feeling well and at Sarah's insistence he went up to bed before his usual time.

The next morning, Saturday, while Ernest was having his breakfast, Sarah went up to see Arthur. He was already awake. When she asked him how he was feeling he complained of a headache and a sore throat. 'Still,' he said, 'I must get ready for work.' He sat up and made to get out of the bed but she put a hand on his shoulder. 'No, you stay where you are,' she told him. 'Lie down again.' She went back downstairs then and put a brick into the oven. Afterwards, returning to the bedroom, she lit the fire in the little fireplace. When the brick was hot she wrapped it in an old piece of flannel and put it beneath the bedclothes against Arthur's feet. 'Now, you stay there, and try to go back to sleep.' 'But I'll be needed at work,' he protested feebly. 'Well, that can't be helped,' Sarah replied. 'You're not going anywhere today.'

On Sunday Blanche stood gazing out of the nursery window while the rain fell with increasing force on the pane. The nursery clock said twelve-fifteen. Nearby on a chair lay her coat. Her mother would be there at any moment to take her to the cottage for the day.

There was 'flu in the village, and because of it she

and Marianne and Mr Savill had not gone to church that morning – and neither would they, Mr Savill had said, until the 'flu had passed. In the room across the landing Gentry Harrow was installed. She and Marianne had called out to him as they had passed his door, but Mr Savill had forbidden them to go near him yet.

Behind her in the room now Marianne sat cutting out fashion figures from a magazine while their new governess, Miss Fenwick, sat nearby mending some linen. Young and attractive, she had come from nearby Frome. With her arrival Miss Timperley, their temporary governess, had gone back to live in the village.

Blanche turned and looked around her. This room would not be her home for much longer. Soon she would be returning to the cottage to live. She wondered what it would be like. She had said nothing to Marianne or Mr Savill about her mother's decision. She didn't want to think about it until the time came. *We'll all be together*, her mother had said, *and that's how families should be. You'll be happy, I promise you . . .* She thought of her mother's words; the promise. They brought little comfort, though.

Turning back to the window she saw a familiar figure come striding across the yard through the rain.

'Here's Ernest,' she said. 'Here's my brother come for me.'

She watched until Ernest had moved out of sight beneath the window then turned and picked up her coat. When she was dressed in her coat, hat and boots she waited for the maid to come for her, but the minutes ticked by and then she saw Ernest moving away again across the yard towards the side door. 'He's going away again,' she said. She frowned, puzzled.

A few moments later there was the sound of footsteps

on the landing outside and then Mr Savill was opening the door and calling to her. She went to him.

'Yes, sir?'

'Your brother Ernest was just here,' he said. Blanche nodded. 'Yes, sir, I know. I saw him from the window. I thought he was here to take me home . . .'

'No. He came to say that it would be better if you didn't go home today – or even perhaps next Sunday.'

'Oh. Why not?'

'Apparently your brother Arthur is sick. Your mother's sure it's the 'flu, and she thinks it best that you don't go home yet – not until Arthur has recovered.'

When Blanche had gone back into the nursery Savill went downstairs to the library. He had thought of going to see Mrs Farrar today. It would have to wait, though. This wasn't the time to go to the Farrars' cottage – not when they had sickness there.

Chapter Seventeen

After Ernest and Agnes had gone from the cottage on Monday morning Sarah went upstairs to the boys' room where Arthur lay in a restless sleep. Earlier she had made up the fire and replaced the brick in his bed. Now she stood beside the bed, looking down at him. At the neck of his old shirt she could see the edge of the brown-paper vest she had made for him the night before, first having rubbed his narrow chest with camphorated oil. After that she had smoothed goose grease on his chest; this she had covered with the brown paper. To combat his cough she had given him honey and vinegar and, last thing the night before, an inhalation of eucalyptus which she had sprinkled on a handkerchief and held beneath his nose. Now as she bent lower to pull the blankets more closely up to his chin the smell of the goose grease and the eucalyptus rose up to her nostrils from his warm, feverish body. He coughed, the sound dry and hacking. It had grown worse during the night and she realized that none of the remedies seemed to be having much effect. She continued to stand there for some minutes then, quietly, so as not to disturb him, she turned from the bed and made her way back downstairs.

Galvanized by the disturbing news of the spreading epidemic, Savill took measures to prevent the admittance of the disease to Hallowford House. On Monday morning he sent a message to his manager telling him that he would not be back at the mill until the epidemic was over. After that he cancelled the few social arrangements he had made and his various business appointments. Then he arranged for certain provisions from the butcher and the grocer to be delivered at once to the house, at the same time instructing the servants not to leave the house on any account. The non-resident servants, such as the gardeners, the odd-job boy and James the groom, he told to continue with their work but not to come to the house. If there was anything he wanted them to know he would put out a note for them, he said. Likewise they could do the same. Savill had no doubt that folk would regard him as fastidious and eccentric for the measures he was taking, but he didn't care. In a matter of hours the situation at Hallowford House was something like a state of siege.

When Ernest got in from the farm that Monday evening he found his brother no better. At Sarah's insistence he at once went next door, borrowed Davie Hewitt's bicycle and rode off to fetch Dr Harmon. The Harmons' maid answered his ring at the door. She told him that Dr Harmon was out, but that she would give him the message as soon as he returned.

When he returned to the cottage he ate his dinner, changed, and then went out to call on Fanny. Fanny's sister Amy answered the door to his knock. Fanny was in bed, she told him – along with her two other sisters, Lottie and Edie. It looked as if they had the 'flu.

As Ernest returned home a little later he found Agnes just on the point of going out to choir-practice.

'Where's Mam?' he asked as he took off his coat. 'Up with Artie?'

'Yes.' Agnes tied the strings of her bonnet. 'The doctor came while you were out.'

'What did he say?'

'Well, it *is* the 'flu, of course. But I s'pose we already knew that.'

She went off then, and Ernest put the kettle on the range. A little later Sarah came into the kitchen.

'How is he?' Ernest asked.

She sighed. 'Oh, I don't know. All we can do is keep him in bed and just – just hope it doesn't – get worse. If it goes onto his chest . . . His cough is very bad. Doctor says he'll call again tomorrow.' She paused. 'What are you doing back so soon? I thought you went out to see Fanny.'

'I did. She's got the 'flu as well, it seems. And Edie and Lottie.'

'Oh, dear.' Sarah shook her head in sympathy. 'How are they?'

'I don't know. I was only there a minute.'

The water in the kettle was boiling and Sarah made some tea. They sat together drinking it at the kitchen table.

'It's such a terrible thing, this 'flu,' Sarah said. 'Doctor said he's had one call after another. There's so much of it about. I mentioned Arthur's boss having caught it, and he said, yes, Mr Grill was very poorly. And Mr Grill's wife now, as well.' She clicked her tongue. 'It's a good thing Blanche didn't come home yesterday. There's no sense in putting her at risk too.'

'Right,' Ernest agreed. 'Anyway, let's hope it all passes soon.'

'Yes.' She looked at him over the rim of her cup. 'And don't you worry about Fanny,' she said. 'She'll be all right soon.'

Ernest said nothing. Sarah continued to study him.

'I think you're mighty sweet on that young lady, aren't you?' she said.

He grinned at her. 'Ah, I reckon I am.'

'It's not hard to see.'

He was silent for a moment, then he said, 'D'you like her, Mam?'

'Oh – yes, I do. She's helpful when she comes round. She's a smart girl, too – in her dress, I mean. And very pretty, there's no doubt about that.'

'Yeh, I think so.' He gave a little laugh. 'I'm really lucky, I know that much.'

Sarah smiled. 'Oh? Well, *I* happen to think that Fanny's the lucky one. Having a nice, handsome, intelligent young man like you – she ought to *think* herself lucky, anyway. She couldn't do better, that's a fact.' Her smile grew wider. 'And there's some typical mother's unbiased talk for you.'

Ernest laughed, took a swallow from his cup, and said, 'Yeh, but like you say, she is a smart, pretty girl, ain't she?' Then he added, 'And she's a sensible girl, too, wouldn't you say?'

'Sensible? Well, yes, I should think she is.'

He nodded, pleased. Sarah watched him and said, 'You really are serious about her, aren't you?'

He looked at her intently. 'Mam, what would you say if I wanted to get married?'

A little silence, then Sarah said: '– When . . . ?'

'Well – soon.'

'And – does Fanny know you feel like this?'

'Oh, yes, she wants it too – very much.'

'More than you, d'you think?'

'Oh, I don't know about that, I . . .' His words tailed off. Sarah reached across the table and briefly pressed his hand.

'Ernest,' she said. 'I know that when*ever* you decide

198

to leave it will be too soon for me. And that's something I've got to be aware of, and I mustn't let it get in the way of what is – right for you. But – oh, Ernest, you're so young. You're both so young.'

'Well – not *so* young. Fanny'll be eighteen in April.'

'And how old will that make you? You'll still be eighteen.'

'Yes, I know, but –' Giving a little groan of hopelessness he turned his head away.

'Ernest, listen to me,' Sarah said. 'At eighteen years old you shouldn't be thinking about settling down. There'll be plenty of time for that in a few years from now. *Then* you'll have time to start thinking about marriage and – everything else – taking on extra responsibilities. Until then you should be having some fun – both of you. God knows, there's little opportunity enough. Have you got any money?'

'Not much, but – I can save.'

'After you're married? That's easier said than done. Why don't you wait – and try to save a little while you're waiting. You won't have much chance afterwards, believe me.' She paused. 'And – are you absolutely sure Fanny's the right girl for you?'

A look of profound disappointment crossed his face. 'You don't think she is?'

'Oh, I didn't say that, lad. It's what *you* feel that counts.'

'Oh, but – I love her, Mam. I do.'

Sarah sighed. 'Well, I don't know what to say to that, Ernest. I reckon there's not much I *can* say – except that – oh, but I do wish you'd wait.'

'I knew you'd say that.'

'I have to, my dear. And if your father were here he'd tell you just the same.'

'But – I'm afraid if I wait I'll lose her.'

She gave a melancholy little smile. 'Fear isn't the best start, is it? And how d'you think you might lose her?'

'Oh, you know – some other chap'll come along. Bound to. A girl lookin' like she does.'

'No – not if she loves you.'

A little pause, then Ernest said. 'Are you saying no, then? That I can't?'

She shook her head. 'No, I'm not saying that, son. I'm saying I'd like you both to wait. But – if you've made up your mind – well, then, you must do what you want. If you're sure you love one another, then – well, I won't stand in your way. I wouldn't do that.'

'Thanks, Mam.' A slow smile touched Ernest's mouth. 'I'll tell Fanny tomorrow, all right?'

Arthur's condition grew worse as the evening wore on and it was agreed that Sarah would sleep in Ernest's bed that night, in order to be near Arthur if he should need anything. Ernest would sleep downstairs on the parlour sofa, or make up a bed in front of the kitchen range; whichever he wanted.

With the little room lit faintly by the glow of the nightlight, Sarah slept only fitfully, each time she awoke her eyes going at once to Arthur in the next bed. Dr Harmon had left a sleeping draught and although Sarah had given a measure to the boy he passed a restless night, turning, muttering in his shallow sleep, mouth open, as if fighting for breath. Next morning it was clear to Sarah that he was much worse.

Dr Harmon called during the late afternoon. An elderly man, he appeared to be tiring somewhat from the now frequent demands on his time and energy. Also he had about him a rather harassed air and his usually slightly impatient manner was more pronounced. He didn't stay long. After examining Arthur, sounding his chest and taking his pulse he shook his head and told Sarah that there couldn't be much doubt that Arthur's influenza had turned to broncho-pneumonia. After giving Sarah further instructions as to the boy's care and leaving with her bottles of linctus and chloral, he left, saying that he would call again the next day.

That night, in spite of the sedative, Arthur remained feverishly wakeful, and Sarah was kept moving about, giving him what help she could, bathing his forehead; giving him doses of the linctus, of honey and vinegar; feeding him warm milk and murmuring softly to him when in his periods of restless sleep he cried out. At long last she saw the curtains lighten with the dawn.

It was clear that Arthur had grown worse during the night, and Sarah remained with him while Agnes got breakfast for herself and Ernest. When Ernest was ready to leave for work he crept up the stairs and came into the bedroom. He stood above Arthur's bed, gazing down at him as he fought for breath. Briefly Ernest laid a hand on Sarah's shoulder. 'Don't worry, Mam,' he whispered, 'Doctor'll be here again soon. He'll look after 'im all right.' Sarah nodded. Exhaustion lay on her like a blanket. Her eyelids felt sore and prickly from her vigil while her emotions seemed so tautly strung that she could hardly trust herself to speak. Turning to him as if only just becoming aware of his presence she said: 'Ernest . . . how are you, son? Did you sleep all right?' He had spent the night on the kitchen floor. He couldn't have slept that well, she knew.

'Oh, I'm all right. Don't concern yourself with me.'

A few minutes after Ernest's departure Agnes came upstairs. She was wearing her coat. As she stood looking from her brother to Sarah her eyes glistened with tears.

'D'you want me to stay, Mam?' she said after a moment.

'No, no, my dear. You go on to work. There's nothing you can do. I'll just wait for Dr Harmon. He'll be here soon.'

Reluctantly Agnes left and Sarah settled herself to waiting again.

Most of the time that followed she spent upstairs with Arthur or in the kitchen where she warmed milk for him, made him broth, and porridge. She could get him to eat but little of it, however. And the hours dragged by, and still Dr Harmon didn't come. When Agnes arrived home from work that afternoon there had still been no sign of the doctor. Arthur's condition seemed to have grown worse. His breathing sounded frighteningly constricted now, and he seemed too weak to bring up any of the secretions that were filling his lungs. Then towards five o'clock the scullery door opened and Dr Kelsey was there. Agnes was sitting at the kitchen table peeling potatoes and she looked up as with barely a knock he came striding into the kitchen and began to take off his coat. Quickly she got to her feet. He had come to see Arthur, he told her, adding that he was taking Dr Harmon's calls as Dr Harmon was sick. She took his coat and, going before him, directed him into the hall and up the stairs.

He was down again ten minutes later, his expression solemn. Sarah followed him into the kitchen. He washed his hands in some warm water that Sarah poured into a bowl, dried them, and then pulled on his coat again. 'I'll look in again tomorrow,' he said as he moved back towards the hall. Just before he went through the door he turned back and looked at Agnes.

'I heard you sing in church a few weeks back,' he said.

Agnes nodded, a nervous little smile touching her lips.

'Very nice,' he said. 'Keep it up.'

Glowing, Agnes thanked him. A few moments later, with Sarah following him to the front door, he was gone.

On the way home from the farm Ernest stopped at the Greenhams' house to ask after Fanny. Mrs Greenham came to the door at his knock. She was a short, wiry little woman with reddish hair and small, neat features. She told Ernest that Fanny, Edie and Lottie were still in bed. She'd ask him in to see Fanny, she added, but she couldn't, not with all three girls being in the one room. They were quite poorly, she added, but were not too bad and were bearing up. Ernest hesitated, then he took from his pocket a sealed envelope containing a letter he had hurriedly written at the farm that morning.

'Would you give Fanny this for me, please?' he said.

Mrs Greenham put the envelope into her apron pocket. 'I'll see she gets it, Ernie. Don't worry.'

'Thank you. And tell her I 'ope she'll be better soon.'

'I will.'

'Here you are – a letter from your young man.'

Up in the girls' bedroom Fanny took the letter from her mother and looked at it. *Miss Fanny Greenham*, Ernest had written in pencil. Fanny tore open the envelope, took out the letter and read what Ernest had written:

Dearest Fan,

I was so sorry to hear you're laid low with the 'flu, and I hope it won't be long before you're well again. I'm looking forward to seeing you. I miss you that much.

I thought you might be interested to know that I talked with my mother last night, and I think I might have some good news for you when I see you next.

As I say, I hope that will be soon. In the meantime, please think of,
Your loving
Ernie

Fanny read the letter again and smiled through the pain in her head. Her sister Edie, lying in the next bed with Lottie, looked across at her and said.

'What is it? What are you smiling about?'

'Never you mind.' Fanny gave her a glance of mock hauteur. 'You'll find out in good time – perhaps.'

Agnes served Ernest his dinner when he got indoors. Their mother was upstairs with Arthur. Agnes told Ernest about Dr Kelsey's visit, and then, looking round at the door to make sure that she wouldn't be heard, gave a little shake of her head and added,

'I didn't tell Mam. But I heard this afternoon that there's a couple have died in the village. Mr Grill was one of 'em.'

Ernest was asleep in the kitchen that night when he suddenly heard his name being called. He sat up abruptly and saw his mother standing in the doorway.

'Quick, Ernest! Quick!' she shouted to him. 'Quick! You must get up and go for Dr Kelsey.' There was fear in her voice.

Throwing back the blankets he swung his legs off the cushions and stood up. 'Is it Arthur?' he said.

'Yes. Oh, be quick. *Please*.' With her words Sarah turned back into the hall and the next moment he heard the sound of her feet as she hurried back up the stairs.

As he quickly got dressed he saw that the time was

just after two o'clock. Minutes later he was letting himself out of the back door and starting off at a run along the lane.

'All right, Arthur. It's all right, my darling. Mam's here. Mam's got you.'

Agnes, in her nightdress, was standing in the doorway helplessly looking on as Sarah sat on Arthur's bed holding him in her arms. His breath was rasping through his open mouth and in the light of the candle and the nightlight she could see that his skin had a strange, cold look about it.

Sarah had watched over him as the evening had worn on, but with the night exhaustion had taken over and she had begun to doze. Then, suddenly, she had awakened and realized that the sound of Arthur's breathing had changed. Getting up from the chair she had moved to his side. His breathing had been bad before, but now it was so much worse; now she could also hear in it a terrifying, strange, fine crackling sound. It was then that she had run downstairs to waken Ernest.

Now as she held Arthur in her arms he coughed his dry, painful, hacking cough and she felt the spasms shake his body before he went limp again in her arms. Then, his body tightening, clenching again, he struggled to draw in a harsh, tortured breath of air and coughed once more. The mucus bubbled out of his nostrils and Sarah took a cloth and gently wiped him clean. He was unaware of it; he seemed unaware of everything. Sarah, tears streaming down her cheeks, had no idea what to do. She could only sit there, murmuring to him over and over and praying that the doctor would soon arrive. Dr Kelsey would know what to do, she muttered to Agnes. He would know.

And then Arthur briefly stiffened in her arms again

and opened his eyes. They were unfocused for some moments, but then they lighted on Sarah's face and she saw the light of knowing in them. The breath was whistling from his lungs and the cold, mauvish look of his skin seemed to have grown stronger. 'Mam . . .' He gasped hoarsely on a terrifying intake of air and Sarah involuntarily cried out and wrapped her arms more firmly about him. He seemed to be turning blue before her eyes. *'Dear God, help me!'* She almost shrieked out the words while at the same time she half rose from the bed, still clutching him in her arms, as if she would run somewhere for help, carrying him with her. Then, sinking back onto the bed she held him close while his breathing grew even more tortured and eventually stopped.

Chapter Eighteen

John Savill stood without moving in the hall, the letters in his hand forgotten. In his ears he could still hear the postman's words as they had come to him through the crack of the partly opened door. One of the Farrar children was dead, the man had told him, and Mrs Farrar herself had also been stricken with the 'flu. Savill remained there for some seconds longer, then slowly turned and made his way across the hall.

The reports of the disease in the village had been filtering in as the days had gone by, sometimes by means of the postman, sometimes by means of James who left the occasional note on the back doorstep, and at other times by means of the tradesmen who, when leaving their produce at the back door, had called through to Florence or one of the maids.

This was the fifth day that Savill and the other inhabitants of Hallowford House had been in isolation, and while the reports from the outside world had grown more disturbing with each day, the house's occupants had so far remained healthy and free of the disease's symptoms.

And the news from outside *was* disturbing, with the newspapers giving regular reports of the toll of the disease in London and other cities. They told of fire brigades being understaffed, of communications being hampered by the high number of absentees among postmen and telegraph operators. And the number of sufferers went on mounting.

Closer to home the reports were no less saddening and alarming. Dr Harmon was seriously ill, it was said. As was poor, little, ineffectual Miss Timperley, the girls' erstwhile temporary governess. The butcher, Grill, was dead, as was his wife. Also the wife of Webster, the blacksmith. And now one of the Farrar children.

At the library door Savill came to a stop. Blanche would have to be told. He moved to the foot of the stairs, came to a halt and hesitated there. Looking at his watch he realized that she would be having lunch. He would tell her later, when she had eaten.

As he stood there he thought of the birthday party that had been planned for next Tuesday, Marianne's birthday. It was to be a joint party, for both girls; Blanche's ninth birthday had fallen on the Tuesday past. The party the two girls were looking forward to would not now take place.

A little later Savill joined Gentry in the dining room for lunch.

Gentry, remaining free of any symptoms of the disease, had had the run of the house for several days now, and Savill, sitting facing him across the table, realized that he was glad of the boy's presence. Confined as he himself was, it was good to have someone to talk to, even someone as young as Gentry; for all the boy's youth and inexperience, he had found him to be intelligent and entertaining. And Gentry had helped considerably with Marianne and Blanche, too, saving them from a good deal of the boredom that might otherwise have been theirs in their confinement to the house. Since Monday when he had been released from his own incarceration he had done what he could to keep them amused, not only in the nursery, where he had played endless games with them, but also in the schoolroom where he had sometimes helped Miss Fenwick with their lessons.

When lunch was over Savill went back into the library, sat there for a while, then got up and went up the stairs to the schoolroom. When he reached the door he raised his hand to knock – and let his hand remain there, poised, his knuckles clenched. From the other side of the door he could hear Blanche's voice; the girls were going through their French lesson. As he listened he heard Blanche stumble in her reading, upon which there came a murmured comment from Miss Fenwick followed by a general little burst of laughter.

He lowered his hand, turned on the landing and went back downstairs to the library. His news could wait.

It had been clear to both Agnes and Ernest on the night of Arthur's death that Sarah herself was coming down with the 'flu as well, though Sarah herself had refused to acknowledge it. After the undertaker's wife had been to lay out Arthur's body Agnes had stayed up with her mother for several hours. When, eventually, Sarah had fallen asleep, Agnes had herself slept. On the morning of the following day, Friday, seeing her mother so much worse, Agnes had announced her intention of staying at home with her.

Throughout that day Sarah had remained in bed. The next day, Saturday, Ernest prepared to go off to work as usual, again leaving Agnes at home with Sarah. On his way, he said, he would leave a note at Dr Kelsey's house, asking him to call at the cottage.

When Ernest had gone Agnes took from the oven the brick she had placed there a little earlier and went back upstairs to the rear bedroom where her mother lay in bed. Sarah lay on her back with her head towards the wall, her eyes open. As Agnes entered Sarah turned her head on the pillow and looked up at her. 'Hello, my dear,' she said.

'How are you feeling now?' Agnes took the brick from beneath the bedclothes and replaced it with the hot one.

'I'm all right. I thought I might get up soon.' Sarah's voice was dull, lifeless.

'No, no. You must stay there.'

Agnes moved to the fireplace then and raked out the ashes and relit the fire. That done she went back downstairs and warmed a little milk over the range. Dutifully, although protesting that she wasn't hungry, Sarah drank a little of it. Later that morning, insisting that she was all right, she got out of bed and came downstairs. It was madness, Agnes told her. Her mother wouldn't be stopped, though. 'I can't just lie there, Agnes,' she said. 'I can't.'

In the kitchen in her chair before the range Sarah sat covered with a rug and watching dully while Agnes cleaned the room. Sarah was silent for most of the time but once when Agnes came near her she said:

'Agnes – there are things to arrange. Arthur . . .'

'Now don't you worry about that,' Agnes replied. 'Ernie's looking after everything. You just think about getting well.'

'The – the funeral – d'you know when it's to be?'

'– On Wednesday.'

Coming into the kitchen from the garden a little later, Agnes found her mother standing at the kitchen table preparing to make pastry. 'Oh, *Mam*,' Agnes said, 'you should be resting.' As she spoke she saw her mother sway against the table and the next moment Sarah was falling to the floor. Agnes, crying out, stepped quickly to her side and bent over her. Sarah's arm had caught the bag of flour as she had fallen and now its contents lay scattered like fine snow. Kneeling in the spilled flour Agnes called to her, then, sobbing with fear, she fetched water and dabbed it on Sarah's face. After a few seconds Sarah came round, opening her eyes and looking about her in a dull, bewildered way. When she was well enough to stand she let Agnes help her up the stairs and into bed.

'Now you rest,' Agnes said as Sarah laid her head back on the pillow. 'I can do whatever needs to be done about the house. I can get on with the washing and get Ernest's dinner when he comes in.' She drew the blankets up around her mother's shoulders. As she did so Sarah lightly grasped her hand. 'You're a good girl, Agnes.' She shook her head. 'It's too much on your shoulders, a girl of your age. Only eleven. It's too much.'

'I'm all right.' Then, softly but firmly Agnes urged her to rest. 'Please – try to get some sleep, Mam. The doctor'll be here later.'

'Sleep,' Sarah repeated, her eyes shifting to gaze unseeingly at the window. 'I sometimes wonder whether I shall ever sleep again.'

Ernest returned from the farm later than usual that evening and on entering the cottage he went straight upstairs to look in on Sarah. He came down again almost immediately. Coming into the kitchen he looked at Agnes as she stood before the range. She turned and glanced at him over her shoulder. 'Is she still asleep?' she asked.

'Yes.'

'Good. It's what she needs.'

'Did Doctor come?'

'Yes, late this afternoon. He left some medicine to give her, and some stuff to help her sleep. It's very important, he said, that she sleeps. Apart from that she must be kept warm – try to stop the infection going to her chest. He said he'll call again tomorrow when he can. But he's that busy, poor man.' She was silent for a moment, then she said, 'You're late in, aren't you?'

He nodded. 'Ah, I am. Mr Harker's come down with the 'flu, and so's Benjamin. So that left me to do most of the milkin'. One of Harker's daughters – Polly – come out to give me a hand, but she's not much good. Still, it was better 'elp than no 'elp at all.'

'You're going to have a long day tomorrow then, as well.'

'Oh, ah. I'm gunna 'ave to go in earlier, and stay later – there's nothin' else for it.'

They spoke almost casually, yet each knew what was in the other's heart and mind. Although they faced one another their eyes met only fleetingly. They had both wept so much, and now it was as if they feared acknowledgement of their continuing grief; as if they were afraid that, looking into those answering eyes, they would see there an echo of the grief that was their own, and would be overwhelmed.

As Agnes turned back to the range she heard Ernest's step as he turned and went back into the little hall. Then there came the sound of the opening and closing of the parlour door. How could he bear it? she wondered. Arthur lay in there in his coffin, waiting for Wednesday's funeral. After a little while Ernest came back into the kitchen. Turning, glancing fleetingly at him, Agnes could see the stain of tears on his cheeks.

As she set the kitchen table Ernest told her that he had called at the Greenhams' cottage on the way home. He had learned, he said, that Fanny and her sisters were feeling much the same.

'Ah, well,' Agnes said, 'at least they're no worse. That's good to hear. No doubt Fanny'll be up and about again any day now.'

She put Ernest's dinner on the table a little later and he sat down to eat. She had prepared a meat and vegetable pie with potatoes and cabbage. She watched him as he ate. 'Is it all right?' she asked.

'Oh, ah.' He nodded. 'One day you're gunna make somebody a tidy little wife, our Aggie, or I'll be very much surprised.'

She smiled faintly at his words, feeling for an instant a small, brief glow of gladness that for a second pierced the cloud of sadness that enveloped her. Ernest ate in silence for a while, then, raising his glance to hers, he said:

'We shall be all right again one day, Ags. You'll see.'

'Yes,' she whispered. She felt relief suddenly, knowing that it was true. If Ernest said it then it would be so. Obliquely she continued to watch him as he ate, and as she sat there she suddenly became aware that in so many ways he had taken the place of her long-departed father. In her memory over the years her father had become just a vague, shadowy image, a picture unformed, without outline. Ernest was real, though; constant and dependable; tall, strong, male, her unacknowledged support and champion, always there. As he had been when she was younger. It was usually to him that she had run when she was unhappy. She and Arthur. And now Arthur was dead.

Through her thoughts she became aware that Ernest had paused in his eating again and was looking at her.

'Aren't you eatin' too?' he said.

'No, I'm not that hungry. Anyway, I had something a little while ago.'

'You sure you're all right?'

'Yes, really.'

'You ought to eat something.' He grinned, teasing. 'There's nothing of you as it is – sittin' there knee-high to a grasshopper. And you must keep your strength up. We don't want you gettin' ill too.'

'I told you, I'm all right.'

Preparing for the next morning's earlier start, Ernest said goodnight just after half-past-eight and went upstairs. After he had looked in on Sarah again he went into the front room and climbed into the double bed. A few minutes later Agnes herself wearily climbed the stairs.

After replacing the brick in her mother's bed she banked up the fire and placed the guard in front of it. Then, moving back to her mother's side she gave her a little of the medicine the doctor had left, followed by a few drops of the sleeping draught. After that she took up the basin containing the last of the goose grease. Bending over her mother, Agnes smoothed in the grease, rubbing it gently over Sarah's upper chest and between her breasts. Sarah sighed, murmured her thanks, adding, 'You're a good girl, Aggie. You're the best daughter a woman could have.' Agnes smiled down at her and, firmly but gently, laid the brown paper back in place and pulled Sarah's nightdress down and made her comfortable again. Then she drew up the bed covers and tucked them up around Sarah's chin. 'You go to sleep now, Mam,' she said. 'I'll be right here if you need me.' After kissing Sarah goodnight she got undressed and climbed into the other bed.

It was a long time before she fell asleep.

It was still dark the next morning when Agnes came awake to find Ernest crouching before the little fire-place. He had raked out the ashes and now he was laying the fire. He had already lit the nightlight on the chair at her side and in its pale glow she lay listening as he carefully went about the work, hearing the rustle of the paper and, after a while, the striking of the match and the welcome crackle of the flames. A few moments later he came to stand beside her. 'Ah, you're awake,' he said softly. 'Sorry – I tried to do it without waking you.' He turned and glanced towards the curtained window. 'It's a very cold mornin'. It's been snowin' all night. Mam's gunna need the fire today.' Agnes nodded as she looked up at him. He was dressed ready for work. 'What time is it?' she whispered.

'Just on 'alf-past four.'

'Have you had your breakfast?'

'Yeh, don't worry. And I've wrapped up something for me dinner too.' He stepped closer to the other bed and peered down at Sarah in the faint light.

'How does she look?' Agnes asked.

'She's sleepin' pretty sound. We mustn't wake her.'

'No.' She nodded. 'You better get off to work . . .'

'Ah.' He nodded. 'Anyway, 'ow are *you* feelin' this mornin'? All right?'

'Yes, I'm fine, thanks.'

'Are you sure?' He bent lower, peering a little closer. 'If you're not, our Aggie, you tell me. You don't look that grand to me.'

'No, really, I'm all right. I feel fine.'

'Yes? If you're not well, you say and I'll stay 'ome.'

'Oh, no, you can't do that. Who'll do the milking if you're not there?'

'To 'ell with the blasted milkin'.'

'No, I'm all right, Ernie, believe me. You get on off to work.'

'All right.' He looked back at the fire. 'That'll be all right for a while. I've lit the range too, and I've got some logs and some coal in, so you won't need to go outside. I've left another brick in the oven for Mam, as well, so

215

you won't 'ave to wait too long for one to get 'ot.' He started to turn away, then turned back to her. 'Listen, if you need me you come and get me, all right? Or get somebody else to come and fetch me.'

'Yes, all right.'

'Well, don't you forget, then. If you need me for anything – *anything at all*. Understand?'

'Yes. But we'll be all right, Mam and me. I'll stay in bed for a while longer then get up and get us some breakfast.'

'Right-o.' He stood there for a moment then reached out and touched her shoulder. Giving her a little pat he added, 'Anyway, you remember what I said, my girl.'

He went then, and Agnes listened to the light sound of his boots as he crept down the stairs. She closed her eyes. She had lied to him when he had asked how she was feeling. She had slept so badly, waking frequently at odd hours throughout the night. And when she *had* slept her restless sleep had been troubled with dreams of sharp, quick-moving images. Now at the back of her nose and throat she could feel a harsh, dry sensation whilst at the same time there was a dull, heavy ache in her head. She would feel better soon, though, she told herself, once she had had some breakfast – although she didn't feel in the least hungry. And she would stay in the warm and get as much rest as she could. She would be all right again before long.

Hard as she tried, she couldn't get back to sleep, and eventually, just after six, lying there with her eyes open, she saw Sarah awaken. She got out of bed, and as she stood up she felt the room suddenly swim about her. She held herself rigid for a moment until the weakness had passed then put on her worn old slippers. From a hook on the back of the bedroom door hung an old coat that had belonged to Arthur. She took it down and wrapped it around her. Then, moving to the window she drew back the curtains and looked out. The snow lay thick over everything while up above the sky was a greyish yellow. After a moment she moved to her mother's bedside. Sarah lay with her eyes half-open, as if her lids were dragged down by weights.

'How are you feeling, Mam?' Agnes asked.

'Oh – well, not too good, my dear. How are you?'

'I'm all right.' Agnes realized that her mother's breathing sounded restricted. The next moment Sarah turned her head on the pillow and coughed. She had coughed frequently during the night, but now the cough had a dry, hacking sound. It was the same sound that Arthur had made, Agnes realized, and she felt her heart lurch with fear.

'Come on,' Agnes said, 'let's get you a bit higher in the bed. It'll help your chest.' When Sarah's position had been adjusted Agnes took the now cold brick from beneath the bedclothes and moved towards the door. 'I'll get you a hot one,' she said, 'and get us some breakfast too.'

'Oh, no, no food for me, thank you, my dear. But you must have something.'

'And you must eat something too. A little gruel perhaps.'

Ignoring her mother's feeble protests Agnes went downstairs, put the brick in the oven and took the hot one out. When she had placed it in Sarah's bed she returned to the kitchen where she cooked some oatmeal, spooned some into a bowl and added a little milk and sugar. Upstairs she wrapped a shawl about her mother's shoulders and gave her some of the gruel. A little later she helped her from the bed onto the chamber pot. Afterwards she took the pot downstairs. In the scullery she put on her boots and, wrapping the coat more closely about her, braved the snow and the cold air to hurry outside and empty the pot into the privy. Back in the kitchen she fed the fire in the range. She felt she should take some medicine, but there was only that which the doctor had left for her mother. After a moment she went to the dresser-cupboard and took from it the precious little bottle of brandy that was always kept there. Pouring some warm milk into a cup she added a spoonful of the brandy to it. The taste of the brandy made her shudder slightly, but she took comfort from its diffusing warmth in her body. It would do her good, she was sure.

When she climbed the stairs again a couple of minutes later her limbs felt weak; it was as much as she could do to lift one foot up behind the other.

In the times between caring for her mother Agnes spent as much time as she could in bed over the next few hours, and all the while her headache grew more painful along with the feeling of increasing congestion in her nose and chest. There was no sign of the doctor.

Sarah, lying in the next bed, was unaware of Agnes's own sickness for some time, until, taking a little of the milk and brandy that Agnes had prepared for her she looked into Agnes's eyes and said, 'Oh, my dear God, child, you're ill too! Get back into bed, do.' In answer Agnes shook her head, insisting that she was all right. After a moment or two Sarah ceased her protests and weakly lay back on the pillow again.

It began to snow again just after one o'clock. Later on Agnes got up from the bed to make up the fire. When she had finished she straightened, stretched her aching limbs and looked out at the whirling flakes that skimmed past the window. As she stood there she felt the dizziness sweep over her again, and she clutched at the iron bedstead to steady herself. The pain in her head was like a split in the lining of her skull, a wound played on by a hammer that pounded away without pause, sometimes quite lightly, but at other times so violently that it was all she could do not to hold the sides of her head and cry out. She stood there for some seconds, clutching the bedstead until the dizziness began to recede, then she moved back and sat down on the side of the bed. Pulling back the covers she lay down again. After a while she fell into a fitful sleep.

When she awoke a little less than an hour later she sat up, looked across at the other bed and saw at once that her mother was much worse.

Chapter Nineteen

'Mam . . . Oh, Mam . . .'

Agnes threw back the bedclothes and struggled out of bed. As she put her feet onto the cold floor and stood up the familiar dizziness swept over her again so that she staggered slightly and had to brace the backs of her legs against the side of the bed. Her legs ached and her knees were weak.

Recovering after a few seconds she stepped across the small space to the other bed and leaned over her mother. Sarah had pushed back the bedclothes and lay on her back. Sweat had broken out on her forehead and ran down her face, dampening the hair at her temples. Her mouth partly open, her breath came rasping, as if torn from her lungs. And then suddenly she began to move her head wildly from side to side while from her dry, cracked lips a torrent of muttered words spilled out, staccato, disjointed, stumbling over one another. She cried out something about the Cut and then, 'Ollie . . .!' and then her words faded and she lapsed back into her stertorous breathing once more. As Agnes looked down at her Sarah began to cough. 'Oh, Mam!' Agnes cried out and, quickly, using all her strength, she forced her mother to sit up, and then held an old piece of a torn sheet for her to cough into. Then, gently, she helped her to lie back on the pillow again, covered her up, then turned and hurried from the room.

Her legs were so weak that she staggered slightly

halfway down the stairs. She was hardly aware of it, though. She went on down into the kitchen where she put some more wood into the stove and poured a little milk into a saucepan. Skipping from one foot to the other with cold and impatience she waited for the milk to heat. Looking at the clock, she saw that it was twenty-past-three. *Where was the doctor?* When the milk was warm enough she poured it into a cup then carried it upstairs to the bedroom where, sitting on the side of Sarah's bed, she got her to drink a little. Afterwards she dabbed at her mother's sweat-damp brow with tepid water. Now she could see about her mother's nose and mouth the faint bluish look that she had seen on Arthur just before he died. As she straightened, a sob welled up in her throat. She spun, helplessly, on the little piece of matting, turned back to gaze at her mother's face again, and then began to snatch up her clothes.

When she had put on her dress she pulled on Arthur's old coat again. It was much too big for her but she didn't care. After whispering a few hurried words of comfort to her mother she went down the stairs and out into the scullery where she pulled on her boots. Then she went out into the yard. The snow was still falling but not so heavily now, and the air seemed not so bitterly cold as it had earlier. Hurrying across the narrow back yard she climbed over the low fence into the Hewitts' yard and rapped at the scullery door. To her relief the door was opened almost immediately and Esther Hewitt stood there in her apron, holding a dish in her hand. At the sight of the expression on Agnes's face she said, frowning:

'Oh, Agnes, my dear, what's the matter? Is it your mam?'

'Yes!' Agnes burst into tears. 'Mrs Hewitt, please come! She's that bad and – I'm afraid. I've been waiting for the doctor but he hasn't come and I don't know what to do anymore. Will you come and see 'er?'

'Yes, of course, my love.' Esther was all quick nods as she spoke. Then, turning away, she set down the dish and took up her shawl. A few moments later she was following Agnes into the Farrars' cottage.

Up in the bedroom Agnes stood by while Esther bent over Sarah and put the back of her hand on her brow. Esther clicked her tongue and muttered, 'Ah, she've got a tempitcher all right.' Then, listening to the harsh sound of Sarah's obstructed breathing she shook her head. 'I'm afraid that – well, I reckon your mam's got the broncho-pneumonia, Agnes.'

'Oh – what can we do, Mrs Hewitt?'

'Well – there's not much you *can* do till the doctor gets 'ere – 'cept keep her warm, and try to help her to sleep.'

As she spoke Sarah began to mutter, lifting her head from the pillow, opening her eyes and gazing around her. Then, her eyelids fluttering, she sank back again. Esther turned and took up one of the blankets from Agnes's bed and added it to those that covered Sarah. Agnes stood beside the bed looking down at her mother. Sarah's breathing had grown harsher, while the dusky-red look about her mouth, nose and ears was more pronounced. Agnes's fear grew stronger. 'Why doesn't the doctor get here?' she whispered with a little cry. 'Where is he? Why doesn't he come?' Aimlessly she moved across the room a couple of paces, then came back to Esther's side. 'We can't just stand here and wait,' she said. 'With all those other people to see he might be all day.' She had started to take off the coat, but then, her mind made up, she pulled it back on and began to do up the buttons. 'Mrs Hewitt,' she said, 'I must go for the doctor. Will you sit here with Mam while I'm gone?'

'Well – yes, of course, my dear, but I doubt you'll find the doctor at 'ome, will you? 'E's bound to be out somewhere, visitin'.'

'That doesn't matter. They'll know where he's gone. I'll find him.'

'Ah, all right, then.' Esther watched as Agnes did up the last of the buttons. 'That's it – you wrap up warm. It's very cold out.' She frowned. 'And you don't look well yourself, my little wench.' As she spoke she reached out and laid her hand on Agnes's brow. 'You're very 'ot, Agnes. You're burnin' up, child.'

'No, no – I'm all right.' Agnes was moving away from Esther's touch, stepping towards the door. 'I must get the doctor. I'll be as fast as I can.' With her final words she was moving out onto the landing and down the stairs.

In the kitchen she paused only long enough to put on her old woollen hat and muffler. Then, snatching up her mittens, she hurried from the cottage.

Agnes started off at a run towards the centre of the village. It was not quite so cold now, and the falling snow had changed to a steady drizzle of rain, softening the snow beneath her feet so that her boots sank into it. At the end of the lane she turned left into Elm Road, ran along it and, turning right at the Temperance Hall, entered Peters Lane. As she did so she slowed her pace and then came to a stop. Her heart was thudding beneath her ribs and her face felt burning hot. Her legs felt weak and rubbery. She began to cough, a dry, hacking cough, whilst in taking in the cold air she could hear a harsh sound in her chest. She spat onto the snow some rusty-brown stuff that was like the stuff that Arthur and her mother had brought up. After steadying herself for another moment against the rough stone wall she took another painful breath and started off again, hurrying on towards Bridge Street.

By the time she reached Dr Kelsey's house on Stainer Street ten minutes later she was wet through and so out of breath that she was afraid for a moment that the little breath she had would fail altogether. At the entrance to the drive she stood holding the gate post while she painfully sucked great draughts of air down into her lungs. Then, recovered a little, she hurried up the path to the front door and rang the bell.

As she stood there she realized that she should have gone round to the back, to the door which led to the doctor's surgery. She should also have put on her own coat, she thought. She must look a sight. Arthur's old, patched, darned coat hung on her like a sack, the shoulders coming almost halfway down her upper arms and the cuffs hanging below her fingertips. It was too late to do anything about it now, though.

As she hitched up the coat's sleeves the door was opened and the doctor's young maid stood there, small and freckle-faced. Agnes, between gasps of breath, asked her if the doctor was in. The girl shook her head. No, she said, he was out visiting some of his patients. Agnes asked then when he would be back.

'I'm sorry, I got no idea.'

'Oh, but – I've got to find him,' Agnes said. As she spoke tears sprang into her eyes. 'It's my mam, she's very bad and she needs the doctor as soon as possible.'

'Well, I'm sorry.' The maid gave a sympathetic shrug. ''E's not 'ere. But if you wait I'll tell Mrs Kelsey . . .' She turned away then and went back into the house. A few moments later Mrs Kelsey was coming to the door. She was a tall, fair woman; pretty, in spite of her spectacles and plain dress. When Agnes had given her name Mrs Kelsey said kindly, 'Listen, my dear, if you go on back home the doctor will be there as soon as he can. But he has so many patients to see.' She had a piece of paper in her hand. 'Farrar, did you say?' She consulted the paper then gave a little shake of her head. 'I'm sorry, but it doesn't appear as if he'll be getting to your house for some little while. He has a number of other patients to see first.'

'Oh, but it's so urgent,' Agnes said. 'My mam's so bad. If I could just see him and tell him . . .'

Mrs Kelsey gave a sympathetic little shrug. 'I'm so sorry, my dear.' She looked back to the paper, reflected for a moment then added, 'Listen, he hasn't been gone long, and his first call is at Woodseaves House. Near the bottom of Lowbridge Hill, d'you know it?'

'Yes, yes.' Agnes nodded; she was already starting to turn away.

'You might catch him there,' Mrs Kelsey said after her. 'If not he's due then to call at the Dillons' house in Forge Lane.'

Woodseaves House was on the very outskirts of the village, near the river. As Agnes hurried back along Bridge Street she could feel the cold rain in her eyes and chilling her neck. Putting up her mittened hands she drew her muffler closer at her throat and ran on.

Fifteen minutes later as she reached the foot of Lowbridge Hill the high stone wall and gates of Woodseaves House came in view and thankfully she slowed her pace. Outside the gates she came to a stop. She held a hand to her side. The stitch from her running was like a knife wound. She stood there for a few seconds while her heart pounded against her ribs, then entered onto the drive. As she did so the imposing façade of Woodseaves House came in view and, standing on the forecourt before the front door, a phaeton with a brown mare between the shafts. The feeling of relief brought a sob to Agnes's throat. The phaeton must be Dr Kelsey's; it had to be.

Moving up the length of the drive to the carriage she came to a stop at its side and stood there trying to get her breath back. All she had to do now was wait. The doctor wouldn't be long, and she would catch him when he came out. Surely, then, when she had told him how sick her mother was he would go at once to the cottage.

As she waited beside the horse she became aware of how wet she had become. The water was running from her shapeless woollen hat and trickling down beneath her muffler. The coat, too, was wet through. She realized, to her relief, though, that the rain had stopped – although the air seemed to have grown colder. Still, the running had kept her fairly warm – in spite of the rain. Inside her mittens her fingertips were tingling.

'You! You there . . .! What do you want, child, hanging about here?'

Agnes turned at the sound of the voice and saw that the front door of the house was open and a woman was standing in the doorway. Agnes went hesitantly towards her. She recognized the woman; she had seen her at the market on occasions; a tall, handsome woman, always imposingly dressed. The woman was gazing at her now with an expression of wariness and suspicion, and Agnes vaguely realized what a strange sight she must present, wearing Arthur's old coat and with her hair coming from beneath her hat like rats' tails. She came to a stop before the woman.

'Well, what do you want?' the woman asked.

'Please, ma'am – I hope you don't mind – I was waiting for the doctor.' Still breathless from her running, Agnes's words were punctuated by gasps for breath. Half turning, she gestured, indicating the phaeton. 'This is – Dr Kelsey's carriage, isn't it, ma'am?'

'Yes, it is. But this isn't the doctor's surgery, you know.' The woman's tone was imperious. 'If you want him I suggest you go to his house like everyone else.'

'Oh, but – ma'am, we need him and I wanted to –'

The woman broke in: 'I told you, go to his house – as other people have to. I'm sorry you've got illness, but so have many others in the village. And I doubt that your need is any greater than anyone else's.'

'Oh, but, please, I –'

'No.' Then, as Agnes opened her mouth to speak again, the woman added sharply: 'Now – be off. Be off with you.'

Agnes hesitated still, as if unable to comprehend the woman's words, then, slowly, she began to back away. After she had gone a few paces the woman spoke again.

'Go on. Get away from here. I don't want you loitering about the house.'

Turning with tears of pain and frustration welling in her eyes, Agnes walked back across the forecourt and up the drive. When she reached the gates she turned and looked back. The woman was still standing in the doorway. Quickly Agnes averted her gaze, turned back and stepped out onto the road.

She walked back up Lowbridge Hill away from the house until, when she turned back, the gates of the house were no longer in sight. She came to a stop. It didn't matter about not being able to wait for him there, she told herself; Dr Kelsey would be leaving the house soon anyway. She panicked for a moment as the thought came to her that he might turn left at the gates and return to the village by Crop Row, but then she remembered that he was going on to Forge Lane to the Dillons. She relaxed again; if he went straight to Forge Lane then he would come back up the hill. So, she would wait for him here and catch him as he drove by; this was as good a place as any, now that she knew where he was. And perhaps, she thought, he would let her ride back with him. Her legs felt so weak that she was afraid they would not carry her much further. She coughed and spat out more of the rusty-brown stuff. It left an unpleasant taste in her mouth and she spat again, trying to rid her mouth of it. Close to the hedge were the remains of a fallen tree trunk and she moved to it, brushed off the snow and sat down, not caring about the damp coldness, only grateful for the relief it afforded. She closed her eyes and instantly inside her eyelids little shapes began to dance in ragged patterns and her head began to swim. She opened her eyes again and tried to concentrate on the things she saw. Up in the top of a nearby oak tree pigeons were sitting, plump, motionless, swelling out their feathers against the cold. A robin flew down and alighted on a twig of the hedgerow, stayed for a few moments then took off again, winging away over the cheerless fields. To help the time pass she began to count the seconds, marking them off into minutes one by one until, after six minutes had gone by she lost count and gave up. A sharp, biting wind swept down the hill towards the river and she pulled the coat more closely about her. She realized then that the air was growing colder. Inside her thin boots she could hardly feel her feet anymore. The doctor must come by soon.

After a little while longer she got up from the log, staggering slightly as she put her weight onto her weak legs. She stood still for a moment clenching her hands, willing herself to keep her balance, then, recovered a little, she turned and began to make her way back down the hill.

The walls of Woodseaves House came in sight after

a short distance and, keeping close to the hedge, she walked towards it. She came at last to the gates and there, after hesitating for a moment, she leaned forward, put her head around the gate post and looked up the drive.

Dr Kelsey's phaeton was not there.

No longer caring whether or not anyone saw her, she stepped out into the centre of the drive and stared up towards the house. No, there was no sign anywhere of the carriage. Then, her eyes moving to the ground beneath her feet, she saw in the hardening snow the marks of the carriage and horse as they had come back down the drive and turned onto the road – turning left, moving away towards the north. Agnes stared at the prints in the snow and groaned with weariness and despair. He had not gone in the direction of Forge Lane, but in another direction.

Shoulders bowed, she turned and began to walk slowly back the way she had come. After she had gone a few yards she quickened her steps and began to run again. Dr Kelsey might have gone to some other house right now, but he would be going to Forge Lane at some time. And, if she hurried, she might get there in time to catch him. Her breath sobbing in her throat she hurried on up the hill towards the village.

The last reserves of strength that had taken her to Woodseaves House were failing quickly as she reached Green Street. She had run most of the way, though covering the last few hundred yards in little bursts of running between pauses for breath. Now, with Forge Lane just ahead of her she was gasping for breath, snatching at the cold air with her mouth gaping. Her course was erratic and her footprints in the freezing snow showed the irregular pattern of a staggering gait.

Forge Lane was a narrow little way connecting Green Street and Church Row. Although she had sometimes played with one of the Dillon girls when she was at school she didn't know which of the terraced cottages was occupied by the family. Now, entering the lane, she saw no sign of Dr Kelsey's carriage. She didn't know what to do. She could wait, but for all she knew he might already have been and left again. She couldn't take the chance of waiting; she must find out where the Dillons lived and then whether or not the doctor had been.

She was just moving to the front door of the nearest cottage when she heard the sound of a horse and carriage and, turning, she saw Dr Kelsey's phaeton enter the lane from the other end. A great surge of relief swept over her, and with tears springing to her eyes she ran towards it as it came to a stop outside one of the far cottages.

'Doctor . . . Dr Kelsey . . .'

She called out to him as he stepped down into the freezing snow, and he turned at the sound of her voice. She got to his side a few moments later.

'Oh, Doctor . . . Doctor –' Then, relief and exhaustion sweeping away her control, she burst into tears. She stood there looking up at him, her whole body shaking with her sobs while the tears poured down her cheeks. In moments Kelsey was putting down his bag and was crouching before her.

'Now, now, what is it? What's the matter?'

She couldn't speak. He put his hands on her shoulders and said gently, looking into her distorted face, 'It's Mrs Farrar's little girl, isn't it?'

She nodded, her sobbing going on and on, as if it would never cease, as if there was no limit to the well of her tears.

'Agnes? Is it Agnes?'

She nodded again. Then, her hands hanging limply

at her sides she leaned forward so that her forehead rested on his shoulder. His hands came up and held her.

'Now, Agnes – tell me what it is. Is it your mother?'

She nodded against the comfort of his shoulder, feeling the rough softness of the fabric of his warm coat against her skin. Then she managed to say,

'Yes, it's my mam, Doctor.'

Drawing back her head a little so that she could look into his face she told him of her mother and of how worried she was for her. 'I didn't know what to do anymore, Doctor . . .' She told him how she had run to his own house and after that to Woodseaves House where she had seen his carriage. When she told him how the woman had sent her away her crying burst out anew. She told him then how she had waited for him at the side of the road and of how she had gone back to the house only to find that his carriage was gone. He nodded. Yes, he said, he had gone a little out of his way to call on another patient.

'Anyway,' he added, 'you've found me now, Agnes, and as soon as I've looked in on Mr Dillon we'll go together and see your mother. How's that?'

Silently she nodded at him through her tears and he took off his glove and, taking from his pocket a neatly folded white handkerchief, wiped away her tears. Afterwards he put the handkerchief into her mittened hand – 'Here, you keep it,' – and then put his hand in a little warm, comforting touch to her cheek. His fingers lingered there, and then the back of his hand was touching her forehead.

'Agnes,' he said, frowning, 'you're running a fever. How do you feel?'

'I – I got so out of breath with running and . . .' A cough took away her last words and she stood with her head bent, alternately coughing and sucking in the air.

She spat into the snow, then turned and looked guiltily into the concerned face of the man. As she looked at him his face wavered before her and a slight greyness crept about the edges of the image. And then, suddenly, she was vomiting. Bending low, her small body contorted in spasms, she retched some dark brown stuff into the snow at her feet. Kelsey reached out and held her. After a moment she straightened and put the handkerchief to her mouth. The next moment the doctor was taking her up, feather-light, in his arms, lifting her and placing her in the carriage. He took a rug and wrapped it about her, tucking it in. 'I'll be as quick as I can,' he said. 'Then we'll take you home. You're wet through and you're freezing cold. We've got to get you to bed as soon as we can.' He took a step back. 'Will you be all right while I'm gone?'

'Yes, sir. Thank you.'

'That's a good girl.' He paused, looking at her with his head a little on one side, then turned away, moving towards the door of the nearest cottage.

Agnes watched as the door was opened by one of the Dillon boys, then as the doctor went into the hall, the door closing behind him. The greyness that had come over her a few moments ago kept on coming back, in waves, and each time she set her teeth and clutched at the blanket, waiting for the wave to pass.

Kelsey came out of the house in just a little over ten minutes. As he emerged he looked at the phaeton and saw Agnes move slightly, turning towards him. In just a few strides he was beside the carriage and getting in next to her and taking the reins. 'Now,' he said, 'we'll get you home, and see your mama and get you to bed where you belong.'

It was quite dark now and the lamps on the sides of

the carriage reflected yellowly in the icy crystals of the banked snow at the roadside. The mare made a slow but steady progress, and when the carriage was suddenly jolted in the freezing ruts in the roadway Kelsey put his arm around Agnes and drew her a little closer to him. He talked to her as they rode. 'How are you feeling now?' he asked, and she answered, 'Quite well, thank you, sir.' 'Good.' He nodded. 'I'm looking forward to hearing you sing again in church before too long has gone by.' She didn't answer at this, and he turned and looked down at her in the light of the lamp and she looked up at him and gave a faint little smile. He asked her how old she was and she replied:

'Eleven, sir. Twelve next June.'

He left her in silence then, just murmuring occasionally to the mare as they made their way. Just before Church Row became Elm Road the phaeton was brought to a crawl behind a herd of cows bound for a nearby farm. But then at last the cattle had moved on and the carriage was free to turn into Coates Lane. As it did so it was jolted by a pothole in the road and Kelsey held on to Agnes's slight form at his side, tightening his arm about her and saying with a little chuckle, 'Hey-*up*!' Then, turning, he looked down at her. Her head was bent low, her face obscured by the woollen hat. He pressed his encircling hand into her arm. 'We're almost there now, Agnes. Nearly home now.'

She didn't answer. He spoke again. 'Agnes . . . ?'

She didn't move.

'*Agnes.*' His voice was sharper now, imperative and touched with fear. 'Agnes!'

Holding her fast with his left hand he pulled on the reins with his right, calling out, 'Who-o-a-a-ah, Janie,' and brought the mare to a halt. Then, letting fall the reins he turned and lifted Agnes's face, his fingers

233

beneath her chin. The glow from the lamp reflected in her dull sightless eyes as they gazed past his collar into the bitter evening air.

Chapter Twenty

The snow fell intermittently over the following days, adding to the silence within the walls of the cottage. There seemed to be no words to say and Ernest and Sarah went for hours at a time hardly speaking. For a time Ernest was deathly afraid that Agnes's death would be the final blow to his mother, but it was not so. Somehow, it was as if the death of Arthur had filled up the capacity of Sarah's grief, and when she learned of Agnes's death too she just seemed to retreat into a kind of numbness. Lying in her bed, so ill herself, it was as if some cocooning shield slowly enwrapped her, keeping her from a total awareness which, Ernest was sure, should it find her when she was so weak, would surely be too much.

The days passed. Ernest, having no choice, continued with his work at the farm while Esther from next door came in during the days to stay with his mother. On Wednesday while Sarah, too ill to move, had remained in her bed, Ernest had taken the morning off and, following the coffin of Arthur, had helped carry Agnes's coffin to the churchyard. There beside Mary and their father the two were buried. After the funeral Ernest changed back into his working clothes and left for the farm. No matter what happened livestock had to be fed and watered, cows milked.

Each evening on leaving the farm Ernest hurried back home to be with his mother. And slowly, slowly, with no effort on her own part, Sarah began to recover. It seemed to Ernest that his mother had no real will to keep living, yet at the same time she showed no wish to die. She just didn't seem to care what became of her. Lying silent and uncomplaining on her bed she obediently did as she was told, almost childlike in a way, as if the matter of what became of her held no interest for her and was outside her own control.

With the death of Dr Harmon, Dr Kelsey had continued to make frequent calls at the cottage, attending Sarah with gentleness, firmness and understanding. Ernest, on meeting the doctor there, knew that he would never see his face without it bringing back to him the memory of the afternoon when Agnes had died. That Sunday, increasingly concerned about his mother, Ernest had asked for an hour's leave from his duties at the farm and had hurried home to see how she was. Finding Esther Hewitt sitting with his mother, and learning that Agnes had gone off to fetch the doctor he had sat waiting for his sister's return. When, after half-an-hour there had been no sign of her he had announced his intention of going to find her. He had put his coat back on and was just opening the scullery door when he had seen a dark figure moving towards him across the yard. In the darkness he hadn't been able to make out who it was – someone carrying a bundle in his arms. Then, in the faint light from the lamp-lit kitchen window he had made out the figure of the doctor. 'Ah, Dr Kelsey,' he had said with relief as the man came towards him, '– our Agnes has gone off to find you and –' Coming to a stop he had seen then what was the burden in Kelsey's arms. A child. And then some part of his brain had registered the coat the child was wearing. But – it was Arthur's old coat. Then, a moment later, he had recognized the child's old woollen hat and realized who it was.

*

Savill had pondered on when to tell Blanche of the deaths of her brother and sister. But then, realizing that everyone in the house but the two girls knew of it, and fearing that it would only be a matter of days before word got to Blanche in some oblique way and perhaps made the shock even greater, he decided she would have to be told.

On the day of the funerals he sent word to Blanche that he would like to see her, and two minutes later she entered the library.

After Savill had told her she just remained there, standing in silence for what seemed to him a long time, occasionally glancing up at him and then looking away again. There was a perplexed expression on her face, a slight creasing of her brow, as if she did not understand. Then, looking up at him again she said,

'Arthur, sir?'

'Yes . . .'

'And Agnes?'

'Yes . . . Oh, Blanche – I'm so sorry.'

A further little silence. 'And my mama, sir? How is she?'

'Your mama – she's going to be all right, I'm sure. It may take some time, but I would think now she must be over the worst. She'll be all right again soon, don't worry. You'll be seeing her again soon.'

She nodded, still frowning. 'But – Agnes – and Arthur – I shan't be seeing them again, shall I, sir?'

'No, Blanche – I'm afraid not.'

She glanced dully from the window. 'It's snowing again,' she said. Savill watched her.

'You do understand what I've been saying, don't you, Blanche?'

She nodded. 'Yes, sir.' She half turned on the carpet. 'May I go back now, sir . . . ?'

'Yes – yes, of course.'

She moved to the door, opened it and looked back at him. 'I must go and see my mama,' she said.

'No – not just yet, my dear.' He shook his head. 'She'll be all right. You just wait a little longer, till she's better.'

'But – she'll want to see me. Won't she?'

'Well, yes, but – what if you catch the 'flu as well? How would she feel then, d'you suppose?'

She nodded her understanding. Then she said softly, her eyes gazing into the distance:

'Arthur and Agnes . . .'

Savill said nothing. After a moment she raised her eyes to his.

'What happens to them, sir?'

'What happens? What d'you mean?'

'When people – die. Where do they go?'

'Do you mean when –'

She broke in quickly: 'I don't mean when they're put in – in the graves. I mean – what happens to *them* – the – the *persons* – *inside*. Do they just – stop?'

Savill frowned, gazing down at her. Then he said, 'You mean – well, you're talking about a person's *soul*, Blanche.'

She was silent, waiting.

'Well, it – it goes to – to God . . .'

'To God . . .'

'Yes . . .' He felt stupid and ineffectual. 'Yes . . . God takes them.'

The frown on her brow was deeper. 'God took them? Arthur – and Agnes?'

'Well – yes.'

'*Why*, sir?'

'Why . . . ?'

'Yes.' She nodded. '*Why?*'

She waited for some moments for an answer that never came, then turned and went from the room.

*

A week after the funeral it was Christmas. At the Farrars' cottage the time came and went with barely any acknowledgement. On the way to and from the farm Ernest passed by some dwellings where lighted windows gave glimpses of Christmas trees and holly and decorated rooms. In deference to the sickness and deaths in the village there were fewer this year. What there were, though, he observed dully; they had no relevance for him.

Over the days messages had come from various people in the village. Mr Savill had written several times, on the occasions of the deaths of the children and also to say that Blanche was perfectly well. For Ernest, too, there had been letters from Fanny, offering sympathy and saying that she herself was recovering well. She looked forward to seeing him again soon, she told him. He had not seen her since before she herself had been taken ill, though he had called at her home on a few occasions to ask after her and to convey his affection and good wishes.

On the Sunday evening just a few days after Christmas she came round to the cottage. Ernest was sitting up in the bedroom reading to Sarah when he heard his name softly called from below the stairs. Leaving Sarah with some murmured words he left the room, turned onto the landing and saw Fanny standing at the foot of the stairs. When he reached the hall he led her back into the kitchen where he turned up the flame in the lamp. They stood facing one another. He smiled at her and she smiled back at him, a slow, melancholy smile like his own.

'Hello, Fan,' he said.

'Hello, Ernie. I knocked but I couldn't make you hear. I hope it's all right – my coming in.'

'Oh, yeh, course it is.' He paused. 'I'm right glad to see you.'

'I'm glad to see you too. How's your mam?'

He gave a little shrug. 'I think she's gettin' better – slowly.'

Fanny nodded. 'Good . . .'

'Should you be out yet, Fan? You sure you're well enough?'

'Oh, yes, I'm feelin' all right now.' She smiled. 'I liked gettin' your letters, Ernie. It was so nice.'

'Ah – well . . .' After a moment he held out his arms and she came to him. He wrapped his arms around her, drawing her close. She sighed, laying her head against his shoulder. 'Oh, Ernie,' she said, 'it's such a – terrible, terrible time.' She paused. 'Still – at least we've got each other.'

He bent his head and she lifted her face to him. As he kissed her he was aware of a greater warmth in her kiss than he had known before. After the kiss she said, looking up at him:

'What did you mean – in your letter?'

'– Mean?'

'In your first letter. You said you'd talked to your mam and that you had some good news . . .'

'Oh – yeh – that . . .'

She waited. 'Well? What was the good news?'

For the briefest moment he felt himself touched by a little shadow of disappointment. But he brushed the thought aside and shook his head. 'Oh, yeh – well,' he said awkwardly, 'this – this ain't the time for it, Fan. Not right now.'

'Oh . . .' She frowned momentarily, then gave a shrug. 'I was just lookin' forward to hearin' it – the good news, that's all . . . Whatever it is . . .'

'Yeh, I know, but – well, like I said, this ain't the time for it.'

'Oh, well – when will be the time for it?'

'Later on. A bit later. We'll talk about it later on. There's time.'

She nodded. 'Yes, of course. Just so long as you don't forget, though.'

'No, I won't forget.'

She sighed and stepped away. 'Anyway, Ernie, I must get back home. I told our mam I'd just slip out for a few minutes.'

'Ah, right.' He followed her to the scullery door. 'Will you be all right, going back on your own?'

'Yes, of course. I got 'ere, didn't I?' She stretched up and kissed him. 'Shall I see you soon?'

'Yes – soon as our mam's a bit better I'll come round.'

She pulled her coat collar more closely about her throat. 'You won't leave it too long, will you?'

'No – course not.'

'– It's New Year's Eve day after tomorrow. Shall I see you then?'

'I'd like to but – I don't know. I doubt I'll be able to come out.'

She nodded. 'Anyway – I'll see you soon, Ernie.'

'Yes, soon.' He bent and kissed her. 'And don't forget, Fan – I love you.'

'I love you too.'

On Wednesday evening Sarah insisted that she would be perfectly all right on her own and when Ernest had shaved and changed he went to Fox Lane to the Greenhams' cottage. Fanny herself answered the door.

She smiled at him. 'What are you doin' here?'

'I just come to wish you a happy new year,' he said.

From behind Fanny came the sound of voices, that of her sisters and brothers. She frowned. 'Wait a minute, Ernie, and I'll get my coat.'

He waited while she went back into the cottage. Five minutes later she had returned wearing a dark brown

241

coat with trimmings of squirrel at the collar and cuffs. 'You got a new coat,' he said.

'You like it?'

'Ah.' He nodded. 'Looks champion.'

She took his arm and together they set off along the lane, the snow crunching beneath their boots. It was too cold to keep walking, though, and they made their way to Coates Lane. When they got to the cottage Ernest led Fanny inside, lit the lamp then took off his coat and went upstairs to look in on his mother. Finding her sleeping he crept out of the room again and went back down to the kitchen where Fanny had taken off her coat and now stood warming her hands before the range. Ernest moved up quietly behind her, put his arms around her waist and held her, laying his cheek against the top of her head. She turned in the circle of his grasp, lifted her face to his and kissed him gently on the mouth.

'Just think,' Fanny said, 'we could be in our own 'ome like this, couldn't we?'

He smiled. 'Yeh, I s'pose we could at that.'

'Be nice, wouldn't it? Though not here – in Hallowford, I mean. Though I s'pose at the start we'd have to, wouldn't we? Till we decide where we want to go, and get a few things up together.'

Ernest didn't answer. He put on the kettle and made tea. As they drank it Fanny looked at him over the rim of her cup.

'All right, Ernie Farrar, what's this news you've got for me, eh? You said you'd talked to your mam.' She paused. 'Come on now. You can't expect me to wait for ever.'

He sighed, smiled at her. 'Oh – well . . .' He felt somehow a reluctance to talk about it. But then, seeing the look on her face, he went on: 'Well, you know what I meant, didn't you?'

'Per'aps.'

He shrugged. 'It's just that I talked to our mam about
– about gettin' married . . .'

'– And?'

'Well, she thinks I'm too young but –'

'Oh, drat!' Fanny said. 'I was afraid she'd say that.'

'No, wait,' Ernest said, '– let me finish. She said I was
too young – she thinks we're *both* too young, come to
that – but that if it's what I want – well, she won't stand
in my way.'

'Oh, Ernie!' Fanny put down her cup, got up and
came to him. She took his own cup from his hand and
set it down on the table beside her own, then sat on his
lap, putting her arm around his neck. She kissed him
on the cheek, on the ear, on the forehead. Then, laying
her face against his, she said, 'That's wonderful news,
Ernie. Just about the best present a girl could 'ave.' She
drew back a little and looked into his eyes. Her own
eyes were sparkling. 'So – there's nothing in the way
now, is there.' She laughed suddenly. 'So now you'll
have to go and talk to my dad.'

'Oh, now, wait a bit, Fan . . .' He frowned.

'What's up? What's the matter?'

'Nothing – just – well, I don't think we should be in
too much of a hurry.'

'What d'you mean?'

He shrugged. 'Let's wait a little while yet, before we
go talking about it to anybody, all right?'

'Why? Oh, Ernie, I want to tell *everybody*.'

'No, come on now, Fan. It's too soon.'

'Too soon? You already told me your mam says it's
all right.'

'I know that. I mean it's too soon after – well, after
what's 'appened.'

'Oh . . . yes . . . of course.' Her expression became
grave. 'I'm sorry, Ernie, I should've realized.'

'That don't matter. But anyway – what with – that, and with Mam still bad – I'd just like to keep it to ourselves for a spell yet, all right?'

'All right. It'll be our secret. I won't tell anybody yet. We'll wait till your mam's better.'

'Right. There'll be time enough then.'

A little over an hour later, when Ernest had walked Fanny back to her home, he went upstairs to see his mother again. Standing beside the bed he looked down at her. Her eyes were closed. When she opened them she looked up at him without surprise.

'Ah, you're back now, lad.'

'Yeh, back now.' He smiled at her. 'Ow're you feelin'?'

The shrug was in her tone. 'Oh – all right. What time is it?'

'Just on nine. I'll make your fire up then get to bed. I'll change the brick, too. T' other's in the oven.' He grinned. 'Good and 'ot now.'

When he had taken the brick from the foot of her bed and replaced it with the one hot from the oven he made up the fire and put the guard back in front of it. Then, returning to Sarah's side he sat down on the edge of the bed. 'Is there anything you need?'

'No, nothing, thanks.' Taking her hand from beneath the covers she laid it on his own as it rested on the patchwork coverlet. 'How's Fanny?' she asked.

He smiled. 'Oh – very well.'

'That's good.' Shifting her glance towards the window she added, 'I suppose the two of you will want to be naming the day soon, won't you? You'll want to start making your plans.'

'Ah, we'll talk about that later.' Gently he pressed her hand in his. 'You just think about gettin' well again. That's all you got to think about.'

Sarah said nothing to this. Then as Ernest watched her he saw the silent tears run from her lowered eyelids and course slowly down her cheeks.

'– Oh, Mam, don't – please.' Taking up a handkerchief from beside the pillow he dabbed gently at her tears. When her tears had stopped he said softly, earnestly:

'It will get better, Mam. It will. Soon you'll be well again, and then the spring'll be 'ere before you know it. Things will look different then.' He gave a little shake of his head. 'Oh, I know it's no good my saying it'll be like old times again. We both know it won't. But it *will* get better – in time. We'll be all right again, you'll see.'

Chapter Twenty-One

The rain, driven by the early March winds, lashed the window panes. Savill had just returned from Trowbridge, from the mill. Now, sitting beside the library fire in his carpet slippers, he drank the tea that Annie, the maid, had brought him. When his cup was empty he sighed and leaned back in his chair. He had been back at work for more than a fortnight now. The worst of the influenza had come and gone. Throughout the country by the end of January the effects and the number of instances of the disease had passed their peak and begun to wane. The situation had started to get back to normal again; the workers going back to their jobs, and the students – Gentry among them – to their schools. By the end of February only a few cases of the sickness were being reported in the village, none of which, according to Kelsey, gave any real cause for alarm. The toll, however, had been great. About one in four of the villagers had been affected – among whom there had been seven deaths.

Savill sighed again. The deaths of the two Farrar children had touched him more than he might have guessed and he wondered increasingly about the effect it had had on their mother. She had not been to the house since before the epidemic had begun, and although he and the other members of his household had been going about their business for over a month now, no one had seen anything of Sarah Farrar about the village. Earlier, in January, Ernest had called at the house and told Mrs

Callow that his mother would not be able to do the Hallowford House laundry again until she was strong enough once more. When that would be, he had said, he didn't know. Since that time Ernest had visited the house on several occasions to see Blanche, but of his mother at such times he had said little. Savill's only sources of information with regard to Sarah Farrah had been Robert Kelsey, and the vicar, Tupper, who had called on her on a number of occasions. Kelsey had reported that she had recovered quite well from her illness, although it had left her somewhat weak. With regard to her emotional and mental state, however, he, like the vicar, had shown himself far less satisfied.

Over Christmas Blanche had confided to Savill her mother's intention of taking her back to live in Coates Lane. He had not been surprised at the news, though seeing the unhappiness in the child's face he had for a moment been at a loss as to what to say and could give her no words of comfort other than to tell her that she would soon settle down and be happy again. He knew well how difficult it would be, though. His own hopes regarding Blanche had been finished by the influenza. He had had to dismiss from his mind every thought he had ever entertained about her adoption. Sarah Farrar had lost two of her four children in the space of a week. He couldn't think of taking away a third.

With regard to Mrs Farrar's decision to take Blanche back to the cottage, however, there had been no word since that which had come from Blanche herself . . .

On Thursday Ernest called at Hallowford House and left word that he would call for Blanche on Sunday afternoon.

When the day came Blanche changed her clothes after lunch and went into the hall to wait.

She sat there nervously, viewing the visit to the cottage with mixed feelings. There had been no further word from her mother about her, Blanche's, returning to live at the cottage, but she felt sure it wouldn't be long now. And although she felt that for her mother's sake she should go, still, in her heart she didn't want to. To her Hallowford House was home.

The minutes went by. The hall clock struck three, three-thirty. As she sat there Mr Savill appeared from the library. 'What's this?' he said, with a little frown. 'Still no sign of your brother, Blanche?' Blanche shook her head: 'No, not yet, sir.'

Alone again, Blanche continued to sit there, her guilt lying on her like a cloak. She had not wanted to go to the cottage – and now, as if in answer to her prayer, no one had come to take her. She continued to sit there for some moments longer and then suddenly she got up, snatched up her coat and hurried from the house.

At the foot of the hill she turned into Coates Lane, slowing her pace as she approached the first of the cottages. Reaching the gate she stood for a moment of hesitation, then entered the front garden and went round to the back.

Entering the kitchen she found her mother sitting by the range, darning socks. At Blanche's appearance Sarah lowered her hands and looked at her. After a moment she said awkwardly:

'Hello, Blanche. What are you doing here?'

Blanche stood and gazed in silence. Her words, her greeting, had died on her lips. Her mother looked different, so different. She looked smaller than Blanche remembered. She looked thinner, somehow shrunken – and older; there were lines in her face that Blanche had never seen before. Her hair, once a rich chestnut, now had streaks of white in it. Turning, closing the door, Blanche said:

'Ernest didn't come – up to the house . . .'

Sarah lowered her eyes to the half-darned sock in her hands, then, looking at Blanche again she said: 'You came out without your bonnet. You must take care. This weather's treacherous.'

Blanche frowned. 'I was waiting for Ernest but he didn't come. I didn't know what had happened.'

Sarah gave a little shake of her head. 'Oh, my dear, forgive me – I've had so much to do. I thought it would be better to wait until another day. I should have let you know. I'm sorry.'

Blanche continued to stare at her. It wasn't only the way her mother looked; there was something else different about her. She seemed almost cool – offhand. Their meeting again after all these weeks – it was not at all the way Blanche had expected it to be. She had expected her mother to take her in her arms, to kiss her. Instead her mother remained in her chair, the sock and the darning needle in her hands.

'I was waiting,' Blanche said. She paused. 'I – I thought you'd want to see me. I knew how – how sad you must be.'

Sarah didn't speak for a moment, then she said, 'Does Mr Savill know you've come out?'

'I didn't tell him. I just – ran out.' Blanche felt bewildered. 'Didn't you want to see me today, Mama?'

'Oh, yes, my dear, but –' Sarah sighed. 'But you'd better not stay, though. I think it would be better if you go on back up to the house. But next time. Stay with me for a little while next time. Not today.'

Blanche stood there for a few seconds longer then turned and moved back to the kitchen door. She opened it and looked back at her mother. 'Goodbye, Mama,' she said softly.

Sarah just nodded, her eyes lowered to her still,

clenched hands. After another second Blanche stepped out into the yard.

As she emerged from the front garden she saw Ernest coming up the lane from the direction of the village. When he caught sight of her he waved and quickened his steps. She stood waiting for him. As he reached her side he said, smiling,

'So you came down after all. I wasn't expecting to see you today. We thought you were going off some-where with Mr Savill.'

She didn't know what he was talking about. 'Going off? With Mr Savill?' She shook her head. 'I wasn't going anywhere. I waited for you, Ernest, but you didn't come.'

He frowned. 'But Mam said she got a note from him – Mr Savill – saying that you would be . . .' He let his words tail off. Then he smiled. 'Anyway, where are you off to now?'

'Back to the house.' She nodded in the direction of Gorse Hill. She could feel tears starting in her eyes and she blinked them back.

'Ain't you gunna stay for tea, then?'

'No . . .'

'No? Why not?' He studied her for a moment or two then crouched before her so that his face was on a level with hers. 'What's the matter, Blanche?'

Shaking her head, she said, 'I don't understand. I don't understand.'

'What? What don't you understand?'

'Mama – she's – she's so different. Why?'

'– Oh, Blanche, you must remember – she's had so much unhappiness lately.'

'Yes, I know that. I mean she's different with me. She's not the same with me anymore.'

His hands moved from her shoulders and gently

touched her cheeks. 'Listen,' he said. 'I'm afraid she's different in lots of ways lately. But just – give it time, eh? She'll be all right again. Just give it time.'

She nodded. He straightened before her and said, 'You want me to walk up the hill with you?'

'No, thank you, I'll be all right.'

'You sure?'

'Yes.'

'Fine. We'll see you soon, then, yes?'

'Yes, see you soon, Ernest.'

Something was wrong, Savill thought. First of all Blanche's brother had not come to collect her, and later, after her return from her visit alone to the cottage, she had seemed troubled, unhappy. On Savill's questioning her, however, she had said nothing. Afterwards, bearing in mind what Kelsey and Tupper had told him, he decided to call himself and see the child's mother.

Now, sitting facing Sarah Farrar in the kitchen of the cottage, he thought he had never seen such a change in a person in so brief a time.

As she poured the tea – he had accepted the offer more for her sake than his own – he brought up the subject of Blanche. 'I understand, from Blanche,' he said, 'that last year you spoke of wanting her to come back and live here with you again.'

She didn't answer for some moments, and in those moments, watching her, thinking of all that she had so recently been through, he gained some inkling of the situation. For some reason or other she didn't want Blanche back yet; she wasn't ready.

When at last she spoke she kept her eyes fixed on the cup in her hand and said simply: 'I – I want what is best for Blanche.'

'Yes, of course you do.' He couldn't get over the

change in her. And it wasn't only in her looks, the way she had aged, it was everything about her. In the past he had always been so aware of a certain indomitability of spirit that had somehow shone through, whatever had happened. Not now. Not anymore. Now to his eyes she looked beaten, utterly defeated.

'Mrs Farrar,' he said carefully, 'I know how much you want Blanche to come back to her home but – why not wait until you feel quite well again? A few months isn't going to make any difference, is it?'

At his words she looked up at him and he saw a faint but unmistakable flicker of relief in her dull eyes.

'I'm sure it would be better for both of you,' he added. 'For both you *and* Blanche.'

She gave a slow, brief nod, then, frowning, she said:

'But – to give you responsibility for her still . . . You've already done so much for her – for us.'

'Oh, please, please.' He raised a hand, palm out. 'I shall never be able to repay you for what you've done for me. Never. I have so much to be grateful for where you're concerned. For so much – for all you've given me and Marianne. Mrs Farrar – you *gave* me my daughter. You *gave* her to me. You gave me her life, and since that time, through Blanche and through your own kindness, you – you have added to the quality of that life – of Marianne's life. Please, I ask you, don't speak of what I have done for you.'

She said nothing to this, but continued to gaze down at her cup.

'So,' he said, 'will you allow Blanche to remain where she is – until you're well again?'

'Well – it would be better for her,' she said. 'I know it would be, of course.' She raised her eyes to his. 'And if it – suits you, sir . . .'

'Oh, indeed. We shall be happy to have her with us

for as long as you want, Marianne and I.' He paused then added softly, 'We love her, Mrs Farrar. We love her – very much.'

That evening Sarah told Ernest of Mr Savill's visit.

'And now Blanche is going to stay there?' he said. 'Up at the house?'

'Yes.'

'But – I thought you wanted to bring her back.'

She paused before she spoke again. 'Bring her back,' she said. 'Bring her back to what, Ernest? Don't you realize – the only thing that saved her was being where she is now. If she hadn't been up at the house during the sickness . . .' She let her words trail off. Then she added, her words seeming to echo in her mind from some past time:

'Leave her where she is. She's better off there.' She paused. 'And anyway, it's where she belongs – now. She hasn't been mine for a long time.'

On Sunday afternoon while Sarah prepared the tea, Ernest and Fanny walked across the heath to the river. March was drawing to a close and new buds could be seen on the trees, and in the springing grass the first signs of awakening life. Beside a gnarled old oak Ernest drew Fanny to his side and they stood in silence while she nestled into his warmth. After a while they set off again, arms linked, walking back through the copse towards the road. On reaching the cottage in Coates Lane Fanny helped Sarah set the table and afterwards the three of them sat down to eat. This was only the second time Fanny had gone to tea with Ernest and his mother since before the epidemic. As on the last occasion a week before, the meal that afternoon was a fairly quiet, subdued affair. When it was over Fanny helped

Sarah wash the dishes. Afterwards they sat around talking for an hour, until Fanny said that she had better get back home. Ernest set off to walk back to Fox Lane with her. As they left Elm Street, heading for the green, Fanny said,

'I've been waiting for you to say something, Ernie.'

He knew what she meant, but he said vaguely, 'Oh, what's that, then?'

'*What's that, then?* Ernie, you know very well what I'm talking about. The last time we spoke about our gettin' married you said it was too soon to think about it – because of your mam, you said.'

'Ah . . . yes.'

'Well – is it still too soon? I mean, she's a lot better now, ain't she?'

'I dunno.' He sighed. 'It's changed her – a lot.'

'Well – bound to, a thing like that. How could it not? But she's getting better now, you can see she is.'

'I dunno,' he said again. 'I thought she was getting to be all right. She seemed to be. But then it was like she reached a particular point and just – sort of stayed there. She don't get any better and she don't seem to get any worse. She just stays the same.'

They walked on in silence for a few paces, then Fanny came to a halt. As Ernest stopped at her side she looked up into his face.

'Tell me, Ernie, what's gunna happen to us? When d'you reckon we can get married?' She laid her head against his shoulder. 'Oh, I'm that impatient to be wed and have my own home. I'll be eighteen next month and – oh, I don't want to wait for ever.'

'Course you don't. Neither do I, but –'

'But what?' She raised her head, looked up at him. 'Tell me the truth, Ernie, you're just not ready to get married, are you?'

He didn't answer.

'Are you?' she insisted.

'– I love you, Fan . . .'

'*I love you, Fan*,' she echoed scornfully. 'Yes, you love me, but not enough, right?' She paused, then said evenly, 'Tell me, are we getting wed or not?'

'I want to,' he said. 'Believe me, I do.'

'But . . . ?'

'Please,' he said, 'try to understand. Our mam's gone through hell these past weeks. I can't leave her now, Fan, I just can't.'

Sudden tears sprang into Fanny's eyes. At the sight of them Ernest reached out for her hand but she snatched it away. 'You really mean that, don't you?' she said.

He was silent.

'So how long do we wait for your mother?' she went on. 'We could wait for ever till you think she's well enough.'

Still he said nothing.

The tears brimming over and starting down her cheeks, she raised her fist and struck him on the chest. He closed his eyes, not from the pain of the blow, but from some other hurt. When he opened his eyes she was standing back, glaring at him.

'So, that's it, then, Ernie Farrar,' she said, spitting out the words. 'You've made your decision and that's it. That's it, *mama's boy*.' He flinched at the words. She went on: 'Well, if you think I'm sitting around waiting you've got another think coming. I'm not. If you don't want me, there's others that do.'

'Fan – please.'

'There's others that do,' she repeated. With these words she spun and began to walk away. Ernest started after her.

'Fan – wait . . .'

'Go on back,' she said without looking at him. 'Get on back to your mother.' Then, turning to face him, her eyes cold with contempt, she added, 'And tell 'er she's welcome to you – because *I* don't want you.'

When Ernest called at the Greenhams' cottage in Fox Lane the next evening her sister Lottie came to the door and told him curtly that Fanny wasn't in. He knew she was lying.

Two weeks later while walking in a Trowbridge street after the market he saw Fanny's father, Arthur Greenham. A meek little man, he came over to Ernest and asked how he was. After a couple of minutes of awkward conversation Ernest asked after Fanny. Greenham shook his head.

'I wish I knew,' he said.

'What d'you mean?'

'She've gone. On Sat'dy last. Packed her box and went.'

'But – but where . . . ?'

'Up to London. She've been walkin' out these past few days with some feller from the factory – Higham. She've gone with 'im, I reckon.'

That evening Ernest told his mother of Fanny's leaving. As he sat staring into the fire Sarah put her hand on his shoulder.

'Oh, son – I'm so sorry . . .'

He reached up and patted her hand. He couldn't bring himself to look at her. After a moment he said:

'Ah, well – I daresay I'll manage.'

PART THREE

Chapter Twenty-Two

On a July Friday in 1897 Blanche and Marianne sat gazing from the windows of the 2.20 from Bristol as it moved through the green countryside towards Trowbridge. Both girls wore the uniform of their school, white blouse and deep green skirt; brown capes and light-toned straw boaters lay on the seats beside them.

Their clothing apart, the two sixteen-year-old girls could not have looked more different. Marianne's hair was woven into two heavy plaits that encircled the crown of her head, and its rich dark brown, along with the darkness of her eyes, set off the delicate pink of her skin. In contrast, Blanche's own thick, corn-coloured hair hung past her shoulders, secured back from her face by a ribbon. Her eyes, usually appearing of the richest blue, had taken on a slight hint of green as they reflected the grass of the verges beside the line.

The trees, bridges, hedges and fields swept by, the green splashed with the colours of summer flowers: thistle, elder-flower, cow parsley, the trumpets of bindweed. Faded bunting festooning one or two of the stations they passed through gave lingering signs of the Queen's Diamond Jubilee celebrations from the month before, a time when the Queen had driven in her carriage through the streets of London to the tumultuous cheers of her subjects, while throughout the rest of the country bonfires had been lit and flags hung from windows. At their school in Clifton Blanche and

Marianne had celebrated along with the other pupils; but the celebrations were over now, and the pageantry and patriotic songs seemed very far away from the peace of the gently rocking railway carriage.

Feeling a touch on her knee Blanche turned her head to Marianne, who, seated opposite, smiled and gestured towards the far corner of the carriage where Mrs Callow sat. The housekeeper had travelled to Clifton that morning to collect the girls, taking a cab from Bristol station to the school, and then returning with them in time to catch the train back to Trowbridge. Now, the warmth of the July day and the rhythm of the train had lulled her into a doze and she sat with her cap a little askew and her mouth slightly open. With a faint, smothered giggle Marianne leaned closer to Blanche. 'It seems such a shame to wake her, poor dear,' she whispered. 'She obviously needs her sleep. Perhaps we should leave her.'

'Yes,' Blanche nodded, 'she might appreciate an unexpected afternoon in Westbury.'

They smiled affectionately towards the sleeping woman. Mrs Callow, now in her fifties, had been as much a constant in their lives as anyone they had known. The governesses and other servants had come and gone at Hallowford House, but Mrs Callow had always been there.

The train rattled on. Blanche and Marianne had taken the journey between Trowbridge and Bristol so many times since the September of 1893 when they had first gone away to The Towers, as the school was named. Blanche would not easily recall the journeys made since that time, but she could remember that first one well enough. Even now she could remember her sensation of excitement, the odd, unaccustomed feel of the new school uniform, see the dully gleaming leather of the new satchel on the seat at her side. She could see Mrs Callow again, as she had been then, absorbed in her book in the corner seat diagonally across the compartment; Marianne sitting opposite, dark braids reaching halfway to her waist. She would see again in her mind's eye the reflection of herself in the carriage window as the train had passed through one of the several tunnels between Trowbridge and Bristol – herself at twelve years old, wide eyes peering at her reflection in the sudden mirror of the glass. That had been four years ago, and come September she and Marianne would begin their final year at Clifton. And then – France. Finishing school in France. It was a whole year away but the time would eventually come.

As Blanche sat there in the gently rocking carriage she felt full of hope for her future, and in control of her destiny. In her complacency she thought back to the start of her schooling at The Towers. She was happy there now, but it had not always been so, even though she had gone there in such excitement and hope. It had not taken long before there had come the assault on the bubble of her dreams.

The Towers, with no sign of a tower in sight, was a large Georgian house of three storeys near the edge of the Somersetshire town of Clifton, boasting accommodation and facilities for some fifty-five girls. Owned and run by the two principal teachers, two maiden sisters, the Misses Carling, the house stood in grounds that stretched behind and to either side for several acres.

There were four dormitories, all on the top floor, one of which Blanche and Marianne – who had adjacent beds near a window – shared with ten other girls.

The two had settled in well on their arrival and had quickly made friends with many of the other girls. They had done well in their lessons, too, and although Blanche had sometimes found herself in trouble over minor infractions of the rules, nevertheless she had been happy and successful.

The threat to her happiness had come the following autumn with the arrival at the school of a new girl, Helen Webster. Some two years older than Blanche, and a few inches taller, she was a beautiful girl with a mass of dark brown hair and long, angular face and limbs. At fifteen years old her breasts were full and she had possessed a self-assurance that was daunting.

Blanche had come face to face with her for the first time in the second week of that term.

The Towers looked out – beyond its front garden – over a surprisingly narrow street, on the other side of which stood a row of tall, terraced houses. Early on that bright September morning Blanche, Marianne and five other girls had finished dressing and now stood peering down from the window towards the central house opposite. They had learned to watch at this time for the awakening of the sleeper there in the room just below the level of their own. He was a short, squarish young man who on fine, warm days would draw back the curtains and open the window, then, leaning out, would close his eyes and deeply breathe in the morning air. On cold mornings his window remained closed – or he would soon retreat from it – but on warm mornings he would take off his nightshirt and, before getting washed and dressed, would walk naked about the room for a minute or two. Did he know that he was being watched? the girls asked each other. He never gave a sign of any awareness; never looked up towards the window from which they peered through the lace net curtains. The watching girls, having made the discovery, were now as interested in the sun as he was, for when it shone they would be afforded a brief, distant glimpse of his genitals before he retreated into the shadows of the room again. They named him Adam. For some of the girls the sight of him naked was a totally new addition to the fragments of fact and myth which went to make up the limited sum of their sexual knowledge. To others who had learned the truth, or who had seen similar sights before, the sight was no less thrilling. To all of them, with their new awareness of sex, it was – whether or not they would have admitted it – totally compelling.

On this particular morning the young man was there, opening the window. A moment later as he took off his nightshirt Marianne giggled, bit her lip and flicked a swift glance at Blanche who stood beside her. Before Adam Marianne had never in her life seen a naked male body, young or old, her sexual knowledge resulting from conversations with Blanche and two or three children from the village and the occasional sight of mating dogs or other animals. Blanche, with vague memories of having seen her brothers naked when she was much younger and once on a walk with Ernest in the woods having stumbled upon a near-naked couple lying in the grass, had gained a minor advantage over her friend. Now, as the young man tossed his discarded nightshirt onto a chair the girls stared, seven pairs of eyes fixed on his nakedness, his hairy chest, his penis like a root in the dark of his pubic hair.

Suddenly a girl's voice called to them from the open doorway behind them: 'What are you looking at?' No one answered. The voice came again: 'I asked what you were looking at.'

Blanche, half-turning, saw that the speaker was Helen Webster, the new girl who slept in the dormitory next door. One of the younger girls, Amelia Robson, whispered to her with a giggle, 'There's a man in the house opposite. He's got no clothes on.'

'No clothes on!' Helen said, raising her voice. 'What disgusting little wretches you are.'

'Sshh!' Amelia said sharply. 'You'll have Miss Carling coming in.'

'Don't you *shush* me,' Helen said contemptuously, and stepping forward she roughly thrust the small girl out of the way and took her place at the window. 'Don't do that,' Blanche said at once. 'Don't *push*. If you want to see then *ask*.'

Helen turned to her at this. '*Ask?* Ask who? Ask *you?*' Her tone was incredulous. 'I should ask *you* for permission?' She laughed into Blanche's face then turned again to the window.

Blanche felt anger rising within her. 'Get back to your own dormitory,' she said sharply. 'Look out of your own window. Don't come in here throwing your weight about. We're not impressed.'

As she spoke there came the sound of the breakfast bell. Helen straightened and turned to face her again. 'You're Blanche Farrar, aren't you?'

Blanche looked at her coldly. 'So?'

The other girl nodded. 'I know about you. You're from Hallowford, aren't you? My aunt lives in Hallowford. She told me all about you – the charity girl from Hallowford House.' She smiled coldly. 'I shall remember you, Blanche Farrar.' With a little toss of her head she turned and went from the dormitory.

From that time onwards Helen seemed to do what she could to make Blanche's life a misery. Whenever she and Blanche came together for any purpose Helen behaved towards her with a contemptuous and ridiculing manner. Sometimes she would start away from Blanche with a grimace, as if Blanche were infected with some unspeakable disease; on other occasions, if it should become necessary for their heads to be close, she would, with eyes rolling, hold up her hands as a screen between Blanche's head and her own, indicating to her few sniggering cronies that she was terrified of catching lice. If Blanche should just happen to be passing by, then without glancing in her direction, Helen would suddenly begin to talk loudly of 'peasants' and 'upstarts' and 'charity', after which Blanche would be followed by gales of laughter.

And through it all Blanche was determined not to react. She was only too aware of Mr Savill's generosity in providing for her schooling, and she would do nothing to disgrace him or put his faith in her in doubt.

And the taunts went on, after a while beginning to come from Helen's friends as well, as, encouraged by her, and growing stronger in the immunity that she seemed to enjoy, they took up the war she had waged.

'I shall tell Papa when we see him next.'

Marianne spoke as they walked in the school grounds during Recreation. Over luncheon in the refectory Helen had done her best, unseen by the mistresses, to humiliate Blanche again. 'He'll tell Miss Carling,' Marianne added. 'It's bound to stop then.'

'No,' Blanche said at once. 'Uncle John mustn't know of it.' She put her hand on Marianne's arm. 'I must deal with it myself. And I will – in time. Till then I shall just have to put up with it.'

Helen's assaults continued. On one occasion Blanche returned to the dormitory and found on her pillow a note in Helen's hand. 'There is a strong smell of cow manure in this area,' the note said. 'When you go home, please ask your brother to keep his distance.' Saying nothing, Blanche tore up the note and threw it away. The following afternoon she found on her bed a pile of dirty clothes. She stood staring – and then from behind her came the sound of Helen's raucous laughter. She turned to see her standing there flanked by her three cronies.

'We were just wondering if you'd mind taking it back home with you next week,' Helen said sweetly as she gestured to the clothes. 'We thought your mother wouldn't mind putting it in with the rest of the village's washing.' For a moment Blanche stood there, then, whirling, she snatched up the collection of soiled drawers, petticoats, nightdresses and stockings and, running to the window, pitched the lot out onto the forecourt. Her action, however, in no way constituted anything of a victory. Miss Carling, not knowing the reason for her actions, punished her for them.

That October, with Blanche and Marianne back at Hallowford for the half-term holiday, it was clear to John Savill that something was wrong and he asked Blanche what it was. 'Nothing, sir,' she answered, avoiding his eyes. He knew, though, that something was the matter.

Returning to school Blanche found herself once again the victim of Helen's taunts. Now, however, there was a slight difference; now Helen had widened the aperture of her focus to include Marianne.

One warm Saturday morning in late October Blanche and Marianne had been set to work on their garden plots, to clear away the dead summer growth and begin to prepare the ground for next spring's sowing. Miss Bassington, the horticultural mistress, had just gone back into the school building, leaving them to their work. They had been busy for some time when Helen and four other girls came towards them from the direction of the side gate. Helen and her friends, Blanche guessed, were returning from doing various jobs of work at the nearby church, tasks which were a privilege which they guarded with jealousy. They went to the church regularly each Saturday morning after breakfast, where, joining two or three local women, they gave their help in the cleaning of the brasses, arranging the flowers and doing other odd jobs that needed to be done. They went happily, not for the sake of the work they did, but mainly for the chance of escaping for a few hours from the confines of the school and Saturday morning lessons.

Blanche, having seen Helen's approach, turned to concentrate on her work. But it did no good. While two of the girls went on by, Helen and the other two came to a stop nearby. There Helen, after trying without success to get a response from Blanche, turned her attention to Marianne.

'You never have a word to say for yourself, have you?' she said. 'All you can do is hover around the peasant.' She reached out a contemptuous hand and stroked Marianne's cheek. 'Little Miss Goody Goody.'

Marianne stood silent for a moment but then, finding her courage, said: 'Why don't you leave us alone, Helen. Just go away and leave us alone.'

The 'O-o-o-o-h' from Helen's lips was a long sound of surprise. 'So the little worm has a voice, too, has she?' She stepped forward, looking down at Marianne from the advantage of her greater height. 'Where did you learn such manners? From your friend here?' Marianne said nothing, and suddenly Helen was stooping, picking up from the earth a long, writhing worm. She laughed. 'A worm for a worm.' Suddenly reaching out, she thrust the worm into the neck of Marianne's blouse. As Marianne squealed in horror Helen gave her a push and the next moment Marianne was sprawling on the earth.

Blanche, seeing Marianne fall, felt rising within her all the pent-up rage that had been growing ever since she and Helen had first come face to face. With a little cry she rushed forward, hurling herself at the taller girl. Taking her completely by surprise, her hands reached out, grasping, snatching at Helen's long hair. In another moment, using all her strength, she had thrown her onto the soft, newly-dug earth. Then while Helen screamed out and the other girls stood gaping and silent, Blanche threw herself on top of her and, sitting astride her, began to rain blows down on her face. '*Never, never, never,*' Blanche shrieked, punctuating her words with blows, 'never touch me or Marianne again! Never, never speak to me again as you have done! Never, never, *never . . .!*' Then, eyes frantically casting around her, she reached down to the earth near Helen's head. And there was a worm. Before the shrieking Helen had realised what was happening. Blanche snatched up the worm and pushed it into the girl's gaping mouth.

It took both Miss Bassington and the younger Miss Carling to drag Blanche off when they came rushing onto the scene a few minutes later.

Afterwards Blanche and Marianne, and Helen and her two friends were taken before the senior Miss Carling. Helen and her friends testified that Blanche had instigated the trouble and had attacked Helen for no reason at all. Marianne told the true story. Blanche remained silent.

The following week Savill arrived at the school, his presence requested by the elder Miss Carling. After his interview with her he was shown into a small private room and Blanche was sent for. 'Mr Savill, your guardian, is here to see you,' Miss Lessing, the art mistress, told Blanche as she emerged from the school-room. Blanche was puzzled. Why had she been sent for and not Marianne?

Mr Savill kissed her when she entered the room. Then when she was seated facing him he told her that he had been summoned there by the headmistress. 'She's concerned about your behaviour,' he said gravely. It was what Blanche had feared. He went on to speak of the attack on Helen and also of the incident when Blanche had thrown the clothes from the window. 'Why did you do it?' he asked. Blanche, however, would say nothing in her defence.

When Blanche had gone from the room Savill went back to the headmistress and asked to see Marianne. When Marianne came to him she told him the true story. It was Miss Baker all over again, he said to himself.

Blanche's attack on Helen had subdued the latter for a few days, but not for long. Blanche, although she had humiliated Helen had, nevertheless, lost the battle. She it was who had remained in the greater disgrace, who had suffered the ignominy of having a guardian summoned to the school. Helen, escaping from the episode with a sharp reprimand – and a threat that her church duties would be suspended – was still bitter. She could still taste the worm that Blanche had thrust into her mouth, and she did not forgive easily. In a matter of only a couple of weeks she took up her cudgels again.

But things were to change.

One Saturday morning Blanche watched as Helen got up from the breakfast table and prepared to leave for her work at the church. Blanche saw the way she held herself as she walked to the door, tall, proud and beautiful. She looked invincible.

When Blanche and Marianne had finished breakfast they put on their smocks and, along with other girls from the class, went to the art studio where they were to have a drawing lesson. When Miss Lessing came into the room a few minutes afterwards she announced that as it was such a bright day they would take their drawing pads outside into the garden. So, clad warmly against the autumn coolness, the twelve girls collected together their materials and trooped out into the sun where Miss Lessing instructed them to choose some particular scene and render it in their sketch books.

Blanche and Marianne left the others and started off down the garden path, walking beside the croquet lawn, the kitchen gardens and the orchard, moving towards a distant part of the grounds. After a while, with the more formal area of the grounds behind them, they came to a glade that was situated close to another in which stood a small summerhouse. The little building was out of bounds to the pupils and kept locked, and neither Blanche nor Marianne had ever set foot inside. Once, for a brief time, the land in its immediate vicinity had been cultivated – but that had been long ago. Now the surrounding shrubs and other plants grew wild, and the summerhouse itself, so long uncared for and forgotten, was dilapidated, rotting and falling apart.

Standing on the edge of the smaller clearing, Blanche and Marianne looked around them. This would do, they agreed. Two minutes later they were sitting side by side on a small hillock drawing the twisted roots and branches of an old beech tree.

They concentrated steadily for the first fifteen minutes or so, silent, intent on their work. Looking appraisingly at her drawing, Blanche sighed with disappointment; she hadn't inherited her father's talent for draughtsmanship. At her side Marianne put down her pencil, stretched, and idly looked around her. And then suddenly she froze. Next moment, reaching out, she put an arresting hand on Blanche's arm. Blanche opened her mouth to protest but Marianne said quickly, softly, 'Sshhh . . . don't make a sound.'

Marianne had turned on the hillock and, screened by

the foliage of the evergreens, was peering through at the main clearing. Silently she raised a beckoning finger to Blanche. Blanche moved to her side.

Before them in the clearing was the summerhouse. A little further away, and drawing nearer through the trees, was a figure.

'What's Helen doing here?' Marianne whispered. 'She's supposed to be at the church with the other girls.'

They watched as Helen came closer. She carried her smock over one arm. There was caution in her movements. Looking anxiously about her she crossed the clearing towards the summerhouse and stopped at its door. There she stooped, fumbled at the ground for a moment, then reached up to the lock. She had a key. In another moment she had opened the door and gone inside. The door closed behind her.

Marianne and Blanche turned to one another, wide eyes showing their surprise.

'What's all that about?' Marianne whispered. 'And why is she being so secretive?'

Blanche shrugged. 'She's not supposed to be there.'

Their drawing forgotten, the two girls continued to gaze at the entrance to the summerhouse. 'If Miss Carling knew about this there'd be trouble,' Marianne murmured with a faint smile and a sidelong glance at Blanche. Blanche shook her head. 'But not *enough* trouble, I'm afraid. No. When I cook Helen Webster's goose I'm going to make sure that the oven's really hot.'

As Blanche finished speaking their gaze was attracted by a moving shape over to the right; the wall to the side lane lay in that direction. As they watched a young man came in view. Tall, dark-haired, he looked to be about seventeen or eighteen. He wore the uniform of the nearby grammar school, St Michael's. The pupils of St Michael's were the bane of the elder Miss Carling's existence; they were for ever making nuisances of themselves, pestering the older girls when they went out into the town, or hanging over the wall and whistling at them. Miss Carling was always complaining about the nuisance they caused and instructing the girls to have nothing to do with them.

Now, standing at the edge of the trees, this St Michael's pupil looked about him for a moment or two and then, very quickly, ran across the open ground to the summerhouse door. Next moment he had opened the door and gone inside.

When the door had closed behind him Blanche murmured, 'So now we know the reason.' Another moment and she had started to move away, creeping through the shrubbery. 'Where are you going?' Marianne whispered after her.

'To see what's going on.' Blanche flapped a hand at her. 'You stay here and keep watch.' Then, to the sound of Marianne's whispered protests she crept away.

Emerging from the cover of the trees and shrubbery, Blanche covered the little distance of open ground in a swift, rushing scurry. Reaching the summerhouse she glanced down at the spot from which Helen had taken the key. There was a large stone there; obviously she had kept it hidden under that. Then, swiftly and silently she began to creep around the shabby little building, searching for some aperture that would allow her to look inside; the windows, uncurtained, would not allow her any shield. Then, beneath one of the windows she saw that one of the rotting feather boards had begun to fall away. Carefully, without making a sound, she bent and peered through the gap.

In a very little time she learned more than she could ever have done from a dozen occasions watching the waking man across the street from the school.

The boy had taken off his jacket and he and Helen were standing wrapped in each other's arms. They were kissing, their faces moving on one another's. Blanche could hear their sighs, their faint, breathy moans. The young man began to stroke Helen's breast, then after a moment he took her hand and pressed it to the front of his grey flannel trousers. Eagerly Helen held him there, feeling, kneading, and he lifted his head, closing his eyes in ecstasy. And then both Helen's hands were there, fumbling at the buttons, quick and impatient. The boy hitched off his braces and pushed down his trousers and drawers. His member, tumescent, rigid, sprang up. As Helen eagerly grasped him his own hands worked at the buttons of her uniform dress. For a few seconds as the pair undressed they were a picture of feverishly moving limbs, and then they were standing naked, pressed against one another.

There was a covering on the floor, made of what appeared to be an old blanket and Helen's smock. They lay down on it together, Helen supine, her knees bent and slightly apart. The boy, at her side and leaning over her, ran his hands over her naked body, his fingers lingering on her full breasts. He bent, taking first one red nipple and then the other into his mouth. As he did so Helen sighed, reaching down to his groin, taking him in her eager hand again. As he bent with his mouth closed over her breast his left hand moved down over her smooth, flat stomach, lingered for a moment in the little bush of hair at its base and then closed over the mound of her sex. His fingers moved, probing, stroking, manipulating, and Helen gripped the back of his head and opened her legs wider.

In the next moments the boy moved his slim, muscular body onto the girl's, her knees rising wide and high to accommodate him. Then, to the accompaniment of the couple's gasps and groans the boy's smooth, tight buttocks moved up and down as he repeatedly thrust himself into the girl's body.

At last, with a loud, shuddering sigh from the boy, it was all over. The pair lay still for a moment and then the boy was rolling from Helen's body and lying down at her side.

That night Blanche and Marianne lay in their beds and looked at one another across the little space between. 'Next Saturday,' Marianne silently mouthed, and Blanche mouthed in return, 'Next Saturday,' grinned at her and slowly nodded her head on the pillow.

The following Saturday morning dawned cloudy and Blanche was afraid that there would be rain and they would be confined to the indoors. Over breakfast, though, the clouds disappeared and the sun came out bright and warm. Covertly as they ate she watched Helen at the next table. Helen's hair had been brushed till it shone, and there was a faint blush on her cheeks. Like last Saturday she had once again taken particular care with her appearance. Blanche smiled to herself.

'May we go outside to sketch again today, Ma'am?' Blanche asked Miss Lessing when breakfast was over. 'Marianne and I would like to finish our drawings of the beech tree.' Miss Lessing looked at her keenly. She was a short woman and her eyes were not far above the level of Blanche's own. 'All right,' she said after a moment, 'and I hope that you'll accomplish a little more than you did last week. You didn't have much to show for your time.'

'Oh, I'll do well this time, Ma'am,' Blanche assured her. 'Really I will.'

Blanche's final words to Miss Lessing echoed in her

mind as she gathered her drawing materials together. She *would* do well. She turned to Marianne, grinned at her, and together they went out into the sun.

At the edge of the smaller clearing they waited for Helen to appear, and as the time went by Blanche began to fear that she would not come. After all, she said to herself, perhaps the incident with the boy had been an isolated one. And then she would remind herself of the key – the key to the summerhouse which Helen had somehow got hold of and which she had kept hidden under the stone. However Helen had come by it, whether it had been stolen or copied, it made clear that her visits to the summerhouse were regular events.

Helen arrived some twenty minutes after Blanche and Marianne, and they watched through the leaves as she stepped quickly across the clearing to the summerhouse door. A moment later she had vanished inside and the door had closed behind her. At once Blanche got to her feet and started off at a run towards the schoolhouse.

She found the elder Miss Carling and Miss Lessing talking together in the hall. Miss Carling turned her red face towards the sound of Blanche's hurrying feet. 'Walk, young lady,' she reprimanded. 'You're not outside now.' Then her tone changed as she asked, frowning, 'What's the matter? Is something wrong?'

'Well, Ma'am,' Blanche said ingenuously, 'it's just that we saw someone go into the summerhouse.' Please, God, she prayed, let Helen's young man have turned up. 'One of the boys from the grammar school,' she added.

Her words, as she had hoped they would be, were like a red rag to a bull. Miss Carling and Miss Lessing exchanged sharp looks. Miss Carling's face had grown a little redder. 'Are you sure?' she said, turning back to Blanche.

'Oh, yes, Ma'am. Marianne and I were sketching nearby when we saw him. We saw him go inside.'

'But – the place is locked.'

Blanche shrugged. 'Well, he went in, Ma'am. We saw him. He's there now.' A brief pause then she added, 'You'll catch him if you hurry. And if you're very quiet.'

Miss Carling, tight-lipped and preparing to move away, was already lifting the little chain which, suspended from her belt, held a heavy bunch of keys. 'Does this boy know that you saw him?'

'Oh, no, Ma'am. Marianne and I – we were very careful not to let him see us. But I thought you'd want to know.'

'Thank you. You did right to tell me.' Miss Carling exchanged a further glance with Miss Lessing and then they were striding away towards the door.

Moments later Blanche was walking some way behind the two women as they moved across the grounds; they walked at such a swift, determined pace that Blanche had no trouble keeping her distance. *Please, God, let Helen and the boy be there*, she prayed as she left the field and entered the woodland. And then up ahead she saw the smaller, nearer clearing, and there was Marianne, sitting where she had left her, on the little hillock in the shrubbery. Watching anxiously she saw the women stop at Marianne's side, exchange a few brief words with her and then slip quietly out of sight into the larger clearing beyond. As Blanche approached Marianne a moment later Marianne turned and gave a slow smile and nodded.

A little later as Blanche and Marianne hovered in the shrubbery, pretending to get on with their drawing, Miss Carling reappeared and told them to go back to the schoolhouse. Miss Carling's face was almost purple. Neither she nor Miss Lessing put in an appearance at the refectory for luncheon, and of the two only Miss Lessing, looking nervous and shaken, was at dinner. When one of the girls enquired after Miss Carling she was told that she was unwell and was lying down.

And of course neither was Helen Webster at luncheon or dinner that day – or on any other day that followed.

Now, in July, three years later, sitting in the train bound for Trowbridge, Blanche smiled to herself at the memory, the pictures as clear in her mind as the images thrown by Miss Lessing's magic lantern.

She had been a little sorry at first about the boy; whatever had happened to him she didn't know. She was not unduly perturbed, though; she had quickly thrust aside any feelings of sympathy. So often a trap needed live bait, and like any angler, if one spent too much time feeling sorry for the fly, one would never catch the fish.

Chapter Twenty-Three

John Savill had lunched with his brother Harold at
Hallowford House. They had talked at length of the
worsening situation in the Transvaal, discussing the like-
lihood of another war with the Boers. Now, though, it
was just after four o'clock, Harold had gone, and Savill,
sitting in the library, heard the sound of the carriage on
the drive. At once he got up and went into the hall,
opening the front door just as the carriage drew up
before the house. He was sixty-six now, and the years
had whitened his grey hair, and made leaner the fine
lines of his face. His bearing was still upright, though,
and his step still firm, and as the girls got down onto
the forecourt he hurried towards them, smiling, reaching
out in welcome. He had not seen them since the Easter
holidays and the house, as always, had been a duller
place for their absence. Embracing them, first Marianne
and then Blanche, he kissed them, then, arms around
their shoulders, led them into the hall.

When the girls had taken off their capes and hats and
washed their hands, they joined John Savill in the library
where afternoon tea was served, over which they talked
lightly of this and that – mostly about their recent days
at Clifton.

As they talked Marianne touched at her hair and then
got up from her seat and moved to a small, ornate
looking-glass beside the fireplace. Standing almost in
profile to her father she took a couple of pins from her

braided hair, placed them between her even, white teeth and readjusted the loosened braids. As she reached to the back of her head, elbows lifted high, Savill saw the swell of her breasts, a sudden anachronism against the dull green of her uniform school dress. He became aware suddenly of the neatness of her small waist, the curve of her hips – and it was as if he was suddenly seeing her with new eyes. She's no longer a child; she's a young woman, he thought with a little shock of mingled joy and sadness. His glance rising he took in her face, the fine arch of her eyebrows as she concentrated on her reflection, her dark, wide eyes, the pink blush of her cheeks, her lips a deeper pink, drawn back over the remaining hair pin between her teeth. Savill's glance lingered on her in a kind of wonder, and then Blanche was asking him whether he wanted more tea. His eyes moved to her. 'No, thank you,' he said. He watched as she leaned forward slightly in her chair and poured tea into her own cup. Blanche, too, of course ... With similar fascination he found himself watching her movements with the teapot, the cup and saucer, the milk jug – everything she did was casually deft and sure with the assurance of her nascent maturity. He saw then the way her pale, heavy hair fell against her shoulders; he saw the line of her lip, the fringe of her lashes on her lowered lids; the smoothness of her cheek, the curve of her delicately pointed chin. Marianne was telling some story about one of the teachers at the school, but Savill's mind was on his discovery. The girls had been growing up and he had not realized it until now.

When tea was finished Blanche changed her clothes and went out to the stables where James had saddled one of the cobs. Mounting the pony she rode it out of the yard and away from Hallowford, heading for Colford, a small village a short distance to the north. Three years earlier Ernest had changed his employment, moving as stockman to a farm a little further afield. Following the change he and his mother had left the Hallowford cottage to rent one in Colford. The move had had varying effects, among them on the relationship between Blanche and her mother and brother. With them all living in Hallowford their very different social circumstances had created certain tensions and problems – although they were unacknowledged. To a degree the move of Mrs Farrar and Ernest to Colford had eased these tensions – but at the same time the greater distance meant that Blanche had seen less of them over recent times, and consequently had grown further away.

Reaching Colford, Blanche dismounted near the end of Hummock Lane, tethered the pony and walked the short distance along to the cottage, there going around to the rear where she entered by the scullery and went into the kitchen. Her mother was standing at the kitchen table, a pair of scissors in her hand. Beside her, spread out on the table, was a large piece of white cotton to which was pinned a dressmaker's paper pattern. Putting down the scissors, Sarah smiled warmly at her.

'Hello, Blanche. I thought that would be you.'

'Hello, Mama . . .' Blanche briefly wrapped her arms around her mother and kissed her on the cheek. Then she stepped back and looked at her. 'Well – how are you?'

Sarah nodded. 'Oh, quite well, thank you, dear. And you?'

'Yes, very well.'

Sarah rolled up the cotton. 'It's just an apron I'm making,' she said. 'I'm not sorry to put it away. I think I need to get some spectacles . . .' She smiled. 'I'll make some tea.'

Blanche filled the kettle and put it on the range. She didn't want more tea but the ritual came as welcome assistance. As Sarah set out the cups Blanche looked around her. Although the interior of the cottage was clean and neat, she was struck – as she was every time she entered – by its lack of any kind of luxury.

When the tea was made Blanche and her mother sat facing one another beside the range, Blanche taking Ernest's chair. Beside it stood a small bureau holding a number of well-read books, and as Blanche set down her cup she took in the titles; there were volumes of Keats's and Shelley's poetry, a copy of *Measure for Measure*, and two or three medical books. Sarah, observing Blanche's interest, said, 'Oh, Ernest's books are all over the place.' She glanced up at the clock. 'He should be home soon.'

As they drank they spoke of Blanche's days at Clifton and events in Hallowford, but the conversation did not flow and its course was dotted with little pockets of silence.

Blanche studied her mother as the desultory conversation progressed, noticing the lines in Sarah's face, the grey in her hair. Sarah was forty-eight now, and Blanche was aware of the fact that her mother was ageing. Thrusting the realization from her mind, she said:

'Mama – Mr Savill wants me to go away with Marianne to finishing school. In France, so he says.'

Her mother looked at her in surprise. 'Oh, Blanche, really? What a wonderful opportunity for you.'

'You don't mind?'

'Of course I don't mind. If it's what you want.' She paused. 'Is it?'

Blanche nodded. 'It would be lovely to – to have the experience of another country.'

'Oh, indeed. And if Mr Savill wants you to go and you want to, then of course you must.'

'Thank you. Mr Savill said he's going to talk to you about it, but I said I wanted to speak to you first.'

'When would you go?'

'Not for another year. Next summer, Mr Savill says.'

They talked for a little while about the proposed year in France but then silence fell again, so that the ticking of the clock sounded unusually loud in the small room. Blanche found herself wishing for the time to pass when she could leave and return to Hallowford. In spite of the smiles and the enthusiasm, somehow all the conversation had about it the faint ring of politeness, and Blanche found herself wondering, once more, whether she and her mother would ever be really close. But perhaps, she said to herself, it had all gone beyond that. She thought of earlier times; in times past her mother had been warm and approachable. Now there was a distance between them, a distance which had grown wider with the passing years. Was it, Blanche asked herself, all due to their move here to Colford?

Soon after six o'clock Ernest came in after finishing his work for the day. He kissed his mother and then with a smile moved to Blanche as if he would embrace her, but then, as if becoming aware of his rough working clothes he dropped his arms. He stood before her, a tall, handsome young man of twenty-five, with level grey eyes, thick, chestnut hair, straight, blunt nose.

'Oh, my, Blanche,' he said, gazing at her, 'I notice such a difference every time I see you.' He shook his head in a little gesture of wonder and approval. 'You're a real young lady now.'

Blanche felt a sense of awkwardness as they faced one another. She didn't know what to say. Then as Sarah set about making fresh tea for Ernest, Blanche prepared to leave. Ernest said, 'I don't know what we've got for supper, Blanche, but will you stay?'

At his words Sarah began to add her own words of invitation, but Blanche thanked her and said that she was expected at Hallowford House for dinner. Perhaps on another day, however, she said; they would arrange it.

She wished her mother goodbye then, and Ernest, saying that he would see her to her mount, followed her out of the cottage.

As they walked together towards the waiting pony Ernest looked up at the evening sky, sighed and said, 'It's a beautiful evening. You should come for a walk with me on an evening like this. It's beautiful round here in the woodland at this time of year.'

'I will,' Blanche said.

They came to a stop some yards from the pony. 'You'd better get back,' Blanche said, smiling. 'Mam will have your tea ready.'

Ernest nodded. 'Ah, in a minute.'

They stood facing one another. Blanche thought suddenly of the girl, Fanny Greenham, who had left Hallowford long ago. Blanche wondered whether Ernest ever thought about her. Had he loved her? Such a question had never occurred to her before, at those times when Fanny had been there and they had all walked together and played on the hill. Was there anyone now he loved? She knew that over the years he had walked out on occasions with two or three young women from the area, but the relationships had never lasted.

Blanche thought suddenly of the medical books she had seen at the cottage.

'I saw your books, Ernest,' she said.

'My what?'

'Your books. Your medical books.'

'Oh – those . . .' He straightened, dismissing her words with a wave of his hand. 'I picked them up 'ere and there.'

She smiled. 'You haven't given up, have you?'

'Given up?'

'– Well – those medical books. You've never forgotten, have you? – what you wanted to be – a doctor.'

'Oh, I'll never be a doctor now. But I can't help but be – interested.'

'No more than interested?'

He laughed. 'Ah, well – per'aps. I've learned a good deal working with the animals at the farm. And I've 'elped the vet on a few occasions.' He gave a little snort of derision. 'Not that it'll ever do me any good.'

'Are you happy, Ernest?' she asked.

He frowned. 'Happy? Oh – Blanche – it's not a thing I ever think about.' He narrowed his eyes slightly. 'I s'pose I'm happy enough, all right. Are you?'

She shrugged. 'Oh, yes. Like you, I suppose I'm happy enough.'

'Still getting on all right at Clifton?'

'Yes, thank you.'

'How much longer have you got there?'

'Another year.'

'That'll go soon enough. Will you be sorry to leave? I expect you will – a clever girl like you.'

'Oh, I don't know about that – being clever.'

He smiled. 'No Miss Bakers there.'

'No, no Miss Bakers.'

She told him then about Mr Savill's proposal to send her to finishing school with Marianne when they had finished their studies at Clifton. He gave a low whistle. 'Going to France, eh? Well, if that don't beat all.'

Blanche gave a deprecating little laugh. 'Well,' she said, 'it's not like a real education, is it? I mean, it's not like going to university or anything like that, is it?'

'Is that what you'd like to do – go to university?'

'Oh, fine chance of that for a girl. Haven't you

realized that no one takes education seriously for females? No, girls have to learn deportment and such fascinating things.'

A little silence fell between them. A movement to her right drew her eyes and she saw the red shape of a squirrel come to a halt on the branch of an oak and stay for some moments, tail flicking, before leaping away again. She watched the squirrel until it had gone from her sight. When she moved her glance back to Ernest she found him studying her. She smiled. 'What's the matter?'

'Nothing.' He returned her smile. 'I was just thinking that Mary would have looked just like you.'

'I wish I could remember her. I was too young.'

'Yes, of course you were. But you're very like her. And Dad. You've got their colouring.'

A little silence, then Blanche said:

'How is Mama, Ernest? I can't tell. She never talks much about herself when I go to see her, or in her letters when I'm away at school.'

Ernest shrugged. 'Oh, she's all right, I s'pose. She gets about a bit more now.' He paused. 'Though I don't think she's that strong.'

'She – she's not ill, is she?'

'No, she's not ill. But, as I say – I don't think she's that strong.' He gazed at her in silence for a moment, then he said, 'Come and see her soon again, will you?'

'Yes, of course I will.'

'You promise?'

She felt touched by a little irritation at his words. 'I said I would,' she said.

'Sorry – I didn't mean to push you. It's just that . . .' He let the rest of his words go unsaid.

Blanche said suddenly, 'When I go to see Mama there's – there's no real – closeness between us anymore.'

He frowned. 'Oh, Blanche, what a melancholy thing to say.'

'It's true.' She shook her head. 'I wish it were otherwise.'

He paused. 'Have you any notion as to why it should be?'

'No.'

He pondered the problem for a few moments then said, 'It'll be all right, you'll see. And in the meantime don't worry about it.' He gave a little smile. 'Fancy – you going away to France. You'll be so grand when you come back it'll be a wonder if you ever speak to us again.' He laughed, and Blanche laughed with him.

As she rode away on the cob a few minutes later, heading back towards Hallowford, the sound of his words lingered in her mind.

At noon the following day Ernest filled a mug with fresh milk from the dairy and, taking up the tin containing his dinner, left the farmyard. When he had crossed over the narrow road between the farm buildings and the meadows he passed through a stile into a field where a number of Palmer's cows were grazing. Walking beside the hedge he made his way to a clump of trees on the far side, a small thicket in which was a clearing through which flowed a narrow stream. Near the stream he sat down at the foot of an oak. It was the usual spot in which he ate when the weather was fine, and this July day was warm and bright.

The varying shades of green of the sundrenched copse about him was splashed here and there with the pink of dogroses. Through the screen of leaves he could watch the cows grazing in the meadow. From his pocket he took a small volume and opened it on his knee. As he read he slowly drank the milk, and ate the bread-and-cheese and bread-and-dripping his mother had prepared for him.

A little later as he took from the tin one of the two hard-boiled eggs packed there his eye was caught by a movement to his left and, looking over, he saw an animal slink by in the foliage. A second or two later the creature came more clearly into his view and he saw that it was a dog.

As he looked at the animal it came to a halt and turned to face him. For some seconds they stared at one another, then Ernest leant back against the tree and began to eat.

When both eggs were gone a few minutes later he looked over and saw that the dog was still there, watching him. It had moved a little nearer now, lying in the long grass beside a bramble bush. After a moment Ernest said gently, 'Hello, there, dog. What're you doin' 'ere, then? Are you lost?' The dog remained still. Ernest put out a hand. 'Here, boy . . .' Seconds went by. Ernest spoke again: 'Here, boy. Come on, now . . .' And slowly, cautiously, the dog raised itself and, limping slightly on its right foreleg, moved a few feet towards him. Ernest began to speak again, a gentle, continuous, coaxing murmur, and eventually the animal was crouching just six feet away.

Keeping his eyes on the dog, Ernest reached down to the tin at his side. At the movement the dog backed away a foot. 'It's all right, it's all right . . .' Ernest kept up the soothing words as he slowly took the lid from the tin and laid it on the ground. There was only some cold meat left now, some mutton left over from yesterday's supper. He picked it up, unwrapped it and broke off a small piece. With a soft word he tossed the morsel towards the dog, which quickly stepped back in alarm. 'It's all right,' Ernest said. 'It's all right, it's all right . . .'

The dog stayed there for a few seconds, eyes lifted to Ernest's face. Ernest gazed back. The dog was of medium size, of some indeterminate mixture of breeds. Its dull and dirty coat was white with a black patch over its right eye and ear. One or two bits of twig and dried grass clung to the matted and tangled hair. Beneath the dog's coat its frame looked thin and starved, and obviously the creature's limp had been caused by some injury.

After remaining still for some seconds the dog lowered its head and cautiously stretched its neck towards the smell of the meat.

'Come on, boy,' Ernest said. 'Come on. Eat it. It's good. Come on, boy . . .'

And suddenly the dog moved forward, snatched up the scrap of meat, wolfed it down and backed away again.

'Was that good, boy?' Ernest kept his voice to a soothing monotone. 'You want more?' He threw another scrap towards the dog. This time the dog hesitated for only a second before moving forward and snatching it up. Timidly it backed off again. 'It's all right,' Ernest said. 'You don't need to be afraid – not of me.' He tossed another morsel of meat and now, almost without hesitating, the dog moved forward and ate it. And this time instead of backing off afterwards it merely wavered a little on the spot, its head lifted to Ernest, its dark, moist, fearful eyes gazing into his own.

'Come on, boy . . . You and I can be friends, I reckon.'

Ernest took another scrap of meat and this time tossed it so that it fell only a yard away. The dog hesitated again, then timidly moved forward, its cringing body low to the ground. It took up the meat slowly, aware of the shortened distance between itself and the man. Afterwards it didn't move. Ernest too remained still.

'Come on, boy.'

Ernest tore off another piece of the meat – there was little of it left now – and slowly bent forward and placed it on the grass near his feet. He remained there, bending over, watching the dog. After a few seconds the animal moved forward. When it had eaten the meat it looked up at Ernest. Moving slowly, Ernest tore the last of the mutton in two and slowly, slowly reached out, one of the remaining pieces of meat on his outstretched palm. A few moments later he felt the dog's warm breath on his hand as it took the meat gently into its mouth. Ernest held out the last piece and watched as the dog carefully took it.

'I'm afraid that's all, boy,' Ernest said. 'There's no more.'

The dog stayed a while longer, waiting, looking up at him, while once again Ernest took in the creature's sorry condition. Turning, the dog moved away, limping down to the bank of the shallow stream where it began to drink. Afterwards it stepped away, moved across the grass a few feet and urinated against a tree. Then Ernest watched with a little surge of happiness as the dog came back to his side and, after a moment, lay down in the grass at his feet.

A little later when Ernest got up to go back to the farm the dog rose too and moved after him. And walking along the edge of the field Ernest glanced back and saw the dog still there, walking steadily behind him. For a moment Ernest feared that the dog might go after the cows, but it paid no heed to them, continuing to limp along, keeping to the hedge. Reaching the stile beside the gate Ernest stepped through it onto the roadside. When he had crossed to the entrance to the yard he looked back and saw the dog sitting beside the stile. 'Ah, that's right,' Ernest said. 'You'd better not come in 'ere, lad. A stranger like you – you come in 'ere you're likely to find yourself in trouble.' He turned away again, opened the gate to the yard and went in, closing the gate behind him. Just before he turned out of sight by the cowshed he glanced back and saw the dog still sitting there.

Later on, when he crossed back into the field to help Lizzie, the young milkmaid, with the milking, there was no sign of the dog. He was aware of a slight feeling of disappointment.

At six o'clock when he left the farm dark clouds were gathering and there was the scent of rain in the air. He set off briskly, heading for home. As he moved along the road he glanced over his shoulder and saw that the dog was there again, following him at a distance of about twenty yards. By the time he got to Hummock Lane the dog had shortened the distance between them. When he reached the cottage gate he left it open behind him, and reaching the scullery door a moment later he turned and saw that the dog had followed him into the yard.

In the kitchen he found his mother preparing his supper. 'Come and look,' he said, nodding towards the door. Sarah, busy at the range, said, 'What is it?'

'Come and look.'

She came towards him and looked past his broad back at the dog. It backed away a little at the sight of her and then stayed there, looking nervously from her to Ernest.

'Where did he come from?' Sarah asked.

'God knows. He's been following me around half the day.'

As Ernest spoke the first drops of rain fell. In just seconds it was raining heavily. The dog didn't move; it remained there, seemingly oblivious, eyes fixed on Ernest's face.

'Well,' Ernest said, 'we can't leave the creature out

there, can we?' He bent, stretching out his hand. 'Come on, boy. Come on inside, in the dry.'

After a moment's hesitation the dog moved forward. As it came through the doorway, Sarah said:

'You make sure he stays in the scullery.'

The first thing Ernest did was to dry the animal and then feed him. Only then, and with much impatient admonishing from Sarah, did he change his clothes and eat his own supper.

Afterwards he gave his attention to the dog once more, first of all examining his injured paw. He found there was a thorn deeply embedded in the soft pad, and with the dog flinching and whimpering he carefully extracted it.

In the corner of the scullery he laid down an old, worn-out coat and a bit of an old blanket. He set the dog down on the makeshift bed and stood back watching as it circled, lay down and began to lick its paw.

'He'll be all right now,' he said.

Sarah, watching from the kitchen doorway, said: 'Have you any idea where he's come from?'

'None at all. I've never seen him around before.'

'He's a funny-looking thing,' Sarah said.

Ernest nodded. 'Ah, I doubt he'll win any prizes for looks.'

'How old is he, d'you think? He's not a pup. You can see that.'

'No, but he's not very old, I don't reckon.'

'He looks half-starved.'

'He does. I should think he's been on the move for a good while. Wandering about . . . Either that or he's been very badly mistreated by his owner. Still – we'll soon put him right.'

At the implication of his words Sarah turned to look at Ernest. He shrugged.

'Well, we can't turn him out, can we?'

She frowned. 'You want him to stay? But he's so – so dirty and –'

'He won't be in a day or two, you'll see. Just let 'im get his health and strength back.'

Sarah said: 'He might not want to stay. Surely he must have a home somewhere.'

Ernest looked back at the dog which now lay sleeping, head on its paws.

'Ah, I reckon he has,' he said with a nod. 'And I reckon it's 'ere, with us.'

Under Ernest's care there was a marked difference in the creature's appearance and behaviour in only the space of days as its health and strength improved. Ernest called him 'Jacko'. Blanche, calling at the cottage a week after the dog's adoption, was surprised to see him there. She sat watching as Ernest brushed the animal's coat. Seeing the love and trust in the creature's soft, dark eyes as it looked up at Ernest she reflected that she had never before seen such naked adoration.

'Is he yours?' she asked.

Ernest nodded, smiling. 'In a way. Though I think it might be nearer the truth to say that *I* am *his*.'

Chapter Twenty-Four

That Christmas guests were expected at Hallowford House. Edward Harrow and Gentry were to spend the holiday season there. Gentry was to visit from Oxford where he was a student at Trinity College, while his father planned to travel over from Sicily, both to see his son and to visit his old friend. Edward Harrow's wife having died some two years earlier, he would be travelling alone. Another reason for his visit was to meet Marianne. She would be seventeen that December, and, like Savill, Edward Harrow had long had dreams of her and Gentry making a match.

Gentry, who had not been to Hallowford for several years now, was due to arrive at the house two days after the girls' own arrival. The last time Blanche and Marianne had seen him they had been only twelve years of age. They recalled him as a tall, dark young man who had sometimes teased them, had sometimes played a few games with them, but who, for most of the time, had virtually ignored their presence. Since that time, when not able to return to Sicily, he had chosen to spend his school vacations with one or other of his fellow students, either going to stay with them at their homes, or else going off with them on various travelling holidays.

Now, on the day of Gentry's planned arrival Savill had to go to Bath on business and he left instructions with James to drive to Trowbridge in the phaeton to meet Gentry at the station and bring him to the house. Savill had suggested to Marianne that she and Blanche go along to welcome him, but Marianne had resisted the suggestion. She was well aware of her father's unspoken wish with regard to herself and Gentry and silently she balked at the idea. Although she had no particular feelings at all for Gentry Harrow – she was nothing if not indifferent to him – she was quietly determined, on principle, to resist any thought that, simply because their respective fathers wished for it, there could ever be anything between them.

When the phaeton with Gentry inside eventually drove up Gorse Hill towards Hallowford House Marianne and Blanche were standing at the window of the first floor landing half-concealed behind the curtains, watching for his arrival. A minute or two later the phaeton was entering through the gates and coming up the drive.

'Oh, Lord,' Marianne whispered, 'here he is. I can't bear it.' With her words she moved back behind the curtain. Blanche, continuing to gaze out, said, 'Aren't you curious as to what he's like?'

'Not in the least.'

The phaeton came to a stop on the forecourt below. Marianne said:

'What's happening?'

'The phaeton's stopped – and now he's just stepping out. I can't see what he looks like; his hat is hiding his face.'

'Who cares what he looks like, anyway?'

'He's very tall.'

'Who cares.'

'Oh, you must give him a chance, Marianne. I'm sure he can't be *that* bad.'

'Are you? How can you be so sure?'

'– Anyway, you'll have to go down and welcome him.'

Marianne gave a resigned sigh. 'I suppose so.'

As Marianne moved across the landing towards the stairs Blanche continued to gaze down, watching as the young man waved aside the offered help of the groom and took up his box. As he turned towards the house he glanced up and for a moment he and Blanche were looking into one another's eyes. For a split second her gaze was held as she looked into his dark eyes; then the next moment, feeling the blood rushing to her cheeks, she was stepping back out of sight behind the curtain. Marianne, half-way down the first flight of stairs, turned to her and whispered:

'Aren't you coming with me?'

Wild horses could not have dragged Blanche down the stairs at that moment. 'Not for a minute,' she said. 'I'll join you in a moment or two.'

Marianne shrugged, touched at her hair with a nervous hand and went on down the stairs. Blanche lingered there. Unlike Marianne she had been not a little curious about Gentry Harrow. Now, having been caught looking at him from the window, spying on his arrival, she felt she would be happier if they never met.

In seconds, however, she could hear the sound of Gentry's entry into the hall below; Marianne's voice and then his own – stronger and deeper than she remembered it. Turning to the mirror on the wall at the foot of the upper flight of stairs she ran a palm over her hair and ran a smoothing fingertip unnecessarily over the arching line of one eyebrow. Then, moving towards the stairs – she couldn't stay up there forever – she started down.

As she neared the foot of the stairs she saw Gentry, his back turned to her, handing his coat and hat to the maid. She had a swift impression of black hair and broad shoulders, and then Marianne was catching sight of her and saying, a trifle over-brightly:

'Ah – and here's Blanche, too.'

He turned to Blanche at the words and she found herself looking into his eyes once more – eyes almost as black as his hair – while he smiled at her, his teeth very white against the Medditerranean tan of his skin. He stepped towards her, hand outstretched.

'Blanche,' he said. 'Hello. Was that you up at the window?' Then, before she could frame a reply, he added, 'Imagine – Blanche Farrar – still here after all these years.'

She felt the colour suffusing her cheeks for the second time in minutes. She gazed at him, horrified by his words. And he was still smiling at her, not knowing – or not caring – how his words had hurt. Then, still gazing down at her, he put his head a little on one side and said with a little nod:

'And you've grown up as well, I see.'

Blanche, glaring at him, lifted her chin and said coldly: 'I'm afraid I can't say the same for you.'

With her words she turned, moved across the hall and walked quickly up the stairs.

Upstairs in her room, Blanche sat before her dressing table. *Still here*, he had said, *after all these years*. And his words had brought to the fore the constant awareness of Mr Savill's generosity to her, reminding her too of all the Miss Bakers and the Helen Websters in the world. He, Gentry Harrow, she said to herself, was no better than any of them.

As she sat there there came a knock at the door. She called out, 'Come in,' and Marianne entered, closed the door behind her and came to her side.

'Don't be upset by it, Blanche.'

'I'm not upset.'

'He didn't mean anything by it, I'm sure.'

'It doesn't matter to me. Forget it.'

'He was just being thoughtless, that's all. Don't take any notice. What does it matter what he says, anyway?'

'I just told you – it *doesn't*. It doesn't matter to me in the slightest.'

'Good. It certainly doesn't matter to *me*.'

'Oh,' Blanche said, 'he thinks he's so grand, walking in here in his new Chesterfield and his bow tie. Who does he think he's impressing? Certainly not me.'

'Me neither.' Marianne gave a little snort of contempt. 'Anyway, it's only for this Christmas – and he'll be gone soon afterwards.'

Later, over dinner, and afterwards in the drawing room, Gentry tried to entertain Savill and the girls with a few well-chosen and amusing stories of life in Messina and at Oxford. Although Savill clearly found the anecdotes amusing Gentry tried in vain to elicit a similar response from Marianne and Blanche. With secret signs to one another across the table the girls kept a united front against him and refused to be amused, greeting his words with smiles that were clearly nothing more than polite, and damning him with their very faint praise.

In spite of the girls' reservations where Gentry was concerned, that Christmas was an unusually light-hearted time at Hallowford House. Marianne and Blanche – helped by Gentry – spent a good deal of time putting up festive decorations and trimming a tall tree which Gentry brought in from a nearby wood, and the house echoed with the sounds of laughter and animated voices. Two days before Christmas Gentry's father arrived, and he and Savill, after being apart for so many years, had a warm reunion.

After church on Christmas morning Savill, Edward Harrow, Marianne, Blanche and Gentry exchanged Christmas gifts – and once again Savill's kindness was brought home to Blanche, for with his allowance to her she was able to give presents which were on a par with those she received. Afterwards, Savill sent her, carrying a hamper and various packages, off in the phaeton, driven by James, to see her mother and brother in Colford. When they reached the cottage James let her off, saying he would go on to have a drink at The Plough and come back to pick her up in an hour.

Blanche had written to say she would be coming that morning, and her mother and Ernest were expecting her. As she entered the cottage to be greeted by them she found that its small front parlour had been decorated with homemade paper trimmings and sprigs of holly and mistletoe. Sarah and Ernest asked her at once whether she could stay for Christmas midday dinner. She was afraid she couldn't, she said. James was coming back for her in an hour, and she was expected back for Christmas luncheon at Hallowford House. Sarah nodded understandingly, and after Blanche was seated before the bright fire they brought her the carefully wrapped gifts that had sat waiting on the piano. From Ernest she received a little book of Shakespeare's sonnets. From her mother came some lengths of ribbon and a pair of combs. After she had thanked them she gave them the presents she had brought, sitting eagerly watching as they unwrapped the finely-wrapped packages. Ernest first, who took from a box a fine wool muffler and six silk handkerchiefs. As he exclaimed over the gifts Blanche watched as her mother unwrapped a fine cotton nightdress with intricate lace at the throat and down the front.

Sarah shook her head in wonder, saying that she had never before had such a fine nightgown. For Jacko, Blanche had brought a fine meaty bone from the Hallowford House kitchen, and he at once lay down and began to gnaw away at it.

Sarah, meanwhile, clicked her tongue over the gifts they had given Blanche; they were so poor in comparison, she said. Brushing aside such comments, Blanche presented them with the hamper containing various consumable items, including a plum pudding, a cooked ham, an assortment of preserves, gentleman's relish for Ernest and sugared almonds for her mother. 'It's too much,' Sarah protested, but Blanche said laughingly, 'No, no, it's not too much at all.'

Ernest poured glasses of cider for them then and Sarah brought out some little spiced cakes which she had made early that morning. And as they ate and drank, the cider and the occasion lent to the meeting a light-heartedness that Blanche realized had not been there for some time. But even so, one part of her mind was aware, the camaraderie was only on the surface; the underlying reserve was still present.

When James knocked at the door close on noon Blanche put on her coat, kissed her mother and Ernest goodbye and, saying that she would call again soon, left the cottage. As the carriage drove along the lane she looked back and saw the two of them, Jacko at their side, standing at the gate.

The numbers at Hallowford House were swelled that evening by the arrival for dinner of Dr Kelsey and his wife, and also Savill's brother Harold from Trowbridge. Marianne went downstairs to join her father in greeting them as they arrived; a few minutes afterwards Blanche herself went down. Wearing a new dress bought for the occasion – a long gown of deep blue brocade with lace at the throat – she entered the drawing room where the walls were festooned with the decorations that she, Marianne and Gentry had spent so long arranging. As she gazed at the splendour of the room, the elegantly dressed guests assembled there, and the firelight reflecting in the crystal of the chandeliers and in the tinsel that hung in swathes from the tree, she could not help but contrast it with the little parlour of her mother's cottage in Colford.

After all the greetings were over she helped Marianne in handing out canapés and refilling the sherry glasses. When that was done Gentry pointed out that the candles on the tree were still unlit and Marianne brought him a packet of Lucifers and stood beside him watching as, one by one, he lit the array of tiny candles.

Blanche, standing near Edward Harrow at that moment, noticed how he turned and caught the eye of John Savill; she noticed the brief, subtle glance they exchanged, and how their eyes then turned back to take in the pair at the tree – Gentry, tall and handsome in his dinner jacket, and Marianne beside him looking small and slender in her dress of lilac and lace.

When dinner was announced Blanche went in on the arm of Harold Savill, who was lavish in his compliments on her appearance. Over dinner he talked to her of his interest in the motor car, saying that on a recent trip to London he had seen numbers of them on the streets. It was the transport of the future, he said, and anyone with the opportunity should waste no time in investing in its promotion and manufacture. Later, the subject got around to the Jubilee celebrations of the previous summer, and Dr Kelsey spoke of the possibilities of the Empire's expansion. 'But where else is there to go?' Savill asked. 'To the north, south, east and west – a quarter of the earth's surface, and almost a quarter of its people, are beneath the Queen's domination. We've got to stop somewhere.'

'Why?' said Harold. 'There's South Africa yet. The Transvaal. Though if things had been handled properly twenty years ago it would be part of the Empire already. Those wretched Boers – thinking they can deny English settlers their rights like that. They've got a few surprises coming to them.'

Robert Kelsey said, 'You don't think there'll be another war, do you?'

His wife groaned. 'Oh, no. Wasn't one war with them enough?'

Harold said, 'That was seventeen years ago, Mrs Kelsey. And a few skirmishes like that don't amount to very much.'

Gentry said, 'With all due respect, sir, I should think they amount to a great deal when it was Britain who got the bloody nose. And of course we've never got over our defeat.'

'You don't know your history, young man,' Harold said. 'We were not beaten. We continued to hold the reins when it was all over. We were victorious.'

'Victorious after a fashion,' Gentry said. 'And after some very, ignominious defeats. Look at the battle of Majuba. What a disaster that was. To be beaten by a ragbag of Dutch farmers. For that's what it amounted to.' He shook his head. 'Oh, that kind of *victory* in our history can leave a very sour taste in the mouth.'

Harold Savill said, a slight edge to his voice, 'For a young, inexperienced man you seem to hold strong views on the subject.'

Gentry hesitated then replied: 'Well, if there is a war, sir, then I shall be very much involved. Therefore I think I *should* hold views on such a matter.'

'I agree,' Edward Harrow said, nodding, at which Mrs Kelsey said:

'What I don't understand is why there is all the talk of war now? What has changed since the last one?'

Robert Kelsey replied, 'Well, dear, not to sound too cynical, you mustn't forget that since the first war there's been the discovery of gold in the Transvaal.'

'Meaning what?' said Harold sharply.

Gentry said, 'I agree with the doctor. Britain couldn't really have cared less about the fate of her settlers there before the discovery of the gold.'

'But it's been the Britons who have gone in and *mined* the gold,' Harold said. 'And they're as much a part of the country now as the Boers. And they have a right to have a say in the running of the place.'

'With Britain stepping in to make sure that they have that right,' Gentry said. 'And of course, with all that gold to be had it would suit her purpose to take over the place on the pretext of putting the country to rights.'

Blanche spoke up then.

'Allow us *some* worthy motives, please,' she said. 'Have you forgotten that even now the Boers would like to continue slavery? Don't let your cynicism blind you to everything.'

Gentry looked at her in surprise as she spoke, then said,

'– Anyway, let's talk about something else.' He turned to Marianne. 'I don't think you ladies want to discuss such matters, do you? I'm sure you'd much rather talk on some other subject.'

Blanche said lightly, jokingly, but meaning every word:

'What do you think we'd be happier discussing, Gentry? The latest Paris fashions? – or perhaps a little scandalous gossip concerning the Prince of Wales? Don't think because we're female we've got no interest in what goes on in the outside world.'

Savill chuckled at this. '*Touché*, Blanche.' Then, to Gentry: 'You don't really know Blanche as yet, Gentry. But one thing you must learn is not to underestimate her.'

Gentry nodded, smiling lightly at his host. 'No, sir, I'm learning that already.'

When dinner was over the three women left the men to their port, brandy and cigars and retired to the drawing room. Later when the men joined them Marianne poured coffee and Blanche handed it round. As she came to Gentry he said very softly as he took his cup, 'Don't you think we should call a truce, Blanche?'

'I wasn't aware that there was a battle,' she said, unsmiling, equally softly.

'But you're not the one who's constantly in the firing line.'

She said nothing, but stood waiting with the tray as he spooned sugar into his cup.

'Don't you think,' he said, 'that you can be a little too sensitive where some things are concerned?'

She shook her head. 'No, I don't. And as for being sensitive, I'm surprised you even know the meaning of the word.'

A week after Christmas Edward Harrow prepared to leave to return to Sicily. During dinner on his last evening – a bright, happy affair – he invited Marianne and Blanche to spend the next summer in Messina with Gentry and himself before they went on to their finishing school in France. Graciously they accepted the invitation.

That night Blanche was lying in bed just on the point

of drifting off to sleep when she heard her door opening, followed by the sound of soft footfalls across the carpet. Then came Marianne's voice:

'It's only me. Are you awake?'

'I am now.' Sitting up in bed, Blanche struck a match and put the flame to the nightlight on her bedside table. 'What is it?' she asked as Marianne sat on the edge of the bed. In the light of the little candle flame Blanche looked at her friend. Marianne was clad in a blue dressing gown, her hair falling in a cascade over her shoulders. In the soft light her eyes were in shadow and Blanche could not read their expression. 'Is something wrong?' Blanche said.

Marianne smiled at her. 'No, nothing at all. I just wanted to see you for a moment.'

'What for?'

Marianne shrugged. 'Oh, nothing really, I suppose.' She was silent for a moment or two, then she said: 'We couldn't do anything else but accept Uncle Edward's invitation, could we?'

'No, I suppose not. But when the time comes we can always think of some excuse.'

'Yes – I suppose so.'

Marianne sounded doubtful. Blanche looked at her a little keenly. Marianne added:

'– Although of course it might be fun.'

Fun? Blanche frowned.

'Are you still angry?' Marianne said after a moment.

'What about?'

'Oh, Blanche, you know what I'm talking about. With him – Gentry – for what he said when he arrived.'

'Of course not.' Blanche thought she would be glad when the Christmas holidays were over and Gentry went back to Oxford.

'I thought he was quite – funny over dinner this

evening, didn't you?' Marianne said. 'Telling the story of his school Shakespeare production.'

Blanche gave a shrug, allowing a faint, contemptuous smile to touch her mouth. 'Yes, I suppose so – if you find that kind of thing amusing.'

'Well – it was all right . . .' Marianne was avoiding her eyes. After a moment she said, 'Do you thing he's – nice-looking?'

Blanche studied her, and all at once she realized that Marianne's continued indifference was nothing but a front – it had been bogus for days. She thought back to dinner that evening and to other occasions over the past week. And she could see now that all the time Marianne's feelings had been changing. As she sat there she examined various little memories as they flitted through her mind; and now she could see the way Marianne hung on Gentry's words, the way she laughed at his jokes, the way her eyes followed him as he moved across the room. I must have been blind, she thought. Marianne's antipathy for Gentry was clearly a thing of the past.

Blanche narrowed her eyes, looking at her friend with contempt. *How quickly people change,* she thought.

'Well,' she said, '– you've certainly changed *your* tune, haven't you? You were singing a very different song not so long ago.'

Marianne said nothing, but sighed and studied her fingernails.

Blanche nodded. 'Oh, yes, a very different tune.'

Marianne gave a reluctant little shrug. 'Well, yes – I suppose that's how it seems.'

There was a brief silence in the room, then Blanche said:

'I can't believe it. I thought we were both freezing him out – and all along you're falling in love with him. You are, aren't you?'

'Oh, don't be silly, I —'

'Yes, you are.'

'No, no.' Marianne shook her head. 'Love — I don't even know what love is like.' But she sounded uncertain. Then she added, 'But I have to admit: I do think he's nice.'

'Nice.'

'Yes. And he *is* handsome, isn't he? Any girl would think so.' She paused. 'Don't *you* think so?'

'Is that what you came in here to ask me?'

'Oh, come on, Blanche. And he's very amusing, too. Don't you think?'

Blanche shrugged. 'Well, obviously *you* do.'

Marianne looked Blanche in the eyes. 'I know what you must think of me — especially after all I said. D'you think I'm an idiot, Blanche? You do, don't you?'

'— I don't think anything. It's nothing to do with me.'

'Oh, Blanche, please . . .'

'Look, I'm tired,' Blanche said.

Marianne remained there. 'I really do like him,' she said. 'I have to admit it.'

'Good. Now — may I get to sleep?'

Marianne got up off the bed and started across the room. Near the door she turned and looked back. 'Goodnight, Blanche.'

'Goodnight.'

Marianne reached out for the doorknob, stopped. 'Blanche . . . ?'

'Yes . . . ?'

'Do you think I've made it obvious — that I liked him? Do you think he'll have — noticed it?'

'Would you notice a snowstorm in August?'

'Oh, Blanche — *please*.'

Blanche gazed at her for a moment and then forced a faint smile. 'Goodnight, Marianne.'

'Goodnight, Blanche.'

Blanche leaned towards the nightlight. As she took a breath to blow out the flame Marianne's voice came again, softly: 'Listen . . .'

'Yes . . . ?'

'Do you think he likes me?'

Blanche felt a little flash of irritation which she swiftly quelled. 'Yes, Marianne,' she said. 'I'm sure he does. How could he not?'

Marianne smiled at her across the room, and gave a little nod of pleasure. 'Goodnight, Blanche. Sleep well.'

'Goodnight.'

And, Blanche told herself, she was right – as was made very clear to her over the following days before Gentry left for Oxford and she and Marianne left for Clifton. She was right – Marianne was falling in love with him. *Was* in love with him, already. And was clearly past saving.

Though the knowledge that she was right brought her no pleasure. She felt betrayed. She would watch how Marianne looked at Gentry across the dining table, dark eyes gazing into his; she would observe Marianne's shyness in his presence, the way she would sometimes be at a loss for the right thing to say and would end up stumbling over her words like a selfconscious child; she would observe how the most minor incident of teasing from Gentry could be enough to make Marianne all fingers and thumbs – and she felt contempt. For herself she was determined to maintain her position. If Marianne wished to make a fool of herself that was her affair.

And Marianne seemed to be content to do just that, and as the few remaining days of the vacation went by her feelings for Gentry seemed to become stronger. And as for Gentry, he was obviously fond of her, too. The result was that although she was not physically excluded, Blanche often felt very much in the way. She would be glad, she said to herself, to get back to school.

On the day Gentry left – the day before Marianne and Blanche themselves left for Clifton – Marianne accompanied Gentry to the station in the landau. Blanche was asked to go with them but had declined. She was in her room when Marianne returned, and Marianne went to her there, sat down on Blanche's bed and sighed. Blanche turned from her packing and looked at her. 'What's the matter?' she asked, knowing full well.

Marianne gave a little smile – which Blanche found infuriating – and sighed again. 'Nothing,' she said. Then she added, as if the thought had just occurred to her:

'I shall probably write to Gentry when we're back at school. He gave me his address.'

Blanche nodded. 'Good – that will be nice for you.'

Marianne shrugged, a gesture of near-indifference that was not in the least convincing. 'Well – it will be something to do – someone to write to.'

'Yes, indeed.' Blanche turned back to her packing.

After a moment Marianne said: 'Papa's invited Gentry to come here at Easter for part of the holidays. He'll be spending the first two weeks in Scotland with friends from university, but then he'll come to us for the last few days. That'll be fun, won't it?'

'Oh – yes.'

Marianne's words brought Blanche no pleasure. Gentry's remark to her on his arrival just before Christmas still rankled. *Blanche Farrar – still here after all these years.* She could not forget his words and she would not forgive him. And, further, she felt that his sentiments must be echoed by any number of other people who were aware of her situation. Everything she had, or had ever had, she owed to Mr Savill's generosity – and, she realized, there would always be those who would be ready to remind her of the fact – either doing it maliciously – as by the likes of Helen Webster and Miss Baker – or insensitively, and nonetheless cruelly, by people like Gentry Harrow.

Turning back from her packing she caught a glimpse of Marianne's face as she sat on the bed gazing unseeingly out of the window. There was a faraway look in her eyes. Blanche felt she could have slapped her.

Chapter Twenty-Five

Early in April Blanche and Marianne returned from Clifton to Hallowford for the Easter break. Blanche did so with mixed feelings. Not only did she resent the fact that she would have to spend part of the holiday in the company of Gentry Harrow, but also, at the back of her mind, she was aware of a growing problem connected with her family.

Where her mother and Ernest were concerned, Blanche had become increasingly aware that their move to Colford had changed the situation between them and herself. With the distance being so much further, and a visit requiring a carriage ride, a ride on horseback, or a rather long walk, her visits had become less and less frequent over the years – and this was in addition to the already-present reserve that had so long ago taken root.

Now, when Blanche visited the cottage at Colford she did not expect any closeness. Over the years she and her mother and brother had drifted further and further apart.

The exposure of the growing estrangement between them came about towards the end of the Easter holidays that year, 1898. It was on a Friday, the day of Gentry's expected arrival at the house, a bright, mid-April day when the sun shone with an unseasonal warmth. James was to drive Marianne in the landau to Trowbridge to meet Gentry from the train. Marianne had asked Blanche to accompany her, and although Blanche did not really want to go, she had nevertheless agreed, saying that the journey would give her the opportunity to call on her mother, whom she had not visited since returning from Clifton at the start of the holidays. With this in mind she would get James to drive back via Colford and let her off there.

Not long before three o'clock Blanche and Marianne, driven by James, set off for Trowbridge. Gentry's train was due in just after four. They got to the station as the train pulled in – but without Gentry on board. Marianne, clearly very disappointed, said he had either missed the train or had changed his mind about coming. Whichever way, the next train was not due for at least another hour; there was nothing for it but to get back into the carriage and return to Hallowford. If Gentry was on the next train, she said, he would hire a cab from the station.

They set off back, reaching Colford close on 5.15 where, at the end of Hummock Lane, James brought the carriage to a halt and Blanche got out. Marianne asked if they should send the landau back for her in an hour or so, but Blanche said that it was not necessary; it was a fine day and she could easily walk the three miles back to Hallowford. With a basket over her arm, Blanche left the carriage to continue on to Hallowford while she walked along the lane to the cottage.

She found her mother in the small rear garden, crouching over a vegetable patch pulling up weeds. As Blanche approached down the narrow path Sarah heard her step, and turned and smiled a greeting at her. She stood up and, keeping her soil-stained hands well away from Blanche's cape, kissed her on the cheek.

'I should have thought Ernest would have been doing this,' Blanche said, gesturing to the little pile of weeds that lay on the garden path near her foot. Sarah shook her head at the idea. 'Oh, Ernest has enough to do at the farm. He has so little time to himself I wouldn't want to see him spending it all in working about the house. Anyway –' she vigorously brushed her hands together, removing some of the dark, rich soil, '– come on inside and we'll have some tea.'

In the little kitchen Blanche put on the kettle while Sarah washed her hands. For the next few minutes as they made the tea they talked of this and that, politely though, with the conversation never going far below the surface. And then:

'Oh, I was forgetting,' Blanche said, and took from her basket a package containing some little gifts she had brought back from a trip to Bristol. There was a pot of expensive marmalade, some potted meat, and a little jar of dressed crab. Blanche smiled as she set the items on the kitchen table. 'I thought that you and Ernest might like a little treat,' she said.

Sarah's smile was faint and strained. 'You always bring presents,' she said. 'You never visit but you bring something – why?'

Blanche gave a little laugh. 'Why not? If it's something you like, why not?' She paused. Suddenly she felt awkward, a little embarrassed. 'Perhaps,' she said, '– perhaps it's just a token. Besides, I want to make you happy.'

'But we don't want your gifts,' Sarah said.

Blanche looked at her, all trace of her smile gone from her face. 'I don't understand,' she said.

Slowly Sarah shook her head. 'No, Blanche, you don't understand. I don't think you ever have – ever will.'

Silence in the room. Sarah added:

'Why do you keep bringing us things? These little gifts. We don't need them. We're all right as we are.'

312

'All right?' There was a note of incredulity in Blanche's echoing words. 'Mama, you don't realize – I have so much. I want you to have things too. Is that wrong?' Then before Sarah could respond Blanche went on: 'You have so few comforts here, you and Ernest. Every time I visit you I'm so aware of it. And you *could* be more comfortable if you wished, you *know* you could. At Hallowford you didn't even have to pay rent, and Ernest has told me since that Mr Savill has offered to help in – in various ways, and if you –'

'*No!*'

The vehemence of Sarah's tone shocked Blanche into silence. She sat there at the kitchen table, open-mouthed, facing her mother, seeing a new side to her, her anger, an anger which she had never really seen before.

'Why do you think we left Hallowford?' Sarah said. 'It wasn't only because of Ernest's work. One reason was to get out of the trap of Mr Savill's charity.' She shook her head. 'God knows, he is a kind, well-meaning man, but where does it end? There had to be a limit at some time. So – we came here. And we pay rent here, as the other tenants do. Good God, it's hard enough to see him paying for everything for *you*, but we don't have to be a part of it as well.'

Blanche continued to stare at Sarah. Her mother too was resentful of all that Savill had done for her over the years. Blanche said, her own voice growing sharp:

'The way you talk, it's as if you regret what he has done for me.'

Sarah didn't answer. Blanche waited a moment then went on:

'Don't you realize the advantages I've had? Aren't you aware of it all? He's given me a good education. I've learned about the best things in life. I shall travel, see foreign lands. Do you begrudge me all that?'

'No, I don't begrudge it. But I sometimes regret that it ever happened.'

'Mama –'

'Listen to you,' Sarah said. '*Mama, Mama*. My other children called me *Mam*. Ernest, Mary, Arthur, Agnes. *Mam* they called me. Not you.' She got up from the table, moved to the window, stood looking out over the narrow back garden. 'But it's not your fault,' she said at last. 'It's the way you've been brought up. Why should you talk to me as the others did? You're not like the others. You never have been. You never will be. That was all decided long ago. It's out of my hands now – and out of yours too.' A silence, then, her voice bitter, she went on:

'No, I only regret that I ever agreed to your staying up at the house. It was no place for you. You belonged with me, with us, your family. But it's too late now. You'll never belong to us now.' She turned, and suddenly reached out and pushed across the table towards Blanche the pot of marmalade, the jar of potted meat. 'We don't want your charity,' she said. 'Keep it for those who are grateful for it. Don't come round here with your gifts – acting like some Lady Bountiful giving out her largesse to the deserving and unfortunate poor. Keep it for those who appreciate it. Your gifts – your nightgowns and your silk handkerchiefs – we don't need them.'

She straightened. 'Go on back to your friends up on the hill,' she said. 'Don't be kind to us; there's no need. And there's no need for you to *honour* us with your occasional visits. Because I know your heart isn't in them. You don't want to come, and I'd rather not see you than that you come under some sense of obligation.'

With her final words Sarah turned away. Blanche continued to sit there, her face pale, fingers gripping the handle of the cheap teacup. After long, long moments she put down the cup, got up from her chair and picked up her basket. Standing, facing her mother's back, she said:

'Yes, Mama –' She caught herself on the familiar word, and began again. 'I'm going now.' Her voice was very low in the little room, measured against the ticking of the clock. 'I'm sorry I brought you so much unhappiness. I shall try not to do so in the future. But tell me – Mother – why were you so content to leave me in Mr Savill's care? You must have had some reason. Was it because you resented me? Resented that I was having chances the others were denied? Or was it because I lived when Agnes and Arthur died? And they meant so much more to you than I did – than I ever could. I didn't ask to stay with the Savills, Mama. It was you who made the decision. You and my father and Mr Savill. I had no say in the matter. Is it any wonder, then, that now, after seventeen years, I regard Hallowford House as my home; *that* kind of life as my own – *that* as the circle where I belong. I didn't ask for it, Mama. I didn't. You made me what I am.' She nodded, the tears so close to the surface now. 'You have every reason to reproach me. I could have been a better daughter to you, but – but did you make it easy for it to happen?'

She turned and stepped towards the door. She could feel the tears swimming in her eyes; her throat was so constricted she felt pain. In the open doorway she turned to her mother again. Sarah's back was still turned towards her.

'You said I don't belong here anymore, Mama. But I don't belong *there* either – at Hallowford House.' And now the tears spilled over and coursed down her cheeks. She struggled to get her words out. 'I've had that knowledge forced upon me many times in the past, and I have no doubt that I shall be made aware of it again in the future.' She shook her head. 'I don't belong anywhere, it seems.'

With her last words she turned, went into the yard, around the house and out of the gate.

At the end of Hummock Lane Blanche started off along the road, leaving Colford behind her. Her tears still ran, but determinedly she fought them back. A hundred yards along she turned left onto a bridle track that marked a shortcut to Hallowford.

Leaving the main road behind her, she walked swiftly for some minutes as if eager to reach her destination, but then slowed and came to a stop. Across the fields from the direction of Hallowford she heard the sound of the striking of the church clock. Six o'clock. Not far from the side of the track in a little bower formed by silver birches and some shrubs was the stump of a fallen tree, and she moved to it and sat down, putting her head in her hands.

After a while she raised her head and sat looking dully ahead. Then, with a gesture of anger and determination she wiped a hand across her tear-stained cheek. She would never return to the cottage, never.

Half-turning, she glimpsed, through the screen of leaves on her right, a figure, a man, approaching along the bridle path. Instinctively, not wanting any encounter with anyone at that moment, she shrank back into the shelter of the foliage. But even her brief glimpse of the man had been sufficient for her to recognize him. It was Gentry Harrow.

He was the last person she wanted to see at that moment, but there was no way she could escape. Her only hope was that he might pass by without seeing her there, though it was a slim hope, she knew.

Unable to do anything but remain there, she watched

as he came on, coming closer, moving along the track in the direction of Hallowford. He walked with an easy stride, a tall young man with broad shoulders, his hat in his hand, his black hair shining in the April sun.

And then he was drawing almost level with her and she shrank further back into the shadow of the leaves. Watching him, she could see the very moment in which he caught sight of her on the periphery of his vision, drawn by the pale blue of her blouse, the deeper blue of her cape. Next moment he was turning to her, recognition dawning in his eyes.

He came to a sudden stop. 'Blanche.' The surprise was evident in his voice. 'Blanche – what are you doing here?'

She felt like a child caught in some forbidden act. For a moment she gazed at him, conscious of having been found lurking, hiding from him, and of her unhappiness which, she was sure, must show in her face. She opened her mouth to speak to him, but no words would come, and, after a moment's hesitation she picked up her basket and hurried away.

With Gentry's voice calling out behind her, she left the track and, quickening her pace, ran off into the thicket that ran beside it, her feet uncertain on the uneven, bramble-strewn ground – which threatened at any moment to send her sprawling. And all the time she was desperately aware of the indignity of her action. Once embarked upon it, though, she was committed and her shame only drove her faster, deeper into the wood.

She didn't get far. She was brought to a halt by a meandering stream that wound through the thicket, and stopping beside its bank she stood there unmoving, hearing the sound of Gentry as he came through the trees in her wake. Then, above the sound of the surrounding birdsong, and that of her own breathing, heavy after her exertion, she heard his approach close behind her, and then silence as he came to a stop. She could hear too, then, the sound of his own breathing.

'Blanche . . .'

She didn't turn to him. She couldn't, but remained there, facing out across the little stream with its high banks, her emotions a turmoil of shame, pride, hostility and grief.

'Blanche – look at me.'

It could have been anyone coming by, she said to herself – but it had to be he. She was reminded of the time of his arrival at Hallowford House when she had peered down at him from the landing window and he had caught her looking . . .

'Blanche . . .' And now after the sound of her name there came the touch of his hand on her arm. 'Blanche – please . . .'

And in his voice there was a softness, a tenderness that she had never been aware of before. After a moment she turned and faced him. He was gazing at her with concern clouding his dark eyes.

'Why did you run from me?' he said.

She shook her head dumbly, unable to trust herself to speak. The encounter, coming so soon after the painful meeting with her mother, threatened all her feelings of resolve.

Gentry spoke again, the same note of concern in his voice:

'Are you all right?'

She nodded. They stood there in their own silence surrounded by birdsong, in particular that of a black-bird who sat in a tree close by singing fit to burst its breast. Behind Blanche's feet the stream rippled by. After a few moments she said lamely:

'Marianne and I – we went to Trowbridge to meet

you.' She found it difficult to look him in the eyes. 'Did you miss the train?'

'Yes. I had to catch the next one. But I couldn't find a cab at Trowbridge so I left my box there and set off to walk. It's not that far across the fields. Anyway, I was lucky: I got a ride in a trap a good part of the way.' He smiled. 'I never expected to see you there – sitting beside the bridle path like that.' He grinned. 'You gave a fellow quite a start.'

Gazing at her, so close, his dark eyes burning into her own, his smile faded as he said:

'There *is* something wrong, isn't there?'

'Wrong? No, of course not.'

She shook her head and attempted a small laugh, which didn't quite work. He continued to look at her, his own mouth unsmiling. 'Yes, there is,' he said; and then: 'Is it me? Have I said something else to upset you? I seem to have a talent for it.'

'No. No, Gentry, it's not you. Please – it's nothing.'

'It's something. And you're on the verge of tears because of it.'

'Please. I told you – it's nothing.'

He shrugged, then: 'What were you doing here, anyway?'

'I'd been to see my mother.'

'Ah.' He nodded. 'And is she well?'

'Quite well.'

'Good. And pleased to see you, I imagine.'

Blanche nodded. After a few seconds Gentry said:

'I think this is the first time you and I have ever really been alone, isn't it? At other times there have always been others about, somewhere or other.'

Blanche said nothing. He went on:

'It gives me the chance – which you've never allowed me before – to say to you that – well, that I'm so sorry we got off on the wrong foot when we met again last Christmas.'

Blanche shrugged. 'It doesn't matter.' It didn't. Somehow her antipathy for him seemed very unimportant and unreal. 'It doesn't matter,' she said again.

'Well, it did at the time,' he said. 'And very much. Of course afterwards I thought about it and I could see why. I realized then how it must have sounded to you – as if I was – making some kind of *comment* on your still living at Hallowford House. Almost as if you – you had no right to be there.' He shook his head. 'God, how crass I was. How insensitive I must have sounded – not to mention *cruel*.' He paused, then added earnestly, 'But, Blanche – I meant nothing by it. Please believe me. They were just – empty words.'

He stood waiting for her response, then she said softly, a little note of bitterness in her voice:

'Perhaps you were right.'

'I beg your pardon?'

'Perhaps I *do* have no right to be there – at Hallowford House.'

He stared at her blankly. 'What do you mean?'

And suddenly the tears she had kept back were springing to her eyes, overflowing and running down her cheeks. Letting fall her basket she lifted her hands to her face.

'Don't. Oh, Blanche, don't.' Gentry stepped towards her and she saw him, his form distorted by her tears, as he reached out to her. Briefly she held out her hands, as if she would ward him off, but then let them fall to her sides. The next moment she was held in the circle of his arms.

For a little while she stood there with his arms around her while she wept against his neck. Afterwards, when her tears had stopped she told him, haltingly and with prompting, something of the scene that had ensued between herself and her mother. He listened in silence. Afterwards Blanche said:

'I don't know why I'm telling you. And I'll get over it in time, I don't doubt. And if I don't the world won't stop turning.'

Standing there in silence, held in his arms, she suddenly became aware of the situation. Quickly she broke free and stepped away from him. 'God, what am I doing?' she breathed. 'I must be mad.'

He moved to her side again, once more reaching out to hold her, but she thrust his arms away, avoiding his grasp and, bending, took up the basket where it lay in the grass. Straightening, she raised the basket before her, as if it were a shield against his nearness. He stood looking at her, a slight frown on his brow, his dark eyes troubled as if by some sudden awareness that had found him unprepared. After a moment she turned away and started off through the trees, only to find that she had lost her direction. She came to a stop on the edge of a clearing where a grassy slope, dotted with clumps of primroses, rose steeply to join the denser woodland above. As she stood there Gentry came to stand beside her again.

'Blanche . . .' He reached out, took the basket from her hand and placed it in the grass. Then his arms were rising again, encircling her, drawing her to him. As he gazed into her eyes she said hoarsely:

'Gentry – no. There's Marianne. You have Marianne.'

She became suddenly aware that her whole body was trembling, just as she was aware that nothing in her life had prepared her for the sensation she knew in those moments as Gentry bent his head and kissed her on the mouth. Any feelings of guilt, of shame, fled almost before they had even registered in her spinning brain.

She was only aware of Gentry's nearness, of the scent of him, the feel of his mouth on hers, the ungiving strength of his arms that held her to him. For some moments, under the frantic urging of her mind, she resisted him, trying to draw back out of his embrace, but she had not the power or the will, and after a few seconds of ineffectual struggle, she gave up.

Eyes closed, and held fast in the circle of his left arm, she felt his free hand move to her face; felt the touch of his fingers on her skin – trembling against her cheek, her chin, then moving lower to her throat – his touch so soft, so gentle, but so insistent and not to be denied. His hand gently brushed the swell of her breast, moved back, rested there, feather-light, and her breath caught in her throat as she tried to summon some movement, some word of protest. But no protest came and the moment passed and his hand was cupping her breast and she gave herself up, willingly, to his greater power. When she felt his fingers releasing the clasp of her cape she made no effort at all to stop him. Moments later she lay in the grass, Gentry beside her, bending over her, kissing her mouth, her throat, her breast.

Soon afterwards, following the feverish, hurried movements of fingers on buttons she felt the freshness of the evening air against her naked skin, and opened her eyes to see him gazing down at her nakedness. Then, moments later, she felt his hardness against her naked thigh, and she reached down her trembling fingers and, guided by his own hand, touched him, held him. Then he was moving above her, lifting her knees, and slowly, slowly entering her. And from first to last there had been no moment when she could have stopped him, when she had desired, truly desired, to stop him. In those long, everlasting, brief moments as they lay together in the grass, their bodies crushing the primroses, Blanche felt that the whole of her life so far had been leading to this event. She would never, she knew, be the same again.

Afterwards Gentry held her in his arms and they sat side by side in the falling dusk. For a long time neither spoke, but then he moved his head and looked down at her.

'Blanche . . . ?'

'Yes?' She lifted her head slightly. His dark eyes were all a shadow in the fading light.

'You're not sorry, are you?'

'Sorry? About what happened?'

He nodded.

She gave a slow little shake of her head. 'I shall never be sorry about it,' she said. 'I'm glad. I always shall be.'

'And I.'

There was a little silence, then she said, 'This time will stay with me – forever. It must – for it can never happen again.'

'But Blanche . . .' There was a note of protest in Gentry's voice. She broke in quickly:

'It can't. You belong to Marianne. You know that as well as I do.'

'No,' he said. 'I don't belong to anyone. I belong to whoever I choose to belong to.'

She took his hand, pressed it between her own. 'Oh, Gentry, no matter what you might feel right now – no matter what I might feel, we both know that nothing can come of it. You know very well that one day you and Marianne will marry. It's what your father wants for you – and what Mr Savill wants for Marianne.'

'I'm not a puppet,' Gentry said. 'What others want of me is no concern of mine. I'm my own master.'

'Are you?'

She gazed up at him. Raising his hand to her mouth, she kissed his fingers. Then, lifting her face to his, she kissed him softly on the mouth. Their immediate passion spent, she felt a great tenderness for him. It was an emotion as powerful in its way as that of that all-consuming ecstasy that, minutes before, had brooked no hesitation and had swept her up like some great ocean wave. Now one part of her was all happiness at what had happened between them, while another part of her threatened to bring tears springing to her eyes as she suddenly became aware of the gulf that separated them.

And as if Gentry had somehow been able to read her thoughts he said:

'You said you didn't know where you belonged, Blanche. I know where you belong. You belong with me.'

She gave a little groan. She pressed his large hand between her fingers. 'Don't,' she said. 'Don't make it more difficult.' She released him, got up, adjusting her skirt, brushing down her clothes. 'We must get back,' she said. 'It's getting late.'

Chapter Twenty-Six

Fortunately for Blanche, with less than three days remaining of the Easter holidays the time that had to be spent in Gentry's company was limited and she was able to get through the time without giving herself away, without giving out any clue as to their meeting and what had passed between them. For the little time that remained there were no outward signs of anything untoward; on the contrary, on the surface – and much to Marianne's pleasure – Blanche warmed to Gentry a little, giving the impression that some kind of truce had been called, that they had buried their differences. In reality the new colour of their relationship, seemingly quite friendly and easy-going, hid in Blanche an unease and lack of understanding that left her bewildered and confused. In one way she was glad when the vacation was over and it was time for Gentry to return to Oxford, and for Marianne and herself to return to Clifton; at least then she would not have to see him.

Gentry left Hallowford first, and Blanche and Marianne stood on the forecourt while his box was placed in the carriage. Gentry had said goodbye to Savill earlier that day. Now he kissed each of the girls lightly on the cheek, and, after saying that he would see them in the summer when he would come to escort them to Sicily, he wished them goodbye and got into the carriage.

As the carriage moved out of the gates Blanche turned and moved back towards the house. Marianne remained there, watching as the carriage rolled out of sight. Only then did she turn and follow Blanche. As she came to stand at Blanche's side on the step she sighed, and Blanche looked questioningly at her. Marianne gave an embarrassed little laugh.

'I can't wait for summer,' she said. Then, reaching out, pressing Blanche's hand, she added, 'Blanche, I'm so pleased that you and Gentry are seeing eye to eye a little better. Can you imagine – Sicily would be wretched if you and he were warring all the time.'

Upstairs they got on with packing their boxes ready for their own departure in the morning. Blanche had just finished when the maid came to her door saying that her brother was there and wished to see her. He would not come in, the maid added, but was waiting for her in the yard. At once Blanche went downstairs and out of the house by the rear door.

As she appeared Ernest came towards her, smiling gravely, Jacko at his heels. She saw that he had ridden over on one of his employer's ponies, which was now tethered at the side of the yard by the stables. After they had greeted one another she asked if he would come inside. He shook his head. 'I just wanted to see you for a minute or two,' he said.

Side by side they walked from the yard into the rear garden. For a while neither spoke, then Ernest said:

'You'll be going back to school soon, won't you?'

'Tomorrow morning. I've just finished packing my things.'

'Are you looking forward to it?'

She shrugged. 'In a way, I suppose. I enjoy it.' Looking at Ernest she could see that he was ill-at-ease.

'Have you come about Mama?' she said.

'Yes. She told me a little of what happened between you.'

Blanche nodded, silent.

'Will you come and see her before you go?' Ernest said. 'To say goodbye?'

A little pause, then Blanche shook her head. 'I – I'm sorry – I can't.'

'You mean you won't.'

'She told me not to bother coming back, so –' Blanche shrugged, 'so I shan't.'

'And that's how you're going to leave it, is it?'

'She said it, Ernest; I didn't.'

He sighed, shook his head. 'She's proud, Blanche. You know that.'

Blanche said nothing. Ernest gave a nod. 'And you are too.' After a moment he added:

'But she can't come here to see you, can she?'

Not answering his question, Blanche said: 'Does she know you've come here today?'

'Yes. I've got some errands to do for Palmer, my guv'nor. I told her I'd call on my way.'

'And she sent no message – no word with you?'

'– No.'

Blanche shrugged. 'Then I have no word for her, either.'

'Blanche, please . . . just for a few minutes.'

'I'm sorry.'

'You're as stubborn as she is.'

Blanche gave a little shrug. After a moment Ernest sighed and said:

'Well, I must go. I've got things to do.' He put out his hand. 'Goodbye, Blanche.'

She put her hand in his and for a moment she thought he would draw her to him and kiss her on the cheek. But he did not. Their touch was awkward and the distance between them remained, much greater than the little patch of gravel between their two sets of feet. Then he was turning, moving across the yard to the pony. Moments later, with Jacko loping at the pony's side, Ernest had ridden through the side gate and was out of sight.

The estrangement from her mother had stayed at the forefront of Blanche's mind for the rest of that day, and was still there the next morning when she and Marianne were in the carriage driving to Trowbridge. The situation could not, Blanche knew, continue, and as they drew near to Colford she suddenly said:

'Marianne – may we go near Hummock Lane? I want to see my mother for a moment. Have we got time?'

James, questioned, said they could spare a few minutes, and at the next junction he turned the horse's head. On reaching Hummock Lane Blanche got out and hurried along to the cottage. Entering through the back door she found her mother scrubbing the kitchen table. Sarah looked up as she entered and the two of them stood there, facing one another.

'I came to say goodbye.' Blanche spoke the words softly, awkwardly.

Sarah nodded silently, then put down the scrubbing brush and wiped her hands on her apron. 'I'm glad,' she said. 'And I'm – I'm pleased to see you.'

Still they gazed at one another, then Blanche quickly stepped forward and held out her arms, and in the same moment Sarah moved to meet her. They stood holding one another for some moments and then Blanche broke free.

'I must go. The carriage is outside. We're on our way to Trowbridge to get the train.' There were tears in her eyes. 'I couldn't go without seeing you.'

The tears now shone in Sarah's eyes too. She reached out her hands and Blanche took them.

'I'm so glad you came,' Sarah said.

'I had to. I'm sorry, Mama – for everything.'

'No, no, my dear. It wasn't your fault. I'm to blame if anyone is.'

'Don't say that.'

They stood there for some moments longer, then, with a final pressure on her mother's fingers, Blanche turned and moved to the door.

'Goodbye, Mama. I'll see you in the summer, when I get back.'

From The Towers over the following weeks Blanche wrote to her mother frequently, and Sarah wrote back, and through their letters they seemed to begin to regain some of their lost ground, to begin making up some of the lost time, and by doing so to come closer than they had at any time in years past. That this was so became evident through Ernest's letters too, as he wrote to Blanche of his mother's new-found contentment.

And the brief time afforded by the half-term holiday from school added to the closeness and understanding between Blanche and her mother. They spent more time together, and they talked together, and their conversation gradually developed a greater ease as the few days of the vacation passed by. By the time Blanche had to return to Clifton she and her mother had reached a greater understanding of one another. They would never be, Blanche knew, as other mothers and daughters were – their histories denied this – but at the same time they now knew a relationship in which they felt an increasing respect and affection for one another.

That summer Blanche and Marianne left The Towers for the last time. In September they would leave for

France, for the finishing school in Brittany. First, though, the summer was to be spent in Sicily.

In preparation, it was decided that they would accompany Marianne's father on a trip to London where he had arranged to meet Edward Harrow – over from Sicily on business – and whilst there spend a day shopping in the West End. Consequently on the morning following their arrival the two girls took a cab from their hotel to Oxford Street where they spent some happy, carefree hours browsing in the fashionable shops, and making up their minds on what they should spend the allowance that Savill had made to them for the occasion. London for them was an exciting place; with all the electric light, the trams, and the motor cars, it offered a pace of life they had never experienced before.

Later that afternoon, exhausted, but with their purchases made, they returned to the hotel to rest and prepare for dinner, which, at Harrow's invitation, was to be at one of London's top restaurants.

They were five at dinner that evening, the fifth being one Alfredo Pastore, a Sicilian with property and business interests in Palermo and Messina and known to Edward Harrow who had run into him by chance in London that day. Pastore, whose father had once been a business associate of Harrow's, was a good-looking man in his mid-thirties. He had travelled extensively, and seated next to Blanche, he kept her amused throughout the meal with various anecdotes garnered from his travels.

The evening marked a further new experience in the lives of the two girls. They drank champagne and afterwards stayed up late in the hotel lounge, talking with the men. They had truly come of age now, it appeared, a fact further acknowledged by the attentions paid them by the handsome Pastore. When they got up to take their leave of the men and go to their room he escorted them to the lift, there smilingly bowing and kissing their hands. He hoped, he said, that he would have the pleasure of meeting them again one day, perhaps during their visit to Sicily.

Lying in bed that night in the room which she and Marianne shared, Blanche thought back over the excitement of the day and its culmination in the dinner at the restaurant. She could see again Alfredo Pastore's eyes upon her, feel the slight pressure of his hand as he had lifted her own hand to kiss. She doubted that she would ever see him again, but that did not matter. The certain knowledge that he, a wealthy, sophisticated man, had found her attractive had given the occasion an added sparkle that had nothing to do with the champagne.

The following morning Savill and the girls said goodbye to Edward Harrow before returning to Hallowford. He had further business to attend to in London before returning to Sicily, but, he said, he would see them there, and in his absence Gentry would look after them.

Gentry . . .

Later, as Blanche sat beside Marianne in the train bound for Trowbridge, Gentry's name kept going through her mind – just as his face kept appearing before her. She had tried to keep all thought of him away from her, but now she could do so no longer. Tomorrow he would arrive in Hallowford, and the day after that they would set off together, the three of them – he, Marianne and herself, to travel to Messina for the summer. And it mattered not at all that she told herself that the only reason she had been invited was to keep Marianne company; all she could think of was that she would be seeing Gentry again, that she would be spending time in his company. At the prospect she could see before her nothing but a kind of sweet agony – she knew nothing could ever come of it – but whatever it turned out to be she knew that she could not give up the promised experience.

At the cottage in Hummock Lane that afternoon Sarah was baking cakes. She expected Blanche for tea. Blanche would call, she had said, on the way back from Trowbridge station after the trip to London. It was arranged that the carriage would let her off at the cottage and call back for her a couple of hours later.

As she busied herself about the neat little kitchen Sarah reflected that these remaining summer days could well be the last time that she and Blanche would really be together. Blanche was moving on. In a few days Sicily for the summer – and then France for the following year. And after that? The two girls would not remain in one another's pockets forever. Marianne would marry. And perhaps, with luck, Blanche too would soon meet someone suitable – someone from the circle in which she moved.

Sarah looked at the clock. Just after three. Blanche would soon be there. Moving to the table she glanced briefly, approvingly at the two short ranks of small sponges that were cooling on a tray, and then began to set out cups and saucers and plates. Stopping momentarily, she put a hand to her head. She had a slight headache, which had been with her all day, a dull throbbing sensation that had continuously made its presence felt. She realized now that the headache was worse; not only that but there was a strange feeling of fullness in her head, added to which she felt slightly sick, as though she could vomit.

She swallowed hard, trying to force back the sensation of nausea and, setting down the little pitcher of milk on the tablecloth, moved to a chair and sat down. The pounding in her head grew stronger.

As Blanche got out of the carriage at the end of the lane Mr Savill said he would send the phaeton for her at the appointed time. Blanche thanked him, said goodbye to him and Marianne and, as the carriage set off once more, made her way towards the cottage.

Rising with difficulty from her chair, Sarah walked slowly from the kitchen into the scullery, from which window she could look along the lane to the junction with the main Hallowford to Trowbridge road. Now, standing before the window, she gripped the small table in front of it as a wave of giddiness washed over her. On the lane she could see the slim, elegantly-dressed figure of Blanche as she came towards the cottage. Sarah registered the sight for a moment but then her awareness was swiftly dissolving under the pressure from the throbbing pain in her head. It was stronger than ever, and now she could hear strange noises in her ears, like the rushing of water. She staggered slightly and, reaching out, clutched desperately at the sink. Her fingers grasped it, but in the next moment her grasp was slipping away as consciousness left her and she fell to the floor.

Ernest, summoned quickly from his work by the son of a neighbour whom Blanche had sent to the farm, ran back to the cottage, the dog at his heels. He got there to find his mother lying insensible on the old couch, with Dr Kelsey in attendance and Blanche waiting worriedly close by. Their mother had suffered apoplexy, Ernest learned, and was paralysed down her left side. On hearing this he at once burst into tears. Blanche comforted him, after which Dr Kelsey told them that their mother had a chance of recovery with careful nursing. But great care would have to be taken, he said. The stroke had been caused by a haemorrhage in the brain, due to the bursting of a blood vessel, and great care would have to be exercised to ensure that it didn't happen again. The vital time, Kelsey added, would be over the next two or three days, during which time she must be kept extremely quiet and disturbed as little as possible. Any undue disturbance, he said, could bring about a recurrence of the attack.

'Her – her paralysis . . .' Ernest said. 'Will she get over that?'

Kelsey paused before he answered. 'We don't yet know the extent of it – and won't until she recovers consciousness. But if she's much affected it's very doubtful that she'll make anything like a full recovery – though she might make a very good *partial* recovery. The next three or four weeks will tell. At the end of that time she should, with care, be out of danger. Also at that time you'll see any signs of recovery of her powers.'

Before the doctor left he gave instructions for Sarah's nursing – though there was little that could be done for the present during her state of unconsciousness, he said, except to maintain extreme quiet and keep her lying down.

When the doctor had gone – with the promise to call again the next morning – Ernest and Blanche brought Sarah's bed downstairs and erected it in the front parlour. Then, gently and carefully, they laid Sarah upon it. With nothing more they could do for their mother for the present, Blanche set about making tea for Ernest and herself.

As they drank it there came a knock at the front door

and Ernest opened it to find there James, the Savills' groom, come to take Blanche back to Hallowford House. Blanche told him that her mother was ill and that she would have to stay with her. She would, she said, send Mr Savill a message the next day.

When James had gone, Ernest noticed dully that Blanche had changed into one of Sarah's frocks; her own dress and cape, which she had worn to London, were now hanging behind the door of Sarah's bedroom.

As Ernest sat at Sarah's side, watching over her, Blanche prepared a meal for him, then sat near him as he ate, the plate on his knee, beside Sarah's bed.

Later on Mr Savill himself came to the cottage to inquire after Sarah's condition. Blanche brought him into the kitchen where they talked quietly. After a little while, exacting the promise from her to let him know if there was anything her mother needed, he left.

That night Ernest prepared to sit beside Sarah and watch over her. Blanche tried to persuade him to go to bed, but he would not, insisting on remaining there, sitting on the chair at Sarah's bedside. Just after eleven o'clock Sarah showed signs of regaining consciousness, and minutes later she opened her eyes. Ernest, trying to keep back the tears, held her hand while she tried to ask what had happened. As he and Blanche had feared, she had difficulty in speaking; her speech was thick, as if her tongue would not obey her commands, while the left side of her face, particularly the muscles around the left side of her mouth, seemed to have fallen and to have lost their power.

Ernest told her that she had had a slight stroke, quickly adding, however, that she would be all right in time with careful nursing. The doctor, he added, would be calling to see her again in the morning. 'Meanwhile you'll have to put up with Blanche and me looking after you,' he grinned.

A little later Blanche again tried to persuade him to go to bed. 'I'll sit with her,' she said. 'You must have your sleep. You have work to go to in the morning.'

He shook his head. 'How can I go to work? Someone's got to be with her.'

'I'll stay with her. Don't worry, I'll care for her. And if she needs you I'll send for you. In the meantime you go on to bed.'

He nodded and got up from the chair. Sarah was sleeping again now. After whispering a goodnight to her he moved silently away from her bedside. In the doorway he said softly to Blanche, a perplexed frown on his brow:

'How are you going to make your arrangements – about going away?'

Blanche shook her head. 'We won't discuss it now. You go on to bed.'

'But you're leaving the country in a day or two.'

'Go to bed, Ernest. Please.'

'Right.' He nodded. 'Goodnight, Blanche. Wake me if – if anything happens.'

'Don't worry – I will. But she'll be all right.'

Sitting in a chair beside Sarah's bed, Blanche spent the night in alternate periods of sleeping and wakefulness. And even during the times when she slept it seemed that half her mind was alert for any sign of alarm from Sarah. When Ernest, followed by Jacko, came downstairs just on five-thirty he crept into the parlour and found both Blanche and his mother sleeping. After spending a few silent moments at Sarah's bedside he went softly out of the room again. A faint noise from the kitchen a little later awakened Blanche and she went out there to find Ernest washing. She told him that their mother had spent a restful night, after which he urged her to go back and try to get some more sleep. She would not, but set about preparing his breakfast. Following the long, uncomfortable night Blanche's limbs ached and felt stiff, but after moving about the room for a few minutes she felt better. After feeding Jacko, Ernest ate the breakfast of oatmeal and eggs which Blanche had prepared for him and then, after looking in on Sarah once more – she was still sleeping – he called the dog to him and together they left the cottage.

Sarah awoke later on. In her strange, thick voice, she said she was in no pain and that she felt comfortable. After helping her to wash, Blanche prepared her a very light breakfast and, with difficulty, persuaded her to eat a little. After that, Sarah lay quiet again.

Blanche was tidying the cottage later that morning when Dr Kelsey called. After examining Sarah he accompanied Blanche into the kitchen. The extent of the paralysis showed that the haemorrhage had been severe, he said, and once again emphasized the need for very careful nursing over the next few days and also over the weeks that followed. 'It will be necessary for someone to be with her all the time,' he said.

Blanche nodded. 'And after that time?'

He shrugged. 'We shall see. But you must understand – she'll never be as she was.'

Marianne called that afternoon, on the way to meet Gentry's train at Trowbridge. She had brought with her various dishes prepared by the cook at Hallowford House. Blanche repeated to her what Dr Kelsey had said. Marianne nodded; they both knew what it meant – it would be impossible now for Blanche to think of going to Sicily.

That evening John Savill came to the cottage again. There he told Blanche and Ernest that he had found a nurse for their mother – 'A reliable woman,' he said, mentioning the name of a Mrs Melcome, a woman in the next village. He would pay for her to come and care for their mother. Ernest looked at Blanche as she sat there.

'It's up to you, Blanche,' he said.

Savill added: 'If Mrs Melcome comes in you would still be able to travel to Sicily if you wish, and, later, to France.'

Blanche gave a little smile. 'I thank you, Uncle John,' she said, 'but I can't go now. My place is here.'

A few minutes later she followed him out to the carriage. 'Are you sure?' he said. 'If you wish to go I'd make certain that your mother got the best care.' He paused. 'Or perhaps you could stay with her for a while until she's making a good recovery – and then join Marianne in Sicily at a later date.'

She thanked him again, then said, 'I can't. My mother needs *me* right now. I was never here at any other time when she needed me. I can't leave her now.'

The next day, Thursday, at mid-morning, the Savills' carriage stopped at the end of the lane. It was taking Marianne and Gentry to Trowbridge where they would take the train to begin the journey to Sicily.

Marianne had come to bid Blanche goodbye. In the cottage doorway they embraced and then Blanche walked out with her to the front gate and stood watching as she walked back along the lane and climbed into the carriage. And then suddenly Gentry was there, climbing down, coming quickly towards her. Reaching her side he stood before her for a moment in silence then held out his hand.

'Goodbye, Blanche.'

'Goodbye, Gentry.'

They kept their voices low, although they could not be heard by Marianne in the carriage.

Gentry released her hand. 'I'm so sorry,' he said, '– about everything.'

She nodded.

'Oh, Blanche,' he whispered suddenly, 'I wish you were coming with us. I wish you were going to be there.'

'Gentry – please. Marianne will be there – and that's the way it should be.'

'I know, but –'

'We couldn't do anything to hurt her.'

'No. It's just that . . .' He let his words trail off.

Blanche sighed. 'What happened between us was never meant to happen, Gentry. Now we must forget that it ever did.'

He said nothing. After a moment she held out her hand again. Perhaps, she thought, we shall never meet again.

'Goodbye.'

Gentry did not miss the note of finality in her voice. He took her small hand in his. 'Goodbye, Blanche Farrar.'

Then he was walking back along the lane and a minute later the carriage was disappearing out of sight on the Trowbridge road.

Chapter Twenty-Seven

The days, the weeks went by. Summer mellowed and the harvests were brought in. In the hedgerows hazelnuts, elderberries and blackberries ripened, while on the heath the bracken grew shoulder high. At the cottage when Sarah recovered sufficiently to leave her bed the old couch was brought into the kitchen and she spent the greater part of her days there in the company of Blanche.

Towards the end of August Marianne returned, suntanned and radiant after her summer in Palermo and Messina. At the cottage in Hummock Lane she visited Sarah and Blanche and sat in the small kitchen telling of her experiences. And so many times in her narrative Gentry's name came up, and Blanche could see – who could have missed it? – how much in love she was. Blanche did not want to hear about Gentry, though, did not want to hear about all the wonderful times they had had together, and looking at Marianne as they sat opposite one another, she reflected on how much everything had changed. It was as if her own life had come to a stop, while Marianne's was suddenly beginning. Her own life had come full circle; now she was back with her mother – where she had begun. Where, she said to herself, she belonged.

A little later she walked with Marianne from the cottage to the front gate. There Marianne turned to her and took her hand. 'Let us know if there's anything you want, anything we can do,' she said.

'I will.' She would not, though, Blanche knew. She could never now go to them at Hallowford House, asking for their charity. She had taken enough during her life, and now she had come to a turning point, and she would ask for nothing more.

Back in the kitchen she spent some time manipulating her mother's left leg and left arm. It was a regular twice-daily routine, when for a period Blanche would try to encourage a greater degree of life into Sarah's sluggish limbs. It was a slow business, though, but even so, it had shown results, and Dr Kelsey had admitted himself surprised at the extra mobility which Sarah had gained over the weeks since her attack. She could walk now – albeit with an ungainly swinging of her left leg – but even her gait was improving. Now when Blanche had finished helping her mother with the day's exercises Sarah took a child's rubber ball in her left hand and sat trying to squeeze it in her grasp – another means of trying to coax additional life into her wasted muscles.

As Blanche worked in the kitchen she looked at Sarah manipulating the rubber ball and reflected how much a part of their routine it now was. And her own life had settled into a routine, she said to herself – up in the morning to get Ernest's breakfast and then help her mother to wash and dress. That done she would start on the chores around the cottage – the cooking, the cleaning. And so the days would go by, only Sundays showing any variance of the pattern, for on that day Ernest would not spend long at the farm. For the rest of the time the days melted one into another with hardly anything to mark the difference between them.

That December Blanche was eighteen. Marianne's birthday was a week later, and Blanche was invited to Hallowford House to join in a celebration dinner. She was undecided as to whether to go, but in the end, after considerable urging from Ernest and her mother, she accepted the invitation and on the evening in question the phaeton came for her.

On her return she was quiet and uncommunicative, and Ernest and Sarah looked at her with concern.

'Is something wrong?' Ernest asked. 'Didn't you have a good time?'

She shrugged. 'Yes, it was fine.' She got up and, making some excuse, went into the front parlour. After a moment Ernest followed her in.

'What happened?' he said.

'Happened?'

'Did something happen?'

'No. We had a very nice dinner. Mr Savill, Marianne, her Uncle Harold, and I . . .' She paused. 'And I should not have gone.'

'Why not?'

'Because it's not a part of my life anymore.'

'How can you say that? Marianne's like a sister to you. And Mr Savill's like a father.'

She nodded. 'I know. And here am I with a foot in both camps. And I can't keep my balance, Ernest. And if I try to keep it up I shall fall over.'

Following the dinner party at Hallowford House Blanche decided not to go there again. That part of her life was over, she said to herself. There had been all those years when she had grown up beside Marianne, but now those years were over. It was time now that they separated and led their separate lives. In any case, Marianne would probably be leaving Hallowford one of these days when her year at finishing school was over – probably to go to Sicily to live – as Gentry's wife. Blanche had to recognize the fact: she had no further part to play in the lives of the inhabitants of Hallowford House, and it was time she began to think of her own life. And she would have to with it as much as she could. Not that she had any reason to complain, she said to herself – after all, she had had a good start, and a good education – which alone should fit her for something.

Sarah was in the kitchen when Marianne called at the cottage a few days later to invite Blanche to tea, but Blanche, she was surprised to see, declined the invitation. Sarah looked at the two young women as they talked together – Marianne in her fashionable dress, Blanche with her hair tied back, and wearing one of her oldest frocks. After Marianne's departure Blanche turned to find Sarah looking at her with a little expression of concern. Blanche smiled at her.

'Are you all right, Mama?'

'Yes, thank you, dear.' Sarah nodded, then said, 'Don't cut yourself off from everything, Blanche.'

'I'm not.'

'And don't do it on my account.'

'Oh, Mama.'

As Blanche came to her chair, Sarah reached out her right hand and took Blanche's wrist. Blanche frowned, smiling: 'What is it?'

Sarah looked into her eyes. 'I never understood you, Blanche. And I underestimated you.'

'What do you mean?'

'You have a strength I never knew you possessed.'

Blanche smiled at her. 'No, no . . .'

'Yes.' Sarah sat in silence for some moments, then she added:

'I know what you've given up for me.'

'I haven't given up anything.'

'Ah, yes, I know.' Her fingers around Blanche's wrist tightened. 'But it will all come to you in time, Blanche.

343

You'll see. You deserve the best – and it will come to you in time.'

One bright day in mid-June of the following year, 1899, Blanche answered a knock at the door to find John Savill standing on the doorstep.

'Uncle John . . .'

He smiled at her. 'Is it convenient, Blanche . . . ?' He was taking off his hat.

'Of course.' Beyond his shoulder, at the end of the narrow lane, she could see his phaeton. 'Please – come in.' She stepped back and allowed him to enter. When she had closed the door behind him he said softly: 'Perhaps I might see your mother in a little while, but may we talk privately first for a minute or two?'

'Yes, of course . . .'

She led him into the front parlour where they sat facing one another.

'How is your mama?' he asked.

'Going on quite well, thank you. She seems to be improving, but her progress now is very slow.'

'She can't be left.' It was almost a statement.

'Oh, no. I'm afraid not.'

He frowned.

'What is it, Uncle John?'

He gave a little shrug. 'I worry about you, Blanche.'

'Oh, you have no need to worry about me. I'm all right.'

'Are you? Truly?'

'Yes, believe me.'

'I wonder about you – what's happening to you.'

'I'm managing.'

'Are you happy, Blanche?'

'Happy?' She paused for a moment then smiled at him. 'I think I'm – coming to terms with – with reality.'

'Oh, dear. That makes it sound quite a feat.'

'No, no. It's time I did.'

He said nothing for a moment, then: 'Blanche – I want you to remember something . . .'

'Yes?'

He sighed. 'I have a responsibility towards you, you know.'

'There's no need.'

'Oh, indeed there is. I took you from your home and – and gave you a kind of life that was different. Don't think I'm unaware of that.'

'I don't,' she said. 'But how far can it take me, Uncle John? It won't keep me forever. At some time or other I have to be responsible for myself. And I am now. I'm eighteen years old, and what I do now is my own decision.'

He gave a little nod. 'I just want you to know, Blanche, that if you ever want anything – anything at all – you have only to ask.'

'I'll remember that. And thank you.'

'You have no need to thank me. I owe it to you. But apart from that – I would want to help you if I could. You know that.' He reached out and took her hand in his. 'You mean a great deal to me, Blanche. You're like a second daughter to me. You've given me so much over the years – not to mention what you've given to Marianne.'

'No, Uncle John,' she pressed his hand, '– it's what you've given *me*.'

They sat in silence for some moments, then Blanche said:

'I hear from Marianne quite regularly. She seems to be reasonably happy at school in Brittany.'

Savill smiled. 'I think "reasonably" is the right word. She's managing well enough, I suppose, anyway. Though

I know she'd be happier if you were with her. Did she tell you that we're going away in the summer, to Sicily?'

'– Yes, she mentioned it.'

'Just for a while. We think – Gentry's father and I – that Marianne and Gentry should see a little more of one another – get to know each other a little better.' He smiled. 'I'm sure you're well aware of the fact that we'd like Marianne and Gentry to marry one day. If they find they're suitable, of course. And there's no doubt that they're very fond of one another – but as it is, with Gentry now living in Sicily again, and Marianne in England, they don't get that much opportunity to meet.' He shrugged. 'So, as I say, we're going out to Messina to stay for a while.'

'When do you leave?'

'In a couple of weeks – when Marianne returns from Brittany. We shall stay in Sicily for a few months. Harold will look after things for me here while we're gone.' He gave a little sigh. 'You know, I'm not getting any younger, Blanche, and I'm getting tired. I find I let things get on top of me as I never used to, and I'm looking forward to doing nothing at all for several weeks.'

Marianne came to visit Blanche when she returned from Brittany and again a week later before her departure for Sicily with her father. On that second occasion the two girls sat for a while in the kitchen with Sarah. When Marianne got up to go Blanche walked with her out into the lane.

Beside the carriage they stopped, facing one another. It was a bright, warm day, and Marianne was wearing a new summer dress of pale blue linen which she had bought on a trip to London. She looked very elegant and very beautiful and Blanche was suddenly very much aware of her own worn dress and apron.

'I wish you were coming with us, Blanche,' Marianne said. She and her father were to leave early the next morning. Savill had already called to say his goodbyes.

'Yes, but I'm afraid it can't be.'

'Perhaps another day.'

'Perhaps.'

'I don't want us to – to lose touch,' Marianne said. 'We won't let that happen, shall we?'

'No, of course not.'

'It's strange sometimes without you, Blanche.'

'Oh?'

'I'm getting used to it now, but at the start, when I went to Brittany on my own – it was odd not having you there.' Marianne smiled. 'I was so used to having you with me all the time. Like a sister.'

Blanche nodded. 'It's what we get used to, I suppose.' She added to herself: *And I'm getting used to a different life now.* It was a time of goodbyes. She was saying goodbye to all the connections with her old life. Marianne was going away, and soon she would have gone away for good. Even sisters went their own ways eventually . . .

Marianne stepped forward, putting her arms around Blanche, drawing her close, pressing her cheek to Blanche's cheek. 'I love you, Blanche. Don't forget me, will you?'

Moments later as the carriage was moving away towards Hallowford Blanche thought of Marianne's words. It's more likely, she thought, that you, Marianne, will forget me.

The knowledge that Savill as well as Marianne had gone from Hallowford that summer left Blanche for a while with a strange feeling of being cut off from much of her past. Their departure also placed her even more firmly in her present situation, and she wondered what would be the outcome. Perhaps she would just remain there, she thought, caring for her mother and her brother. As it was, her future was a mystery. She could see nothing beyond her present situation.

Beyond the confines of Colford, Britain was occupied with larger matters than Blanche's future, and as the summer wore on the worsening situation in South Africa was the subject of daily reports in the newspapers. With so much indignation on behalf of the British immigrants in the Transvaal who were being denied their rights, there was no shortage of those who believed that Britain should go out there and teach the Boers a lesson.

To Blanche, living and working in the cottage, it all might have been going on in another world, on another planet. It was no part of her own life. And even when Ernest came home in mid-October to announce that Britain was going to war with the Boers, she found that she was barely touched by the news.

'It won't last five minutes, though,' Ernest said. 'Not with England on the side of the immigrants. They'll soon teach those damned Boers what's what.'

The next day all possible thoughts of the war, and of anything else that was happening beyond the walls of the cottage were wiped away.

Sarah had felt discontented that morning, as she was wont to do at times – a discontent due to her inability to do all the things that had previously come so easily to her. She felt sometimes that she would never get used to it, her new situation. Having led a very active life, she often found her enforced sedentariness frustrating and depressing. Not only could she not walk with the unquestioned ease of the past, but the continuing weakness in her left arm denied her so many of her past occupations. And it seemed now that she would get no better. For a while with all the manipulating and exercising of her limbs she had made astonishing progress. But after a certain time the progress had ceased, and she had been left as she was now, with her strange, ungainly gait, a much diminished power in her left hand and arm, and the muscles of the left side of her face pulled down.

That morning Blanche had entered the kitchen to find her standing beside the range looking at herself in the small mirror that hung there, her hand covering the left side of her face. At Blanche's entrance Sarah quickly dropped her hand and started almost guiltily away. Then, turning, she caught Blanche looking at her. She gave a sad little smile that lifted only the right side of her mouth.

'I'm just a foolish woman,' she said.

'Nonsense. Don't say that.'

'It's true. To still be thinking on how things *were* – how they used to be. Lord, I've known enough disappointments in my life to realize by now that there's no changing the past. Good God, if I could I wouldn't know where to stop.' Her hand moved back to her face, her fingertips touching the flesh over the immobile muscles. 'I used to be pretty once . . .'

'– I'm sure of it.'

'Once. Your father certainly thought so.' Into Sarah's mind came a sudden picture. Trowbridge on an evening in winter. Ollie writing with his finger on a window. Mist on the glass as she breathed upon it. Words appearing. *Love me, love me, Sarah Keane.* 'Once,' she said.

She turned and looked out through the window to where the grey October sky hung over the little strip of garden. 'And now I feel I'm keeping you back – you and Ernest.'

'No, that's not true.'

'Oh, Blanche – I might have had a stroke, but it hasn't affected my knowledge of what is the truth. Without me you might be – anywhere now. You'd be in Sicily.'

'No. There's no place for me there.'

'There would be if it weren't for me.'

Blanche avoided her eyes. 'Anyway, it's a good thing I'm not there – in Sicily.'

'Why?'

Blanche shrugged, raised her eyes. 'I'd be in the way there now.'

'In whose way?'

Blanche did not answer. Sarah's eyes gazed into her own. There was a little shadow of knowledge in them, of concern. 'It's that young man, isn't it? Gentry.'

Blanche hesitated then said: 'It doesn't matter if it is. I'll never see him again.'

Sarah watched her turn away, opened her mouth to speak but was overwhelmed by a sudden rushing in her ears. With the sudden fullness in her head, the feeling of nausea, she was all at once aware of what was happening. She gave out a choking cry, and was vaguely aware of Blanche spinning to face her. She lifted her hands to her head, her eyes rolling up in their sockets. The next instant the darkness swept over her.

It was what they had feared, a second haemorrhage.

All that afternoon and evening Blanche and Ernest sat beside Sarah's bed as she lay unconscious. Dr Kelsey, calling at midday, had looked grave after his examination of Sarah, and had left giving precise instructions for her care. Everything, he had said, would depend on the next few hours.

350

Side by side at Sarah's bed, Blanche and Ernest sat through the night, waiting for some sign, the movement of a hand, the blinking of an eyelid. There was nothing. Then, as the first light of day crept into the room through the gap in the cheap curtains, Sarah slipped away.

She was buried on a late October day in the Hallowford churchyard, beside Ollie and the children. The morning had been frosty and cold, but later the sun had shone through surprisingly bright and warm. Beside the grave Blanche and Ernest stood with bowed heads, while on the nearby yew tree the mistle thrushes ate the scarlet berries. Later, when Ernest's tears had ended he had seemed somehow numbed.

Back at the cottage Blanche had tried to get him to eat something. He had little appetite, though, and after toying with the meal she placed in front of him he apologetically pushed it to one side. He sat in silence for some moments then said quietly, a note of bitterness in his voice, already hoarse with his grief:

'You mustn't let it get to you, too, Blanche.'

She didn't understand. 'What d'you mean, Ernie?'

'You've been given a chance to make something of yourself. Don't throw it away. Don't be like Mam.' He sat staring ahead of him, his mouth a thin, tense line. 'It's the poverty. It takes everything away and gives nothing in return. And it's that that took Mam. It wasn't any apoplexy – not really. It's the loss, the continuing loss. And seeing it, you think to yourself sometimes that it's a wonder that a person can go on as long as they do. Mary, Arthur, Agnes, Dad. How much can a person take? You have a life like ours, with all the losses – and those losses chip away at you, long after they've happened. And in the end it's like there's not enough to keep you upright. And you know that with just one more it will all go. But it doesn't. And you keep on. But even so it eventually wears you down.' He reached out, his large hand closing gently around Blanche's wrist. 'You mustn't let it happen to you, Blanche. You must get out as soon as you can. Stay in this situation and it will only drag you down too.'

She said nothing, just gave a slight nod. His eyes burned into hers. 'You listen to what I'm telling you,' he said fiercely. 'You've got to get out while there's time.'

Chapter Twenty-Eight

'Well, I have to say that as regards your education you seem well qualified for the position, Miss Farrar. But on the other hand you are rather young.'

Having already been interviewed by Mrs Andrews – and presumably having passed the test – Blanche now faced the woman's husband. She sat in a wing chair before him in the library of Highfield, the Andrews's house on the edge of Ashton Wick, a village two miles to the west of Colford. In his early fifties, David Andrews was a solicitor, a tall man, lean and angular, with a heavy moustache. 'When we advertised the post,' he said, 'my wife and I rather had in mind someone a little older.'

'I shall be nineteen next month.'

'Even so . . .' He looked perplexed. 'And how will you get here every day, from Colford?'

'Walk.'

'You won't mind that?' He gestured to the window, beyond which a November sun shone down on a well-kept lawn. 'It's a fine day today – but what about when the snow comes. Two miles isn't far – but in very bad weather it might seem a very long way.'

'I'm young, sir. A two-mile walk won't mean much to me.'

He smiled. 'Well, I can't say much to that, can I? And I daresay we would manage somehow if the weather grew really severe. Right. We'll agree then, shall we?'

'Thank you.'

'And you can start immediately?'

'Tomorrow if you wish?'

'That will suit us fine. And the salary is acceptable to you?'

Seventy pounds a year was not a fortune, but it would keep her independent, and added to Ernest's wages they would manage very well. 'Yes, sir.'

'Good.' He got up. The interview was over. Blanche rose and took his outstretched hand. 'We have a bargain, Miss Farrar. And we'll start tomorrow sharp at nine, yes?'

'I shall be here.'

He showed her to the door. As she turned to take her leave she saw beyond him, standing in the hall, the two children, eight-year-old Robert, and his seven-year-old sister Louisa, who were to be her pupils.

She walked the two miles to Colford with a light step. Finding the position as daily governess to the Andrews children had lifted a great weight from her mind. After her mother's death she had remained at the cottage caring for Ernest, but it was not a full-time job, and anyway, she had wanted to get out and find work of her own. And now she had a position; she was making a start, at last – a start with her own life. And it would still enable her to care for Ernest – as she wanted to. With lessons for the two Andrews children ending each day at three, she could still get back well in time to prepare Ernest's evening meal and keep the cottage in some sort of order.

When Ernest returned from work that evening, Jacko at his heels, Blanche told him of her acquisition of a job. He was pleased for her.

'Mr Andrews was concerned about my age,' Blanche said, '– but on the other hand, I think they had not had many responses to their advertisement. So – I was lucky.'

'Don't sell yourself short,' Ernest said.

The following morning, just before nine o'clock, Blanche was admitted to Highfield and shown to the schoolroom on the second floor. A few minutes later her two pupils were brought into the room by Mrs Andrews, a short, nervous-looking little woman, who – rather reluctantly, it seemed – left them alone with her. Then, with the two children taking their seats at a table facing her own, the lessons began.

And Blanche found herself enjoying the work far more than she had expected to. At first the children were very shy with her, but as the day wore on and their shyness receded, they began to emerge as bright and affectionate, eager to please and to do well, and possessing keen, inquiring minds and lively personalities. At the end of that first day Blanche left the house with a feeling of hope and confidence.

In her continuing quiet life, Blanche, like most of the British, found herself relatively untroubled by events in such a far-off place as the Transvaal.

But the conflict there was gathering momentum. With the continuing improvements in international communications the reports of the war's progress were not long in reaching British shores, and after the early reports of success – the defeat of the Boers at Glencoe – to the general surprise there came astonishing news of victories for the enemy. Not only did Pier Joubert win a decisive battle against British forces under George White, but the very next day he presided over the surrender of Ladysmith. The British, to the great surprise of everyone but their enemies, were not getting things all their own way. Even so, it was said all over England, the British troops were experiencing only a temporary setback. Once they had come to terms with the new terrain, they would easily win through. That not everyone in high places concurred with such sentiments, however, was evidenced by the fact that before November was out Canadian and Australian volunteer forces were on their way to South Africa.

In her work at Highfield in Ashton Wick, the only slight disturbance to Blanche's new-found equanimity came two days before her nineteenth birthday in the shape of a letter from John Savill in Sicily. Writing that he had just heard from his brother of Sarah's death, he extended to Blanche and Ernest his deepest sympathies, after which he went on to say:

> Our host, my friend Edward Harrow, urges me to invite you to come and stay here for a while. And of course it goes without saying that it would please Marianne enormously, and me, too, but more importantly than that, I think it might give you a much-needed respite from your recent responsibilities, and help to ease the sadness you must be feeling. Marianne is also writing to you, but she still urges me to press you to come here where, she says, she will make you enjoy yourself, and where, she is sure, you will be able to relax.
>
> Please let us know at once whether you can come, and if so we will make the necessary arrangements for your journey. If we move quickly you might even be here in time for the New Year celebrations.

The letter ended with John Savill suggesting that when he and Marianne returned to England perhaps Blanche would like to return to live at Hallowford House once more. Enclosed with the letter was one from Marianne who voiced her own hopes that Blanche would travel to Sicily to stay with them.

Blanche had found the letters waiting for her on her return from Ashton Wick, and Ernest saw the envelope on the dresser when he came in later and sat down to eat. Blanche handed him the letters and he read them as he ate. Afterwards, pushing the letters across the table towards her, he said, 'Well? Will you go?'

'To Sicily? No, of course not.'

'Why not?'

'I have a job to do here. Or had you forgotten?'

'You're a daily governess. D'you think that's going to make you your fortune?'

'Is that what I'm after? My fortune?'

'Mam was a daily governess when she was young. And where did it get her? And I'm sure she had no lack of hopes and dreams.'

'No.' Blanche shook her head. 'I can't leave here, Ernie.'

'It might mean another start for you. And if you go back to Hallowford House too . . .'

'To what purpose?'

He shrugged. 'Mr Savill must have something in mind, otherwise he wouldn't ask.' He gazed at her. 'Give it some thought, Blanche.'

'I've given it some thought. Besides . . .'

'– Besides what?'

She smiled. 'I'm getting used to you, Ernie . . .'

'Oh, yeh?' He grinned at her. 'Well, likewise. But what does that mean?'

'Who would look after you, Ernie? Who would cook your meals, wash your clothes?'

'Who? Why, I'd do it meself, wouldn't I?'

'When? You spend so many hours at the farm. I've seen how you get home in the evenings – exhausted and worn out. Besides, you never learned to cook worth a fig.'

'Oh, I'd manage, you'd see.'

'Yes, after a fashion.'

'True,' he said, 'but that's life, isn't it? That's how we do most things.' He paused, the food before him momentarily forgotten. 'But you've got to leave sometime, Blanche. Or d'you see us growin' old together, eh? One of those eccentric pairs of brother and sister, getting more cranky and bent as the years go by.' He shook his head. 'I don't see you in that role, Blanche. Nor me for that matter.' He grinned. 'Anyway, I don't know as I want you around me all the time. I mean – a chap likes a bit of privacy.'

Blanche laughed and playfully raised a hand as if she would box his ears. He laughed with her. 'Eat your dinner,' she said. 'I'll go make some tea.'

The next day she replied to the letters from Marianne and John Savill. She thanked them, but said that she could not, regretfully, think of travelling to join them. She had taken a position as governess, she said, besides which, she did not wish to leave her brother just yet. However, she finished, she looked forward to seeing them on their return to England.

A few days later Ernest asked her if she had responded to the letters. She told him she had, and that she had declined the invitation. 'I think you're makin' a mistake,' he said. He shrugged. 'But if you can't see it, there's nothing to be done.'

Christmas arrived bringing news of further humiliating British defeats in the Transvaal, but the great British soldiers, Frederick Roberts and his Chief of Staff, Lord Kitchener, were on their way out there. They, said the optimists, would soon put the whole matter in order. In the meantime, at the cottage in Colford the time for Blanche and Ernest passed quietly. On Christmas morning they went to church, after which, with Jacko accompanying them, they walked across the fields to Hallowford, there going to the little churchyard of St Peter's where they stood together beside the graves of their parents and siblings. Afterwards they walked slowly home together to the cottage where they shared the work of preparing Christmas dinner.

And the days and the weeks passed, and the war continued, and in England the snows came and went, and spring came again to the West Country.

One March day Ernest came home from the farm with the surprising news that Palmer was selling up; growing old and with no sons of his own, he planned to retire. Ernest looked grave as he sat at his dinner that evening.

'Who are the new owners to be?' Blanche asked him.

'That's the trouble,' he answered. 'He's selling to Hanworth on the next farm.'

'Where will that leave you?' Blanche asked. 'Surely Hanworth will want you to stay on, won't he?'

'He might. Who can say? He's already got men of his own, and I hear talk as he intends to get rid of the sheep and cattle and turn all of Palmer's land over to grain crops.'

'Will that be so bad, Ernie?'

'I'm a stockman, Blanche. I know about livestock. I don't know about the raising of crops.' He forced a smile. 'Anyway, we'll see what happens . . .'

Some days later John Savill returned to Hallowford. He wasted no time in coming to see Blanche at the cottage. It was late afternoon, and he found her in the garden, working on the little vegetable plot. She brushed the soil from her hands and came to him, and he bent, put his arms around her and kissed her on the cheek.

'Hello, Blanche, my dear.'

'Hello, Uncle John.' She studied him. 'Your holiday's done you good. You look very well.'

'So do you.'

He declined her offer of tea, and they remained standing on the garden path. He had left Marianne in Sicily, he said, at which Blanche said: 'She must be having a good time there.'

Savill nodded. 'I think so.' He gave a satisfied smile. 'She and Gentry are to be married in the summer.'

Involuntarily Blanche caught her breath. Marianne and Gentry – to be married. She had expected it for so long; known for so long that it was inevitable, but nevertheless it still came as a shock.

'I'm sure you must be very happy, Uncle John,' she said.

'Oh, indeed.' He paused. 'There's one other thing that would give me happiness . . .'

'What's that?'

'Have you given any further thought to my proposal? That you come back to stay at Hallowford House?'

Blanche was silent for a few moments then said that she had thought the matter over, but that she could not do so.

'But why?' he said. 'I don't understand. You've got nothing to stop you now.'

'I'm still doing my teaching,' she said.

He shrugged. 'So? What is the problem there? If you're set on continuing with it you could as easily do it from Hallowford.'

'Ashton Wick is a good bit further away, Uncle John.'

'Then you could ride one of the cobs – or James could drive you in the phaeton in the mornings, and bring you back later.'

As she was about to reply Savill raised his hand. 'Don't answer me now,' he said. 'Give it some thought. I'll ask you again in a few days.'

'There's something *I* don't understand,' Blanche said after a moment.

'What's that?'

'Why are you asking me back? I don't understand. Marianne will marry soon and go to live somewhere else with – her husband. Why are you inviting me to live at Hallowford House again?'

'Well – you belong there, Blanche. You belong there as much – if not more – than you do here. And another thing – I feel I owe you a better kind of life than you have at present.' He looked around him, gave a little shake of his head. 'You've no idea how it grieves me to see you here.'

'Working? I'm not ashamed of it.'

'No, of course you're not. And there's no reason you should be. There's every reason for pride in honest work well done. But it's – it's seeing you in these – reduced circumstances. For such they are, Blanche. It grieves me to see you like it.'

'How would you see me?'

'Oh . . .' He gave a little shrug, a little smile. 'Oh, I don't know. Meeting some young man who, if not wealthy, is at least comfortably off – someone who could provide you with the kind of life you've been used to – with what you deserve. And if I could I'd like to do my best to see that it happens.'

He stepped towards her, bent, embraced and kissed her. 'Anyway, I'll come and see you again in a few days.

361

Think about it in the meantime. Give me your answer then.'

When John Savill had gone Blanche went into the cottage. She was in the kitchen washing her hands when Ernest came in. 'I saw Mr Savill's phaeton just leaving the lane,' he said. 'When did he get back?'

'A day or two ago. Marianne's still there – in Sicily. He just called to see how I was.'

'I see. And does that mean that you'll be leaving here? Going back to Hallowford?'

She looked at him sharply. 'What makes you say that?'

'Ah.' He nodded, a faint smile on his lips. 'I got close to the mark, did I?'

She didn't speak for a moment, then she said: 'Why should you think we spoke of such a thing?'

He shrugged. 'It's not hard to imagine. He asked you to go back when Mam was alive, so now – and knowing how close you are to him . . .' He was looking at her intently. 'Are you going, Blanche? There's nothing to stop you now.'

She didn't answer. He said: 'What did you tell him?'

'I didn't tell him anything. He's going to come back for my answer.'

'What do you *want* to do?'

'Well, I don't want to be dependent on anyone, that's for certain. This way I'm not. I know that my work at Highfield isn't about to make my fortune, but at least I've made a start at living my own life.'

'But couldn't you still do that from Hallowford House? You could live in comfort at the same time.'

'That's what *he* said.'

'Well, it's the truth.' Ernest cast a hand around him. 'You can hardly say that we're living in the lap of luxury here.'

'I know that, but . . . Anyway . . .' she turned from him, began to busy herself at the stove, 'I don't have to make any decision yet. Let's see how things go on.'

At Hallowford House John Savill told his brother Harold of his talk with Blanche.

'And what did she say to your proposal?' Harold asked.

'I told her I'd ask for her answer a little later.'

Harold nodded. 'You can't bear it, can you? Marianne staying in Sicily, soon to be married and out of your sight for good, and Blanche also living away.'

'Is that how it seems to you?'

'Is it that you just can't bear to have them both gone at the same time?'

Savill sat in silence for a moment or two, then he nodded. 'Perhaps it is that – partly. That and a little guilt.'

'Guilt? What do you feel guilty for?'

'To see Blanche having had everything throughout her life, and now, suddenly, having to see her with nothing.' He frowned, gazing ahead of him, as if unseeing. 'I want to make it up to her,' he said. 'I wanted to adopt her when she was a child – but I had to give up that idea. Now, though . . .'

'You still think you want to adopt her?'

Savill smiled. 'Perhaps it's a little late for that. But at least I can make sure that she's provided for.'

'Ernest – is there anything wrong?'

It was a Thursday, two weeks after John Savill's visit. At the cottage Blanche watched her brother as he readied himself to leave for the farm. The Hanworths were his employers now, though how he was getting on with them he had not volunteered. Blanche had the feeling, however, that all was not well. Ernest was not the most talkative person first thing in the mornings but over the past few days he had gone off to work with hardly a word. In addition, on returning home in the evenings he had appeared subdued and uncommunicative.

Now at her words he shook his head, a trifle impatiently. 'No – no, of course not. Why should there be?'

'I thought *you* might be able to tell me that.' She paused. 'Is it something I've done?'

He halted momentarily in the act of shrugging on his coat. 'No, Blanche, don't think that.' He gazed at her for a moment, then, smiling, he added: 'It's nothing.'

A few moments later, standing at the door and watching his tall figure move along the lane, Jacko trotting along at his side, Blanche knew that he was lying. Something was wrong. Ernest was such a private person, though; he always had been. Whatever it was that was troubling him he would not tell her until he was ready.

Following his departure Blanche washed the dishes and then set about tidying the kitchen. And it did not take her long to discover that Ernest had gone off without taking his midday dinner. There it was on the kitchen table where he had forgotten it, a tin containing bread, cheese, cold meat, and a wedge of cold apple pie. After weighing the situation for a few moments she decided to take it to him at the farm. She had time enough. Her services were not required that day at Highfield; she had not taught there for almost a week now, the two Andrews children having gone to spend the Easter period with relatives in Oxford.

Just after eleven o'clock she set off from the cottage. Soon after noon she was back again, still carrying Ernest's dinner tin, its contents still intact.

When he returned that evening and washed and changed, she set his evening meal before him as usual as he sat at the kitchen table.

'Is there anything you want to tell me, Ernie?' she said as she sat in the chair facing him across the table.

He looked at her. '– No. Why should there be?'

'There's obviously something on your mind. For one thing you forgot your dinner tin when you went off this morning.'

'Oh – yes,' he said. 'Anyway, I managed all right.' He paused. 'I got something at the farm.'

Silence. Blanche watched him as he gave his attention to the food on the plate before him. He ate as if he had not eaten all day – which, she thought, was probably the case. When he had finished eating and she had made the tea she said suddenly, unable to keep it back any longer:

'Ernie – you weren't at the farm today. I know that because I went there to take you your dinner.'

He looked at her, a child caught out. He said nothing.

'I called at the farmhouse to ask where you were,' Blanche said. 'I saw Mrs Hanworth in the yard. I asked where I could find you and she said she had no idea – you were no longer employed there.'

After a moment Ernest nodded. 'What else did she say?'

'She said you hadn't been at the farm for a few days.'

He stared down at his cup. 'Hanworth asked me to take less money,' he said after a moment. 'I told him I couldn't. Good God, it was hard enough to manage on the little I was getting as it was. He had his own men, though, he said. And he had me over a barrel – he said there's plenty without work on the farms these days – that's why so many are flocking to the cities. I told him I couldn't accept less, though.'

'– And . . . ?'

Ernest shrugged. 'So – I'm out of a job.'

'Oh, Ernie . . . Why didn't you tell me?'

'I couldn't. I thought I'd get another job first – then I could tell you about it – once the other business was all behind us.'

'Have you had any luck – finding other work?'

Gloomily he shook his head. 'There's so much unemployment around these days. Too few jobs and too many men looking for 'em.'

'So what have you been doing during the days while I thought you were at the farm?'

'Well – I've been going the rounds of the other farms – and the rest of the time I've just been sitting on the heath.'

'Waiting till it was time to come home – so I wouldn't suspect the truth.'

'Something like that.' He gazed at her for a moment, his eyes intense, then he added: 'I'll find something soon, Blanche, don't you worry.'

'I'm sure you will. Anyway, until you do at least we've got my bit coming in. It's not much but it'll help till you get something.'

She was smiling at him, but seeing his own grave expression her smile disappeared. 'What is it?' she said. 'There's something else . . .'

'The cottage,' he said. 'We've got to leave. Hanworth said he wants it for his own employees.'

She felt her heart sink. 'How long . . . ?'

'The end of next week. Saturday noon at the latest. I was going to tell you all this tonight, anyway. I couldn't have kept it back from you any longer.'

'Oh, Ernie.' Blanche felt overwhelmed by the weight of the depression that fell, settling on her. 'What are we going to do?'

'What am *I* going to do? you mean. Don't worry, I shall be all right.'

'It's both of us, Ernie. It's not just you.'

'You'll be all right, Blanche. You can go back to Hallowford House. You won't be homeless.'

'Well, I'm sure I could, yes, but – without you? I can't leave you with nowhere to go.'

'I told you – don't worry about me, Blanche. I shall manage all right. And if I can't find any work I can always go for a soldier. The way things are going out in South Africa it looks like they could do with all the help they can get.' He reached across the table and briefly pressed her hand. 'We'll be all right, Blanche, you'll see.'

Late in the morning a few days afterwards John Savill arrived at the cottage. He had expected to find Blanche ready to agree to his proposal, but to his surprise he found her reluctant even to discuss the matter.

'I don't understand,' he said. 'What's the matter? Has something happened?'

They stood facing one another in the little front parlour. After a little hesitation Blanche told him of Ernest's having lost his employment at the farm. 'He's trying to find another job,' she said, '– *and* somewhere else to live. Uncle John – how can I leave at a time like this? I can't just – forsake him. How could I do that – leave him here to fend for himself?'

'But Ernest is not a child.'

'Of course he's not a child. But I'm all he has left in the world. And how could I leave him to look after himself when I'm living in comfort just a few miles away.'

'I'm sure he wouldn't want to hold you back.'

'No,' she said, '– that's the last thing he'd do. He'd be the first to urge me to go. All his life he's always thought about others.' She shook her head. 'I can't leave him. Particularly now when things are so uncertain.'

'Where is he now?'

'He went to Trowbridge to look for a job there.'

'Well, when he gets back tell him to go and see my brother at the mill. There'll be a job for him there.'

'I've already suggested that this might be a possibility. I'm afraid he's not very amenable to the suggestion.'

'Oh, too much pride, is that it?'

Blanche gave a resigned little nod, then she said brightly: 'But he'll find something. He's very determined and very able. It won't be long.'

'And until he does? What will you do – sleep out in the fields?'

When she didn't answer, Savill said: 'Listen, I've got a cottage in Hallowford that will be empty for a few weeks. At least have that until you find somewhere else to live – if you're both determined to be so stubborn.' He gave a slow shake of his head. 'And what will happen when Ernest *does* find a job, Blanche? When he *does* get back on his feet?'

'Well – then I'll be able to do what I choose. But until then – I have to stay with him.'

Savill said: 'What you feel for your brother is pity, Blanche – and that's not the best foundation for happiness.'

'No, Uncle John,' she said quickly, 'it's not pity. I love Ernest. Not only that, but right now he needs me. Later, when he's settled about his job, then I'll think again about what I want. But for now I have to think of him.'

Savill gave a slow, resigned nod. 'I can see that in your present frame of mind you're not going to see things differently.' He sighed. 'Anyway, let me know if you want the cottage.'

'I will. And thank you, Uncle John.'

He put his arms around her, held her for a moment. 'Don't thank me. I want what is best for you.'

Blanche remained sitting near the parlour window after Savill had gone from the cottage. Then, hearing a faint noise she turned and saw Ernest standing in the doorway, Jacko at his side.

'Hello,' she said, '– when did you get back?'

'Oh – just this moment.'

She smiled at him, but his returning smile didn't quite hide the look of melancholy behind his eyes.

'Did you have any luck?' she asked.

'No – not today.' He came on into the room. 'I'll try again tomorrow.'

'Mr Savill was here,' she said after a moment.

'Oh? Yes?'

'He said there's a job for you at the mill, if you want it.'

Ernest looked away. 'I don't want to work for Mr Savill.'

His answer came as no surprise to her. Nevertheless she asked, 'Why not?'

'Oh, Blanche,' he said, 'how can I go and work for him when things are the way they are with you and him?'

She had guessed that this would be his answer. She said, 'He's also offered us a cottage in Hallowford for a few weeks. Until we find somewhere else.' Seeing Ernest's frown, she quickly added: 'We've got to live somewhere, Ernie.'

'You mean *I've* got to live somewhere. You can go on back to Hallowford House.'

She was silent for a moment, then she said:

'What makes you so sure that I *want* to do that? Where will it get me if I do?'

He sighed. 'We've been through this before. For one thing you'll be living in comfort. Admit it, Blanche, this

369

isn't the right home for you. You deserve something better than this.'

'Meaning that you don't?'

'Ah, but I'm used to it. This is the only kind of home I've ever known. That's not the case where you're concerned.' He moved to the window, stood staring out across the tiny front garden onto the lane. 'Thank Mr Savill for me,' he said, 'but I'll manage without his charity.'

Blanche felt a flash of anger at his words, at his pride. 'How?' she asked. 'How will you manage?'

He remained gazing out. 'I'm going away,' he said.

'Away?'

'Away from Colford. Away from Wiltshire.' He shook his head. 'There's no money in farming – not for a common farmhand, anyway. I'll never amount to anything if I stay here. I shall be twenty-nine come October. Twenty-nine – and what will I have to show for it? What have I got to show for God-knows-how-many years' hard work? Nothing. I ain't even got a roof over my 'ead that I can be sure of. It's no way to live.'

'But – but where will you go? What will you do?'

'I shall go north.' He turned to her now and she saw the determined set of his mouth.

'I shall get work in a factory – in one of the cloth factories there.'

'You could work in a cloth factory here in Trowbridge.'

'Trowbridge!' he said scornfully. 'You don't realize it, Blanche, but the West Country's almost finished now when it comes to wool production. Oh, yes, it's jogging along, but its heydays are *over*. If you want to make money now you've got to go where the big factories are – where they can *really* go into production. And production can only come from machines.'

'There are machines here,' Blanche said. 'Mr Savill has machines at his mill.'

'I don't mean a *handful* of machines, Blanche. I'm talking about the great factories full of them.'

'Well, in time they'll have them here too, won't they?'

'Oh, yes? How will they drive them? You need power to drive machines. Which means coal. Which is why they build the factories where the coal is to be found. In Leeds and Bradford and those other Yorkshire towns. *They're* becoming the centres now. Look at East Anglia – they've got no coal supplies and their wool industry's dying on its feet. And the West Country's not much better.'

'We've got coal in the West Country, Ernie, haven't we?'

'Ah, a bit, but nothing to compete with further up north. And that's where I'm going. Leeds or Bradford or somewhere like that. That's where the money is.'

'You always said you'd stay on the land. You said you'd never work in a factory.'

He shrugged. 'Times change. I've got to do something. I can't stay here and starve. You know, Blanche – I've heard stories of factory men in Yorkshire walking round with pound notes stuck in their 'atbands.'

'You sound – determined, Ernie.'

'I am.'

He sat down, bent to stroke the dog's head. 'We'll have a good life, eh, Jacko, boy?' Jacko's tail thumped the floor. Blanche said after a moment:

'I'm coming with you, Ernie.'

'You? Come with me?'

'Why not? I can work as well as you.'

'Ah, I daresay you can, but . . .' He shook his head. 'I never thought of you coming along, Blanche.'

'Does that mean you don't want me to?'

'No, of course not. It don't mean that at all. It's just that I never considered it.' He paused. 'It might not be easy at first, Blanche. Times might be hard till we got established.'

'That's all right. I'm strong. And I'm as determined as you are. I can put up with a lot when I have to.'

'But, Blanche . . .' He frowned. 'I thought you'd stay on here. Go to live at Hallowford again. Surely that's the best place for you, isn't it? And Mr Savill wants you to go back that badly.'

'Yes, I know, Ernie, but – well, I've thought about it, and I want to make my own life. It's time I did. I can work up north as well as down here. Children need teachers there as well as here. And if I can't teach I'll work in a factory like you. With two of us working in a factory we could earn good money, couldn't we?'

'Oh, ah, I daresay.'

'So . . . ? Will you take me with you?'

He studied her for a moment, one hand abstractedly stroking the dog's head. Then, smiling, he said, 'I reckon you're set on it, are you?'

'Yes, I am.'

'Then we will.'

'Oh, Ernie!' Blanche got up, a brightness in her eye at the thought of the opportunities that were to be theirs. 'When shall we go?' she said.

'What about your teaching at Ashton Wick?'

'I'm not due back there yet. I can write to Mr and Mrs Andrews. I'm sorry to let them down, but it can't be helped.'

'All right, then.' Ernest shrugged. 'We've got to be out of here in another two or three days, so we might as well go straight away. We can start in the morning.'

They spent the rest of the evening making plans.

They would go to Leeds, they decided. As they sat at the table, counting out the little money they had saved, Ernest said, looking at the coins near Blanche's hand:

'That's your sovereign. The one Mr Savill give you.'

'Yes. What about it?'

'Oh, Blanche, you can't use that.'

'Why not? This is no time for sentimentality. We're going to need every penny we can get.'

When they had counted up their money they reckoned they would have enough to take them to Bradford by train and pay for lodgings for a few weeks till they earned their first wages and got on their feet. Later in the evening after Blanche had packed a few belongings into a bag she wrote to Mr Savill and to Mr Andrews, telling them that she was going away. She would post the letters on the way to the station, she said. Looking at Ernest as he stood packing some of his belongings, her attention was suddenly caught by Jacko who stood close to Ernest's feet, clearly bewildered at all the unaccustomed activity. 'Ernie,' Blanche said, 'what shall we do about Jacko?'

'We'll take him with us,' he said.

'Even on the train?'

'Why not? Dogs travel in trains. They ride in the guard's van. And I daresay they've got dogs in Bradford.'

They prepared for bed early that night, ready to make an early start. As they stood facing one another on the tiny landing at the top of the stairs, each carrying a lighted candle, Ernest said:

'I'll wake you at six-thirty. That'll be time enough to get to the station.'

'Yes.'

'So you sleep well.'

'You too, Ernie.'

He put out a hand, gently touched her cheek. 'You're a good girl, our Blanche.'

He gazed at her for a moment then leaned forward and awkwardly kissed her a peck on the cheek. It was such an unaccustomed gesture on his part that it took Blanche by surprise. She smiled and gave a little nod. 'Tomorrow,' she said, 'we'll take the first step, Ernie – towards our fortunes.'

'Ah, that we will.'

'Well – goodnight.'

'Goodnight, Blanche.'

With Jacko at his heels, Ernest turned and went into his bedroom. Blanche watched his door softly close and then went into her own room.

She lay awake in bed with dreams of the future going through her mind. It was time she got away from Colford and Hallowford. No matter how much Uncle John wanted her back at Hallowford House she could not see any future there for herself. She had to make her own future. From now on it was up to her. At last she slept.

She was awakened by the barking of Jacko. She sat up in bed and looked at her watch on the small, cheap bedside table. It was almost seven. Ernest had overslept. Quickly she got out of bed and, pulling on her dressing gown, left the room and knocked on Ernest's bedroom door. There was no answer. She knocked again, and called his name. Still getting no response she opened the door. The room was empty.

Starting down the narrow stairs she called to him. Still no answer. Entering the kitchen she found it empty but for Jacko who stood tied by a rope to the leg of the kitchen table. At the sight of her he strained to reach her as she went past him into the scullery. Ernest was not there, neither was he in the front parlour. Nor was his bag, or his overcoat. There was, though, on the kitchen table, a letter, addressed to her.

Her hand shaking slightly, her heart thumping, she took up the sheet of notepaper, unfolded it and read the words that he had written.

My dear Blanche,

This letter will come as a great shock to you, and I'm sorry to be the cause of so much disappointment. By the time you read this I shall be well on my way, and there will be no point in your trying to catch me up. This is the only way, Blanche – you must realize that – for me to go on my own. It will be easier for us both. You won't be held back by me anymore, and you'll be able to go and live with Mr Savill again, which is what you should have done. I, on the other hand, will do better alone. I shall find success much faster if I'm on my own – and I do intend to find success, you can rely on that. And you can also rely on the fact that once I'm settled and am doing all right I shall write to you. Then, if you care to, you can come up north to join me. It won't be long till I do – and I shall, I promise you that. I promise you faithfully.

In the meantime, look after yourself. I'm sorry to desert you like this, Blanche, but I hope you will understand and won't think too badly of me. And please, look after Jacko for me. I can't explain to him as I can to you, and he'll miss me, I know. Still, I know I'm leaving him in safe hands. If only I could tell him it'll only be a while and we'll be back together again. I must go. Forgive me, Blanche. Just be patient for a little while, then

you'll hear from me and we'll have everything we
want.

Until then you'll always be in the thoughts of
Your loving brother,
Ernest

When Blanche had read the letter she read it through
again. Then she laid it down on the table and, moving
to the dog who was agitatedly whining, pleading to be
set free, she bent to untie the rope that held him. As
her fingers worked at the knot she murmured:

'He's gone, Jacko. Ernest – he's gone without us.'

Chapter Twenty-Nine

When Blanche released Jacko from the rope that tethered him, he ran to the door, scratching at it, whining to be let out. Then, when she opened the door he dashed out into the yard, round the house and into the lane. She stood there watching as he sniffed around, seeking Ernest's scent. And all at once, finding it, he took off, dashing away along the lane.

Later she made her way to Trowbridge station. On her arrival she not only learned that Ernest had been there earlier and had bought a ticket for Bradford before taking the train, but she also found Jacko there, sitting silently and unmoving on the platform, waiting as if at any time Ernest might return. She had taken his lead with her and after attaching it to his collar she coaxed him reluctantly away, bringing him back again across the fields to the cottage.

If she had imagined that that was the end of it where the dog was concerned, however, she was mistaken. Whilst worrying herself over what she should do and where she should go, she also had the added pain of seeing Jacko moping about the house, wandering from room to room. Very swiftly the dog set up a pattern in which he would climb the stairs to Ernest's room, circle the room and then come back downstairs where he would move from the kitchen into the scullery, then pad back through the kitchen and into the front parlour. There he would go to the window where, rearing on his hind legs, forelegs on the window frame, he would gaze out along the lane, eyes and ears alert for the slightest sign. Five or ten minutes later and the whole pattern would begin again. Watching the creature's worried movements, his continual searching, Blanche thought she would go crazy. 'Oh, for God's sake, Jacko, be still!' she cried out to him after observing the pattern of his repeated searching for the tenth time. '*He's gone! He's gone! He's not coming back!*' The dog turned to her, looked up at her with sorrowing eyes, then after a moment moved on again, his search continuing.

From the day Ernest and the dog had found one another they had never been separated. Now Ernest had gone and Jacko's world had come to an end.

As time wore on it was as if the dog realized that his master would not return, and, as if resigned, his prowling ceased and he lay down beneath the old sideboard, head on his paws, dark brown eyes open, looking at nothing. When, later, Blanche put down food for him, he ignored it.

Jacko's lack of appetite, however, was not her only concern; she had other things on her mind – one of which was the problem of where she was going to sleep come Saturday night. Her searches revealed no shortage of rooms available in the area, but it was finding a house where she was also allowed to take the dog that proved the difficulty. She knew very well that she only had to go to Hallowford House and there would be a welcome for her, but she could not bring herself to do so. She must, she felt, strive to keep her independence; she had taken so much from John Savill in the past; she could not go seeking his charity now at the first crisis.

Eventually, after searching around and making inquiries, she at last, late in the afternoon, located a house on the edge of Ashton Wick where there was a room for rent and where she could take Jacko with her. It was a small cottage, humbly furnished, but the middle-aged owner, a widow, a Mrs Grimshaw, had a kind heart, and a soft spot where animals were concerned.

'He can sleep in the shed,' Mrs Grimshaw said. She studied the dog as he stood at Blanche's side, tethered by the lead. 'He'll be all right there, will he?'

Blanche nodded. She was sure he would, she said. Then, looking down at the animal she added, 'He won't eat.'

At the suggestion of Mrs Grimshaw, who was obviously concerned, the dog ended up sleeping in Blanche's room. Not that Jacko seemed to care one way or the other where he was. He showed no interest whatever in his surroundings or in what was happening to him. He was perfectly obedient, as always, but all his accustomed eagerness and energy had gone. And although he drank the water that Blanche set before him he continued to refuse whatever food she offered. As the days passed she watched him wasting away, his strength and energy fading before her eyes. It was as if with Ernest's departure, so had gone all the animal's will to live.

Crouching before him as he lay on the floor beneath the window, Blanche tried to tempt him with some scraps of lean meat that Mrs Grimshaw had brought for him. The dog took no notice. With tears in her eyes, Blanche pleaded with him. 'Oh, for God's sake, Jacko, do eat – *please*. I can't bear it. If you don't eat you'll die.' But still he lay there, only moving to make occasional trips into the garden, and Blanche watched his energy draining away, and the fear grew within her that he would soon be dead.

But then at last, after several days had passed and she had given up all hope that he would eat, she watched one afternoon as he sniffed at the food she placed before him, and then, to her joy, as he took some in his mouth and ate.

With tears of happiness and relief swimming in her eyes, she watched as he finished the meat. She knew now that he would be all right.

Blanche and Jacko remained as lodgers in Mrs Grimshaw's little house until June. And then it was that John Savill discovered something of Blanche's circumstances and at once went to see her. After learning of Ernest's departure he set out to persuade her to return with him to Hallowford House.

She eventually agreed – and not a little gratefully – though making it clear that the dog must go with her, and that she also wished to continue with her teaching of the Andrews children at Ashton Wick. Of course Savill agreed at once – though where the dog was concerned he thought what a sorry-looking thing it was – a lack-lustre, docile creature, lacking in any degree of spirit. Blanche, however, he quickly found, was fiercely protective of it and determined that it should have the best possible care.

On an afternoon in July John Savill and his brother Harold sat in the library of Hallowford House as Blanche entered the hall. Hearing her footsteps John Savill called out to her.

'Is that you, Blanche?'

A moment later Blanche, carrying her light coat, appeared in the open doorway. She had just returned from Ashton Wick. Smilingly she greeted the two men where they sat on either side of Savill's desk.

'How was your day today?' Savill asked, and Blanche replied to the effect that it had been much as other days. After a pause she asked whether there had been any post for her. Savill replied that there had not. She thanked him, and left them, and Harold remained turned in his chair to watch her trim, retreating figure as she crossed the hall and started up the stairs. When she had gone from sight Savill crossed to the door and closed it. As he turned he said with a shake of his head,

'Her brother – Ernest. She's heard nothing from him since he left.'

'That was in the spring, wasn't it?'

'Yes, back in April.'

'And there's been no word from him?'

'Nothing. Blanche believes he went up to Leeds or Bradford – but there's no way of knowing. Naturally she's worried by his silence.'

Savill moved back across the room and stood at the window and looked out onto the lawn. Behind him Harold said:

'What's going to become of her?'

At the words Savill turned to his brother. 'I don't know. I wish I knew.' He paused. 'What I'd like is for her to meet some young man and make a good match. She'll make somebody a fine wife.'

Harold nodded. 'And she's attractive enough.'

Savill turned to him. 'Attractive enough? Harold, she's a beautiful young woman – or haven't you noticed?'

Harold smiled. 'Yes, of course.'

Savill sighed. 'Perhaps I'm hoping for too much too soon for her. After all, she's only nineteen. There's time for her to meet someone. I suppose that with Marianne settled I want the same for Blanche too.'

Harold said, frowning slightly: 'Are you sure that Blanche expects you to be concerned for her in this way?'

'Whether she expects it or not,' Savill said a little

sharply, 'I *am* concerned. How can I not be? She's been a part of our lives here for many years. We love her and I have a responsibility towards her – whether or not she wants it. Which is why I'm going in to Trowbridge to see Baron this afternoon.' He shook his head. 'I should have done it years ago, made legal provision for Blanche, but I always put it off. No more, though. All that business with her going off to live in that little cottage really brought it home to me. I've got to make sure that she's provided for. Marianne's all right now. Her worries should be over. But Blanche's situation is very different.'

Harold nodded then said, 'It won't be long before Marianne and Gentry are here, will it?'

Savill smiled. 'Not long.'

'And then, next month, the wedding.'

'Yes.'

'And then what? Marianne will return to Sicily to live, I suppose?'

'Of course. That's where Gentry's home is – where his future work will be.'

'How does Marianne feel about that?'

'Happy enough, I believe. But there, she's very much in love. I don't think it would matter much where she went as long as she was with Gentry.' He sat down at his desk. 'Gentry, though, she writes, is talking about going off to fight in South Africa – which of course makes her very unhappy. Still, we seem to be having better fortune out there of late, so perhaps the war will soon be over and he'll no longer feel obliged to join in.'

In the kitchen Blanche saw to the feeding of Jacko, after which she took him outside. Leaving the house behind her she walked out onto the road for a little way and then left it to walk on the heath. Walking slowly along one of the narrow, bracken-fringed pathways that bisected the heath, she watched as the dog moved back and forth, sniffing here and there, ambling back to her to check on her continuing presence, and then trotting off again – though never going very far away. Observing him, she thought again of Ernest's departure. Every day she expected to hear from Ernest, wherever he was. There would be a letter telling her how well he was faring, and then he would be sending for her to join him. And when that happened she and Jacko would go to him, and together they could make a new start. So far, though, there had been nothing, no word at all. She was certain, however, that she would hear in time.

In the meantime she could only wait. And the days were passing. It was mid-July now; in a few days the two Andrews children would be leaving to spend a summer vacation at the seashore. Blanche then would be left to her own devices. Later, Marianne would be returning – with Gentry – to be married. After which Gentry would take her back to Sicily.

Blanche thought back to the time when she and Gentry had met on the bridle path near Colford, and with the thought she saw him in her mind again, so clearly. It was not new to her, the memory; it would come to her unbidden, often when she lay wakeful in her bed. And at those times she would think again of how they had lain together in the primrose-dotted grass; for brief, tantalizing moments she would be able to feel again the sensation of his body on hers, his closeness; know again the scent of him, the sweet taste of his open mouth on her own. When the memories dissolved they would leave in their wake a sweet, lingering ache. She would be glad, she said to herself, when Marianne and Gentry were married and were settled in Sicily. Until then, anticipating Gentry's arrival in Hallowford, she found herself increasingly disturbed by the thought of him.

Taking a circular route by means of the network of narrow paths, her steps took her towards the road once more. As she emerged from the wildness of the heath and turned in the direction of Hallowford House she saw a pony and trap coming towards her, with Harold Savill at the reins. As the trap drew near he pulled on the reins and the horse and vehicle came to a halt.

'Hello, Blanche.' He smiled at her and nodded towards the dog that came to her side. 'Taking your friend for a walk, I see.'

'Yes.'

Observing the man, Blanche unconsciously reflected that he was very unlike his older brother. Like John Savill he had always appeared a cheerful and good-natured man, but whereas John Savill's handsome features had aged with a fineness over the years, Harold's face had grown coarse, his complexion florid. Now his appearance was in keeping with his liking for brandy which she had noticed on various seasonal occasions.

Now Harold said:

'John was telling me that you've heard nothing from your brother, Blanche.'

'No, I'm afraid not.'

'Well,' he shrugged, 'it takes time to get settled some-times. And I'm sure he's not finding everything easy.'

'I don't suppose he is.'

'You'll hear in time, anyway.'

She nodded.

'Would you really like to go to Bradford to join him?' he said. 'Work with him?'

She gave a little shrug. 'I've got to do something, Mr Savill.'

'Yes, I know, but . . . Those mills, those factories in Bradford and such places – by what I've heard they don't offer an easy life.'

'I don't expect an easy life.'

'I mean there is a great deal of misery there. You're bound to get it where so many of the poorer people go flocking. They're not all going to make their fortunes.' He studied her, frowning slightly. 'Wouldn't you be better off staying here, Blanche?'

'In Hallowford?'

'It's not perfect, but you know what they say about the devil you know . . .'

She didn't answer. He added:

'And your roots are here.'

'No.' She said the word quickly, and he looked at her in surprise.

'No? You seem very positive about that.'

She gave a sigh, shrugged. 'I don't think anyone could understand, but . . .'

'I might,' he said.

'– When I'm here in Hallowford I don't know where I belong,' she said. 'And where are those roots you speak of? I think I'd have to go away from here before I could think of putting down roots. I need to find a place of my own, somewhere that belongs to me.'

He nodded. 'You'll find what you're looking for one day, Blanche.'

Leaning down from his seat, he reached out and gently pressed her hand. Then, straightening again, he clicked his tongue, flapped the reins, and the pony started forward.

Blanche turned and watched as the trap moved away along the road, then set off back towards Hallowford House, the dog at her heels.

On reaching the yard of the house she found John

385

Savill saddling one of the cobs in readiness to ride into Trowbridge. James, the groom, he said, was ill in bed with the 'flu and it was easier to take one of the cobs than to prepare one of the carriages. He was going to see his solicitor, he said. He wouldn't be long.

When he had climbed into the saddle Blanche walked beside him as he rode the cob across the yard, and opened the gate to let him out into the lane. She watched then until he had ridden out of sight.

At seven o'clock Mrs Callow came to Blanche asking what should be done about dinner as Mr Savill had not returned. They would wait, Blanche said; he would be back soon. She was concerned, however; he had said he would not be long, and it was unlike him to stay out longer than he had planned.

At seven forty-five Blanche told Mrs Callow again to delay dinner and went downstairs and across the yard to the lodge where James lived with his wife and small daughter. James's wife, Annie, who worked as one of the maids at the house, told her that James was in bed. 'Shall I get him up, Miss?' Annie asked, to which Blanche replied no, leave him where he was.

Out in the yard again she debated for some moments on what to do, then hurrying to the stables she saddled up the other cob and led it out of the stable. After mounting she rode the pony out of the yard and set off down the road, after some distance turning left onto a bridle path that led towards Trowbridge.

After travelling on the path for a mile or so she looked across the adjoining fields and, feeling her heart lurch, suddenly caught sight of the cob that John Savill had ridden. It stood alone in the middle of a field, quietly cropping the grass. Turning the head of her own mount she set off, riding beside the hedgerow until she reached the solitary pony. Dismounting, she tethered her own pony and then walked steadily towards the other, speaking calmly to him as she moved. He was unperturbed by her approach, and she was able to take his bridle and lead him back to the edge of the pasture. 'Well,' she murmured as she tethered him to a tree beside the other cob, 'I've found you, but where is Uncle John?'

With the aid of a nearby tree-stump she managed to mount her cob again and leaving the other tied to the tree she set off across the field, all the while casting her eyes about for any sign of John Savill.

It took her over an hour of searching, moving about the adjoining fields surrounding the spot where she had found the cob, but at last she was rewarded. At last, in the late, fading evening light, she came upon him, lying beside a low hedge.

'Uncle John!'

Quickly she dismounted and hurried to his side. His eyes were open and he was looking at her. He gave her a faint smile and murmured her name. Her heart thudding, she bent over him. He lay with his left leg bent beneath him. 'The cob took off with me, and threw me,' he breathed, his breath catching, and Blanche said quickly, 'Don't talk. Don't try to talk.'

She could see at once from the distorted position of his leg that it must be broken.

'Uncle John,' she said, 'I must go and fetch help. I'll have to leave you here for a while.'

'Help me first,' he breathed, grimacing with pain. 'My leg. Help me to straighten my leg.'

Gritting her teeth, she bent and, while he cried out in pain, she pulled the broken leg into something like the right position. The contour of the leg through his trousers was alarming, though, and lifting the blood-stained trouser-leg she could see the bone protruding through the flesh.

Taking his cravat, she tied it around his leg, above the wound, and with the use of a small, sturdy twig taken from the hedgerow, tightened it, secured it there. It would slow or stop the bleeding for now. She pressed his hand, straightened.

'I'm going to fetch help, Uncle John. I'll be as fast as I can.'

He nodded, grimacing as another stab of pain shot through his injured leg. Blanche remained gazing down at him for a moment longer, then turned and hurried away. Minutes later she was riding as fast as she dared back towards Hallowford House.

James, roused from his bed, fetched help from a gardener who lived close by and together they took a cart and brought John Savill back to the house where he was carried upstairs and put to bed. Dr Kelsey was sent for, but he was away, and an ageing doctor, Soames, from Ashton Wick was sent for in his stead. Later, after the bone had been set and Savill had been left in some degree of comfort, the doctor spoke to Blanche in the hall.

The break had not been a clean one, he said, and the setting of it had proved no easy matter. He hoped, however, there would be no complications. He left saying that he would return the next day, and that in the meantime the patient should be kept quiet and warm.

When the doctor had gone from the house Blanche knocked softly on Savill's door and entered. Moving to the bed she stood gazing at him. As she did so his eyes opened and he looked up at her and smiled.

'I thought you might be sleeping,' she said softly.

'No, not yet.' He smiled. 'Has the doctor gone?'

'Yes, a minute ago.'

In the silence that followed Blanche found herself astonished at how old Savill looked. She had not been aware of it till this moment. Now, though, he looked more than his seventy years – suddenly he was a very old man lying back on the pillows.

'I came to see if you wanted anything,' she said.

'No. No, thank you, my dear.'

'Nothing?'

'No.'

'I'll wish you goodnight, then.'

'Goodnight, Blanche.'

'Ring if you want anything.'

'I will.'

She leaned down, kissed his cheek. 'Goodnight, Uncle John.'

The doctor called again the following day. In the meantime Harold Savill had been informed and had come to the house. He was there again, having driven over from Trowbridge, when Dr Soames called once more three days later. This time neither the doctor nor John Savill seemed as happy with the progress of the injured leg.

After spending some time examining the patient, Dr Soames went to the library where Harold Savill waited.

'How is he?' Harold asked. 'I noticed a – a faint smell when I was in his room. Coming from his leg.'

Soames's expression was grave. 'The trouble is,' he said, 'the break was not a clean one – which is surprising in a man his age. With a fracture like that, though, where the bone is virtually splintered . . .' His voice trailed off, and he shook his head. 'I'm afraid the healing process is not so efficient as one grows older. And you must understand that the flesh was badly lacerated by the broken bone, and –'

'What do you mean?'

The doctor looked at him for a moment then said: 'I'm afraid the wound has begun to mortify.'

When the doctor had gone Harold went into the bedroom where his brother lay in bed, propped up against the pillows. A nurse had been brought in, a woman from the village, and on Harold's entrance she excused herself and left the room. Standing near the bed Harold could detect again the faint smell coming from the bed. Savill's voice came to him.

'Don't stand there. Come on in.'

Harold moved to the bed, Savill gazing at him as he approached.

'Has Soames gone?' Savill asked.

'Yes, a minute ago.'

'What did he say?'

Harold said nothing. Savill looked up at him for a moment then shook his head on the pillow and gave a deep sigh. 'Oh, Christ,' he breathed.

'It'll be all right,' Harold said. 'Give it a little time . . .'

'Time.' Savill shook his head. 'Time will do for me. I knew what he was about there. Prodding at my leg like that. In some places I couldn't feel a thing. I can smell it too. The flesh is dying on me.'

'He's going to bring a surgeon in – a Mr Tindal. He's one of the best surgeons around.'

'What's he going to do that Soames can't? It's too late.'

'Maybe they can stop it.'

'Maybe.'

'Anyway – Tindal will know what to do for the best.'

The surgeon, George Tindal, completed his examination of Savill's leg, and then, his expression grave, told Savill that the gangrene had gone too far to be halted. The only thing to do was to amputate the leg.

'I suppose there's not much choice,' Savill said after a few moments.

'I'm afraid there's *no* choice,' said Tindal.

'– When will you do it?'

'This afternoon. It must be done as soon as possible if it's to be effective.'

'Where will you do it?'

'I can do it here – if there's a room downstairs I can have prepared.' He laid his hand on Savill's shoulder. 'You'll have the best possible treatment, I promise you.'

'Thank you.'

There was a little silence, then Tindal said: 'I understand you have a daughter . . .'

'Yes. She's in Sicily right now. She's due home very soon.'

'When? When is she due back?'

'Well, not until –' Savill's words halted, and he gave a brief nod and an ironic smile. 'Yes,' he said, 'I suppose it's as well to be prepared for all contingencies.'

When Soames and Tindal had gone away to make their preparations Harold went into the room. The smell was so much stronger now, and he swallowed against the sickening odour. Savill said as he drew near:

'You'd better send a wire to Marianne. Nothing to alarm her, but ask her to come home.'

'Yes, of course.' Harold paused. 'Did the doctors suggest it?'

'Tindal did.'

'Oh, but, John – don't you –'

'Tindal's a realist. And I must be too. Or try to be. I know that modern medicine is a wonderful thing. And I won't feel anything, I know that. But I also know that

I'm not a young man, and that it's possible that my body won't survive such an assault. I'm seventy, Harold – not seventeen.' He paused. 'Send a wire to Marianne, like a good fellow, will you? Not that it would do much good in the long run, I'm afraid, it – if something went wrong. She couldn't get back in time.'

Harold left the room and returned a little later to say that he had written a wire and that James was riding into Trowbridge with it. Savill thanked him, then, gesturing, said:

'Close the door and sit down. I have to talk to you.'

Harold did as he was bidden. When he was sitting at Savill's bedside, Savill said to him:

'If anything should happen to me I shall expect you to take care of Marianne's interests until she marries or comes of age – whichever is first. Her marriage, almost certainly.'

'Whatever you wish.'

'It's all set out in my will, anyway.'

'Yes.'

Savill paused. 'And there's also the matter of Blanche . . .'

Harold waited. Savill went on:

'As you know, when I fell I was on my way to keep an appointment with Mr Baron, my solicitor. I wanted to make sure that Blanche is provided for.'

'I know.'

'It's got to be taken care of. As I said to you, I should have done it a long, long time ago, so it's imperative that it's done now – before it's too late.'

'Of course. What do you want me to do?'

'There's no time to send for Baron from Trowbridge now. So if you could get some paper and a pen – I must make a codicil to my will.'

Harold fetched paper, pen and ink and then at his

brother's dictation, wrote down a codicil to his last will and testament. In it provision was made for Blanche, to the effect that upon Savill's death the sum of £10,000 was to be placed in trust for her until she came of age. In the meantime the interest on the sum would bring her an income which would make her life considerably easier. When the document had been completed, and John Savill's signature on it witnessed by the cook and Mrs Callow, he handed it to his brother asking him to put it safely with his other papers.

'You'll probably find that I'll outlive you all,' he said; then, with a sigh of relief and satisfaction, he added, 'I should have done that years ago. Still, it's done now, and now I can feel easy in my mind.' Later on Savill sent for Blanche. She knocked, entered the room and moved quietly to his side. The smell of mortifying flesh was stronger than ever, in spite of the disinfectant with which it had been treated.

'You know they're going to operate on my leg,' he said as she stood beside him.

She nodded. 'Mr Harold told me.' She had to fight back the tears. Seeing them shining in her eyes, Savill raised a hand. She took it between her own two hands.

'I've had a wire sent to Marianne,' he said. 'Though I shall be all right.' He gazed up at her. 'You've been like a daughter to me, Blanche. And like a sister to Marianne. I won't forget it.'

'Uncle John . . .' Blanche swallowed over the lump in her throat.

'Don't worry about me. I told you – I shall be all right – and I'm in very good hands.'

Savill was operated upon late that evening, in the wash-house which had been temporarily adapted to an operating room. Afterwards, still unconscious, he was taken

393

back to his room and put to bed. Blanche, going quietly to his bedside at the suggestion of the surgeon and Harold, looked down at him as he lay there, an old man, pale and shrunken, a shadow of his former self.

Soon afterwards, with precise instructions to the nurse as to Savill's care, Tindal, accompanied by his assistant, left the house. After seeing the surgeon off the premises Harold Savill sent the servants to bed and went into the hall where Blanche sat alone.

'Everything depends on the next few hours,' he said.

Blanche nodded. 'He *will* be all right, will he not?'

'We can only hope and pray.' Harold looked at her, seeing the concern and sorrow in her eyes. 'Go to bed,' he said. 'It's almost midnight. You can't do any good sitting up worrying. Go and sleep.'

She shook her head. 'I don't think I could.' She sat staring ahead of her. If Uncle John died . . . The changes in her life were occurring so fast. Her mother's death, Ernest's going away . . . and now, John Savill . . .

'What are you thinking?'

Harold's voice broke into her thoughts and she raised her head to find him gazing down at her, a strange, rapt look in his eyes. She shook her head. 'I think I'll make myself some tea,' she said, 'and then perhaps try to get some sleep.'

Getting up, she went to the kitchen where she boiled a kettle and made a pot of tea. She was sitting on a chair waiting for the tea to brew when suddenly the door opened and Harold entered. She gave a little smile of relief.

'I'm sorry,' he said. 'I startled you.'

'It's all right. It's just that the house is so quiet.'

'I thought I might join you – as you were making tea.'

'Of course.' She set out another cup and saucer,

poured the milk. Harold, watching her actions, said quietly:

'My brother's always much concerned about you, Blanche.'

She shrugged. 'Oh – he has no need to be. I manage all right.'

'Oh, I'm sure of it.' His eyes had not left her face. 'What do you plan to do?'

She shrugged. 'I'm not sure that I have any plans.'

'Perhaps you'll marry . . .'

She smiled. 'Oh, I should think that's most unlikely.'

He moved towards her as she spoke and she found herself a little disconcerted at his proximity.

'You haven't got anyone in mind?' he said.

'No.' Avoiding his eyes she picked up the teapot. 'I should think this must be ready now.' She poured the tea, aware all the while of his eyes upon her. 'Will you have sugar?'

'No, thank you.' He gave a melancholy grin. 'We must have taken tea many times together over the years, and you haven't noticed even that about me.'

She said nothing. After a moment he said:

'If anything should happen to my brother I –'

Blanche broke in, saying: 'Oh, don't say that. He'll be all right.'

'Well, I hope so. But if he's not . . . Blanche, you're going to need someone to look after you, aren't you?'

She gave an awkward little laugh. 'I told you, I shall be all right. I can look after myself.'

'So you say. I'm not sure that you can, though. And a pretty girl like you . . .'

His hand came out and lightly brushed her hair. She flinched, but, sitting on the chair, could not escape.

'Don't be afraid,' he said. 'I'm not going to hurt you.'

'No, no, it's just . . .' She shrugged, at a loss. She

pushed one of the teacups nearer to him, but too quickly so that the tea slopped over into the saucer. He took no notice of the action, his hand moved to touch her hair again. 'You're a very beautiful young woman, Blanche – do you know that?'

She shrank back in the chair, and his hand left her hair, gently touched her cheek, lingering, caressing. She brushed his hand away and got to her feet. 'Please . . .'

'You're afraid of me,' he said. 'Don't be, please. I wouldn't hurt you, you must know that.' His hands came out towards her and she backed away. 'On the contrary – I'd take care of you. Would you let me do that? Take care of you?'

And suddenly he was right there beside her, his arms enveloping her, drawing her to him. As he bent his head to her she could smell on his breath the scent of brandy. Then his mouth was opening and his lips were pressing down on hers. She struggled in his grasp, twisting her body to escape, but he held on. With his face only an inch from her own, she was dimly aware of the mesh of broken veins on his nose and over his cheeks. 'Let me go,' she said, '– please.' He ignored her plea and held her closer, bending his head to kiss her again. Twisting her head to avoid his mouth, she said sharply, her anger erupting:

'Get away from me! Let me go!'

'Blanche . . .' His mouth was there again, wet and repellent. With difficulty she lifted her hand, placed it as a shield over her mouth. '*Let me go.*' She put into her voice all the loathing she could muster. 'You disgust me.'

His movements ceased. He held her for a few moments quite still, then, his hands moving to grasp her upper arms he held her from him, fingers digging into her flesh.

'Who do you think you are?' he said, his mouth twisting with his words. 'Who are you to act like some fine lady? *I disgust you*? Who are you?'

Blanche, seeing his hatred of her, was suddenly afraid. He went on:

'You're brought here, out of squalor – taught how to use a knife and fork, given an education, given fine clothes to wear and the society of your betters, and you think it entitles you to put on airs.' He shook his head. 'You're *nothing*. You've always been nothing, you always will be nothing, and you'll always *have* nothing. There's only one thing you're good for.'

With his last words he yanked her roughly towards him and pressed his mouth on hers once more, at the same time roughly fondling her breasts. For a moment Blanche was forced to suffer his kiss and his touch, but then, managing to pull back her head, she drew the saliva into her mouth and spat full in his face.

He froze and then drew back from her. As the spittle ran down his cheek he put up his hand and wiped his face.

'You're going to be sorry you did that,' he said.

As she watched him he turned and strode towards the door. Only then did they see the figure of the nurse as she hovered in the doorway. Harold came to an abrupt stop before her.

'What are you doing here?' he said sharply. 'How long have you been standing there?' Blanche could see his face turning scarlet with embarrassment.

'Oh, sir,' the nurse said breathlessly, 'I – I've been looking for you. It's Mr Savill . . .'

'Yes – what is it?'

She gave a shake of her head. 'I'm sorry, sir, but I'm afraid – he's gone.'

*

Later, in his room, Harold Savill took from his pocket the codicil to John Savill's will. He read through its contents and then carefully tore it into shreds.

Chapter Thirty

'There is something I have to ask you,' Harold Savill said. And then: 'Would you mind telling me what you plan to do?'

It was the morning of the day following Savill's death. Blanche, her eyes reddened from weeping, was going downstairs when she had come face to face with Harold who was on his way up. Coming to a halt before her, blocking her way, he had asked her the question, speaking very quietly, keeping the sound of his voice from the ears of any servant who chanced to be near.

'What do you mean?' Blanche replied coldly, at the same time backing slightly away from him towards the landing window.

'You don't need to be afraid,' he said. 'I'm not going to touch you again. I just need to know what you intend to do.'

'About what?'

'– Do you intend leaving?'

'Leaving here? The house?'

'Yes.'

'Do you wish me to leave?'

He was silent for a moment, then he said, avoiding her eyes, 'It would be awkward – when Marianne arrives. If you moved out suddenly just before her arrival she would wonder why.'

Blanche nodded. 'Indeed she would.'

'So?' He was looking at her now. 'Unless you intend to tell her what happened . . . ?'

Facing him, hating and despising him as she did, she wanted to say yes, she would tell Marianne, she would tell everyone – but she knew she could not. 'No,' she said. 'Marianne is my friend, and she'll have enough to concern herself with without adding to her grief.'

'How noble!' Harold said. 'But even if you told her d'you think she would believe you?'

Making no attempt to disguise the contempt that coloured her voice, she said, 'Oh, yes, she would believe me. You need be in no doubt of that. Marianne might be inexperienced, and naive, but even she has not escaped hearing some of the stories about you that have circulated over the years.' She paused. 'Also, she is very capable of forming her own opinions. Rest assured, she knows you better than you are aware.'

At her words his face paled and he made a sudden half-step towards her. She flinched, fearing for a moment that he might strike her. For a few moments they stood there in silence, then Blanche said:

'Don't worry – Marianne will not learn of it from me, you can be sure of that. For *her* sake I shall say nothing about it. Also, I shall remain here until she arrives, and then for as long as she needs me.'

Harold nodded while Blanche continued to gaze at him coldly. 'When she's here,' she said, 'we can put up the pretence for her sake. But make no mistake; don't be under any misapprehension as to my feelings for you. I loathe you, and the less I have to see you the happier I shall be.' Then after a pause she added, her voice very low, 'And if you ever come near me again I shall really make you regret it.'

His mouth moved in the cold semblance of a smile.

'Regret?' He shook his head. 'It's not I who's going to have regrets.'

'What else can you do to me?'

'It's not what I can *do*, but what I have *done*.'

'What do you mean? What have you done?'

'Ah,' he said, 'and that is where my true regret comes in – in that I can never tell you, and that you'll never know.'

With his words he turned from her and continued on up the stairs.

Marianne, accompanied by Gentry and his father, arrived in Hallowford to be greeted with the devastating news of her father's death. The wire informing her of his accident had intimated the gravity of the situation, but she had left Sicily before the wire relating the news of his death had arrived and had come to Hallowford in the desperate hope that he was still alive.

That night, not wishing to be alone, she shared Blanche's room, and in the silence she wept on Blanche's shoulder.

The wedding, of course – there was no question – would have to be postponed until some later time, and instead of shopping for her trousseau, Marianne and Blanche were driven into Bath to buy mourning.

After the funeral Blanche joined Marianne, Harold, Gentry and Edward Harrow and the servants in the library where Mr Baron, Savill's solicitor, made known to them the terms of Savill's will. Apart from small bequests to the servants and other individuals, the bulk of the estate went to Marianne, all property to be held in trust for her until her marriage or her coming of age at twenty-one – whichever was first – by Harold Savill, who was appointed her legal guardian. Harold, apart from being suitably rewarded under the terms of Savill's will, was also, on Marianne's behalf, to take complete control of the mill and all her other industrial and financial interests.

When the business was done Mr Baron replaced his papers in his briefcase. As he did so the others began to move out of the room. Marianne remained where she was for a moment or two, then, rising, went to the solicitor where he stood behind the desk, and indicated that she wished to speak to him privately. She waited until they were alone in the room and then said:

'Is that all – in my father's will? Is that the extent of it?'

He gave a little nod. 'That's the *essence* of the will. I avoided giving it all in strictly legal terminology as –'

Marianne interrupted him: 'There was nothing about Blanche – Miss Farrar . . .'

He shook his head. 'No, nothing. Your father's will was made many years ago, when you were a very small child.'

'Yes, I understood that. But there's nothing about Miss Farrar . . . ?'

'No, miss – she's not mentioned.' He opened his briefcase. 'If you wish to examine the document yourself you –'

Marianne waved away the suggestion. 'No,' she said. 'I have no reason to doubt your word. It's just that I always thought that he would make some provision for her. She was – very dear to him.'

Baron said, 'Well, unfortunately, miss, he didn't do so. I don't know whether you're aware, though, but when he met with his accident he was on his way to Trowbridge to meet me in my office. We had an appointment that afternoon. I don't know what he wished to see me about, but it is quite possible that it was about the terms of his will.' He shook his head. 'I'm afraid now that we shall never know.'

'No, I suppose not.' Marianne sighed, then smiled at him. 'I thank you, Mr Baron.' Then, assuming her unaccustomed role as mistress of the house, she asked him if he would stay to drink a glass of sherry before starting back to Trowbridge. He thanked her, but said he had other pressing business to attend to. With that Marianne showed him from the house.

Later, when the funeral guests had gone, Marianne spoke to Harold alone in the library. 'I don't understand,' she said. 'Papa made no provision for Blanche.'

Harold shrugged. 'So it appears.'

'But he loved Blanche. You know that. Why would he ignore her in his will?' She paused. 'Apparently he was on his way to see Mr Baron when he had his accident. If so, perhaps he intended to take care of the matter then. It's possible, isn't it?'

'Oh, indeed it is.' Harold spread his hands before her. 'But he did nothing, in the event. And if he did wish to make any changes in Blanche's favour we shall never know of them.'

'He never spoke to you on the matter?'

'No, never.'

Marianne was silent for some moments then she said:

'Uncle Harold, I know Papa would have wanted Blanche to benefit at his death. I know that as well as I knew him.' Briefly she paused, summoning the courage to assert herself. 'And – I want something to be done.'

He raised his eyebrows; her forthrightness was unexpected. 'Oh? Exactly what do you have in mind?'

'I don't know.' She gave a helpless little shrug. 'But *something*. Some interest in the mill, or some of my capital. Something has to be made over to Blanche, and as soon as possible.'

Harold said nothing. Marianne went on:

'I'd like you to write to Mr Baron so that we can

discuss it and make the best arrangement. Please – will you see to it?'

Harold sighed. 'Marianne, my dear,' he said, 'I don't want you to think that I'm being unsympathetic, but I'm afraid I can't allow this to happen. For your own sake I –'

She broke in, forcing herself not to lose her assertiveness: 'Uncle Harold, it's – it's my money, and I can do with it as I please.'

'It *is* your money indeed,' he said, 'but as for your being able to do with it as you please, I'm afraid that that is not so – and it will not be so while I'm your legal guardian. And I shall be your guardian until you marry or until you're twenty-one years of age. At the moment you are only nineteen, in addition to which your wedding plans have been postponed. Until the situation changes you must recognize the fact that you do not have control over your inheritance.'

She gazed at him wide-eyed. 'But – but it is what Papa would have wanted. You know that.'

'*How* do we know that, Marianne?'

'Of course we know it. You know how he loved Blanche. He loved her as a daughter.'

She waited. After a moment he said, a little stiffly:

'I'm sorry, Marianne. And I'm sorry that this has had to come up on such a sad occasion. But I think later on you'll understand – that I'm doing what I'm doing for *your* sake; I'm carrying out your father's wishes. As I said, when you are independent of my control you may do what you wish with your money and your property, but until then, and I must make it very clear, whatever decisions are made will be entirely up to me.'

He turned and started to the door. As he opened it Marianne said, her voice causing him to halt and turn back to face her:

'I shall have my way eventually, Uncle Harold. My marriage *has* been postponed for the present, but it will happen. And even if it should not, in a year and a half I shall be twenty-one. One way or the other I shall have control of what is mine – and when that happens I shall see that Blanche gets what is rightly hers.'

Harold did not answer. With the merest nod he turned and left the room.

Two days went by, days when to Blanche the hours seemed to drag. There was no lightening of the gloom that had prevailed since John Savill's death, and Blanche observed Marianne, Gentry and Harold Savill each in a different mood of melancholy and preoccupation.

Then, one afternoon when she sat alone in her room, there came a knock at the door and a moment later Marianne entered.

'Oh, Blanche . . .' Marianne came towards her where she sat by the window, mending a stocking.

'What is it?'

Marianne gave a deep sigh and sat on the edge of Blanche's bed. She looked on the verge of tears. 'Tell me,' Blanche said, '– what is it?'

'Oh, Blanche, Blanche,' said Marianne wistfully, 'I don't know what's happening any more.'

'What do you mean?' Blanche put down the stocking and the needle and thread. After a moment Marianne said:

'Gentry – he's thinking of going away.'

'Back to Sicily? But that's where his work is, where his home is.'

'No, not Sicily. To South Africa. He's talking about going off to fight the Boers.'

Blanche sat up in her chair. 'D'you think he will?'

'I don't know. He's talking about it – and he won't

405

let the subject go. He says that the war is dragging on and – and every man should do his part. I told him that it's not his responsibility, but he said it's every man's responsibility. Oh, Blanche, what shall I do if he goes?'

Blanche said nothing. The reports from South Africa were horrifying; the number of deaths from disease seemed to be taking a greater toll of the British forces than was the enemy. And if Gentry should go out there . . .

'You must tell him,' Blanche said, 'that he's needed at home.' She paused. 'What does his father say?'

'Oh, Uncle Edward talks against it, but I'm sure a part of him secretly approves. Anyway, whatever he said, it wouldn't make any difference to Gentry. I've discovered that much about him – he always goes his own way.'

Listening to Marianne's words, and thinking of Gentry's manner since his arrival she felt somehow that there might be another reason behind his talk of enlisting, a reason apart from any feelings of patriotism and duty – which naturally had their effect upon him. What it was, though, she did not know; she only knew that she had observed in him a restlessness and an unease that was making it difficult for him to settle. Something was on his mind, was preoccupying his thoughts. What it was, though, she could not begin to guess.

They had exchanged very little in the way of conversation since his arrival; in fact there had been a lack of communication to the point where it almost appeared as if Gentry was avoiding contact with her. On first becoming aware of it the knowledge had hurt, and she had nursed the wound in the silence of her room, wondering what was the reason for his ignoring her so – was it guilt over their past association? Later, attempting to come to terms with it, she had tried to behave as if nothing had happened. In time he would be going back to Sicily, and then later Marianne would go to him, for their marriage – and from that time onwards it was possible that he and Blanche would never meet again.

Now, though, he was speaking of going off to South Africa . . .

'If he goes,' Blanche said to Marianne, 'what will you do? Will you stay here?'

Marianne gave a groan. 'I don't know. I just don't want him to go.' She got off the bed, moved to Blanche's side. 'Blanche, I love him so.'

Blanche said nothing. After a moment she got to her feet, and stood at the window, gazing out. Behind her Marianne turned and said:

'I can't bear to think of him being away. I'm so afraid that – that something will happen to him.'

'You mustn't talk like that,' Blanche said, her voice sharp. Then, more gently, she added: 'It does no good. You must – must think positively about things.'

'I know that, Blanche, but – oh, what's the use. I know that if he's set on it I won't be able to dissuade him.'

After a moment Blanche said, 'Perhaps you should go back to Sicily to stay. After all, you like it there.'

Marianne nodded. 'Oh, yes, I do, and – well, Uncle Edward suggests I do that – if Gentry goes away. And if he *does* go, then my being in Messina, at his home – it would make it seem that I was a bit – closer to him.' She remained still for a moment, then gave a little shudder. 'I know something – I couldn't stay here alone with Uncle Harold.'

'Why?' Blanche turned to her now, looking at her with surprise.

Marianne, thinking of Harold's recalcitrance over her

407

wish to make provision for Blanche, said, 'Oh – I'll tell you one day. But anyway, you know I've never really liked him. And I couldn't bear the thought of having to live in the same house with him for any length of time.'

Marianne stood there for a moment longer, then stepping towards Blanche, reached out and wrapped her in her arms. 'Oh, Blanche, I'm so glad I've got you on my side.'

Blanche gave a little laugh. 'Marianne, it's not as bad as that.'

Stepping back, looking at her, Marianne said, 'Sometimes I feel that it is. Right now – when nothing seems to be going right.' She sighed. 'I do miss Papa so. Nothing will ever be the same now – without him.'

Blanche nodded in agreement. 'I know what you mean, and how you feel. But it will pass, in time. That's what they say: everything passes.'

'I suppose so. But it's waiting for that time for it to pass that can be so painful.'

The following day after luncheon Blanche, with Jacko at her heels, left the house and set off down the road towards the heath. She had asked Marianne to accompany her, but Marianne had an engagement in Trowbridge with Mr Baron, the solicitor.

It was a beautiful, warm day, with the sun shining brightly; against it the remembered atmosphere inside the house seemed dark and constrained. Halfway down Gorse Hill Blanche left the road and took one of the paths that led onto the wild, green acres of the heath. Just before her steps led her in among the dense shrubbery she turned and looked back up the hill, to the hill's brow where Hallowford House stood. It was good to get away from it; it was a place of such unrest. In contrast the heath was peaceful, and she let her footsteps take her along the paths without thought as to direction, at last coming upon a little glade where she found a soft, grassy spot in the shade. There, while Jacko sniffed around in the undergrowth, she sat down, removed her bonnet and then took from her bag a book. It did not hold her interest, however, and after a while she replaced her bookmark between its pages and set it down at her side. Lying back in the soft grass she was aware of Jacko giving up his exploring and coming to lie down at her side, then she closed her eyes against the bright sunlight that filtered through the leaves of the overhanging oak.

Several minutes later, against the sound of Jacko getting to his feet, there came the sound of a whispered voice, very close.

'Are you sleeping?'

She knew the sound at once, and opened her eyes to see Gentry standing above her, gazing down at her with a soft, slightly anxious look in his eyes. Quickly she sat up.

'Hello,' she said, a false note of brightness in her voice as she straightened her hair; then: 'What are you doing here?'

He crouched in the grass some feet away while Jacko came to him, thrusting his nose into his hands. 'It's not a coincidence,' he said after a moment. 'I saw you from the window at the house. I came down after you. I've been looking for you.' He lowered his intense gaze and gave his attention to the dog, stroking him, fondling his ears.

'Jacko,' he said, 'you're a good old dog.'

As Jacko wagged his tail Blanche said, 'Oh, yes, he is that.'

'And loves you a great deal, I'm sure.'

'Oh, well – yes, he loves me well enough. But I'm afraid I'm no substitute for Ernest.'

'No?'

'No. Ernest is his god.'

'Does he still miss him?'

'Oh, yes. I'm afraid a little light went out in him the day Ernest went.'

She watched for some moments in silence as Gentry continued to stroke the dog, then she said:

'Why did you come after me?'

He raised his eyes to hers. 'I had to see you – before I go.'

'You're going, then – to South Africa.'

'Yes.' He nodded. 'In the next day or two. If they'll have me.'

'Can you doubt it?'

He smiled and gave a little shrug. 'I suppose not.'

Silence. Blanche said: 'Why did you want to see me? Since you arrived with your father you've hardly exchanged more than a few words with me. And now here you are, seeking me out. I don't understand.'

Jacko moved away, wandering off into the surrounding shrubbery. Gentry watched him go, then said, 'It's taken me a while to understand it myself.' His hand plucked the blades of grass at his feet. Blanche watched him, taking in the fine lines of his profile, the darkness of his lowered eyes, his black hair, the tan of his hand as it plucked at the grass. Then he said simply, raising his eyes to hers:

'I keep thinking about you, Blanche.'

At the words she felt her heart lurch in her breast. She sat up straighter, gazing at him. 'Oh, Gentry . . .'

A moment later he was crouching at her side, so close. 'I can't get you out of my mind,' he said. 'I never stopped thinking about you.'

As if coming to, out of a dream, she gave a shake of her head. 'Gentry – don't – please. Don't say this.' She moved as if she would rise to her feet, but his hand came out and grasped her wrist. 'Wait, please,' he said.

She allowed herself to be held there, a willing prisoner, but tore her glance from his to look away. He released her from his grasp.

'Look at me, Blanche . . .'

He repeated the words, and after a moment she turned her face to him. His eyes burned into her own with an intensity that brought back to her the time when they had lain together among the primroses; so long ago . . .

'I want you,' he said.

'No,' she said, 'you love Marianne. You're going to be married to her.'

He gazed at her. 'Why do you think I'm going?'

She said nothing. He went on after a moment:

'I knew, as soon as I saw you again, that I was glad that the wedding had to be postponed. Seeing you, Blanche – after so long – it all came back to me. And I realized that all my thoughts of you in the meantime – they were – were based on what is *real*.'

'Gentry . . .'

'It was *real*, Blanche. It *is* real – what I feel for you. I love you.'

Blanche put her head in her hands. 'Oh, God . . .' She had not even dared to hope that she would ever hear such words. But now he was saying the words and, besides the joy she felt, there was pain.

'But Marianne,' she said, '– you love her. You must love her.'

'I love *you*.' He shook his head. 'I can't help it, Blanche. We can't direct our feelings, can we? In a way I do love Marianne – and I thought that those feelings for her would be enough to see us through, to make things work for us. But seeing you again – it's made me aware of so many things I tried to put aside, not face up to.' He gave a deep sigh. 'Do you think I wanted this to happen? Of course I didn't. How much simpler it would have been – for everyone – if I could feel for Marianne as I should, as I'm expected to. But I had to meet you, to fall in love with you.'

Blanche lifted her head and found him gazing at her. She became dully aware of the sound of the birdsong all around them; the rest of the world going on unmoved by his revelation. Then in their own silence he was suddenly falling to his knees, reaching out and wrapping her in his arms, drawing her to him. When he bent his head to kiss her she made no attempt to draw away, and a moment later his mouth was pressed on hers; and once again, after so long, she knew the feel of his mouth on her own. When he drew back from her and looked at her again he gave the smallest nod. 'I had no idea,' he said, 'that you would still feel the same way. But you do. I know you do.'

'*Yes*. Oh, Gentry, my darling, yes. Yes, yes . . .'

He kissed her again and she remained in his arms, she sitting, he kneeling in the dry summer grass. When reality came again, thrusting a way between them, she said, pulling back out of his embrace:

'Gentry, what are we doing? We're like two lunatics. What are we doing, fooling ourselves like this? Nothing can come of this but unhappiness. You know that.'

'Don't say that, Blanche.'

'You know it's true. It doesn't matter what we feel for one another. We'll never be together, you know that as well as I do.'

'It could be,' he said. 'It could.'

'Could it? Could you deny your father? You would get nothing if you turned away from Marianne. Nothing. He's had his heart set on your marriage to her for as long as I can remember. Could you really deny him?'

'– Yes, I could.'

Blanche nodded.

'Could you break Marianne's heart?'

She gazed at him, and watched as with her words he turned away. 'No,' she said. 'You could not. Perhaps you could bring yourself to defy your father, but this other thing . . .'

'Blanche –' he gave a helpless, tortured shake of his head, 'we can't live for other people. Aren't we entitled to find our own happiness?'

She did not answer. He moved his gaze back to her. His eyes were so dark, so intense. His arms moved to draw her to him again. 'I only know that I love you,' he breathed.

Lying in the grass, Gentry made love to her. For some moments one part of her mind resisted, trying to shut out the feel of his hands upon her body, the feel of his fingers removing the barrier of the fabric between them, the warmth and hardness of him as he pressed against her. But her own desire was too strong, and even while an echoing voice in her brain cried out that it was madness, she gave herself up to the overwhelming passion of the moment, to her needs, and to the love she felt.

Later, when it was over, they lay side by side in the grass. Above her own breathing Blanche could hear the sound of Gentry's breathing as it gradually slowed after his exertion. After some time she sat up and began to arrange her hair. Looking down at him, seeing his eyes closed, she said:

'It doesn't change anything, Gentry.'

He opened his eyes to her. 'No, I suppose not.'

'And now you're going away. And going away to fight.'

413

'I shall be back.'

'Will you?' She spoke the words with a sad little smile. Inside her head a voice whispered to him the words she could not say: *You might be killed, Gentry. You might die there of disease. If not you will come back to Marianne. Whatever happens I shall never have you.*

'Yes, I shall come back,' he said again.

'And who will you come back to?'

'Oh, Blanche . . .' He turned his head, closing his eyes, burying his face in the folds of her skirt. 'There's only one thing I'm certain of – and that is that I love you.'

'And I love you too, Gentry. But sometimes love just isn't enough.'

She got to her feet. 'So you go to South Africa to escape the problem for a while. Isn't that what you're doing? And what of Marianne and me while you're gone? Marianne will probably accept your father's offer and go back to Sicily with him. Have you thought of that? Marianne at your home in Sicily, you in South Africa and me here in Hallowford or somewhere close by. And what happens when the war is over and you come back?' She turned to look at him as he sat gazing up at her. 'And in the meantime we both wait for you, and pray for your safe return.'

PART FOUR

Chapter Thirty-One

Marianne and Blanche made their way side by side back up the hill towards Hallowford House, Jacko walking at their heels. They had been to the churchyard, carrying flowers which Marianne had placed upon her parents' grave, and which Blanche had placed upon the graves of her own parents and siblings. It was an early Saturday evening in August. At the roadside the bracken of the heath looked dry, while on the brambles the berries were green.

Hearing Marianne sigh as they walked along together, Blanche turned to look at her. The lingering sadness on Marianne's face was not due only to the visit to her father's grave. That afternoon Gentry had left the house – soon to be leaving England, sailing for South Africa. Once he had set his mind upon it he had wasted no time in putting his plans into action, and within weeks of voicing his determination he had joined the Grenadier Guards and, in the rank of lieutenant – the commission bought for him by his father – had taken leave of those at Hallowford House and set off to join his regiment. Blanche, having said her goodbyes to him in the house – and carefully keeping her feelings in check – had later stood at an upstairs window and watched as he and Marianne had got into the landau in preparation to driving into Trowbridge where he would catch his train.

And soon Blanche and Marianne themselves would

be leaving Hallowford House, Blanche to take up new employment, and Marianne to go back to Sicily in the company of Edward Harrow.

'There's nothing to keep me in Hallowford any longer,' Marianne had said as she had told Blanche of her intentions to return to Sicily. 'And I'd prefer to wait for Gentry's return there with Uncle Edward rather than stay here with Uncle Harold.'

Edward Harrow had tried to persuade Blanche to accompany them to Sicily and spend a holiday there, but with gratitude she had declined the invitation. She had to get back to work, she said, and get on with her life. Besides, she had thought, it was bad enough trying to cope with Gentry's departure on her own; it would be ten times worse having to see her own unhappiness echoed in Marianne's eyes.

Even though Blanche had decided not to accompany Marianne back to Sicily, Marianne's decision to go had nevertheless determined Blanche's actions. Knowing that she could not possibly remain at the house with Harold Savill in Marianne's absence – and he had stated clearly his intention of living there – she had decided to give up her employment as governess to the Andrews children and move further afield. So, to the disappointment of Mr and Mrs Andrews, she had given them a month's notice and set about advertising for another position.

The previous day, Friday, had seen her last day as governess to the Andrews children, and having taken her farewells of them she was now waiting to begin work for her new employer, a Mr George Marsh of Bath, to whose house she was to travel the next day.

Mr Marsh, a shopkeeper in the city, was a widower with an eight-year-old daughter, Clara. After answering Blanche's advertisement he had travelled to Hallowford

House to interview her. She had liked him at once, and had soon accepted his offer of employment – though instrumental in her decision to join his employ was the fact that he would allow her to take Jacko along with her. Had he refused she could not have accepted. Where Mr Marsh was concerned, however, she need have had no worries. He had owned dogs himself in the past, and after seeing Jacko and hearing a little about him he had put up not the slightest resistance to the dog's accompanying her.

'Are you looking forward to going to live in Bath?' Marianne asked now as they turned in at the main gates and started up the drive. She and Edward Harrow had delayed their leaving Hallowford House to coincide with Blanche's departure.

Blanche nodded. 'Yes – I think it'll be a good thing for me to get away from Hallowford for a while.'

'You know,' said Marianne, 'if you had remained with Mr Andrews you could have stayed on here at the house. And for as long as you wish – you know that.'

Blanche nodded. 'Yes, I know – but it's time I moved on.' She paused. 'There's only one thing that bothers me . . .'

'What's that?'

'When Ernest comes back – he'll look for me here in the village and in Ashton Wick and he won't be able to find me.'

'Don't worry about that,' Marianne said at once. 'He'll find you. Uncle Harold will be here and he knows where you'll be – as does Mrs Callow. Ernest will find you all right; don't worry.'

Side by side the two girls walked through the kitchen garden and into the orchard. Blanche said:

'You know – I think it will be good for me to go to a place where not everyone knows me. I'll have a better chance that way.'

'A better chance? Chance for what?'

'To – to make a life of my own . . .'

'Oh, Blanche,' Marianne said, 'I do wish you would come with us.'

'One day.' Blanche linked her arm through Marianne's. 'Not yet – but one day I shall come and join you in Messina for a long, leisurely holiday in the Sicilian sun.'

'Yes,' Marianne said. 'When Gentry comes back, when this awful war is over – and it will be over any day now, I'm sure – then we can be married, and you shall come to us whenever you want, and stay for as long as you like.'

At Marianne's words Blanche was aware of a sudden, sharp stab of resentment. Marianne blithely spoke as if Gentry belonged to her; she was so sure of him. Gazing at her, Blanche said to herself: But he loves *me*. He loves *me*.

Near the orchard wall was a rough-hewn seat and the girls sat on it side by side. The sun was sinking low in the sky. After a little silence Marianne said:

'There's something I want to say to you . . .'

'What's that?'

'Well – I don't know how you felt at the reading of Papa's will – whether you felt any – any disappointment at all . . .'

Blanche opened her mouth to protest, but Marianne continued:

'Anyway, I just want to say that his will did not reflect his true wishes. I know that, Blanche.'

'Marianne, please . . .'

'No, listen to me. I want to tell you that when everything is mine – *really* mine – I shall see that you have a part of it. I know it's what Papa wanted – and what he would have arranged if he'd been better prepared.'

She gave a little shrug. 'But he wasn't prepared, and so . . . Anyway, I shall do what he would have wished.' She laid her hand on Blanche's hand as it rested on her knee. 'Come December of next year we shall be twenty-one. And on my birthday I shall have control of what Papa left to me. When that happens I shall see that some of it goes to you.'

'Marianne, I –'

Marianne lifted her hand against Blanche's protests. 'It doesn't matter what you say. I've already decided. I shall have plenty of money – and Gentry will as well.' She pressed Blanche's hand. 'I want to make sure that you don't have to keep on working all your life.' She smiled, adding, 'And now we'll say no more about it.' Turning on the seat she looked back towards the house. 'You know, Blanche? – I shall probably never live here again.'

'No?'

'No. My home will be where Gentry's home is. And he'll want to stay in Sicily.' She turned back to face Blanche. 'Why do you look like that?'

'– Like what?'

'I don't know. A strange expression on your face.'

Blanche laughed. 'Oh, Marianne . . .'

Going back to her original thought, Marianne said, 'I don't think I'll miss it, though – Hallowford. Does that sound odd? But – oh, the house just won't be the same. Not with Papa gone – and you in Bath . . . And I have no interest in the mill. There's nothing for me here now.'

The next morning Marianne and Edward Harrow left Hallowford House, Blanche and Harold Savill waving them off from the front steps. As soon as the carriage was out of sight Blanche made final preparations for her own departure. Mr Marsh was sending a carriage for her later that afternoon. When it arrived she got in, and with Jacko beside her and her box safely under her feet, she left the house. There had been a brief, tearful scene of goodbye with Mrs Callow, the housekeeper, but she had said no word of farewell to Harold Savill. Where he was concerned she would be happy never to see him again.

Mr Marsh, his elderly mother beside him, was ready to welcome her on her arrival at the house, which was situated on Almond Street, a quiet street on the edge of the city. At once she was shown to her room on the second floor, Jacko afterwards being taken into the yard, to a kennel there that had housed a pet belonging to the family in earlier days.

Apart from Mr Marsh and his mother and daughter, the house held two servants, a cook and a maid. Marsh's draper's shop was situated a mile away near the city centre and every business morning he set off to walk to work. He was a quiet man of forty, with a gentle manner. Of less than average height, with a round face and receding hairline he was by no means handsome, yet Blanche was quick to recognize in him qualities of kindness and consideration. His mother, too, though a little gruff in her nature, was nevertheless of an essentially kind disposition. The personalities of the two were echoed in George Marsh's small daughter Clara, a shy, affectionate little dark-haired girl. In a very short time Blanche was convinced that if she could be happy in any kind of employment then her present situation was ideal.

And installed in her little room in Mr Marsh's house in Bath, she watched the time passing by, and the war dragging on. In the past the reported progress of the war had not really touched her. Now, though, knowing that Gentry was out there, she avidly followed the accounts in the newspapers. Of Gentry himself she learned what news she could in the letters that came from Marianne, who wrote to him regularly and received letters in reply. It appeared, judging by the news that Marianne passed on, that Gentry was making light of his experiences. Further, it was clear to Blanche that Marianne herself, living in Messina with Gentry's father, found it difficult to resign herself to Gentry's absence; her letters to Blanche were full of expressions of her love for him, and of how much she missed him. Blanche, in writing back to her friend, had to stifle any such expressions.

The Marsh household in Bath was by no means a luxurious one, and Blanche soon gained the impression that there was not a great deal of money to spare once all the expenses had been met. George Marsh had inherited the business, Marsh & Son, from his late father. And Blanche suspected that the business could very likely do a great deal better than it did. Marsh was an unadventurous man, however, unwilling to take any chances, and consequently – so it seemed to Blanche – opportunities were passing him by. But it was no concern of hers, she told herself, and for all the lack of luxury in the house she was as happy as she could expect to be under the circumstances.

She asked for very little. During the days she taught Clara, and in the evenings she often spent time conversing with Mr Marsh or his mother. At other times she was alone. Not that she had any wish to be otherwise – not with things as they were. The three people who meant most to her had gone out of her life. Gentry was on the other side of the world, fighting on some South African plain. Marianne was in Sicily, living in some villa in Messina. And Ernest? God knew where Ernest was.

Apart from her continuing concern at the lack of any word of Ernest, all Blanche seemed able to do was think of Gentry's safety and his return. Beyond that she seemed not fully to exist. And it was madness, she said to herself; for she could wait forever for Gentry to return, but when he did leave South Africa he would be returning not to her but to Marianne.

Chapter Thirty-Two

It was 1901, the first year of the twentieth century, and January brought in that first year – what should have been a year of hope and promise – with England still at war, and no sign of the war ending. On the 22nd of the month the Queen died, to be succeeded by her son, Edward VII.

Amid the respective sorrow and excitement generated by the death of one monarch and the advent of a new one the distressing reports continued to pour in from South Africa where the British troops were dying in their hundreds, the majority falling victim not to the actions of the guerrillas – who certainly claimed their share – but to disease, which had become endemic in most of the camps. Where the guerrillas were concerned, they were at last having things a little less their own way; for to combat the success of their actions Lord Kitchener was building chains of blockhouses and was denuding the country of its farms. Without bases at which to muster, the guerrillas were proving to be less effective.

In Messina, in Edward Harrow's villa on the fashionable Via Gabriele, Marianne waited impatiently for the war to come to an end. And she had soon found that being domiciled in Sicily was a distinct disadvantage where news of the war was concerned. The Italians, not being involved in it, gave relatively little space to it in the newspapers compared to the coverage it received in the British press. As a result, Marianne often found herself frustrated at the lack of news – though there was only one piece of news she wanted to hear, and that was that the war was over. And while she waited for such tidings she looked forward impatiently to Gentry's letters, and with the receipt of each one breathed a deep, heartfelt sigh of relief at the knowledge that, at least at the time he had written, he was still safe.

And the days and the weeks and the months passed. And like Blanche in Bath, Marianne felt herself to be in some state of limbo. If everything had gone according to plan she would be married now to Gentry and would be living with him here in the city. But instead everything had changed; everything had gone wrong; her father had died and Gentry had gone off to fight.

Apart from worrying about Gentry's safety, she also knew some other vague unease that touched her when she was least prepared. It had something to do with the tone of his letters. She had hoped for warmer words from him, more evidence of his love for her, in which she so needed to believe, and to which belief she so fervently clung. But then, she would ask herself, how could she expect him to write of passionate love when he was in such a desperate situation?

So, going from day to day, from week to week, and from month to month, she eked out the days of her existence, in a city in which she did not belong – where could she belong without Gentry? – and waited for the time to pass.

In Bath Blanche continued with her life as governess in the Marsh household. And she was happy there – or as happy as her circumstances would allow – and as the months passed she grew increasingly fond of Mr Marsh and his mother, and they of her – which fondness also took in Jacko, who soon had the run of the house. Blanche had developed, too, a warm relationship with Clara, a bright little girl who responded gratifyingly to the affection and care bestowed on her.

In the meantime she and Marianne continued to correspond regularly, but the periods between those times when Marianne was able to pass on news of Gentry seemed to Blanche to be never-ending, and as the days and the weeks stretched on the ever-present fear of his danger often made life seem unbearable. But then at last she would receive another letter from Marianne, and once more she would breathe easily – for a little while – then to begin to worrying again until she received further word.

As it did for many of those who waited through the anxious times of the war, the coronation of the new King that August seemed to Blanche as if it might as well be taking place in another country. How could she become involved in any celebration when Gentry was so far away and in such a perilous situation, and when she had no idea at all of where Ernest might be?

That autumn, however, one of her most heartfelt prayers was answered. Early in October she received a letter from the Transvaal. And at once, on glimpsing the handwriting, she saw that it had come from Ernest.

He had addressed it to her at Hallowford House, and Mrs Callow had sent it on to Bath.

After apologizing for not writing since leaving her in Colford he wrote that after spending a considerable time in Bradford – which experience he did not elaborate upon – he had decided to volunteer to join the fight against the Boers. Following his decision he had subsequently joined the Royal Wiltshire Fusiliers and had recently arrived in the Transvaal. He did not dwell on any of the miseries and discomforts which, Blanche was certain, he must be enduring, but devoted most of the letter to other, less distressing matters. Much of his letter concerned Blanche herself; and he was anxious to know how she had fared since he had left her. His last inquiry was of Jacko.

As winter approached Marianne wondered what to do as regards assuming control of her inheritance, for she would be twenty-one in December. She and Gentry would never live in Hallowford; Gentry had made that clear; his business interests were those of his father in Messina – in property, and in the soap factory. There was no future in wool in England's West Country, Gentry had said, and he was not prepared to give up Sicily for the damp climate of England. Marianne's intention, therefore, on reaching her majority, was simply to sell all her interests in England. But she would do nothing about it until Gentry returned. When he did, they would marry and he would assume control of the matter.

In the meantime, while fretting over what she should do, she received from her uncle, Harold Savill, a letter asking if she intended to return to Hallowford to assume her inheritance on the occasion of her birthday. After this inquiry his letter continued:

... Though, I must add, I hardly think that December would be a particularly good time to travel from Sicily to England. Also, if you intend to sell your property as you have intimated, I feel you would do well to wait until the spring; the dead of winter is never a propitious time for buying and selling in the property or industrial market – and particularly in the West Country right now where the comparative scarcity of certain resources, such as coal, has to an extent already devalued the wool manufacturing industry. Not that you need be concerned about the success of the Savill mills, however, for our progress is good. It is just that the general climate does not make the present time the most advantageous for buying and selling in such a market.

He ended his letter with advice to wait until the spring or summer and then review the state of the market before disposing of her assets.

Marianne was relieved to get his letter and was glad to take up his suggestion. She was regularly receiving her allowance from him, and she was glad now to avoid the necessity of having to take action without Gentry being beside her. Early in December she wrote back to her uncle asking him if he would agree to continue for the time being in his present role. She added:

As you suggest, I shall return to Hallowford in the spring or early summer. Whether or not I come alone will depend upon this dreadful war that just seems to drag on and on. I pray that it will be over soon, in which case I shall soon be married, and I shall of course travel with my husband. In the meantime I feel I cannot ask Mr Edward Harrow for help or advice as I am afraid he is not strong and I do not wish to burden him with my responsibilities. As for him travelling with me, I'm afraid that such a prospect is out of the question. The journey to England on the occasion of Papa's death exhausted him enormously and I could not dream of asking him to undertake the same rigorous journey again. However, as I say, I shall be there at some time in the spring or early summer, at which time, I am sure, you will be very pleased to be relieved at last of your responsibilities.

Thinking then of her promise to Blanche – which had never been far from her mind – she went on to inform him that she had determined upon making a settlement on Blanche, which would help to relieve Blanche's situation in her present limited circumstances. To this end, she added, she would be grateful if he would send her, Marianne, an account of her realizable assets so that during the coming weeks she could determine the extent of the settlement she should make.

Harold replied saying that he would draw up an account of her assets, and that in the meantime he would see that Blanche was provided for.

One December day soon after her twenty-first birthday Blanche and Clara prepared to set off to walk together to the centre of the city. The excursion was to be something of a Christmas treat for Clara, for they were going to see the brightly illuminated store-window displays with all the luxury of their Christmas goods – after which they were to take tea together in one of the tearooms. That done they would meet Clara's father at his shop, following which the three of them would return home.

The December day was mild and the sky was clear. On reaching the crowded town centre Blanche and Clara began to make their way from store to store, gazing into the brightly lighted windows, Clara frequently exclaiming in delight at the goods on display.

When they had looked around the shops for some time they made their way to a tearoom. On entering they found the interior crowded and Clara gave a little groan of disappointment. 'Oh, there's no room for us, Miss Farrar.'

'Be patient, dear,' Blanche said consolingly. 'There'll be a table in a minute or two.'

As her eyes moved over the occupied tables the sweep of her gaze came to a stop and she found herself looking into the eyes of a man who sat alone at the other side of the room. Hastily she looked away again. Standing there, however, she was aware, through her peripheral vision, of the man's eyes still upon her. And then he was rising, moving across the floor in her direction, coming to her side, stopping there.

'Excuse me . . .'

At his words, delivered with a slight accent, she turned to him. Expensively dressed, he looked to be in his late thirties. He was tall, with thick, dark hair; good-looking in a rather heavyset way. As she looked at him Blanche suddenly realized why she had noticed him: there was something familiar about him.

'Excuse me if I'm bothering you,' he said, 'but we've met before.' He smiled at her. 'You don't recall?'

A moment more and then recollection came to her. She smiled and nodded.

'Yes, of course. You're − you're a friend of Mr Harrow's. We met in London.'

He nodded. 'Alfredo Pastore.' His smile grew wider. 'It's Miss − Miss Farrar, isn't it? Miss Blanche Farrar . . .'

'Yes, it is.' With Alfredo Pastore's dark eyes smiling warmly into her own, Blanche put her hand on Clara's shoulder. 'And this is my friend, Miss Clara Marsh. Clara, this is Signor Pastore.'

Pastore bent slightly and briefly took Clara's hand. 'How do you do, Miss Marsh.'

As Clara smiled shyly in return the man said, glancing around:

'It's quite crowded in here. Will you come and join me at my table?' As Blanche hesitated he added quickly:

'Oh, don't refuse – for Clara's sake at least. I'm sure she'd like to sit down.'

Smiling, Blanche agreed, and Pastore turned to lead the way. Taking Clara's hand Blanche followed him as he threaded his way across the room. When they reached his table he took their coats and hung them up, and then asked what he could order for them. Consulted first, Clara, notwithstanding the season, said she would have a vanilla ice. Blanche ordered a tea-cake and some tea. When Pastore had attracted the attention of the waitress and had given the order he turned back to Blanche, smiling at her across the table. 'And now,' he said, 'tell me what you're doing in Bath.'

Blanche told him that she was living in the city where she was employed as Clara's governess. In return Pastore told her that he was in the area on business. 'My father had several commercial connections in Bath and the surrounding areas,' he said. 'But they're more or less finished now. I'm just here to finally wind them up.' When his work was done, he said, he would be returning to London before returning to Sicily.

'Palermo, isn't it?' Blanche said. 'If I recall correctly, your home is in Palermo.'

He nodded, pleased. 'I'm flattered that you remember so much about me.'

Blanche said, 'The trip to London when we met was a very special occasion for me. It isn't likely that I would forget it so soon.'

Pastore went on to say that he would be returning to Sicily in another month when he had finished his business in England. 'January is not the time to be in Britain,' he said. 'I prefer a milder climate.'

The waitress appeared then with the order. When she had gone again Clara concentrated on her vanilla ice while Blanche poured the tea. As they ate and drank she and Pastore chatted pleasantly together, until Blanche looked at the time and exclaimed that they had better be going.

'Oh, please,' Pastore said, 'don't go yet.'

'I'm afraid we must.' Blanche was taking coins from her purse to pay for their order – which payment Pastore refused, saying he wouldn't dream of accepting it. As he got their coats he asked where they were going, and on being told insisted on accompanying them.

The bill paid, the three left the tearoom and joined the throng on the pavements again where Blanche, holding Clara by the hand, led the way through the streets towards George Marsh's draper's store. On reaching its doors Blanche and Clara glanced in and saw Marsh busy at the rear of the shop. Quickly Clara left Blanche's side to go in to see her father. When the door had closed behind the child Blanche held out her hand. As Pastore took it she thanked him for the tea.

'It was a great pleasure for me,' he said.

'Well . . .' She smiled at him, releasing his hand. 'I must go in . . .'

'Oh, but – one moment . . .' He stood aside to allow a customer to get by. Blanche waited. He went on:

'I'd like to call and take you out – if you're agreeable, of course.' As Blanche hesitated he added: 'It would certainly be a great kindness to me, you can be assured of that. I don't know anyone in the area and I get rather tired of eating alone, and spending all my leisure time in my hotel room and taking long walks on my own.' He grinned. 'I enjoy my own company – but only up to a point.'

As he finished speaking the shop door opened and George Marsh appeared. Clara had told him of the man they had met in the tearoom and he had come to see for himself. Blanche introduced the two men and after they had exchanged the necessary pleasantries and shaken hands Pastore added that he was an old friend of Blanche's former guardian's business associate, and that he was in Bath on business for a few weeks before returning to Sicily.

The brief meeting between the men ended with Marsh inviting the other to come for dinner one evening. Pastore accepted the invitation with a little bow, after which they passed some further words of conversation and then Marsh, saying that he must get back to his customers, took his leave and went back into the shop.

When the door had closed behind Marsh, Alfredo Pastore said, 'Well – it appears that I have your employer's approval – so will you agree to help me pass a little of my time while I'm here in the city?'

Still Blanche hesitated. She had enjoyed the meeting, but she could see no point in repeating it. Before she could say anything further, however, Pastore was saying:

'You must have some free time. When is that?'

'Well, tomorrow, Sunday, but –'

'Then may we meet?' He paused, smiling. 'At least for the sake of auld lang syne – as you say.'

'Signor Pastore, I –'

'*Alfredo* – and say – at three o'clock tomorrow? I shall wait for you here.'

'Oh, but –'

He was backing away. 'I'll wait for you tomorrow.'

Without waiting for an answer he was turning, and with a final wave, melting into the throng.

Blanche had no particular interest in keeping the appointment with Alfredo Pastore the next afternoon, nor any special wish to do so; but the engagement had been made and she felt that she couldn't really do anything else but keep it. When she had finished getting ready she left her room and started down the stairs – near the foot to be met by Clara who, seeing her dressed to go out, asked if she might go with her. For a moment or two Blanche was tempted to say yes, but even as she briefly pondered the question it was settled by Mrs Marsh who, coming into the hall and catching the gist of the matter, told Clara that Miss Farrar needed a little recreation and that they would see her later.

Approaching the shop – shuttered for Sunday – Blanche found Pastore waiting for her. Smiling as he caught sight of her he moved forward to greet her, and Blanche, seeing the warmth of his welcoming smile, felt suddenly glad to be there. She had spent too long confined to the house, and it was good to get out for a while. It was good, too, she felt as the afternoon wore on, to be with someone as attentive and solicitous as Pastore proved to be.

Although crisp and cold, the afternoon was bright, and together they wandered into the park and strolled slowly along the paths. Afterwards he took her to a café where they sat over steaming cups of coffee and toasted muffins. He talked to her of Palermo, where he lived – a beautiful city, he said – and something of his business interests – sulphur mining, a growing interest in shipping, and the export of citrus, olives and soap.

He told her a little, too, of his personal life. He had been married once, long ago, he said, but his wife had left him to go away with a singer. He spoke of the man as 'a tenor with a second-rate opera company'. Some years after his wife's departure, he said, he had learned that she had died in a train accident.

His face betrayed little emotion as he spoke of his wife, her desertion of him and her ultimate death.

'You had no children?' Blanche asked him.

He shook his head. 'No.'

Having told Blanche something of himself he changed the subject and concentrated upon Blanche herself. He had been surprised, he said, not only to find her in Bath, but also to find her working as a governess.

Blanche said, 'As regards my work you made the mistake of assuming that I was wealthy, that I had no need for employment.'

'I suppose I did.' He shrugged. 'But – it doesn't matter, does it?'

'Not to me.'

Under some prompting from him, she told him a little of her own life. When she had finished he said: 'And where are you going now?'

'What do you mean?'

He shrugged. 'Perhaps you have certain plans.'

'Plans?' She frowned. 'What plans?'

'I'm thinking of your employer, Marsh.' He paused briefly, then observed: 'He's a widower.'

Blanche responded quickly: 'Signor Pastore – Alfredo – Mr Marsh is my *employer*. Nothing more.'

'Forgive me.' He sounded contrite.

'I have no plans or hopes of becoming the second Mrs Marsh.'

'Please – forgive me. I was impertinent.'

There was a little silence between them, then he said: 'But I still don't have an answer to my question.'

'Which was?'

'Well – what is to become of you?'

When she didn't answer he said:

'You're a very beautiful young woman, Blanche. And you're obviously clever, too. But here you are, working as a governess, while burying yourself in the domesticity of some quiet English family. Is that what you

436

want out of life? You could obviously have so much more.' Then quickly, before she could answer, he added: 'Or am I being impertinent again?'

'No, it's all right.' Avoiding his eyes she gazed down into her cup. He was right, she said to herself. Where *was* she going? Or could it be that she was already there? Could it be that everything that had so far happened had been leading her to this, the situation she was now in – that of governess to the draper's daughter? The uncertainty of her own life seemed to be unending. Was this *it*? Or was there to be more? Was this the end of her particular road?

Over the following days Blanche saw Pastore on several further occasions. On one evening he took her to the Theatre Royal to see Anton Chekhov's play, *Three Sisters*, which had opened in London so successfully earlier in the year. On another occasion he took her to a concert at the Corn Exchange where the pianist and orchestra performed the romantic, beautiful second piano concerto recently written by the young composer Rachmaninoff. When it was over Blanche had come away in a dream.

Now, on New Year's Eve, Pastore was to call for her to take her to dinner at one of the premier hotels in the city.

She had just finished arranging her hair when she heard the sound of a motor car coming to a stop outside the house. Moving to the window she pulled back the curtain and peered down. Such vehicles were being seen more and more frequently on the streets of Bath lately, but she knew no one who owned such a vehicle. Now, as she watched, she saw the driver, dressed in cap and goggles, muffler and long coat, get down from the vehicle and move towards the house. The ring of the front door bell echoed up the stairs, and a minute later the maid was knocking at the door and announcing to Blanche that there was a gentleman to see her.

'It's a Mr Harold Savill, miss.'

When the maid had gone Blanche stood quite still for some moments. What did Harold Savill want with her? She had seen nothing of him since the day she had left Hallowford House sixteen months before – though on her rare trips to Trowbridge she had heard various reports about him – reports of his often being seen in the company of various doubtful women in the area, and of his spending less and less time at the mill. Blanche might have gained some real knowledge of him through the occasional letters she exchanged with Mrs Callow. The housekeeper, however, obviously guided by loyalty and awareness of her position, had never volunteered news of her new master and Blanche had not been interested enough to ask.

Blanche made a final brief check on her appearance then left the room and went downstairs. On the hall table she saw Harold's cap and gauntlets. She found him standing in the library. He had not taken off his coat. As she entered he gave her a small bow. She nodded in return.

'Mr Savill . . .'

'Hello, Blanche.'

She did not ask him to sit. He studied her as she in turn studied him. He looked more dissolute than ever; his nose had taken on a purplish hue, his fleshy cheeks now covered with a mesh of broken veins. While she gazed in distaste at him he said:

'I must say you're looking well, Blanche.'

'I am – thank you.' She had no wish to do more than be polite. She was still wondering why he had come.

'A letter came for you at the house,' he said after a

moment's hesitation. 'Mrs Callow sent it on to you. I hope you received it all right.'

'Thank you, yes.' She did not want to share any joy with him, but she could not stop herself from adding: 'It was from my brother Ernest.'

'Good.' He nodded. 'And he is – safe, I hope?'

'Yes. I trust he is. I'm in touch with him quite regularly now.'

There was a little silence, then she added, 'I saw your motor car from my window. I couldn't think who would be calling here in a motor car.'

He nodded, pleased. 'Ah, yes, the motor car. The transport of the future. You know, in London they even have motor-run omnibuses now.'

'Yes, I know.'

He smiled. 'But that's not why I've called to see you.' Delving into one of his capacious pockets he drew out a roll of notes. 'Marianne,' he said, 'she's written to me from Sicily – asking me to see that you're all right – financially.' He held the money out to her. Blanche made no attempt to take it but instead stepped back half a pace.

'No,' she said. 'No, thank you.'

'Please.' He flourished the notes slightly. 'Take it.'

'I don't want it.'

'It's not from *me*, Blanche. I told you – it's from Marianne. I'm simply carrying out her wishes. I'm only her messenger. She's going to make some legal financial arrangement with her lawyer, she says. In the meantime I promised I'd bring you this. Please, take it.' When she still hesitated, he said, 'It's thirty pounds; it's not a huge fortune.'

After another moment of hesitation, she stepped forward and took the money from his hand. 'Thank you.' Then she added: 'I'd better give you a receipt.'

He waved the idea aside. 'Don't bother. It's not necessary.' Already he was moving past her towards the door. 'I must go.' His mouth twisted in irony as he added, 'I don't want to wear my welcome out.'

Blanche followed him into the hall where she handed him his cap and gloves. Then she stood aside as he opened the door, let himself out and moved towards the front gate.

After she had closed the door she heard the car's engine throbbing into life and then the sound of the vehicle being driven away.

Five minutes later Alfredo Pastore had arrived in a cab to take her to dinner, and after first joining George and Mrs Marsh in a toast to the new year he escorted Blanche from the house.

Dinner at the hotel restaurant was a bright, festive affair, and Blanche enjoyed herself. They remained there till after midnight, on the first stroke of which they joined in the singing of 'Auld Lang Syne' and then toasted one another in champagne. Afterwards, with the first bells of 1902 ringing over the town, they set off to walk back to Almond Street. Pastore was soon to leave for London and Sicily.

'I shall miss you, Blanche,' he said, turning to look at her as they walked.

Looking up at him she saw the intense look in his eyes.

'Will you miss me too?' he said. 'Just a little?'

He had not spoken of, or even hinted at, any kind of special regard for her, and for a while she had naively told herself that his interest in her was as a result of knowing Edward Harrow. She had soon become aware of her naiveté, though, and had come to see him with new eyes.

'Will you miss me, Blanche?' he said again.

'Yes – of course.'

And yes, she would miss him, she said to herself. She would miss him for a while. He was a striking man, in his own way, and he had a warm, outgoing personality. And he was good company in these times when part of her mind was so concerned with anxieties over Gentry and Ernest. But for all that she liked him and enjoyed being with him, she could not return the affection he so clearly felt for her.

They were walking beside a park, and his footsteps paused and halted in the cover of a tall yew tree. Taking her arm he drew her gently towards him.

'Blanche . . .' He was gazing down at her. 'Listen to me . . .'

She wanted to move on, but she had to stand there, his eyes burning into her own.

'Blanche,' he said, 'by this time you must have gained some idea of how I feel for you.'

'Alfredo . . .'

'And you like me too, don't you?'

'Yes – of course I do.'

'You must do – or you wouldn't be here with me, walking with me on this cold night.' He pulled up the velvet collar of her ulster a little more closely about her chin. 'But I more than like you, Blanche. You must realize that by now.' His breath vapoured in the air. After a little silence he said:

'Blanche – I want to marry you.'

She gazed at him in astonishment.

'Will you?' he said. 'Will you marry me?'

She had not been expecting such a question and she was quite unprepared. 'Oh – Alfredo,' she said, shaking her head, 'I can't – I can't . . .'

'Why not?'

'– Oh, Alfredo . . .'

'I know it has come – very suddenly to you. But I mean it, Blanche. With all my heart.' He paused. 'Perhaps I'm being foolish where you're concerned, but I can't help it. I have to speak now because I have so little time. I must return to Palermo, you know that.' He paused. 'Marry me, Blanche. Marry me and come with me.'

She shook her head. 'Oh, Alfredo, I'm sorry. I can't – can't marry you.'

'Don't you feel anything for me?'

'Of course. I like you very much.'

'But you don't love me,' he said. Then he shrugged. 'But that's all right. I don't expect everything at once. You could learn to love me in time, I know you could. Just give it a chance.'

Wrapping his arms around her he drew her close to him, bent his head and kissed her. His kiss was firm, insistent. As he drew back his head a moment later he murmured. 'I love you, Blanche. I never thought I could say that to any woman – after what happened with my wife, but . . .' He gave a wondering little shake of his head. 'From our very first meeting in London I was attracted to you. I never expected ever to see you again, but I did. Suddenly, there you were in the tearoom. It was – as if it was fate. We were meant to meet again, Blanche, I know we were.' His ungloved hands lifted, gently touched her cheeks. 'And now that I've found you I don't want to let you go.'

She did not answer. He said again:

'Marry me, Blanche, please. Tell me you'll marry me, and let's leave for Sicily together. We could get a special licence and be married at once. I'll look after you. You'll never have to work again. Living in Marsh's dingy little house – you deserve better than that. And I can give you better. Come with me. You'll love Sicily.'

'Alfredo – I can't marry you.' She shook her head. 'I'm sorry, believe me.'

He gazed at her with his disappointment in his eyes, then he said: 'Is there someone else?'

How could she speak of Gentry? She shook her head.

'Well, then,' he said with a little nod of satisfaction, 'there's a chance for me. And I shan't give up. I shall ask you again when I come back to England.'

'– Please, I –'

'There's nothing you can say that will deter me, Blanche. I know you'll love me in the end.' His arms came around her again, drawing her to him. 'You will be mine some day, I know that.' He smiled. 'And you might as well accept the idea too.'

Chapter Thirty-Three

When Marianne did not receive her monthly allowance for February at the anticipated time, she was not overly concerned, expecting it to arrive any day. When March came and she had still not received it – and now the March payment was also due – she wrote to her uncle to remind him of the situation. Three weeks went by, however, and there was no word from him. Puzzled at the silence she then wrote to Mrs Callow, asking whether her uncle was sick or whether there was some other reason to account for his silence. Mrs Callow replied to the effect that he had left the house towards the end of February, saying that he had to go away on business. She had heard nothing from him since that time, she added, though a great deal of post addressed to him had been delivered to the house.

Growing a little uneasy, Marianne then wrote to Mr Baron, her father's solicitor, asking him if he knew what was happening. Baron's reply was extremely disquieting. He wrote that he had not handled the Savill legal affairs for some time, and that such matters were being handled by another firm, *Dusop, Marlin and Sams*. He was somewhat surprised, he said, that Mr Harold Savill had not mentioned the matter to her. However, he would make some discreet inquiries as to her uncle's where-abouts, he added, and would communicate with her as soon as he was able to find some answers.

The communications back and forth between Sicily

and England took time and it was the end of May before she heard anything further on the matter. Judging by what he had been able to discern, Baron wrote, the situation appeared somewhat clouded. Certain things were clear, however, he added, among them being that no one seemed to have any idea where Harold Savill was at present, and also that there appeared to be a great deal of confusion over the Savill business affairs. He ended his letter by suggesting to Marianne that she return to England as quickly as possible, and that in the meantime, if she wished, he would assume responsibility for her legal affairs and do what he could to clarify the situation. Marianne replied that she would like him to do this, and that she would return at once.

Saying nothing to Edward Harrow of her real concern, she merely told him that she wished to return to England to take charge of her affairs. He insisted that she take with her one of the maids to assist her on the journey. She agreed and immediately set about preparing for her return.

The next day, *en route* to Calais, she bought a newspaper at one of the railway stations, and discovered that Britain's war with the Boers was over.

The Peace of Vereeniging, on 31 May, had put an end to the conflict. The Boers had accepted British sovereignty, in return being promised representative government and £3 million for restocking their denuded farms. The cost of the war had been high. The vanquished Boers had lost 4,000 killed in action against nearly 6,000 of the victorious British troops. Further swelling the numbers of Britons lost were some 16,000 who had died from disease.

It was George Marsh who brought the news to Blanche and she wept with happiness. The fighting was over. From now on Gentry and Ernest would be safe.

Soon afterwards she received a letter from Ernest saying that he expected soon to be sailing for England. To her great disappointment, however, he added that on disembarking he would go back to Yorkshire for a while where he had a good job waiting for him. 'But you'll hear from me again soon,' he said, adding that he would write to her when he was settled, and then come south to see her.

The day after receiving Ernest's letter Blanche heard news of Gentry's impending return.

That Saturday, having taken Clara to the shop to meet her father, Blanche had got into conversation with one of his customers, a woman whose son, Blanche discovered to her secret joy, was in the same regiment as Gentry. And, she learned from the ecstatic woman, her son – along with the rest of his regiment – was due to sail for Bristol the following day on board the *SS Maine*.

Blanche hugged the news to her. *Gentry was coming back*, and for a little while, before going on to Sicily, he would be in Bristol – so close, so close.

Later, in the solitude of her room, with Jacko lying at her feet, she sat gazing, unseeing, out of the window. It was time now to face up to reality. The war had given her a brief respite from the knowledge of what must happen, but now it had to be faced. With Gentry's marriage to Marianne postponed and his being so far away she, Blanche, had managed to avoid the truth of the situation, hardly looking further than his safe return. Now, though, the war was over, and she must live again in the real world. And in that real world she had to face the truth, and in that truth he had promised himself to Marianne.

Over the following days the newspapers were full of news of the returning victorious troops, and of the movements of the transport ships. If victory had been hard won at least the war had ended and the survivors were returning – albeit many of them wounded, or sick with disease. And Blanche, though so deeply involved, felt left out in the cold. Ernest was going straight to his promised employment in Yorkshire, while Gentry – whose ship, the *SS Maine*, was expected at Bristol within days, and whose imminent arrival was even reported in the morning paper – would waste no time in returning to Sicily.

And then, suddenly, in the schoolroom where she was teaching Clara, she found she could bear it no longer. She would go to Bristol. If she left today, now, she might be in time to meet Gentry's ship. What would happen if she did she did not stop to imagine; she did not think beyond her decision, her determination to meet him, to see him again.

Telling Clara to continue with her work alone for a few minutes, Blanche took the newspaper and went to see Mrs Marsh. Ernest's ship, she told her, pointing to the relevant item in the paper, was due to dock at Bristol. She would like to go and meet him, she said.

Mrs Marsh herself grew excited at the prospect. Of course Blanche must go to meet him, she said. 'Do you know *when* his ship is due?' she asked.

'No, but it must be any time now. It could be today; it could be tomorrow.'

'And you're sure that your brother is on it?'

'Oh, yes,' Blanche lied. 'He wrote that he would be.'

'And if the ship doesn't come in today – what will you do?'

Blanche shrugged. 'I'll find a hotel, and wait.'

In just over half-an-hour Blanche, carrying a small, hurriedly-packed valise, set off from the house. At the corner of Almond Street she managed to get a cab and within twenty minutes of arriving at the station she was on a train bound for Bristol.

As soon as she arrived in the city she took a cab to the docks where, amidst all the seeming confusion, she eventually found someone who could give her the information she sought. To her joy she found that she was not too late. The *SS Maine* was still a day out. It was estimated that it would berth sometime during the evening of the following day.

Holding on to the good news, Blanche then set off to find lodgings for the night, eventually securing a room in a small hotel not too far from the docks. That done it only remained to find some way of passing the hours until the ship's arrival.

She was afraid to stray too far away and the next morning found her making her way back towards the quays, there to begin her waiting. As the day wore on she was joined by others who had arrived to welcome the returning soldiers. Shortly after one in the afternoon she reluctantly hurried off to a nearby hotel to get something to eat, but less than half-an-hour later she was back on the quay, rejoining the burgeoning crowd of watchers who stood looking out across the sea.

And then at last, in the late afternoon, she saw on the horizon a little thread of smoke rising up. Eventually, as the ship drew nearer, she saw that it was the *SS Maine*.

She watched, almost breathless, as the ship slowly hove into the port, as it docked and was secured, and as, eventually, after what seemed an age, the gangplank was lowered. She found herself caught up in a throng that surged like the sea itself, carrying her forward while people cheered and cried out, and somewhere behind her a brass band played. Her head lifted, her eyes ran back and forth over the faces of the uniformed men lined up at the rails who stood looking over at the throng below. She could see no sign of Gentry.

The able-bodied soldiers had to wait for disembarkation, however. Down the gangplank stretchers were carried one after the other by bearers, some with female nurses in attendance. Blanche, trying to get close, but prevented from doing so by the crowd, was terrified in case Gentry was one of those borne on the stretchers and that he should be carried to one of the waiting ambulances without her knowledge.

Then, eventually, the last of the sick and injured soldiers had been helped from the ship and after a short delay the first of the able soldiers came down the gangplank, his kit-bag carried on his shoulder. One by one they descended, and as each one appeared Blanche's anxious eyes lighted upon his face, and she watched as each stranger passed by into the throng, many to be greeted there by anxious families and sweethearts.

And then all at once her heart lurched as her darting, eager eyes lit on the face of Gentry.

Not expecting to be met by anyone he was making no attempt to look into the crowd, but instead was looking ahead of him.

'Gentry . . .'

She cried out his name as she pushed her way through the waiting crowd, but her voice was drowned by the shouts and cheers and the continuing, blaring music of the band. She called out to him again, but still he did not hear. Suddenly there was desperation in her movements to get to his side, and the crowd in her path, hearing her calls and seeing the anxiety in her face, made way for her, and so gradually she was able to find a way through the dense body of waiting people. By the time she came anywhere near the foot of the gangplank, however, Gentry had left it and was striding off across the quay. Blanche hurried after him. Then she saw that he had stopped to say goodbye to one of his comrades.

Coming to a halt some feet away she watched as the two men affectionately clasped hands and clapped one another on the shoulder. A moment later the other young man was walking on and Blanche took a breath and called out Gentry's name again. He himself was just about to move away, but hearing the sound of his name he was held, and he turned.

They stood there looking at one another, Gentry gazing at her with a little frown on his brow, as if he could not believe what he was seeing. He gave a shake of his head. For Blanche the world around them might have ceased; they might have been standing alone, in silence.

Then he spoke.

'Blanche . . .'

She watched his mouth form her name. As if in slow motion she saw him swing his bag down from his shoulder and let it fall beside him. Tentatively his arms lifted towards her. A moment later she was running forward, reaching out for him, touching him. Then she was feeling his arms close about her as he held her fast.

Smelling the unfamiliar soldier smell of him, she raised her head to him, and then his hand, rough but tender, lifted and touched at the tears on her cheek. 'Don't cry, don't cry. What are you crying for?'

'Oh, Gentry, you're back, you're safe. You're back. You're here. I thought it would never happen.'

'Yes, I'm here.' He gave a little laugh, nervous, and kissed her again. They remained there for some moments, holding one another, then he released her, bent and took up his kit-bag and hoisted it up onto his shoulder. Putting his other arm around her waist, he led her from the quay, away from the crowd.

They found a coffee house and inside made their way to a corner table where they sat facing one another in their own silence, interrupted only by the appearance of the waitress who came to take their order. When she had gone away Gentry said:

'I can't get over it – your being here.'

'Are you angry?'

'That you came here?'

'Yes.'

He gave a wondering little smile. 'Oh, can you even think I might be?'

'I don't know anything any more.'

'How did you know I'd be on that ship?'

'I talked to someone – a woman whose son was in your regiment. She told me when your regiment would be returning and by which ship.'

He nodded. 'I thought that – that Marianne might have told you.'

'No.'

And now Marianne's name had been mentioned; the spectre at the feast; already Blanche could feel her presence there.

'I wondered,' she said, 'whether Marianne herself might come to meet you.'

'No, no.' Gentry was avoiding her eyes. 'I told her to wait for me in Messina.'

A little silence, then Blanche said, 'I shouldn't have come.' She looked down at her hands, clasped before her on the white tablecloth. 'What am I doing here? I must be mad.'

'Don't say that.' His large, sunburned hand reached out and briefly pressed her hands. And a simple touch like that was enough to increase the pace and power of her heartbeat and make her catch her breath.

'I couldn't stop myself,' she said after a moment. 'I had to come. Knowing you'd be here, getting off that ship – so close to Bath. I had to come.' She shook her head. 'I don't know why. Maybe – maybe it was just to see you one last time.'

Even as she spoke she knew she was lying – lying to herself as well as to him. She had not wanted to see him for a *last* time. She had wanted to *see* him, to be with him. 'I had to see you,' she said.

Their conversation was marked with little pockets of silence. The waitress brought the tea and scones they had ordered and went away again. Blanche poured the tea, handed a cup to Gentry, and watched as he stirred in the sugar. As he lifted the cup he looked at her over its rim. There was a look in his eyes she could not fathom. I'm treacherous, Blanche said to herself. I am betraying Marianne, my friend, my faithful friend. I am betraying a lifetime of truest loyalty and friendship with treachery. She watched as Gentry drank, set the cup down again.

'Oh, Blanche,' he said, 'what a sight for sore eyes you are. It's so wonderful to see you.'

She could feel the moments slipping away. There was so little time. Soon he would be leaving to continue his journey to Sicily, and she must return to Bath.

'I understand you're working as a governess in Bath, is that right?' he said.

'Yes.'

'And they allowed you a little time off, did they?'

'Yes.' She said nothing about having given the reason that she wished to meet her brother. 'I got here yesterday.'

Watching him across the table, so handsome, she was very much aware of a difference in his appearance. It was not the fact that he was in uniform. There was something about his face that she had not seen before. And it wasn't that he looked older, thinner; there was something else. There was a look of weariness there too;

in his eyes a look of experience, a look that told of the end of innocence; that same look that she had seen in the faces of some of the other young soldiers who had come down the gangplank, a look that told of a knowledge of death and destruction, that they had known happenings that had forever changed them, that ensured that in some ways they would never be the same again. And she cried out in a little choking whisper, while the tears came to her eyes, spilling over like a spring and streaming down her cheeks:

'Oh, Gentry, I love you so much.'

'Blanche, my darling . . .' And he was leaning forward, reaching out to her. 'Don't. Don't cry.' His hand was gentle against her tear-stained cheek. He took her hand and pressed his mouth into her palm. 'I love you too, Blanche,' he murmured. 'I couldn't stop thinking about you. I longed to write to you, to tell you, even though I knew it would have been madness. You were on my mind so much. I love you, Blanche. I love you.'

When she had collected her valise from the hotel they found another hotel where Gentry registered them as husband and wife. Blanche's gloves hid the fact that she wore no ring. In their room Gentry held her in his arms again. After a while in a feverish passion he undressed her, lifted her in his arms and carried her to the bed. Then, taking off his own clothes he lay down beside her, pressing his strong, hard body to her, his hands moving over her breasts, her smooth limbs while he kissed her soft mouth. Blanche, touching him once again, felt that she could never get enough of him, never know enough of the feel of him beneath her reaching, clutching hands as they moved over him, exploring once again, after so long, his lean, muscular form. And through it all the silence in the room was broken only by the sounds of their breathing and the endearments that escaped from their eager lips. And at last Gentry was covering her body with his own, and she felt his hardness enter her, begin to move within her.

When it was over and they lay side by side in the disarray of the linen sheets, their combined breathing slowing, she felt his lips touch her temple, her ear, and then heard his murmured words, 'I love you, Blanche. I always will.'

Later they went out to dine at a nearby restaurant where they sat facing one another across the table. They ate slowly, but savouring the time rather than the food – which was good, but might have been indifferent for all that it mattered. And often, and without apparent reason, they would touch, their hands moving across the tablecloth to light on the hand of the other, fingers brushing, or clasping, anything as long as there was physical contact. And in the light of the candles that flickered and wavered between them they gazed at each other, looking deep into one another's eyes. Once, as Blanche looked into Gentry's dark brown eyes he said to her, 'What are you seeing?' and she replied, without moving her gaze, 'I'm seeing into your heart, your soul.'

'And what do you see there?'

She avoided his question. 'You tell me,' she said. 'You tell me what I can see.'

'You must see that I love you. Anybody could see that.'

Alone once more, in the quiet of the hotel room, he stood at the window with the curtains drawn back, looking down at the gaslit street below. Without turning to Blanche he said, his voice soft, but firm with determination:

'I know now – I can't give you up. I must go to Messina at once and see Marianne. And I must tell her that she and I – we can't marry.'

He gave a deep sigh, and Blanche, watching him, hanging on his words, saw how he bent his head in pain at the prospect. She thought: It will kill her. Such words from Gentry – they'll surely kill her. But she thrust the thought aside, saying nothing. After a moment he went on:

'We'll be married, Blanche. As soon as we can.'

'– Yes, oh, yes.' She felt as if she could hardly breathe.

'You wait for me in Bath, and I'll come back from Sicily as soon as I can. And we'll be married.'

'Oh, Gentry, yes.' They were the words which for so many years she had dreamed of hearing, and although they brought her such joy they brought also the pain that came with the knowledge of the certainty of Marianne's unhappiness.

Gentry's thoughts too were on Marianne. 'Oh, God,' he said. 'if only we could have our happiness without hurting others. If only there were some other way. If only it were not Marianne who had to be hurt.' He sighed again. 'But there's no other way for it.' He turned to face Blanche, reached out for her. She moved towards him and he enfolded her in his arms and they stood there together, her forehead against his warm cheek. 'I've got to do it somehow,' he said after a while. 'I don't know how, but it must be done. It makes it even more difficult with her staying in Messina with my father. He dotes on her so.' He paused. 'You realize, do you, that he might disinherit me?'

'It won't matter to *me*,' Blanche said.

'Will it not?'

'Not if I have you.' She raised her head, kissed him on the mouth. 'I love you. If I'm with you I can put up with anything.'

Gentry said, 'Though in truth I don't think he will – even though he might threaten it. Besides, I have money from my mother. We'd manage all right somehow, without any real hardship. It's the thought of Marianne that brings me so much – so much pain.'

Blanche tried to dismiss the thought of Marianne from her mind, and when that failed, to justify her grasping at happiness. Gentry doesn't love her, she told herself. He loves *me*. And while a protesting voice cried out to her of her betrayal of her friend she closed her ears to the sound and nestled closer into Gentry's warmth.

They made love again, giving themselves up to a passion that swept aside all doubt and fear and promised them that no matter what the obstacles were they would be overcome. But when they awoke in the morning Blanche was afraid, terribly afraid that in the glare of the new day Gentry would see things in a new light, that all the promises of yesterday would count for nothing. She watched his face, listened to his voice, seeking the slightest sign of regret at the vows he had made. But there was no sign. She saw again, as she expected to, his regret over Marianne's certain unhappiness, but in spite of it he appeared to remain firm in his purpose.

They had breakfast sent up to their room and afterwards finished the preparations for their departure. They would go to the station together, Blanche to take the train for Bath, Gentry to go on to London where he would take the boat train for the Continent. When at last they were ready to go Gentry held her in his arms and kissed her. 'I shall write to you and return to Bath for you as soon as I can,' he said.

'I'll try to be patient.'

'Yes. And just keep thinking of me.'

'I shan't be able to do anything else.'

Out on the street they set off to make their way to

the station. As they passed a newsagent's shop on their way Gentry came to a halt at Blanche's side saying that he wanted to buy a newspaper. As he turned into the shop Blanche moved on, idly looking into the neighbouring shop windows. Turning a few minutes later to search out Gentry she saw him standing on the pavement shaking hands with another man. At once she recognized the man as Mr Baron, Mr Savill's solicitor.

Not wishing to be seen with Gentry, she stepped back into the shop doorway and from her concealed vantage point watched as the two men talked for some minutes. Then at last, with a further handshake they parted and Baron walked on down the street. She waited until he was out of sight before she emerged from her cover. On reaching Gentry's side she found him looking grave and preoccupied.

'That was Mr Baron, wasn't it?' she said.

'Yes.' Gentry was standing gazing in the direction the man had taken.

Blanche said, 'What a surprise, your meeting him here in Bristol.'

Gentry nodded. 'He came along just as I came out of the shop. I knew his face but at first I couldn't think who he was. He knew me, though, from when we met at Uncle John's funeral.' Then, turning to Blanche, he said, frowning:

'He asked me if I was going to Hallowford. I said no, I was not – and then he told me that Marianne is there – now.'

'Marianne? In Hallowford?'

'Yes.'

Blanche shook her head. 'I've heard nothing of it. He must be mistaken. She would have been in touch with me if she had come back to England. The last I heard from her she was in Sicily. And she made no mention in her letter of coming back. Surely Mr Baron must be mistaken.'

'No, he's seen her. He's had meetings with her.'

'But – but why is she there? And why should she return without telling me?'

Gentry shook his head. 'Baron wouldn't say very much. But he hinted that – well, that everything is not as it should be.'

'What do you mean?'

'I don't know. He was very noncommittal.'

They stood there together on the pavement in the constant stream of the passers-by. For some reason Blanche's heart began to beat with fear. 'What are you going to do?' she said.

He shrugged. 'What else can I do but go to Hallowford to see her?'

Chapter Thirty-Four

On the train Blanche asked Gentry whether she should go with him to Hallowford. No, he said, it would be better not to. How could they explain their presence together? He would go alone.

'You get off at Bath as originally planned,' he said, 'and when I've seen Marianne I'll be in touch with you.'

And she had to be content with that, though her heart continued to beat with increasing fear at the unexpected and puzzling turn of events.

When they reached Bath Blanche got off and stood on the platform watching as the train started up again and, with the smoke streaming from its stack, moved out of sight.

On arriving at the Marsh house in Almond Street Mrs Marsh asked eagerly whether she had seen her brother. Blanche replied that she had, adding that Ernest had then gone on to Bradford. She volunteered no further information on the matter, and to her relief no more questions were asked. All her thoughts were of Gentry and the surprising development of Marianne's presence at Hallowford. All she could do now was wait to hear from him.

At the door of Hallowford House Gentry rang the bell and waited. As he stood there he looked around him. He was surprised to discover that the place had a rather unkempt look about it. The wide front lawns, in his experience always so well kept over the years, now were overgrown, while the herbaceous borders, once John Savill's pride, had a look of wildness about them, their once-carefully tended plants encroached upon by weeds.

A maid whose face was unfamiliar to him opened the door, and he asked at once to see Miss Savill. The maid said apologetically that she could not see anyone at present. 'She will see me,' Gentry said. 'My name is Gentry Harrow. Please tell her that I'm here.'

At the sound of his name it was clear that the maid knew of him. Yet her expression remained doubtful as she took his hat, showed him into the library and went upstairs.

A minute later Gentry, standing in the library with the door open, heard her coming down the stairs again. He moved to the door at her approach, then came to a halt as he saw the apologetic look on the girl's face.

'I'm sorry, sir, but Miss Savill can't see anyone right now. She – she asked me to tell you that she is writing to you.'

'– Writing to me . . . ?' He frowned. 'She says she's writing to me? I don't understand.'

'Oh, sir, I'm sorry, sir.' The girl looked uncomfortable. She stood before him, twisting her apron between her nervous hands.

'Is Mrs Callow here?' Gentry asked.

'She's not in the house at the moment, sir, but she's expected back shortly.'

Gentry nodded, thanked the girl then walked past her out of the room. In the hall, however, instead of turning towards the front door he stepped towards the stairs, and while the maid protested behind him he quickly climbed up, two steps at a time, to the floor above.

'Marianne?' he called out as he reached the first floor landing. He had no idea which room she might be in.

Coming to a stop in the centre of the landing he called her name again and then stood there listening. There was no sound. Over the soft carpet he moved towards the stairs leading to the floor above. Just as he reached the lower step he heard the faint click of a door catch. He turned at the sound. It had come from a door at the rear. After a moment's hesitation he moved softly towards it, grasped the handle, swiftly turned it and thrust the door open wide.

Although it was not long after one in the afternoon the window curtains were drawn, so that the only light that came in was that from the landing by the open door, and the little that crept in through the cracks between the curtains.

He saw Marianne at once as he entered. She was standing by the window, and although her slim figure was in shadow he saw her physically flinch at the abruptness of his entrance.

He stood in the open doorway, gazing at her while she raised her hands to her face and turned away from him. There was silence in the room, a silence brushed only by the sounds of their breathing, then she said, her voice sounding heavy with the scars of very recent tears:

'Gentry – what are you doing in Hallowford? I was astonished to learn that you're here.'

'By chance I saw your father's solicitor, Mr Baron. He told me you were here. Marianne, what's the matter?'

She turned to face him now and he could see that her eyelids were swollen with weeping, though now there seemed to be a steady calm about her. 'When I heard that you were downstairs I couldn't believe it,' she said. Then she added, 'I wish you hadn't come.'

'Well, I have,' he said.

'I didn't want to see you.'

'Why not?'

She shook her head. 'I don't want to see anybody. I don't want to see Blanche, either. I thought I would; I had intended to, of course, but – no, not now.'

'Marianne –'

'I told Mary to tell you that I would write you a letter.'

'I don't want any letter from you, Marianne,' he said, frowning. 'Why didn't you want to see me?'

Disregarding his question she said to him, 'Oh, Gentry, I'm so happy that you got back safely – now that that terrible war is over, and you're safe again.' She put her head a little on one side. 'You look thinner, you know.'

'Marianne,' he said, 'tell me what's going on. Why didn't you want to see me? Tell me. What's the matter?'

She turned from him again; she appeared to be fiddling with the catch of a small travelling box that stood on a table before her. 'What makes you think there's something the matter?'

He stepped forward. 'D'you think I'm seven years old, Marianne? And look at me. Please – look at me.'

After a moment she turned to him once more, and in spite of her brave smile and the dimness of the light in the room he could see the misery in her eyes, the shock, the emotional bruising.

'Marianne . . .'

She swallowed hard while she faced him, and he saw the way she drew herself up, straightening, squaring her shoulders. 'Gentry,' she said after a second or two, speaking carefully, as if choosing her words, and the manner in which she spoke, '– this isn't the way it was meant to be. This isn't the way I imagined it – your homecoming. I'm sorry.' She took a deep breath. 'I'm

462

trying to be strong. And it's not easy for me. Though you can see how cowardly I am in my refusing to see you. But there, I never pretended to have any great degree of bravery.'

Gentry opened his mouth to speak but she quickly raised a hand. 'Oh, please, Gentry – it's difficult enough for me as it is.'

He nodded. 'Go on.'

She took a breath and said: 'I suppose your coming here – it might be the best thing after all. At least it – it will enable us to make a – a clean break.'

'What – what are you talking about?'

She looked down at her hands as they clenched and unclenched. 'It's all finished, Gentry. All of it. There's nothing left.'

'I don't understand. What do you mean?'

She turned slightly, leaned over and picked up a newspaper. She thrust it into his hand – 'Read it' – and, stepping to the window, roughly drew back one of the curtains. In the sudden harsh light of the afternoon he stared at her, seeing clearly the extent of the misery in her face, the bereft look in her eyes. 'Read it,' she said. 'Read it.'

Reluctantly he moved his gaze to the newspaper in his hand. It was a local, West Country paper. He scanned the columns. 'On the right,' Marianne said, '– at the top of the page.'

He found himself looking at a short column headed, *Hallowford Man Found Dead*. Beneath it he read:

A report has come from a correspondent in Budapest of the discovery of the body of a man which has been identified as that of Mr Harold Savill, of Hallowford, manager of the Savill Mill in Trowbridge in Wiltshire. It appears that Mr

Savill had been staying at the fashionable Hotel Gelert with a certain lady from London. Official reports state that Mr Savill left the hotel during the afternoon of June 4th and did not return. Later, following the hearing of a single gunshot on the banks of the Danube, Mr Savill was found dead, a bullet wound in the head. An inquest is to be held, but the authorities state that they do not believe that any other party is involved in the death.

Gentry stared at the item. 'And did he kill himself?' he said.

'Yes. Apparently a letter was found on him. There's no doubt that he meant to do it.'

'But – why? Why should he kill himself?'

She shrugged. 'He had gone as far as he could. There was nowhere else to run to.'

'What do you mean?'

She nodded. 'You're as ignorant as I was, Gentry. There I was in Messina, impatiently waiting for you to return, while all the time my uncle was going through my money as if there was a never-ending supply. And I was totally ignorant of it all. As *you* were. I had no idea. I was getting my allowance – so I saw no reason to have any doubts. I had no idea of what was happening. Though it appears that the signs were evident for anyone in this area to see.'

Gentry gazed at her in growing incredulity. 'He used your money?'

'All of it. My father gave him power of attorney over everything until I came of age. I've had several meetings with Mr Baron who has found out as much of the story as he could. It appears that my uncle mortgaged the mill to the hilt – and this house and just about everything else – and put everything into motor car manufacturing.'

464

'– Which failed.'

She nodded. 'Which failed. Oh, indeed it failed. A spectacular failure as failures go. And with it went everything my father worked for all his life. And everything he left for me.'

Gentry could hardly take in her words. 'It's gone? All of it?'

'Every penny.'

'But the house, the land, the carriages, the –'

'Gone!' she burst out. 'Please.' And then more softly: 'It's all gone.'

'Oh, Marianne – there must be something that can be done. There must be a way to –'

She broke in: 'There's nothing. Do you suppose I haven't been into it all, over and over, with Mr Baron. And if he could have found a way he would have done.' She shook her head. 'Believe me, there's nothing to be done. It's all finished.' She turned, gesturing to the half-packed travelling box. 'I'm just packing up a few things before I leave. The creditors are allowing me to the end of the week to get out of the house – and to take one or two personal possessions. I have a few little pieces of jewellery that belonged to my mother, some photographs, clothes. Just a few things.'

There was no sign of tears in her eyes. He was astonished that she appeared so calm in the face of such a calamity. And then, looking at her, looking into her eyes, he saw that it was not a calm that was there; it was something else. It was as if a curtain had come down, shutting out the outside world, closing her in. It was the outward sign of a kind of numbness that he could see.

As he looked at her she returned his gaze for some moments then, lowering her eyes, she put her hands together, her fingers working. Next moment she held

465

out her hand. In her palm lay the engagement ring Gentry had given her. 'Take it, please,' she said.

'– Marianne.'

'Please, Gentry, take it. We have no future together any more. We did once, I thought. But in reality perhaps we never did. Perhaps it only existed in the minds of our fathers. I don't think you had much say in the matter, did you?'

He did not answer. He stood as if stunned, Marianne standing before him, the ring lying on her outstretched palm. Then as he remained unmoving she stepped forward, reached out with her other hand and he felt the sharp hardness of the ring as she put it into his palm and closed his fingers over it. 'You were to marry a girl with assets, with property. I have nothing. Anyway,' she stepped back, '– now you are free.'

Blanche was up in the schoolroom giving Clara her lesson when Lily came to the door to say that Mr Harrow was there to see her, that he was waiting in the library.

Thanking the maid, Blanche quickly got up from her chair, a feeling of elation flooding over her. Since parting from Gentry on the train the day before she had waited impatiently for some word from him. And now he was here. 'I must go downstairs for a little while, Clara,' she said to the child. 'Just get on with your lesson, there's a good girl. I'll be back as soon as I can.'

'Yes, Miss Farrar.' Clara smiled at her and obediently went back to the task she had been set.

Entering the library, Blanche found Gentry standing by the fireplace, watching for her appearance. Smiling, she moved quickly towards him, and then came to a halt as she saw the gravity in his expression.

'Hello, Blanche . . .'

466

'Gentry . . .'

Something was wrong. It should not be like this. He should have come to her, taken her in his arms, but he had remained there, keeping his distance. They stood facing one another across six feet of carpet that was suddenly an unbridgeable chasm.

After a little silence she said softly:

'I've been expecting you. Waiting for you to come for me.'

He did not answer, only lowered his gaze and looked away.

'I've packed my trunk,' she said. 'So that I would be ready when you came.' She tried to force a brightness into her tone, but the sound rang hollow in her ears. When he still said nothing she said, her words a melancholy statement:

'– It's not going to happen now, is it.'

Raising his head, looking into her eyes, he said simply:

'No.' And now he moved to her, took her hands in his, holding them to his chest. 'I'm so sorry, Blanche. I'm so terribly sorry.'

He led her then to the sofa where they sat down, and where he told her of his meeting with Marianne at Hallowford House, of how she had tried to avoid him, and of her reasons for doing so; he told her of the suicide of Harold Savill, of Marianne's loss of everything that had been hers; of her giving back to him the ring.

'And God help me,' he said, 'I couldn't take it. In one day she had discovered the loss of everything that had been hers. I couldn't add to it, her misery. And I knew that you wouldn't be able to do so either.' He looked into her eyes. 'Could you, Blanche?'

And seeing the end of all her new-born hopes she could only nod and murmur:

'No.'

The irony of the situation was almost incredible, she felt. Gentry, going to Marianne to break off the engagement, had found his release offered to him. And he had not been able to accept it.

As she sat there she wept, silently, the tears spilling over and streaming down her cheeks. She felt as if her heart would break. For a very little time she had held a promise of happiness in her grasp, and now that promise had gone, leaving only emptiness in its wake.

'What are you going to do now?' she said a little later, looking at him through her tear-stained eyes.

'I shall return to Hallowford. And I shall take Marianne to Messina where we shall be married. She knows of course how I came to learn of her presence in Hallowford, but she doesn't know I was with you at the time. She must never learn of that – from either of us. She agrees that you, as her sister and dearest friend, must be told of her present situation, and I said I would come here and tell you.' He paused briefly. 'And then she would like to see you. She couldn't bear to see you before. She didn't want to see anyone.'

Blanche nodded. 'Of course.' It was all like some terrible dream. She knew, though, that it was only too real. Gentry had been hers, for a very little time, and now she had lost him again. Soon, very soon, he would have gone out of her life for ever.

'You will be happy, Blanche,' he said softly, intently. 'You will be.' And while a voice in her head cried out that such a thing could never be – not without him – he went on: 'You'll find the right man for you. Someone who will be able to love you, and will be free to love you, as you deserve.'

'And you?' Blanche said.

He avoided her gaze, 'Marianne is a good person,' he

468

said. 'And I do love her – though in a different way. And I can make her happy – as she deserves to be – and I hope she can make me happy too. Though it will be a different kind of happiness from that which I'd dreamed of – with you.'

He looked back into Blanche's eyes. 'Perhaps,' he said, 'some things were meant to be. Right from the start it was all planned that Marianne and I should marry – without any real consultation of either one of us. And now – now it's all going to happen, just as our fathers wished. And you and I, Blanche –' he gave a sad shake of his head – 'I don't think we really ever had a chance.'

After a little while he rose to go. At the library door he took Blanche's hand, pressed it briefly and left.

Two days later Gentry and Marianne left Hallowford for the last time. With their going Blanche felt as if a part of her soul had died.

Chapter Thirty-Five

'You've been quiet, Blanche,' George Marsh said. 'Preoccupied. Is there anything wrong?'

At his words Blanche turned, smiling at him. 'No,' she said, 'there's nothing wrong.'

In the late morning sun they were seated on the fallen trunk of a dead lime, Jacko sitting at Blanche's feet on the carpet of last year's leaves. She bent and stroked his head. His tail thumped the earth a few times and she smiled and ruffled his ears.

'He's getting old,' she murmured; then to Jacko: 'You're getting to be an old man, Jacko-boy.' At her words the dog lifted his head and looked up at her with his soft brown eyes.

He was going quite grey, she realized, and his gait had grown much slower of late, with an increasing stiffness in his joints. It occurred to her that not for some time had he chased rabbits or any of the other wild creatures which in earlier times had offered him such irresistible challenges.

Absently stroking him, Blanche gazed off into the surrounding foliage.

It was July, 1903. Marianne and Gentry had been gone from England for over a year now, and Blanche, following their departure, had done her best to come to terms with her situation and get on with her life at the Marsh house. The passing year had had its share of events. In the autumn Mrs Marsh had died. George had recovered his equilibrium after a time, though, and things had again become much as they had been. And the days and the weeks and the months had gone by, most of the time with little to distinguish one day or one week from the next.

One bright happening in the otherwise dull pattern of Blanche's existence had come in the shape of a letter from Ernest with the news that he was doing well in Bradford and that as soon as he was able he would come to Bath to visit her. Perhaps then, he added, if she wished to join him, they could arrange it – but not yet; he still had certain things he wished to accomplish. Blanche had answered his letter at once. She would like to join him *immediately*, she said. He had replied as swiftly that they must be patient a little while longer.

That exchange had been over six months ago. Since that time she had heard nothing further from him, in spite of writing on several occasions. To her great disappointment and puzzlement, the last letter she had written had been returned to her, with *Gone Away* scrawled across the corner of the envelope.

Her thoughts far away she ceased her stroking of the dog and he gently tossed his head, nudging her hand into action again. 'You,' she said to him, 'are an old rascal.' Thinking of Ernest once more, she murmured to Jacko: 'D'you suppose we'll ever hear from him again? Or has he forgotten us?' She patted the dog. 'You haven't forgotten *him*, have you? You still miss him, don't you?' She looked up and caught George Marsh's eye. 'There's no doubt of it,' she said. 'Jacko still misses Ernest so much.'

At the sound of Ernest's name Jacko's head turned slightly, ears pricking, alert. It was always the same.

Whereas there had been no word from Ernest for some time now, she had heard again from Alfredo

Pastore. Following his return to Sicily a year-and-a-half earlier he had written a number of times, but Blanche had not answered his letters and eventually he had given up. But now here he was again, saying that he would be coming to England and the West Country later in the summer. Perhaps, he said, they could meet, to which end he would be in touch with her again about the time of his arrival.

Blanche was not affected in any particular way by his letter. It might be pleasant to see him again, she thought idly, but her feelings went no further, and it was almost a matter of indifference to her whether they ever met again. She put his letter aside and thought no more about it.

Throughout the past year the one person with whom she had corresponded regularly was Marianne, whose letters, frequently arriving from Sicily, had made no secret of the happiness she had found with Gentry. Her last letter had arrived only yesterday.

On this bright summer Sunday Blanche and George Marsh and Clara and Jacko had left the house for a walk, making their way to an area of woodland not too far from Almond Street. There, reaching a clearing, Blanche and Marsh had found makeshift seats on the trunk of the lime while Clara went off to explore the surrounding trees. And now Clara was coming into view again. Blanche watched her as she stopped, crouching to examine something on the woodland floor.

'I think Clara should go away to school,' Marsh said. 'She should be with people her own age. She's eleven now. She's growing up so fast.'

Blanche nodded. Marsh went on:

'I thought perhaps she might go to one of the new secondary schools, but on second thoughts I'd want to wait and see how they turn out first. I think it would be better if she went away – to a good boarding school somewhere.' Behind his spectacles his small eyes focused on Blanche. 'But that wouldn't mean that you'd have to leave,' he said.

She gazed at him, his plain features beneath the balding crown. 'But you'll have no further need of me here,' she said.

'Oh, if you only knew,' he said. He shook his head, the words coming tumbling out. 'I have such a need of you. Oh, Blanche – I'm so much in love with you.'

His words took her completely by surprise. She gazed at him, silent. She had never suspected that he felt for her anything more than friendship, a kind of fatherly affection. Over the period of her employment in the house she had felt growing between him and herself a welcome, easy closeness, a comradeship which she felt she could enjoy without feeling in any way threatened. She felt a great respect for him, the seed of which had begun to grow at their very first meeting – and as time went by it had grown stronger – but she did not love him.

As she tried to frame words to say to him he went on:

'Blanche, if you would marry me it would make me so happy. And Clara, too, you can be sure of that.' He paused. 'I know I'm not a handsome man, and I know that I'm a good deal older than you; I know that. But I would do my best to make you happy. If you would let me.'

'Mr Marsh – George –'

'I'm not a rich man, either. Which is something else you're already well aware of.' A little light of sudden enthusiasm shone in his eye. 'But,' he said, 'if I had someone like you working with me there's no telling where it might end.'

After a few moments Blanche reached out, laying her palms upon the backs of his hands.

'I'm honoured,' she said. 'And I thank you. So very much.'

He gave a melancholy smile. 'But the answer is no . . .'

'I'm sorry. I'm not ready to marry anyone right now. I'm sorry, really I am.'

His eyes searched hers, seeing that she meant her words. 'It's all right,' he said after a moment. He nodded. 'But if you ever change your mind . . .'

'Yes . . .'

'I mean it, Blanche.'

'I won't forget.'

Two weeks later arrangements were made for Clara to go to a school in Crewkerne, beginning in September, and in the meantime Blanche set about placing advertisements in *The Lady* and various newspapers in an effort to find a new position. With Clara gone, and having rejected George Marsh's marriage proposal, there was no longer any reason for her remaining there. The situation as regards work for governesses was changing, however. State-provided, compulsory education had been slowly developing and improving over the years, and with the Education Act of 1902 free secondary education was now also provided.

Blanche, looking for a position as private governess, found that she was offering her services in a diminishing market as more and more parents chose to send their children to the new, much-improved, locally-funded schools. Another problem she had to contend with was that posed by Jacko. He was a clever, affectionate animal, but he was proving a great hindrance in her search for employment. Perhaps the answer to her problem, she thought, was to find work as a teacher in one of the new schools – though unfortunately this seemed to be a common aim among so many young women. Failing that, she could seek work in a factory somewhere. She had to do something. It wouldn't be long before Clara had gone away to Crewkerne. When that happened her own position as governess would be finished.

While Blanche gave her concern to her immediate future Clara was looking forward to a holiday at the seaside. Her father had arranged for her, as a last treat before her departure for school, to go and stay with his sister and her children in their house on the edge of Weston-Super-Mare. Blanche would accompany Clara to her aunt's home and return there three weeks later to bring her home again. Although it was not acknowledged by him, Blanche felt that part of the reason for Marsh's decision was also to help *her*; not only would Clara's absence free Blanche from her duties for a time, but it would also enable her to pursue any possibilities as regards future employment and allow her to be free to arrange any necessary interviews with prospective employers.

It was planned that Blanche and Clara would leave early on the morning of Saturday, July 25th. Two days before their planned departure, however, Blanche received a letter that for a time dismissed from her mind all thought of Clara's trip and her own immediate problems concerning her future employment.

The letter, from Marianne, said that on the death of a distant relative of Gentry he had been left a property in Brighton, and that he was coming to England to see the house and decide what to do with it. While he was there, Marianne said, he intended to come to Bath to see Blanche. Marianne's letter continued:

... And I have given him strict instructions to do his very best to persuade you to return here with him. Surely it's time you had a holiday, so if your employer can spare you it will be our gain, added to which a vacation in the sun will do you a world of good. This, of course, is apart from the great good it will do for me, and the pleasure it will give me, to see you again, dear sister. Please – do think the matter over very carefully. Gentry should be with you within a very short time of your receiving this.

Gentry was coming to England. He was probably already here – and he was coming to see her. Blanche found that her feelings were a confusing mixture of elation and fear. Since his marriage she had tried to come to terms with the fact that he was no longer a part of her life, that he never could be – but it was easier to pay lip-service to such knowledge than to accept it. And now here he was, coming into her life again, stirring up all the old feelings of longing, of frustration and regret. Would she, she asked herself, ever be free of him?

The next day, Friday, there came a short letter from Gentry himself. Writing from Brighton, he said that he would come to Bath the following day, arriving probably late in the afternoon. He would call on her at Almond Street, he said; he looked forward to seeing her then.

Gentry's letter caused Blanche even greater dismay; while she found herself so anxiously looking forward to seeing him at the same time she dreaded the prospect. What could come of it? All that had once existed between them was now a thing of the past. But how could she realistically avoid him even if she could bring herself to try?

And then that evening there came some kind of answer to Blanche's dilemma. After Clara's box had been packed and the child had gone to bed, Marsh said to Blanche:

'I've been thinking – why don't you stay at the seaside too and have a little holiday yourself? Take in a little of the sea air for a few days.'

Blanche was surprised into silence for a moment, then she shook her head. '– Oh, no, I don't think so. I think – I think I should get back.'

'Why? What have you got to hurry back for? Have you got some appointments?'

She mentioned nothing of Gentry's letter. She shook her head. 'Well, no – not at the moment, but –'

'Then why not stay there and relax for a little while? I don't mean with my sister. My God, that would be the last place I'd recommend for peace and quiet. Besides, there wouldn't be room for you in the house. No, find yourself a quiet little hotel near the sea-front. It's time you had a little holiday yourself. Stay on for a day or two.'

In her head the voice of commonsense told her to accept the offer, but at the same time another voice protested. She said quickly, 'No – thank you anyway – but I think I should come straight back.'

The next morning she and Clara were up early – Clara shivering with excitement at the prospect of the unaccustomed adventure, and eager to get away – and Blanche feeling reluctant to leave the house at all.

The cab had been ordered, was expected in ten or fifteen minutes. After breakfast Blanche went back to her room to put on her coat and hat. As she stood before the glass she wondered at her feelings. What's the matter with me? she asked herself. Here she was, afraid to leave the house in case Gentry called. Had she still not accepted the situation?

Ten minutes later when she came downstairs and entered the breakfast room Marsh looked over his newspaper and saw that she was carrying her valise. Answering the question in his eyes, she said:

'– I changed my mind. Perhaps I will stay on for two or three days.'

He nodded his satisfaction. 'I'm glad.'

There was a ring at the front doorbell then and the maid came into the room announcing that the cab had arrived to take them to the station. At once Clara kissed her father goodbye and hurried outside. As Blanche followed her to the front door Marsh took her hand and pressed some money into it.

She frowned. 'What's this for?'

'It's towards your hotel bill. Please – take it.'

She protested for a moment or two but then, thanking him, put the money into her purse. Minutes later she and Clara were being driven away from the house.

The journey to Weston-Super-Mare passed without incident. For the first part Clara kept up an almost constant stream of chatter, but gradually she relaxed and sat quiet, either looking from the window at the passing scenery or trying – without much success – to concentrate on her book. Blanche had also brought a book to read on the journey – a new novel by Arthur Conan Doyle: *The Hound of the Baskervilles*, which everyone seemed to be reading – but with, first of all, Clara's demanding presence, and then her own preoccupations, she did not get far into it.

Eventually they arrived at their destination where Mrs Wilmslow, Clara's aunt, was waiting to welcome them.

After being introduced to Clara's aunt and two young cousins, Bertha and Constance, Blanche was at once invited to the house for luncheon. She gratefully declined, however, saying that she would like to look around the town and find a suitable hotel for the night. Mrs Wilmslow nodded understandingly. 'And I'm sure you'll be very glad of the chance to be on your own for a while,' she said.

Blanche accompanied the little group from the station to where a cab waited to drive them to the Wilmslows' house situated beyond the outskirts of the town. And after a kiss and a hug for Clara – who in her excitement at being there seemed hardly aware of the gestures – she watched and waved as the cab was driven away.

When it was out of sight she stood alone, valise in hand, breathing in the sea air. She was free now, to spend the next days as she pleased.

She set off along the main street, gazing about her with interest as she went. She would walk around for a while and look out for a pleasant little hotel near the sea-front, she decided – and told herself once again how glad she was to be there, free of responsibilities and cares for a while.

At the sea-front she stood at the railing of the promenade and gazed out to sea while the gulls wheeled in the dull sky above her head. Unable to prevent her thoughts from wandering, she imagined Gentry moving to the front door of the house in Almond Street, ringing the bell . . . Angrily, she dismissed the picture from her mind. It was idiocy to dwell on such matters. She turned and started off again along the promenade.

After stopping for a while in a tea-shop where she drank some coffee she went into one of the smaller sea-front hotels and inquired after a room. On being told that there was one available she asked to see it and a maid was instructed to show her to a room on the second floor. Entering the room, Blanche looked around her. The room, with its view of the sea, was pleasant enough, but suddenly into her mind came the question: What am I doing here, staying alone in some unattractive seaside town where I have no desire to be? Turning to the maid, she thanked her, but said she had changed her mind. Then, quickly, she walked out of the room, down the stairs, through the foyer and out onto the street. There she turned her steps in the direction of the railway station. She would return to Bath at once. And it was no good trying to fool herself as to the reason for her return. The reason was Gentry. And now she could only pray that she would get back to the house in Bath in time to see him when he called.

In a little under an hour she was sitting on a train on the first part of her return journey to Bath.

She got there just after five o'clock, and as the train drew into the station she adjusted her hat and prepared to alight. She found that she was trembling and she became aware of the beating of her heart. Part of her emotion now was fear – fear that she was too late.

The train slowed and came to a halt. Following on the heels of another passenger she stepped down onto the platform. And a moment later she glanced up – and there was Gentry standing at the other end of the platform.

She came to a halt so suddenly that the man who had followed her from the carriage stumbled and almost fell over her. She was faintly aware of his muttered oath as he recovered himself and moved on. And she stood there, gazing at Gentry as he, unaware of her, stood reading a newspaper, his suitcase on the ground at his feet. And then after a moment or two, as if he had somehow felt her eyes upon him, he lifted his head and saw her.

For a second he remained still, looking at her, while the other travellers brushed past them. Then he folded his paper and put it under his arm, took up his suitcase, and moved towards her. Standing before her he bent and kissed her lightly on the cheek.

'Hello, Blanche.'

'Hello, Gentry.' She could still hardly believe it, his presence; she had found him.

'I called at the house, Mr Marsh's house,' he said. 'The maid told me you'd gone to take your charge to Weston-Super-Mare. She said she thought you'd be staying on there for a few days.' He shrugged. 'So – I was on my way to London.' With a little smile he said: 'Did you change your mind – about staying there?'

'Yes – as you can see.'

He nodded. 'Good. I'm glad.'

Taking her arm, he led her from the platform.

'Where are we going?' she asked.

'Is there anywhere you would like to go?'

I just want to be with you, the voice inside her head replied. She said aloud: 'I'm not particular. Perhaps we might have some tea and a sandwich.'

'Have you eaten?'

'Not since a very early breakfast.'

He nodded. 'We'll get some tea and something to eat.'

Before leaving the station they stopped at the left-luggage department and Gentry deposited his suitcase and Blanche her valise. Then together they went out into the street.

A little later, in the tearoom of a large hotel nearby Gentry chose the most secluded table available, and when they were settled ordered tea and smoked salmon sandwiches. When the waitress had gone away with their order he turned his attention back to Blanche. Returning his gaze, she said:

'You're looking so much better. When you came back from South Africa you looked very tired, very weary.'

He nodded. 'I've had opportunity to recover since then.' He looked so handsome. She wanted to lean across the table and kiss him on the mouth.

'Yes,' he said, 'I'm well. I'm very well.'

'Married life,' she said – and she could not prevent herself from saying the words – 'Married life obviously agrees with you.'

He let this pass. 'Marianne sends you her fondest love,' he said, 'and demands that I persuade you to come back to Sicily with me. And if you can't be persuaded then I'm to kidnap you, or take some other similarly desperate measures. Anything, apparently, so long as I get you there.'

Blanche laughed. 'Oh, I'd so love to, but – I'm afraid it's just not possible.'

'No?'

'No.'

'Perhaps in a few weeks? Couldn't you arrange it?'

She shook her head. 'I'm sorry.' How could she go to Sicily and live in the same house as Gentry? To be in his presence for hours at a time, for days at a time? Such a thought was not to be considered, no matter how much a part of her longed for such a thing to happen. 'No,' she said again, 'I'm afraid I'm quite committed at present. There's no way that I can get away. But tell Marianne that just as soon as it's possible I shall be there.'

The waitress arrived then, all neat black and starched white lace, carrying a laden tray. When she had gone again Gentry watched Blanche as she ate. 'You were hungry,' he said.

'Yes.'

'You should have eaten something while you were at Weston.'

'No, I couldn't do that.' Then she added, 'I had to get back – in case you called.'

A silence followed her words. In the silence she gazed at him for a few moments, then forced her attention back to the food before her. She was trying to provoke him, she realized, trying to provoke some response from him which, in his present situation, he could not allow himself to make – whatever his feelings. She no longer felt hungry. 'I'm sorry,' she said, eyes lowered. 'I shouldn't have said that. It wasn't fair of me.'

Another little silence. Blanche dabbed at her mouth with her napkin then said, moving onto safer ground:

'Marianne said you had inherited some property – in Brighton. Have you been to see it?'

'Yes. A house there – left to me by a maiden aunt. There's no point in my keeping it. I'm having it sold. I've put it into the hands of agents.'

'So your business in England is finished now.'

'Almost.'

'When will you return – to Sicily?'

'Tomorrow. I have appointments. But I must leave for London tonight.'

'Tonight?'

She had not intended her voice to give away her sudden sense of dismay. Gentry nodded.

'I have a business engagement there late tomorrow morning. I'll start home by the afternoon boat train.'

'Home,' she echoed softly, her tone wistful. 'So if I hadn't come back from Weston today we wouldn't have met . . .'

'I'm afraid not – not this time. I'd hoped to be down here earlier – but the business in Brighton took longer than I anticipated.'

They were silent for some moments. When they spoke again it was if they had determined to speak on matters that did not concern them both. He told her that his father had not been well for some time now, and had more or less given up all active participation in the family business, Gentry having almost completely taken over the running of it. Blanche in turn told him of her work in the Marsh household, and then of Ernest, of not having heard from him in a very long time.

'And you're worried about him, obviously,' Gentry said.

'Of course. I just wish I knew where he was, what he's doing. If I knew where he was I would go to him.'

'Don't worry about him. You'll hear from him again when he's ready.'

'But it's been so long, and – he's all I have left.'

They left the hotel after a little while longer to go back out into the sunshine of the late afternoon. As they emerged onto the street a young man limped into their path, unshaven, dirty and ragged, his open cap in his hand. Blanche recoiled from him, her disgust plain in her face, and she was surprised when Gentry took coins from his pocket and gave them to the man.

As they walked on, the man's thanks ringing after them, Blanche said:

'They come to the house all the time, these wandering navvies, or whatever they are. They come begging food or money, or asking for work. They frighten me. Lily and I, the maid, we send them packing – no nonsense about it.'

Gentry looked at her in surprise. 'There but for the grace of God . . .' he said. He sighed, shook his head. 'There's more than one way of being a casualty of war.'

'What d'you mean?'

He gestured with a nod of his head. 'That young man there – he was probably fighting on some Transvaal plain a couple of years ago. These poor bastards – they're encouraged to rush off for the Queen's shilling, but when the fight's over and they get back and have to cope with the consequences no one wants to know anymore. It makes me sick; there's so much talk about Glory and Patriotism, but when it's over the ones who do all the talking find the survivors an embarrassment. Particularly the injured survivors. It's always the way. I was one of the lucky ones. I survived intact. But when I think of all those poor bastards who were injured, or who died for no other reason than the incompetence of the army doctors . . .' He shook his head. 'Doctors.' His voice was heavy with contempt. 'It wasn't surviving the Boers that was the problem for most men, it was surviving the medical assistance and the army hospitals.' There was a look of bitterness in his eyes. 'Anyway,' he said, '– it's over now. And please God we shan't have to suffer like it again in order to satisfy the whims and the bruised pride of some jingoistic British bureaucrats and politicians. God save me from them.'

Blanche did not want to dwell on such a melancholy subject. A little petulantly, and feeling reprimanded by his words, she said, 'Oh, let's not talk about such things, Gentry, please.'

He smiled down at her. 'No, of course not.'

They walked on. 'What time are you expected back?' he said after a minute or two. 'Will they wonder where you are? Don't you have things to do?'

'No. Not with Clara away . . .' Blanche shrugged. She felt awkward. The atmosphere between them was constrained. 'Oh, by the way,' she said, 'I'm expecting a visit from a friend of yours.'

'Oh? Who's that?'

'Signor Pastore. Alfredo Pastore.'

'Pastore?' And then he nodded, remembering. 'Oh, yes, Pastore.'

She wondered why she had brought up Alfredo's name. If she had hoped to stir in Gentry any sign of jealousy she saw nothing of it. He just shook his head. 'He's not a friend,' he said. 'I don't really know him. His father had business dealings with *my* father at one time – concerned with soap export, I believe.'

They walked on, to what purpose and towards what destination she did not know. As if aimlessly they wandered into one of the city's parks, and as they walked slowly along the narrow paths she thought of that other time and that other park when they had walked together. Gentry, looking at his watch, remarked that it was almost seven-thirty.

'I've booked a sleeper which will get me into London early in the morning,' he added. 'It leaves just after eleven.' He paused. 'Are you able to have dinner with me before I go?'

She nodded, trying to appear casual. 'If you like. I've got nothing to hurry back for.'

'Good. Perhaps if we could find somewhere fairly close to the station . . .'

'Of course.'

Not far from the station they found a quiet restaurant where they were shown to a corner table.

They ordered their food and as they ate they chatted of this and that, keeping to mundane subjects. At last, though, they ran out of conversation and fell silent. And then the moment had come. Gentry put down his coffee cup and took out his watch. He gave a little shake of his head. 'I must pay the bill and get going.'

Out on the street they walked in silence for a while, but as they drew near the station entrance they found refuge in the usual conversational banalities used by parting friends. And all at once they were inside the station. When they had retrieved their cases from the left-luggage department Blanche said, 'I'll come with you to your train.'

486

'You don't need to.' He looked away along the plat-form, as if searching for his train; in truth he was avoiding her gaze. 'Perhaps it would be better if you didn't,' he said.

'As you like.'

Their eyes met, held. Looking up at the station clock, Blanche saw that it was ten-fifty. 'Is your train in?' she said.

'Yes.' He gestured to a waiting train.

'Well . . .' She wanted to step forward, to feel his arms enfold her, draw her close to him. 'I'll go on back now.'

'Right.'

Still they stood there. Ten fifty-five. 'You'll miss your train,' she said.

'Yes, I must go.' Then, giving her a little smile, awkward, only just there, he turned and strode away. She watched him for a few moments then herself turned and made her way towards the station exit. She came to a halt as she reached it, and stood waiting as the remaining couple of minutes passed. Hearing the sound of a train starting up she asked the uniformed officer at the gate: 'Is that the train for London?' He told her that it was. She thanked him and made her way from the station.

Outside on the street she had walked less than twenty paces when she heard a voice calling her name. Quickly turning she saw Gentry moving towards her from the station entrance. He was at her side almost at once. Putting down his case he took her in his arms and held her to him. Then, lifting a hand to her chin he raised her face and kissed her on the mouth.

487

Chapter Thirty-Six

She and Gentry spent that Saturday night at a hotel on the outskirts of Bath. Their naked bodies pressed together, limbs entwined, she told him over and over that she loved him. 'I can't help myself,' she said. 'I shall never stop loving you.'

And she had waited for him to say the same things. Begged him. 'Tell me you love me too, Gentry. Just tell me. It will be breath to me for the rest of my life.'

But he had been reluctant to say such words, and she had tried to understand, but then, in the early morning light, when they had awakened again and made love once more he had said it: 'I love you, Blanche. I do; you must know I do.'

And hearing his words she had said to herself that somehow, *somehow*, everything would work out. Somehow they would find a way to be together. After all, they loved one another. He loved her; he had told her so. It was a commitment from him; he was bound to her now.

When they were both dressed and had eaten a little of the breakfast that had been sent up to their room she went to him where he stood tightening the straps of his suitcase. Reaching out to him she lightly touched his smooth, newly-shaven cheek, and he, taking her hand, kissed it, pressing it to his mouth. She stepped closer, laying her head upon his shoulder.

'When will you come back?' she said. 'Tell me.' He

would have no difficulty in finding reasons for frequent journeys back to England so that they could be together.

'Come back?' he said.

She lifted her head, smiled up at him. 'I don't know how I shall get through the time till you do. Oh, Gentry, tell me how I can live till then.'

'Blanche . . .' His hands lifted, taking her gently by the shoulders, holding her a little away from him so that he could look directly into her eyes. 'I can't come back.'

She shook her head, not understanding. 'What do you mean? You *must* come back.'

'I'm sorry. This mustn't happen again. I won't be able to live with myself afterwards – the feeling of betrayal.'

'You – oh, but – but you don't have to feel that way. No one would ever know.'

'*I* would know.'

'Oh, Gentry, but – but I love you. You love *me*. You told me so.'

'I know. And I shouldn't have done. I'm sorry I did.'

'No, no, don't say that! I want you to love me. I wanted you to tell me so.'

'But what good has it done?' He sighed. 'This should never have happened.'

'No!' she raised a hand, placing it over his mouth. 'Don't say such things.' Then, letting her hand fall she said: 'Perhaps, though, you didn't mean it. When you said you loved me – perhaps it was a lie.'

'No, it's true, Blanche. I meant it. But in the long run it doesn't matter either way, does it? I'm not free to do anything about it. You know as well as I do. It's not only you and me to consider. There's Marianne.'

'Oh, Marianne, Marianne!' she said. 'It's always Marianne. She's had everything in life. She's never had to make an effort for anything.'

'Don't talk like that, Blanche.'

'It's true. Everything's been handed to her on a plate. Even *you*.'

He gazed at her for a moment then, letting his hands fall from her shoulders, turned away to the window. Blanche said, bitterness in her voice:

'Why did you come after me last night? Why did you leave your train and come for me?'

'Forgive me. I wish now I hadn't.'

Sudden tears sprang into her eyes. 'Oh, God, Gentry, don't keep saying you regret it. It makes a mockery of everything that's happened.'

'I can't help it.' He turned back to face her. His hands came up, cupping her face. 'Listen to me,' he said. The tears now were streaming down her cheeks. She nodded. After a moment he went on:

'It's true that I love you, Blanche. But you must know as well as I that nothing can come of it. Not now. It's too late. For both of us. You knew that when I got married. And although you talk now about carrying on some – some clandestine affair – as if it would be an easy thing to do – you know as well as I that we couldn't do it. I love Marianne. Not as I love you, but I love her. And I can't do anything to hurt her.'

'But what about *me*?'

'Yes, I know. And I'm so sorry that you have to be hurt. But I didn't plan it this way, anymore than you did.' He paused, his dark eyes intense in their gaze into her own. 'You're stronger than Marianne. Much stronger. And you'll survive, Blanche. You'll get over it, over this.'

'No, no, I shan't.'

'Believe me, you will. Though you may not think so now. I shall go to the station for my train soon, and I shall go out of your life. And that's the best way for both of us.'

'Gentry —'

'It's a good thing we won't be seeing each other. I have no real reason to come back to England very often now, and it's better that way. We shan't have the opportunity to meet.' He gave a little shake of his head. 'Oh, make no mistake — I wanted to see you this trip. And when Marianne asked me to, and to try to persuade you to come and visit us I realized how glad I was of the chance to see you. And calling at the house and being told that you had gone off to the coast, well — you can't imagine my disappointment. I couldn't believe that I was not going to see you. I realized that I so wanted to. And it was wrong of me. It was selfish. But it's done now, and we have to get on with our lives.'

'Apart. Our lives apart.'

'Yes.'

Through her tears his features were distorted. She said sadly:

'So last night — it was not a new beginning of anything.'

'I'm sorry.'

'And it's over.'

He nodded. 'Yes.'

A few minutes later Gentry held her to him one last time and when she had dried her tears they left the room. He paid the bill and they emerged onto the street. After they had walked some little distance towards the station he came to a halt.

'Don't come with me any further,' he said. 'Just in case you're seen by someone who might know you.'

'I don't care,' she said defiantly, but he shook his head, 'Blanche . . .' in a gentle reprimand. They stood facing one another and he reached out and took her hand.

'Goodbye, Blanche.'

She said nothing. She knew that if she spoke it would release more tears and she had already wept too much.

So, silently she stood and watched as he crossed the street. She did not move again until he had gone out of sight, turning a corner with just one last backward glance. Continuing to gaze after him even though he was gone she said softly,

'It's not over, Gentry. It's not.'

Only then did she move. Taking a grip on her valise, she turned and walked away. Later, after she had wandered around for a while, she returned to Almond Street.

The next day she heard from Alfredo Pastore saying that he would be arriving in England on Friday, August 3rd. He would write to her again from London following his arrival, he said, and would travel down to see her a few days later – if she would allow him to – as soon as his business commitments would permit. His letter barely touched her. Gentry's departure had left in her heart a void that nothing, she felt, would ever fill.

The days passed slowly by. Without Clara's presence the house seemed strange, and in addition Blanche found that she had not enough to do. In attempts to be occupied and useful she took to helping as much as she could in the tasks of the house – giving a helping hand to Mrs Warrimer, the cook-housekeeper. Even so, there was not enough to take up much of her time or engage much of her concentration, and she was left with time on her hands, time in which to brood.

A week following Gentry's departure she received a letter from a doctor in answer to an advertisement she had placed in a local paper. He was seeking a resident governess for his two daughters, he said, and would like to interview her. He suggested that, if convenient, he would call on her on Thursday morning at eleven.

Blanche at once sat down to answer the letter. She would be in at the proposed time, she said, and would be very happy to see him then.

When Marsh returned from the shop that evening Blanche told him of the coming interview with the doctor. But with the problem of Jacko, she said, she didn't hold out a great deal of hope. She had been interviewed on a few occasions already in her search for employment, but in each case when she had stated that Jacko would have to accompany her she had met with no success. Now Marsh said that if it still proved to be a problem she could leave the dog where he was. After all, he said, Clara had become very fond of Jacko, as he was of her. 'And you can come and visit him whenever you want to,' he went on. 'And he'll be well looked after, you can be sure of that.' He paused, smiling. 'Besides,' he added, 'it'll give you a reason for returning to see us.'

The next day, Tuesday, she heard again from Alfredo Pastore. Writing from his London hotel, he said he would travel to Bath on Friday and would call at the house in the hope of seeing her then.

By the time Dr Walsh arrived on Thursday morning Blanche had decided to accept George Marsh's offer and let Jacko remain where he was. Apart from the convenience of the arrangement where she was concerned it would also be better for the dog; it was likely that he would not live for many more years, and it was best that he remain where he was comfortable. So, when, after some discussion, Dr Walsh offered her the position, she made no mention of Jacko. She would be free to begin work at the beginning of September, she said, once her present pupil, Clara, had gone off to boarding school.

And so it was arranged. When the doctor left the house a little later Blanche knew a great feeling of relief. At least she had made some advance. Not only had she secured employment but the problem of Jacko had also been solved.

But for how long was she to know the temporary sense of security that came to her now? she asked herself. The position in Dr Walsh's household would not last for very long, and she would once again be without anywhere to live. And was she to go on like this forever? Without roots, without prospects? Perhaps she should have accepted George's proposal. In no way could he be described as wealthy, but they would live comfortably together, and there was no doubt that, with some imagination and the right application, his shop could have considerable prospects. But George Marsh was not Gentry.

Alfredo Pastore arrived the following afternoon, and Blanche went down to the library where he stood waiting for her. Tanned and looking dashing in his flannel suit, patterned waistcoat and khaki necktie, he came towards her holding out both hands, taking her hands in his, bringing them to his chest.

'Oh, Blanche,' he said, 'it's been worth the wait, seeing you again.'

When she had made tea they sat together talking of this and that, and throughout the conversation it was clear that there had been no lessening of his interest in her.

Why, he asked, had she not answered his letters when he had written from Sicily? She replied evasively that she had been concerned with other matters and that she had not expected to see him again. 'Perhaps,' he said, smiling, 'you didn't *want* to see me again.' But no, she assured him, that had not been the case at all.

He asked later if he might call again that evening and take her out to dinner. She agreed with very little hesitation, finding herself glad of the opportunity for some diversion, for the chance to be released for a while from the dullness of her routine.

There was another reason for her acceptance of his offer, a reason which, though increasingly present in her consciousness, was brought nearer to the surface of her mind that same evening. Having got ready early for Alfredo's visit, she had gone to the drawing room to sit and talk to Marsh for a few minutes. She had told him earlier that she would be out for dinner, adding that Pastore was in town and was coming to take her out. He had made no comment but had simply nodded and said that he hoped she would have a pleasant evening. Now, sitting there in a little silence that had fallen she had become aware that he was speaking to her. 'I'm sorry,' she said, turning to him. 'What were you saying?'

'It's not important.' Smilingly, he added, 'You were miles away.'

'Was I?' Under his scrutiny she turned away.

'Blanche,' he said, 'is anything wrong?'

'Wrong?' She gave a little laugh and shook her head. 'No, nothing at all. What could be wrong?'

'That's what I'm asking you.'

'No,' she said, 'there's nothing wrong.' Getting up from her chair, she moved to the door. 'I must go and finish getting ready.'

In her room she sat on the bed. Marsh's words had touched a nerve, forcing her to acknowledge, albeit tacitly, the reality of her preoccupation. The reason for her preoccupation was that her period was late – and usually it was so regular . . .

She sat there for a few moments longer then, dismissing the threatened nightmare from her mind, got up and smoothed her dress and touched at her hair. As she did so she heard from below the ring of the front doorbell. Alfredo was here. She picked up her coat, her bag. She was worrying about nothing. It would all come right in a day or two. Lots of women were late for no real reason at all. It happened all the time. In a day or two she would find that she had been fretting for nothing. With a few final admonishing words to herself she gave a last look in the glass and went from the room.

To her surprise she found that she enjoyed the evening very much – far more than she had expected to. It turned out to be more than the temporary diversion she had looked for; Alfredo proved a very attentive, thoughtful and amusing companion, and in his company the time passed swiftly and she found that she was able to forget, for long periods at a time, the problem that threatened to preoccupy her mind.

When he escorted her back to Almond Street that night he thanked her warmly for a pleasant evening and asked if they could meet again the following day. If she cared to they could go to the theatre, he said, and afterwards for some supper. Blanche said she was agreeable, and when he leaned forward and lightly kissed her she made no attempt to draw away. Straightening, he said:

'I've thought of you so much since we last met, Blanche. I couldn't understand why you hadn't written; I so hoped you would.' Then, smiling, he said: 'Anyway, that's all over now. I hope this time to persuade you to see things my way. I haven't got much time in which to do so, but I'm hopeful. My feelings towards you haven't changed at all.'

The following evening was fine and warm and Blanche was ready soon after he arrived. In the cab he had hired they drove to the theatre where they saw and enjoyed Barrie's *The Admirable Crichton*. Afterwards they went for supper at an hotel.

When Pastore had given their orders the wine waiter poured champagne. Pastore looked at Blanche over the rim of his glass, smilingly toasted her, drank and then said:

'I have to leave for London tomorrow. But I shan't be gone long. I can be back by Thursday afternoon.' He looked into her eyes for a moment then said, 'Is there any point in my returning, Blanche?'

She did not know what to say. 'Point?' she said. 'I – I don't understand.'

'Of course you understand,' he said. 'You understand very well what I mean. I'm talking about *us*, Blanche – you and me.' He reached out, laid a hand gently on hers. 'Tell me you'd like me to come back.'

'Oh – Alfredo . . . please – let's not get too – too serious.'

'*I am* serious,' he said. 'I'm *very* serious. I haven't got time for your English games.'

The waiter brought the soup. When he had gone again Alfredo said:

'Well? What do you say?'

When she did not answer he raised one eyebrow and gave a sardonic smile. 'Blanche, you're toying with me. Don't, please.' Then, leaning towards her, he said softly:

'I love you, Blanche. I want to marry you.'

She had known what he would say; had been expecting it. Shaking her head she said, 'You move so quickly, Alfredo. I can't keep up with you.'

He raised a hand. 'Don't give me an answer now. As I said, I have to go to London tomorrow, but I can be back by Thursday evening or late afternoon. I shall ask you again then. So, please – give my question very serious thought, I beg you. If your answer is no then I promise I will accept it and you'll never hear from me again; I'll never bother you again. If your answer is yes – and I do so hope it is – then I'll get a special licence and we'll get married and leave for Sicily at once.'

Blanche took a breath, opening her mouth to speak, but he gently touched a finger to her lips.

'No, don't say anything right now,' he said. 'Tell me on Thursday. For now –' he gestured to the soup before her, 'eat your supper.'

Pastore was to leave for London by an early afternoon train the next day. Blanche, however, was not thinking of his departure or of his final injunction to think carefully on his proposal. Preoccupied with her problem, she found herself over and over counting the days. And the more she thought about it the more certain she became that she must be pregnant. She could think of no other reason to account for the time.

Next day, Monday, meant that a week had gone by. Her certainty grew stronger.

She spent the morning in her room, sitting in her armchair by the window, mending her clothes while Jacko lay at her feet. He had seemed slower than ever in climbing the stairs to her room.

The day was very bright with a warm sun, and after a light luncheon which she ate with Lily and Mrs Warrimer in the kitchen she carried a cup of tea and a book out into the back garden. There she made herself comfortable on a garden bench set beneath the spreading arms of an old apple tree in the middle of the lawn. Jacko, having followed her, lay down in the tree's shade.

Blanche had begun reading H. G. Wells's *The War of the Worlds*, but her preoccupation made concentration difficult, and she found her attention continually wandering. Among the leaves above her head the wasps buzzed as they ate the ripening fruit. Idly she watched as a male blackbird chased his brown-feathered offspring from his home territory, and as the younger bird repeatedly returned, only to be driven away again each time. Lily came from the kitchen with a basket over her arm and moved to the kitchen garden beyond the lawn and the flower beds. As she went past the lawn Blanche heard her call out: 'No, we've got nothing to give away, thank you very much, so get away with you.'

Turning, following the direction of Lily's voice, Blanche craned her neck and saw through the screen of the low-hanging apple leaves that the object of Lily's annoyance was another of the wandering tramps who called at intervals in the hope of getting money or work. She could just see him beyond Lily's shoulder; a poor wreck of a creature, an old man who had hobbled up the garden path from the lower gate that backed onto the lane. Unkempt and unshaven, he stood uncertainly on the gravel path, hat clutched in his right hand. Lily flapped a hand at him as if she were shooing away some bothersome animal. 'Go away, go away,' she cried out. 'Go on or I'll set the dog on you.' At her words Blanche immediately thought of the time when she and Gentry had been approached by the young man outside the hotel, of how she had been shamed at her own past reactions. Now, quickly putting down her book, she got up from the seat.

She started to say to Lily that she would deal with the matter, but as she began to speak she heard a strange, almost unearthly sound coming from her right. Startled, she turned and saw that it came from Jacko. She watched as he got to his feet while he emitted the sound again, a loud, lingering howl, followed by a plaintive, whimpering, drawn-out cry, that seemed to go on and on. And both she and Lily, frozen in their actions, watched as the dog, moving unsteadily but very swiftly on his stiff old legs, started across the grass, whimpering as he went. Standing amazed, Blanche watched as Jacko moved across the garden, pushing heedlessly through the shrubbery, ploughing through the flowers of the herbaceous border, body jack-knifing as his violently wagging tail bent his body double, as he moved towards the stranger on the gravel path. And she saw the stranger crouch to meet him, reaching out to him. And she watched as Jacko, giving out yelping, delirious cries of ecstasy, found Ernest again, at last.

Chapter Thirty-Seven

Several hours had gone by now since Ernest's return. Although he had insisted that he was all right, Blanche, weeping, had quickly seen, to her horror, that he was in fact close to collapse out there on the garden path, and together she and Lily had supported him, helping him into the house. Somehow they had got him up the stairs and into Blanche's room where they had assisted him onto the bed. Lily then had gone from the room, saying that she would help Mrs Warrimer to prepare some food for him.

Blanche and Ernest were alone then – alone except for Jacko who stood close by, watching intently, eyes never moving from Ernest's face. Blanche pulled off Ernest's boots and, sitting at the side of the bed, gazed at him while at the same time she had fought to stem the flood of her tears.

'Blanche . . . Blanche . . . Dear Blanche. Don't cry . . .' His hand had moved towards her on the coverlet and she had reached out and laid her own hand over it. And her tears had continued to flow, spilling over in a flood of joy at his return and from grief at his condition.

Through her tears she gazed at him as he lay on the bed, propped up against the pillows. So many, many times over the years she had imagined their reunion. But it had never been like this. In her mind's eye it had taken place against the background of some imaginary house; where, she did not know, but there was a prosperous look about its sunlit exterior. And Ernest's appearance showed that prosperity also, and she saw him always as a happy, healthy, young man, smartly dressed, laughing as he moved towards her.

And how different was this reality. It was hard to believe that this was the same man who had kissed her on the cheek – that kiss of goodbye – that night in Colford not much more than three years ago. Now his body looked thin, gaunt and emaciated, while beneath his days' old beard his face had a disturbing pallor that was relieved only by the unhealthy red of the skin that was stretched over his cheekbones. There was something wrong with his left arm, too, she had been swift to notice; the elbow joint moved stiffly and he appeared to have only limited use of the fingers of his hand.

'Oh, Ernie, love,' Blanche said, 'where have you been all this time? I've been so worried about you.'

'Oh – various places. Bradford mostly.'

'Is that where you've come from now?'

'Yes.'

'How did you get here?'

'Walked.'

'You *walked?* All that way?'

'Ah, it was that or stay where I was. And I – I wanted to see you, Blanche.' He paused for a moment then said hoarsely, the tears shining in his eyes, 'You know, Blanche, this isn't the way I planned it at all. I intended –' His words broke off in a spate of coughing that brought sudden sweat standing out on his brow. Pulling a ragged handkerchief from his pocket he spat into it, looked for a moment at the blood there, then closed it in his fist and lay back again, exhausted.

'Rest, Ernie. Rest – better not try to talk.'

Weakly he smiled at her. 'But – I got so much to say.'

'Later. Say it later. There'll be time. Rest for a while and get your strength back.'

Lily came to the door soon after with a bowl of soup. To Blanche's relief he ate most of it. There was no question, though, but that he was very ill, and after another spate of coughing that again left him sweating and gasping for breath, Blanche asked Lily to run for the doctor.

Dr Quinn, the Marsh family doctor, was out on calls, Lily came back to report, but added that he would come as soon as he could.

Before the doctor appeared George Marsh returned from the shop and Blanche wept while she told him of Ernest's arrival. Then, between them, he and Blanche helped Ernest to bathe, after which Ernest asked for a razor to shave. But the effort exhausted him so that George took the task over. When Dr Quinn eventually arrived just before seven, with apologies for his tardiness, Ernest was lying sleeping between the sheets of Blanche's bed.

Dr Quinn was a tall, lean man in his late fifties, with a seamed face and a direct glance. Standing in the hall, Blanche quietly told him of Ernest's arrival at the house. Afterwards she led him up to the room where Ernest lay, then left him there while she went back downstairs to wait. A little while later the doctor went to Blanche where she sat in the library. His expression was grave as he stood before her.

'Is – is he going to be all right, Doctor?' she asked as she rose to him.

He gestured to her to sit. 'Please – sit down . . .'

At his words Blanche sat back on the sofa; Quinn sat beside her, placing his leather bag near his feet. There was incredulity in his eyes as he said:

'You told me that he walked from *Bradford*?'

'So he said, yes.'

With a little wondering shake of his head, he said, 'Well, God alone knows how he managed it. He must have had some – inner strength driving him on or something – because it wasn't his physical strength, that's for certain.'

Blanche gazed into his eyes, trying to read there the answers she sought. 'Is he – going to be all right? He is, isn't he?'

Quinn placed a hand over hers. 'I'm sorry, my dear. As I say – I don't know how he got this far. He –'

'But now he's here he'll be all right,' she broke in. 'I can look after him. I can make him well again.'

'I'm sure if anyone could, then you could. But I'm afraid that – well, you must know the truth. I'm afraid that your brother – can't live very long.'

She flinched as if she had been struck. She turned her head away. The doctor said after a moment:

'I'm sorry – but you have to know the truth. It would be wrong of me to try to give you any hope – when there is none.'

She nodded. Quinn said:

'I think he said he's thirty-one.'

'Yes. He'll be thirty-two in October.'

'This illness is a – dreadful thing. Do you have any other family?'

'No. I'm all he has. He's all I have.' She turned back to face him. She could hardly speak. 'Is there really no hope?'

'I'm afraid the deterioration of his lungs is already so far advanced. To be truthful I don't know how he's held out for this long. And to walk all that distance. The wonder *is* that he *got* here.'

'So it could be – any day?'

He pressed her hand. 'Or any hour, my dear.'

*

Blanche showed the doctor to the front door, opened it and stood aside. She thanked him, and he gave a little nod and said that he would call the next day. In the meantime he would have some medicine made up; perhaps, he suggested, someone could return with him to his surgery to bring it back. At once Blanche called to Lily and asked her if she would accompany the doctor. Quickly, obligingly, the girl put on her coat and followed Dr Quinn out to the street where his motor car waited at the kerb in the early evening light.

Having closed the door behind them, Blanche leaned back against it for a moment, like a runner pausing for breath. Then, with a sigh she stepped forward, moving towards the stairs. As she stepped onto the lower step George Marsh emerged from the dining room.

'Blanche . . .'

As he came towards her she avoided looking him in the eye, as if somehow he might see past her now calm exterior to the fear and desperation that lay so close below the surface.

'The doctor's just gone,' she said.

'Yes, I heard him leave.'

'He's coming back tomorrow. Lily's gone with him to bring back some medicine. I hope you don't mind.'

'Of course not.' After a moment Marsh said, 'What did Dr Quinn say?'

Blanche shrugged, not trusting herself to speak at once. Then she said, 'I won't give up hope.'

Marsh's hand lifted, rested briefly on hers on the newel post. 'I told you – if there's anything he needs you have only to ask.'

'I know – and thank you.'

She turned then and went on up the stairs.

Entering the bedroom, she softly closed the door behind her and moved to the bed. In the dim glow of the gaslight, Jacko, lying on the floor at the bedside as close to Ernest's pillow as he could get, looked around at Blanche's entrance and thumped the floor once or twice with his tail. Blanche bent to pat him gently on the head and then stood looking down at Ernest who lay with his eyes closed. She could see so clearly now the unmistakable signs of his sickness. But it wasn't too late, she said to herself. He could be saved. He had not come all that way only to die. She would save him.

As she stood there he opened his eyes and smiled at her. She returned his smile and asked softly:

'Did I wake you?'

'No. I wasn't asleep. We were waiting for you to come upstairs, Jacko and I.'

She moved to the chair and sat down. In spite of the haggardness of Ernest's face, the ravages wrought by his illness she could see there now a kind of calm; it had been growing since the moment she had found him again, since that moment when she had run to his side on the garden path, had held him in her arms. It was as if he had found a kind of peace.

'I'm sorry I let you worry so about me, Blanche,' he said.

'Ernest – please don't talk. Please rest.'

'No, I must talk to you. I didn't write because – well, because I'd promised you that I would send for you. I was so sure that I'd be a success – that it would only be a matter of time before everything was the way I wanted it to be. And I thought that when I had everything prepared I could write and – and if you still wanted to you could join me. It didn't work out, though. Nothing worked out the way I hoped it would, the way I expected it to.'

'Ernie, it doesn't matter anymore. Don't talk, please. Please rest.'

506

'I can rest later. I have to talk to you now. Don't stop me. There isn't much time.'

'Oh, Ernie –'

'It's all right, Blanche. I've known for some while now – that's why I came here. I wanted to see you before I – while I still could. Though at times I thought I'd never make it. At last, though, I got to Hallowford and after asking around a bit I found where Mrs Callow lived in her little cottage. She told me where you were.'

As Blanche sat there Ernest continued to talk. She urged him several times to be silent and rest, but he would not and went on, his words a never-ending stream, tumbling over one another in his feverish effort to say to her everything that was on his mind. She heard from him about his early efforts to make good on his first trip to the mills of Bradford and Leeds, of the hardships that abounded there, the squalid living conditions for the thousands who had poured into the towns in search of prosperity. She heard of his eventual disillusionment and subsequent enlistment in the army and going out to the Transvaal. He spoke a little of his experiences there, of how, shortly before the war had ended, he had been shot in the arm and then had become sick with dysentery, returning to England in a weakened condition. 'I couldn't come to you then,' he said. 'I couldn't come to you when I was in such a state. When I came back to you I wanted to be whole and healthy – and have something behind me. I wanted to be able to offer you a home – not the squalor and the – the misery that I found.'

He gazed at her, his hollow eyes burning into hers. 'It's what I told you before, Blanche – it all comes down to poverty. It destroys everything in the end. It will take the strongest person and wear him down, break him down. It makes rogues of good men. It destroys everything in its path.' He paused. 'I'm afraid for you, Blanche.'

'Hush, hush, Ernie.'

As Blanche spoke there came a knock at the door and Lily was there, having returned with a bottle of medicine from the doctor. Blanche thanked her. When the door had closed again behind the maid Blanche poured out a little of the medicine and gave it to Ernest. As she set down the spoon he said, taking up his earlier theme:

'I'm afraid you'll let it happen to you too, Blanche. And believe me, it can – and so easily. You start to go through bad times and you think things will be better. Tomorrow will be better, you say. But tomorrow *isn't* better. Tomorrow's often worse. And in the end you look back on your life and you see nothing but a string of – of empty yesterdays – and each one had been invested with *hope*. And in the end it's all ashes. You mustn't let it happen to you, Blanche. I told you before – you must make things happen for you. You must. Don't accept whatever life cares to offer you; you have to reach out and take what you want. I learned that. Too late. Don't let it happen to you, too. You won't, will you?'

'No, Ernie, I won't.'

'There's a good girl.' He smiled, turned and looked down to his side where Jacko lay. 'And there's a good old boy, too,' he said. 'Ent that right, Jacko?'

At the tone, at the words, Jacko rose, lifting his cold nose to meet Ernest's hand that reached down to him. After stroking the dog's head for a moment or two Ernest laid his hand back on the coverlet. 'I think I shall sleep now for a while,' he said. Then, frowning, he added, 'Where are you going to sleep?'

'Don't you worry about me. I shall be all right. If I need a bed there's a spare one. But I shall stay here.'

He smiled. 'I won't insist that you don't. It's so good to have you near.'

'Blanche . . .'

And she was awake. Suddenly. Sitting in the chair she had thought that she would not sleep, could not sleep. But towards morning sleep had come and she had drifted off. And now Ernest was calling her name and she was awake, alert again.

She was at his side at once, sitting on the bed, arms reaching out, wrapping him in her embrace, for the first time in their lives the stronger in the situation. As she held him she became aware of Jacko moving about the room, prowling in a circle, like some phantom shape in the dim light of the oil lamp's tiny flame, lost, impotent, making little whimpering cries.

'Blanche . . .' Although she was so close Ernest called out her name as if she were far away.

'Blanche . . .!'

And there was alarm in his voice. Her name on his lips was a hoarse, gargled cry. 'I'm here, I'm here,' she murmured. She stroked his hair as she held him, weak as a child in her arms, while she felt the sweat of his forehead wet and clammy against her chin. 'I'm here, I'm here.' She could hear the phlegm rattling in his throat as he sucked in the air. He gasped, called to her again:

'Blanche . . .'

'Yes, Ernie, yes. I'm here.'

'Oh . . . oh . . . oh . . .' Little sighing cries, like those of a lost child; a child waking to find his mother close, the nightmare over. She could hear the sudden sound of relief in his voice. 'Ah, Blanche, you're here . . .'

'Yes – I'm here, Ernie. Always . . .'

'Yes . . .' And then, suddenly: 'Remember – what I said, Blanche.'

'Ernie –'

'Don't – let it – happen to you.'

For a moment she could not think what was he talking about, but then she recalled his earlier admonishings. 'No,' she said, 'no, I won't.'

She held him in silence for some moments, listening while his breath struggled in his raddled lungs. After a while, his voice a hoarse whisper, he asked her to get him some water. Releasing him, she turned to the small bedside table and took up the jug. In the moment that she did so he spoke to her again:

'Blanche – quickly – hold me. Hold my hands.'

Setting down the jug so quickly that the water slopped over onto the table she spun at the sound of his voice, bending to him, reaching out for the hands he raised before him. His eyes were closed. As her hands touched his she felt within each of them a little flicker of life, acknowledgements of her touch. *I won't let you go, Ernie*, a voice cried defiantly in her head. *I won't let you die. I won't, I won't.* But his hands in hers were already still.

On Thursday morning, with the skies heavy with the promise of rain, the coffin containing Ernest's body was conveyed to Bath and placed in the coffin van of a train bound for Trowbridge. In one of the carriages sat Blanche, George Marsh beside her.

Dry-eyed now, Blanche sat numbly gazing out at the passing scenery and the stations through which they passed – Bathampton, Limpley Stoke, Freshford, Bradford-on-Avon. On arrival at Trowbridge she stood silently by while the coffin was taken from the train and loaded onto a waiting hearse. When the two wreaths had been placed on the coffin – one from herself, one from George – she and George climbed into a carriage, which then set off to follow the hearse along the winding road to Hallowford.

At St Peter's church the hearse and carriage came to a halt and Blanche and Marsh alighted onto the grass verge. As the bearers lifted the coffin to carry it to the graveside Blanche left Marsh's side and stooped in the grass to pick a handful of daisies.

A little later she stood at George Marsh's side while the coffin was lowered into the earth. Reaching out, she opened her fingers and let the small white flowers fall onto the coffin. It was over.

The rain came on in a heavy downpour as they drove back to Trowbridge station, lashing the windows of the carriage and distorting the view of the woodland, the fields and the heathland. Blanche had travelled the route so many times over the years. She would never travel it again.

On the train bound for Bath she sat gazing out unseeing from the rain-washed window of the railway carriage. Apart from the grief in her heart she was aware of a feeling of anger. Her mother and father, Mary, Arthur and Agnes . . . and now Ernest. All gone. And Ernest was right, she said to herself. It was the poverty that did it. *It destroys everything in the end,* Ernest had said. *It will take the strongest person and wear him down, break him down.* And he was right. All those stunted, withered dreams – like flowers trying to grow in some city street, starved of soil and sunlight. Her father with his talent for painting – destroyed by poverty – his dreams left to atrophy for want of nutriment – and which lack had also destroyed the others. And now Ernest, cast out by a society that had used the best of him and discarded the rest. *It's what I told you before, Blanche – it all comes down to poverty.* His words rang in her mind, echoing over and over . . . She saw him as he had been all those years ago, a tall, chestnut-haired young man with straight, strong limbs and steady grey eyes, taking Marianne and herself for rambles through the woods and over the hills. All the promise, gone. And then her imaginings would bring him back to her as he had been at the end – broken, and disillusioned with life, and with nothing left to live for. *I'm afraid for you, Blanche. I'm afraid you'll let it happen to you too.*

'No, Ernie, I won't.'

George Marsh turned to her and she realized she had spoken the words aloud. 'It's all right,' she said, giving him a little smile. 'I'm all right.'

But to herself she silently repeated her vow: *I won't, Ernie. I won't.*

In her room in the house on Almond Street Blanche changed her clothes. Standing before the mirror she laid her spread hands over her belly. It had been ten days now, and she knew with an unwavering certainty that there was a child growing within her; she had no doubt of it whatsoever. Gentry's child.

Just after six-thirty Alfredo Pastore arrived at the house. George Marsh himself answered his ring at the bell and showed him into the library, after which he went upstairs and informed Blanche of her visitor's presence. Blanche, though expecting Alfredo's appearance at some time, was not quite ready for him. Telling the visitor that she would be down in a few minutes, Marsh poured glasses of sherry for them both and as they drank he spoke briefly of Ernest's arrival and subsequent death, and of his burial that morning.

When Blanche herself appeared ten minutes later

Marsh excused himself and left them together. Pastore at once went to Blanche, reached out and took her hands.

'Mr Marsh told me about your brother, Blanche. I'm so terribly, terribly sorry.'

She thanked him.

The stilted conversation that ensued lasted for some minutes and then he said:

'What I came to say, Blanche – the answer I came back for –' He shrugged, at a loss. 'How can I ask you now – without appearing insensitive?'

She gazed at him for a moment then turned to the window and stood gazing out over the street.

'It's all right, Alfredo,' she said without looking at him. 'Life has to go on, hasn't it? Such things happen, but life has to go on.'

She thought of the child growing inside her. She had already made up her mind.

He stepped forward. 'I'm glad you understand . . . You see – I have to return to Palermo in a matter of days. I was hoping, that you would – would return with me. But now . . .' He shrugged again. 'Is it – possible?'

'My brother's gone,' she said. 'Nothing I could do could help him.'

'If you would –' He took from his pocket a piece of paper. 'In the hope that you would agree I – I've taken out a special licence. We could be married very quickly.'

Blanche did not answer. He added:

'I know how you're feeling now, Blanche, but you'll get over your grief and I can make you happy, I know I can. If you'll give me the chance.'

She turned to him, seeing the chance he offered. And what were the alternatives? They were too depressing even to contemplate. *I'm afraid for you, Blanche. I'm afraid you'll let it happen to you too.* No, Ernie, no. But it was not only herself now, anyway, to be considered. Soon she would have a child to think of as well.

With a little shake of her head she said, 'There's nothing for me here anymore, Alfredo. I've nothing to stay in England for.' She gave him a grave smile. 'So if you want my answer, then my answer is yes.'

Blanche and Alfredo, as man and wife, left for Palermo four days later. On the afternoon before their departure Blanche, much concerned about Jacko, who was refusing to eat or drink, had gone to seek him in his kennel in which, since Ernest's death, he had taken to hiding away. Usually on going to him, when she would try to coax him to eat or drink something, he would simply raise his head and gaze back at her out of the confined, shadowed interior of his shelter and then lay his head on his paws again.

On this particular afternoon she called his name but got no response at all, not even the flicker of an eyelid. Crouching lower, reaching in and touching him, she realized that he was dead.

When she left Bath the next day with Alfredo she saw Jacko's death as the breaking of her last link with the past.

PART FIVE

Chapter Thirty-Eight

'Has Daddy gone, Mama?'

Adriana's voice came from the open doorway as Blanche sat before her dressing table.

'Yes, darling. He's just left.'

'I looked for him but I couldn't find him. He didn't say goodbye. What time will he be back?'

'– I don't know. We'll have to wait and see.'

'I wanted to talk to him.'

'Oh, yes?' Blanche could guess what it was about. Confirming Blanche's belief, Adriana said:

'I want to talk to him about Betta.'

Blanche said nothing. Adriana went on:

'He's always going away these days.'

'Yes – but I'm afraid he has a lot on his mind right now.'

Adriana nodded, sighed, then: 'Why was he shouting so?'

Avoiding giving an answer, Blanche said, '– Oh, was he?'

'Very loudly.' Adriana gazed at her. 'Are you nearly ready to leave?' Her tone now was a little impatient. She was wearing her coat and hat and carrying a paper bag given her by the cook: scraps of bread for the ducks.

'In a moment, darling.' Blanche's tone gave evidence of her preoccupation as she turned her face to catch the light. As she did so her eyes were drawn to Adriana's reflection beyond her shoulder as the child came towards her across the room.

Coming to a stop at Blanche's side, Adriana looked at her mother in the mirror. Blanche, her own eyes upon her, saw the child's expression change to one of concern.

'Mama, what happened?' Adriana said. 'Your face is swollen.'

Blanche covered her upper cheek with her hand to hide the swelling there, the emerging bruise. 'It's nothing, my dear. I just had a – a little accident.'

Adriana shook her head in an imitation of adult resignation and hopelessness. 'You're always having accidents lately.'

'– Yes, I'll just have to be more careful in the future.'

With her powder puff Blanche gave an additional light dusting to her cheek, then took out her loose hair-pins and secured her hair where it had come loose. The growing strain of the past five years had taken their toll, showing now behind the smile she gave to Adriana, and in the tension that lay behind her eyes as they moved back to take in her own reflection, the weariness in her sigh as, gazing at herself, she gave a final touch to her hair and let her hands fall in a little gesture of resignation and despair.

'Are you nearly ready, Mama?'

'Almost.'

Her eyes moved back to the child. Adriana was four-and-a-half now, small and thin-legged, a little bird of a child. The blue of her eyes was Blanche's own, but the set and shape of them Gentry's; Gentry's too the glossy black of her pigtails and heavy lashes.

In a sudden demonstration of love, and her own need for closeness, affection, Blanche wrapped Adriana in her arms and hugged her. The child suffered the embrace for a moment then said, 'Mama, are we going?'

'Yes, we're going right this minute.'

Blanche released her and got up from her seat. When she had put on her own hat and coat she and Adriana left the room and started down the stairs. They met Betta, Adriana's nurse, on the way up. The plain face of the eighteen-year-old girl was puffed with weeping, while her eyes showed such sadness that Blanche could hardly bear to look at her. We make a good pair, Blanche said to herself. Last night the girl had pleaded with her; did she *have* to go? she had asked. Was there nothing that the signora could do? Blanche, though, had been able to say nothing that was of any comfort.

Blanche went on down the stairs. Reaching the hall she was not surprised to see Edgardo, Alfredo's valet-*cum*-butler, emerge from an ante room near the front door. How he always managed to be so close never ceased to surprise her. In his early fifties, he was a short, lean, swarthy man. Now as Blanche and Adriana crossed the hall his already bent body bent further in the faintest bow, a gesture touched with an insolence that was echoed in the touch of his mouth and the lift of his brows. In his heavily accented English he said, 'The signora wishes something?'

His question came from no feeling of solicitousness, Blanche was well aware, but simply from a wish to know her intentions – where she and Adriana were bound.

Raising a hand to cover – casually – the left side of her face, Blanche replied, 'No, thank you.'

Her tone was cold. She had learned very soon after her initial arrival at the villa that any pleasantness she showed the man was very swiftly construed as a sign of weakness. With the realization she had tried to back-track, to make up the lost ground, but the damage had been done, the mould set, and she knew that she could never win. The situation had been the same now for the years she had lived in the house. He was always unfailingly polite to her, but she always discerned behind his politeness a thinly-veiled contempt that discomfited her and put her on the defensive. At the beginning she had spoken to Alfredo of Edgardo's manner towards her, but he had scoffed at her words, saying that it was all her imagination and paranoia. She knew better, though. Also, she had learned since that it would do no good to make any further complaint about the servant. Edgardo was without question Alfredo's man; devoted to his master, and implicitly trusted by him, there was no doubt where his loyalties lay.

'If the signore should return . . . ?' Edgardo said.

'You can tell him we shan't be long,' Blanche said. 'We're only going to the park.'

'The park?' Edgardo opened the door, frowning slightly at the English word, feigning non-comprehension. Blanche said shortly:

'The *Giardino Inglese* – you know very well where I mean.'

'Ah – yes, signora.'

Blanche ignored the faintly mocking inclination of his head. As she and Adriana moved down the curving flight of stone steps she could feel Edgardo's eyes upon the back of her head. Their feeling of antipathy was quite mutual.

The villa, large and spacious, stood on the southern side of the Via Catania. Reaching the corner where in the spring the flower-seller stood surrounded by his banks of brightly coloured flowers, Blanche and Adriana turned to the left onto Palermo's main *corso*, the Via della Libertà. Hand in hand they walked along the pavement, past the shops – all open-fronted to all winds and weathers – while beside them along the *corso* the motor cars and motor omnibuses – the latter a recent

520

innovation – fought for space with the old horse-driven cabs and the donkey- and mule-carts and carriages.

How different it all was from England, and what a place of contrasts. Palermo, a bustling, dusty city, boasted an opera house that was said to be the largest in the world, while the peasants who lived outside the city's boundaries dwelt in caves and empty tombs. For Adriana, of course, the Sicilian way of life was the only way of life she had ever known, and no part of it seemed to her to be remarkable, but where Blanche herself was concerned she occasionally thought she would never cease to be surprised at the city's ways.

After a few minutes walk they entered the public park. There, freed from the confines of the house, and with space about her, Adriana let go Blanche's hand and dashed away, Blanche quickly calling after her not to run too fast in case she should fall. At Blanche's words Adriana came to a halt and turned.

'I want to see the fish and feed the ducks,' she said.

'Wait for me, then. They won't go away. We'll go together.'

Adriana paused for a moment then ran back to Blanche's side. Hand in hand they strolled on. This early December Saturday morning, with the bright sun reflecting off the cobbles, the weather for their walk was perfect. Before Adriana had started school that past autumn they had taken the walk in the *Giardino Inglese* almost every morning when the weather allowed. Now, however, their excursions were limited to the weekends.

In one corner of the gardens a group of old men congregated – as they always did when the weather was fine – to play chess and backgammon and to talk of the past. Adriana paused in her step as she and Blanche went by, her eyes as always drawn to the scene.

The two continued on, eventually making their way

to the edge of the wide pond, where Adriana took the scraps of bread from the paper bag and tossed them into the water. There was at once a little flurry of activity as the nearby ducks converged on the spot and snapped up the scraps. As the ducks slowly swam away again Adriana straightened, her blue eyes focusing on the stone statue of the two children who, crouching on a rock near the pond's centre, bent eternally over the water, hands reaching out to the golden fish that darted in the shadows beneath their outstretched fingers.

After a while, Adriana asked, turning to her mother, the stone children momentarily forgotten, 'When shall I invite Licia and Paulo and Tonio to the party?'

'Oh, we'll get that done in a day or two,' Blanche said. 'Christmas isn't for nearly three weeks yet.'

'D'you think Papa will be here?'

'At Christmas? I should think so. We'll have to see.'

Nothing was certain these days where Alfredo's movements were concerned. He was going off on his various trips more and more frequently of late. Apart from the fact of his absences, though, Blanche knew very little about his movements; of the purpose of them she knew even less – except, she was sure, that their outcome would not be to the good. Where he was at that moment she had no idea. After the scene following breakfast that morning he had left the house, slamming out of the door, giving her no indication of when he would return. And she had known better than to ask; after what had transpired she didn't want to risk his further anger. He might be still here in Palermo; he might have gone to Messina. Wherever he had gone there was no knowing when he would return. He might not be back for three or four days. As far as she was concerned, she thought bitterly, he could stay away for ever.

There was a vacant bench near the edge of the pond

and Blanche sat down upon it. Act in haste; repent at leisure; the words went through her mind. True. And how hastily she had acted. How swiftly everything had happened. The marriage at the register office; the painful goodbye to a shocked, somewhat stunned George – for Clara, who had still been in Weston-Super-Mare, there had been no goodbye at all – and then the departure for Sicily and Alfredo's villa here in Palermo. And now, that December of 1908, Blanche had been in the city for over five years. Five years. It seemed a great deal longer. And as far as her relationship with Alfredo went, the course of that time had been increasingly downhill.

The pain on her cheek where Alfredo had struck her had now subsided to a dull ache. Perhaps when he returned he would apologize. Not that she cared much. She had long since realized that his apologies made no difference, that they were meaningless – an awareness that even seemed to have touched *him* of late; expressions of contrition from him in recent times were very few and far between.

Thinking about him, about the events of that morning, Blanche thought again how astonishing it was that one could be so deceived by another person – by someone whom one thought one knew. Not that she had ever consciously believed that she had *known* Alfredo – but at the same time the little she had learned about him had never prepared her for what was to come. Though perhaps the signs had been there, she sometimes reminded herself; it was just that in her need for the solution to her own problems she had simply not seen them.

In any event, nothing had turned out the way she had hoped it would or expected it to. Everything had turned to ashes, all of it destroyed by one thing or another: most of their material assets had been gambled away, while any affection that she and Alfredo had ever felt for one another had long since been destroyed by his intolerance and his jealousies.

As far as their relationship went its failure came down to the fact that they were totally unsuited to one another. She had soon come to realize that Alfredo expected a wife to be submissive and compliant – to be there when needed, to be decorative, the perfect hostess, and a constant support for his actions, right or wrong. But to his dismay she saw things differently. And in any case she *could not* fit into such a mould and she had no intention of ever trying to. As a consequence Alfredo saw her as rebellious, defiant, and generally difficult – and as such she was a continuing challenge to his beliefs and his authority.

Apart from his need to dominate her, she also had to suffer his jealousy – a manifestation that further endorsed her growing doubts that they could ever live in harmony.

His passionate jealousy had first reared its head just three weeks after their arrival in Palermo following their marriage. It had been demonstrated with the arrival from England of a letter for her from George Marsh. In it, after voicing his hopes that she was happy, George had told her that Clara had been much affected at returning to find her, Blanche, gone away, and Jacko dead.

Alfredo's reaction to the arrival of the letter had astonished Blanche. On taking it from the maid who had brought it to the salon he had asked Blanche who was writing to her from England. Taking the letter from him and looking at the envelope she had recognized the handwriting. It was from George Marsh, she had said.

Alfredo had watched her closely as she read the letter and afterwards asked her what Marsh had said. She told him what Marsh had written about Clara's reaction to her departure and the loss of the dog.

'And what else does he say?'

'What else?' She looked at him in surprise. 'There's nothing else.'

'Tell me what else he says.'

'Alfredo –' she gazed at him, astonished at the intense expression on his face, his piercing eyes, 'I tell you there's nothing else of interest. He sends us his best wishes and tells me about Clara. There's no more.'

'Clara, Clara,' Alfredo said impatiently. 'What else does he say?'

Blanche looked at him a moment longer in disbelief and then, turning, moved away. He was at her side in an instant.

'Give me the letter.'

And before she could stop him he had reached out and torn the letter from her hand.

'– Alfredo –'

Ignoring her protests, he tore the letter from the envelope, opened it out and quickly read it. Then in one staccato gesture he handed it back to her. She refolded it, replaced it in the envelope.

'Are you satisfied now?' she said disdainfully.

'For the moment, yes. But I know the man is in love with you.'

'Alfredo, please –'

'I'm not a fool, so don't take me for one.' He stood glaring at her, then he said:

'What are you going to do now?'

'Do?'

'Are you going to answer it?'

'Of *course* I'm going to answer it.'

He paused. 'I'd rather you didn't.'

'But I must.'

'Don't I make myself clear? I told you – I would prefer that you did not answer the letter.'

'Don't be foolish; of course I shall answer it. Anyway, it's up to *me*. It's *my letter*.'

His hand came out, snatched the letter from her hand. This time, however, he did not give it back but instead tore it across and across. Then with a contemptuous toss of his hand he threw the pieces at her.

'There is your letter.'

As the pieces fell at her feet he was already turning, striding angrily away. In the open doorway he turned back to face her while she stared at him, aghast.

'You still do not seem to understand,' he said, '– I am master in my house, and *you* are now in Sicily. You're not in England. And the sooner you realize it the happier we shall be.'

He went from the room then, while Blanche stared after him. She could hardly believe what had taken place. The contempt and the anger in his eyes; it had been like seeing a different person. After a moment or two she stooped and gathered up the torn pieces of George's letter.

She and Alfredo had spent the remainder of that day with silence between them. But then that night he had come to her telling her that he was sorry for his behaviour. His contrition seemed total, and as he had held her in his arms and begged her to forgive him she had been surprised to discover the wetness of tears on his cheek. It was then she had hinted to him that she had an idea that she might be expecting a child. In the dim light of the lamp she had watched the joy on his face as he absorbed the news. A little later he had made love to her – though in his passion he had shown little regard for her own feelings. By that time, however, in the few weeks of their marriage, she had learned, and she no longer expected more from him. And, she told herself in moments of solitude, it was part of the price she must pay for the things she wanted – the promise of security and a name for her coming baby; next to such gains her own personal satisfactions were insignificant trivialities. And there had never been a time when she had expected *everything*.

In spite of his self-recriminations, however, Alfredo's exhibition of jealousy over George Marsh's letter had proved to be not an isolated phenomenon. As the days and weeks passed there were frequent demonstrations of it, so that Blanche began to dread any occasions that would bring her into contact with other men – occasions such as dinner parties when some or other of Alfredo's business associates would be invited. Usually, Blanche soon discovered, such events would be followed, when they were alone, by accusations levelled at her of flirting with various guests or encouraging familiarities with them. Her denials made no difference; Alfredo seemed unable to see past his own passionate jealousies and what he imagined to be the truth.

His jealousy and his demand for submission soon proved to be matched by the violence of his temper. On several occasions he had struck her and thrown various items at her; a bureau in the library still bore the signs of one of his violent outbursts, showing the deep scar sustained from the points of a pair of scissors which in his rage he had hurled at her. They had missed her by inches.

In time such incidents had brought to the forefront of her mind the notion that she and Alfredo should separate. How could she continue to live in a situation where her physical safety was at risk? – besides which the atmosphere was not one in which to raise a child. Alfredo, though, she knew, would never agree to a separation, and she was afraid to raise the matter. She was certain that the only way to leave him would be to go without his knowledge, to creep away at some time when he was unsuspicious and unaware. Even that exercise, though, would prove very difficult. When Alfredo himself was present there was never an opportunity to make such a move, and when he was away from the house there was always Edgardo about the place, with his keen eyes and ears, watching, listening.

And anyway, where could she go? What could she do? She had hardly any money to speak of. All the shopping for the house was done by the cook, with money allocated by Alfredo, under his instructions the household's budget and books managed by Edgardo. Blanche received an allowance for clothes and personal expenses, but she had soon found that it was impossible for her to save more than a trifling amount without arousing suspicion. She had been putting aside a little money from time to time, whenever she could, saving it in a purse which she kept in a chest in her room, but the growth of the sum was slow.

As she had no financial means of support in the event of an escape, so neither did she have any nearby friends she could call upon for help in her need. From the very start of their marriage Alfredo had discouraged her forming friendships. It was as if he wanted her to be dependent solely upon himself, and resented her finding amusement or companionship from any other source. So it was that any budding friendships with any other young women in the district that might otherwise have blossomed to the benefit of them both had swiftly been stifled.

Blanche's relationships with all her older friends had suffered in the same way. She had long ago ceased to keep up any correspondence with George Marsh and

Clara; such unpleasant scenes had ensued as a result of her trying to insist on keeping up the friendships that she had deemed it the wiser course to give them up. She had not written to or heard from the Marshes now in over four years.

And with Marianne the situation was almost the same. Since arriving in Sicily she and Marianne had met only three times. With Marianne and Gentry living in Messina, where some of Alfredo's own business interests were centred, it would have been the easiest thing for Alfredo sometimes to have taken Blanche and Adriana along on his occasional business trips, and so to have allowed the two women to be reunited. It had happened just once, not too long after Adriana's birth, but never since that time. On that occasion (as they had done several times since) Marianne and Gentry had invited Blanche and Alfredo and Adriana to stay at their hotel, the luxurious Metropole, but Alfredo had declined, instead reserving a suite for them at another hotel. In the event on that occasion it had still proved satisfactory for Blanche, for while Alfredo had gone about his work during those four days she and Marianne had been able to spend many hours together. Alfredo had clearly resented their closeness, however, notwithstanding that Marianne had done her best to show him a warm welcome by inviting the couple to dinner on two occasions during their stay.

It was clear to Blanche that Alfredo had not viewed her reunion with Marianne and Gentry with pleasure – and neither had he enjoyed either of the dinner parties. Afterwards, returning to Palermo, he had made it clear that such an excursion would not take place a second time, though he refused to go into his reasons for taking such a stand. Blanche simply had to be content with his decision.

The two other occasions when Marianne and Blanche had met had been when Gentry had brought Marianne to Palermo (Gentry had business in the city) and they had called at the villa on the Via Catania. As on both occasions they had arrived unexpectedly Alfredo had been unable to prevent the meetings.

'But Marianne is like my sister, my family,' Blanche protested to Alfredo on one occasion, to which he angrily retorted: 'But she is *not* your sister. And *we* are your family, Adriana and I.'

Was it, Blanche asked herself, that he resented any connection she had with her earlier life, her life before her marriage to him? There were such men, men who wanted to pretend that their wives or lovers had known no lives prior to the lives they shared. Or was his jealousy where Marianne was concerned less to do with Marianne and more to do with Gentry? It was possible. Alfredo was jealous of her where *any* man was concerned.

And yet with Gentry there had never been the slightest hint of the closeness that had once existed between them. On the few occasions on which they had met following Blanche's arrival in Sicily – over those days during her visit to Messina and on the two occasions when he had brought Marianne to the villa on the Via Catania – their behaviour with one another had been the model of propriety. They had never once been alone together, and their conversation had been that of distant friends. In fact, Blanche later said to herself, from Gentry's behaviour now on the few occasions when they met it was almost impossible to believe that there had ever been anything between them. Then, however, looking at Adriana's dark hair and the set of her eyes, it would all come back. It had not been a dream.

And something else now. She was aware now that Gentry also knew about Adriana.

Though he must have wondered, Blanche had often told herself. He must, surely, in observing the date of Adriana's birth, have counted back the weeks, and in doing so he must have seen the significance of the dates.

Blanche's awareness of *his* awareness had come during the second of the two visits that he and Marianne had made to Palermo, when they had arrived without notice at the villa on the Via Catania. On that latter occasion Alfredo was still absent from the house on a trip to the sulphur mine at Sierradifalco and was not expected back till the evening. Marianne had arrived first at the villa, in a cab, and later during the afternoon Gentry, his business concluded for the day, had also appeared at the door.

On seeing Adriana again Gentry had bent to her, smiling warmly, his hand gentle and light upon her dark hair. Then, conspiratorially, he had whispered to her of a gift, and delving into his pocket had brought out a little necklace made of tiny shells and coloured beads. After Adriana had shown her delight over the gift she had happily allowed him to fasten it around her neck, after which Gentry sat back on his heels and exclaimed on how well the necklace suited her. 'But you must see,' he said, and straightening, he lifted her up in his arms and held her up before a glass.

While the little happening took place Blanche and Marianne were sitting over their teacups, Marianne with her head bent as she sewed a button onto her coat, a button which had come off on the journey from Messina. Blanche, however, all observance, had missed nothing. Smiling, watching the little scene with pleasure, her eyes moved from the face of Adriana to that of Gentry as they looked into the glass together, their faces side by side. And then so clearly she saw it, that likeness that was there between them, a likeness about the

531

eyes, the set of the brow. With the sudden realization –
she had known it was there, but had never had it so
clearly demonstrated – her eyes flicked from one to the
other. And then suddenly she had found Gentry's eyes
looking back into her own, focusing on hers in the glass.
And so it was that she knew beyond question that he
knew also.

And as she watched his eyes left hers and he swiftly
and softly kissed Adriana's cheek before setting her
down on the floor again.

And, of course, nothing was said.

Adriana had turned from the pond and was moving
slowly away, her attention taken by the activities of a
small group of children who played with a ball. She
stood on the sidelines, watching them, one part of her
wanting to join in, the other part afraid of them and –
with their dirty faces, their ragged clothes – of their
mystery.

Blanche observed her as she stood on the sidelines.
There was a particular loneliness about the child, she
had sometimes found. It was less marked now that
Adriana was attending school, but even so she still spent
far too much time alone. The melancholy discovery of
Adriana's loneliness would strike Blanche unawares
when she would come upon the child playing her solitary games, joined only by friends conjured from her
imagination.

Ideally, of course, she needed brothers or sisters, but
there had been no more children, no more pregnancies
– a situation that had caused Alfredo great disappointment – a disappointment which had, in its turn,
contributed to their estrangement.

Not that he had ever suspected for a moment that
Adriana was not his daughter. Her birth had been

greeted by him with raptures of delight, and with his first marriage having been childless he had seen Adriana's birth as the advent of a succession of children. But it had not happened. The sons that he had dreamed of had not appeared. Consequently, Blanche often thought, any love that he was capable of was invested now in Adriana. And, as he did with Blanche, he treated the child with a possessiveness that brooked few other claims on her affections.

Getting up from the bench, Blanche wandered over to Adriana and took her hand, and they continued on their stroll. Attracted by the sound of music they idled for a while listening as two ragged men played on a mandolin and an old clarinet a melody that Blanche recognized as the Serenade from Bizet's *La Jolie Fille de Perth*. When the tune had ended she gave Adriana a few centimes to drop into the clarinet-player's misshapen old hat which he held out to them. 'We'll go on home now, shall we?' Blanche said, adding, 'If you like, we'll go by the *pasticceria* and buy some pastries. We can have them with our morning coffee.'

Emerging from the park they stopped by the equestrian statue of Garibaldi where Blanche retied the lace on Adriana's boot and then set off back along the wide Via della Libertà, after a short distance stopping at a small pastry cook's shop where Blanche bought two little tarts filled with cream and candied fruit. Leaving the shop they moved back towards the main street, as they did so passing a young goat boy who crouched beside an open doorway milking his goat for the customer who stood waiting nearby, the money for payment in her hand. There was no fresher goat's milk than that bought by the Sicilians.

Reaching the villa on the Via Catania Blanche let Adriana and herself in. As they entered the hall Edgardo appeared with his usual ghostlike silent steps, and Blanche told him to tell Anita the maid that she could serve the coffee now, and that signorina Adriana would have her hot chocolate.

'Si, signora.' With a slight inclination of his head, Edgardo turned away. Watching as he moved silently across the cool tiles of the hall floor, Blanche asked herself once again why it was that Alfredo almost invariably left Edgardo behind when he went away on any of his business trips. Did the answer lie in the tangled skeins of Alfredo's jealousy? Did Edgardo remain behind in his master's absence in order to keep a watch on her? It was, she felt, in view of what had transpired over the years, more than likely.

Blanche and Adriana sat in a small room overlooking the sunlit courtyard to drink their coffee and chocolate and eat the rich little pastries. As they sat there Adriana rocked in her arms a little golden-haired doll that she had been given for her fourth birthday in May.

Looking out onto the courtyard the thought went through Blanche's head that she could not foresee any way in which things would change now. Not for the better, anyway. She had made her bed, as the saying went, and now she must needs lie on it. Though the question had often insinuated itself into her consciousness as to whether she had indeed had no alternative but to marry Alfredo. She could have married George Marsh, whose love for her had been tried and tested and shown to be real. But then the thought would come to her of the baby. Could she have married him and allowed him to believe that Adriana was his own daughter? And in her moments of greatest honesty she knew the answer to that as well; had he had sufficient money then the answer was *yes*. Poverty had wrought enough havoc in her life and in the lives of those she had loved and lost, and with Ernest's death she had determined that it should have no further power over her as long as she could prevent it. But even so, who was to say that she could not have been open and honest with George?

Sometimes, looking back, she felt that had she told him of her expected child he might well still have married her. He had loved her, she had never been in any doubt of that. Nevertheless, she had chosen Alfredo, the richer man; and in doing so she had chosen to live here in Palermo, Sicily. And, she had to admit in her more honest moments, the thought that not only Marianne but also Gentry was living on the same island had never been that far from her consciousness.

That evening after Betta had put Adriana to bed, Blanche went up to the child's room to hear her prayers and tuck her in. Afterwards, sitting on the edge of Adriana's bed she leaned down and kissed her.

'Goodnight, darling.'

'Goodnight, Mama.'

As Blanche straightened, Adriana added:

'Betta was crying again.'

Blanche sighed and shook her head. 'Oh, dear.'

'Has she really got to leave?'

'Well . . .' What could she say? 'I'll talk to Papa,' Blanche said.

'Yes.' Adriana's hand came from beneath the covers, reached up and very gently touched Blanche's cheek.

'Your poor face.'

Blanche's smile was ironic. 'Yes, I know.'

A pause and then: 'It was Daddy, wasn't it? Papa did it, didn't he?'

Adriana's words took Blanche by surprise so that her lie – 'No, no, of course not' – came too late to be convincing. With a little sigh, Adriana simply said once again:

'Poor face.'

Blanche held on to Adriana's little hand, kissed its soft palm. 'Now, you go to sleep.'

Later, in her own room, Blanche sat before the glass and looked again at her cheek. The swelling had gone down now, but the flesh over the cheekbone and near her upper lip was discoloured by the bruise. The words went through her head: 'I don't know how much more I can take' – and she realized that she had spoken the words aloud.

Sometimes, when she found herself dwelling on her lot, she would tell herself that she had no reason to complain. After all, she had never loved Alfredo. She had used him, used him to escape from the threat of a situation that had promised nothing but destruction – used him to ensure that Adriana had a start in life free from opprobrium and any stigma. Even so, in committing herself to her role as Alfredo's wife she had tried to be a good wife. *A good wife*. The words echoed in her mind. But it was true. Her own efforts, however, had not been enough; so swiftly everything had gone sour.

And the reasons, she knew well, were not only due to Alfredo's jealousies and intolerance. In fact, she sometimes said to herself, they were probably the symptoms of other ills. And she didn't need to look far for those.

Ever since their marriage the feeling had slowly dawned upon her – she found it inescapable – that Alfredo was being increasingly *driven* by some compulsion within him. And it was all to do with their financial situation. But piecing together bits of information gained over the period of their marriage she had learned that the money and assets Alfredo owned had all come from his father, an ambitious man who had started with nothing, but who with great imagination and flair had ended up making a fortune from various interests. Sadly, although Alfredo had inherited his father's money and material assets he had inherited none of his business acumen. As a result – and so creating one of the greatest ironies for Blanche – that financial security she had so desperately sought was now slowly but surely draining away like water through a sieve.

Alfredo, of course, had taken steps to halt the downward slide of his fortunes, but his lack of sound judgement had continued to prove a great disability and he had ended up in a worse situation. Consequently, in desperation, he had sought some other means of turning the tide – and had turned to gambling.

His growing addiction to the gaming tables had taken a disastrous toll and Blanche had seen their finances going steadily downhill. She had watched helplessly as he had disposed of more and more of his assets; already his interest in the sulphur mine at Sierradifalco had gone, as had much of his export business here in Palermo. And the changes, the losses, were continuing, the effects on the lives of those at the villa showing in various ways. Adriana's young nurse was only one of the servants who had been given notice to quit in recent times. Several of the servants had been dismissed over the past few weeks, and some of them after years of faithful service – and all the dismissals had taken place without any consultation of Blanche.

It was the matter of Betta that had led to the quarrel that morning. Blanche, trying to make conversation, had asked him how his business had gone in Messina. He had replied non-committally.

Covertly she observed him as he drank from his coffee cup. He looked different in many ways from when they had married. He had put on a good deal of weight for one thing, his body having thickened considerably, particularly about the waist and neck. He looked older than his forty-five years. It was not so much the coarsening of his body that she observed now, however, but his expression; there was a haunted look on his face, which, she realized, had been growing stronger over recent weeks.

Carefully choosing her words – aware that the morning was never the best time to approach him on any difficult matter, but necessary in view of his impending departure from the house – Blanche at last brought up the subject of the young nurse. Betta was so upset, she said. Would he not reconsider her dismissal?

No, he replied, he would not.

'But she's been here three years, and she's so good with Adriana, and so trustworthy and obliging.'

'Adriana's at school now,' he said. 'She doesn't need a nurse.' He shook his head and added: 'Don't interfere.'

'I'm not interfering. It concerns me too. I'm not a guest in this house.'

He said nothing to this. Blanche added:

'Alfredo – Betta has nowhere to go. She has no family. She has no one. Please don't send her away at a time like this. Couldn't we at least keep her till after Christmas? Wait till the spring; she'll find it easier then to get employment.'

'The decision has been made. The subject is not for discussion.' He pushed away his half-full plate and got up. Blanche, trying to recover the lost ground, said:

'You haven't finished your breakfast –'

'I'm not hungry any more.'

'Alfredo, please . . .' She rose from the table and moved to him. 'Reconsider it, please. Let Betta stay – at least till the spring.'

'I told you – the subject is not for discussion. The girl has to go.'

'Yes,' Blanche said angrily, '– you'll send her away, as you've sent away the other servants, but Edgardo you allow to cling to you like a leech.'

'Don't push me too far,' he said quietly.

'Have you no heart? At least let her stay till after Christmas.'

'The girl is going. She's an unnecessary expense.'

'Expense?' Blanche said incredulously. 'She eats like a sparrow and you pay her a pittance.' Then, her growing anger at the injustice driving all her caution away, she added with a sneer: 'The truth is that the pittance you pay her might finance an hour or two for you at the casino. We mustn't lose sight of that, must we!'

It was then that Alfredo had stepped forward, hand lifting, and struck her the blow in the face.

Chapter Thirty-Nine

It was on Alfredo's return that Blanche learned that they were to leave the house on the Via Catania, that they were, in fact, to leave Palermo altogether.

Alfredo, it transpired, after storming out that morning after striking Blanche, had gone back to Messina. He stayed away for three days. On his return to Palermo he took a cab from the railway station and entered the house tired and irritable after the long train journey along the coast. He was met in the hall by Edgardo who took from him his travelling bag and at once went to run a bath for him and set out clean clothes. Blanche, hearing Alfredo's voice, went into the foyer as he started up the stairs. He gave her a brief greeting, not meeting her eyes, then brusquely told her to delay dinner until he was ready to eat.

Over dinner he and Blanche sat facing one another across the dining table, waited on by Edgardo and Anita, one of the two remaining maids. They ate for much of the time in silence, when they spoke keeping their conversation to safe matters. When dinner was over they retired to the library where Alfredo sat smoking his cigarettes and reading his newspaper while Blanche sewed. She was in the last stages of making a dress for Adriana, with coloured threads of silk working on a complex pattern of smocking on the yoke. Pausing in her work, glancing up over her needle, she caught Alfredo looking at her. It was then that she learned about their coming departure.

'We shall be leaving here soon,' he said, lowering his newspaper, 'if everything goes right.'

Her needlework forgotten she said after a moment's pause: 'Leaving here? You mean, this house?'

'Palermo.'

And that was the way it was done. No consultation. Just the bald statement: they would be leaving soon. There was no warmth between them at all now, Blanche said to herself.

'Leaving Palermo,' she said.

'Yes.'

'And going where?'

'Messina.'

'Messina?'

'Am I not speaking clearly?' he said. 'Must you repeat everything I say?'

She bit back the retort that rose to her lips and said instead: 'Am I allowed to ask why we're going?'

He sighed. 'It's a matter of economics. It's pointless to keep this up – this interminable travelling back and forth, dividing my time between Palermo and Messina. I've long thought it would be better to concentrate all my interests in one place, and now the opportunity's here, and I'm going to take it.'

Blanche said nothing. She was sure that his decision had come not as the result of choice but very likely as the result of necessity. At the start of their marriage he had appeared to enjoy travelling between the two cities, overseeing the export and distribution of the citrus fruit, the olives, the soap, and the sulphur that were his stock in trade. Other journeys had taken him regularly to Sierradifalco near Caltanisetta where the sulphur mine was situated. Now, with the mine disposed of, he was left with his depleted interests in Palermo and Messina – whatever such interests were; Blanche did not know;

he had long ago ceased to take her into his confidence and there had never been a time when he had discussed with her anything connected with his business that did not directly affect her.

Now, continuing with the fantasy, he went on to say that there was little scope left in Palermo, whereas Messina offered untold opportunities. All the necessary space was available, he said, and also labour was cheaper.

'So,' Blanche said, 'when shall we be leaving?'

'In two or three weeks. I'd like to be there by Christmas. I'm finalizing arrangements now – as regards the business, I mean, in Messina. That's what I've been doing there this trip. I've also been selling up the rest of the property here in Palermo. All I have to do where you and Adriana are concerned is find somewhere suitable for us to live.'

'Oh, let me help,' Blanche said quickly. 'Oh, I would love to, Alfredo. Let me come with you to Messina and help find a nice house for us.'

After a pause he shook his head. 'Leave it to me,' he said. 'Trust me. I'll take care of it.' He went back to his newspaper.

The exchange between them, Blanche thought, just about illustrated the sum of their marriage: the increasing distance between them, the lack of communication and trust, the complete lack of affection. Thinking about the reversal of his fortunes she could not help but ask herself, as she had done many times in the past, whether she was in some way responsible. Had she, in some subtle, insidious way, done this to him, or contributed to it? But then she would remind herself that he had already been set on this downward slide at the time of their marriage – the information she had gleaned over the past five years showed that clearly enough.

She was distracted from her thoughts by Alfredo putting down his newspaper and rising from his chair. He was going out, he told her; he would be back later on. He would go to the Casino Nuovo, she guessed, a gambling club in the Palazzo Geraci on the Corso Vittorio Emanuele.

It was very late when he returned.

Over the past year he had, much to Blanche's relief, taken to sleeping in an adjoining room, only disturbing her when he required a response to some alcohol-inspired maudlin need for affection or release for his sexual needs – though, Blanche was quite sure, he had long since habitually sought this release in other quarters. On this night, in the early hours of the morning, he entered his own room noisily, waking her from her sleep. Some minutes later he was opening the connecting door and coming into her room.

For a little while she feigned sleep, but soon gave up and opened her eyes to him, seeing him standing silhouetted against the light that came through the open door.

He sat on the edge of her bed and smiled at her. He was dressed in his nightshirt. 'Did I wake you?' he asked, knowing that he had.

'It's all right.'

He was in a good mood; he had obviously hit a winning streak at the tables. There would, she said to herself, be a price to pay. There always was when he showed any degree of warmth these days.

She yawned, hoping that the gesture would deter him. It did not. His hand came out and touched her shoulder.

'Blanche . . .'

As he leaned forward and spoke her name she could

543

smell the whisky on his breath. His hand rose, touched at her cheek below the bruise.

'Listen,' he said, '– I'm sorry I hit you.'

'It's – it's all right.'

'– But sometimes you make me so angry.'

'Obviously.'

There was a little silence. She waited, wanting him to go, but knowing that he would not.

After a little while he said,

'I've been thinking. Betta can stay till the spring. She'll be useful with the move to Messina and getting settled in there.'

'Thank you. May I tell her tomorrow?'

'Yes, of course.' A little pause, and then: 'I'm getting cold.' Pulling back the covers he got in beside her while she was forced to move over in the bed.

A little while later she lay beneath him and as he thrust away at her she felt she could shriek aloud at the invasion, reach up, take him by the hair and wrench him away from her. But she suffered it, the assault, almost counting the strokes until his heavy breathing quickened and he at last collapsed on her unresisting body. She lay there, saying nothing, not moving. After a while he raised himself from her and, without a word, got out of the bed and moved back to his own room.

Long after she had heard the sound of the communicating door clicking shut behind him she lay awake, gazing into the dark.

Without any consultation of Blanche, Alfredo bought a villa just off the Via Varese in the southern area of the city of Messina. It was smaller than their home in Palermo, he said, but it was adequate, and, anyway, with fewer servants they would not require so much space.

Blanche had mixed feelings about the planned move.

She had grown attached to the villa on the Via Catania, and was fond of Palermo. Messina, from what she had seen of it, was very much a town of industry, with fewer concessions to culture. On the other hand, Marianne was there – and Gentry – though she never allowed herself to think of him. She wasted no time in writing to them both to say that she, Alfredo and Adriana would shortly be taking up residence in the city.

With regard to her anticipation of a reunion with Marianne and her hopes that they would be able to spend time together, it appeared that Alfredo had considered the same possibility, for he said, with no ceremony:

'But if you see the move as enabling you to spend all your days with your friends from England you can get rid of the idea at once. I don't propose to entertain it.'

Blanche protested briefly, but then remained silent. She would not be denied her friendship with Marianne, she was determined. And she would find a way to achieve what she wanted.

The villa on the Via Catania was in a chaotic bustle as, under the direction of Edgardo, years' accumulation was sorted and either discarded, put aside for sale, or packed in preparation for the move to Messina. Although Blanche took part in the work at the start she soon felt herself redundant in the situation and left the few remaining servants to continue it alone. Alfredo's final business links with Palermo were severed as he divested himself of the last of his interests there, including the house – and then, at last, came the 20th, a Sunday, the day when she, Alfredo and Adriana were to leave their Palermo home for the last time. The furniture and other effects that had not been sold by auction had already been sent ahead to Messina. Blanche, Alfredo and

Adriana would spend the night at an hotel and start for Messina first thing in the morning. By the time of their arrival much of the furniture and other items would be in place in their new home.

Wandering through the rooms of the house on the Via Catania, Blanche knew without doubt that any brief happiness she had known in the marriage had long since passed by. The best was not to come. The best, such as it was, was gone. The marriage was far beyond saving now.

Later that day, with Edgardo remaining behind to continue in his role of directing the move and the closing of the house, Blanche, Alfredo and Adriana climbed aboard a horse-drawn cab and drove away from the villa for the last time. Blanche did not look back. She knew she would never see the house again. She could only look forward; though what lay before her she could not imagine.

After an uncomfortable night at an indifferent hotel they took a cab to the railway station where they caught a train for Messina. The journey, along the northern coast, much of the time with the sea in view, seemed to Blanche to be interminable, added to which, with Christmas so close there were so many travellers that the train was packed to bursting.

At last, after many hours, they arrived at Messina and Alfredo hailed a cab to take them to their new home. Set on the Via Imera, a narrow street leading off the Via Varese, the villa was small and drab, the street itself dirty and unkempt. Alighting from the cab and standing before the house, Blanche's spirits sank. She tried not to show it, though, and squeezing Adriana's hand, she smiled down at the child's doubtful expression and, with appropriately encouraging comments, led her inside.

In the villa she and Adriana wandered from the dark, narrow vestibule into the adjoining rooms. The servants had been busy and a good deal of the furniture and other items were in place, though there was still a great amount of work yet to be done. As they stood looking around them Alfredo came and directed them to the rooms that he had allotted to them on the floor above. Leaving him busy with other matters, Blanche and the child went upstairs. Blanche saw that Adriana's room was at the rear of the house, across the landing from her own and Alfredo's which, adjoining one another, were at the front. Entering her room, Blanche found Betta there, adding some last minute touches to it in preparation for her mistress's arrival. On Blanche's entrance with Adriana behind her, Betta straightened from polishing the top of a small bureau, turning her plain face to Blanche and smiling and murmuring a shy greeting. Since Blanche had told her that it was arranged that she might stay until the spring – combining her duties of nurse to Adriana with those of housemaid – Betta seemed to have done everything possible to please her. Her gratitude now was evident in the appearance of Blanche's room. Many of Blanche's favourite things were in evidence – two or three particular pieces of porcelain, a specially favoured cover on her bed, even the framed photograph of Adriana carefully placed on the bedside table, while from somewhere the girl had managed to get some roses. Not expensive roses, obviously; they stood in a vase by the window, looking a little bedraggled and sorry for themselves, but roses, nonetheless.

Blanche stepped forward, bending to take in the delicate scent. 'Betta, what lovely flowers.' As Betta spoke no English Blanche always addressed her in Italian. 'Where did you get them?' she asked.

Betta gave a little shrug. Oh, they were nothing special, she said; they were nothing at all, really . . .

Blanche looked at her. 'Betta,' she said, 'you *bought* them . . .'

Betta, embarrassed, shrugged again. They had cost only a few centimes, she said, and, apologizing for their poor appearance, she moved to the door, gave a little half-curtsy and left.

After the sound of the girl's feet had faded on the stairs, Blanche remained gazing at the flowers, touched by the girl's thoughtfulness.

In Alfredo's absence Blanche spent the rest of that day helping to unpack and supervise the placement of the remaining items. She could see how irritated Edgardo was by what he regarded as her interference, but she closed her eyes and ears to his barely-hidden superciliousness and, with Betta's help, got on with her task. In the meantime Adriana slept, exhausted after the journey from Palermo. That night after Alfredo had left the villa – obviously for gaming tables somewhere in the town, Blanche thought – she herself, exhausted after the long day, went early to bed.

She was awakened in the early hours of the morning by the sound of her door opening. Gritting her teeth she kept her eyes closed as Alfredo padded across the floor towards her.

'Blanche . . .'

She heard the slurring sound in his tone. She kept her eyes closed.

'Blanche . . .' His voice came again.

She opened her eyes in a simulation of waking and saw him standing there.

The edge of the mattress gave as he lowered his weight heavily onto it. She looked at him for a moment in the dim light and then closed her eyes again, turning her head away on the pillow. He was drunk. Go away, she wanted to say, go back to your own room and leave me in peace.

'Look at me,' he said. 'Open your eyes.'

She gave a little groan, opening her eyes briefly and then closing them again. 'I'm tired, Alfredo.'

'Open your eyes.' His tone was a little sharper now as he leaned over her. 'Look at me.'

She turned her head on the pillow to face him, opening her eyes as she did so. His breath was overpowering; she could smell on it whisky and the sour smell of vomit. There came from him also the scent of cheap perfume. 'What is it?' she said. 'I want to sleep.'

'You always want to sleep.' His tone was now aggrieved. 'You never give a thought to what I want. Why are you always so damned cold to me?'

So tonight it was to be the deprived, unloved, misunderstood child. Go back to bed, Alfredo, she cried inwardly. Go to sleep. Aloud she said wearily, 'Alfredo, please. Let's not quarrel now. It's so late.'

'I don't want to quarrel,' he said sulkily. 'I just want a little – attention. A little wifely affection. Is that too much to hope for? You *are* my *wife*. You're supposed to be, anyway.'

Giving up all hope that he would leave her in peace she sighed, pulled herself up in the bed. 'What is it you want?'

'Don't say it like that.'

She gave a little shrug. He frowned, then reached out to her. She moved her head, avoiding his touch.

'Don't,' he said, '– don't move away from me.'

'I'm sorry, but – I'm tired and I want to go back to sleep. I've had a very long day.'

He continued to gaze down at her. His expression now had darkened.

'What's the matter with you?' he said at last.

'I told you, I'm *tired*.'

He studied her for a while, then: 'Let me get in. Move over.' He reached to pull aside the bedcovers. Blanche pressed her hands flat upon them, holding them in place.

'No.'

He halted, frozen in his movement. '– What . . . ?'

'I said *no*.'

She forced herself to look him in the eye while he gazed back at her in disbelief. Never in five years had she ever denied him so categorically before. In the face of his swiftly rising anger she could not sustain the baldness of her denial, however, and in an attempt to blunt its harshness and appeal to some reason that still might be there she shook her head distractedly and said, 'Alfredo, *please*. Let me rest. That's all I want.'

For long moments they remained as they were, looking at one another, while she sensed that the eruption of his anger was being held back by a thread. Then, at last, sighing, he straightened and lurched up from the bed.

'*I'm* tired as well, anyway,' he said. 'And if you're tired too . . .'

He turned from her, moved across the floor. In the doorway he turned and looked back at her, a long look, then turned away again.

When his door had closed behind him Blanche lay in a turmoil of mixed emotions. She had won a battle. She had defied him, outright, though the act had left her with her heart fluttering and her palms damp. She was well aware, though, that it didn't matter how strong her spirit might be; when it suited him he would not hesitate to use his superior physical strength – he never had in the past – and against that she could do very little.

Even so – and as she lay there she set her lips in

determination – she would do all in her power to see that he never touched her again. She had denied him and got away with it and she could to it again. She was determined – she would never allow him to use her as he had done in the past.

She saw very little of Alfredo the following day. When she went in for breakfast – finding Adriana already sitting at the table – she learned from Edgardo that Alfredo had already eaten and left the house. His stamina could only amaze her. It could only come from that compulsion that was continuously driving him on, she thought.

She had thought that she might take Adriana and call on Marianne, but it began to rain heavily soon after breakfast and the rain kept up for the rest of the morning. In the end, immediately after luncheon, she put on her hat and cape, picked up her umbrella and, leaving Adriana in the care of Betta, prepared to set out alone. In the hall she was met by Edgardo – who as usual just appeared to be passing through at the same moment. He expressed surprise that the signora wished to go out in such weather, but Blanche merely told him that she would be back later.

Turning west onto the Via Varese, she walked to the end of the street and turned right onto the Via Porta Imperiale, one of the main streets in the city. There, after making enquiries, she caught an omnibus as far as the Palazzo Reale. By the time she got off again the rain had stopped and with its cessation the Christmas shoppers had begun to appear, crowding the pavements as they jostled by with their loaded bags and baskets.

It was only a short walk to the Via Gabriele, and in just a few minutes Blanche had reached it and was making her way along to number 27. On reaching it she rang the bell and a minute later she was inside the hall and she and Marianne were holding one another.

Blanche stood at one of the tall windows of the library looking down onto the Via Gabriele. The rain had begun again. She sighed. Behind her, Marianne said, from her seat on the sofa:

'What are you sighing for?'

'I was just thinking,' Blanche said, '– how the time goes by. How swiftly. It's hard to believe that it will be Christmas Day in just three days.'

She moved back to the sofa, bent and replaced her teacup on the coffee table. She smiled down at Marianne.

'It's so good to see you,' she said.

'And you, Blanche.' Marianne reached out and took Blanche's hand, pressed it briefly before releasing it. 'And such a lovely surprise.'

With Gentry out on business, the two women had spent the time talking of this and that, their conversation, however, where Blanche was concerned – she had seen to it – never getting out beyond the shallow, safe waters.

Looking at Marianne, Blanche thought again how well she looked – and prosperous, too – from her simple ochre home gown to her casually dressed hair and the few pieces of simple jewellery she wore. By contrast Blanche felt that her own day dress was out-of-date and had been worn a few times too many. And if Marianne's appearance reflected the happiness she had found with Gentry – which it was clear that she had – then Blanche felt that to anyone with half an eye her own appearance must be a good indication of her own situation.

Not that she would have admitted it for a moment, her unhappiness. Faced with the evidence of Marianne's happiness she found herself even more anxious to conceal the reality of her own state. Over the years she had never admitted to Marianne the existence of the rift between herself and Alfredo – though Marianne would have to have been blind not to realize that it was there, even though she was unaware of the extent of it. Even when Alfredo had denied Blanche visits to her friends she had made excuses for him. The result was that she had given her marriage a façade that bore little relation to the substance beyond. And while Marianne and Gentry were almost certainly aware by now that there were problems in Blanche's marriage, they knew nothing of Alfredo's gambling, the losses he was incurring, the continual eroding away of the material of their livelihood; they knew nothing of his bouts of drunkenness, his intolerance, his passionate jealousies.

Looking at the clock on the mantelpiece, Blanche said with a shake of her head: 'Half-past four. I must get back to Adriana – and to make sure I'm ready for dinner.'

'Is Alfredo expecting you?' Marianne got up from the sofa.

'Let's say that he expects me to *be there*,' Blanche replied quickly, '– whenever he wants me.'

Immediately she had spoken she felt that she had said too much. Marianne said nothing, but was looking at her with sympathy – a look that Blanche could not suffer. Blanche remained standing there, as if undecided whether to go or to stay. Marianne said:

'Listen, on Boxing Day we're going to the opera house to see *Aida*. Madame Karalech is singing. We've got a box there. Why don't you and Alfredo join us? We can have supper afterwards, the four of us.'

Blanche said, 'I remember we saw Madame Karalech in Palermo, Alfredo and I, when we were first married.'

'Will you come? Ask Alfredo. It would be lovely if we could all go together.'

Blanche nodded. 'Oh, it would.' She was sure that Alfredo would not agree. Nevertheless she said, 'I'll ask him. I'll let you know.'

'If not, perhaps we can meet for dinner over the Christmas season.'

'Yes, I hope so.'

'And I do so want to see Adriana. What a shame you couldn't bring her today. Still, you're living here now, so there will be plenty of opportunities. I'm sure we'll see quite a change in her since we saw her last.'

'Oh, yes. She's a tiny, solemn little creature.' Blanche smiled. 'But she's beautiful.'

'It's my one regret,' Marianne said, lowering her eyes,' – that Gentry and I have no children.' She sighed. 'I don't know whether it's me or . . .'

She let her voice fade, and Blanche, looking at her, could see what the words had cost her. And, knowing Marianne, she was sure that it was unlikely that she had made any such admission to anyone before.

Marianne raised her eyes to Blanche. 'Still,' she said, with a little smile, 'we're young, we're strong, we're healthy. There's still plenty of time.'

'Yes, of course.'

And it was as if Marianne's words had freed Blanche from her own self-imposed restraint, for suddenly, reaching out, she took Marianne's hands, gripped them.

'Why am I pretending, Marianne?' she said. 'Why with you, of all people? I hate him! I hate him! I can't stand to live with him another moment.' She stood there, holding Marianne's hands while the tears welled up in her eyes, spilled over and ran down her cheeks.

They stood holding one another. After a time Blanche grew calmer, and Marianne asked:

'What are you going to do about it?'

'There's only one thing I *can* do,' Blanche replied. 'I must leave him. I must just take Adriana and go.'

'Where? Back to England?'

'Yes. I'll find work there. I can support us both.' She paused. 'The trouble is, there's no one there for me any more.'

'What about Mr Marsh? He'd help you, wouldn't he?'

'Oh, yes, I'm sure he would.' Blanche shook her head. 'But how could I go to him for help?'

Marianne said, 'Well – if you decide to go, then you know I'll help in any way I can. Gentry and me – you can depend on us, you know that.'

'Yes, I know. Thank you.'

And, Blanche was determined, if things got any worse then that was what she must do. And if she still did not have enough money then she would have to ask Marianne and Gentry to lend her what she needed. It might be the only way.

Chapter Forty

Alfredo came in late for dinner that evening, sat uncommunicative at the table and left again soon afterwards so Blanche had no real opportunity to tell him of her visit to Marianne and of Marianne's invitation to the opera. He was off to the casino, she assumed. For how much longer, she wondered, would he be able to hang on to their few remaining assets? With some irony she reminded herself that if she was dissatisfied with their present home in Messina, she might find that they were in an even worse situation come a year or two. The only certain thing about Alfredo's gambling was that it always eventually ended with loss.

What time he returned from his club she had no idea; he did not awaken her. He joined her at breakfast the next morning – complaining of a headache and yawning over his newspaper. Knowing that she must have an answer for Marianne, she waited for the right opportunity to bring up the matter of their meeting. She did not need to wait for the right moment, though; Alfredo himself brought up the subject.

She had said to him that she wanted to go into the town to buy some Christmas gifts, and asked if she might have some money for the purpose. In response he took out his wallet, counted out some notes and grudgingly pushed them across the table towards her. 'I thought you'd already gone out shopping,' he said. 'Didn't you go yesterday?'

No, she said, she did not.

'Then where did you go to in the rain in such a hurry?' he said, and the tone of his voice and the look he gave her up under his eyebrows told her plainly that the matter of her departure from the house had been on his mind.

Angered by his question and its implication, Blanche said:

'If you're so intent on watching my every move I wonder you don't get your spy to follow me. I'm sure Edgardo wouldn't object.'

Alfredo gave a shrug. 'Perhaps I shall.'

The scene having taken such a turn for the worse, Blanche tried to recover some of the lost ground. In a conciliatory tone she said:

'I only went to see Marianne. I just wanted to call on her briefly, to say hello, and to let her know that we had arrived safely.'

'You didn't waste any time, did you?'

'Alfredo, isn't it natural that I should want to go to see her? We grew up together, you know that. You know how close we are.'

'You mean you and Marianne?'

'Of course I mean me and Marianne. Who else would I mean?'

Alfredo disregarded the question. 'Was her husband there?' he asked.

'No, he was out. Why?'

He simply looked at her for a moment in silence, then picked up his coffee cup and drank down the sweet liquid in one swallow. As he set down the cup Blanche said:

'She's invited us to the opera the day after Christmas.'

He nodded. 'Boxing Day, as you English call it.'

'Yes.' Blanche nodded and waited for him to go on, but he did not.

'May we go?' she said. 'Paola Karalech is singing in *Aida*. Marianne and Gentry have a box. And we can all go to supper afterwards. Oh, it would be such a lovely evening – and I'd so like to spend some time with them. May we go?'

'– No, I'm sorry.'

As she gazed at him in dismay he shook his head. 'You'll have to see them another time. I have other plans for Christmas. I want to invite some friends here on the 26th.'

'Well – in that case, may we invite Marianne and Gentry for dinner on some other evening?'

He did not answer for a moment, and then he said: 'We'll see.'

And she suddenly realized that he was punishing her. He was punishing her for having refused him when he had come to her bedside.

So be it. She would not beg him. She gave a little nod of understanding and went back to her breakfast, although her appetite had quite gone.

Later that morning, after sending a message with Anita to Marianne regretting that they would not be able to join her and Gentry on Boxing Day, she and Betta and Adriana went shopping. It was a bright dry day, and the streets of Messina – so much narrower than those of Palermo – were crowded with Christmas shoppers. For Alfredo she bought some tobacco and a silk necktie. Then, while Betta led Adriana to another part of the street, she went into a toyshop where she bought for the child a little doll in a cradle (Adriana could not have enough dolls), a colourfully illustrated story book of *La Bella Addormentata nel Bosco* (Adriana spoke Italian – not to mention the Sicilian dialect – as naturally as she spoke English) and a drawing pad and a little box of crayons. Afterwards she bought little gifts for the servants, Betta, Anita, and Anna the cook. For Edgardo she bought nothing. For Marianne she bought a box of lace handkerchiefs, and for Gentry a silk cravat. She also bought various coloured papers and baubles and a small, rather lopsided fir tree. She and Betta and Adriana returned to the villa on the Via Imera loaded down with the purchases. The excursion had been a positive one, though, and Blanche felt bright and buoyant from its effects.

During the afternoon (Alfredo was at his office in the city) Blanche and Adriana made trimmings from the coloured paper – yards of brightly coloured paper chains which they hung from the pictures and along the mantelpiece. The fir tree they set in a little tub of earth – which Betta brought in from a nearby park – and then decorated it with the baubles and with decorations they had made from the paper.

When their work was finished she and Adriana stood and gazed around them in delight and satisfaction. In her earlier years Adriana had been too young to appreciate the magic of Christmas but she was old enough now, and was much affected with the excitement of it all.

The next day, Christmas Eve, Blanche and Adriana spent the morning in the kitchen where they worked with Anna helping to prepare the Christmas fare. Alfredo had left the villa that morning – to work, Blanche assumed – and after luncheon, acting on a sudden whim and the need to get out into the air, she got Adriana into her coat and hat and, taking her by the hand, left the house to see something of the ancient city. And, wonder of wonders, Edgardo was not there to witness their departure, which, Blanche was sure, would be for him a matter of some regret. But let him fret, she said to herself with satisfaction; let him wonder where she and Adriana had gone.

From the Via Varese they took a cab past the university to the main part of the centre where Blanche bought an inexpensive little illustrated English guide book. With its help, she and Adriana spent some pleasant hours wandering the streets in the mild afternoon air.

Blanche had read that in the past the city had suffered from a lack of society and a lack of concessions to society, and as a result had not been a popular resort for tourists. The situation was changing swiftly now, though. There were many tourists visible, she found – and many of them busy with their Kodaks. And, certainly, she soon discovered, there was no shortage of interesting and beautiful sights for new arrivals – herself and Adriana included – to see, although few of the artefacts were as old as the city itself. Messina had been destroyed so many times that few of its ancient sights and treasures remained. Over the centuries it had been ravaged by the most devastating wars, plagues and earthquakes, but from each disaster the city had miraculously risen, its survivors picking themselves up, burying their dead and rebuilding their houses, their churches. To Blanche, reading of the city's past, it seemed to her to have a wondrous kind of indomitability of spirit. It had faced up to all the calamities with which man and nature had been able to assault it, and it had withstood them all.

Together, and enjoying the comradeship, she and Adriana wandered through the museum, looking at the paintings and the sculptures. Afterwards they strolled along the narrow streets, pausing once to drink hot chocolate and to eat wickedly rich little pastries at a small café before going out again into the December sunshine. There on the street they saw a young boy in a scarlet satin tunic performing impressive contortions, standing on his hands and bending his lithe young body backwards until his feet almost touched the ground. As passers-by paused to watch and then applaud, the boy's smiling father moved about with his open cap in his hand. Blanche gave Adriana a coin to give for the boy's performance and then they moved on again. 'Are you tired, sweetheart?' 'No, no, Mama.'

Blanche was aware of a light-hearted atmosphere in the air as all around them the citizens of the town hurried about completing their business in preparation for the coming holiday, moving in and out of the shops on final shopping excursions or, their work finished for the day, getting down to the serious business of beginning their revels.

Beside the Duomo Blanche and Adriana stood and looked at the beautiful Fountain of Orion while inside the ancient cathedral itself they gazed in awe at the rows of magnificent columns. It being Christmas Eve there were many who had come there to worship, to light candles and say prayers. Blanche joined them. On her marriage to Alfredo she had, as a concession to him, embraced the Catholic faith, and now she and Adriana each put a few centimes into the offering box and lit candles and offered up prayers. Sadly, Blanche felt that the little prayer she offered up – that she and Alfredo could find some kind of peace that would eventually save them – had no hope of fulfilment.

Outside the Duomo again they gave a few centimes to a blind beggar who sat on the steps, and then set off again, wandering along the Corso Vittorio Emanuele. To their right beyond the shabby customs houses and the low buildings of the market lay the port and the sickle-shaped tongue of land that held the lighthouse; beyond these the waters of the Messina Straits stretched away to the distant shadow of Reggio di Calabria on the opposite shore. The left of the *corso* was flanked by a uniform row of palaces with soaring colonnades, magnificent still in their grandeur, but squalid now from the constant assault from the rigours of the harsh and humble life of the port.

Reaching the area of the Palazzo Reale Blanche hesitated, briefly considering going on to call again on Marianne. But there was no time. They must start back. Besides which, Adriana was growing tired.

They took an omnibus along the Corso Cavour, and not too long afterwards were back at the villa.

That evening there was no difficulty in getting Adriana off to bed and shortly after Blanche had returned downstairs from tucking her in, Alfredo returned.

Over dinner he said that he had invited a business associate and his wife for dinner on the 26th, and asked Blanche to make the necessary preparations. She said she would, adding that she had sent a message to Marianne declining her invitation. He merely nodded. A little later, as she anticipated he would, he got dressed and went out for the evening, as usual not saying where he was going or at what time he would return. Blanche did not care; she was glad of his absence, relieved to know that he was no longer in the house.

She spent the evening alone, first packing the gifts she had bought, and then trying to read. From time to time she would hear the sound of revellers going by on the street. Once, moving to the window, she drew back the curtain and looked out at them as they went straggling by, laughing and singing, the intermittent cries of 'Buon natale' ringing out in the cold night air.

That night as she lay awake in the silence of her room she thought back to her meeting with Marianne, and how she had unburdened herself to her – something she had never intended to do. And in doing so she had wept – wept not only at the misery she felt in her situation, but from frustration at her inability to change it. For she was sure now that it would never change.

Christmas Day dawned chilly and dull with a light rain falling.

Soon after breakfast Blanche discreetly sought out Betta, Anita and Anna and gave to them the little gifts she had bought for them. She was touched by the warmth and sincerity of their thanks, while her happiness at bringing them each a little pleasure was blunted by the sadness of her conviction that come next Christmas not one of them would be serving in the household. At the rate that Alfredo's fortunes were diminishing, by the time next Christmas came it was unlikely that she and Alfredo would have any servants at all.

Alfredo remained at home for most of the early part of the day, and for Adriana's sake appeared for a while to make an attempt to relax. Anita had lit a fire in the sitting room and Adriana sat on the rug before it and played with her doll and cradle, her story book and her crayons and drawing pad. Delighted with her gifts she had thanked Blanche warmly and now went to Alfredo where he sat in the opposite chair. Reaching out to him she put her arms around his neck.

'Thank you, Papa.'

As Alfredo warmly returned Adriana's embrace he glanced up and caught Blanche's gaze over the top of the child's head. Their glances held for a moment and then his eyes fell away and he patted Adriana on the shoulder and released her. Blanche, also lowering her gaze, thought how sad, how strange it was, the obvious restraint that was within him.

At luncheon, which was accompanied by a mixture of Sicilian and English traditions, Blanche tried to create something of a spirit of brightness and – for Adriana's sake – some feeling of camaraderie. Whether her efforts worked as far as the child went, however, she could not tell. She doubted it. Alfredo made very little effort towards creating any kind of jollity on which they might build and Blanche soon found her own light laughter sounding hollow in her ears, while her attempts to bring him into any casual, everyday conversation very swiftly sounded meaningless and false.

When Alfredo eventually left the house after dinner that evening to go to his club she relaxed for the first time in the day.

When she herself went to bed shortly before eleven she lay awake while from the street came the sounds of horse-drawn cabs and the cracks of whips, the occasional motor cars and noisy, homeward-bound revellers. She thought back to past Christmases, seeing herself as a child again, with Marianne, or with her mother, brothers and sisters. She saw herself decorating the tree with Marianne at Hallowford House; at the cottage playing games of bob-apple and blind man's buff; Ernest and Agnes laughing; songs around the piano with her mother playing and Agnes's sweet voice floating on the air. She knew well that distance lent enchantment to her memories, but there was no denying her present unhappiness. It couldn't continue, and the situation now seemed to be growing worse by the day.

At last she slept. At what time Alfredo came into the house she had no idea; at least his return was quiet and did not awaken her.

Blanche stood before the cheval glass in her room and gazed at her reflection. Her evening gown was almost three years old. As Alfredo's assets had diminished so her clothing allowance too had shrunk to the point where now it didn't allow her to buy much more than the merest essentials.

Even so, the dress looked well on her. Of a creamy white satin, with draped bodice hung with a wide satin bow, its heavy, trailing hem and hanging sleeve drapery were trimmed with net frills and ribbon. Betta had helped her to arrange her hair, which as usual Blanche wore swept up; this evening she dressed it with a tiny ribbon of black velvet.

Alfredo's guests were expected around seven and well before that time Blanche had gone down to the kitchen and the dining salon to check that everything was going well. Alfredo had said nothing of his reasons, but it was clear from his edginess that the occasion was important to him. It was some time since they had entertained at home, and Blanche inferred now that he was hoping that the coming evening would be instrumental in the furtherance of some business negotiation or other – though at what it was he never hinted; nor did she make any inquiry.

The guests, a couple visiting from Catania, were a certain signor Francesco Marino and his wife Elena. The man turned out to be short, heavy-set, in his early fifties, with a paunch and a pock-marked skin. His loud laugh was matched by the tones of his waistcoat. His wife was a mousy little creature in her forties who looked incongruous in her ultra-fashionable gown of lavender silk crêpe-de-Chine. Without knowing anything about her, Blanche felt a certain sympathy for her, while for the woman's husband she soon felt a growing antipathy.

Of course she hid her feelings, however, and for the sake of Alfredo (and her own comfort which was so dependent on his mercurial moods) did her best in her duty as hostess to make the evening a success. One thing she was very relieved to find, and that was that Marino and his wife spoke English to a degree. Even so, she found the evening a long and tedious affair, the dinner itself stretching out interminably during which time both she and signora Marino were effectively excluded from much of the conversation – which for the early part dwelt on discussion of the olive and citrus trade but later degenerated into a general review of various, and somewhat risqué, theatrical performances which, it appeared, signor Marino had appreciated at different times on his travels.

Later, over coffee, as a result of Blanche's being English, the conversation somehow got round to the subject of Mrs Emmeline Pankhurst and her followers, the suffragettes who, members of Mrs Pankhurst's Women's Social and Political Union, were constantly in the news – even at times in the Italian press – on account of their violent demonstrations in the cause of women's suffrage.

Signor Marino, having recently returned from a trip to England, was able to give something nearer to a first-hand account, and he proceeded to regale the company with reported stories of some of the more recent scandalous actions of the women. Blanche, failing to see any humour in his loudly-delivered anecdotes, sat silent.

Alfredo, turning, catching Blanche's cold expression, said with a laugh and barely-hidden curl of his lip:

'Oh, dear, my wife, I'm afraid, my friends, is obviously not amused. But there, as we all know, the English are not known for their humour.'

Signor Marino joined uncertainly in Alfredo's laughter, laughter which Blanche brought to an end as she said, her voice heavy with contempt:

'I wish I could say that you surprise me, Alfredo – but I can't.'

She knew well that with her words she was skating on thin ice, but she could not remain silent. Alfredo, after the barest moment's pause, tried to make light of the situation and save face. He leaned across to Blanche.

'Don't take it all so seriously,' he said; he spoke as if she were a child. 'You must learn to laugh, my dear. Dear God, if you cannot see the humour in such goings on then there's no hope for you that I can see. Come on now, try to relax.'

As he finished speaking he raised his hand and gently patted her on the head. Blanche, infuriated at his words and at the humiliating gesture, flung up a hand and violently slapped his own hand away. The sound of the slap rang in the room. 'Don't you patronize me!' she said sharply, the words ground out between her tight lips.

There was a sudden silence. And then Alfredo laughed into the quiet, but it was a laugh that was too loud and only demonstrated to Blanche his own sudden anger and feeling of humiliation. For once, though, she remained untouched by it.

'You must excuse my wife.' Alfredo turned expansively to the guests. 'Obviously she has not yet learned how to behave in company.' Then to Blanche he added, hardly bothering to disguise his sneer, 'Do you think your background fits you for such superiority, my dear? Do you think you're above us? Would you be more content in different company? Perhaps you would be happier being chained to some railings in London somewhere, would you?'

Blanche, who had turned her head away from his piercing eye and curling lip, now swung back to face him.

'You can't insult me by allying me with such women and such beliefs,' she said incredulously. 'Don't fool

567

yourself there. But you see such humour in it, don't you? In women wanting equality. But why shouldn't they fight for what is rightfully theirs? But no, you see it as comical – to you it's *funny*, a joke – women suffering the most appalling degradation and humiliation for their beliefs. Don't you think women have the right to equality?' She shook her head. 'Though I don't need to ask that question; I've learned well enough the answer to that.' She gazed at him, at his face so close to hers as he leaned towards her. 'You amaze me still,' she said. Her voice was icy, calm. 'Are you totally insensitive? Women chain themselves to railings to have their cause recognized. They do no harm to anyone but themselves. They go to prison where they're subjected to suffer the most painful forced feeding – and you see it all as a music hall turn.' She turned away from him. 'You make me sick.'

Throughout her words Alfredo's face had told her that she should halt, but she had been unable and unwilling to stem the flow. Now, as she finished speaking she became aware of the quiet vehemence with which she had spoken. And she looked at the glassy eyes of the signor and signora Marino (Alfredo's eyes were now lowered – in embarrassment, humiliation?) and saw that, for all their smiles, they were not regarding her with approval.

How Blanche got through the rest of the evening she did not know. Whatever lightness and enjoyment had been created the mood now was gone, and it was not long before Marino and his wife got up to leave. Blanche, having tried in the meantime to recover the lost ground, had known that she could not succeed. The damage had been done.

She remained in the living room while Alfredo saw the pair to the door, and she stood listening to the distant murmur of their voices as they said their goodbyes, followed soon afterwards by the closing of the front door.

At the sound of Alfredo's approaching steps as he came back across the tiled hall she tensed. Knowing him she knew how he would have nursed and nurtured his anger for this moment when they were alone. Even so, she was not prepared for the eruption of his fury.

Entering the room by the already open door he strode across the carpet towards her, and as he reached her side he raised his hand and struck her hard across the face. She reeled from the blow, but before she even had time to cry out his arm swung back and with the back of his hand he struck her on the opposite cheek.

The force of the blows made her head swim and she staggered back, fetching up heavily against a bureau, her flailing arm striking a vase of roses that rocked and toppled with a dull crash to the floor. As she straightened, her head still reeling, she was dimly aware of the taste of blood in her mouth.

'Alfredo – please –' she managed to say, but he would not be halted, and he came after her, his hand rising again, striking out at her again.

'Don't you ever dare to humiliate me like that in front of my guests again,' he said. He spat the words at her, punctuating them with violent blows from his swinging hands.

Desperately, while shrieking out pleas and little cries of protest, Blanche tried to protect herself, but her hands as she fought to ward him off were ineffectual against his strength and his fury. At last, sent spinning from a particularly savage blow from his fist she careered backwards over the coffee table and crashed to the floor.

The violence of the fall drove the breath from her body and she sat up gasping. As the seconds passed she recovered her breath, but her humiliation and her suffering were not yet over. Lifting her face and opening her eyes she gazed up through the mist of her pain and saw Alfredo unbuckling his belt as he stood above her. In a daze she was dimly aware of him unbuttoning his trousers, wrenching them down. Next moment he was bending, kneeling, his hands reaching out for her. Through the waves that brought her consciousness receding and returning over and over she was aware of him throwing back the fabric of her dress and her petticoat. His hands fumbled for a moment at the waist of the lace combinations she wore, and then with one furious movement gripped the front buttoned edges and ripped the garment open from her chest to her knee. His hands moved to her ankles, roughly clutching them, thrusting them apart so that she lay with her legs bent and splayed, open to his assault. 'Yes!' he hissed, '*and I'll teach you never to refuse me again.*' Following his words he threw himself upon her and in one movement thrust himself up inside her body. She had not the strength to resist him. For a few moments as she lay there the strange, unreal thought went through her mind that it was not really happening; it was all a nightmare. Then, still lying there under his weight, she found herself unable any longer to hold at bay the creeping darkness and, almost welcoming the dark, she drifted into oblivion.

Chapter Forty-One

'Signora . . .'

She felt cold, and there was a voice, soft, concerned, whispering close to her ear.

'Signora . . .'

She was aware of hands pulling down the skirt of her dress, covering her bare legs. Then the voice again:

'Signora . . . please . . .'

She tried to close her ears to the voice but it remained there, insistent. At last she opened her eyes – her right eye was rapidly closing – and saw Betta's homely, worried little face close to her own.

'Betta . . .'

Betta, frowning, gave a little smile, the relief sounding in her voice. 'Oh, signora.'

With the pain coming back with her returning consciousness Blanche remembered what had happened. With Betta's help she sat up, struggled to her knees and somehow managed to get to a chair nearby. Sitting, she leaned forward, dipping her head low over her knees. 'Where is he?' she muttered through her swollen lips, '– the signore . . .'

'Gone up to his bedroom.'

Whispering encouragement, Betta urged Blanche to sit up. Blanche did so. Then Betta's gentle hands were dabbing gently with a damp cloth, sponging away the blood – though, Betta said, the signora's beautiful dress was ruined for ever. When Blanche's cuts had been treated with iodine and her bruises with some soothing balm, she was helped out of the chair. Now, Betta said, she would help her upstairs to bed.

Quietly, Blanche and Betta set off up the stairs. Blanche's ribs had been bruised in her fall and she was aware now of their sharp ache as she moved. At last, however, she reached her room and Betta helped her to get undressed and into bed. There was a sofa on the other side of the room and Betta whispered that she would sleep there for the rest of the night. Blanche wanted to say that the girl should go back to her own bed beside Adriana's in the nursery – which would surely be more comfortable – but she had not the energy or the strength to protest. She merely nodded, 'Yes.' The hands of her bedside clock pointed to two-fifteen. She must have been lying downstairs for hours. Closing her eyes against the memory and the pains that nagged at her, she at last slept.

She did not go down to breakfast the next morning, and Betta brought to her a tray with some toast, some scrambled egg and some coffee. Blanche ate a little of the food and drank the coffee. Where was the signore? she asked, and Betta replied that he had already breakfasted and left the house. She had heard him say that he was going out on business and that he would soon be back.

Blanche heard of Alfredo's absence with relief. Where was signorina Adriana? she asked, to which Betta replied that the child was playing downstairs and had been asking when she could visit her mama.

Blanche asked Betta to fetch her a mirror, and Betta took the tray, set it down and brought to Blanche her little looking glass. Blanche gazed into it. Her left eye was discoloured and almost closed, while the left side of her upper lip was also very swollen. There were other bruises on her face, and a few minor cuts, other than the cut on her lip. Most of the rest of the pain was in her rib-cage, from the bruising sustained when she had fallen.

When, with Betta's help, she had done as much as she could towards patching up the damage to her face, and had dressed her hair, Blanche asked Betta to let Adriana up to see her. After that, she said, she would get up.

A few minutes later, when Adriana entered the room and looked at her mother she burst into tears.

'Oh, Mama . . .'

'I'm all right, my darling. I'm all right.'

Sitting up in the bed, holding the child in her arms, Blanche knew that she must come to a decision. She either had to put up with it, to suffer whatever Alfredo cared to do to her, or else take Adriana and get away.

The day passed slowly, the hours drifting by without any sign of Alfredo, though all the while Blanche expected to hear the sounds of his return. And evening came and there was still no sign of him. She said to herself that if she had known that he would be away for so long she would have packed a bag and taken Adriana and gone – and she would have sought help from Marianne and Gentry. Their home, though, would surely be the first place Alfredo would go looking for her. And in any case it would be very difficult to get out of the house during Alfredo's absence without Edgardo knowing of her escape. The only answer would be to wait for a time when she was sure that Alfredo was going to be away for some hours. Then, where Edgardo was concerned, she would just have to look for the right opportunity.

*

After she had tucked Adriana into bed that night she got into the warm bath that Betta had drawn for her and lay there while the soft water soothed her stiff muscles and sore bruises. She felt better afterwards, though her face with its bruised mouth and eye was still a shocking sight.

Betta came to her room to help her prepare for the night. Was there anything she could get for the signora? she asked. Blanche thanked her but said there was nothing. She wanted only to get to bed again, to take refuge in the blessing of sleep, for a while to be able to forget.

When Betta had gone from the room Blanche lay for a while in the dark listening to the occasional sounds coming from the street. 'Please God, let me sleep before Alfredo returns,' she murmured. She didn't even want to hear him, let alone see him.

After a while she slept.

She was lying awake, brought back to wakefulness by the sound of a carriage going by beneath the window and by the ache in her ribs. After lying there for a while she gave up hope of going back to sleep and pulled herself up in the bed, struck a match and lit the lamp. Glancing at the clock she saw that it was just after four. She would go downstairs and make herself some tea, she decided. With the decision she got out of bed and put on her dressing gown and slippers.

Quietly, so as not to risk waking Alfredo, she opened her door and moved out of the room. The landing was lit by the small flame of a gaslight that was kept burning throughout the night at the head of the stairs. In its pale glow she turned and glanced towards the door of Alfredo's room. Earlier, when going to her own room to sleep, she had noticed that his door had been left ajar.

574

It was still so. She turned from it and moved across the landing.

She was halfway down the stairs when a sudden thought brought her to a halt, and after hovering for a moment she turned and made her way up again. Silently moving back across the landing she came to a stop outside Alfredo's door. Had he still not returned? Without making a sound she slowly pushed the door open wider and looked in. By the dull light that spilled from the landing she could see that his bed was empty; it had not been slept in.

Turning from the door she stood on the landing and wondered at his continued absence. It had been shortly after breakfast when Betta had heard him say as he was leaving that he would soon return. Had something unexpected happened to delay him? And then the thought came to her that perhaps he had *never intended* to return so soon. Perhaps he had known that he would be away for several hours. Yes . . . Perhaps he had spoken in front of Betta about soon returning in the knowledge that she would relay the information to her, Blanche. Perhaps she, Blanche, had been *meant* to expect his return – for in doing so she would not entertain any thoughts of escape.

Blanche stood quite still on the landing. Perhaps Alfredo's words and actions meant that he would *not* be returning tonight.

She was aware all at once of her heart thudding in her breast, while her palms were suddenly damp. *She could go now*. She and Adriana, they could leave now, while Alfredo was out of the house and before Edgardo and the other servants were up. *Yes*. She would go to Marianne and Gentry. They would help her to get away.

One after another the thoughts spun through her mind. But how would she get to the Via Gabriele, she wondered. She wouldn't easily be able to find a cab at this hour – and it was too far to walk with Adriana. And if they did attempt to walk they would soon be found by anyone who cared to come after them.

She must do it, though. It might be a very long time before she had another chance.

Another minute of pondering on the problem and she had decided on a plan. Turning, she moved silently across the landing to the nursery where she noiselessly turned the door handle and crept into the room.

Betta lay asleep in the bed nearest the door, Adriana near the window. The room was faintly lit by a night-light that burned on a little table near Betta's bed. Silently closing the door behind her, Blanche moved to Betta and, leaning down, whispered the girl's name into her ear and gently shook her. Betta came awake almost at once, and as she did so Blanche put a finger to her lips, signalling to her to be silent.

Betta nodded, and Blanche whispered to her that she needed her help, that she should get dressed at once, put on her coat and come to her room. 'But don't make a sound,' she urged. 'We mustn't wake anyone else.'

'Yes, signora.' Betta nodded; she was already pushing aside the covers.

Returning to her own room Blanche hurried to her little table beneath the window, opened the drawer and took out writing paper, an envelope and a pen. Her hand shook so as she wrote the note that she paused to take a deep breath and try for greater control. There was no time to go into detail in her letter; she had to be brief. In it she asked Gentry to get a cab, or bring his carriage at once to the Piazza San Bernardo which was close by. She and Adriana would meet him there. There was, she wrote – and she underlined the words – no time to lose. She folded the note and slipped it into the envelope. As she did so the door behind her silently opened and Betta slipped into the room. She was wearing her outdoor coat. Blanche turned to her, gave her a nod, then bent over the table and wrote on the envelope Gentry's name and address. Turning back to the girl she paused briefly then whispered:

'Betta – I'm taking Adriana and I'm leaving the signore. I can't stay here any longer. Will you – will you help me?'

'Of course, signora.' Betta nodded firmly. 'What do you want me to do?'

Blanche held out the letter. 'Take this to the Via Gabriele, number twenty-seven. You must give it into the hands of signor or signora Harrow – to no one else, you understand?'

'Yes, signora.' Betta took the envelope.

'Give it to no one else. Everyone's sure to be asleep when you get there, but you must wake them up.'

Betta nodded.

'Oh, Betta,' Blanche said, 'I know it's a long way and in the dark, but – but you'll be as quick as you can, will you?'

Betta nodded again. 'Of course, signora. I'll run all the way.'

Blanche put her arms around the girl, quickly hugged her. As they broke apart Betta said:

'Signora – will you take me with you?'

'– Do you want to come with us?'

'Oh, yes, signora. *Please.*'

Blanche saw tears in the girl's eyes. She gave a nod. 'Of course.' She put her hands to her mouth for a moment in frantic thought, then added: 'In that case, don't try to return here on your own, but wait for me with the signora Harrow at the Via Gabriele – you understand?'

'Yes, signora.'

'– But Betta – if you come with us – I'm afraid there's no time for you to pack anything. The rest of the servants will soon be awake. We've got to get away.'

Betta gave a shrug. 'That's all right, signora – I have nothing to pack.' Another little shrug. 'I have nothing.'

Blanche said: 'Leave the house by the rear door and go by the courtyard. It will be quieter than using the front door.'

'Yes, signora.' Betta was already turning, moving away.

As soon as Betta had gone Blanche got dressed as quickly and quietly as she could – though she could not move about too hurriedly for fear of disturbing the servants on the floor above. When she had finished putting on her dress she took a key from a vase, went to the chest beneath the window and opened it. She had not saved very much money, but the little she had she would need.

At once, however, as she bent over the open chest, she could see that something was wrong. The contents of the chest had been disturbed. Pushing her hand down the side, she located there the purse where she had kept the money she had been accumulating. She brought it out. The clasp was undone. The purse gaped open, empty.

Alfredo, anticipating what might go through her mind, had forestalled her. It must have happened last night; while she had lain unconscious on the floor downstairs he had come up here and gone through her things. She felt that she could weep. It had taken her so long to amass that small sum, and now it was gone. In a passionate flurry of movement she began to snatch at the other items in the chest until they lay scattered about her knees on the floor. At the bottom of the chest she found a few odd coins – a couple of franc pieces, some centimes and the sovereign. The rest of the money – all the notes – had gone. Almost sobbing with frustration, she scooped up the few coins and dropped them into her pocket.

A sudden thought occurred to her and she rose from her knees and opened the top drawer of the chest of drawers in which she kept a small jewel box containing trinkets and the few pieces of jewellery she owned – her mother's wedding ring and a few other small pieces she had acquired over the years, some from Alfredo. If necessary she could sell some of it; it might bring enough to help her and Adriana once they were back in England. The box, however, was no longer in the drawer. Alfredo had thought of everything.

Taking a small travelling bag from the wardrobe Blanche began to pack it with a few clothes and other essentials. She worked feverishly, aware of the minutes swiftly ticking by. When she had packed what she needed she put on her coat and hat, picked up the half-full bag and went across the landing to the nursery. After silently closing the door behind her she shook Adriana awake and, urging her not to make a sound, pulled her up in the bed. Still half-asleep, Adriana was like a rag doll, and it took all Blanche's patience to handle her calmly.

With Adriana's movements infuriatingly slow and languid, Blanche took off the child's nightgown and began to get her dressed. 'Come on, dear – wake up.'

'What's happening, Mama?' Adriana's words were a slurred, sleepy whisper.

'We're going away.' And Adriana was already sagging against her again. 'Please,' Blanche pleaded, 'Adriana, wake up. Help me.'

Adriana opened her eyes, making an effort. 'Where are we going?'

'On a long, exciting journey. Just you, me and Betta.'

Adriana looked over at Betta's empty bed and yawned. 'Where's Betta now?'

'Hush – not so many questions. We're going to meet her in a little while.'

At the Harrows' villa on the Via Gabriele the butler, Carlo, had answered the door to Betta's persistent ringing and at once had fetched his master who, also awakened by the bell, was already out of bed. Putting on his dressing gown, Gentry went downstairs to Betta where, breathless after her run through the streets, she stood in the hall. On reading Blanche's note he gave orders for the groom to be awakened and the carriage to be prepared immediately. That done he hurried back upstairs to get dressed. By the time he came down again some minutes later the groom was bringing the carriage around to the front of the house.

In the meantime Marianne, also awake and having learned from Gentry of the impending arrival of Blanche and Adriana, rang for her young maid, Lisa. When the girl appeared she asked her to make some tea.

Downstairs Betta, who had told Gentry that she had been instructed to wait for her mistress, had given up her coat and been shown into a small sitting room off the hall where Carlo lit the gaslight and put a match to the fire.

As Betta sat nervously waiting and warming her cold hands before the flames Marianne came to her, clad in her dressing gown, and introduced herself. She was soon followed by Lisa carrying a tray of tea. As Marianne and Betta drank the tea Betta nervously spoke a little of her mistress's stated determination to leave signor Pastore. And she herself, she told Marianne, with some little pleasure, would also be leaving with her mistress for England.

*

When Adriana was at last ready and wearing her coat and hat Blanche took some of the child's clothes and put them into the bag along with her own. Then she closed the bag, took it up and silently opened the bedroom door. Seconds later she and Adriana were out on the landing.

Outside the door to her own room Blanche came to a halt, trying to remember if there was anything she had forgotten. She could think of nothing. Tightening her grip on the travelling bag and giving Adriana's hand a little squeeze she turned and led the child silently down the stairs.

Reaching the hall below she turned towards the rear of the house, and as she did so Alfredo appeared before her.

They came to a stop, facing one another.

Alfredo, having just entered the house, stood before her wearing his coat and hat and carrying a travelling bag. As Blanche looked at him she said to herself: *We're too late. Just a few more seconds, another minute, and we would have been safely away, but we've left it too late.*

There was silence. Then Alfredo said softly:

'It looks as if I returned just in time.'

Blanche, not speaking, merely held on to Adriana with one hand and gripped the bag in the other.

'May I ask where you think you were going?' Alfredo said. In the dim light of the gas lamp Blanche could see that his face was pale with shock and growing anger.

Her heart thudding furiously she briefly closed her eyes while she tried to collect herself. Summoning her courage, she said, 'Alfredo – please – I must talk to you.'

He gave a nod. 'Well, obviously some explanation is necessary. I can't imagine you were taking Adriana out for her health. It's dark and cold outside. Hardly the right time, I would have thought, for a pleasant stroll around the town.' He paused, waiting. 'Well? What have you to say?'

Frowning, she glanced down at Adriana who stood looking from one to the other. Clearly the child could sense the great tension in the situation and her lower lip quivered as she fought back her tears.

'Please –' Blanche said, '– not before the child.' She turned, gesturing to the door on her left that led to the dining room. '– Can't we sit down and talk about this?'

Without waiting for a reply she put down her bag then opened the dining room door and led Adriana inside. Taking a match from a little jar she struck one, turned on the gas lamp and put the flame to the mantle. 'There –' she gestured to a chair, '– will you sit down while Daddy and I have a little talk? – Will you?'

Unconsoled, Adriana burst into tears. Blanche bent to her, wrapping her arms about her. 'There's nothing to cry about, my darling – nothing, I promise you.' Taking her handkerchief she gently dabbed at Adriana's wet cheeks while the child clung to her. When Adriana was calmer, Blanche touched a gentle finger to the tip of her nose. 'Trust me. You just sit there for a moment like a good little girl, all right?'

'Yes, Mama.'

Blanche straightened. 'There's a good girl.'

With an encouraging smile, Blanche backed out of the room and closed the door behind her. Alfredo was still standing there, arms folded, waiting. After a moment's hesitation she moved towards him, came to a stop before him. She drew a breath to speak but he broke in, saying:

'Before you tell me anything . . .'

She waited. '– Yes?'

'Listen –' He shook his head. 'I've been in Palermo.

I had some business to do there. But I came back because . . .' He let his words trail off, then he added, avoiding her eyes:

'I'm sorry. For what I did. I'm very sorry.'

Keeping her voice low she said:

'It's too late, Alfredo.'

Now he raised his eyes to hers. She added:

'You – you've got to let me go.'

He said nothing. She went on:

'We're both unhappy, you and I, you know that. It was a mistake, our marriage. You must see it.'

Still he said nothing. She continued:

'We should never have married, Alfredo. I'm not the right kind of wife for you. I don't fit in with your life. I never have; I never will.'

'Go on,' he said. 'I'm listening.'

'– Alfredo, you know that what I'm saying is true. We can't even talk to each other any more. The only thing is for us to separate. We must go away – Adriana and I.'

He shook his head. '*Never.*'

She gave a groan. 'Oh, why do you want to keep me here? – when it only brings such unhappiness to us both?'

'Look,' he said, '– I told you: I'm sorry.'

'It's too late for all that. It doesn't make any difference any more. I'm leaving you.'

'You're all the same,' he said, and now his voice was bitter. 'That first whore I married went off, and now you tell me you're going to do the same.'

'I don't want to leave you for anyone else,' she protested. 'I want to leave because I can't see any other way out – for either of us.'

'And if I hadn't come back when I did you would have left by now. You would have taken my child and gone. Just – stolen her away. I would never see her again. I was afraid of this happening.'

'You think this is a good atmosphere in which to rear a child? With mistrust and – and hatred between her parents?'

'I love her. And she is my daughter – just as you are my wife.'

'I'm your wife, yes – but that doesn't make me your property. I don't belong to you. I belong to *myself*. And Adriana, too. She doesn't belong to you, or to me – or to anyone. Parents don't own their children. They have the responsibility for their care – but they can't own them.'

'It doesn't matter what you say – I'm not letting you take our child away.'

They stood there facing one another. In the silence Blanche became aware of the ticking of the hall clock. She turned, looked at its face. Almost five-twenty. Betta would have reached the Via Gabriele ages ago, and surely Gentry would be well on his way to meet her by now.

Turning back to Alfredo she said quietly:

'Let me go, Alfredo. Please.'

His eyes were piercing in his pale face. He glared at her for long moments and then lurched forward, stooped and picked up her travelling bag. Turning, he swung his arm and pitched the bag violently along the hall; it landed near the front door.

'Go on,' he said. 'Get out. It you want to go, then go.'

'Alfredo –'

'But you're not taking Adriana with you.'

The nightmare was growing worse. 'I *am* taking her,' she said. 'And no one's going to stop me.' She turned to move towards the door of the dining room, but Alfredo was quicker, and he stepped before her, barring her way.

'*I'm* stopping you,' he hissed. 'And if you try to take my daughter I tell you I shan't be content with beating you; I shall kill you. I told you – go if you want to, but if you go you go alone.' He leaned forward, punctuating his words. 'Adriana is my daughter and she's staying with me.'

He straightened. There was a little moment of silence, then Blanche said:

'She's not your daughter.'

'– What?' He frowned, curling his lip.

'It's the truth, Alfredo.' Blanche took a breath, braced herself. 'Adriana is not your child.'

He glared at her for a moment then gave a short, hollow laugh. 'You can't tell me that. I know differently.'

'Then you don't know the truth.' She kept her voice very even. 'You don't know anything.'

His eyes narrowed. 'Don't you make up such things,' he said warningly. 'I know what is the truth.' But there was less conviction in his voice. She knew that the seeds of doubt had taken root, and her fear grew along with his doubt. She could not go back now, though. After a moment she said:

'I never wanted you to know it. I never intended that you should. But when –'

Abruptly her words broke off. The floor beneath her feet had begun to shake, moving with an increasing violence. The windows rattled, a picture fell from the wall and fell onto the tiles of the hall with a loud crash of breaking glass. Blanche gave a little cry while in almost the same moment there came a scream from beyond the dining room door.

'Holy Christ,' Alfredo muttered, '– an earthquake.'

Chapter Forty-Two

The first tremors of the quake were felt just after five-twenty that morning of December 28th, 1908. Many further shocks were felt during the rest of the day and over the days that followed, gradually diminishing in number and intensity as the days and the weeks passed by. But it was during the first minutes of the appalling catastrophe that the greater part of Messina, second largest city in Sicily, was utterly destroyed.

In the worst earthquake in Sicily's recorded history Messina and her surrounding towns and villages about the eastern coast were razed to the ground, with varying degrees of devastation occurring as far inland to the west as the town of Caltanisetta, almost at the centre of the island and over two hundred miles away. On the far side of the Messina Straits to the north-east, on the toe of the mainland of Italy, the town of Reggio di Calabria also suffered the most terrible destruction. It was at Messina, however, where the catastrophe reached its most devastating heights and where loss of life was at its worst. Prosperous, popular Messina, ancient city of treasures – with all its history of earthquakes and other disasters it was totally unprepared for the horror of that night and for what was to follow.

Just before dawn the sleeping inhabitants were awakened by a sudden upheaval of the earth. The first violent tremor lasted several seconds, the shock racing north-east and south-west from the quake's centre in the middle of the Straits. It was, however, a mere presage of what was to follow. After an ominous lull of only a moment or two there came the major part of the catastrophe.

Suddenly, accompanied by a dull rumbling sound, the earth began to move again, a convulsive shaking that seemed to go on and on. This, the greatest of the shocks, lasted for some thirty-two seconds. It was in this period that the city of Messina was destroyed.

With the warning given by the first, short upheaval, some of the city's people were able to scramble from their beds and make a run for safety before the more calamitous effects of the major quake took their toll. While the earth shook people poured from their houses, their cries of 'Terremoto' (earthquake) and their prayers to God and the saints quickly drowned by the terrifying sounds of the collapse of buildings. Beginning with a series of loud, thundering crashes which grew in intensity, the noise culminated in one prolonged, stupendous crash as most of the city fell in ruins.

Out into the streets streamed thousands of terrified people, while all around them bricks and mortar, roofs and walls and chimneys crashed down. Of those citizens who escaped safely from devastated houses, hotels and other buildings, many ran for the open spaces of the docks where there would be no risk from falling masonry. Within minutes they were pouring onto the quays, running to the water's edge, as far from the town's collapsing buildings as they could get. It was then, just when they thought they were safe, that they encountered a new danger.

The middle of the Messina Straits being the core of the shock, the seabed suffered unseen and unimagined distortion. Only on the surface could its effects be discerned as great gaping troughs appeared in the sea, great yawning caverns of water that sucked down ships and boats and spewed them up again on mountainous waves.

A further result of the massive disturbance of the seabed and the water's displacement was that the sea itself was caused to be drawn from the shoreline of Messina for hundreds of yards – only to go rushing back again minutes later. With a great roar, hurtling forward at incredible speed, a huge seismic wave of water, like some gigantic tidal wave, hurled itself at the Messina shore.

Cargo steamers and mail boats sailing in the Straits were carried shoreward on the wave as if by some unseen giant hand, their crews fighting with all their might to prevent their vessels from capsizing. Of the shipping moored at the docks the smaller craft were picked up and carried inland to be tossed amongst the ruins of the devastated city like so many children's broken, discarded toys. Larger vessels were wrenched from their moorings, their anchor chains snapping like thread, and, at the total mercy of the wave, were sent crashing into other ships.

On the quays the people who had just arrived in their desperate bid for safety saw the wave approaching. But too late. Rearing high above them, it struck the shore and crashed onwards, carrying with it not only the debris of the ruined harbour buildings but the people themselves who, only seconds before, had glimpsed salvation. Pounding inland for several hundred yards, the wall of water did much to complete the destruction of the buildings and carried everything with it. With its recession it swept not only a mass of debris but also hundreds upon hundreds of drowned and crushed bodies into the sea.

Any work of destruction left undone by the quake

itself and the giant wave would be completed by the fires that swiftly broke out all over the city.

No one in living memory had ever known such devastation, such loss of life. As for the city itself, it appeared to be gone forever.

Signor Marino and his wife, who had been guests of Blanche and Alfredo only two days before, were sleeping in their third floor room of their hotel off the Corso Cavour when the quake struck. The bed on which they lay rose up and began to rock violently. Signora Marino screamed out, clutching at her husband, and the next moment the floor was giving way beneath the bed and the bed was falling. Minutes later signor Marino regained consciousness and found himself lying in a small space amid the rubble, pinned down by a beam. From a few yards away he could hear his wife calling out to him. He tried to move towards her, to help her, but he could not. He began to cry out for help, but his voice was only one of so many voices calling, and no one came. After a few minutes his wife's voice ceased, but by this time signor Marino himself was dead.

In another, poorer part of the city the tumbler, the little boy with the bright smile and the scarlet tunic, to whom Adriana had given the coins, was snatched from his bed by his father and carried out into the street. Seconds later they both lay dead, killed in an instant by a huge falling block of masonry as the father had hovered, undecided, not knowing where to run for safety.

At the villa on the Via Gabriele Marianne, in her petticoat, was sitting at her dressing table when the quake happened.

A few minutes earlier, downstairs, she had put down her teacup and got up from her chair saying to Betta that she had better get dressed as her husband would be arriving shortly with signora Pastore. Then, leaving the girl alone by the fire, she had gone upstairs to her dressing room where Lisa came to help her to dress and do her hair.

Lisa, a slight, pretty seventeen-year-old from Catania, had been with Marianne for three years. She was speaking of the Christmas festivals in the city when the first tremors came, and her voice at once came to a halt. The floor beneath them shook, the shaking going on for what seemed endless seconds, while the windows rattled so violently that it seemed that in another moment they must shatter. Marianne and Lisa held their breath. Then, after the slightest pause, the protracted, crescendoing shaking began.

And then everything seemed to happen at once. To the accompaniment of a distant roar, the floor began suddenly to heave and shake at the same time, while the room started to sway. The rattling of the windows became so violent that several of the panes shattered and fell in. The whole earth was being shaken like a rat in a terrier's mouth. The chandelier above their heads danced crazily, while on a table a little porcelain figure suddenly moved across the polished surface in a weird, vibrating shuffle, a second later falling to the floor with a crash.

Marianne leapt to her feet crying out, 'An earthquake!' while Lisa screamed and turned on the spot, helpless in her fear. Rushing to the door, Marianne clutched at the handle.

'It's stuck!' she cried. 'I can't open it!'

The handle turned in her grasp but the door would not budge, and she stood pulling at the handle while Lisa screamed and the violent shaking of the room went on and the walls cracked and the mirrors and the pictures began to fall.

Suddenly there was a deafening crash as a nearby house collapsed and fell – and then a series of crashes, each one coming faster upon the heels of the ones before, thousands of crashes eventually mingling in what sounded like one stupendous, prolonged thunderclap as all over the square mile of the city the bricks, mortar, plaster and stone of the roofs and chimneys and walls of the city's buildings came down.

In those moments when the greater part of the city fell, so most of the walls about Marianne and Lisa fell too, along with those of the adjoining houses giving way to the barrage and collapsing in a cloud of choking dust.

In the little sitting room below, Betta had leapt from her seat as the floor beneath her feet first began to shake, the table rocking and the teacups rattling in their saucers. The door that had been closed suddenly sprung open, and in seconds she was dashing into the hall. Another moment and she was opening the front door and rushing down the steps and out into the night.

While the buildings fell and the earth continued to shake beneath her feet she ran on, as she did so being joined by other terrified people as they dashed out of their collapsing houses. Unlike Betta, most of the panic-stricken citizens had been in bed sleeping when their homes had began to fall about their ears, and now they spilled onto the pavements for the most part clad only in nightclothes or underwear or else completely naked. The narrow streets into which they poured, however, offered them little safety, for there was no space available in which to escape from the falling masonry. And, as the buildings crumpled and fell, so thousands more were crushed to death as they ran.

Betta had reached the end of the Via Gabriele and was just turning, seeing before her the open space of a small piazza, when a loud cracking report sounded above her head. It spelt the end for her. Before she could dash out of the way, she was struck. A second later she lay dead, crushed beneath the broken stone of a collapsed wall.

In the eastern part of the city Gentry had just arrived in the Piazza San Bernardo in his carriage when the disaster happened. At the first tremors the horse whinnied with fear, kicking at the air with its right forehoof, and Gentry heard the groom's alarmed mutter of '*Earthquake*'. Then, seconds later, as the long, violent shaking of the earth began, making the vehicle shake and rock like something possessed with life, the frightened driver urged the terrified horse into the square's centre away from the surrounding buildings.

As the cab moved forward, still pitching and tossing, the buildings began to fall and Gentry heard the air filling with cries as people swarmed out into the open, the houses collapsing behind them. A minute before there had been lights in many windows, lights from the oil lamps that customarily burned throughout the nights in many Sicilian homes. Now, with those lights extinguished, the city was momentarily plunged into near darkness. But then, only a moment later, somewhere over to his right a sudden blaze of light sprang up as a fire broke out, a broken oil lamp igniting the escaping gas from a fractured pipe.

With a jerk on the reins the driver had brought the horse to a halt. As he did so a crack appeared in the earth beneath the creature's belly, and in seconds a fissure was opening, gaping wider, and the horse, with a scream of fear, was falling down, being swallowed up. Gentry, watching in horror, threw open the carriage door and leapt from the lurching vehicle. Falling heavily on his left arm he felt pain shoot up to his shoulder. There was pain too in his right leg. As he turned, rolling on the ground, he was just in time to see the driver and the carriage follow the horse down into the abyss.

In the glare of the leaping flames Gentry watched, helpless, as others fell into the crevasse – a woman running with a child in her arms, an elderly man, another woman, a dog barking wildly and dashing madly round and round in circles – all toppled into the abyss. And then, amazed, he saw the jaws of the earth close again, and then open once more, widening by the second, its split running across the piazza and claiming yet more victims in its wildly zigzagging course.

'Quick! Outside!'

Alfredo shouted the command at Blanche, and she cried out, '*Adriana!*' but he was already turning, moving to the dining room. The door rattled as he turned the handle and threw it open, while at the same time there came Adriana's voice again, her frightened cries ringing out against the terrifying rumbling and shaking of the earth. A second later Alfredo was sweeping Adriana up in his arms and, out in the hall again, was turning and running for the front door. 'Quick!' he cried, 'the house is going to fall!' Blanche dashed ahead of him, snatching at the bolts, wrenching them back. In another moment they were running down the steps into the street. As they fled there came the first sounds of cracking masonry, brick, plaster and wood, soon to be followed by the terrifying noise of the falling walls, chimneys and roofs.

In the dark they dashed on, while all around them buildings were beginning to collapse upon each other, the thundering crashes of their fall drowning the terrified screams of their panic-stricken occupants who tried to run from them into the open. Not knowing the city well Blanche had no idea where Alfredo was going, though he appeared to be heading towards the sea. Then he was crying out to her, 'Down to the quays – where there's open space. We must get to the quays.'

Against the thundering crashes of the falling city they ran on through the narrow streets while the houses crumpled and fell on either side, stone, brick and concrete smashing onto the pavement within feet of them, raising clouds of dust that filled their throats and made them cough and choke. Fires were breaking out everywhere, lighting up the scene as the streets filled with half-naked, screaming people, running, staggering, limping, all trying to escape from the falling buildings. At Blanche's right a young girl emerged from a dust-clouded doorway of a partly wrecked house. In the glare of flames Blanche saw blood streaming down her face. As the girl staggered against the wall the balcony high above her head tilted and fell. In an instant she lay crushed. Wherever the light was sufficient Blanche could see people lying among the ruins.

Caught up among the stampeding hordes, she and Alfredo continued on their dash towards the sea, very soon leaving the ruined houses behind and emerging onto the seafront. There the magnificent row of uniform palaces with their great soaring columns was now only a façade; behind their standing faces there lay only ruin.

Alfredo was gasping for breath as he came to a stop, while Adriana clung to him, wailing. All about them people were pouring onto the docks, running from every direction, all of them terrified of remaining in the area of the buildings in case there should be further shocks.

'We – we'll be safe here,' Alfredo gasped.

Blanche, also gasping for breath, nodded. Before them lay the sea, the Messina Straits, but like no sea that she had ever seen before. Now beneath the dark sky she could see it heaving and dipping while on its surface the moored boats and anchored ships were tossed about like tethered corks. Instinctively she stepped back and, turning; looked back at the ruined city behind them. Most of it had already collapsed, while here and there on the seafront, as far as she could see along what remained of the Corso Vittorio Emanuele, fires were breaking out.

Alfredo's voice came, breathless, staccato:

'Forgive me, Blanche. For everything.'

She turned to him. He stood gazing intently at her over Adriana's head.

'*Please* . . .' he said.

'Yes – yes . . .'

He nodded, then: 'It wasn't true, was it?'

'What . . . ?'

'– About Adriana – and me. You said that I was – was not –'

She broke in quickly: 'No – it was a lie. I – I wanted to hurt you. I'm sorry.'

'I thought so,' he said, and he smiled, but in spite of his smile Blanche could see in his eyes that he knew she had spoken the truth.

The very next moment she heard him cry out in awe and horror, 'Dear God!' – and turning back she followed his gaze and saw far out on the sea a wall of water rushing towards them. In the same moment she realized that most of the other people on the docks were unaware of it; nearly all of them were standing with their backs to the sea while they gazed at the ruins of the city.

'*Quick!*'

Alfredo turned and, with Adriana held tight in his arms, began to run from the sea front. In seconds Blanche was with him as he dashed towards the façades of the ruined palaces. Reaching the nearest one he ran between the cracked columns and in through an open doorway. Beyond it the rest of the once-magnificent building lay in total ruin, a mass of plaster and broken stone.

Alfredo did not hesitate. Climbing over the heaps of debris he struggled towards the broken remains of a once grand and elegant staircase that still reared a few feet above the wreckage. Gasping for breath from his exertion he struggled through the dust and rubble and, reaching up, thrust Adriana onto the stair above him where still clung some of the carved stone balusters and the remains of the sweeping marble rail.

'Hold on!' he ordered her. 'Hold on!'

He turned and grabbed at Blanche's arm, pulled her roughly towards him and then half-pushed, half-lifted her up onto the step where Adriana knelt holding on. Scrabbling up behind the child – there was only just enough room for her – Blanche knelt at her back, her arms reaching out on either side of her, clutching at the supports.

Alfredo had no chance to get up beside them. Even as Blanche's hands closed around the stone balusters the wall of water came roaring onto the shore. Through the open spaces in the building's façade Blanche saw in the dim light hundreds of people running before the wave, their mouths opening in cries of terror, cries drowned by the roar of the water and the splintering and cracking of timber as boats were picked up from the water and hurled forward on the crest of the wave.

With Adriana held fast in the circle of her arms Blanche braced herself and held on. And then the wave, over thirty feet high, came roaring over the quays and was upon them.

The wall of water struck the remains of the palaces. Some gave beneath the force, the columns and the façades cracking, toppling back to fall on the masonry that had already been brought down by the quake. Other façades shuddered under the onslaught and miraculously held, the water rushing around them and through their open windows and doorways, carrying in its flood the remains of wrecked boats, tons of debris from the ruined customs sheds and other port buildings, and the bodies of the drowned men, women and children.

As the water struck the façade behind which Blanche, Adriana and Alfredo cowered, Blanche took a deep breath and closed her eyes against the onslaught. The wall held. And the water, ice cold, poured into the space behind the wall through every possible aperture. As it struck Blanche and the child, pounding over them, several feet above their heads, Blanche gripped the rails with all her might, at the same time pressing her arms together and her body forward, imprisoning Adriana within the rigid circle of her arms.

Head well down, eyes shut tight against the force that threatened at every moment to tear her hands from their grip, she felt as if the rolling wave of water would never come to an end. She could not breathe, and her whole body was buffeted by the debris that was carried on the current. After what seemed an age (but was in fact only seconds) when she felt that she could hold out no longer, the power of the water slowed, and changed direction. Then, its pace increasing again, it began to run back to the sea. And this time Blanche felt the strength of the current at her back, pressing her and Adriana against the banister, threatening to sweep them both away and into the sea.

At last, feeling the level of the water running lower, Blanche opened her eyes and her mouth and breathed again. The water was below the level of her feet, and draining away, the last of it running back through the openings in the façade of the ruined building. To her right floated the body of a child, a little boy, his nightshirt drifting behind him as he slowly turned in the current. She watched as he floated out through the wide, paneless window. The body of a young woman came floating by, naked to the waist, and came to rest against a pile of rubble that lay against the inner wall of the façade. It remained there, caught. Blanche shifted her gaze, eased herself back from Adriana's body and looked down at her. Adriana was crying. But she was safe. Turning, Blanche looked at the spot where Alfredo had been standing. He was no longer there.

When Marianne opened her dust-clogged eyes she did not at first realize what had happened. Then memory returned. She coughed, feeling that she would choke on the thick dust that seemed to fill her mouth and nose and lungs.

All around her there seemed to be darkness, though further away she could see the glow of flames. She realized that she was half-covered with bricks and pieces of broken plaster. Her head hurt and there was pain in her shoulder. From all around she could hear the sounds of wailing and weeping. She opened her mouth to call out for Gentry, but then recalled that he had left the house. Further recollection came back to her and she called out 'Lisa?' several times but there was no answer. After a while she kept silent and just lay there, waiting for daylight to come, the air all around her filled with the continuing sounds of crying voices and the occasional crash as the standing remains of buildings toppled and fell. Sometimes the surface on which she was lying trembled as the earth was shaken by further tremors. *It's the end of the world*, a voice in her head kept repeating. *It's the end of the world.*

*

Gentry's left arm hung useless at his side, the humerus broken just above the elbow in his plunge from the carriage. Also in the fall he had wrenched his right leg. He had to move, though; he had no choice.

After picking himself up he had stood in a daze, unable to fully comprehend the reality of what had happened. *There's been an earthquake,* he said to himself, the realization coming through the fog of his pain and his dulled senses.

He looked around him. The only light on the scene came from a fire that had taken hold nearby and was beginning to blaze in the ruins of a fallen building. Just yards from where he stood the crushed remains of the carriage were visible above the rim of the gaping fissure that had split the piazza. From all around him came the screams and moans of people in agony, people who cried out over and over for help. No vision of hell had ever prepared him for this.

After he had stood there helplessly for a few moments he told himself that he must get back home. Marianne would need him.

As he started painfully away he suddenly remembered that he had been on his way to meet Blanche. He came to a halt. She might be close by – perhaps even in the piazza. He opened his mouth and called out: 'Blanche . . . Blanche,' but his voice was lost amid the continuing ragged chorus of cries and screams that rang all about him. There was no knowing where she might be. She and Adriana might still have been at the house when the shock came . . . He started off again. The Via Imera was on his way to the Via Gabriele . . .

Making his painful way by the occasional light from burning fires was a continuation of the nightmare. Once out of the piazza he found that the surrounding streets were almost totally impassable. There was not a square foot of pavement or roadway that was not covered by dense rubble. Where rows of tall houses had once stood facing each other across the narrow streets there now lay only piles of ruins. In many cases the buildings had been completely razed and lay as pyramids of wreckage, while here and there the shells of buildings still stood, some of their floors intact.

Skirting the fragile walls that still remained upright, he slowly, painfully picked his way along, climbing over shattered beams, slabs of stone and piles of bricks and plaster. His broken arm throbbing, his wrenched knee crying out in protest against the effort of his exertion, he fought his way forward, clambering over smashed armchairs, sofas, chests, ovens – the wrecked remains of the lives of so many, and all the while as he struggled along the cries of the desperate, the injured and the dying continued to rend the air. The voices came from all around him, from before and behind, and from left and from right; they came from above him, from people stranded high up in the remains of their houses and from below, from those who lay buried beneath his feet.

By the time he reached the place that had been the Via Imera it was daylight. The house – in fact the whole row of houses – had been completely demolished. Only the odd broken walls here and there showed where one house had been divided from its neighbour. For the rest it was one long, uneven hill of wreckage. Standing before the pile of ruins that had once been Blanche's home, he looked at it and knew that no one caught inside could have survived such destruction.

As the creeping light of dawn came Marianne found that she was lying on the floor, half propped against a wall – one of only two walls remaining. The others had gone, fallen away. In the burgeoning light she looked out over the rubble-strewn carpet to open air, air grey with a lowering cloud of smoke and dust, and saw the devastation before her. Gone were the streets of tall houses, theatres, palaces and civic buildings. As far as she could see, in whichever direction she moved her disbelieving gaze, there was nothing left of the city but piles of rubble.

Closer at hand, down below in the ruined streets, she could see people moving about, crawling, limping, staggering, dragging themselves from the wreckage or lying in it, partly buried in the debris, unable to pull themselves free. And all the while the air was filled with their screaming and sobbing and wailing.

A sighing groan from her left brought her head around and she saw movement among the rubble a few yards away.

'Lisa . . .'

Coughing, choking on the dust that hung in the air, Marianne pushed aside some of the bricks and plaster that lay upon her and moved towards the young girl. Lisa was sitting up, groaning. Lifting the girl's head Marianne saw that her face was almost black with dust, while bits of plaster, brick and stone lay thick in her hair. She could see traces of blood on her face, her hands.

'Lisa – are you all right?'

She put her arms around her and spoke her name again. Lisa did not reply; she seemed stunned. After a while she bent her head and began to weep, the crying of a child. Marianne drew her closer, drawing her head down onto her own shoulder, trying to comfort her.

Releasing her after a few moments, Marianne carefully got to her feet, as she did so the brick- and plaster-dust falling from her in a cloudy shower. The door of the room – that door that had jammed and prevented their escape – was now open and hanging crazily on its broken hinges. She moved unsteadily to it and looked through into the bedroom beyond. It remained, though with its rear and side walls torn away, leaving it open to the cold morning air. The bed remained too, and most of the rest of the furniture – except for the huge wardrobe. Having once stood against the rear wall it had, along with the wall, fallen with the rest of the house. The bed and the remaining furniture were covered in rubble and dust, and looking up Marianne saw that only part of the ceiling remained. Through the gap she saw that part of the upper house still stood, two walls at right-angles, cracked and split and leaning inward, still supporting part of the roof. For how much longer it would all remain so, she had no idea.

Treading carefully, she stepped through the bedroom to the door leading to the landing and the stairs – only to find that the stairs were no longer there. At the end of the landing the floor had sheared away in a tattered edge of broken timber and torn carpet, and where the stairs had been there was now only an abyss, a hollow well that plunged down into the ruins below.

Looking up she saw that the stairs ended abruptly some yards above her, just below the floor of the upper landing. Something dripped onto her hand, like rain – but then she saw that it was red in colour. Standing back slightly, she saw through the gap in the ceiling the fabric of a dress, a bare arm steadily dripping blood. She thought at first that it was one of the other maids, Maria or Stella, but then she saw that it was the cook, Anunziata. She called the woman's name, at the same time knowing there would be no reply. She turned and moved unsteadily back to the dressing room.

'Lisa . . .' She bent over the girl who sat there, moaning, making little crying sounds. 'Lisa, we must try to get down.'

The girl looked at her dumbly, making no reply. Marianne repeated her words, but there was no response. Irritated, impatient, she spoke more sharply and then, taking the girl by the shoulders, shook her. '*Lisa* – listen to me. We have to get down from here. Do you understand?'

Lisa looked vacantly at her and Marianne gave her another shake. 'We've got to get down! We must! Do you understand me?' She shook her again and then, raising her hand, sharply slapped her cheeks. Lisa shuddered, sucking in her breath and jerking her head back from the small, sharp pains. Now, though, there was something approaching comprehension in her eyes. She gazed around her in horror and then came back to focus on Marianne.

'Do you understand?' Marianne asked her again. 'We've got to get down before the rest of the house falls. You understand?'

'Yes . . .' Lisa nodded. 'Yes . . .'

'*Now*. We've got to get down *now*.'

'Yes.'

Rising again, moving away, Marianne made her way carefully from the dressing room and through the bedroom to the edge of the sheared-off floor that looked out onto what had once been the Via Gabriele. There were people about, some trying to pull others from the ruins while others limped and staggered by; some just sat looking dazedly into space. She called out to them. 'Help us,' she cried out. 'We are trapped. We can't get down.' But those who heard her cries merely looked up at her with blank looks in their eyes, and in the moment that they looked away again she was already forgotten.

As she gazed desperately around her the tottering remains of a building in the next street fell with a crash. Similar sounds were coming at intervals from every direction. It would not be long, she was sure, before the remains of the house in which she stood fell also.

'Lisa – come here! Quickly!' As she called to the maid she was already bending to the bed, tearing at the covers, and by the time Lisa had appeared in the doorway the sheets had been torn from the bed. 'Quickly,' Marianne said to her, 'we must tear the sheets to make a rope.'

Lisa shook her head. 'We can't,' she said. 'It's all finished.'

Marianne rounded on her angrily. 'It's not impossible, and it's not all finished. We're *alive*. We can get down if we try.' Although she gave Lisa the impression of strength she felt like weeping; she wanted Gentry there to take care of everything, to make everything all right. She didn't know where he was, though, and there was only herself and Lisa. 'Come and help me!' she shouted. 'At *once*!'

Lisa came to her side and they quickly set to work. First biting at the linen, they tore the sheets and then tied the pieces tightly together. When they had finished Marianne bent to the bed and tied one end of the long makeshift rope securely around one of the legs. 'It will hold our weight easily enough,' she said, 'and it's not that far down.'

Gentle persuasion did not work with Lisa and it took stern words before the girl eventually sat on the rubble-strewn floor and inched her way to the edge. Then, very much afraid, she gripped the sheet-rope and slowly, slowly, her feet finding support where they could on the shattered dividing wall, began to lower herself down.

Marianne, watching from above, was terrified that the girl would fall, but after a few moments Lisa was safely down and standing in the rubble. At once Marianne began to draw up the rope.

As she did so she felt the floor quiver beneath her

feet as a tremor shook the earth. The quake was met by frightened cries from those about her while from across the street came a crack and crash as the surviving walls of another wrecked house fell in a cloud of dust and rubble. Almost in the same moment there came from above her a loud crack like the report of a gun. It was followed in a split second by a further crash as a great piece of one of the chimneys came crashing through the ceiling above her head and plunged onto the bed at her side. Under the impact the bed collapsed like a toy. In another moment the wall beside her was cracking, splitting, bellying, tilting inwards. A beam from somewhere above fell and hit the floor on the far side of the bed while a shower of plaster and brick fell in a heap beside the open door. The remaining part of the building was coming down around her head. There was no longer time to let herself down by means of the sheet-rope. Even as the realization went through her mind there came another deafening crash from above her head. With a cry she ran to the edge of the sheared-off floor and leapt off into space.

She hit the rubble below heavily and awkwardly and fell sideways into a well formed by fallen beams and collapsed masonry. Seconds later the remains of the house began to fall. Lisa, standing open-mouthed, saw Marianne lying there one moment; the next, in a thundering crash of bricks, beams, plaster and stone, the remaining walls and floors fell in. When the dust had cleared Lisa could see nothing there but the rubble.

Chapter Forty-Three

When at last Blanche and Adriana left the shell of the wrecked palace daylight had come.

Emerging from the ruins Blanche stood and looked out to the Straits. Although the sea was calmer it was still turbulent. In the harbour floated hundreds upon hundreds of bodies – men, women and children, all drowned when the wave had swept them from the quays. Naked, half-naked, they lay in the water, moving with the swell of the waves. Blanche tore her eyes away, but there was no escaping the sight. The bodies of the crushed and the drowned lay all about her on the quays, too. Death was everywhere.

Adriana, standing at her side in the thick mud left by the wave, was crying softly, a low, mournful little wailing sound. Blanche bent to her and quickly stripped her of her soaking wet clothes. Then, wrapping her for the moment in her own wet, wrung-out coat, she wrung the water from Adriana's clothing as well as she could and then dressed her in them again. At least now they would dry more quickly.

'Come,' she said. Taking the child's hand she led her away from the sea, towards the ruined town.

And all of a sudden Blanche was catching at Adriana's hand more tightly, drawing her towards her. Adriana made no protest, and Blanche turned their steps, leading them along a different route, away from the clutch of bedraggled bodies that lay in the mud of the ruins, away from the body of Alfredo as he lay there, grotesquely twisted in death, eyes half open as if casually contemplating the sky.

Walking on, they felt further tremors of the earth. It appeared that there were no longer any buildings left intact to fall, but the tremors caused the standing remains of some already wrecked buildings to totter and collapse into the rubble-strewn streets. The extent of the mud showed that the water had gone many yards inland, and still there were the bodies, the dead and the dying. In whichever direction Blanche looked she could see ruins burning, flames and smoke leaping into the air. Everywhere was ruin and devastation. An old woman came limping along. 'Messina is finished,' she muttered as she slowly passed by. Blanche could hear her voice continuing into the distance: 'Messina is finished . . .'

Blanche and Adriana walked on. If anyone had asked Blanche where they were going she could not have answered with any certainty. The only thing she knew was that they could not remain still. Somewhere in the city were Gentry and Marianne. Perhaps she could find them. Where were they, though? Even when the city had been whole she had not known her way about its streets. Now that the whole place was nothing but rubble she had no real idea of where she was. She had a vague idea of the direction in which lay the Via Gabriele, but it was doubtful that Gentry would be there. Surely by the time the quake had come he would already have left to meet her. She must keep going; it was the only thing to do.

As she walked on through the mud and the debris a woman, wearing a torn nightdress, came to her, clutching at her sleeve.

'I've lost my son,' she said. 'Help me find him, my Paolo.'

Immediately she had spoken she turned and walked quickly away, stopping in front of a man who sat, head bowed, in front of the ruins of a house. She tugged at the man's arm. He did not respond and after a few moments she gave up and went on her way.

A man came by carrying a young girl in his arms, weeping as he walked, the girl's head lolling back. A middle-aged woman knelt near a pile of ruins while she stretched out her arms hurling curses at the sky. 'There is no God,' she cried out; 'there is no God.' As they passed the ruins of a house Blanche's eye was attracted to a dark shape and she saw a crow swoop down to the body of a young man who lay with only his head and shoulders above the wreckage. He was obviously dead. She saw the crow alight on a stone in front of the dead face, and in one swift, easy movement the crow's head drew back and darted forward, sinking into the eyesocket of the corpse. With a little cry of horror Blanche closed her eyes and turned away. And all the time she could hear the sounds of the groaning and wailing, and the cries for help, many of them muffled and distant, coming from below the surface of the ruins, from those who lay trapped beneath them.

'There's nothing left,' a man observed to her with a strange, dazed smile on his face as she walked past him. Sadly she shook her head in agreement. Others called out to her as she went by. One chorus of voices came from above her head, and looking up she saw a little group of people standing precariously on a narrow balcony of a ruined hotel, The Trinacria. Help us, they called down to her; they were trapped; there were no stairs. What could she do, she asked herself. She could do nothing. Holding Adriana's hand more tightly she walked on.

After a time Blanche found herself on the Via Imera,

standing beside Adriana and gazing at what had once been their home. A section of the lower part of the front wall was still standing, to a height of about eight feet, part of its window frame still in place. On the left side a curtain moved in the breeze. In the tangled wreckage of the rubble Blanche could make out the remains of a picture that had hung on the wall of the dining salon.

'Wait here,' she said, letting go Adriana's hand. But Adriana snatched at her hand again, holding on, crying out in a mournful, keening sound.

'Only for a moment, darling,' Blanche said. 'And I won't leave your sight.'

Pulling her hand from the child's grasp she climbed up over the heap of rubble, casting her eyes about her and calling out: 'Anna . . . Anita. Anna . . . Anita. Anna . . . Anita . . .'

There was no response. Standing quite still in the midst of the ruins Blanche listened for the voices of the maid and the cook. There was nothing. After a moment she called out:

'Edgardo . . . ?'

No answer. After a few seconds she turned and moved back to where Adriana waited, took her hand and led her away again.

The previous day Blanche and Adriana would have been able to walk the distance between the Via Imera and the Via Gabriele in less than half an hour. Now Blanche thought they would never come to the end of their journey. Since her arrival in the city only days before she had seen its streets busy with traffic of all kinds – not only its people, but its vehicles – trams, horse-drawn cabs, mule- and goat-carts, motor cars. Every sign of transport had gone now. Roads and vehicles had been destroyed, and buried under the ruins. Now there was only one way to move, by foot. And even this means of travel was fraught with difficulty and peril. Not only was there danger from overhead with the ever-present risk of collapsing buildings, but underfoot the way was also full of danger. Like everyone else in the ruined city, Blanche and Adriana found that in order to go anywhere they had to pick their way carefully and laboriously through acre upon acre of wreckage, to climb one hill of debris after another.

Blanche came upon the remains of the Duomo without at first being aware of what it was. And then she realized. The magnificent cathedral lay in ruins. The great granite columns, once part of Neptune's Temple at Faro, and which Blanche had gazed at in awe, now lay shattered, covered in the debris of priceless mosaics, frescoes and cornices. Only one wall was still standing – that in the apse at the east end. And on it still the serene, mosaic figure of Christ remained, hand uplifted in blessing, as it had been for the past five hundred years; now, Blanche thought, a terrible irony among the ruins.

On the shattered steps of the cathedral stood a woman, beating her bare breast with one hand while she clutched a naked dead baby in the other and screamed her misery to the skies. Beyond her at the side of the piazza men and women worked pulling away the rubble, and as Blanche watched she saw them bring out a young girl of seventeen or eighteen, covered in blood and with her nightclothes hanging from her in shreds. There seemed no end to the suffering and the death and destruction, and suddenly, as if reaching the point where she could take no more, she sat down on a stone and buried her head in her arms.

In seconds, though, she lifted her head once more. She couldn't give in to despair. She started to rise, and as she did so there came to her a voice, calling from some distance away.

'Blanche – oh, Blanche . . . Thank God . . .!'

Turning her head she saw the figure of Gentry moving slowly and unsteadily towards her over the debris.

'Gentry . . .!'

Blanche got quickly to her feet and hurried towards him. She could see that he was walking with difficulty, limping on his right leg, while his left arm hung at his side. They met and Gentry put his right arm about her and drew her to him. Feeling his touch, his strength, her own arms encircling him, her last resolve went and she burst into tears. Alfredo, she told him, was dead, killed by a great wave that had come onto the shore. Her head against Gentry's shoulder she remained there, weeping.

He released her after a while and bent to Adriana and she came to him and he put his arm around her and pressed his begrimed face to her own.

'Your arm –' Blanche said as he straightened, and he nodded and told her briefly how he had come to injure himself. It must be set, he said: he knew how it had to be done, but he couldn't manage it himself; she would have to do it for him.

Searching among the wreckage he found a short piece of wood, and Blanche found some fragments of cloth which she tore into strips. Then, while he gritted his teeth and clenched his eyes against the pain, she helped him off with his overcoat and his jacket, after which he sat down among the broken stone of the cathedral steps. Laying his coat and jacket down at his side she unbuttoned the cuff of his shirt sleeve. That done she tore his sleeve from wrist to shoulder to expose the bare flesh. As she looked at it she was suddenly, for a moment, back in England, in a field in Wiltshire, bending above John Savill as he lay in the grass.

Gentry's upper arm was very swollen, and as she ran her fingers over the skin she could feel the form of the broken bone beneath. After a little time, however – though a time of great pain for Gentry – the shattered bone was in place and she began to bind the splint to his arm. She was halfway through when suddenly there was a cry from Adriana at her side and she turned to see a young man, his naked body almost black with dirt and dust, snatch at Gentry's overcoat and dart away again. Before she could do anything to stop him he was hurrying off among the ruins, the garment clutched in his hands.

'Stop!' Blanche cried out. 'Stop!' But the man took no notice. In seconds he was out of sight behind the ruined walls of the cathedral. Blanche was about to go in pursuit, but Gentry held her with his free hand. 'Leave him; he's gone. You won't catch him now.'

'But your coat –' Blanche said, shaking her head.

'It's gone now – there's no getting it back.'

'But you'll be cold come the night.'

He shrugged. There was nothing to be done about it.

When Blanche had finished binding his arm she improvised a sling for him from part of a tablecloth that she pulled out of the debris nearby. She did not know what to do about his leg, however. While nothing was broken he appeared to have badly wrenched and bruised his knee. It would be all right in time, he assured her. For the moment what he needed was some piece of timber that he could use as a support to aid him in his walking. When this was done Blanche draped his jacket about his shoulders, with his right arm through the sleeve, and the three of them set off together, making their way slowly among the ruins in the direction of the Via Gabriele.

Adriana must be hungry, Blanche thought as they

walked, and she murmured to Gentry that they would have to try to find some food soon, and something to drink.

That, he replied, could be a problem, adding that it was inconceivable that the water pipes and the reservoirs had remained undamaged. It was possible they might find some food, but where they would find drinking water he didn't know.

Reaching a small piazza near the Via San Cristoforo a little while later, Gentry recalled that there had been a baker's shop on the corner. On coming to the spot they found the front part of the shop lying in ruins while the ground floor rooms towards the rear looked to be still comparatively whole. There might be bread there, Gentry said. With due warnings to take care – Gentry could be of little physical help due to his injured leg and arm – Blanche moved carefully through the rubble towards the back part of the ruined house.

As she slowly made her way she passed by the bodies of a man and a woman who lay in the hall, close to one another, still in their aprons, and quite dead, crushed beneath fallen stone and a huge beam. She went on past and came at last to the kitchen, a mass of broken beams and masonry, but nevertheless recognizable and just navigable. Seeing the huge old ovens ahead of her she had to stoop and crawl to reach them, but she got there at last. The oven fires had long since burned out and the ovens were quite cold. Moving aside some of the debris she managed to open one of the doors. The baker and his wife had been busy that morning, and the oven's interior was packed with loaves of bread, overbaked, but fresh. She took up three of the loaves and thrust them into the bodice of her coat. Then, looking around her she saw lying in the dust and debris that covered the floor two oranges and a lemon. Snatching them up she put them into her pockets. There was nothing else she could see that might be of use. After a moment she turned and, bending, began to make her way back towards the front where Gentry and Adriana were anxiously waiting.

Outside she tore a piece from one of the loaves and gave it to Adriana. Then she gave some to Gentry and took a piece for herself. The bread tasted good and they ate as they walked. When Adriana had eaten her piece of bread she tugged at Blanche's coat: 'Mama – Mama . . .'

Hearing the child's voice Blanche halted beside her, crouched down and looked into her eyes. It was the first time Adriana had spoken since their dash to the quays. Her heart full, Blanche lifted a hand and gently touched it to Adriana's soft but grimy cheek.

'What is it, darling?'

'I'm thirsty.'

'Yes, I'm sure you are.'

Taking one of the oranges from her pocket, Blanche peeled a part of it. With Gentry's words in mind about a possible water-shortage she gave Adriana just two segments of the fruit, gave one to Gentry and ate one herself. The remainder of the orange she put back into her pocket.

As they moved away a small, dirty street urchin came by. Seeing the bright pieces of orange peel lying in the dust he snatched them up and ate them.

There were two further earth shocks as they continued on their way. On each occasion it brought cries of fear from many of those who moved about the ruins, causing little flurries of sudden movement as the frightened survivors instinctively began to run, desperate to escape the possibility of further harm. Very quickly, however, they all came to a halt, realizing that there was no longer any safe haven they could run to.

On some occasions Blanche and Gentry stopped to help in the rescue of some poor individual, though Gentry's disabilities made their assistance of limited effect. Also, he and Blanche were anxious to get to Marianne in the Via Gabriele, so often they shut their eyes and ears to the pleas.

Due to the delays, and Gentry's injuries and the difficulties caused by the conditions of the terrain, their journey took many hours and it was mid-afternoon before they eventually reached the remains of the Via Gabriele. Turning into it – what had once been a street of tall, elegant houses – they picked their way across the rubble. As they did so a figure suddenly appeared hurrying towards them – a young girl, sobbing, crying out, 'Signore, signore . . .'

Gentry came to a stop. 'Lisa . . .'

The girl came to him, stopping before him and bursting into tears. In between her sobs she told him that the signora had jumped from the house and that the house had fallen, and now the signora was buried in the ruins.

At her words, hearing what he had been so afraid of hearing, Gentry gave a groan. But then as he raised his hand to cover his eyes Lisa said that the signora was still alive; she had heard her crying out from underneath the debris. At her words Gentry began to hurry forward across the rubble.

Reaching the ruined remains of the house that had been his home, Gentry asked where Marianne lay, and Lisa guided him to a spot at the front. Then, against the continuing background of moans and screams from the trapped and the injured, he picked his way through the debris, came to a stop and shouted out Marianne's name. They stood listening, and then faintly from below the rubble came the muffled sound of Marianne's voice:

'Gentry . . .'

She was alive.

Bending as much as his injured leg would allow, Gentry called out to Marianne again, asking whether she was all right and what was her situation there. She replied faintly that she was trapped in a hollow in the debris, that she could not move but that she was all right. Gentry replied that they would get her out as soon as they could. Turning quickly, seeing a man who stood gazing nearby, Gentry called out to him to come and help. 'My wife is buried here beneath the ruins,' he called. 'Please help me get her out.' At Gentry's call the man turned to him, eyes blank, registering nothing, and then looked away, to gaze dully upon the devastation before him.

In spite of the number of people about and notwithstanding Gentry's pleas there was no help forthcoming. Many of those nearby were already involved in scrabbling at the debris with bloody hands, trying to release trapped relatives and friends. Others lay there among the ruins, too injured to do anything even to help themselves. Others, like the man whom Gentry had appealed to, just sat or walked about in a daze, as if their senses had been stunned by the calamity.

So, Gentry, one-handed, helped by Blanche and Lisa and Adriana, set to the task of trying to extricate Marianne from her prison beneath the ruins of the house. It was like digging bare-handed into the side of a hill, a hill of stone and wood and bricks and plaster and broken glass. Adriana was soon too exhausted to continue and Blanche took off her coat, which was now nearly dry, wrapped the child in it and laid her down out of harm's way in a small hollow in the debris nearby. She had given a piece of the bread to Lisa and the remaining loaves she hid beneath the coat at Adriana's feet. Leaving Adriana with a small piece of bread to eat, she turned back to continue in the work of setting Marianne free. Later, when she moved back to look at Adriana she found her sleeping soundly among the rubble.

Removal of the smaller bits of debris presented no difficulty; they could easily be lifted. Larger pieces, however, required all their combined strength, while there were some pieces that they found impossible to shift. Their work also needed great care, for there was always the danger that they would dislodge some of the heavy debris and that it would fall upon Marianne as she lay trapped.

Working without tools, using only their bare hands, the work was not only extremely slow, but very painful; in a short time their hands were torn and bloody from manhandling the rough stone and brick and timber, and Blanche searched among the debris until she found some fabric – the remains of a cotton sheet. Tearing it up, she carefully bound the hands of Lisa, Gentry and herself as a protection against further injury.

And the work continued, laborious and exhausting. Every now and again they would be forced to stop and rest and catch their breaths. At these times Gentry would bend and call out to Marianne and she would call back to him. Later in the afternoon Blanche took some of the bread and shared it out between them. Afterwards they ate the rest of the orange. Having eaten they resumed their work, and so, gradually, bit by bit, they fought their way nearer.

A bitterly cold wind was blowing, and as the light began to fail a few spots of rain fell. At this Gentry broke off work to say that they must erect some kind of cover for the night in case the rain grew worse. In many of the ruined buildings around them shelter was offered from the cold and wet in rooms where parts of ceilings remained intact. It was not safe to go into them, though; many were so unsound that there was a danger that at any second they might come crashing down. To remind them of the situation, every few minutes as they worked there would come a crashing thud as the standing remains of another building fell in a heap.

At Gentry's suggestion they erected a small, low, very crude, three-sided shelter which they put together from a door propped up on supports made from various items taken from the debris. Into this they put a mattress which they had managed to salvage. Though torn and with its stuffing bulging from its sides, it was a welcome acquisition and would at least provide a bed for Adriana.

After making the shelter they at once went back to work removing the debris, though they were forced to halt not long afterwards when darkness fell. By now they were almost too weary to move. Lisa moaned and cried in misery and exhaustion as she sat down, and Blanche sat beside her and put an arm around her, drawing the girl's head onto her shoulder. 'I want to go home,' Lisa cried. 'I want to go home.' Blanche held her tighter and murmured that she should go home soon. Everything would be all right, she said; they had survived the worst and they would go on surviving.

In the glow of a fire that Gentry made from bits of timber that Blanche had collected and which he had lit with matches he had found in his pocket, the four of them sat together, warming themselves at the flames. Blanche shared out more of the bread. Afterwards Adriana and Lisa crawled in under the rough shelter and lay down on the mattress side by side, snuggling close for warmth in the cold night air, Blanche's coat wrapped around them both.

Apart from their own, controlled little fire Blanche could see the glow of fires that burned here and there in the ruins about them. Some were quite near, others off in the distance, some quite small, others infernos in which the raging flames lit up the area around them and sent up showers of sparks into the night sky.

Gentry sat a few feet away from her, his begrimed face bathed in the light of the flames before them. He looked cold, disconsolate and unutterably weary. Blanche leaned across to him and adjusted the jacket over his shoulder. She laid her hand briefly on his. 'Get some rest, Gentry. You must rest. There's no more you can do tonight.'

He said nothing. After a few moments he got up from the stone on which he was sitting and moved once more towards the hill of rubble beneath which Marianne lay. In the faint light cast by the fire he began to pull at the debris. Blanche got up and went to him.

'Gentry, don't. We can't get her out tonight, you know that. Besides, it's more dangerous in the dark. Wait till the morning. We'll all be rested then and we'll be able to do so much more. And there's sure to be help available too. There will be help coming from outside. People with the right equipment. If we can all just get through this night everything will be all right, I know it will.'

He gave a weary nod. 'Yes, I suppose so.' He bent, directing his voice down to Marianne where she lay trapped.

'Marianne . . . ?'

Marianne heard Gentry's voice calling to her. Ever since he and Blanche had arrived on the scene she had been able to hear their voices, faint murmurs coming from above her, sounds mingling with the sounds of brick scraping on stone, stone scraping on wood, wood moving on plaster, sounds resulting from their efforts to free her. But now those other sounds had finished and she could only hear Gentry's voice as he called down to her. It was night, he called; they had to stop and rest. Night, day – they were all one to her. To her it had been night since early that morning when she had leapt to the ground and the bricks, stone and timbers of the house had come crashing down upon her.

She was lying on her side, her cheek resting on her upper right arm, which was flung out ahead of her. Her left arm was bent at her side, her hand close to her chest. She could see nothing – and knew nothing except discomfort and terror. She lay in a hollow formed by a configuration of a doorframe, part of a beam and a section of a stone wall. Across these had fallen a heavy beam which had formed a roof, protecting her from the rest of the debris that had fallen. She could move hardly at all, though she was afraid to try, fearful that any shifting of her weight might bring tons of rubble down upon her.

Gentry's voice came to her again:

'Are you all right still, Marianne?'

'Yes,' she called back. 'Yes . . .'

'Try to bear it for the night, can you?'

She could hear his voice waver as if he was close to tears.

'Yes,' she replied, she could bear it – though secretly she wondered how she would.

'In the morning,' called Gentry, 'we'll get help. And we'll soon have you out.'

'Yes, yes . . .'

A pause, a silence broken only by the sound of distant cries, moans of fear and pain. Then Gentry's voice again:

'Marianne . . . ?'

'Yes . . .'

'Try to sleep. Try to sleep and make the night go faster.'

'Yes.' She felt her own terror well up again. 'But don't leave me. Don't go away. Don't leave me.'

'I shan't leave you. I shall be here, very close.'

After that there were no more voices calling to her; the only voices were the distant cries of others who were trapped, and they continued on and on without respite.

Dear God, she prayed, *let me get through the night . . .*

Chapter Forty-Four

That night, while Marianne lay beneath the rubble, unable to move in the cold confines of her prison, Blanche and Gentry kept their vigil above, huddling close for warmth in the bitter cold. Side by side they sat staring into the crackling flames and waiting for the night to pass. All about them continued the cries of the trapped and injured, the sounds such a constancy that Blanche almost ceased to register them. At the same time she saw that several fires were continuing to rage in many of the devastated buildings. What ruin the quake and the wave had failed to accomplish the fire would complete.

Every so often as Blanche and Gentry sat there, numbed in the stupor of their misery, they would hear Marianne's voice joining the ragged chorus of other voices that sounded in the night. Distant, muffled through the debris, she called first to Gentry and then to Blanche, wanting the comfort of their voices. And each time they called back to her, assuring her that they were present and would remain so.

To add to the horror of the situation, the earth tremors continued. There were at least a dozen minor quakes during the night, and although they were not severe enough to cause any new, major damage they were often of sufficient power to cause the collapse of some of the standing ruins and bring them tumbling down in showers of dust and rubble. Such happenings brought terror to Gentry and Blanche who were afraid that the tremors might bring a further fall of the debris that lay above Marianne's trapped body.

It came on to rain towards morning, an icy, driving rain that quickly soaked their clothing, doused their meagre fire and left them in such a state of misery and discomfort that Blanche despaired that they would ever get out of the nightmare. She could only keep telling herself, over and over, that help was bound to come from some quarter soon.

As the first light of dawn lit up the landscape Gentry was already moving to resume work on the removal of the debris. Blanche got up to help him. As she did so she looked about her. While the driving rain had put out their own little fire it had done nothing to halt the spread of the flames that raged in the ruins, and many of the half-standing buildings had now become smoking, burned-out shells or had collapsed into piles of smouldering rubble. Up above her head crows and ravens circled, occasionally swooping down to scavenge on the bodies of the dead. Many more people had died during the night, perishing as they lay trapped beneath the debris, or, lying out in the open had died from their injuries and the bitter cold. The dead lay everywhere. Turning from the sight, Blanche bent her head against the rain and moved to Gentry's side.

Later, when Lisa and Adriana awoke, Blanche shared out some of the bread between the four of them. As they ate they heard the sounds of gunshots in the distance. Blanche and Gentry looked at one another, baffled. 'What is it?' Lisa asked. Blanche shook her head. 'I don't know.'

Afterwards she and Gentry got back to their labours again. A little later they heard a voice, a man's voice calling out to them, asking whether they needed some help. Straightening from their back-breaking task they saw a young sailor approaching among the ruins, and then it was that Blanche registered the fact that he had spoken in English.

They called back to him at once: yes, they would like his help – and he in turn shouted to someone else. The next moment another young man had appeared, like the first clad in a merchant seaman's uniform – though now filthy with grime and dust. Happy to meet some English people, the two sailors, who carried saws and ropes, wasted no time but took charge of the rescue operation and immediately bent their backs to the task of helping to remove the debris. With great relief Gentry watched their efforts for a moment or two and then called to Marianne that it would not be long now before she was free.

As they worked the young men referred to one another by the names of Reid and Smith. They appeared to be in their mid-twenties. Reid, red-haired and the taller of the two, and more heavily set, was clearly from somewhere in Wales, while the accent of the dark-haired and wiry Smith betrayed his origins in London.

They were from a British merchant ship, the *Afonwen*, they said, which had been steaming into port with a cargo of coal when the quake had struck. Miraculously the ship had escaped any serious damage from the wave. All the previous day they and the rest of the crew had been out in the ruined city, distributing the little food and water they had to spare and giving whatever help they could. They were due to set sail again that afternoon, taking some of the survivors to Naples.

Blanche asked if, once Marianne was free, they could return with them to their ship and be taken to Naples along with the others. At her words Lisa, who stood nearby, began to wail and, very much afraid, clutched at Gentry, crying, 'Oh, don't leave me, signore. Don't leave me, please. How shall I get back to Catania?'

Gentry tried to pacify her. 'Don't cry, Lisa. We're not going to leave you alone here. We'll see that you get back to your mother somehow.'

Reid, the Welshman, said apologetically to Blanche, 'I'm sorry but – I'm afraid we can't take you on board ship. There just isn't room. She's already packed to the portholes with survivors. We've got strict orders from the captain not to bring anyone else on board.'

Blanche cried out, 'But what shall we do? We can't stay here.'

'Other ships are coming into port,' said the young man, adding that three ships of the British navy had arrived that morning, called from Syracuse to come and help in the rescue of survivors. There were Russian ships too. Already, he said, boats were coming ashore bringing surgeons and medical supplies and food and blankets. A temporary hospital was being set up in the Piazza Mazzini near the Palazzo Reale. It would only be a matter of time before rescue came. 'You'll get help soon,' he added.

As he finished speaking there came the sounds of more distant reports, gunshots.

'Looters,' said the young man. 'Apparently they're being shot.'

As Blanche looked at him in alarm he remarked that the whole city was in chaos. The quake had broken all telegraph lines and all communications with the outside world had been severed. Furthermore, there was no way of travelling out of the city by train as all the railway lines had been wrecked.

After much hard work the two young men eventually succeeded in digging a tunnel through the debris, after which the lithe, wiry Englishman, Smith, carrying a rope, bravely crawled through to Marianne's side. There, suffering constant danger that the tunnel would fall and trap them both beneath the mountain of debris, he worked to set her free.

It was a long and exhausting and exacting task, and one that the young Cockney had to do alone. Eventually, however, just after one o'clock that afternoon, he re-emerged into the cold, rain-swept day, crawling backwards, and slowly, painfully, inch by inch, dragging Marianne after him, holding her by her shoulders and with a rope bound around her and underneath her arms.

Holding their breath, Gentry and Blanche hovered, watching tensely as the young seaman drew Marianne out of the debris and into the open. And moments later she was lying free.

She was quite naked, her petticoat and other underwear having been torn from her in the process of her escape, while her body was smothered in dirt. As Smith straightened, Blanche laid her coat upon Marianne's naked body while Gentry hobbled to Marianne's side and stood looking down at her, tears streaming from his eyes and murmuring little words of endearment. Miraculously, apart from the cuts and grazes and bruises that covered her body, she appeared to be physically unhurt. She was alive, and she was free.

Turning to the young men, Gentry asked if they would take her to the shelter out of the rain. Without hesitating Reid gently lifted Marianne into his arms, carried her to the makeshift shelter and laid her down on the mattress. Gentry followed and, with difficulty, crawled in after her. As she lay there the tears ran from her eyes, making little channels in the grime that covered her face. She spoke not at all, but just lay shivering in the cold while her silent tears coursed down her cheeks.

Blanche murmured that they must try to find some shelter from the wind and the rain where they would be safe until they could leave. The two young men said they would help her to find somewhere suitable. She thanked them and, telling Gentry of her intention and leaving Adriana in the care of Lisa, she and the two young men set out.

After exploring the ruined remains of several buildings nearby, a suitable place was eventually found. On one side of a piazza Smith had clambered over piles of bricks, timber and masonry of what had once been a fine villa, and discovered an open way to a flight of steps that led down to a basement. Minutes later he had led Blanche to the spot and she was descending the stairs behind him to a passage, from there turning to the right through an open door into a room. There, by the faint light that crept in from above, she found that she was standing in a large kitchen.

There was an oil lamp on a table, with fuel, and Smith set the match to the wick. By its light they looked around. The room appeared to be quite dry. There was a smaller room opening off, and in it they found racks holding dozens of dusty bottles of wine along with two or three bottles of brandy and Scotch whisky. Also they found a container of oil for the lamp and some kitchen candles. At least, Blanche thought, they would be provided with light if nothing else.

Back in the main room they looked in cupboards and found food – some stale bread and cake, and a quantity of macaroni and some vegetables – potatoes and swedes. They also found a large cooking pot full of water which, Reid said, nodding with satisfaction, would be safe to drink.

'You'll be all right here for the night,' he added, 'or until you can all get away.'

After putting out the lamp, they returned up the steps to the surface. There the young men pointed out that as most of the walls of the house had already fallen there was very little chance of any further peril from falling masonry.

When they got back to the others Blanche greeted them with the news that they had found a place of shelter. Then, with Marianne wrapped securely in Blanche's coat, Reid took her up into his arms again. With Smith helping Gentry, Blanche and Lisa picked up the mattress and together they all set off through the teeming rain towards the piazza.

Reaching the ruined house Smith went ahead and lit the lamp again. Minutes later the rest of the little group had followed him down into the basement kitchen, the mattress was set down on the floor and Marianne was laid upon it. At Blanche's urging Gentry loosened the buttons of his waistcoat, laid his watch on the floor at his side and lay down next to Marianne.

The seamen left them then to see what other necessities they could find, returning a little while later with two rather torn blankets and another mattress which they had managed to salvage from ruins nearby. They also brought in their pockets a quantity of fruit which they had taken from a garden in the vicinity.

At Blanche's direction they set down the mattress on the far side of the room from where Gentry and Marianne lay, and Adriana and Lisa were urged to lie down on it and get some more rest. Blanche covered them with one of the blankets and laid the other over Marianne and Gentry in addition to her coat.

Afterwards the young men told her they had been informed that nearly every single member of the carabinieri at the Military College had perished and that martial law had been declared. And it was necessary, they said, for already numerous ghouls were entering the ruined city from the surrounding countryside, peasants and bands of wandering gypsies who had come to loot and pillage.

The two young seamen then announced that it was time for them to return to their ship which was due to sail shortly. Reluctantly they said their goodbyes and, turning to Blanche, wished her luck. She went with them into the passage to the foot of the stairs where she quietly begged them to take Marianne and Gentry with them. They needed medical attention, she said: surely there was room for them on board the ship. Reid said sadly and apologetically that there was not. Well, then, said Blanche, could they not be taken to the Piazza Mazzini where the field hospital was being set up? Reid said it could not be done. 'Nothing's organized there yet,' he said, 'and so many injured people are arriving there wanting treatment and food and shelter. Wait till tomorrow. Until then you're better off staying here where it's dry and warm.'

Reluctantly Blanche had to accept the advice. Solemnly the young men shook her hand. She thanked them for all they had done. 'I'll never forget you,' she said.

They were just about to start up the stairs when Smith stopped and, turning back, advised Blanche that it would be as well if neither she nor her friends did anything to advertise their presence in the basement. Hundreds of desperate people were roaming about the city, he said, and there were many of them who would not stop to kill for a warm bed and a piece of bread.

Reid nodded agreement. They didn't want to alarm her, he added, but also with the collapse of the prison hundreds of dangerous criminals had been released, many of whom were actively engaged in looting the remains of the wealthier villas. Like many of the ghouls from the countryside, some of them were actually stripping the dead of the jewellery they wore. And not only the dead; there had been reports of some injured survivors being attacked for the sake of their possessions. Some had been murdered, while others had had hands and fingers hacked off to enable their attackers to get at rings and bracelets. Now, though, Reid said, with martial law and with help beginning to come in, the situation would soon be under control.

They left her then, and she stood watching from the foot of the stairs as they climbed back up into the pouring rain.

Returning to the kitchen Blanche went to Adriana and Lisa where they lay awake and hungry on the far side of the room and gave them some of the bread – very stale now – and some pieces of swede which she sliced off with a sharp knife. She also divided half an orange between them. In one of the cupboards she found glasses, and breaking open a bottle of wine she poured a little into two glasses, to which she added a little of the water.

Leaving the girls to eat and drink she took some of the food and wine to Marianne and Gentry. Marianne, however, although awake, would not eat. With a shake of her head she turned her face away.

Placing the oil lamp nearby, Blanche took a bottle of Scotch whisky, poured a little into a saucer and did what she could to clean the many cuts and grazes that covered Marianne's body. Marianne lay there in silence all the while, occasionally sucking in her breath as the spirit stung her. The worst of the cuts Blanche bandaged with a tea cloth which she found in a drawer and then tore into strips.

Blanche was relieved to see that in spite of the number of cuts and bruises Marianne had suffered there still appeared to be no sign of any serious injury. It was a miracle. The greatest harm seemed to have been done to Marianne's mind, the experience obviously having caused her the severest shock. But she would recover in time.

Blanche's ministrations over for the time being, she once more covered Marianne with the blanket and the coat and then tried again to persuade her to drink a little, to eat a little of the bread. Marianne silently shook her head and turned her face away and closed her eyes. After a while she drifted off into sleep.

Blanche poured a little wine and water for Gentry, which she gave him along with some of the bread and a hunk of the swede. Sitting on the edge of the mattress beside him she drank some wine and water, and ate the bread and the swede, carving off slices with the knife. Neither she nor Gentry spoke. When she had finished she set down the glass and the knife on the floor and moved quietly across the room to where Lisa and Adriana lay. They had eaten and drunk everything she had given them and now lay sleeping. She tucked the folds of the blanket about them and then moved back to Gentry. Softly, so as not to waken Marianne, she inquired as to his own injuries. His arm was all right, he said, but he had to admit that his knee was very painful. He pushed aside the covering of the blanket, sat up and tried to pull up his trouser-leg. He could not; the fabric was too tight. When Blanche touched his knee he flinched and she saw that his leg was very swollen.

Having no alternative, Blanche took the knife and slit the seam of his trousers – and was horrified to see that his knee was swollen and inflamed to the extent where it ballooned out grotesquely. Clearly he had wrenched it so badly that he had torn ligaments and muscles.

Taking another of the tea cloths, she tore it into strips and bound his knee. Then, at her urging, he lay back down on the mattress beside Marianne, and she covered him again with the blanket and the coat. Try to get some sleep, she urged him.

He nodded and closed his eyes. Blanche remained standing there. She felt absolutely helpless. Four people – Adriana, Lisa, Marianne and Gentry – all were dependent upon her – and she did not know what to do for any of them. And she was so tired. She sighed with weariness; she seemed to ache in every bone and muscle of her body. It would be so easy to lie down beside Adriana and Lisa and just sleep. She could not, though. There were too many responsibilities. Standing there with the low-burning oil lamp in her hand she thought back over the events of the past two days. And it was not finished. The horror was continuing. She raised her left hand and pressed it to her eyes as if she would blot out the images that ran through her brain. For a moment there was the threat of tears; she forced them back; tears at such a time would be an indulgence, and there was no time for such a thing.

Gentry lay with his arm across Marianne's body. As Blanche gazed down he opened his eyes and looked up at her. 'Try to sleep,' she whispered. 'We'll be safe here. And tomorrow we'll go away.' He gave a little nod and closed his eyes again.

Her gaze shifted to take in Marianne's still face, and as she looked at her she thought back to how she had been in earlier days. She saw her as she had been that Christmas, when she had fallen in love with Gentry, so pretty and so full of hope for the future. She saw her as she had been as a schoolgirl at Clifton, as a child on the heath around Hallowford . . .

She moved away, walking on soft feet towards the passage, and the stairs that led up to the street level. Setting down the lamp she climbed the stairs. The atmosphere of the subterranean kitchen was oppressive; she felt she had to get some air.

At the top of the stairs, emerging from the shattered doorway into the devastation of the ruined villa, she found the rain still teeming down and driven by a hard, cold wind. Up in the sky the crows and ravens flapped, occasionally swooping down towards the earth where lay the bodies of the dead. A movement over to her left drew her eye and she saw a large rat scuttle out of sight amid the debris. And still could be heard the cries of those who lay buried beneath the ruins, voices sharp with pain, dull with despair. Raising her hands, she pressed them over her ears, blotting out the sound. Would the voices never be still?

After a few moments she turned from the lashing rain and made her way back down the stairs and into the kitchen. Moving to where Marianne and Gentry lay together on the mattress she stood gazing down at them. As she did so Marianne suddenly opened her eyes and gave a little cry, while her features were distorted in a sharp spasm of some mental anguish. Gentry awoke, raised himself on his elbow and looked at her in concern. Perspiration stood out on Marianne's brow while at the same time she shivered. With her eyes closed again, her head turned from side to side on the mattress while her hands, the knuckles white, clutched at the blanket.

Crouching beside her, Blanche laid her hand on Marianne's cheek and murmured her name. After a moment Marianne turned her head and looked at her. At first she gazed at her blankly with no recognition in her eyes. But then, quite suddenly, it was as if some curtain in her mind was lifted, and the blank, empty look left her eyes and they were filled with fear.

'Blanche . . .' As her dry, cracked lips opened to speak Blanche's name, her hand loosed its grasp on the blanket and clutched at Blanche, gripping so tightly that the rings on her fingers pressed into the bones of Blanche's wrist.

'Blanche . . .' she muttered, 'Blanche . . .'

And then her hand left Blanche's wrist and fell back, spasmodically gripping the blanket, while her eyes clenched tightly shut again.

Over her prostrate body Blanche's eyes caught Gentry's and she read there the plea in his gaze.

'I'm going for help,' she said softly. 'I'm going to see if we can get on board a ship today. We can't wait for tomorrow. We need help now.'

Gentry nodded. 'What can you do?' he whispered.

'I'll find somebody from one of the English ships. Those young sailors said there were doctors and other men from the ships bringing all kinds of supplies ashore, and setting up a hospital in the Piazza Mazzini. It's not far. I'll go there and bring somebody back. They must come and fetch you and Marianne and take us on board one of the ships so that we can leave.' She straightened. 'I'll go now, before it gets dark.'

With a final glance down at Marianne, she turned and hurried softly to the shadowed place on the far side of the kitchen where Adriana and Lisa lay. She was relieved to see that they were still asleep. Seconds later she had set down the lamp and was out in the passage and moving towards the stairs.

As she emerged into the open the driving rain struck at her, and in minutes her hair was plastered to her head and her dress was wet through. Unaware of the

634

discomfort, though, she pushed on, making her way over the piles of rubble that choked the narrow streets as she headed for the Piazza Mazzini.

As she picked her way among the ruins her attention was drawn to two dogs digging in the debris. They were wet, bedraggled, and covered in mud, and she was afraid of their wild appearance as they snapped and scrabbled at something in the rubble. But they were not interested in her. As she watched, the larger of the two dogs backed away, dragging something held in its jaws, while the other dog, snarling, tried to wrest it away. Then Blanche saw that they were fighting over the corpse of a baby.

She trudged on. And still as she passed there came to her the muffled cries of those still buried, while in whichever direction she looked she could see dead bodies, corpses either lying on top of the rubble, or partly buried beneath it. Sometimes just a foot or an arm would be visible above the debris. In the end such sights ceased to shock.

Even though the Piazza Mazzini was situated not very far away, traversing the almost impassable streets took a very long time. As she continued on her way she passed many little groups of people effecting rescue operations, many of them trying to dig out survivors who were still buried beneath the rubble. The shock of the catastrophe had initially stunned many of the citizens into a numb apathy, but in some cases this had now, thankfully, given way to a realization of the necessity for action. Not in every case, though; far from it; many still wandered or sat about, silent, with dull, vacant looks in their eyes. It was the same look that touched Marianne, Blanche thought. Others, pushed even further by the horror of their experiences, had gone quite mad. One man whom Blanche came across was moving about the ruins in the rain singing and doing some strange dance; his mind, unable to take any more, had given way, saving him from knowledge of the continuing horror.

As she drew nearer to the Piazza Mazzini there were more and more signs of activity. At one point she came upon some Italian soldiers collecting the dead for burial, loading the corpses onto a donkey-driven cart. Frequently she came across rescue parties hard at work, and she heard the familiar and comforting sounds of English voices from blue-uniformed British sailors working there, and the strange tongue of those seamen whom, she assumed, were from the Russian ships. As she passed by the groups of men she saw them digging perilous tunnels through the rubble, sawing through beams, carrying away heavy pieces of masonry. They worked tirelessly, drenched in rain and sweat, and covered from head to foot in dirt and mud. In some instances she saw them bringing out survivors from the ruins, and she gazed in awe and admiration at the tenderness displayed. As she passed she heard the words of comfort murmured by two young Scottish sailors as they carried out from the ruins an old man and covered his nakedness with a blanket. Further on she saw a burly Russian sailor emerge from the wreckage carrying a tiny naked child, a little creature looking so small in the arms of his saviour whose bearded face, streaming with tears, bent over the baby.

Entering the open space of the Piazza Mazzini she found that the rescuers had erected makeshift canvas shelters from the pouring rain, and that as many as possible of the injured had been placed beneath them. There was not room for all of them beneath the shelters, however, and many of them were forced to sit or lie out in the rain. They were there in their hundreds, sitting and lying in row upon row, while the air was filled with their cries and their moans; and all the time more of them were appearing, either limping in on the arms of others or borne on stretchers.

Amongst all the figures moving about Blanche could see the ships' surgeons going back and forth. Accompanied by attendants they were doing whatever they could with their limited resources to bring some kind of succour to the poor creatures who lay in such desperate straits. And witnessing the scene, Blanche knew that all her hopes of getting immediate help for Marianne and Gentry would be in vain. Nevertheless she had to try, and after a moment's hesitation she hurried to a tall, bespectacled man whom she took to be one of the surgeons. As he straightened from his examination of a woman who lay on the ground Blanche spoke to him in English.

'Sir – please – forgive me for bothering you, but – is there someone you can send to help me . . . ?'

He frowned, while observing: 'You're English . . .' and then added: 'Help you? In what way?'

'I've got two friends who are both lying injured, and I need help for them.'

'Injured? How badly?' He spoke quickly, impatiently, as if resenting even the time it took to converse with her.

Blanche replied, the words pouring from her:

'One of them has a broken arm. And his leg is wrenched so badly that he can't walk. He's in a great deal of pain. His wife is hurt in some other way. I don't know – she's in great shock. Oh, please, can you help . . . ?'

'Where are they? Are they near by?'

'Well – they're some little distance away, but –'

He broke in: 'Are they under cover right now? Have you got blankets for them? And food? Water?'

'Well, yes, but –'

He frowned. 'They're under cover – and you've got food and water for them?' He shook his head in astonishment. 'Good God, young woman, don't you realize what's happening here?' He gestured with a swift, short movement of his arm. 'Look around you. There are people dying here for want of attention – and we can't even bring most of the poor wretches under cover! Look at them – lying out in the rain – and they've already spent almost two days out in the open, in near-freezing conditions! Even with *our* ships and the Russian ones we haven't got enough blankets or enough food for those who are already here. And they're still being brought in every minute.' He bent slightly to her, lowering his voice to an intense whisper. 'So many of these poor devils are going to die – d'you realize that? And there must be two or three thousand who are still trapped. Did you hear me? Two or three thousand, they reckon. And we haven't got a hope of getting them out before most of them die of their injuries or cold and starvation and madness. Oh, yes, other help will be here soon, we can only hope and pray, but until then whatever we do isn't enough.' He shook a hand in front of her, as if brushing away some bothersome creature. 'Look at you – you've got *clothes*. You're even wearing a *dress* – when most of these poor people haven't got a pair of drawers to cover their nakedness. You don't know how fortunate you are. And your friends are in the dry, you tell me – and they've got blankets and food.' He shook his head. 'How can you come here asking me for help? Can't you see? – we haven't got it to give.' He turned away from her.

Blanche had stood in silence throughout the onslaught, and all the time she had known he was only speaking the truth. Then, in a great trembling gasp she sucked in the air and sobbed, and stood there in the rain while the tears poured down her cheeks.

The man turned back and saw her standing there, a young woman with a bruised face, clenching and unclenching hands that were cut and raw; a young woman in a torn and filthy dress, her wet hair hanging loose and in strings about her shoulders. His face softened suddenly. He reached out, put a hand on her saturated, muddy sleeve. 'I do understand,' he said. 'I'm sorry for speaking so harshly – but if you knew how desperate our situation is . . .' He shook his head in a little gesture of hopelessness, then asked: 'Are they British, your friends?'

She nodded, unable to speak.

'And you obviously want them taken off the island. Well, maybe tomorrow it will be possible – but at present . . .' He patted her shoulder. 'Go on back to them. Perhaps tomorrow real relief will be here – hospital ships, more supplies. Or perhaps you can get them aboard one of the ships that will be leaving. Until then they're better off where they are. There's nothing that can be done today.'

He gave her shoulder a final pat and moved away. She stood looking after him for a moment and then turned and started off through the rain.

It was almost dark. The woman moved on near-silent feet over the rubble that strewed the corner of the piazza. As she moved past one ruined villa her eye was attracted by the faintest glow of light amid the ruins. She halted and stood there, peering into the shadows of the house's shell. There was no doubt; a very faint glow of light was coming from somewhere. After a further moment she moved quickly and quietly forward. In her mid-fifties, she was heavily built and wore the coarse clothing of a gypsy. In her hand she carried a stout piece of wood.

After clambering over the ruins she found herself standing at the opening to the villa's basement. There were steps leading down, and a pale glow of light coming from below. After a moment she took a grip on the piece of wood and silently began to descend.

The stairs ended in a passage, but there was a room to the right, and it was from here that the light shone. On her silent feet she came to a halt in the doorway and stood there, taking in the scene. The room, what looked to be a kitchen, was very large, and with only one small lamp burning on a table nearby the space was so dimly lit that it was difficult at first to make out what was there. Then she saw that there were two figures lying on a mattress. They lay very still. Without making a sound she crept forward. As she drew near she saw that the figures were those of a man and a woman. They lay with their eyes closed, unaware of her presence. Was anyone else near? She turned, looking about her. The other side of the room was in shadow but after a moment or two she could make out what appeared to be the shape of another mattress lying on the floor. She froze, waiting to hear from it some cry of alarm – but none came.

After some moments of absolute quiet, in which she could hear the breathing of the couple who lay nearby, she became emboldened and took a step nearer to them. In the dim light she could see that the woman was young. Her eyes flicked to the man and she saw that his arm was in a sling. Also in the faint light she saw the gleam of metal at his side and saw his watch lying on the floor beside the mattress. She moved forward and bent to pick it up. As she did so there came the child's cry, a scream of fear. At once it brought the man's eyes open.

As the woman grasped the watch, his hand shot out and clutched at her wrist, and in the same moment he cried out in alarm.

With the watch still in her hand, the woman struggled to pull away, but the man's grip was too strong and he refused to let go. She did not hesitate another moment. Raising the piece of wood in her free hand, she swung it, bringing it down with a cracking thud across his skull.

While the child screamed again, the man groaned with the shock and pain of the blow. But still he held on. She raised the wood again. In the same moment there was a flurry of movement beside him, and more screams, and the young woman, quite naked, was rising up, reaching for her. Easily evading her clutching hands, the gypsy brought down the piece of wood again onto the man's head, and this time his grip on her wrist relaxed and he fell forward, sprawling half off the mattress, half on the floor. Not content, the woman raised the wood again.

'No! No! No!'

Her shrieks of denial rending the air, the younger woman launched her feeble strength at the attacker, leaping forward, one hand snatching at her arm, the other hand clutching at her face, nails digging into the soft flesh. The watch fell, smashing on the tiles. Ignoring the man, the gypsy turned her attention to the younger woman. Raising the piece of wood she struck out with it with all her force.

Twilight lasted so little time. It was almost quite dark by the time Blanche reached the piazza. Relieved to have got back safely, she picked her way across the rubble towards the entrance to the stairs.

She heard the voices from below as she started down

641

the stairs – a sudden eruption of sound, screaming from Adriana, joined immediately by cries from Gentry and Marianne – all the voices set against the sounds of violent movement.

Without stopping to think Blanche rushed down the remaining steps into the passage and swung into the kitchen. And the sight that met her eyes brought the fear welling up as if from a fountain, and her knees felt weak and the sweat broke out under her arms.

In the meagre light of the little lamp she saw a writhing mass over the mattress on which Marianne and Gentry had lain, making a large, amorphous shape that moved and separated and fused again. There were the figures there of Marianne and Gentry – and another, a woman. While the kitchen echoed with their cries, the screams of Adriana and Lisa, and the noises of the struggle, Blanche saw the woman strike violently at Gentry's head with something in her hand. She heard the crack of the blow and saw Gentry fall while the woman raised her hand to strike him again. And then Marianne, shrieking out 'No! No! No!' was hurling herself at the woman and the woman was striking at her instead, swinging her arm, bringing down the weapon with all her might, the blow smacking against the side of Marianne's head with a sharp cracking sound that rang in the cavernous room.

In the next split-second Blanche was rushing forward.

Having had her back to the door, and with the noise drowning the sounds of her feet, Blanche had the advantage of the element of surprise.

She threw herself at the woman with such force that they both went thudding onto the floor beside the mattress. As they did so the woman released her hold on the piece of wood and the weapon went sliding across the tiles. Blanche, recovering first, forced herself up, the woman's body pinned beneath her own. Holding her by the wrists, Blanche tried with all her force to keep the woman down, struggling to remain astride the thick body while the woman rocked beneath her, spitting and shouting curses at her. Blanche quickly realized that although the woman was years older, she was infinitely the fitter. Further, Blanche realized that she was fighting for her very life, and not only her own life but for the lives of the others in the room.

But she didn't know what to do. In that moment while she had the advantage the thought flashed through her mind that she should take the woman by the hair and strike her head against the floor – but she could not bring herself to do it. The next moment it was too late. The woman had given a heave and thrown her violently to one side, sending her sprawling.

Driven by desperation which gave her a strength and energy she had never known, Blanche swiftly recovered her balance. Then, as the woman rose on her knees and stretched for the piece of wood. Blanche reached out for the woman's hair and caught at it, gripping, wrenching her head to one side. The woman cried out with pain. Seconds later the woman's own hands were reaching out and Blanche felt the fingers clench in her own hair, and she screamed as they pulled with a strength that threatened to tear out her hair by the roots. Stretching up, she found her mouth pressed against the woman's wrists and she opened her mouth and bit down, hard. With a grunt the woman relaxed her grip on Blanche's hair, and the next moment they were rolling over on the floor, struggling for supremacy. Blanche knew, however, that she was fighting a losing battle. With a sudden, terrifying realization she knew that in a very short time it was going to be all over, and she would be dead.

Against the chorus of screaming from Adriana and Lisa, the two women rocked together, entwined, gasping and grunting with their exertions. And then suddenly the woman twisted, wrenching herself free. The next moment she was rearing above Blanche and then throwing the weight of her body on top of her. Blanche gasped as the air was knocked out of her lungs. Then, while the strength was draining out of her limbs she felt the woman's hands reaching forward, grasping at her throat.

The hands clutched, gripped, and began to press. Blanche tried to push her away but the woman, in command, was oblivious to her efforts. In the dim light Blanche could see the gleam of the black eyes as they stared into her own, and she could smell the strong, spicy smell of the woman's breath. In desperation Blanche dug her fingernails into the backs of the woman's hands, drawing blood, and for a moment the grip about her throat was loosened. It gave Blanche only an instant's respite; in another second or two the hands were about her throat once more.

As Blanche's head began to swim she flung out her arms, scrabbling with her hands on the floor to find something to grip, some purchase that would enable her to throw the woman's weight from her body. Her fluttering right hand came in contact with the mattress, brushed the flesh of Gentry's unmoving shoulder as he lay there. And then there was something else beneath her fingers, hard and metallic – the knife she had used earlier in the day. Swiftly grasping it, turning it so that the handle was in her palm, she brought it between herself and the woman and pushed upwards with all her strength. She felt the resistance of the woman's clothing, of muscle and cartilage, and she withdrew the knife and gave another thrust, this time using every last ounce of her remaining strength.

As the knife pierced the woman's heart she made a little sound, half grunt, half moan, at the same time loosening her grip about Blanche's throat and expelling her fetid breath in one long sigh. Her eyes, only inches from Blanche's own, suddenly fixed and dulled as the spark of life was extinguished. In the same moment Blanche felt the woman's body, like that of someone suddenly falling asleep, relax heavily onto her own.

With the sounds of Adriana's and Lisa's hysterical screams still ringing in the room, Blanche lay without moving for a moment or two, the dead weight of the woman's body upon her. Then, still fighting to recover her breath, she thrust the body aside and freed herself of its weight. Head hanging, mouth open, gasping, she got to her knees. Then there came Adriana's cry – '*Mama* . . .' – and the next moment Adriana was beside her, wrapping her in her arms.

'It's all right . . . It's all right . . . my darling . . . I'm all right . . .' Blanche felt as if she would never fully catch her breath, never stop trembling. After holding Adriana to her for a few moments, she called to Lisa – who was growing calmer now – beckoning to her to come and take Adriana away. Hesitantly the girl did as she was bidden, carefully skirting the body of the woman on the floor. Blanche watched as Lisa led Adriana back to the mattress, then she struggled to her feet and turned and walked unsteadily towards Gentry and Marianne.

Gentry lay prone, his face resting on his cheek, blood running from his head. Blanche knelt beside him and put her hand on his heart. Although he was unconscious he was still alive; she could feel the beating of his heart. She turned to Marianne.

Marianne, naked, lay supine on the tiles, one leg on the mattress. Blanche spoke her name, but there was no answer. She put her hand to Marianne's breast, but there was no heartbeat there.

'*Marianne . . .*'

Falling to the floor beside her, Blanche cried out Marianne's name while she lifted up her body, cradling it in her arms, bending her head to look into her face. Marianne's dark eyes, once so bright with warmth and spirit, gazed back dull and lifeless into her own.

Chapter Forty-Five

Many hours had passed.

Blanche sat on a hard wooden chair close to Gentry where he lay. Immediately after the attack she had bound his bleeding head. Since that time he had lain on his side on the mattress, silent, his eyes closed. She had done all she could to bring him to consciousness, but all her efforts had been to no avail.

Throughout the night in the pale light of the lamp she had sat on the chair, keeping her vigil, the deep silence of the room broken only occasionally by the distant sounds of gunshots. For all the long hours of this seemingly endless night she had sat looking into the shadows. She had wanted to sleep, to find some way of escape from the nightmare, but she could not. Rather, she had sat there as in some kind of trance, as if the events of the past two days and nights had numbed her senses.

Now, trying to shake the stultifying dullness from her, she got up. Her joints were stiff from the hours of sitting, and her eyes itched from lack of sleep, but she was hardly aware of such negligible added discomfort. Standing there in the dim light, looking down at Gentry's unconscious body beneath her, the full impact of the reality came back to her. Tomorrow they must get away; she knew it. If they did not, she was afraid they would never survive.

Turning, she walked on silent feet to the mattress at

the far end of the room where Lisa and Adriana lay fast asleep. She could only thank God that Adriana was not really aware of what had happened the evening before. Held in Lisa's arms during the fight, terrified and screaming, she had hidden her face and so had seen neither the knife nor the blow that Blanche had struck with it. When Adriana had eventually found the courage to look upon the scene, upon the corpse of the woman lying prone upon the floor, the knife had been hidden from her sight.

And Blanche had endeavoured to ensure that the child was not further enlightened. To enable her to tend to Gentry and the girls she had first covered the woman's body with an old tablecloth. Later, when the situation was calmer and the two girls were sleeping, she had removed the knife and wiped it clean. Then, struggling with the heavy weight, she had dragged the body into the small room leading off the kitchen. Securely closing the door behind her she had moved back to the place where the body had lain. There was blood there. Taking a cloth she had wiped it up as well as she could, though from then on she had skirted the spot whenever she crossed the room.

Now she moved back across the floor and stood looking down at the tiled floor. Even in the dim light she could see the clean patch where the blood had fallen and where she had wiped away the stain. The words went through her mind: *You have killed another human being. You have taken a life.* But she had had no choice in the matter. And she knew that were she faced with the same situation she would have to do the same thing again.

She turned away and stood unmoving, hands hanging at her sides. After a while she raised her head and forced herself to look over to that part of the kitchen where the shadows were deeper. It was there that Marianne lay.

Softly, Blanche moved to her side.

Marianne lay on her back on a small piece of matting that Blanche had found and laid there. Her body was covered by a tablecloth.

Blanche lowered herself and knelt on the tiles. Gently she pulled back part of the cloth to reveal the still face. She had closed the dead eyes. Now Marianne looked as if she were sleeping, and for a brief moment the strange, desperate thought flashed through Blanche's mind that Marianne could wake, could open her eyes and turn to her. And Marianne would smile, and in that moment everything would be behind them. All the horror of the past two days would all be gone, and they would once again be as they were in happier times.

Lifting her hand, Blanche softly touched the back of her fingers to Marianne's cold cheek. Then she let her hand fall back to her side and bowed her head. Marianne was dead. She had gone for ever, and with her going a part of Blanche's life had gone too.

Remaining on her knees, she turned her head and looked back to where Gentry lay. When he recovered consciousness he would have to learn what had happened. And a voice in her head said perversely: *If he recovers consciousness.* She thrust the voice away. *No.* He might be gravely injured, but he would be all right. He would be. He needed medical help, though, and he needed it soon. She must get help for him as soon as it was light. If he didn't get it . . .

Slowly, she got up off her knees. Moving back to the hard wooden chair beside the mattress she sat down. Staring into the gloom that was relieved only by the little flame of the lamp, she sat and waited for morning to come.

*

Standing at the head of the stairs, facing out into the surrounding ruins, Blanche watched as the dawn revealed the devastated landscape. Mercifully now the rain had stopped. There was something else, though; a pervasive smell of decay that drifted on the cold wind.

When the sky was light she turned and went back down into the kitchen. Moving to the mattress where Adriana and Lisa lay, she bent and touched Adriana on the shoulder and whispered her name. The child awoke at once, and Blanche saw a shadow of alarm appear in her eyes.

'Mama . . .'

'It's all right, my darling. It's all right.'

As Blanche spoke Lisa stirred and opened her sleepy eyes, and Blanche watched as the memory of all the horrors quickly touched the girl and brought her fully awake. Blanche laid her hand upon Lisa's shoulder, patted her.

'Listen,' she said, 'I must go out. I'm –'

Adriana broke in at once, her voice sharp with fear: 'Oh, Mama, don't leave us.'

Lisa added her protest, sitting up beside Adriana: 'Oh, please, signora –'

'Listen to me,' Blanche said. 'I've got to go and get help so that we can get to the docks. Once there we can find a ship to take us away.' She gestured to where Gentry lay on the other mattress. 'We need a stretcher to carry the signore. *We* can't do it, and if we just stay here he'll die.'

Adriana began to wail. 'Oh, don't leave us. Don't leave us.' And then a new, plaintive cry: 'Daddy. Where's Daddy?'

Blanche could hear the beginnings of hysteria in Adriana's cries. 'Hush, hush,' she said soothingly. Then, ignoring the question regarding Alfredo she said, 'All

650

right – all right, you can come with me.' Then to Lisa: 'But Lisa, you must stay here and keep a watch over the signore.' As Lisa's face showed her swiftly growing fear at being left alone in the place Blanche put her hands reassuringly on her shoulders.

'No one else will come in. You'll be safe, and we shan't be gone long. And if the signore should waken, then tell him we shall be back soon.' She pulled aside the blanket. 'Come, Adriana – put on your coat.'

A few minutes later she and Adriana emerged from the stairs into the open air. At once Adriana wrinkled her nose at the unpleasant, pervasive smell – and in the same moment Blanche realized what it came from. It was the smell of rotting flesh. Briefly she put a hand up to cover her nose and mouth, but then she realized that there was no escaping from it; and not only would she have to put up with it but it was going to get worse.

Hand in hand, she and Adriana set off, clambering over the debris in the direction of the docks.

Near the Palazzo Reale she came across two young sailors carrying a rolled-up stretcher under their arms. She could see from their uniforms that they were British, and much relieved she hailed them and hurried towards them. On learning that she was English the men at once asked her if they could be of service. They were two of a team from HMS *Euryalus*, they said, seeking out injured survivors to take to the Piazza Mazzini for medical help. In answer to Blanche's questions they told her that there was a British ship, the *Blake*, anchored in the port, which was shortly to leave with survivors for Naples. At that very moment, they said, survivors were being ferried out to the ship where she lay at anchor. At the words Blanche begged them to go with her. She had a friend who had to be taken to the docks, she said. He was unconscious, he had been so for many hours, and she was afraid that if he didn't get attention soon he might die.

The taller of the two bluejackets put a hand on her shoulder. Don't worry, he assured her, they would see that she and her friend got to the docks all right.

Feeling that she could weep with relief, Blanche thanked them and, turning, took Adriana by the hand and led the men back towards the piazza.

A while later she stood in the kitchen watching as the two young men lifted Gentry onto the stretcher and turned to bear him up the stairs. Blanche called after them: 'I'll catch you up.' She turned to Lisa and Adriana: 'Go with the men. I'll join you in a moment.'

They would not, though, but hovered beside the doorway. Blanche, her control at breaking point, snapped out angrily and sharply: 'Go – now! Do as I say!' And the two girls looked at her wide-eyed for a moment and then turned and went up the stairs behind the sailors.

Blanche moved across the kitchen floor to where Marianne's body lay. Kneeling on the tiles she pulled aside the cloth that covered Marianne's dead face. She still looked as if she were asleep. Words formed in Blanche's head: *Marianne, I have to leave you . . .* There was no choice; she had to go; she had to care for the living. As she was about to replace the cloth her eye was drawn to the gleam of the rings on Marianne's fingers. She couldn't leave them for any looter or anyone else who chanced by. After a moment's hesitation she lifted Marianne's small hands, first the left, then the right, and then, with some difficulty, removed the rings. She put them into her pocket. Later she would give them to Gentry . . .

Carefully she laid the cloth back over Marianne's face and got to her feet.

'Goodbye, Marianne . . . my dear, dear friend.'

She took a breath, turned away and moved across the

floor to the doorway. Seconds later she was climbing the stairs for the last time.

As she emerged into the open air she could see the little procession not far ahead, the two sailors bearing Gentry on the stretcher, followed by Lisa and Adriana walking hand in hand. Their progress was slow. As she looked at them she saw Adriana turn and glance back anxiously over her shoulder. Blanche waved to her and the child waved in return.

As she set off, picking her way over the debris, Blanche's glance was drawn to movement over to her right and she saw a little group of Italian soldiers moving about among the ruins not far away. They had a small, mule-drawn cart which somehow they were managing to manoeuvre through the congested streets. The soldiers were collecting up the dead. On the cart the bodies lay one on top of the other. On a sudden impulse Blanche changed her course and hurried towards the group. As she drew nearer two of the soldiers emerged from the ruins of a house carrying on a stretcher the body of an old man. Reaching the cart they laid the body on top of the others and then set off again bearing the stretcher between them.

Blanche reached the cart just as the other two soldiers appeared carrying the body of a teenage girl. She waited until the corpse had been deposited with the rest and then stepped forward. The soldiers looked at her inquiringly. 'Yes, signora . . . ?'

'Please – signori,' she addressed them both, '– can you tell me – what is to become of the – the dead?'

One of the soldiers was several years older than the other. He, the nearer of the two, gave a little shrug. 'They're to be buried. Graves are being dug. At the English Cemetery – near the port. The bodies are being taken there . . .'

'The English Cemetery?'

'Yes. They're digging mass graves.' He shrugged again. 'There are so many bodies.'

The thought went through Blanche's mind: *Marianne, to be buried in a mass grave.* She could see pictures, images flashing. They were too horrible, and briefly the thought touched her that it might be possible for Marianne's body to be taken back to England. After all, if there were ships arriving and taking people away, then perhaps . . . But then a second later she knew that it was a foolish thought; with so many injured to be taken away, no one would allow valuable space on board ship to be taken up with the transport of the dead.

The young soldiers were leaning against the side of the cart (they were inured to death now) taking a brief respite from their task. Having discerned from Blanche's accented Italian that she was a foreigner, they asked her where she was from. England, she replied. They nodded; she should go down to the docks, they said. Perhaps she could find a ship to take her home. Yes, she said, that was her intention.

They straightened, preparing to get back to work. Briefly turning, Blanche saw that Adriana, Lisa and the two seamen carrying the stretcher had come to a halt and were waiting for her.

'Oh, just a moment, please,' Blanche said to the soldiers. '– Please wait.'

They halted and she turned and pointed off to the ruins of the villa above the basement kitchen. When would they be going there, she asked them.

They shrugged. Soon, quite soon.

She nodded, hesitated for a moment and then began to work at her hand, trying to take off her wedding ring. When it wouldn't come off she spat on her finger in an effort to ease the ring's removal. After a few moments the ring was free. Holding it in the palm of her dirty hand she held it out to the soldier nearest to her.

'Please,' she urged him, 'take it. Take the ring.'

He frowned. 'What for . . . ?'

She gestured again to the ruined villa where Marianne lay. In the basement kitchen there, she said, there was the body of a young woman. 'Please, please,' she said, 'be gentle with her.'

The soldiers looked at her with sympathy. The elder lifted his hand and gently closed her fingers back over the ring.

'No, signora – it's not necessary. We don't want your wedding ring. I promise you – we'll be very gentle with her.' He patted her hand. 'Obviously she's someone close to you . . .'

Blanche nodded. '– My sister.'

She stood there with her hand outstretched, the ring closed in her palm. The soldier, lifting his hand higher, softly touched her cheek in a little gesture of comfort. 'Listen, signora – you'll get over all this one day. This terrible thing.'

He smiled at her, a grave little smile, then turned and gave a little nod to his companion. Then together, taking up the stretcher between them, they moved away.

Wetting her knuckles she pushed the ring back onto her finger and turned and moved back over the debris to where the little procession waited. When she had joined them they set off together towards the docks.

On arriving at the docks Blanche found the situation to be one of the most incredible chaos. Word that ships were shortly to leave the port had spread and from every direction the survivors, both wounded and able-bodied, were pouring onto the quays, walking, limping, or being carried – all anxious to get away from the scene of the disaster. Many of them were covered only in blankets, while others wore only the remnants of underwear or nightclothes. Once she had seen these quays alive with happy, busy people – seamen going about their work, porters running about with baskets or produce on their heads, tourists and other passengers arriving from an endless stream of ships coming into the once prosperous harbour. Now wherever she looked she could see only despair, anxiety and suffering. Injured survivors were everywhere, some sitting on pieces of debris, others lying on stretchers or on the bare, muddy ground. And still more were arriving at every moment.

Walking behind Gentry's stretcher, Blanche held tightly to Adriana's hand as they were jostled by the surging crowds. Coming to a halt before them, the seamen set the stretcher down and one of them pointed out into the harbour where the British ship, the *Blake*, rode at anchor. The seaman pointed again, this time to the edge of the wharf where crowds were converging around a lighter. 'You'll board from there,' he said, and then: 'Wait here. I'll try to find one of her crew.'

He went off, pushing through the throng at the water's edge, and came back a few minutes later to say that he had talked to one of the *Blake's* crew and that there was still a little room on board her if they didn't wait too long. With his words he and his companion bent to take up the stretcher again. As they did so Blanche said quickly. 'Wait – please –' and she turned to Lisa who stood looking lost and afraid. Taking Lisa's hand, Blanche turned back to the seamen. 'This young girl has to get to Catania, to her family. I can't just leave her here.'

Straightening, one of the men indicated another steamer that lay at anchor a little further to the south. 'You want the *Piemonte*,' he said. 'She's an Italian ship and bound for Catania.' Turning, he cast about with his eyes for a moment and then yelled to a tall, burly seaman who was passing, and who at once came hurrying through the throng. 'This young girl has to get on the *Piemonte*,' said the first sailor. Without wasting a moment the newcomer nodded and reached out for Lisa's hand. 'Come with me, young lady,' he said kindly. 'I'll see you get on board.'

Lisa looked nervously from the seaman to Blanche. Speaking in Italian, Blanche quickly reassured her. 'Go with the signore, Lisa,' she said to the girl. 'You'll soon be home again.'

Lisa nodded, her eyes shining with relief, and stepping to Blanche she threw her arms around her neck. 'Goodbye, signora.' Then, with a swift goodbye for Adriana, she turned and, escorted by the sailor, was hurried away through the crowd.

'Now,' said one of the remaining seamen, 'we must be quick about it. The *Blake*'ll be weighing anchor soon. And she's about full as it is.' With his words he and his companion bent and took up the stretcher again.

Blanche had never had experience of a crowd such as that which swarmed over the quays at Messina that morning. Of those that were not desperately trying to get on one of the ships that were leaving, there were many who had come simply in search of provisions, and they hurried about crying out for bread, water and clothing.

Forcing her way through the mêlée and holding tightly to Adriana's hand, she followed in the wake of the two sailors as they bore Gentry's stretcher onto the wharf off which lay the *Blake*.

As she and Adriana moved towards the edge of the crowd that seethed over the wharf she suddenly found herself confronted by a man who stepped out in front of her and grasped her roughly by the shoulders. Covered in mud and dirt, his rags of clothes hung about his bent form as his fingers dug into her flesh and his mouth opened in a wide, humourless grin. It took a moment for her to realize that it was Edgardo.

'Signora!' he cried out, and pulling her towards him clasped her in a hard embrace. 'Signora, signora!'

'Let me go!' Screaming at him, Blanche struggled to free herself. But she could not, and she felt herself being lifted up and then swung around in some kind of crazy dance while he sang odd snatches of a popular song, his voice cracked and wavering in his insanity. Then, putting her down, but still holding her tightly in a vice-like grip, he leaned towards her and asked: 'Where is signor Alfredo? Where is he?'

Blanche had no opportunity to answer. Even as he finished speaking he was releasing his hold on her, and, turning, bending to Adriana, was snatching her up. Then, with the child shrieking in his arms he was turning and dancing away.

Blanche leapt at him, screaming, clutching at Adriana. And all the while it was happening the people milled about, unconcerned, caught up in their own problems of survival. Edgardo, now on the edge of the wharf, turned on the spot, evading Blanche's reaching arms, keeping Adriana out of her grasp. Then, breaking away again with the child held in his arms, he started off across the quay.

As Blanche tried desperately to prevent his escape she suddenly found that there was help at hand. To her indescribable relief a tall British sailor, his attention drawn by the action and Blanche's cries, suddenly appeared and, barring Edgardo's way, reached out and took the child from him. Moments later the sailor was at Blanche's side, Adriana safe in his arms.

Blanche told him that they were to board the *Blake*, and the man said sharply, 'Then you'd better hurry up, lady.' He tipped his head towards the wharf. 'The lighter's just about full. I don't know if there'll be room for you.'

Turning, he hoisted Adriana high in his arms and moved to the crowd. On its edge he said sharply to Blanche, 'Hold on to my belt.' And she did so and the next moment he was moving forward, thrusting his way through the dense throng.

It was a struggle but they came at last to the water's edge where the crowded lighter was moored and a few last passengers were hurriedly being taken on board. There was a feeling of great nervousness and tension in the air as the last few anxious evacuees were helped down into the boat as it rode gently up and down on the swell of the waves. A number of armed sailors stood guard at the wharf's edge, standing between the vessel and the general crowd, preventing the more desperate from pouring onto the boat and swamping her as they were in danger of doing.

Already the large, flat-bottomed barge was packed to bursting with survivors lucky enough to have been granted a place. They stood or sat in every available space, while in the centre, cheek by jowl, lay several stretchers. Blanche's anxious eyes saw with relief that Gentry's was there among them.

As she stood nervously behind the sailor at the wharf's edge, her heart thudding in her chest, the air around her was filled with a cacophony of wails and cries coming from the other desperate survivors clamouring to be allowed on board. Blanche felt sure that the only reason she was being allowed on the lighter was because she was English. She didn't care. Standing beside their protector, the young English sailor, she watched as he held Adriana out in his arms and she was taken into the arms of another sailor who stood in the barge. The next moment Blanche herself was being helped down from the wharf. Then she and Adriana were standing holding one another in the crowded boat. One or two other passengers were helped on board and then to a chorus of protests from the wretched people on the wharf, the men were casting off and the boat was slipping out into the water. She turned, looking into the crowd to seek out the figure of the young sailor, at least to call out her thanks to him, but already he had melted into the crowd at the water's edge.

Some minutes later when the lighter reached the *Blake* the passengers were helped from it onto the gangway and up onto the deck of the ship. The survivors on stretchers were the last to be brought on board, and Blanche, with Adriana beside her, stood watching, anxiously waiting for Gentry's stretcher to be lifted up and carried onto the deck. But then at last he was there, his stretcher carried by two sailors and set down at a spot near the ship's rail where several other stretchers had been placed. Holding Adriana tightly by the hand, Blanche pushed through the throng to Gentry's side. She got there just as a young medical attendant from the ship was bending over Gentry, lifting his eyelid and peering into his eye. He turned to Blanche as she and Adriana came to his side.

'Do you speak English?' he asked.

She nodded. 'I *am* English.'

He gave a grave little smile then looked down at Gentry. 'You're with this gentleman, are you?'

'Yes.'

He nodded, looked into Gentry's still face. 'He looks as if he's concussed, is he?'

'I – I think so, yes.'

'How long has he been like it? Since the quake?'

'No – it happened later. Yesterday evening.'

The man sighed. 'Well – let's hope he'll be all right. At least he'll get some treatment once you get him to Naples. How about you? Are you all right? And your little girl?'

'Yes, we're all right. We were lucky.'

'Lucky . . . Yes . . .' He nodded, then: 'You're all going back to England, are you?'

'Yes.'

'You'll be put in touch with the British consul at Naples. They'll help you.'

'Thank you.'

He shrugged. Turning to Adriana he said: 'Are you hungry?'

She nodded.

He touched her gently on the cheek. 'We'll bring you some food in a minute. Be patient.' With a little smile at her and then at Blanche he straightened, turned and moved away.

Blanche crouched beside Gentry and looked into his still face. He lay perfectly still, only his regular breathing showing that he was still alive. At the edge of the bandage the blood had dried in his hair. She put her hand to his grime-covered cheek, gently stroked it. She called his name two or three times, but he made no response, gave no sign that he had heard. The terrifying thought came to her that perhaps he would remain unconscious; she had heard of people remaining in comas for days – eventually dying without ever regaining consciousness.

She closed her eyes for a moment in a little gesture of despair. When she opened them again she found Adriana looking into her eyes, her gaze shadowed with concern. 'It's all right, darling,' she said. 'I'm all right.'

She patted a corner of Gentry's blanket. 'Here – come and sit down. Get some rest.'

Adriana sat down on a corner of the blanket that covered Gentry. Blanche straightened and stood at the rail. Every inch of space of the deck around her was taken up with survivors. There were hundreds of them, injured and uninjured, standing, sitting and lying over all the decks.

Sounds of commands among the ship's crew rang out. Beneath Blanche's feet the deck gave a little shudder. She felt relief pour over her as slowly the *Blake* began to move. She stood looking out over the water, and over the swarming quays to the scene of destruction beyond. The view of the city as it lay in front of her was a wide panorama of complete and utter devastation. In whichever direction she cast her eyes she could see nothing but ruin; wherever she looked she could not see one building standing whole.

Beside her a little old woman wrapped in a blanket murmured to no one in particular, 'Messina is finished. Messina is finished.' Blanche silently nodded agreement. The Messina she had known for that brief space of time was gone for ever.

The ship with her melancholy cargo moved slowly out of the harbour, each second leaving the devastation further behind. Gone were Messina's luxurious hotels – not only Gentry's hotel, the Metropole, but also the Victoria, the Trinacria and the France. Gone were the factories; gone were the theatres, the Vittorio Emanuele and the Munizione. Gone was the Civic Hospital, its patients calling out for their nurses as the walls had collapsed around them. Gone the university, the convent of San Gregorio, the museum of the Castel Durante, the Bank of Italy, the American consulate, the Municipal Palace, the Central Station. And in that once prosperous city of some 112,000 souls, over 80,000 had perished, while a similar number had died in Reggio on the other side of the Straits and in the surrounding towns and villages.

As Blanche looked back towards the shore she saw a large crowd of crazed survivors attacking one of the customs buildings which still stood partly intact, breaking down its doors. She looked away.

The ship moved out of the harbour, past the sickle-shaped tongue of land on which stood the lighthouse and where lay the remains of the *Cimitero Inglese* — the English Cemetery, where bands of soldiers were to be seen at work, digging. And the thought went through Blanche's mind: *Marianne will be buried there today* . . . She tried to close her mind to the thought; there would be a time later for remembering . . .

As the shore receded with its view of the devastation growing more and more indistinct there were no sounds of jubilation; there were no words or cries of relief from the passengers who huddled on the decks. For the most part they lay or sat or stood in silence, gazing dully ahead, only the occasional moans of the injured breaking the melancholy silence.

Turning from the rail, Blanche looked down at Adriana where she sat on the blanket at Gentry's side. Adriana had not asked again for Alfredo, but it would be only a matter of time before she did. And then Blanche would have to give her some kind of answer. But perhaps, she told herself, news of Alfredo's death might not come as such a dreadful shock; for Adriana as for everyone else in the devastated city, death and destruction were the norm.

From Adriana, Blanche's glance moved to Gentry. He had nothing now. His factory had gone. As had his hotel. All of it reduced to piles of rubble. As had Alfredo's properties. All gone. Totally destroyed along with everything else in the city.

Moving on from Gentry's still face, Blanche looked around her at the other passengers, and she realized dully that there was no way of knowing who had been rich, who had been poor. Now for the most part they were all the same. Men who had once been millionaires now sat side by side with those who had had nothing; hardly any of them now were able to claim more than the blankets or ragged clothes that covered their nakedness.

How transitory everything was, Blanche thought. One could spend a lifetime searching for some kind of security and it could be lost in a moment. Could nothing material be depended upon? In a single night a whole city had been wiped out, and along with it the happiness and hopes and fortunes of thousands upon thousands of people had been destroyed. And so many dead. She thought again of Alfredo. And it seemed now that perhaps she could understand him. Ever since she had known him he had been constantly driven to recover what, through his lack of ability, he had lost. And his desperation had wrought changes in him that had almost destroyed him even before the wave had taken him.

And Marianne. Gone too. Beautiful, warm, generous Marianne – who had had everything to live for. Now to be buried in a mass grave with no one there to mourn for her.

Blanche's eyes shifted back to rest once more on Gentry's face. And there was a bitter irony here. There had been so many times in her life when she had dreamed of such a situation – that of finding herself with Gentry – and at a time when they were both free.

And it had happened. And now that it had happened it somehow did not matter any more. She loved him still, desperately, but beyond that she seemed to feel nothing. And she felt that she could not even weep over her loss.

She stood holding on to the rail, a young woman in the remains of a torn, filthy, bloodstained coat, blonde hair hanging loose and matted about her shoulders, the skin of her hands cut and grazed beneath their covering of grime, one eye bruised and discoloured, her gaze dull with a weariness that was close to a weariness of life itself. Sighing, she thrust her hands into her pockets. In her left pocket she felt the rings that she had taken from Marianne's fingers. In her right pocket she found the loose coins she had put there when preparing to leave Alfredo. She withdrew her hand. There were three centimes, and the gold sovereign that John Savill had given her when she was a baby.

She stood staring at the gold coin. It was what she had begun with . . . She had come full circle.

'Blanche . . .'

It was Gentry's voice – a little cracked, a little hoarse, but still his voice. Putting the coins back in her pocket she turned and bent to him. 'Gentry . . .' He was gazing up at her. He was going to be all right.

He looked from her face to that of Adriana who peered at him. After a moment he asked, frowning:

'– Marianne . . . ?'

Blanche was silent for a moment then she fell to her knees beside him.

'Oh, Gentry . . .'

His hand came out from beneath the blanket, closing around hers, gripping her tightly. Tears flooded his eyes and spilled over, running down over his temples to be lost beneath the blood-stained bandage. Blanche felt her own tears spring to her eyes, distorting the image of his face.

They remained there like that while Blanche wiped at his stained cheeks with the tips of her fingers. At last their tears ended, dried in the salt wind. They would survive. They were safe now. They would be all right. She clutched more tightly at his hand. *We shall survive*.

Adriana had moved to the rail and now stood looking out across the waters of the Straits.

'Mama, look,' she said, '– you can hardly see it anymore.'

Turning, still holding fast to Gentry's hand, Blanche saw that the ship had swung around, that the Messina shore was swiftly receding behind them. Up above her head the gulls wheeled in the clear sky.